THE
MOMENT

ALSO BY DOUGLAS KENNEDY

FICTION

Leaving the World
The Woman in the Fifth
Temptation
State of the Union
A Special Relationship
The Pursuit of Happiness
The Job
The Big Picture
The Dead Heart

NONFICTION

Chasing Mammon
In God's Country
Beyond the Pyramids

THE
MOMENT

A NOVEL

DOUGLAS KENNEDY

ATRIA BOOKS

New York   London   Toronto   Sydney

ATRIA BOOKS

A Division of Simon & Schuster, Inc.
1230 Avenue of the Americas
New York, NY 10020

First Atria Books hardcover edition May 2011

ATRIA BOOKS and colophon are trademarks of Simon & Schuster, Inc.

For information about special discounts for bulk purchases, please contact Simon & Schuster Special Sales at 1-866-506-1949 or business@simonandschuster.com.

The Simon & Schuster Speakers Bureau can bring authors to your live event. For more information or to book an event contact the Simon & Schuster Speakers Bureau at 1-866-248-3049 or visit our website at www.simonspeakers.com.

"The Layers." Copyright © 1978 by Stanley Kunitz, from THE COLLECTED POEMS by Stanley Kunitz. Used by permission of W. W. Norton & Company, Inc.

Alabama——song from *Mahagony Songspiel*, lyric by Bertolt Brecht, music by Kurt Weill, copyright © 1927 by European American Corporation and Universal Edition.

Designed by Kyle Kabel

Manufactured in the United States of America

10   9   8   7   6   5   4   3   2   1

Library of Congress Cataloging-in-Publication Data

Kennedy, Douglas.
　　The moment : a novel / Douglas Kennedy. —— 1st Atria Books hardcover ed.
　　　p. cm.
1. Travel writers——Fiction. 2. Americans——Germany——Fiction. 3. Cold War——Fiction. 4. Foreign agents——Fiction. 5. Berlin (Germany)——History——1945–1990——Fiction. 6. Spy stories. gsafd 7. Love stories. gsafd I. Title.
　　PR6061.E5956M66 2011
　　823.914——dc22

2010048577

ISBN 978-1-4391-8079-2
ISBN 978-1-4391-8080-8 (ebook)

For five great friends:
Noeleen Dowling of Grangegorman, Dublin,
Anne Ireland of Falmouth, Maine,
Howard Rosenstein of Montreal, Quebec,
Judy Rymer of Sydney, New South Wales,
and Roger Williams——across the street from me in Wiscasset, Maine.

And to the memory of another great friend,
Joseph Strick (1924–2010).

Oh, I have made myself a tribe
out of my true affections,
and my tribe is scattered!
How shall the heart be reconciled
to its feast of losses?

—Stanley Kunitz, *The Layers*

THE
MOMENT

PART ONE

ONE

I WAS SERVED WITH divorce papers this morning. I've had better starts to the day. And though I knew they were coming, the actual moment when they landed in my hand still threw me. Because their arrival announced: this is the beginning of the end.

I live in a small cottage. It's located on a back road near the town of Edgecomb, Maine. The cottage is simple: two bedrooms, a study, an open-plan living/kitchen area, whitewashed walls, stained floorboards. I bought it a year ago when I came into some money. My father had just died. Though broke by the time that his heart exploded, he still had an insurance policy in place from his days as a corporate man. The policy paid out $300,000. As I was the sole child and the sole survivor——my mother having left this life years earlier——I was also the sole beneficiary. My father and I weren't close. We spoke weekly on the phone. I made an annual three-day visit to his retirement bungalow in Arizona. And I did send him each of my travel books as they were published. Beyond that, there was minimal contact——a long-ingrained awkwardness always curtailing any ease or familiarity between us. When I flew out alone to Phoenix to organize the funeral and close up his house, a local lawyer got in touch with me. He said that he'd drawn up Dad's will, and did I know I was about to receive a nice little payoff from the Mutual of Omaha Insurance Corporation?

"But Dad was hard up for years," I told the lawyer. "So why didn't he cash in the policy and live on the proceeds?"

"Good question," the lawyer said. "Especially as I advised him to do that myself. But the old guy was very stubborn, very proud."

"Tell me about it," I said. "I tried sending him some money once, not that I had much to offer him. He returned my check."

"The few times I saw your dad, he bragged to me about his son the well-known writer."

"I'm hardly well known."

"But you *are* published. And he was very proud of what you had accomplished."

"That's news to me," I said, remembering how Dad had hardly said anything about my books.

"That generation of men——they often couldn't articulate a damn thing they were feeling," the lawyer said. "But he obviously wanted you to have some sort of legacy from him——so expect a payout of three hundred grand in the next couple of weeks."

I flew back east the next day. Instead of returning home to the house in Cambridge that I shared with my wife, I found myself renting a car at Logan Airport and pointing it in the direction of places north. It was early evening when I left the airport. I guided the car onto Interstate 95 and drove. Three hours later, I was on Route 1 in Maine. I passed through the town of Wiscasset, then crossed the Sheepscot River and pulled into a motel. It was mid-January. The mercury was well below freezing. A recent snowfall had bleached everything white, and I was the only guest at the inn.

"What brings you up here at this time of year?" the clerk at the reception desk asked me.

"No idea," I said.

I couldn't sleep that night and drank most of the fifth of bourbon I had packed in my travel bag. At first light I got back into my rental car and started driving. I followed the road east, a narrow two-lane blacktop that snaked its way down a hill and around a curvy bend. Once that bend was negotiated, the payoff was spectacular. For there in front of me was a frozen expanse, shaded in aquamarine, a vast sheltered bay, fringed by iced woodlands, with a low-lying fog hovering above its glaciated surface. I braked, then got out of the car. A boreal wind was blowing. It chafed my face and nettled my eyes. But I forced myself to walk down to the water's edge. A meager sun was attempting to light up the world. Its wattage was so low that the bay remained dappled in mist, making it seem both ethereal and haunted. Though the cold was brutal, I couldn't take my gaze off this spectral landscape. Until another blast of wind made me turn away from it.

And at that precise moment I saw the cottage.

It was positioned on a small plot of land, elevated above the bay. Its design was very basic——a one-storey structure, sided in weatherbeaten white clapboard. Its little driveway was empty. There were no lights on inside. But there was a "For Sale" sign positioned out in front. I pulled out my notebook, writing down the name and number of the Wiscasset real estate agent who was handling it. I was going to approach it, but the cold finally forced me back to the car. I drove off in search of a diner that served breakfast. I discovered one on the outskirts of town. Then I found the agent's office on the main street. Thirty minutes after I crossed his threshold, we were back at the cottage.

"Now I have to warn you that the place is a bit primitive," the real estate agent said. "But it's got great bones. And, of course, it's right on the water. Better yet, it's an estate sale. It's been on the market for sixteen months, so the family will accept a reasonable offer."

The agent was right. The cottage was the wrong side of rustic. But it had been winterized. And thanks to Dad, the $220,000 asking price was now affordable. I offered one eighty-five on the spot. By the end of the morning, the offer had been accepted. The next morning I had——courtesy of the real estate agent——met a local contractor who was willing to redo the cottage within my budget of $60,000. By the end of the same day I finally called home and had to answer a lot of questions from my wife, Jan, about why I had been out of contact for the last seventy-two hours.

"Because on the way back from my father's funeral I bought a house."

The silence that followed this statement was an extended one—— and, I realize now, the moment when her patience with me finally cracked.

"Please tell me this is a joke," she said.

But it wasn't a joke. It was a declaration of sorts, and one with a considerable amount of subtext to it. Jan understood that. Just as I knew that, once I informed her of this impulse buy, the landscape between us would be irreparably damaged.

Yet I still went ahead and bought the place. Which, in turn, must mean that I really did want things to turn out this way.

But that moment of permanent schism didn't happen for another eight months. A marriage——especially one of twenty years' duration——rarely ends with a decisive bang. It's more like all the phases you go through when confronting a terminal illness: anger, denial, pleading, more anger, denial . . . though we never seemed to reach the "acceptance" part of the "journey." Instead, during an August weekend when we came up to the now-renovated cottage, Jan chose to tell me that, for her, the marriage was over. And she left town on the next bus.

Not with a bang, just with a . . .

Subdued sadness.

I stayed on at the cottage for the rest of the summer, only returning once to our house in Cambridge——when she was away for the weekend——to pack up all my worldly goods (books and papers and the few clothes I owned). Then I headed back north.

Not with a bang, just with . . .

Months passed. I didn't travel for a while. My daughter, Candace, visited me at the cottage one weekend per month. Every second Tuesday (her choice) I would drive the half hour from my house down to her college in Brunswick and take her out for dinner. When we got together we talked about her classes and friends and the book I was writing. But we rarely mentioned her mother, except for one night after Christmas when she asked me:

"You doing okay, Dad?"

"Not bad," I said, knowing that I was sounding reticent.

"You should meet someone."

"Easier said than done in backwoods Maine. Anyway I've a book to finish."

"Mom always said that, for you, the books came first."

"Do you agree with that?"

"Yes and no. You were away a lot. But when you were home, you were cool."

"Am I still cool?"

"Way cool," she said, giving my arm a squeeze. "But I wish you weren't so alone."

"The writer's curse," I said. "You have to be alone, you have to be obsessive, and those nearest to you frequently find that hard to bear. And who can blame them?"

"Mom once said that you never really loved her, that your heart was elsewhere."

I looked at her carefully.

"There were many things before your mom," I said. "Still, I did love her."

"But not always."

"It was a marriage——with all that that implies. And it did last twenty years."

"Even if your heart was elsewhere?"

"You ask a lot of questions."

"Only because you're so evasive, Dad."

"The past is very much the past."

"And you really want to dodge that question, don't you?"

I smiled at my far too precocious daughter and suggested we have another glass of wine.

"I have a German question," she said.

"Try me."

"We were translating Luther the other day in class."

"Is your professor a sadist?"

"No, just German. Anyway, while working our way through a collection of Luther's aphorisms, I found something pertinent . . ."

"Pertinent to whom?"

"No particular person. But I'm not certain if I got the quote exactly right."

"And you think I can help you?"

"You're fluent, Dad. *Du sprichst die Sprache.*"

"Only after a couple of glasses of wine."

"Modesty is tedious, Dad."

"So, go on: tell me the quote from Luther."

"*Wie bald 'nicht jetz' 'nie' wird.*"

I didn't flinch. I just translated.

"How soon 'not now' becomes 'never.'"

"It's a great quote," Candace said.

"And, like all great quotes, it speaks a certain truth. What made you single it out?"

"Because I worry I'm a 'not now' sort of person."

"Why do you say that?"

"I can't live in the moment; I can't let myself be happy with where I am."

"Aren't you being a little hard on yourself?"

"Hardly. Because I know that's how you are, too."

Wie bald 'nicht jetz' 'nie' wird.

"The moment . . . ," I said, as if trying out the word for the first time. "It's a very overrated place."

"But it's all we have, right? This night, this conversation, this moment. What else is there?"

"The past."

"I knew you'd say that——because that's your obsession. It's in all your books. Why 'the past,' Dad?"

"It always informs the present."

And because you can never really escape its grip, any more than you can come to terms with that which is terminal in life. Consider: my marriage may have started to disintegrate a decade ago, and the first sign of the endgame may have been that day last January when I bought the cottage in Maine. But I didn't really accept the finality of it all until the morning after my dinner with Candace, when a knock came on my cottage door around eight fifteen.

Now the few neighbors I have do know that I am not a morning person. This makes me rare in this corner of Maine, where everyone seems to get up an hour or so before dawn and where nine a.m. is already considered the middle of the day.

But I never emerge into the world before noon. I'm a night man. I usually start writing after ten in the evening and generally work until three, at which point I nurse a nocturnal whiskey or two, watch an old film or read, and eventually climb into bed around five. I've been living this way since I started writing twenty-seven years ago——a fact my wife found somewhat charming at the beginning of our marriage and a source of great frustration thereafter. "Between the travel and the all-night work binges, I have no life with you" was a common lament——to which I could only reply, "Guilty as charged." Now, with my fiftieth birthday well behind me, I'm stuck with my vampiric lifestyle, the few times I ever see the dawn being those occasional nights when I'm on a roll and write until first light.

But on this January morning a series of loud authoritarian knocks snapped me awake just as the tentative rays of a winter sun were cleaving the night sky. For a befuddled moment I thought I was in the middle of a mad Kafkaesque reverie——with the forces of some sinister state about to arrest me for unspecified thought crimes. But then I came to. Glancing at my bedside clock I saw that it was just after seven thirty a.m. The banging intensified. There really was someone pounding on the front door.

I got out of bed, grabbed a bathrobe, and wandered to the front door. When I opened it I saw a squat man in a parka and a knitted hat standing outside. One hand was behind his back. He looked cold and aggrieved.

"So you're here after all," he said, a fog of frozen breath accompanying his words.

"Sorry?"

"Thomas Nesbitt?"

"Yes . . ."

Suddenly the hand behind his back emerged. It was holding a large manila envelope. Like a Victorian schoolteacher using a ruler to discipline a child, he slammed the envelope right into the palm of my right hand.

"You've been served, Mr. Nesbitt," he said. Then he turned and got into his car.

I stood in the doorway for several minutes, oblivious to the cold. I kept looking down at the large legal envelope, trying to come to terms with what had just transpired. When I felt my fingers going numb I finally went inside. Sitting down at the kitchen table I opened the envelope. Contained within was a petition for divorce from the State of Massachusetts. My name——Thomas Alden Nesbitt——was printed alongside that of my wife——Jan Rogers Stafford. She was named as the Petitioner. I was named as the Respondent. Before my eyes could take in anything else, I pushed the document away from me. I swallowed hard. I knew this was coming. But there a vast difference between the theoretical and the hard-faced typography of the actual. A divorce——no matter how expected——is still a terrible admission of failure. The sense of loss——especially after twenty years——is immense. And now . . .

This document. This definitive statement.

How can we let go that which we once held so essential?

On this January morning I had no reply to such a question. All I had was a petition telling me that my marriage was over, and the relentless disquieting question: could we——*I*——have found a way through this dark wood?

"Mom once said that you never really loved her, that your heart was elsewhere."

It wasn't as facile as that. But there's no doubt that the historic so informs everything in our lives, and that it is so hard to break free of certain immutable things that continue to burden us.

But why look for answers when none will balm anything? I told myself, glancing across the table at the petition. *Do what you always do when life gangs up on you. Run.*

So while waiting for a pot of coffee to percolate I worked the phones. A call to my lawyer in Boston, who asked me to sign the petition and send it back to her. She also gave me a fast piece of advice: *don't panic.* A call to a small hotel five hours north of here to find out if they had a room available for the next seven days. When they confirmed they had a vacancy, I told them to expect me around six that evening. Within an hour I had showered and shaved and packed a bag. I grabbed my laptop and a set of cross-country skis, then loaded everything into my Jeep. I called my daughter on her cell phone and left her a message that I would be away for the next seven days but would see her for dinner two weeks from Tuesday. I closed up my cottage. I checked my watch. Nine a.m. As I climbed into my vehicle snow had begun to fall. Within moments the conditions were near-blizzard. But I still forced my vehicle out onto the road and carefully navigated myself toward the intersection with Route 1. Looking in my rearview mirror, I saw that my cottage had vanished. A simple climatic shift and all that is concrete and crucial to us can disappear in an instant, whited out from view.

The snow remained heavy as I turned south and stopped at the post office in Wiscasset. Once the now-signed documents were dispatched, I drove on, heading due west. Visibility was now nonexistent, making any sort of speed impossible. I should have abandoned ship, finding a motel and holing up until the blizzard passed. But I was now locked into the same ornery frame of mind that would overtake me when I found myself unable to write: *you will push your way through this . . .*

It took almost six more hours to reach my destination. When I finally pulled into the parking lot of my hotel in Quebec City, I couldn't help but wonder what I was doing here.

I was so tired from all the events of the day that I fell into bed at ten. I managed to sleep until dawn. When I woke up, there was the usual moment of befuddlement, followed by the arrival of anguish. Another day, another struggle to keep the pain tolerable. After breakfast I changed into the appropriate clothing and drove north along the St. Lawrence River to a cross-country skiing center I'd once visited with Jan. The temperature——according to the gauge in my car—— was minus ten. I parked and climbed outside, the chill lacerating and vindictive. I pulled my skis and poles out of the hatchback door and walked over to the trail head. I stepped into the skis, my boots slotting into the bindings with a decisive click. Immediately I pushed off into the dense forest through which the trail had been cleaved. The cold was now so severe that my fingers stiffened. It was impossible to close them around the poles. But I forced myself to gain speed. Cross-country skiing is an endurance test——especially in subzero temperatures. Only when you have gained enough forward propulsion to warm your body does the unbearable become acceptable. This process took around a half hour, each finger gradually thawing with the buildup of body heat. By the third mile I was actually warm and so focused on the *push-glide-push-glide* rhythm of the ski movement that I was oblivious to all around me.

Until the trail turned a hairpin bend and suddenly sent me charging down a vertiginous hill. *This is what you get for choosing a black run.* But my past training clicked into gear and I carefully raised my left ski out of the rutted track and positioned it on the groomed snow. Then I turned its tip inward toward the other ski. Normally this maneuver should reduce your speed and allow you to control the dips and dives of the track. But the trail was so frozen, so slick with the travails of previous occupants, that I simply couldn't slow down. I tried dragging my poles. No use. That's when I suddenly pulled my ski back into the track, lifted my poles, and let go. I was now on a ferocious downhill trajectory——all speed, no logic, no sense of what was up ahead. For a few brief moments there was the exhilaration of the free fall, the abandonment of prudence, the sense that nothing mattered but this plunge toward . . .

A tree. It was right there, its massive trunk beckoning me forward. Gravity was sending me into its epicenter. Nothing to stop me slamming into oblivion. For a nanosecond I was about to welcome it . . . until I saw my daughter's face in front of me and found myself overwhelmed by one thought: *she will have to live with this for the rest of her life.* At which point some rational instinct kicked in and I threw myself away from sudden impact. As I crashed into the snow, I skidded for yards. The snow was no pillow, rather, a sheet of frozen tundra. My left side slammed into its concrete surface, then my head, the world went blurry, and . . .

I was aware of someone crouching down beside me, checking my vital signs, speaking fast French into a phone. Beyond that, all was hazy, vague. I wasn't aware of much, bar the fact that I was in pain everywhere. I blacked out, waking again as I was hoisted onto a stretcher, loaded onto a sled, strapped down, and . . .

I was now being dragged along undulating terrain. I regained consciousness for long enough to crane my neck and see myself being pulled along by a snowmobile. Then my brain began to fog in again and . . .

I was in a bed. In a room. Stiff white sheets, cream walls, institutional ceiling tiles. I craned my neck and saw assorted tubes and wires emanating from my body. I began to gag. A nurse came hurrying toward me. She grabbed a pan and held it in front of me as I retched. When everything was expunged, I found myself sobbing. The nurse put an arm around me and said:

"Be happy . . . you're alive."

A doctor came around ten minutes later. He told me I'd had a lucky escape. A dislocated shoulder——which, while I was unconscious, they'd managed to "relocate." Some spectacular bruising on my left thigh and ribcage. As to the state of my head . . . he'd run an MRI on my cranium and could find nothing wrong with it.

"You'd been knocked cold. A concussion. But you evidently have a very hard head, as there was no serious damage whatsoever."

Would that my head was so hard.

I subsequently discovered that I was in a hospital in Quebec City. I would remain here for another two days as I underwent physiotherapy for my battered shoulder and was kept under observation for any "unforeseen neurological complications." The physiotherapist——a Ghanaian woman with a rather wry take on everything——told me I should thank some divine force for my well-being.

"It is evident that you should be in a very bad place right now. But you came away with very little damage, so someone was watching over you."

"And who might that 'someone' be?"

"Maybe it's God. Maybe it's some extraworldly power. Or maybe, just maybe, it's all down to you. There was a skier behind you . . . the man who called for help . . . who said that you were racing down the hill, as if you couldn't care less what happened to you. Then, at the very last minute, you jumped away from the tree. You saved yourself. Which evidently means that you wanted to see another day. Congratulations: you are back with us."

I felt no exhilaration, no pleasure in having survived. But as I sat in that narrow hospital bed, looking up at the pockmarked ceiling tiles, I did keep replaying that moment when I threw myself into the snow. Up until that split second, I was in thrall to the declivitous, as there was a part of me that welcomed such existential purity, an immediate cure to all that plagued me.

But then . . .

I saved myself, ending up with nothing more than some bruising, a sore shoulder, a sore head. Within forty-eight hours of being admitted to the hospital I was able to make it out to a taxi, return to the ski area, and collect my abandoned Jeep. Though I wasn't in a sling, my shoulder hurt every time I had to turn the wheel sharply all the way down to Maine. But the journey back was otherwise uneventful.

"You may find yourself becoming depressed now," the physiotherapist told me during our last session together. "It often happens in the wake of such things. And who can blame you? You chose to live."

I reached Wiscasset just before dark——in time to collect my mail at the local post office. There was a yellow slip in my box, informing me an oversized parcel was being held behind the main counter. Jim, the postmaster, noticed me wincing when I picked up the package.

"You hurt yourself?" he asked.

"That I did."

"An accident?"

"Something like that."

The package he handed over was, in fact, a box——and came from my New York publishers. I made a mistake of tucking it under my left arm and winced once more as my weakened shoulder told me not to do that again. As I signed the form acknowledging that I had collected it, Jim said:

"If you're feeling poorly tomorrow and can't get yourself to the supermarket, call me with a shopping list and I'll take care of it all for you."

There were many virtues about living in Maine——but the best of all was the way everyone respected each other's privacy, yet were also there for you if needed.

"I think I'll be able to push a cart around the vegetable aisle," I said. "But thanks for the offer."

"That your new book in the box?"

"If it is, someone else must have finished for me."

"I hear ya . . ."

I walked to the car and drove on to my cottage, the January darkness augmenting my gloom. The physiotherapist was right: escaping death turns you more inward, more alive to the melancholic nature of being here. And a failed marriage is also a death——a living one, as the person you are no longer with is still sentient, still walking among us, very much existing without you.

"You were always ambivalent about me, *us*," Jan said on several occasions toward the end. How could I explain that, with the exception of our wonderful daughter, I remain ambivalent about *everything?* If you're not reconciled with yourself, how can you ever be reconciled with others?

The cottage was dark and drafty when I arrived. I carried the box in from my car and placed it on the kitchen table. I cranked up the thermostat. I built a wood fire in the potbellied stove that took up one corner of the living room. I poured myself a small Scotch. As I waited for all three forms of central heating to kick in, I shuffled through the handful of letters and magazines that I had retrieved from the mailbox. Then I turned my attention to the package. I used scissors to cut through the thick tape that had sealed it shut. Once the lid was pried open I peered inside. There was a letter from Zoe, my editor's assistant, positioned on top of a large, thickly padded envelope. As I picked up the letter I saw the handwriting on this envelope——and the German postmark and stamps. In the left-hand corner of this package was the name of the sender: *Dussmann*. That stopped me short. Her name. And the address: *Jablonski Strasse 48, Prenzlauer Berg, Berlin*. Was this her address since . . . ?

Her . . .

Petra . . .

Petra Dussmann.

I picked up the letter from Zoe.

> This showed up here for you c/o us a few days ago. I didn't want to open it in case it was personal. If it's anything questionable or weird, do let me know and we'll deal with it.
>
> Hope the new book goes well. We all can't wait to read it.
>
> My best . . .

"If it's anything questionable or weird . . ."
No, it's just the past. A past that I had tried to entomb long ago. But here it was again, back to disturb an already troubled present.

"Wie bald 'nicht jetz' 'nie' wird."

"How soon 'not now' becomes 'never.'"

Until a package arrives . . . and everything you have spent years attempting to dodge comes rushing back into the room.

When is the past not a spectral hall of shadows?

When we can live with it.

TWO

I'VE ALWAYS WANTED to escape. It's an urge I've had from the age of eight onward, when I first discovered the pleasures of evasion.

It was a Saturday in November and my parents were fighting again. There was nothing unusual about this. My parents were always fighting. Back then we lived in a four-room apartment on Nineteenth Street and Second Avenue. I was a Manhattan kid, born and bred. My dad worked as a midlevel executive in an advertising agency——a "business guy" who wanted to be a "creative guy," but never had the "word talent" to write copy. Mom was a housewife. The apartment was cramped. Two narrow bedrooms, a small living room, and an even smaller dinette/kitchen, none of which could contain the frustrations that both my parents vented on a daily basis.

It was only years later that I began to comprehend the strange dynamic that existed between them, a profound need to combust over anything, to live in an endless winter of discontent. But at the time all I knew was: my mom and dad didn't like each other. On the November Saturday in question, an argument between them escalated. My father said something hurtful. My mother called him a bastard and fled into the bedroom. The door slammed behind her. I looked up from the book I was reading. Dad was gripping the front doorknob, no doubt wanting to pull it open and walk away from all this. He fumbled in his shirt pocket for his cigarettes and lit one up. A few deep inhalations of smoke and he got his rage under control. That's when I posed a question I'd been wanting to pose for days.

"Can I go to the library?"

"No dice, Tommy. I'm heading into the office to catch up on some work."

"Can I go alone?"

It was the first time I'd ever asked to leave the apartment by myself. Dad thought this over.

"You think you can walk there all by yourself?" he asked.

"It's only four blocks."

"Your mom won't like it."

"I won't be long."

"She still won't like it."

"Please, Dad."

He took another long drag on his cigarette. For all his tough-guy bluster——he'd been a Marine during the war——he was in thrall to my mother, a diminutive, angry woman who could never get over the fact that she was no longer the princess she'd been raised to be.

"You'll be back here in an hour?" Dad asked.

"I promise."

"And you'll remember to look both ways when crossing the street?"

"I promise."

"If you're late, there'll be trouble."

"I won't be late, Dad."

He reached into his pocket and handed me a dollar.

"Here's some money," he said.

"I don't need money. It's a library."

"You can stop at the drugstore on the way back and get yourself an egg cream."

Egg creams——milk and chocolate syrup topped up by soda water——were my favorite drink.

"They only cost a dime, Dad." Even back then I was always cognizant of the price of things.

"Buy yourself some comics or put the change in your piggy bank."

"So I can go?"

"Yeah, you can go."

As I was getting into my coat, Mom emerged from the bedroom.

"What do you think you're doing?" she asked me.

I told her. Immediately she turned on my father.

"How dare you give him permission to do that without first consulting me."

"The kid is old enough to walk a couple of blocks by himself."

"Well, I'm not allowing it."

"Tommy, run along," Dad said.

"Thomas, you're to stay here," she countered.

"Scram," Dad told me. As Mom began to shout things at my father, I made a beeline for the door and was gone.

Once outside I felt a moment of fear. For the first time ever I was on my own. No parental supervision; no outstretched hand to guide, restrain, or discipline me. I walked to the corner of Nineteenth and Second. I waited for the light to turn green. I looked both ways many times. I crossed the street. When I made it to the other side, I didn't feel a great sense of accomplishment or freedom. I was simply aware of the promise that I made to Dad to be back within an hour. So I continued north, exercising great prudence at every street crossing. When I reached Twenty-third Street, I turned left. The library was halfway up the street. The children's section was on the first floor. I browsed the stacks, finding two new Hardy Boys detective books I'd yet to read. I checked them out, then hurried back to the street, retracing my steps home. Halfway there, I stopped at the drugstore on Twenty-first Street. I took a stool at the lunch counter and opened one of my books and ordered an egg cream. The soda jerk took my dollar and gave me ninety cents change. I looked at the clock on the wall. I still had twenty-eight minutes before I was due home. I nursed my egg cream. I read my book. I thought: *this is nice.*

I made it home five minutes before the deadline. In the time that I was absent, my father had stormed out——and I found my mother sitting in the kitchenette with her big Remington typewriter in front of her. She was smoking a Salem and clattering away on the keys. Her eyes were red from crying, but she seemed focused and determined.

"How was the library?" she asked me.

"It was good. Can I go again on Monday?"

"We'll see," she said.

"What are you writing?" I asked.

"A novel."

"You write novels, Mom?" I asked, really impressed.

"I'm trying to," she said and continued tapping away. I adjourned to the sofa and read one of my Hardy Boys books. Half an hour later Mom stopped writing and told me that she was going to have a bath. I heard her pull paper out from the typewriter. As she disappeared into the bathroom and turned on the taps, I approached the dining table. She had left two manuscript pages facedown next to the typewriter. I picked them up. The first page just contained the title of the book and her name:

THE DEATH OF A MARRIAGE

A Novel

by

Alice Nesbitt

I picked up the next page. The opening sentence read:

> The day I discovered that my husband didn't love me anymore was the day that my eight-year-old son ran away from home.

Suddenly I heard my mother shout:

"How dare you!"

She came racing toward me, tight with rage. She pulled the pages out of my hand and slapped my face.

"You must never, *never* read my work."

I burst into tears and ran into my room. I grabbed a pillow off my bed and did what I often did when things got out of hand at home: I hid in the closet, locking the door behind me. With the pillow clutched tight, I sobbed into it, overwhelmed by the feeling that I was all alone in a very difficult world. Ten, maybe fifteen minutes passed. Then there was a knock on the closet door.

"I've made you chocolate milk, Thomas."

I said nothing.

"I'm sorry I slapped you."

I said nothing.

"Thomas, please . . . I was wrong."

I said nothing.

"You can't stay in there all day, you know."

She tried opening the door.

"Thomas, this is not funny."

I said nothing.

"Your father will be very cross . . ."

Finally, I spoke:

"My father will understand. He hates you, too."

This last comment provoked a terrible sob from my mother. I heard her stumble away from the door and head out of my room. Her crying escalated. It became so loud that, even from within my self-incarcerated lair, I could hear her weeping. I stood up and unlocked the door and opened it. Immediately I had to readjust to all the afternoon light cascading through the windows of my room. I followed the sound of Mom's lament. She was lying facedown on her bed.

"I don't hate you," I said.

She continued crying.

"I just wanted to read your book."

She continued crying.

"I'm going out to the library again."

The crying instantly stopped. She sat up.

"Are you planning to run away?" she asked.

"Like the boy in your book?"

"That was make-believe."

"I don't want to run away," I lied. "I just want to go back to the library."

"You promise you'll come home?"

I nodded.

"Be careful on the street."

As I turned to leave, Mom said:

"Writers are very private about what they do. That's why I got angry . . ."

She let the sentence die.

And I headed for the door.

Decades later, during our third date, I remember recounting this story to Jan.

"Did your mom ever finish the book?" she asked.

"I never saw her typing again. But perhaps she worked on it while I was at school."

"Maybe's there a manuscript hidden in some attic box somewhere."

"I found nothing when Dad asked me to clear out all her stuff after she died."

"And it was lung cancer that got her . . . ?"

"At the age of forty-six. Mom and Dad never stopped fighting and they never stopped smoking. Cause and effect."

"But your father is still with us?"

"Yeah, Dad's on his fifth girlfriend since Mom's death and still puffing twenty a day."

"And meanwhile, you've never stopped escaping."

"More cause and effect."

"Maybe you've just never found a good reason for staying put," she said, covering my hand.

I just shrugged and didn't reply.

"Now you have me interested," she said.

"Everyone has an old ache or two."

"True. But there are aches you can live with, and ones that seem to never fade away. Which is yours?"

I smiled and said:

"Oh, I live with most things."

"And now you're sounding far too stoic."

"Nothing wrong with that," I said and changed the subject.

Jan never did learn about that ache——as I always dodged discussions of it. In time, however, she did come to believe that it still impacted on the present and colored so much between us. Just as she also came to the conclusion that there was a significant part of me that was closed off to any real intimacy. But that analysis was reached some time down the road.

And on the next date——the night we also first slept together——I could see her deciding that I was . . . well, *different*. She was a lawyer, an associate at a major Boston firm. She earned her money representing big corporations but also insisted on handling one pro bono case per year "to salve my conscience." Unlike me, she'd been in a long relationship, a fellow lawyer who took a job out west and used the move to end it between them.

"You think things are solid, then you discover otherwise," she said. "And you wonder why your antennae didn't pick up the fact that all was going wrong."

"Maybe he was telling you one thing and thinking another," I said. "Which is often the way these things happen. Everyone has a part of themselves they prefer not to reveal. It's why we can never really fathom even those close to us. The unknowingness of others and all that."

"'And the most foreign place is the self.' That's a direct quote from your book on Alaska."

"Well, I'd be a liar if I didn't say I was flattered."

"It's a great book."

"Really?"

"You mean, you don't know that?"

"As I have the usual writerly distrust of anything I've ever committed to paper . . ."

"Why such incertitude?"

"It just goes with the territory, I suppose."

"In my profession incertitude is not allowed. In fact, an uncertain lawyer is never trusted."

"But surely you have a measure of uncertainty?"

"Not when I'm defending a client or making a closing argument. I have to be indisputable. In private, on the other hand, I'm unsure about everything."

"Glad to hear that," I said, covering her hand with mine.

That was the real start of things between us, the moment we both decided to let our defenses down and fall for each other. Is love often predicated on good timing? How often have I heard friends say that they got married because they were *ready* to get married? That was my dad's story——and one that he related to me just after my mother died. And it went like this:

It was 1957. He'd been out of the Marine Corps for four years, having then gone to Columbia on the GI Bill. He'd just landed a junior executive job at Young & Rubicon. His sister was marrying a former war correspondent turned PR man——a marriage that went south right after the Palm Beach honeymoon but dragged on until her husband drank and raged himself into a fatal coronary fifteen years later. But on the happy day in question, Dad saw a diminutive young woman across a crowded function room at the Roosevelt Hotel. Her name was Alice Goldfarb. Dad described her as the antithesis of the "corned beef and cabbage" Irish girls he knew growing up in Prospect Heights, Brooklyn. Her father was a jeweler in the Diamond District, her mother a professional yenta. But Alice had gone to the right schools and could talk about classical music and the ballet and Arthur Miller and Elia Kazan. And Dad——being a smart but intellectually insecure Brooklyn mick——was charmed and just a little flattered that this Central Park West cutie was interested in him.

So there he was, the altar boy turned Korean War vet turned young ad exec. Aged twenty-six. No responsibilities to anyone but himself. The world was his for the taking.

"And what do I do?" he told me as we sat alone together in the limousine that followed the hearse en route to the cemetery with my mother's coffin. "I go for the princess, even though I knew from the outset that I would never make her happy, that she belonged with some Park Avenue ophthalmologist with a weekend place near a Jewish country club on the Island. But I still had to send myself in her direction. And the result was . . ."

But he never finished the sentence, sinking back into the thickly upholstered seat and reaching for his cigarettes while muffling a deep, anguished sob.

"And the result was . . ."

What? Disappointment? Unhappiness? Sadness? Entrapment? Anger? Rage? Disquiet? Despair? Resignation?

Take your pick of any of the above to fill in the blank. As any thesaurus will show you, there are a vast number of synonyms in the language that reflect our grievances with life.

"And the result was . . ."

Can we ever really predict what that result will be? Consider the random nature of an encounter: a look across a room; a casual conversation on a subway train. Consider, a little further on from this initial meeting, the decision to take the hand of this person as she sits opposite you in a restaurant. Your companion may pull away. She may allow you to keep it there. She may take this as a sign of intent or nothing more than a come-on. She may think you're worth spending a night with and change her mind ten minutes later. She may be wanting something more. She may be wanting something far less. In the aftermath of whatever happens, there is one undisputable fact surrounding the event: when you took her hand, you were after something. Though you might think, at the time, that this "something" is rooted in an obvious need (sex, romance, or other variations on an amorous theme), the truth is: you won't understand what the true meaning of the moment was until long after it has been stored in that cluttered room we litter with memory. Even then, the hindsight that we bring to this incident will only serve to heighten the conflicting emotions surrounding said memory . . . if, that is, there is any memory to begin with. Everything's interpretation, after all. As such, we can look back on an action, a gesture, several words uttered without premeditation, and find ourselves wondering: *did everything change because of that?* Or are we simply rendering the past in such a way to explain the uncomfortable realities of the present?

"And the result was . . ."

A bad marriage that lasted twenty-four years, that saw the two players in this melodrama play endless self-destructive games and my mother commit suicide on the installment plan, courtesy of cigarettes. Say my mother——who had finally broken it off with a certified public accountant named Lester Hamburger only a week before——hadn't shown up at the wedding? Or say she had arrived with Lester in tow? Would that look across the room have ever happened? Would Dad have met someone more caring, more loving, less judgmental? Would Mom have ended up with the rich bohemian she always talked about wanting to marry——though Lester Hamburger and my Nixon-supporting dad weren't exactly the Rimbaud and Verlaine of Manhattan. But one thing is for certain: had Alice Goldfarb and Dan Nesbitt not have hooked up, their shared unhappiness would have never existed——and the trajectory of their lives may have been completely different.

Or maybe not.

Similarly, if I had not reached for Jan Stafford's hand on that third date . . . well, I would certainly not be sitting here in this cottage, glancing anxiously at the petition for divorce that still occupied the same place on the kitchen table when I fled from it days ago. That's the thing about a tangible reality like a divorce petition. You may shove it to one side or walk away from it. But it's still there. It does not go away. You have been named as the respondent. You are now answerable to a legal process. You can't dodge this fact. Questions will be asked, answers demanded. And a price will be paid.

My lawyer had been in touch with me by email a few times since I'd been served with the petition.

"She's asking for the house in Cambridge and wants you to pay Candace's graduate school tuition, should your daughter decide to go that route," she wrote in one of her dispatches. "Considering your wife's income is five times larger than yours——and that yours is completely predicated on what you write——we could argue that she is in a far better financial position to . . ."

Let her have the house——and I will find a way of paying Candace's tuition. I don't want costly legal disputes or further rancor. I just want a clean break.

I pushed the petition away. I still wasn't prepared to engage with it. Instead, I stood up and negotiated the narrow staircase up to the second floor of my house. Once there I opened the door to my office: a long, narrow room with bookshelves covering most available space and my desk facing a wall. Dragging my ankle behind me, I reached for the bottle of single malt Scotch located on the filing cabinet to the left of my desk. I poured a shot into a glass and sat down in my desk chair. As I waited for the computer to illuminate, I sipped the whiskey, its peaty warmth numbing the back of my throat. Memory is such a jumble of emotions. An unexpected package arrives——and the past comes cascading in. But though this rush of remembrances and associations may, at first, seem random, one of the great undisputable truths about memory is the fact that there is no such thing as a random recollection. They are all somehow interconnected——for everything is narrative. And the one narrative we all grapple with is the life we call our own.

Which is why——as the whiskey drips down my gullet and my computer screen bathes the otherwise darkened room in an electronic glow——I'm back again at the drugstore lunch counter on East Twenty-first Street, my book propped up against my egg cream. It's the first moment when, perhaps, I understood the necessity of solitude. How many times since then have I found myself alone somewhere——in a place familiar or strange——with reading material propped up against a bottle of something, or an open notebook in front of me, awaiting that day's quota of words. In these instances——no matter how distant or difficult the locale——I've never felt isolated or alone. Then, as now, I often quietly think: whatever about the collateral damage that my parents' unhappiness may have visited upon me, I am enormously grateful to them for sending me off on that November Saturday forty-two years ago, and allowing me to discover that sitting somewhere on your own——outside of the maelstrom of things——has an absolute clean ease to it.

But life, of course, never really leaves you in peace. You can shut yourself away in a cottage on a back road in Maine and a process server will still find his way to your door. Or a package will arrive from across the ocean——and try as you might, you find yourself transported back twenty-five years to a café in a corner of Berlin called Kreuzberg. You have a spiral-bound book in front of you——and the vintage red Parker fountain pen that your father gave you as a going-away gift is in your right hand, blitzing its way across the page. Then you hear a voice. A woman's voice:

"So viele Wörter."

So many words.

You look up. And there she is. Petra Dussmann. From that moment on, things change. But that's only because you yourself answered back.

"Ja, so viele Wörter. Aber vielleicht sind die ganzen Wörter Abfall."

Yes, so many words. But perhaps all the words are crap.

If you hadn't attempted that bit of self-deprecation, might she have moved on? And had she moved on . . . ?

How do we explain the trajectory of things? I haven't a clue. All I know is . . .

It's 6:15 on an evening in late January. And I have words to write. Having just driven six hours in the snow——and having just been sprung from a hospital——I could make sundry excuses to dodge work for the night. But this rectangular room is the one place in which I can exercise dominion over the shape of things. When I write, the world proceeds as I would like it to proceed. I can add and subtract what I want to the narrative. I can create any denouement I desire. There is no legal process to address. There is no sense of personal inadequacy and crippling sadness looming over everything. And there is no shipping box downstairs, the contents of which remain unopened.

When I write, I am in control.

Except that's a lie. As I punch out the first sentence of the evening——and tip back the last of the whiskey——I keep trying to excise my anxiety about the box downstairs. And I keep failing.

Why do we hide things from others? Could it be because, at heart, we all have one central fear: the horror of finally being found out?

I was suddenly out of my desk chair and heading up into my attic. Once there I unlocked one of the filing cabinets in which I keep my old manuscripts. The cabinets had been shipped here from my old house in Cambridge——and had remained untouched since my arrival in Maine. But I still knew immediately where the manuscript I wanted was stored. Pulling it out I had to blow off a decade's worth of dust from the thick folder into which it had been stuffed before I interred it here. Ten years had passed since I'd typed the final word. As soon as I had finished writing it all, I couldn't bring myself to read it. So in it went, interred in the filing cabinet. Until now.

I came downstairs into my study. After dropping the manuscript on my desk I poured myself the second Scotch of the evening. As soon as the whiskey was in the glass, I was back in my chair, inching the manuscript toward me . . .

When is a story not a story?

When you've lived it.

But even then, it's just your version of things.

That's right. My narrative. My rendering. And the reason, all these years later, I find myself where I am now.

I pulled the manuscript out of its folder, staring down at the title page which, all those years ago, I had left blank.

So turn the page and get started.

I downed the whiskey. I took a deep steadying breath. I turned the page.

PART TWO

ONE

BERLIN. THE YEAR was 1984. I had just turned twenty-six. And, like the majority of people residing in that still-juvenile district of adulthood, I actually thought I understood so much about life and its attendant complexities.

Whereas now, more than fifteen years on from all that transpired, I see how unschooled and callow I was when it came to just about everything . . . most especially, the mysteries of the heart.

Back then I always resisted falling in love. Back then I always seemed to sidestep all emotional entanglements, all big-deal declarations from the heart. We all reenact our childhoods repeatedly during adult life—— and every romance struck me as a potential trap, something that would ensnare me in the sort of marriage that drove my mother to death by cigarettes and left my father feeling as if his existence had been limited, circumscribed. "Never have kids," he once told me. "They just cage you into something you never really wanted." Granted, he'd had about three martinis in him when he said all this. But the very fact that he could openly tell his only son that he felt trapped in his life . . . bizarrely, it made me feel closer to the guy. He had confided in me, and that was huge. Because during the majority of my childhood he was a man who spent much of his life working out ways not to be at home. When he was there, he was so often enveloped in a cloud of silent rage and cigarette smoke that he always struck me——even when I was very young——as someone who was endlessly struggling with himself. He tried to play the typical dad but couldn't pull it off, any more than I could play the average American boy. When it came to sports or the Boy Scouts or winning prizes for civics or joining the Marines——all of the all-American stuff that my dad embraced as a kid——I was a strikeout. I was always the last kid chosen for teams at school. I always had my head in a book.

By the time I was well into adolescence, I was out roaming the city every weekend, hiding myself away in movie theaters and museums and concert halls. That was the thing about a Manhattan childhood: it was *all there*. I was the sort of kid who went to seasons of Fritz Lang films at the Bleecker Street Cinema, who bought student tickets for Boulez conducting Stravinsky and Schoenberg at the New York Philharmonic, who haunted bookshops and Off-Off-Broadway theaters that always seemed to be run by Romanian madmen. School was never an issue, because I had already begun to develop certain diligent habits when it came to work . . . perhaps because I had begun to figure out that work was the one source of equilibrium at my disposal, that by applying myself and getting on with the tasks at hand, I could keep all the dark stuff at bay. Dad approved.

"I never thought I'd tell my only kid that I like the fact he's always studying, always reading. But the truth is, it's kind of impressive, considering the C's I got at your age. The only thing I worry about——all these movies and plays and concerts you go to . . . you're always on your own. No girlfriends, no pals you hang out with . . ."

"There's Stan," I said, mentioning a math whiz in my class at school who was also something of a movie addict and, like me, thought nothing of seeing four films during a Saturday. He was hugely overweight and awkward. But we were both loners——and very much outside the team player ethic that was such an integral part of the prep school to which we had both been dispatched. We often look for friends who can make us realize that we are not the only person in the world who feels maladroit with others, or who doubts himself.

"Stan's the fatty, right?" Dad asked. He'd met him once when I had him over after school.

"That's right," I said, "Stan's kind of large."

"Kind of large," Dad said. "If he was my son, I'd send him to a boot camp to get all that blubber off him."

"Stan's a good guy," I told my dad.

"Stan's going to be dead by the time he's forty."

Actually my father got that one right. Stan and I stayed friends over the next thirty years. After a brilliant academic career at the University of Chicago, he ended up living in Berkeley, teaching wildly advanced calculus at the university there. We made a point of seeing each other whenever we found ourselves on either of our respective coasts. When I returned to the States in the summer of 1984 we must have phoned each other every two weeks. Stan never married, though there was always a string of girlfriends, most of whom didn't seem to mind his ever-augmenting weight. He was the only person I ever confided to about all that went on in Berlin in 1984, and I always think about his comment to me after he heard the story: *You'll probably never get over it.*

Jan was never particularly comfortable around Stan, as she knew that he considered her far too cool and distant for me.

"You've really constructed an interesting marriage there," Stan said after the last weekend he spent with us in Cambridge. He was in town to address some conference at MIT. We had dinner after he read a paper on binary number theory. It was a breathtakingly obscurantist lecture. Stan being Stan, the talk also highlighted his pedantic quirks, a performance which, being his friend, I found endearing, but which Jan considered showboating. Over dinner at an Afghan restaurant (his choice) to which we repaired afterward, she dropped one or two hints that she wasn't impressed by his displays of erudite exhibitionism. When Stan congratulated me on the publication of my most recent book——about venturing into the Canadian Arctic——Jan attempted a witticism:

"It's possibly the first book written about the interrelationship between dogsleds and a writer's deep-rooted solipsism."

Stan said nothing in reply. But afterward, as Jan pleaded an early start in the morning in court, I walked my friend back to his hotel near Kendall Square. Halfway there, he noted:

"You're a man who runs away all the time, despite the fact that what you want more than anything in life is to emotionally connect with someone. But like the rest of us, you've been counterintuitive. You've married someone who——as you've intimated over the years——has never really let you near her. Which, in turn, has made you travel more and fabricate the necessary distance to protect yourself from her coldness. Funny, isn't it? She complains that you are away all the time——yet she has always done everything possible to keep you at one remove. And now you're both locked into a pattern of behavior which only a divorce will break."

He fell silent for a moment, letting that last comment sink in. Then, with just the slightest hint of irony in his voice, he asked:

"Of course, what do I know about such things, right?"

When his corroded arteries finally exploded a few weeks later——and I found myself crying uncontrollably in the wake of learning about his death——that final conversation en route to his Cambridge hotel continued to haunt me. Because even when others point out an essential verity about ourselves to ourselves we often reinterpret it in a way that makes it palatable. As in: "Jan may be distant and critical, but who else would put up with my absences and my need to live in my own head?" Whereas I now understand what my great and good friend was really telling me: that I deserved someone who loved me for what I was . . . and if that arrived in my life, I might just stand still for a change

Still the pattern of flight was established early on. Once I started getting involved with women, I could never really stick around. If anyone ever came too close to me, if I sensed interest or love, I would find an excuse to duck and dodge. I was expert at detaching myself from all entanglements. This became even more pronounced after I graduated from college and moved back to New York, determined to try to become a writer. What's that old line of Edna St. Vincent Millay's about childhood being the kingdom where nobody dies? I was a member of a generation that didn't know economic deprivation and wasn't shipped off to a war, so my early twenties were still a time when—— outside of my mother's death——my existence seemed detached from larger realities. I wasn't thinking about the rapidity of passing time or the need to focus on life's bigger pictures. Rather, I lived in the moment. As soon as I was handed my college diploma, I was on the next bus to New York and a job as an editorial assistant at a publishing house. It was 1980 and my starting salary was $16,000 a year. I had little interest in the world of publishing——and I certainly never saw myself as an editor. But the job allowed me to rent a small studio on Sixth Street and Avenue C and live a loose, louche life. I showed up for work. I carved my way through huge stockpiles of unsolicited manuscripts. I went to five movies a week and used a still-valid student ID to get cheap seats for the Philharmonic and the New York City Ballet. I stayed up late most nights, trying to write short stories, often heading·

out of my tiny apartment to catch the last nocturnal set at a jazz club. And I found myself——much to my surprise——involved with a cellist named Ann Wentworth.

She was a young woman who could best be described as willowy. Tall and willowy, with flowing blond hair and skin that was translucent (could skin be that perfect?). I remember when I first met her at a makeshift brunch at a friend's apartment near Columbia University. Like my own downtown garret, the apartment was small. But it had four picture windows that bathed this one room in almost ethereal light. When I first saw Ann, she was dressed in a gossamer skirt that, in the honeyed glow of a summer morning, showed off her long legs. I remember immediately thinking that this was the New York bohemian girl of my dreams . . . and one who played the cello to boot.

Not only did she play the cello, she was gifted. A student at Juilliard, she was mentioned by even her fellow students as a musician to watch, serious talent with serious intelligence.

But what I remember most of all about Ann at the outset was her mixture of worldliness and innocence. She was wildly knowledgeable about books and music. As such, our conversation was always animated—— with me being the intellectual show-off (well, that was my style back then) and Ann always sounding more thoughtful, more considered. I loved that about her. Just as I loved the way her smile was always couched in a certain wistfulness, a hint that, for all her outward optimism (as Ann herself told me, she preferred to see the glass half-full and life as an enterprise full of possibility), she also had a pensive side to her. She would cry easily in bad movies and during certain passages of music (the slow movements of the Brahms sonatas would always get her). She would cry after making love——which we did at every moment possible. And she cried terribly when, four months into our relationship, I put an end to things between us.

It wasn't as if something had gone terribly wrong, or that we ever had the sort of disagreement that led to this permanent fracture. No, Ann's only mistake was to let me know that she genuinely loved me. She had organized a long weekend for us in the family cabin way up in the Adirondacks. It was December 30. A foot of fresh snow had fallen overnight. A fire was burning in the grate, the cabin was fragranced with pine, and we'd just eaten a wonderful dinner and had finished a bottle of wine. We were on the sofa, our arms linked around each other. Looking deep into my eyes she told me:

"You know, my parents have been together since they were twenty . . . and that's over a quarter of a century ago. As my mom told me a few years ago, the moment she saw my father she knew that he was it. Her destiny. That's what I felt when I first saw you."

I smiled tightly, trying to mask my unease. But I knew that I didn't react well to this comment——as sweetly rendered and loving as it so evidently was. Ann saw this and put her arms around me, saying that she wasn't trying to trap me, that, on the contrary, she was willing to wait if I wanted to buzz off to Paris and write for a year, or didn't feel like getting married until we were both twenty-five.

"I don't want you to feel under pressure," she told me, all quiet and loving. "I just want you to know that, for me, you are the man of my life."

The subject was never raised again. But when we returned to the city a few days later, I spent an entire night writing a proposal for a travel book about following the Nile from Cairo to Khartoum. I spent the next week punching out a sample chapter, based on a two-week trip I'd made to Egypt in the summer after leaving college. Thanks to my work in publishing, I knew several agents and interested one of them in the proposed book. She shopped it around to several editors——one of whom informed her that she rarely took a risk on a new and very young writer, but he would be able to part with a paltry $3,000 as an advance for the book. I accepted on the spot. I asked for a four-month leave of absence from work. My boss refused, so I quit. Then I broke the news to Ann. I think what disturbed her most wasn't the realization that I was about to disappear to the far side of North Africa for several months, but the fact that I had been working toward this goal for the past eight weeks and never once intimated to her that I had been plotting my escape.

"Why didn't you tell me?" she asked quietly, the hurt so evident in her eyes.

I just shrugged and looked away. She reached out and took my hand.

"I mean, on one level I'm so happy for you, Thomas. Your first book, commissioned by a major publisher. It's fantastic news. But I just don't understand why you kept it all a secret."

Again, I just shrugged, hating myself for playing the coward.

"Thomas, *please*, talk to me. I love you, and there is so much that is good between us."

I let go of her hand.

"I can't do this anymore," I said, my voice barely above a whisper. Ann was now looking at me, wide-eyed.

"Can't do what?"

"This, *us*."

"But I am not asking you to marry me."

"Even though it's what you want."

"Yes, it is what I want . . . but only because I think you are a wonderful man."

"You don't know me."

She stared at me as if I had slapped her face.

"How can you say that, *how* . . . ?"

"Because it's the truth. Because you'd be much better off with a nicer guy who wants the little life that you . . ."

As soon as the words *little life* were out of my mouth, I regretted them. Because I could see the effect they had on Ann. It was as if I had punched her.

"*Little life?* Is that what you think I want for us?"

Of course, I knew that Ann wasn't a reproduction of my mother. Just as I knew that she would never press me into the sort of domestic hell that so enraged my father (even if he was the co-architect of that hell). No matter how many reassurances she would give me about not pressuring me into an early marriage, the thing was . . . she had told me she loved me. She had told me I was the man with whom she wanted to spend her life. I simply couldn't cope with such knowledge, such responsibility. So I said:

"I'm not ready for the sort of commitment you want or need."

Again she reached for my hand. This time I wouldn't let her take it. Again the hurt and bewilderment in her eyes was vast.

"Thomas, *please*, don't push me away like this. Do your three, four months in Egypt. I'll wait for you. It won't change anything between us. And when you come back we can——"

"I'm not coming back."

Her eyes filled up. She began to cry.

"I don't understand," she said quietly. "We're . . ."

She paused for a moment, and then said the word I knew she'd say, the word I'd dreaded all along:

". . . happy."

A long silence followed as she waited for a response from me. But none was forthcoming.

Some months later, I woke up in a cheap hotel room in Cairo, very much alone, the solitude and sense of dislocation enormous. I found myself replaying that final conversation with Ann, over and over again in my head, wondering why I had so pushed her away. Of course, I knew the answer to that question. I tried to tell myself that it was better this way. After all, I had made the less conformist, more daring decision. I was a man without all those damnable ties that bind. I could float my way through life, have adventures, flings, even run off to the ends of the earth if I felt like it. And I was just in my early twenties, so why tie myself up with someone who would keep me tethered to a life that would limit the proverbial horizon?

But the question that so gnawed at me that night in that Cairo hotel room was: *But did you actually love Ann Wentworth?*

And the answer was: had I been open to the idea, the love would have followed. But as I had an abject terror of what it meant to love and be loved . . . best to detonate the relationship and kill off all possibilities of a future together.

So after that painful *nuit blanche* in Cairo, I decided to put all such difficult sentiments out of my head. I threw myself into my Egyptian travels with a vehemence that surprised even me. Every day I sought out the new, the strange, the extreme. This being Egypt I could find all of the above. I spent time in the City of the Dead——a vast ghetto made up of families so impecunious, so unable to find dwellings in a city of sixteen million citizens hemmed in by the desert, that they had to rent tombs in Cairo's vast necropolis. I took a train down to Assyut——a university town that was Egypt's primary breeding ground for Islamic fundamentalists——and loitered with intent among members of the outlawed Muslim Brotherhood. I hitched a ride with two felucca men, floating down the Nile from Luxor to Aswan, sleeping on a mattress and a plain sheet every night on the deck of the boat, purifying Nile water to drink. When I reached Aswan I met a French anthropology student named Stephanie, who was heading south to Khartoum. So we traveled down the Nile to the Sudanese border, and then spent a mad week on a series of buses that never traveled more than 150 kilometers a day. They deposited us in nowhere villages with primitive hotels that cost, on average, two dollars a night. I remember making love with Stephanie on a series of straw mattresses, in mud-brick buildings that frequently adjoined an outhouse, in nighttime temperatures that were never lower than ninety degrees. When we reached Khartoum, I had economized so rigorously during the five months on the road that I insisted we splurge and check into the fanciest hotel in town: the Grand Holiday Villa, best known as one of those sunstruck spots where Churchill holed up against the English winter to paint those mediocre watercolors for which he was less than famous. The desk clerk looked at Stephanie and me with suspicion, as we hadn't bathed for days and were both covered in a thin film of dust. But after some dickering I managed to bargain us into a large, airy room with a king-sized bed and a huge bathtub for $35 per day (one of the few things that I liked about the Sudan was its cheapness). Stephanie was a small, sinewy woman with excellent English and a worldview that could be best described as sardonic. She was pretty in a severe sort of way and very passionate whenever we made love. But there was also something clinical to her worldview; the physical heat between us turning into detached dispassion afterward.

"I sense this is all far too colonial and bourgeois for me," she said as we shared the huge bathtub in the room, soaking our bedbug-ravaged bodies. "Eric would not approve."

"Who's Eric?"

"The man I live with in Paris."

"I see."

"Does that bother you?"

"Not at all," I said.

She reached over and stroked my head, smiling wryly.

"Try not to be so sad, Thomas."

"Who said I'm sad?"

"You are always sad, Thomas. Just as you are also so amusing and engaging. It's an intriguing combination: so bright, yet so vulnerable and alone. It's been a fantastic quinze jours. I've loved traveling with you, being with you. When you get back to the States, you should look up the woman you left behind. You obviously miss her a great deal."

"I never said anything to you about someone back in the States."

She gave me a small kiss on the lips.

"You didn't need to," she said, then reached over and pulled me on top of her.

Stephanie caught a plane back to Paris the next day. The last I saw of her was when she boarded a taxi to Khartoum Airport. After a light final kiss on the lips, she wished me a good future and vanished off into her own. Life has many such encounters, an individual who comes into your existence courtesy of the music of chance, with whom you are intimate for a short moment or so, and who then drifts out of your ongoing narrative, never to appear again. You travel down this ever-changing line of human geography known as your life. People fall into your path. Some do you good. Some do you bad. Some become friends. Some become people you never want to see again. You fall in and out of love. You reach out for certain people and they reject you. Others reach for you and you flee. Often you are ignored, just as you ignore others. And in the midst of all these missed and made connections, you try to travel hopefully, always in search of that person who might just make you feel less alone in the world, always cognizant of the fact that, in searching for love, you are also opening yourself up to the possibility of loss. Sometimes these losses are tolerable and you can justify them with bromides like: "It was never meant to be." Or: "Better that it ended quickly." But sometimes you find yourself facing up to a regret that——no matter how hard you attempt to negotiate with it——simply will not leave you in peace.

I had no such lasting regrets about Stephanie. But when I headed to Khartoum Airport a few days later——and began a series of flights via Cairo and Rome that eventually deposited me in New York twenty-four hours later——the sense of emptiness hit me. I returned to my apartment——sublet in my absence for six months to an actor friend——to discover that this gentleman had the personal hygiene of a water rat. I spent the first week fumigating the place and solving a ferocious cockroach problem. Once the apartment was habitable again, I then killed another two weeks repainting it, resanding the floor, and retiling the entire bathroom. I knew the underlying purpose behind all this home renovation: it allowed me to dodge the obligation to kick-start the book into life, and it also stopped me from phoning up Ann Wentworth and gauging whether she wanted me back.

The truth was, I myself didn't know what I wanted. I missed her, but I also knew that a single phone call to her would indicate a desire to accede to her wish. The temptation was a profound one, for so many obvious reasons. A lovely, talented, and (above all) truly nice woman who adored me——and only wanted the best for me, for us. No wonder I stared at the phone so many nights and willed myself to call her. But to do that, I told myself, would be a form of surrender.

Only now do I see the younger man convincing himself that further adventures were awaiting him in the big churning world, that stability and happiness were two synonyms for entrapment.

So the phone remained in its cradle and Ann's number at her little apartment near Columbia was never dialed. Anyway I had a book to write. So once my apartment was freshly painted and general order restored to my tiny slice of Manhattan real estate, I began to work. I had around thirty-five hundred dollars in the bank and figured it would take six months to reshape my many notebooks into something resembling a cogent narrative. Back then, you didn't have to be a corporate player to afford a Manhattan life. My studio set me back $380 a month in rent. You could still go to the movies for five dollars. You could get cheap seats at Carnegie Hall for eight bucks. You could eat breakfast at the local Ukrainian coffee shop on my corner for two-fifty. Knowing that the money I had in the bank would, at best, pay for four months of life, I found a job at the now-vanished Eighth Street Bookshop. Four dollars an hour, thirty hours a week. The pay covered food, utilities, even a couple of nights out every week.

I mention all this because the eight months it finally took me to write *Sunstroke: An Egyptian Journey* now strikes me as a time of great simplicity. I had no commitments, no debts, no ties that bind. When I typed the last line of my first book——on a January night while a blizzard was raging outside——I celebrated with a glass of wine and a cigarette, then fell into bed and slept for fourteen hours. There followed several weeks of excising all the repetitions, misfired ideas, hackneyed metaphors, and all other testaments to bad writing that always make their way into my first drafts. I delivered the manuscript by hand to my editor. Then I took off for two weeks to a college friend's place in Key West: a cheap break in the American tropics, in which I sat in the sun, drank in bars, avoided all novels by Ernest Hemingway, and tried to keep my worry about the book at bay (a worry that has since plagued me every time I've submitted a manuscript, and based on a simple fear: my editor is going to hate it).

As it turned out, Judith Kaplan, my editor of the era, thought the book "most accomplished for a debut" and a "good read." Its publication eight months later resulted in around six reviews nationwide. However, there was a crucial, positive "In Brief" notice in the *New York Times*. It got me several phone calls from assorted editors at good magazines. The book sold four thousand copies and was quickly remaindered. But the fact was: I had published a book. And Judith——deciding that I was worth encouraging (especially in the wake of the mention in the *Times*)——took me out for a good lunch at an expensive Italian restaurant a week after I had come back from Addis Ababa for *National Geographic*.

"Do you know what Tolstoy said about journalism?" she asked after finding out that I was flush with magazine commissions and had long since quit my bookshop job. "It's a brothel. And like most brothels, once you become a client, you keep returning regularly."

"I'm not looking upon magazine writing as anything but an excuse to travel the world at somebody else's expense and get paid a dollar a word."

"So if I was to inquire if you were thinking about a new book for us . . ."

"I would say: I already have an idea."

"Well, that's an excellent start. And what may this idea be?"

"It's one word: Berlin."

Over the next half hour I sketched out how I wanted to spend a year living in the city——and write a book that would be very much "a fiction that happened . . . twelve months in that western island floating within the Eastern bloc; the place where the two great isms of the twentieth century rubbed up against each other like tectonic plates; a town that prided itself on its anarchism, its demimonde credentials, its ongoing whiff of Weimar Republic decadence. Yet it was also a center of gravity for a certain kind of outsider who wanted to exist amidst the edgy, walled-in realities of a metropolis with a storied and hideous past, now rubbing shoulders daily with the monochromatic bleakness of Communism."

For someone who has often been accused of being a little closed-off, I've always had a certain talent when it comes to pitching an idea, especially in the knowledge that it could get me on a plane somewhere. Having carefully thought through this spiel before heading out to lunch with Judith, I reeled it off with a fluency and a confidence that I hoped didn't sound too rehearsed.

"Now don't tell me all that came to you just now," she said when I finished. "But it does sound like the makings of a damn good book . . . especially if you can do what you did with the Egypt book and make us interested in the people that you meet. That's your greatest strength, Thomas: the fact you are fascinated by other people's worlds, the way you really do get the idea that every life is its very own novel."

She paused to take a sip of her wine.

"Now go home and write me a slam-dunk proposal that I can get past those stiffs in the sales and marketing department. And tell your agent to give me a call."

The proposal was written and submitted within a week. I had a thumbs-up from my publisher three weeks later (oh, for the days when publishing was so straightforward, so willing to back a modest idea, so writer-centric). And my agent did well with the deal, garnering me a $9,000 advance——half of which was to be paid up front. Given that it was three times my first contract, I was elated. Especially as I was able to wave this new contract under the noses of several magazine editors and come away with three commissions from Harper's, National Geographic, and The Atlantic Monthly, which added another $5,000 to my kitty. I started doing proper research about minor details like the cost of living and discovered that in a scruffy area like Wedding I could prob-ably find a room in a shared apartment for around 150 deutsche marks a month——which, at the time, was around one hundred bucks. And thinking that it might give the book an interesting texture if I were to be somehow tangentially involved in the city's Cold War complexities, I also sent my résumé and a copy of my Egyptian tome to Radio Liberty in Washington. They were the US-government-funded broadcasting network that beamed in news and the American worldview to all countries behind the Iron Curtain. Along with my book, I attached a résumé and a cover letter explaining that I was planning to spend a year in Berlin and might there be some sort of opening for a writer in their offices there.

I didn't expect to hear back from them, filing the whole thing away under "long shot." I also figured they were probably the sort of organization that only hired rabid anti-Communists who were also bilingual. But a letter did arrive from Washington one afternoon. It was from a gentleman named Huntley Cranley, the director of programming, who informed me that he found my book and my résumé most interesting, and he was dispatching them on to Jerome Wellmann, the head of Radio Liberty in Berlin. Once there I should inform him that I was in town. After that, it was all down to the discretion of Mr. Wellmann whether he granted me an audience or not.

A week later——my apartment sublet again, my one suitcase packed, a heavy army greatcoat on my back——I folded this letter into a German-English dictionary, which I then threw into my shoulder bag. After turning off the lights and double locking the door, I took the bus out to Kennedy Airport on a grim January evening when sleet simply wouldn't transform itself to snow. There, I checked in my bag, accepted a boarding pass, passed through the usual array of detectors and security, squeezed myself into my assigned seat, watched the skyline of Manhattan recede into nocturnal midwinter gloom, and quietly drank myself to sleep as the plane achieved cruising altitude and journeyed east.

When I awoke many hours later, my head was still thick and gloomy after far too many miniatures of Scotch. I peered out the window and saw nothing but the gray density of cloud.

That's the thing about finding yourself in the clouds, I remember thinking at the time. *You are in somewhere which looks like nowhere. You are flying through a blank page . . . and you have no idea what's to be written on it.*

Then the cloud turned to mist, the mist burned away, and down below there was . . .

Land. Fields. Buildings. The outline of a city on the curved edge of the horizon. And all refracted through the numbness of a night spent sleeping sitting up in a cramped seat. We had another ten minutes or so before touchdown. Reaching into my jacket pocket, I pulled out the bag of tobacco and rolling papers that had been my constant companion since my final year at college——and which had, without question, helped me negotiate all the nervy moments at my desk over the past year. Put simply, I had become a serious smoker during the course of writing my first book and needed at least fifteen cigarettes to carry myself through most days. And now——even though the "No Smoking" sign had been switched on——I was already pulling out my smoking paraphernalia and quickly fashioning a cigarette, which could be lit up as soon as I was inside the terminal building.

Land. Fields. Buildings. Specifically: the high-rise outline of Frankfurt, that most mercantile and aesthetically flat of German cities. I had studied German since my freshman year at college. It had always been a complex relationship: a love of the language's density of form and structural rigor coupled with the desperate grind of the dative case and the *longueurs* that accompany trying to drill a language into your head, especially when you are living largely outside said language. I had toyed with the idea of spending an entire year studying in Germany——but instead chose to spend my junior year editing the college newspaper. How could I have thought that being editor in chief of a student newspaper was in some way more important than having a year playing the student prince at Tübigen or Heidelberg and knocking around assorted European capitals? It was the last time I ever made a deliberately careerist decision, and it was one which taught me a lesson: whenever the choice was between doing something practical and self-advancing or the chance to disappear out of town, always go with the latter decision.

Now——as if to prove that point once more——I had again slammed the door on the life I was leading and jumped a plane heading eastward. After we touched down and dealt with the attendant frontier formalities in Frankfurt, I boarded another flight venturing even farther east. Less than an hour later, I peered out the window. There it was, directly below us.

The Wall.

As the plane dipped its wings and began to circle over the eastern front of Berlin, that long, snaking concrete edifice became more defined.

Even from this high altitude, it was so formidable, so severe, so conclusive. Before the clouds broke and The Wall became a scenic reality, we had spent the previous thirty minutes bouncing through turbulence over German Democratic Republic airspace, brought about (as the American pilot explained) by having to fly at just 10,000 feet over this foreign country.

"They worry that if the commercial planes fly any higher," the woman next to me said, "they'll engage in surveillance. For the enemy. Who is everyone outside the Warsaw Pact and the 'fraternal brotherhood' of fellow socialist prison camps, like Cuba, Albania, North Korea . . ."

I looked at this woman. She was in her early fifties——dressed in a severe suit, slightly heavy in the face, puffing away on an HB cigarette (the pack displayed on the armrest between us), her eyes reflecting a tired intelligence; someone, I sensed immediately, who had seen a great many things she would have preferred not to have seen.

"And might you have had experience of such a prison?" I asked.

"What makes you think that?" she asked, taking a deep long drag off her cigarette.

"Just a hunch."

She stubbed out her cigarette and reached for another, telling me:

"I know they will put on the no-smoking sign in two minutes, but I can never fly over this place and not light up. It's almost Pavlovian."

"So when did you get out?"

"Thirteen August, 1961. Hours before they sealed all the borders and began to build that 'Antifascist Detection Device' you see below you."

"How did you know you had to leave?"

"You ask a lot of questions. And your German isn't bad. You a journalist?"

"No, just someone who asks a lot of questions."

She paused for a moment, giving me a quizzical look, wondering if she could trust me with whatever she was about to say, yet also very much wanting to impart her story to me.

"You want a real cigarette?" she asked, noticing that I was rolling yet another one on top of my Olivetti typewriter case.

"That would be nice."

"Fancy typewriter," she said.

"A going-away gift."

"From whom?"

"My father."

On the night before my departure, I'd arranged to see Dad at his favorite "Jap joint," as he called the Japanese restaurant he frequently patronized in the Forties off Lexington Avenue. While there he threw back three saka-tinis (a martini make with sake), then asked the waiter to get him something he'd left in the cloakroom. He ended up presenting me with a fountain pen and a fancy new red Olivetti typewriter, an emblematic piece of modern Italian design. I was both thrown by his generosity and impressed by his good taste. But when I told him this, he just laughed and said:

"Doris——the broad I'm banging right now——she picked it out. Said a published writer like you needs a swanky machine like this one. Know what I told her? 'One day I gotta read my kid's book.'"

Suddenly he flinched, knowing he'd just revealed something he would have preferred to not have revealed.

"Shit, did I say something stupid or what?" he asked.

"It's fine, Dad."

"It's just the booze talking, Tommy."

"Of course it is. And thanks for the cool gift."

"You write well with it, got me?"

I nodded, keeping my hurt to myself, wishing myself anywhere but here.

"He must be a nice man," the woman next to me said, eyeing the seriously stylish red plastic case in which the typewriter was housed.

I said nothing. I just smiled. She noted that.

"So he's not a nice guy?" she asked.

"He's a complex guy."

"And he probably loves you very much . . . and doesn't know how to express it. Hence the nice gift. If you're not a journalist, then you must be some sort of writer."

"So who told you to leave the GDR?" I asked, quickly changing the subject.

"No one did. I overheard talk."

She lowered her head, lowered her voice.

"My father . . . he was a senior member of the Party in Leipzig. And he was part of a top-secret group that had been briefed by the hierarchy in Berlin. I was thirty at the time. Married, no children, wanting to leave my husband——a functionary in a government bureau in which I had a job. As my father was high up, my position was considered glamorous by GDR standards: a senior receptionist at one of the big international hotels in the city. I had Saturday lunch every week with my parents. We were close, especially as I was their only child. My father doted on me, even though, given his Party connections, I could never express what I silently thought: our country was becoming more and more of a place where you were either with the Party or shut out of anything the society could offer you. I wanted to travel. That was simply impossible, except to other gray fraternal socialist states. But I articulated none of this to my parents, as they were both true believers. Until I heard my father, on that Saturday, tell my mother that she should stay indoors Sunday and not answer the phone, as there was going to be a 'big change' happening overnight.

"I had heard rumors for weeks, months, that the government was going to finally seal the borders——which, in Berlin, still remained porous. Walter Ulbricht——he was the general secretary of the Party at the time——was always going on about the 'leakage' at the frontier; the traitors who turned their back on our 'humane, utopian' society for the 'nightmarish filth of the capitalist West.'

"I was returning from the bathroom when my father told my mother about staying inside the next day, and only overheard it as I approached the sitting room where we were taking coffee. I froze when my father's voice whispered to her about the 'big change overnight.' I felt as if I was in free fall. Because I knew what this meant. And I knew that I had only hours to act if I wanted to . . .

"I checked my watch. It was twelve minutes to three. I steadied myself. I went back into the sitting room. I finished drinking coffee with my parents, then excused myself, telling them I was going swimming with a girlfriend at the public baths. I kissed them both good-bye and resisted the desire to hold them close, especially my father, because I sensed I would not be seeing them again for a very long time.

"Then I rode my bicycle home. Happily, Stefan, my husband, was playing football that afternoon with the other functionaries from the housing department where he worked. So he was away from the sad little apartment we shared together. I always thought that one of life's greater ironies. Stefan worked in the department in charge of allocating apartments in Leipzig, and he could only get us this depressing little place. But that was Stefan. He always thought very small. Anyway, I let myself into our place. Once inside I collected a few small items: a change of clothes, a small stash of actual west deutsche marks, my passport, and whatever eastmarks I could find. I was there no longer than ten minutes. Then I rode my bike to the Hauptbahnhof and boarded the three-forty-eight express to Berlin. Within two hours I was there. I had a friend in the city, a man named Florian with whom——I can talk about this now——I was romantically linked. Not love. Just occasional comfort. But available whenever he came to Leipzig or on the rare occasions when I was in Berlin. He was a journalist with the party newspaper, *Neues Deutschland*. But, like me, he was also, in private, someone who had grown more and more doubtful about the regime, about the future. He also told me, two weeks earlier when he was in Leipzig, that he had a friend in Berlin who knew of a place where you could cross over from Friedrichshain to Kreuzberg without detection . . . not that the frontier between the two cities had been sealed off as of yet.

"So as soon as I reached Berlin I called Florian. As luck would have it, he was in. He'd just been recently divorced, and had been spending the afternoon with his five-year-old daughter, Jutta. He'd just returned home after dropping her back to her mother's when I called. His apartment was in Mitte. I walked over from Alexanderplatz to his place. When I arrived, I asked him to step out into the street, because I was worried his place might have been bugged. Then I told him what I knew, that a 'big change' was going to happen late tonight and I was certain this meant the border would be sealed. Like me, Florian went into immediate panic when he heard my news. The thing was, his editor must have been also informed by the Party hierarchy, as all staff leave had been canceled for the weekend and he had been told to report to work by eight a.m. Sunday morning——rather than midday, which was when everyone started work on the Monday morning edition.

"Florian never once said to me, 'Are you sure about this?' He believed me one hundred percent. And he started thinking out loud. 'You know that my ex-wife is very high up in the Party. If I went back for Jutta now, she might get suspicious. But when they close the border tomorrow . . . Then again, what is better? That my daughter comes with me to the West or stays here with her mother?'

"This monologue went on for several minutes. Night had fallen. It was almost eight in the evening. Time was running out. I looked at my watch and told him that we had to go now. He nodded and told me to wait outside. It was a warm August night. I smoked two cigarettes and looked at the street. Gray buildings, all in a run-down state, all painted in the bleak, functional palette of Communism. I thought about my father and whether my departure would hurt his career. I thought about Florian and hoped that he would invent some excuse to pick up Jutta and bring her with us. But when he came outside, he looked ashen.

"'I just called Maria's apartment. They've gone out. If we wait until they get back . . . well, there's no way she will hand Jutta over to me at eleven at night without wondering what is up. So . . .'

"He hung his head——and I could hear him catch a sob in his throat. Then, wiping his eyes, he said:

"'I have an extra bicycle here. We ride to Friedrichshain.'

"And we cycled the twenty minutes from Mitte to a place near a road that ran on both sides of the frontier. There were two Volkspolizisten standing guard on the GDR side——and a simple gate separating the East from the West. But we could see that the Volkspolizisten were checking papers very thoroughly and holding people up and not letting anyone through, even though it was still marginally legal to cross from one sector to another. So we slipped down a side street and up to a block of apartments that faced onto a street that ran parallel with the border. Florian's friend had told him the key to the apartment was atop a fuse box in the hallway. I held my breath as Florian searched for it. When he found it and opened the door, we found ourselves in a place that had been abandoned: a few mattresses on the floor, a filthy toilet, and a cracked window. There was a rope ladder attached to the window frame. Florian peered outside. He said the coast was clear. He threw the ladder outside and told me that I had to go down it now.

"I was terrified. I hate heights——and we were three floors up. The ladder was so feeble, so dangerous, that as soon as I put my weight on it I knew it wouldn't hold me . . . and I only weighed fifty kilos at the time. I told Florian that I couldn't do it . . . that I was just too scared. He literally grabbed me by the scruff of my neck and forced me out the window.

"The descent only took perhaps thirty seconds——because once I had grabbed hold of the ladder it was clear that I only had a few moments before the rope gave away. When I was about ten meters above the ground, the whole thing collapsed. I was suddenly falling——and, believe me, a ten-meter fall is a long one. I landed on my left foot and completely broke my ankle. The pain was indescribable. From up above, Florian began to hiss:

"'Run. Run now!'

"'You have to come with me,' I hissed back.

"'I need to find another rope. You cross now——I'll meet you in a few hours at the Kaiser Wilhelm Gedächtnis-Kirche on the Ku'damm.'

"'I can't move,' I yelled back. 'My ankle.'

"'You have no choice. You go now.'

"'Florian . . . jump!'

"'Now. Now.'

"And he disappeared. My ankle was killing me. I could put no weight on it. But somehow I managed to drag myself the thirty meters across the barren area that was no-man's-land and into the West. As there was still no Wall——still no trip wires or armed guards that would shoot to kill——there were also no Western soldiers awaiting me as I staggered into Kreuzberg. Just a Turkish man who was walking home and found me collapsed on the street, sobbing in pain. He crouched down beside me and handed me a cigarette. Then he told me that he would be back as soon as possible with help. It must have been a good hour before I heard the roar of an ambulance, by which time I was drifting in and out of consciousness. The next thing I knew, I was waking up in some hospital ward. There was a doctor there, telling me I hadn't just broken my ankle, but also tore my Achilles' tendon, and I had been knocked out with anesthetics for over eight hours. Beside him was a policeman who welcomed me to the Bundesrepublik. He also told me that I was a most lucky young lady, as the GDR had sealed the borders just after midnight.

"'Did a man named Florian Fallada make it over?' I asked the policeman. He just shrugged and said: "'I don't have any knowledge of who crossed over last night. What I do know is that it is absolutely impossible to leave the GDR now. It has become a hermetically sealed state.'"

Our plane banked suddenly, its nose headed toward the ground. Then, suddenly, the cloud cover lifted and I could see that we were moments from touching down . . . the last ten minutes of this flight blurred from my memory by the narrative force of this woman's story.

"So what happened next?" I asked as the plane's engines entered reverse thrust mode and our forward progress began to slow.

"What happened? I was in hospital for a week. During that time several Bundesrepublik functionaries visited me and, with great ease, facilitated my passage into their country. I asked several of them if they had any news of Florian Fallada. One of them actually wrote his name down and promised me that when she returned to see me again in several days' time she would have some news for me.

"When she did come back, she had with her my Bundesrepublik identity card and the following information: no one by the name of Florian Fallada was registered as having crossed the frontier before it was sealed on thirteen August 1961."

"And do you know what happened to Florian?" I asked, sounding a little too eager, like a reader who——having been plunged deep into a story——wanted to skip a hundred or so pages to find out what happened next.

"I had no word of him for over ten years," the woman said. "Myself, I found a job in Frankfurt in the hotel business——and within ten years was married and divorced. I also became the sales director of Intercontinental Hotels in Germany. During the Leipzig Trade Fair in 1972, I returned to my former country on business. And although he wasn't there the only newspaper available at my hotel was the Communist Party rag, *Neues Deutschland*. On the masthead, whom did I discover was the new editor in chief? Florian Fallada."

The plane had come to a halt. Snow was falling outside. Steps were being pushed toward the forward door of the aircraft.

"And you never tried to contact him? Never tried to find out what happened to him when he didn't cross over with you?"

She looked at me as if I was the most naïve man in the world.

"Had I contacted Florian I would have destroyed his career. And as I did rather love him . . ."

"But surely you wanted to know why he didn't make it over?"

Again she regarded me with a sort of amused skepticism.

"Florian didn't make it over because the ladder broke. Perhaps he didn't have enough time to find another rope to get him down into no-man's-land. Perhaps he couldn't bear to leave his daughter behind. Perhaps he simply decided that he had a duty to remain in the place he called home, despite all the limitations that decision imposed. Who knows? But that secret——the secret that he was minutes away from escaping——stayed with only one other person: me.

"But now you know that secret, too. And perhaps you are wondering why this stranger——this middle-aged woman who is smoking and talking far too much——decided to tell you, Mr. Young American Writer, this very private story? Because I read today in the *Frankfurter Allgemeine Zeitung* that Florian Fallada, the editor in chief of *Neues Deutschland*, dropped dead two days ago of a heart attack at his office in East Berlin. And now, I say good-bye to you."

"What's your name?" I asked.

"My name is my business. But I've given you a good story, *ja*? You'll find many stories here. The conundrum for you will be discerning which tales are true, and which are built on sand."

A telltale *bing* was played over the loudspeaker system. Everyone began to stand up and ready themselves for the world beyond here. I hoisted my typewriter while putting my army greatcoat back on me.

"Let me guess," the woman said. "Your father acts as if he doesn't approve of you, but brags behind your back about His Son, the Writer."

"My father lives his own life," I said.

"And you will never get him to appreciate yours. So don't bother. You're young. Everything is still a tabula rasa. Lose yourself in other people's stories and gain perspective on your own."

With that, she nodded good-bye to me, heading off back into her own life. But once we were inside the terminal building——and waiting by the luggage carousel for our bags——she caught sight of me again and said:

"*Willkommen in Berlin.*"

TWO

KREUZBERG.

The woman on the plane fell from a ladder in the East Berlin district of Friedrichshain and then staggered the thirty yards or so into Kreuzberg. Whereupon a Turkish gentleman came across her, crumpled in the street, writhing in pain. Within hours of this one small incident, the terrain she had just crossed became the most contentious border on the planet.

Friedrichshain to Kreuzberg. Just steps.

Until a wall is put up. And the steps become impossibilities.

On my third morning in Berlin I took the U-Bahn to Moritzplatz and found myself looking at the border crossing that now existed at Heinrich Heine Strasse. Heinrich Heine. I'd read him in college. One of the patron saints of German Romanticism——and now the name of the principal border crossings between East and West. No doubt, the GDR authorities latched onto Heine's antibourgeois poems as proof of his impeccable "workers of the world unite" credentials. No doubt, there were those in the West who simply looked upon him as one of those flighty nineteenth-century literary personages whose work was largely divorced from quotidian realities and, as such, had to be dismissed as the height of bourgeois narcissism. Whatever the interpretation, when I came upon the Heinrich Heine Checkpoint, all I could think was——as it was for him in life, so it continues one hundred and twenty-eight years after his death. For he remains a writer who traversed the contradictions of the German consciousness——and, as such, deserved to belong to both sides of this now-divided land.

However, upon arriving in Berlin three days earlier I was geographically far away from Heinrich Heine Strasse, as I'd taken up temporary residence in a pension off the Ku'damm . . . right in the heart of an elegant square called Savignyplatz. The place was recommended in a "Berlin on the Cheap" guidebook I'd found in New York. It was a small, immaculate bed-and-breakfast place with rooms for forty deutsche marks a night——which, in 1984, worked out at around $12——affordable for a week or so, but not a long-term prospect for a writer with a small advance, working on a tight budget. Facing the green leafy plaza that was Savignyplatz, the Pension Weisse was a soft landing into Berlin. My room——with its firm single bed, its simple, Scandinavian-style furniture, its spotless en-suite bathroom, its ample heating, its spacious desk upon which I parked my typewriter, its soundproof windows——was a delight. I was punch-drunk after thirteen hours of travel via New York and Frankfurt, but the matron at the reception desk——none other than Frau Weisse——immediately endeared herself to me by letting me have access to the room a full three hours before check-in time.

"I have given you a room with a very nice view," she told me. "And knowing you were arriving today we turned up the heating in it early this morning. Berlin has been arctic for days. Please do not risk frostbite and venture outside. I would hate to have to rush you to hospital on your second day here."

Of course, I did venture outside——around three hours later when the wind and the blowing snow subsided. I made it out to the newspaper kiosk right next to the Savignyplatz S-Bahn station where I bought an *International Herald Tribune*, a packet of Drum rolling tobacco and cigarette papers, and a half-bottle of Asbach Uralt brandy (the idea of buying alcohol at a newspaper shop always pleased me). I then ducked into a pasta place. I ate a bowl of spaghetti carbonara, washed back with a glass of rough red wine. I read the newspaper and smoked several roll-up cigarettes with two espressos. I studied my fellow clientele. They were divided into two groups. There were businesspeople in suits who worked in the offices that lined the nearby Kurfürstendamm. There were also——judging from such standard-issue urban art house gear as their leather jackets, their black turtlenecks, their Bertolt Brecht eyeglasses and their packets of Gitanes——well-heeled members of the creative classes. I'd no doubt these were the sort of people who spoke the same *lingua franca* in which all cultured metropolitan people were fluent. And after lunch——when I was able to manage twenty minutes out of doors before the cold sent me back to my room——my walk around the quarter brought me past the elegant left-behinds of nineteenth-century burgher apartment blocks, and expensive, amply stocked local delicatessens, and fashionable clothing boutiques, and excellent bookshops and emporiums of classical music. The result of this hurried arctic dance around these well-heeled streets was to inform me that I had landed myself in one of West Berlin's most pleasing neighborhoods. Coupled with the ease and comfort of the Pension Weisse, it was clear to me that I would have to get out of here fast. I wanted to write a book that reflected the edgy rhythms of this edgy city. But how could I simply commute into such edginess, then return home to an area that exuded the good life? I needed to wash up in a tough part of town.

Perhaps the reason I was already getting so absorbed with the question of "residence"——when I hadn't even begun to work out the basic geography of the city——had to do with the book I was reading right now. With the blowing snow and the cold keeping me largely indoors, I spent much of the first few days in my room, listening to jazz on some local station and enveloped in a Christa Wolf novel, The Quest for Christa T. What intrigued me most about it was that——though the author was a much celebrated and sanctioned writer in the GDR——the novel was in no way an "official" East German text. Rather, that this tale of an essentially decent, commonplace woman living a decent, commonplace life in East Germany was mired in quiet desperation. As such it was a novel in which so much was left unsaid. As you read it you could begin to discern its subtext: the fact that it spoke about the oppressiveness of uniformity in a society that demanded absolute obedience. Its theme was the subjugation of the individual. But the way it stated its theme, by never stating its theme, both fascinated and unnerved me. Because it made me wonder: Will I ever get a handle on this place? Have I arrived in a landscape where everything is not what it seems, where the divisions, the isolation, the geopolitical schizophrenia, run so deep and are so multilayered that I will never be able to penetrate its many skins, the cloaks behind which it veils itself?

In this sense I was suffering from a writerly form of stage fright. Doubt——that great monolith that frequently positions itself in front of all of us——had arrived. Though I knew there was an irrational aspect to such doubt——that I was panicking even before I had begun to really nose around the city——it was only years (and five books) later that I came to discover this was all part of the process by which one of my travel books was written. So, on these first days in Berlin, I began the daily grind of keeping a journal. I'd arrived here with eight old-style school notebooks——the ones with laminated black-and-white cardboard covers. I'd written in them throughout prep school and college. They also came with me to Egypt. I so liked writing in these books. They brought me back to hours spent in home rooms and lecture theaters, doodling my own thoughts as I listened to some professorial type spouting off. As a result, they became an essential part of what little I packed with me whenever I traveled. I was just a little obsessive when it came to guarding their safety. My notebooks never left the hotel or the room where I was billeted at a given time. Anytime I was outside said room, I had a small pocket-sized jotter with me. Whenever I returned back to the place I was sleeping I would immediately begin to write down, in narrative form, all that happened to me that day——including as much dialogue as I could remember.

This tedious task became an essential discipline. I simply had to keep writing. For I worried often that if I didn't keep up with the story it would slip away from me.

My first two indoor days in Berlin didn't give me much in the way of material. And I decided, on the third night, that I would ignore all the advice given me by Frau Weisse to stay off the frostbite-inducing streets. So I did venture out that evening, daring to walk the two miles from Savignyplatz to Potsdamer Platz and the Philharmonie. The snow that had blanketed the city for the past seventy-two hours had stopped, but the wind remained polar. After traversing the bright lights of the Kurfürstendamm——with its illuminated department stores and modern office buildings, its air of mercantile buzz——I began to regret my decision to sludge through the ferocious cold, especially as I was heading to the Philharmonie ticketless. The concert was long since sold out. Even Frau Weisse, who seemed to have connections everywhere, couldn't pull the necessary strings to get me a single seat.

"This is always a problem when von Karajan is conducting. But maybe if you get there early there will be a return."

It took me almost an hour to wend my way to the Philharmonie. But before I got there I walked around what was left of Potsdamer Platz——it so looked like an abandoned no-man's-land——and got my first hard look at The Wall. Touching it with my gloved hand only seemed to magnify its hardness, its impregnability, its profound ugliness. In the distance I could see, on the Western side, the bright lights of a vertiginous office building, defiantly profit-oriented and looming. Axel Springer's publishing empire was based here. Looking up at what appeared to be a newsroom on a high floor, all I could think was: the people on the other side of the divide were able to stare up at journalists at work in a country not their own, and to which they were forbidden to travel. Meanwhile, the journalists working above them in the West had, no doubt, a clear view over the no-man's-land that separated The Wall from the actual streets of East Berlin. Were they able to see the trip wires, the guard dogs, the armed sentries who were under orders to shoot to kill if the fleeing citizen didn't give himself up? Or did they come to regard this high-rise view as uninteresting? Was that the inherent dichotomy of an infamous structure like this one? To the newcomer like myself, its blank, solidified reality gripped my imagination. As a child of the Cold War I also couldn't help but think: *I'm actually staring at the Berlin Wall!* But if you lived and worked by it, did you come to regard it as just part of the urban scenery, a prosaic fact of life?

The cold forced me to move on. With my head down to the wind I walked the ten minutes to the Philharmonie. I arrived there just a few minutes before the start of the concert and got immediately lucky, as there was a woman standing out front, holding up a spare ticket. It was a very good ticket——and, at 130 deutsche marks, way beyond my budget. But there are moments when extravagance is no bad thing——such as the opportunity to hear von Karajan and the Berlin Philharmonic play the *Ninth Symphony* of Gustav Mahler. So I put aside my budgetary concerns and snapped up the ticket, rushing inside.

The house lights were fading as I fell into my seat. The concert platform was now bathed in a yellow glow, the orchestra and the audience silent, waiting. A simple sculptural object was positioned center stage——a curved steel stand. A side door opened——and the figure of Herbert von Karajan appeared. He was seventy-six at the time. Though hunched and stooped——his face granitic and stern, his hair as white and stiff as a frozen blizzard——what was so immediately apparent was his defiance in the midst of the ravages of age. Though his spine was failing him, he still insisted on comporting himself like a man who had spent his life facing the world with a ramrod-straight demeanor, and was still determined to maintain his patrician hauteur. His progress to the front of the orchestra was slow but still majestic. He acknowledged the voluminous applause from the sold-out hall, then grasped the hand of the first violinist and favored the musicians of the Berlin Philharmonic with a grave, knowing nod. As he positioned himself on that sculpted stand, his back now absolutely rigid, his shoulders held high, the physical effort of simply getting onto the concert platform was now replaced by an imperial bearing. He raised his head, letting both the orchestra and the audience know that he was ready. The hall fell silent and von Karajan held the silence for a good half-minute, forcing us to divest ourselves of all peripheral white noise and simply listen to the hall's immense quiet. Then he raised his baton and made the smallest of gestures, indicating a downbeat. One of the double basses played a low pizzicato note, underscored by a tremolo on a French horn, and then came the emergence of a theme that was so plaintive, so full of tristesse, that it felt almost like a melancholic remembrance of things past. Then again, this symphony——Mahler's Ninth and the last one he was to complete before his shockingly premature death at the age of fifty-one——was very much an extended premonition about encroaching mortality. Over the next ninety minutes Mahler engaged us in a sort of existential summing up of what it means to have lived a life: all the aspirations, all the passions, all the setbacks, the reversals of fortunes, the love that came and went. But, most of all, there was this sense of time's rapid diminishment, how we are helpless in the face of its relentlessness, and the way, at the end of every individual narrative, there is the fade to black that is death.

Throughout the symphony's duration I couldn't take my eyes off von Karajan. Whatever about the curvature of his spine, once positioned on that stand, once deep into the vast musical architecture of that symphony, he was nothing less than mesmeric. Even in the symphony's final pages——when it was clear that, through Mahler, von Karajan was also rendering a profound reflection on the inescapability of human mortality——I couldn't help but feel that he was also letting it be known he would not surrender easily to eternal darkness. When the final strings faded away, he held the silence for a good minute——his arms aloft, his head bowed, the immensity of that final moment——the heartbeat now forever stilled——enfolding all present.

When, with great, deliberate slowness, von Karajan finally lowered his arms, the silence in the hall lingered——as if everyone there was hushed and thunderstruck by that which they had just heard. Then, as if a signal had been given, the Philharmonie erupted into convulsive applause.

Thinking back on that concert now, it remains, quite simply, one of the great musical experiences of my life: a testament to the sheer volcanic and visceral power of live performance. After multiple ovations, von Karajan finally led his musicians off the platform. The entire audience then filed out quietly. After such a profound and transcendental experience, there was something humbling about returning to our individual lives. But perhaps this is the way I now choose to remember the night in question. You only begin to grasp the import of an event——and its larger implications vis-à-vis your life——long after it has entered into that realm marked "memory."

I left the Philharmonie. Making my way to the S-Bahn station at Anhalter Bahnhof, I decided that, with all that Mahlerian complexity still swirling around in my head, it was far too early to return back to the Pension Weisse and my pristine room. So I headed south until I reached Moritzplatz——thinking I should find my way to the place where that woman I met on the plane came over to this side of the world.

But all I could see in front of me as I emerged into Kreuzberg for the first time was swirling snow, as a new storm had erupted while I was on the U-Bahn. It was now blowing so hard that visibility was a near impossibility. I glanced at my watch. It was just after ten p.m. and part of me wanted to execute an about-face and disappear again into the subterranean depths, catching the first U-Bahn back to Savignyplatz. But there was a bar up ahead——Die schwarze Ecke (the Black Corner)——and the U-Bahn ran until three in morning, so why should a minor blizzard keep me away from a dive with a pulp fiction name?

My head down against the blowing snow, I negotiated the street and entered Die schwarze Ecke. It lived up to its name. The interior was painted black. A long chrome bar ran the length of the joint. The only lighting provided was glowing blue tubes that served to illuminate the Day-Glo murals that covered the otherwise black surfaces. They were all pseudo-erotic in nature——depicting a bearded biker guy and some blond biker chick in assorted sexual positions. They were beyond bad taste. But judging from the tattoos on the biceps of the biker guy behind the bar (one of which showed a woman going down on an erect penis), they were an aesthetic theme beloved by its staff members. I ordered a Hefeweizen and a shot of vodka on the side, grabbed a bar stool, and began rolling a cigarette. There was heavy metal music playing on the sound system——the usual sonic air raid of crashing guitars and percussive pyrotechnics——but it was kept at a level where conversation was possible. Not that there were many candidates for chat on this snowy night in January. Just a young punky type at the bar and an equally young woman with a small black bobby pin fastened through a pierced corner of her left nostril. The guy had spiked black hair, a wispy beard, and a permanent scowl. He was smoking Lucky Strikes and doodling in a sketchbook. When he heard me order my beer and vodka chaser, he looked up at me with disdain and asked:

"American?"

"That's right."

"The fuck you doing here?" he asked in English.

"Having a drink."

"And making me talk to you in your fucking language."

"I'm not making *you* do anything."

"Fucking imperialist."

I immediately switched into German and said:

"I am *no* imperialist——and I hate being labeled certain things simply by nature of my nationality. But, hey, since you obviously like nationalistic clichés, maybe I should start calling you a Jew killer . . ."

I said all that without much in the way of premeditated thought. From the wide-eyed look of the artist guy and the biker behind the bar, I now wondered if I would get out of Die schwarze Ecke with my teeth and fingers intact. But then the punky girl with the bobby pin in her nose spoke:

"You're an asshole, Helmut," she hissed at the artist guy. "As always, your attempts to show off simply demonstrate how stupid and limited you are."

The artist guy favored her with a scowl. But then the bartender said:

"Sabine is right. You are a clown. And you are now going to apologize to the American."

The artist guy kept scribbling away in his sketchbook, saying nothing. I decided it best to look away. So I tossed back my vodka, then returned my focus to the cigarette I was forming between my fingers. A very long moment passed, during which I licked the rolled cigarette paper, placed the butt between my lips, and lit it up. At which point the artist guy was standing beside me with a glass. He set it down beside me and said:

"We tend to be a little too confrontational in Berlin. No hard feelings."

He proffered his hand. I took it and said:

"Sure. No hard feelings."

And raising the fresh shot of vodka, I said "Prost" and threw it back.

Were this a movie, the guy would have introduced himself to me; we would have become instant and firm friends. And my guide into the complexities of Berlin. And I would have met a bevy of funky artists and writers. And we would have gone on a very Wim Wenders motorcycle trip with his girlfriend and sister around the Bundesrepublik. And his sister——let's call her Herta——would turn out to be a gifted jazz pianist and we would fall madly in love with each other. And there would be an afternoon in Munich when I would suggest we take a side trip to Dachau. And standing there in the empty camp grounds, regarding the crematoriums as a silent snow falls, there would be a moment of shared silent understanding about the horrors that the world can . . .

But life is never a movie. Having bought me the vodka and made the demanded apology, the artist guy scooped up his sketchbook. Raising his middle finger in the direction of the bartender, he turned and headed out into the cold. The bartender uttered a low laugh, then turned to Sabine and said:

"He'll be back tomorrow——as always."

"He's such a shit."

"You're only saying that because you used to fuck him."

"I used to fuck you, too——and I still drink here. But maybe that's because I got wise and it only happened once."

To his credit, the bartender smiled. Then Sabine shouted down to me: "Buy me a drink and I'll fuck you."

"Now that's the first time I've ever been offered that deal," I said.

"It's not a deal, American. You're here. And I have only three deutsche marks left in my pocket and want to buy cigarettes with them. So I need you to buy me a drink. Just as I need you to fuck me tonight, as I don't want to sleep alone. You have a problem with that?"

I worked hard at masking my bemusement.

"No," I said, "no problem at all."

"Then come over here and buy me a drink. In fact, you can buy me many drinks."

Sabine drank rum and Coke——a treble shot of Bacardi splashed into the dark waters of the cola.

"I know it's pretty fucking teenager to drink a *cuba libre*," she said. "The thing is, I like what alcohol does. But I don't like the taste."

I discovered that Sabine was from Hannover, and that she made sculptures in papier-mâché, and that her father was a Lutheran pastor with whom she no longer spoke, and that her mother had run off with a man who sold agricultural supplies and whom she found to be *petit bourgeois* and insufferable. She asked few questions about me, asking me simply where I was from ("Yes, I've heard of Manhattan") and what I did ("Every American in Berlin is a writer"). But from the disinterested tone of her voice, she was simply engaging in basic niceties. This didn't bother me, as she seemed happy to talk about herself in a manner that veered between self-loathing and ironic detachment. She drank two triple shot *cuba libres* and smoked six cigarettes in the forty-five minutes during which we propped up the bar. Then when the bartender made noises about wanting to close up, I turned to Sabine and said:

"You know, if you'd rather not invite me back, that's okay."

"Is this your way of saying you don't want to spend the night with me?"

"Not at all. I was just saying that I didn't want you to feel obliged about . . ."

"Are Americans always so fucked up about sex?"

"Absolutely," I said, flashing her a smile. "How far do you live from here?"

"Around two minutes."

I threw some money down on the bar and we were out the door, holding each other up against the combined force of blowing snow and an excessive amount of alcohol. Her place was located in a shabby building dabbled with graffiti. It was a room on the fifth floor of a walk-up, a very large room with a mattress on the floor, a stereo, carelessly stacked records and books, a makeshift kitchen consisting of a hot plate and a small fridge, and clothes scattered everywhere. Tidiness was evidently not one of Sabine's strong points. But I was less interested in her strewn garments and overflowing ashtrays than in her papier-mâché sculptures of mutilated animals hanging from the walls. Had I not been so drunk they would have unsettled me. Instead I took them all in with a bemused grin.

"George Orwell lives," I said.

She laughed and produced a small pipe and a chunk of hashish. As the Scorpions blared on the stereo, we smoked several bowlfuls of hash——and then took each other's clothes off and made very stoned love on the mattress. I remember little about the act itself——except that, courtesy of the hash, it went on for a very long time. It had the sort of intensity that, in other, more sober circumstances, could make you think that this was something more than two strangers losing themselves in the pleasure of each other's bodies on a lonely night in a snowbound city locked deep within Eastern Europe. When we finished we both passed out, waking sometime after noon to the sounds of traffic and a domestic argument in Turkish emanating from an adjoining flat. Sabine raised herself up on one elbow, squinted at me with curiosity, then asked:

"What's your name again?"

I told her. She glanced at her watch and said:

"Shit. I was due in work ten minutes ago."

We were both dressed and out the door within five minutes. It was a bright, cold morning——the snow plowed up into huge drifts by the side of the pavement.

"Got to dash," she said, giving me a quick peck on the lips.

"Can I see you again?" I asked.

She looked at me and smiled. Then said:

"No."

And she disappeared around the corner and was gone.

Had it not been so cold and I not so hungry I might have stood on that street, reeling from the morning-after brush-off that had just been administered to me. Instead I decided that a late breakfast was needed. But when I spun around, looking for a café at the end of the street, I found myself facing The Wall. Catching sight of it this way was the visual equivalent of a slap in the face. Spinning around again, I spied the grubby buildings, the overflowing trash bins, the hunched Turkish women heading toward an open-air market, the dude in torn leather trousers with chains clanging off his right calf, the elderly German woman blinking madly into the sun while trying to negotiate the icy footpath with her cane, the two young toughs with shaved heads looking like they were en route to break into someone's apartment . . . the whole strange Breughel-like street scene that was this corner of Kreuzberg.

Then spinning back again I stared right at the solemn triteness that was The Wall. And I thought: *yes, this is where the book will get written. Yes, this is where I belong.*

After a quick pilgrimage to the Heinrich Heine Checkpoint, I turned west again into the middle of Kreuzberg, determined to find a place here to call my own before nightfall.

THREE

NEVER UNDERESTIMATE THE way happenstance governs so much of human existence. Never underestimate how being in a certain place at a certain time changes the entire trajectory of things for you. Never underestimate the way we are all hostages to life's random rhythms.

Just consider:

I leave the Philharmonie, thinking I will return to my hotel. Instead, I decide to seek out a bar in Kreuzberg. Upon emerging from the subway, I almost turn back due to blowing snow. But I cross the road into a bar. A nasty exchange with an artist leads me to talking with a woman with a bobby pin in her nose. We spend the night together. When we get up the next morning, she dumps me. I find myself on a street. I wander up to gaze at the local checkpoint. Then I turn into the first café I find. There is a notice on the wall in English as I walk in:

FLAT SHARE: Artist with Extra Bedroom in his Atelier seeks tenant. Rent reasonable. So too is the premises. Only louche souls need apply.

There was a name——Alaistair Fitzsimons-Ross——on the announcement. There was also a telephone number. I copied both down. *Fitzsimons-Ross. Must be a Brit. And a pretentious one at that, given his "only louche souls" comment.* Then I drank several glasses of thick, coagulated Turkish coffee and ate a slice of baklava and asked to use the phone. The man behind the counter——hangdog eyes, a loopy moustache, stained teeth embedded around a cigarette——charged me twenty pfennigs for the privilege. I checked my watch. Twelve forty-nine p.m. I dialed the number. It rang fourteen times. I was about to hang up when a voice answered. From the sound of profound stupefaction that accompanied this voice, I immediately realized that, like me, the gentleman on the other end of the line had also had something of a late night.

"Do you *always* phone people so fucking early?"

The voice was tobacco-cured, posh. What I would have described as a BBC accent, except with a less clipped layering to it.

"It's nearly one p.m.," I said. "And is this Alaistair Fitzsimons-Ross?"

"Who the fuck wants to know?"

"My name is Thomas Nesbitt."

"And you're a fucking American . . ."

"That's most insightful of you . . ."

"And like the majority of fucking Americans, you're up with your fucking cows every morning at five, so you have no fucking compunction about ringing someone this fucking early."

"I happen to be from Manhattan, so I know nothing about cows. And having just gotten up at midday myself . . ."

"Is there a point to this call?"

"I was calling about the room. But since we don't seem to be getting off to such a great start . . ."

"Hang on, hang on . . ."

A ferocious bout of coughing followed, the same cough I had whenever I had overdosed on cigarettes the night before.

"Bloody hell . . . ," he finally said once the coughing subsided.

"You okay?"

"Nothing an organ transplant wouldn't cure. You said you were interested in the room?"

"That's right."

"Do you have a name?"

"I told you it already."

"So you did, so you did. But it's so fucking early in the morning . . ."

"Maybe I should call you at another time."

"Mariannenstrasse 5. Name's on the bell. Third floor, links. Give me an hour."

And the phone went dead.

I spent the next hour wandering around Kreuzberg. I liked what I saw. Nineteenth-century residential buildings in various states of scruffiness, but still imposing in their burgher solidity. Graffiti everywhere——much of it either related to Turkish government human rights abuses (I wrote down assorted dabbled slogans in my notebook and had them translated later on) or what I came to discover was the usual German anarchist stuff about eviscerating the capitalist, bourgeois state. There was absolutely nothing bourgeois about Kreuzberg. I could spy a couple of small coffee shops, but they all reminded me of German versions of the old beatnik joints that lined the Greenwich Village of my youth. The bars I noted were either the sort of heavy metal joints that I ventured into last night, or the occasional old-style local *bierstube*, or Turkish enclaves. These were lit by fluorescent tubes and peopled by hollow-eyed men in flat caps, smoking furiously, drinking shots of raki chased by coffee, and either talking conspiratorially or staring ahead blankly: that vacant look of the lonely, the exiled, the dispossessed. These men could be seen everywhere on the streets. So too could groups of Turkish women, wearing the Muslim headscarf (or, very occasionally, the full chador), pushing their children in strollers or baby carriages, and gabbing incessantly with each other. There were skinheads and Sabine-style punks everywhere——all shaved scalps or spiked hair, and tattoos adorning their cheekbones. There were the evident druggies——sallow, emaciated, with the toneless, sunken expression of the junkie awaiting his next fix. There were scores of falafel places and cheap pizzerias and the sort of boutiques that sold army greatcoats and biker jackets and shit-kicker boots. The chic, the well heeled, the *au courant* had no place in Kreuzberg. It was cheap. It was raffish. It was motley and profoundly heterogeneous. It was properly bohemian——not one of those alleged bohemian quarters where the moneyed professional classes had moved in and the only artists now in residence were the seriously rich ones. Rather, after this short inspection tour, it was clear that this was a neighborhood where outsiders had gathered, where it was possible to find some sort of foothold in an otherwise diffident and difficult world. During my long stroll through its spindly streets, I couldn't help but think: this is one of those places that affords inexpensive shelter and *no questions asked* to all comers. You could land here and survive here for very little. You could leave ambition behind you and simply exist. It was an urban tabula rasa, upon which you could draw your own set of rules, your own *modus vivendi* for passing this time of your life.

Mariannenstrasse 5 was an intriguing building. It was twice the size of all the other apartment blocks on the street. And it appeared to have been condemned by the local planning board. The windows on the ground floor were boarded up. The front door looked as if someone had repeatedly tried to kick it in. The walls had been so oversprayed with graffiti that none of the slogans were legible. The building was next to a little grocery store——*ein Lebensmittelgeschäft*——that looked like it was gunning for a health code violation, as the fruit and vegetables on display had mold growing on them. There was a diminutive middle-aged Turkish man behind the counter (or, at least, I presumed he was Turkish) making a sandwich for a customer while simultaneously smoking a cigarette. Beyond this, at the end of the street, beyond a small park, loomed The Wall. From this distance I could see the tops of what looked like large Soviet-style apartment buildings only several hundred yards on the other side of this international barrier. That was the other thing about Kreuzberg. Its eastern frontiers completely abutted The Wall. It was everywhere you turned.

I pushed the bell marked Fitzsimons-Ross. No response. I pushed it again and waited thirty seconds. I pushed it a third time. Now, finally, a low buzz indicated that entrance through the front door was possible. I went inside. The entrance hall was cavernous and cold. As I stepped inside and the door closed behind me, I could see my breath fog up in front of me. The first thing that caught my attention was the walls. They were unpainted masonry, chipped and porous, and not exactly inspiring structural confidence. There was a cluster of battered postboxes next to a stairwell. The tiled floor beneath my feet followed the general theme of architectural detrition. The only illumination was a single fluorescent tube.

I headed up the stairs. On the first floor was a single door with a dollar sign crudely painted across its portals and a huge red x crisscrossing it all and the words *Kapitalismus ist Scheisse!* dabbed next to it. On the next floor the door was covered in barbed wire, with a small aperture made to access the lock and the door handle. Either the owner was sending a "Do Not Enter" signal to the outside world or he was a sadomasochist who liked to gamble with the possibility of torn flesh every time he entered his apartment. Either way I was relieved this wasn't the portal to the Fitzsimons-Ross residence.

That was on the following floor. As I reached it I saw that its door was the same style of door as the others, only this one had been whitewashed in a way that allowed its old brown finish to underscore the artfully swabbed white paint. I could hear something loud and baroque——a *Brandenburg Concerto?*——emanating from within. I banged heavily on the door. It opened. I put my head inside and smelled the distinctive, medicinal aroma of paint. I was in a huge room. As with the front door the walls here were also whitewashed——the wide brushstrokes clearly visible everywhere. There were large industrial spotlights focused on all four walls. There were two oversized canvases: moody geometric studies of color——bright ultramarine blues shading into azure, cobalt, navy hues——adorning two walls. On the farthest wall, a good forty feet away, was a long table full of paints, splattered drop cloths and several canvases in varying states of development. But what struck me most forcibly about this vast atelier-style room——besides the evident talent of the painting on the wall——was its orderliness. Yes, it was a rough-hewn space——the floorboards bare and unsanded, the galley kitchen near the studio area this side of basic. The only furniture was a zinc café table, a couple of plain bentwood chairs, and a broken-down sofa over which had been thrown a white linen cloth. There was meager heat here——the space so large that it was, no doubt, prohibitively expensive to keep warm. Despite its austerity I took to it immediately. The artist in residence here was serious about his work and hadn't given in to *La Bohème* squalor.

"So you let yourself in."

The voice——that BBC intonation, raised to a loud bark over the blaring Bach——came from a staircase in a corner of the room. I turned around and found myself staring at a man around thirty-five, exceedingly tall, rail thin, with sallow skin, sunken cheekbones, terrible teeth, and electric blue eyes that matched the ultramarine in his paintings. He was dressed in a pair of faded jeans, a heavy black turtleneck sweater that did nothing to hide his evident emaciation, and a pair of expensive tan leather lace-up boots that were dappled with paint. But, again, it was his eyes that were so magnetic. They had the coldness of permafrost, offset by deep crescent moon rings. They hinted at a worldview both defiant and vulnerable, just as I sensed from the outset that his verbal haughtiness was also a veneer. Arrogance always masks doubt, after all.

"You let yourself in," he shouted over the Bach.

"The door was open . . ."

". . . so you simply decided to make yourself at home."

"I'm not exactly brewing coffee in your kitchen."

"Is that a hint? Your way of telling me you'd like a cup of something?"

"I wouldn't say no. And if you wouldn't mind turning down the music . . ."

"You object to Bach?"

"Hardly. But I find shouting over a *Brandenburg Concerto* . . ."

A slight curl of the lip from Alaistair Fitzsimons-Ross.

"A cultivated American. How surprising."

"Not as surprising as an arrogant Brit," I said.

He thought that one over for a moment, then went over to the record player in his studio area and lifted the tone arm off the record.

"I'm not a Brit. I'm Irish."

"You don't sound it."

"There are a handful of us still left in the country who sound like this."

"West Brits?"

"You are up on your Irish argot."

"There are Americans who read and travel."

"Do you all get together once a year in some restaurant and exchange stories?"

"Actually we meet in a diner. How about that coffee?"

"So rude of me. But I'm afraid all I drink is tea. Tea and vodka and red wine."

"I'll go with the tea."

"But you do drink?"

"That I do."

He moved toward the kitchen, picking up a rather battered and rusted kettle.

"That's a relief. I had some of those strange compatriots of yours at my door the other day. They looked like smiling zombies in very ugly blue suits and had name badges on their lapels."

"Mormons?"

"Precisely. I offered them a cup of tea and they looked at me as if I had asked to sleep with one of their sisters."

"They have a thing against all things caffeinated. Tea, coffee, Coca-Cola. Cigarettes and booze are also a no-no."

"So that explains why they went pale when I lit up. You don't have a thing against fags?"

"By which you mean cigarettes?"

"Oh yes, I forgot you Americans have a different interpretation for that word."

"Why don't you drop the 'you Americans' line right now."

I said this without anger or edge——rather with what I hoped was an ironic smile on my face.

"You are so profoundly direct, Mr. New Yorker. And I must admit that I've forgotten your name."

I told him. Then he said:

"Let me guess? Being a rather serious chappie, you prefer Thomas to Tom or, God forbid, Tommy."

"Thomas works."

"Then I shall call you 'Tommy.' Or perhaps 'Tommy Boy,' just to be contrary. So Tommy Boy, do you smoke?"

"I'm not a Mormon . . . and yes, I roll my own."

"How John Wayne of you."

"You really do talk a load of bullshit for an evidently talented man."

That last part of my statement caught his attention. After lifting the now-boiled kettle, then scalding a large brown porcelain teapot before reaching for a dark green tin, opening it, and heaping three spoonfuls of tea into the pot, he asked:

"What makes you think I have any talent whatsoever?"

"The two canvases on the walls."

"You want to buy one?"

"If I'm here to inquire about renting a room, I doubt I can afford your prices."

"How do you know that I'm so expensive?"

"Just a hunch."

He now poured the boiling water into the pot, covered it, and glanced at his watch.

"It needs four minutes to draw properly . . . unless you are one of those unfortunates who like your tea the color of weak piss."

"Dark piss will do me fine."

He tossed me a half-crumpled pack of Gauloises.

"Here, have a proper smoke," he said.

I caught the pack, helped myself to a Gauloises, lit it up, took a long, deep drag——and had that metallic, exhaust pipe gustatory sensation which always accompanies smoking a Gauloises.

"How much do you think one of these paintings goes for?" Fitzsimons-Ross asked me.

"The art market is something I know nothing about . . . especially the European art market."

"If this was in the Kirkland Gallery in Belgravia——where I usually exhibit——you'd be paying just under three thousand pounds for the privilege of hanging a Fitzsimons-Ross on one of your walls."

"That's serious money."

"Semi-serious. I'm not in the Francis Bacon or Lucian Freud league. Still David Sylvester did once compare me to Rothko. You know Sylvester?"

"I'm afraid not."

"Possibly the most influential postwar art critic in the UK."

"Bravo to you. And he's right. There's a decided *Rothko Goes Greek Island* color spectrum to those two paintings."

"That's facile."

"You don't like being compared to Rothko?"

"Not when I am completely opposed to everything that Rothko stood for."

"Which was?"

"Geometric gloom. Fucking portals in every corner of his fucking funereal paintings. All those blood-red earth tones shaded downwards into shadow and somber self-pity."

"I think I was talking about your use of rectangular shapes and color."

"And that makes me like cut-my-wrists Mark *Götterdämmerung* Rothko?"

"You're the first artist I've ever met who doesn't admire him."

"So you've lost your Rothko virginity. Congratulations. I deflowered you."

"Am I supposed to snicker quietly——or get all offensive——about such a profoundly stupid comment? I mean, I hate to break it to you:

your paintings show real talent. Your repartee, on the other hand, is crap."

Fitzsimons-Ross paused for a moment to stub out his Gauloises and pour the tea. He then opened the small fridge, in which were kept several bottles of wine, several bottles of beer, an open freezer compartment from which protruded a Russian bottle of vodka (or, at least I presumed it vodka, as it had Cyrillic lettering on the label covering its plain glass bottom), and a single bottle of milk. He reached for the milk, pulled out the stopper, and poured such a considerable amount of white liquid into my cup of tea that it suddenly went a particularly pedestrian shade of brown——the color of a street puddle.

"Don't look horrified," he said. "This is how tea is meant to be drunk. Sugar?"

I accepted a heaped teaspoon. He pointed to one of the bentwood chairs. I sat down. He fired up another Gauloises, then asked:

"So, let me guess. You write. And you're here to write the Great American Novel or some such tosh."

"Yes, I write. But not novels."

"Oh God, don't tell me you're a fucking poet. Met far too many fucking poets in the one year I was at Trinity College Dublin. They all smelled and had bad teeth and sat around pubs like McDaid's, begrudging the world, telling each other how brilliant they were, berating the editor of some pathetic little magazine for daring to suggest an editorial cut or two, and generally making everyone in earshot never want to read a fucking poem again."

"Not that you have a strong opinion about such things."

"Glad you noticed that."

"Anyway, I'm not a 'fucking poet.'"

I briefly told him what I did——mentioning the book that was published, and the book that had been commissioned.

"Might I see a copy of this book?" he asked.

"Yes, you might. And you're from Dublin?"

"Just outside. Wicklow. Ever been there?"

"Once. Powerscourt. Glendalough. Roundwood."

"That's my parish, Roundwood."

"A very beautiful one at that."

"Roundwood House was the family manse. Classic Anglo-Irish Big House. Before my father lost it all."

"And how did he do that?"

"The usual Irish way. Drink and debt."

"That sounds like a good story. Tell me more."

"Are you going to take all this down afterward and perhaps use it against me?"

"I'm a writer——so, yes, there is that risk. But does that really worry you?"

"Hardly. Then again, who's going to read what you write?"

"My last book sold eighteen hundred copies——so you do have a point there . . ."

He studied me with care.

"I can't rile you, can I?"

"No doubt you'll continue to try. A fast question before I even look at the room. And the question is one word: quiet? Though I approve of your taste in music . . . do you blare it all the time?"

"Frequently, yes."

"Then there's no real point discussing anything to do with the room, as I won't be able to live in a place where there's loud music."

"A sensitive artiste, are we?"

"I need silence when I write, that's all."

"And I need the rent money you'll pay me——so perhaps we can work out an arrangement. Especially as I usually paint in silence."

"Then why did you say you blare music?"

"Because I felt like being a cunt . . . which I am most of the time."

"So if I take the room . . . do I have your assurance that, when I'm writing or sleeping . . ."

"There will be quiet."

Given his prior need to prod and poke at me with his sardonic banter, it surprised me to hear him say this last statement so reassuringly. For all his talk about his big-deal London gallery, money was obviously a problem . . . the mention of his wastrel daddy a further hint that this was a man who might be worried about keeping this roof over his head.

"And how much is the room per month?" I asked.

"Let's talk about that after you've seen it."

Then putting his cup of tea down, he said, "Ready for an inspection tour?"

We stood up.

"Down here is my realm. The studio, the kitchen, the living area. I sleep in there . . ."

He pointed to a door off a far corner of the studio area. It was open——and I could see a simple double bed, immaculately made, the sheets crisp, ultra bleached.

"You've lived in Greece, haven't you?" I asked.

"Is it that obvious?"

"Absolutely. The white walls. The sky and azure blues of your canvases. What the hell are you doing here, all so cold, so gray . . . with The Wall just yards away?"

"The same thing you're doing here. Running away. Existing in an affordable place with edge. Oh, Spetses was pretty damn affordable. The year I spent there, it was pretty fucking sublime. But it was also devoid of interest. It was like so many men I slept with there and elsewhere. So beautiful, so empty."

So there was a fact dropped into the conversation, even though it was one I had already surmised.

"Are all your lovers like Greek Islands?" I asked.

A hard laugh from Fitzsimons-Ross, followed up with a bronchial cough.

"In my dreams," he said. "But you already know too much. Let's head upstairs where I can show you where you'll live."

"What makes you think I'm moving in?"

"Because you can't resist the complexity of it all. And because you're not a squalor junkie, and what I'm offering you here is tidy debauchery."

"*Tidy debauchery,*" I said, trying out the phrase. "I might have to steal that."

Behind the kitchen was a small spiral staircase that led up to a sort of half-floor, made up of three rooms: a large studio space with a tiny kitchen, a bedroom, a bathroom. The kitchen was nominal: a small fridge, a hot plate and tiny oven, a sink. The bathroom was equally minuscule, but still had enough space for a shower stall. There was a simple double bed in one corner of the small bedroom and a wooden wardrobe.

But the studio space was enviably large at around four hundred square feet. An old sofa, draped with a cream linen cover. A plain table that would serve more than adequately as a desk. What was most pleasing about this space was the fact that all the furniture had been stripped of its paint and varnished in its natural state. Coupled with the white walls it had an ascetic cleanness. It struck me as an ideal neutral refuge from the disorder that lurked in the streets beyond, let alone in Fitzsimons-Ross's downstairs lair.

But that was the intriguing thing about my roommate-to-be. On first sight he'd strike the most indifferent of observers as this side of dissolute, with a mouth on him like a leaky latrine. But from the small glimpse I'd had of his living and working spaces——and of the apartment I was to call my own (and which he so evidently designed to mirror his downstairs space)——he was deeply fastidious. Which led me to wonder: was he, like me, someone who understood that there was profound reassurance to be found in the surfaces of things, and that a disciplined approach to housekeeping allowed you to be saturnalian in so many other areas? But again, this insight is not one which I probably had at the time. All I saw was the fact that Fitzsimons-Ross had the air of an Irish Isherwood about him and knew how to demonstrate good taste on a nominal budget.

"Pretty nice," I said. "I hope I can afford it."

"You're staying where right now?"

I told him about the Pension Weisse and how it suited me so well.

"So remain in Savignyplatz and write about your neighbors the merchant bankers. Or the gallery dealer who's doing a five-million-deutschemark turnover per annum. Here, in Kreuzberg, you get to watch junkies shit on the street and Turkish brutes beating their wives. And you get to see me in *flagrante delicto* with whatever rent boy or Finnish depressive I've picked up at Die schwarze Ecke."

"I know that place well. I fell into it last night."

"And fell out of it with company?"

"How did you guess?"

"Because it's Die schwarze Ecke——where everyone in Kreuzberg goes to score weed and to pick up whoever's sitting at the bar that night and doesn't look too insane. That's the thing about that kip. We all know it's toxic. But everyone frequents it for exactly the same reasons. If you want to score some hash, the only guy there to trust is Orhan. A Turkish dwarf——and fat. Looks like he belongs doing a stint as Snow White's Big Boy. But the hash he peddles . . . *premier cru*."

He fired up another cigarette. Then:

"So are you taking the place?"

"How much do you want for it? I don't have much money."

"You mean, you didn't grow up in a Park Avenue household with a black maid named Beulah?"

"Home was a small two-bedroom apartment on an unfashionable corner of Second Avenue."

"Ah, a boy with something to prove."

"Just like you. You still haven't told me the story of how your father squandered all the family money."

"Maybe I never will."

"So how much do you want per month?"

"One thousand deutsche marks."

"That's a lot more than my apartment in New York . . ."

"But this is a virtually self-contained apartment . . ."

". . . in a less than savory corner of Berlin, where I know I could rent a studio for three hundred. Which is what I am prepared to pay for this place. Inclusive of heat."

"No can do."

"Nice meeting you then."

I turned and headed toward the stairs.

"Five hundred," he said.

"Three-fifty. Final offer."

"Four hundred twenty-five."

"I'm not budging on this. But thanks for an entertaining cup of tea."

"You truly *are* a New York cunt, aren't you?"

"By which you mean . . . ?"

"Money grubbing."

Is that a synonym for "Jewish"? I wondered but decided to say nothing. Except: "You know something, chum . . . I really don't like your tone."

"Three-fifty then," he said, the hint of desperation coming out again.

I held out my hand. He took it.

"We have a deal?" I asked.

"I suppose so. One thing: I'd also like a month's deposit, just in case . . ."

"Do you own this place?"

He coughed out a lung full of smoke.

"Me Own Anything?" he said, giving emphasis to every word. "What an extraordinary idea. I have a very unpleasant Turkish landlord——a real Mister Big, with gold chains and minions and a very black Mercedes in which he cruises the streets of Kreuzberg. He despises me. The feeling is mutual. But I've had this place for three years, and he let me renovate it in exchange for a reduced rent. But now that it is much improved over the dump I first obtained from him . . . naturally, he has increased the rent by four hundred a month."

"Hence the need for a roommate."

"I'm afraid so. And don't take this the wrong way——but how I loathe the idea of having you upstairs. Not that you're bad news. It's just, I really don't want the company."

Fitzsimons-Ross evidently had this need to play the one-upmanship card at every possibility. I knew from the outset that my relationship with this gent would be less than easy. But like Kreuzberg itself, I sensed that his disquietude——and the need to compete with me on everything—— might just prove bracing.

"Hey, you want to be alone," I said, "you can play Greta Garbo if you fucking want."

This time I did walk down the stairs.

"All right, all right," he shouted after me. "I'll shut my bloody mouth."

"I'll be back in a few hours with some cash," I said.

"Can you pay me the deposit and one month up front?"

"I suppose so. Will you be here at six?"

"If you're coming back with cash, absolutely."

I showed up at six fifteen——having returned to the Pension Weisse and collected a handful of traveler's checks from my suitcase, then cashed them all in a nearby bank. After spending some time in a café, writing all that had transpired earlier with my roommate-to-be, I took the U-Bahn back to Kreuzberg. Fitzsimons-Ross had given me the front door code before I left. So this time I didn't ring the front doorbell. When I reached the door to his apartment I heard Miles Davis from his "cool" period ("Someday My Prince Will Come") blaring on the hi-fi. So much for his assurances that loudness was not his style. I banged once on the door. It swung open. I stepped inside.

"Hello?" I shouted.

No reply. I walked toward the studio area. Still no sign of him. Then I glanced in the direction of his bedroom. The door was wide open here——and the sight that filled my field of vision caused me to take a sharp intake of breath. For there, on the bed, was Fitzsimons-Ross. He was bare-chested, with a thick rubber tourniquet encircling his upper left bicep. A needle was sticking out of the bulging vein in the crook of that same arm. Though his voice was otherworldly, it still had a strange cogent clarity to it.

"You bring the rent money?"

Why didn't I turn and walk out right then and there?

Because I knew I had to see how this would all play out. And because I was already thinking: it's all material.

"Yes," I said, "I brought it."

"Just put it on the kitchen table. And if you wouldn't mind putting the kettle on . . . I could use a cup of tea."

"No problem," I said.

Fitzsimons-Ross looked up at me with eyes that, though glassy from the narcotic hit, still shone with arctic-blue incandescence.

"Don't forget: the tea needs to be steeped for a good four minutes," he added.

"Fine," I said.

I turned away from the man with the needle in his arm, thinking: Welcome to my new home.

FOUR

I AM A RATHER fastidious junkie," Fitzsimons-Ross told me.

I made him his cup of tea, which he drank silently. Then I proffered the seven hundred deutsche marks. He reached into his pocket and fished out a metal object that he placed on the table, then slid toward me.

"Here's a key," he said. "Move in whenever."

"I thought I'd come by tomorrow with my stuff, then move in on Friday."

"Whatever works. Don't worry about any of this. I've got it all very regulated. Very under control."

I said nothing. But I did notice how he was working very hard at being lucid right now, despite having mainlined what I presumed to be a significant amount of smack. This, I came to discover, was the strange, infernal duality of Alaistair Fitzsimons-Ross. It didn't matter that I had walked in on his shooting up. It didn't matter if he called me a cunt or made some less-than-vaguely anti-Semitic comment (as he was prone to do). It didn't matter if he had woken up next to some Kurdish rough trade he'd picked up in the toilets near the Hauptbahnhof. Appearances had to be maintained. He was always determined to see himself in the best possible light——even though, as I also came to discover, the hardened, foul-mouthed veneer with which he cocooned himself was easily permeated.

But all that was future knowledge. For the moment I had that strange heady thrill that comes with tossing yourself into a situation that you know to be, at best, dangerous. Writers——as somebody once noted—— are always selling somebody out. I knew I had struck pay dirt the moment I'd spent five minutes with Alaistair. I had my opening chapters, and could only hope that the shooting-up episode was the start of many a low-life moment to be witnessed chez Fitzsimons-Ross.

So the next morning I gave notice at the Pension Weisse. Then I went to KaDeWe——the big department store on the Kurfürstendamm——and bought two sets of white sheets and equally white towels and a desk lamp and a basic set of plates and cutlery and a kettle and a coffee maker. I loaded it all up into a taxi and gave the address on Mariannenstrasse and hauled everything up the three flights of stairs to the atelier. Fitzsimons-Ross was nowhere to be seen. I unpacked my bags and made up my bed. Afterward I adjourned to the café nearest to Mariannenstrasse 5——the Istanbul——for lunch.

The Istanbul was run by a diminutive chain smoking man with a perpetual hack cough named Omar (he finally introduced himself around a month after I starting using his place as my outer office). It was a dump. A very basic zinc bar. Cheaply laminated tables and chairs. Cheap liquor decorating the bar. There were yellowing travel posters featuring scenic views of the Blue Mosque, the Bosporus, Topkapi Palace, and other Istanbul highlights. The cassette player by the till always seemed to be quietly playing some dirge sung by a Turkish woman about (I imagined) the swarthy Lothario who'd ditched her. But I immediately took to the place largely because——bar the low hum of the music and the whispered conversation of the middle-aged men who always seemed to be huddled at a rear table, plotting the downfall of some enemy——the place was ever-calm. More tellingly Omar came to know me as an habitué. Even when I told him my name he seemed to ignore this piece of information and continued to refer to me as *Schriftsteller*. Writer. He also started to lower the music whenever I came in, and seemed to approve of the two hours I would spend every afternoon at a corner table, writing in my notebook, getting everything that had transpired in the past twenty-four hours down on paper. Trying to write it all while the details were still bouncing around the inside of my head.

I would end up living much of the time in the Istanbul. Courtesy of my age back then, I didn't have to concern myself with such pedestrian matters as diet or weight gain or the damage I was doing to my cardiovascular system with the cigarettes that seemed such an essential component of the writing process. The Istanbul had a cheap and cheerful food menu. The "we cook everything" staples it served (spaghetti Bolognese and carbonara, lamb kebabs, stuffed vine leaves, Wiener schnitzel, kofti, assorted pizzas, and even that most Greek of dishes, moussaka) had two essential qualities: (1) they were always, at worst, edible, especially when washed down with two half-liters of Hefeweizen beers and a Turkish coffee to follow; (2) the meal would never cost me more than six deutsche marks. As I hated to cook back then——and even now, as a middle-aged man on my own, prefer not to expend a great amount of time in the preparation of something to eat (maybe I've just never fallen in love with the so-called poetry of food)——the Istanbul was an ideal refuge for me.

On that first early afternoon——as I settled myself down for a plate of pasta at what was to become my corner table——I surveyed the small confines of the café: the coughing, diminutive proprietor behind the bar; the elderly man, his face expressionless, who sat at a table in the window, smoking, staring blankly ahead at the street; the sweaty behemoth with a beer belly the size of a bowling ball who was currently drinking shots of raki, his face awash in tears, singing an aria of woe to the impervious barkeep. I smoked three cigarettes, and scribbled away about discovering Fitzsimons-Ross with the needle in his arm, then recording this scene around me in the Istanbul, and thinking: so many residents of Berlin were refugees——if not from totalitarian regimes or impoverished countries, then from lives they wanted to flee, or things that trapped them elsewhere, or even, quite simply, themselves. It took work to land yourself in Berlin. Once you were here you were geographically boxed in. Even though residing in the western sector gave you the right to travel, it meant taking a train that went nonstop through the German Democratic Republic. Otherwise the only other option was a plane west. That was, I sensed, the inherent contradiction of life here. West Berlin stood as an island of individual and political freedom amidst a landscape of dictatorship. The city afforded those who came here a degree of personal latitude and flexible morality. It allowed you to construct whatever variation on life you wanted within its confines. But "confines" was the operative word. For you found yourself boxed in by geopolitical realities and a barrier that could not be breached. As such, you were free and caught at the same time.

I went to the small Spar supermarket located near the Kottbusser Tor U-Bahn station and bought some basics: cereal, milk, orange juice, and coffee and sugar, a selection of cold meats and two loaves of pumpernickel bread and mustard, two bottles of Polish vodka (cheap) and a half-dozen bottles of Hefeweizen beer (I actually wrote this entire shopping list down in one of my notebooks, as I was that obsessed back then with recording every detail). Later that night, as I climbed into bed for my first-night sleep at the apartment and began to doze off, I had an interesting wake-up call. Loud driving orchestral music, with a gypsy edge to it, blaring from downstairs. It was so full-volume, so deliberately deafening, that I couldn't help but think (once I had cast off middle-of-the-night sleepiness): he's doing this to test me, to show me who's boss around here. I sat on the edge of my bed, rubbing sleep from my eyes, trying to think about my next move. I grabbed my robe and put it on over my T-shirt and pajama bottoms, then took a deep steadying breath and headed downstairs.

Fitzsimons-Ross was standing in the studio area, dressed in a paint-splattered T-shirt and jeans, bare paint-splattered feet, a cigarette sticking out of his mouth, applying an azure-blue paint with hyper-rapid brushstrokes to an otherwise empty canvas. The effect was like watching a brilliant Greek sky being created in front of you——and I was mesmerized by his bravura technique, the assertive skill with which he wielded his brush, the force of his evident concentration. Part of me was furious at being awoken by this blast of music——and wanted to play the prickly lodger, ready to take on my equally prickly landlord. But the other part of me——the writer who knew those moments when a creative reverie suddenly subsumed the world outside of me——knew that to interrupt the flow of his work now by ripping the tone arm off the record would be nothing short of monstrous. So I simply retreated back to my room, leaving in such a stealthy manner that he was never aware of my nearby presence. Once upstairs I did what I always did when sleep eluded me: I worked. Opening up my notebook, I sat down on the hard bentwood chair by my desk, uncapped my fountain pen, and started to write. I checked my watch. It was 2:15 a.m. The orchestral music (was it Bartók?) ended and was replaced by Ella Fitzgerald singing Cole Porter and then John Coltrane's *A Love Supreme*, that long dark journey into the spiritual blur. Whatever I felt about this middle-of-the-night roar, I had to concede that Fitzsimons-Ross's musical taste was high-end.

The music abruptly stopped at four. There was a long silence, during which I put down my pen, rolled up another cigarette, plugged it in my mouth, grabbed the half-full bottle of wine and two glasses, and went downstairs. But when I reached the studio area, Fitzsimons-Ross was otherwise engaged, as he was seated on the sofa, an elastic tourniquet around his upper arm, a needle sticking out of his bulging vein. He was just depressing the plunger as I came into view.

"The fuck do you want?" he said in a hoarse, extraworldly voice. "Can't you see I'm busy?"

I retreated upstairs, smoked my cigarette, drank a glass of wine, then fell into bed. When I woke it was eleven in the morning——and from downstairs came the loud telltale grunts and moans. Drifting into consciousness it took me a few befuddled moments to realize that I was listening to two men having sex. As wake-up calls go, this was a first-of-a-kind for me. After a minute or so of this graphic sexual soundtrack, I reached over and turned on my radio, spinning the dial until I found a rock station. I blared The Clash as I got up and made coffee and smoked two pre-breakfast roll-ups and thought: today is the day I contact Radio Liberty and tomorrow is the day I cross over to nose around East Berlin.

After I had finished breakfast and washed up the dishes, I snapped off the radio and was relieved to hear that the performance downstairs had also ended. Grabbing my parka and scarf, I scooped up my notebook and pen and tobacco and ventured out.

When I reached Alaistair's studio area I started heading directly toward the door. But I was stopped by a voice saying:

"So be a rude little fuck and don't say good morning."

I turned around and saw Fitzsimons-Ross sitting at his long kitchen table, sipping coffee and smoking a Gauloises with a thin, olive-skinned man who I guessed was in his late twenties. He had close-cropped hair, a small earring in his left earlobe, and a gold wedding band on his left index finger. He was dressed in a light brown distressed leather jacket trimmed with white fur——the sort of jacket I always associated with low-level thugs. Naturally I wanted to know everything about him, given that he had just been sharing a man's bed and was also wearing a symbol that informed the world: *I'm a married man.* I saw him as another component of the ever-expanding narrative of my time in Berlin, and wondered what sort of involvement or arrangement he had with my landlord.

"Good morning," I said.

"The cunt speaks." Then, switching into impressively fluent German, Fitzsimons-Ross told his companion:

"He's American, he's my lodger, but he's not really that odious."

In German "odious" is *abstossend*. Fitzsimons-Ross spat that word out with such relish that his friend seemed to almost flinch as the word landed in his ears.

"This is Mehmet," he continued on in German. "Say hello to Thomas."

A quick "*morgen*" from Mehmet, then he stood up and said:

"I must go."

"Really? So soon?" Fitzsimons-Ross asked.

"You know I start work at one."

"See you in two days then?"

Mehmet simply nodded. Then, still not making eye contact with me, he gathered up his coat and walked quickly out the front door. When it closed behind him, Fitzsimons-Ross asked:

"Tea? There's still a cup left in the pot."

I accepted the offer and sat down in the chair that Mehmet had vacated.

"I sense you surprised the poor boy," Fitzsimons-Ross said. "As you may have noted . . ."

"He's married . . ."

"My, my, you are the observant one."

"A wedding ring is a wedding ring."

"And these poor Turkish boys, they have families who essentially map out their lives for them from the moment they emerge into the world. Mehmet's wife is his second cousin——and a most plump girl. Mehmet told me he knew he liked boys from the age of fifteen onward——but imagine if he had admitted such a thing to his father. Especially as he works for his father at the laundry the old man runs right off Heinrich Heine Strasse . . ."

"Am I right to presume that you didn't meet Mehmet there?"

"My, my, Tommy Boy, your deductive reasoning is so impressive. No, I met Mehmet in far more romantic circumstances . . . in the toilets at

Zoo Station, which is a well-known pick-up spot for those of us who practice 'the love that dare not speak its name.'"

"So you know your Oscar Wilde."

"I'm an Irish Protestant shirt lifter. Of course, I know my fucking Oscar Wilde. Did we wake you up this morning, Mehmet and me?"

"Actually you did."

"And were you shocked, horrified?"

"You forget——I'm from New York."

"Ah yes, a worldly American, even if the sound of that phrase has a profoundly oxymoronic feel to it. Well, you'd best get used to Mehmet's presence here, as we have a rendezvous three days a week. Usually in the late morning. And he's always gone after ninety minutes. He comes at no other time, as that might cause suspicion among his all-knowing, all-fascist Islamic family. Anyway, the arrangement perfectly suits me. Mehmet and I get exactly what we need from each other within carefully delineated boundaries. That means there's no fuss, no trouble, no ties that bind."

"Speaking of fuss . . . we need to talk about the music . . ."

"What music?"

"The music you were playing last night."

"You object to my taste?"

"What I object to is being woken at two in the morning . . ."

"Well, I'm afraid that I do my best work from midnight to four. And I can't paint without music blaring. So . . ."

"When we discussed this earlier, you assured me that there would be no blared music here if I moved in."

He reached for his cigarettes and fired one up.

"I lied," he finally said.

"Evidently. The thing is, I cannot sleep if you blare music like that."

"Change your sleeping habits then. Keep vampire hours like me."

"That's not a satisfactory answer."

"Do you expect me to care?"

"I want my seven hundred marks back."

"It's all spent. I had debts, you know. And now . . ."

"Now you have to keep your end of the deal."

"I don't have to do a damn thing, Tommy Boy."

"Yes you do."

"Are you going to get all legal on me, American? 'You'll be hearing from my attorney' and some such shit."

He uttered that "attorney" line in the sort of reedy version of an American accent that a certain type of Brit always turns on whenever he wants to cut us colonials down to size. At that point I found myself getting angry——but anger with me is never expressed. Instead I go all quiet and begin to plot.

"The deal we had," I said in a voice just barely above a whisper, "is that there would be no music playing while I'm here. I'm holding you to it."

I turned and left the apartment.

Outside I had to fight off the desire to punch a window out with my fist. I get overly aggrieved when crossed——especially when I sense I have been treated unfairly or have been simply looked upon as a dupe. Standing outside my new abode, I pondered how to deal with Fitzsimons-Ross and his duplicitous tactics. There were several options here. I could return to the Pension Weisse and ask Madame if she was still willing to cut me a long-term residency deal. The problem with this was twofold: I would lose the seven hundred marks that I had already forked over to Fitzsimons-Ross, and I would also lose the chance of bearing eyewitness to all that went on at his place and in Kreuzberg. I could find another apartment in the district, but the fact was that my set of rooms here were absolutely ideal. Fitzsimons-Ross was right: I had been naïve handing over that sum of money to a junkie. But I think a very large part of me subconsciously knew I was asking for trouble by paying so much rent up front——and did so just to see how everything would play out. Now I had to find a way of getting what I wanted——silence at night——yet not compromising Fitzsimons-Ross's work. So that afternoon, while taking an extended hike through the rarefied streets of Charlottenberg, I happened upon a hi-fi shop and bought a pair of decent headphones and a huge ten-meter extension cord for them. The shop assistant looked at me warily when I asked for such a long lead.

"It's a big room."

Then, toward the end of the afternoon, I stopped in at the Istanbul and asked Omar if I could use their phone . . . and, indeed, if I could have people leave messages on their number (as I sensed it best to not have anyone trying to contact me fall into conversation with Fitzsimons-Ross).

"You willing to pay a little money for the service?" he asked.

"How much?"

"What I charge the five or six other people for whom I take messages: five marks a week. You get good service, I promise that. And you get to make five local calls a day, no extra charge."

"That sounds like we have a deal then. Can I make one of those five phone calls right now?"

Omar motioned for me to come over to the bar, where he pulled up a heavy black Bakelite phone from the lower depths behind him. I dug out my notebook, into which I had copied the name and phone number of Jerome Wellmann, the Radio Liberty station head in Berlin. Dialing the number I reached the switchboard and was put through to Mr. Wellmann's secretary——who was very no-nonsense.

"Does Mr. Wellmann know what this is about?" she asked.

"Huntley Cranley suggested I call."

The fact that I answered her back in her language and also dropped the name of a very serious honcho at Radio Liberty back in Washington seemed to make her pause for thought.

"Anyone can mention Herr Cranley's name. We have people looking for jobs here all the time, and they always tell us the same thing: that they met with someone high up in the organization in Washington, whereas the truth is . . ."

"Mr. Cranley informed me that he was writing Mr. Wellmann himself on my behalf."

"Then I will read through all telexes that Herr Wellmann received recently from the head office. If it turns out you are telling the truth . . ."

"Are you implying that I might be lying?"

"For reasons that I am certain are evident to you, were you to ponder them with care and intelligence, we must be very careful when it comes to vetting any potential employee, or indeed anyone who simply wishes to see Herr Wellmann for an appointment. You should understand that, given the nature of our work, we must be vigilant at all times . . . especially in this city."

"Point taken," I said, then added that messages could be left for me at the following number——and I read off the six digits printed in the plastic holder on the center of the phone.

"And what is this place where we are to leave messages . . . that is, if we even do leave a message for you?"

"It's a café in Kreuzberg called the Istanbul," I said, knowing immediately that the very name and locale of this joint probably sounded like some sub-Cold War spy rendezvous center.

"Why are you having messages taken for you there?"

"Because it's around the corner from where I'm living . . . and because I don't have a phone."

"If you don't hear from us within forty-eight hours, then this means that Herr Wellmann has chosen not to get in touch with you. Good day."

So much for that avenue of possibility. The woman made officiousness her creed, her raison d'être. If she had her way I was certain she would block any work possibilities at Radio Liberty——and, as such, access to an entire world of narrative possibilities for my book. Naturally, I would inevitably fall into other worlds while here in Berlin. But I so wanted the chance to work among Cold Warriors playing the propaganda game for the West.

"Doesn't sound good," Omar said as I handed him back the phone.

"You'll let me know if they phone back," I said, handing over the first four marks for the Café Istanbul telephone exchange.

"You pay for a service, you get a service."

And, I could have added, a deal is a deal. Or, at least, that how I viewed the world . . . and, more specifically, the arrangement I had with Fitzsimons-Ross when I rented his upstairs rooms. So when I returned back to the apartment that night, I discovered him still out and deposited the headphones and the ten-meter lead by his stereo, alongside the following note:

> I bought you these. I sense the lead should be long enough
> for you to move around the studio without encumbrance. The
> sales guy assured me they produce very high-quality sound.
> Happy listening . . . Thomas.

Then I went upstairs and decided to make it an early night, falling into bed by eleven.

The music cranked up just after midnight. Only tonight it wasn't Bartók or John Coltrane or something in a similar rarefied vein. No, tonight it was the loudest heavy metal imaginable——the sort of sonic screech that was the aural equivalent of a five-car pileup and chosen, no doubt, to let me know that Fitzsimons-Ross had rejected the headphones compromise. I sat up and reached for my robe and walked downstairs. Fitzsimons-Ross was already fully engaged in front of his canvas, with his back to the place where his hi-fi equipment was stacked. So he didn't see me approach the turntable and lift the tone arm off the record. The sudden silence made him spin around just as I yanked the turntable free of its cables and approached the window. As I hauled it open he screamed:

"What the fuck do you think you're doing?"

"We had a deal."

"You wouldn't fucking dare . . ."

"Will you keep your part of the deal?"

"I don't go in for blackmail."

"And I won't negotiate with a bully. You either abide by what we agreed, or you return me the seven hundred marks, or your turntable takes the plunge."

"Do you think you can tell me how to fucking behave?"

"Have it your way then."

And I tossed the turntable out the window.

Suddenly Fitzsimons-Ross's face fell. He looked genuinely stunned by what had transpired. Sitting down on the floor in front of his half-finished canvas he stared ahead, saying nothing. There was now something Little Boy Lost about him. I felt strangely guilty about playing so rough, causing him evident distress, even though I also knew that if I hadn't called his bluff, the music would have continued at a deafening volume all night long.

I crept upstairs, leaving him sitting there on the floor. I drank several glasses of red wine and smoked two roll-ups. I paced by the door, trying to discern if he was creeping up the stairs with a hammer in his hand. All right, I was bit paranoid . . . but the guy was a junkie and an emotional pinball, so (I told myself) anything was possible. I decided, then and there, to move out the next afternoon.

I finally crawled into bed at two and passed out. When I woke it was nearly midday. A rare winter sun was shafting in through the venetian blinds. After the usual first befuddling moments of consciousness, I began to assemble a mental checklist:

I need to go to the Café Istanbul within the hour and call the Pension Weisse and negotiate that long-term rate, then phone Radio Liberty and tell Frau Charm that the phone number to reach me on has changed, then come back here and pack up, leaving Fitzsimons-Ross a good-bye note, telling him that I hoped the seven hundred marks would buy him a better turntable (and simultaneously salve my conscience).

After the morning ritual of cheese on pumpernickel bread, followed by two strong espressos and the first roll-up of the new day, I gathered up my coat and headed downstairs. As I moved toward the front door, I caught sight of Fitzsimons-Ross. He was already at work, standing in front of his easel, his brush dancing across the canvas as he layered and relayered a new azure blue rectangle. On his head were the headphones I bought him. The lead stretched across the room to his bank of hi-fi equipment, which now included a replacement turntable.

As I shook my head with bemusement, Fitzsimons-Ross spun around and caught sight of me. Pulling off the headphones he uttered one word:

"Cunt."

Then he favored me with the smallest of smiles.

"Lunch on me at the Café Istanbul?" I asked.

He thought about this for a moment.

"I suppose I have nothing better to do."

It looked like I wouldn't be moving out just yet.

FIVE

ONE OF THE many intriguing aspects of Fitzsimons-Ross was his ability to exist totally in the present. I envied him this talent——and the way he let things go so quickly, never dwelling on past grievances or perceived inequities. Yes, he could groan about an unkind review or one of the many Dublin "begrudgers" (a favorite word of his) who hated him for "the nominal success I've had to date." But he rarely railed against life's manifold injustices or his place in the world. During our détente lunch at the Café Istanbul he never once mentioned the unpleasantness of the previous night, his subsequent distress, or how he had managed to find a new turntable before twelve noon today. On the contrary, his countenance was ironic, witty, engaged. The fact that we were sitting in a public arena seemed to engage some sort of self-censorship device that simply stopped him from uttering the stream-of-consciousness scatology that so marked his normal conversational style. As we began to demolish a liter of the house wine that the Istanbul served up, I asked a question that I had been wanting to pose for several days:

"So how long have you been a junkie?"

The question didn't faze Fitzsimons-Ross whatsoever. Instead, lighting up a fresh Gauloises, he smiled and said:

"Four years."

"And it doesn't impede your work?"

"Clearly not. In fact I would say that my dependence on smack has aided and abetted my career."

"By which you mean 'creatively'?"

"Hardly. But let me ask you this, as someone who's evidently never tried smack, have you ever experimented with hallucinogenics?"

"I did LSD once in college."

"And?"

"Well, besides being up for around twenty-three hours, yes, it was very trippy, very Technicolor."

"Smack is anything but that. What it does is send you to a most sedate and splendidly introverted space and encourages you to feel nothing . . . which, given the horror that is so much of life, is no bad thing. And I don't want to sound like a salesman for the drug, but it is the most profoundly blissful high going."

"Except for its equally profoundly addictive qualities."

"My, my, Tommy Boy, you really do have Calvinistic tendencies."

"Maybe that's why I'm not a junkie."

"Do yourself a favor and never get involved with it. You're far too structured to be a junkie."

"You're not structured?"

"In a surface way, absolutely. But I can give in to my dissolute side—because I have worked out a way of being anally retentive at the same time. Which must make me unique among junkies . . ."

"Perhaps you should give motivational speeches on being such an organized addict."

"Perhaps you'll write them for me. But you can't do unbridled, can you? I'm certain you smoke a little dope from time to time, and you drink a bit. But there's a part of you that simply doesn't like being out of control. Too bad you're not Jewish. You have that Yid responsibility thing."

"That's because I'm a Yid."

Fitzsimons-Ross looked like he'd just walked into an empty elevator shaft.

"You are joking, yes?" he asked.

"In Judaism the mother carries the religion . . . and as my mother was Jewish, that makes me a Yid."

My pronunciation of that expression made it clear how detestable I found it. Fitzsimons-Ross's unease was a pleasure to behold.

"It's just a turn of phrase," he said, reaching for his cigarettes.

"It's an ugly word. And it makes me think you're an anti-Semite."

"You want an apology, don't you?"

"Why should a 'Yid' like me ask such a thing from a fine gentleman like yourself?"

"I will excise that word from my vocabulary immediately. But I need to ask you something: do you regret being circumcised?"

I shook my head and failed to repress the smile that was crossing my face. Fitzsimons-Ross was, at worst, ever amusing.

"I don't think I'm going to answer that question," I said.

"And my gaucheness still doesn't get you off the hook for lunch."

"You mean, the way a 'Yid' would naturally try to stick you with the check?"

"Touché."

Our lasagnas arrived. They were most edible. Fitzsimons-Ross even seemed impressed.

"This is bloody good. Don't know why I managed to bypass this place before."

"Perhaps you have enough Turks in your life already."

"My, my, we are a bitch."

"You still haven't explained to me how you manage to work with smack."

"'*How did the devil drug take possession of me?*' You should write dime-store novels, Tommy Boy. *Smack Faggot Unchained!*"

"I'm stealing that title immediately."

"I tried the Big H shortly after I moved here. Smoked it initially——and then the biker boy, Martin, whom I was with at the time, turned me on to the needle. When that first rush hit me . . . well, there is a damn good reason why it is so addictive. Now I started shooting up in 1980. And I must bow the knee toward Papa who, for an out-of-control member of the failed squirearchy, still imposed on me the idea that 'appearances must be maintained.' You can destroy your family fortune, you can kill all the things you love, but never, *never*, appear in public with an unpressed pair of trousers and scuffed shoes. Anyway, courtesy of Papa, I was rather scrupulous when it came to junkie hygiene. So I never got into sharing needles. Which, as it turned out, saved my life and cost poor Martin his. I speak of 'the plague,' of course. I must have lost a good two dozen friends here and elsewhere because of it. Then again, I was also rather rigid——pun intended——when it came to the use of French letters. So, Papa, *Vielen Dank.* You turned me into a facsimile of you——and, in the process, saved my life."

"When did your father die?"

"Three years ago. Cirrhosis of the liver, not that there isn't much of that in County Wicklow."

"Were you close to him?"

"Immensely, even though he hardly approved of my sexual predilections. But, to his credit, he did rate me as an artist. In his final year——and he was only fifty-eight when he left this life——he did try to, shall we say, make amends for all the absurd tirades, the name-calling, the general dissolution and dissatisfaction which so characterized the major part of his life. By this point my mother——who was totally Anglo and the epitome of cold bitchdom——had long since left him. With what little money he had left, he was living in the gate lodge of the big house of one of his old chums down in Roundstone. When the doctors told him that he had, perhaps, three months tops, he wrote to me here in Berlin and asked if I would 'come home' for a while and 'see him through.' Which, of course, I did——and fortunately had a painter friend in Dublin with a contact on the north side of the city who kept me supplied with smack. Not that I ever once let my dying father in on my nasty little habit. Then again, had he known, I think he would have been more sad than furious. Papa was, at heart, a rather nice man who just wanted to love and be loved. But that eluded him during the course of his life. Just as it eludes most of us."

He stubbed out his cigarette and lit another.

"You've never been in love?" I asked.

"Only about ten times. And you?"

I paused, trying to think this one through. And that troubled me.

"Your silence speaks volumes," Fitzsimons-Ross said.

"There was one woman who was very much in love with me."

"And——let me guess——she was far too nice for you?"

"Perhaps."

"So you too had a mother who found your presence the gravest mistake of her life . . . outside, that is, of marrying your father. And ergo, here you are in Berlin, still running away from the woman who found you wanting . . ."

"'The woman' in question smoked herself to death seven years ago."

"And you're still running. Let me inform you this: it never goes away. You're always fighting it. I haven't seen my mother in fifteen years. She walked out on my father to marry some Colonel Blimpish retired army type and live in one of those repulsive Cotswold villages named Chippendale-on-Tweed——where she was, as she always put it, 'among people of her own standing' . . . the implication being, us Paddys were so beneath her. The thing was, my father was dependent on her. She fulfilled his 'mummy' needs——because, from what I gathered about my paternal grandmother, she was as cold and disapproving as my mother. So . . . let me guess: the woman who loved you——"

I interrupted.

"Have you ever considered reducing your financial outgoings by, perhaps, weaning yourself off smack?"

"It's very intriguing to see how deftly you attempt to change the subject whenever it crosses into something painful or awkward. No, I have no interest in freeing myself of the proverbial 'monkey on my back.' That's what you Yanks call it, right? It keeps me working, and it keeps reality tolerable."

"Because you too are resistant to love?"

A deeply ironic smile from Fitzsimons-Ross.

"You are a most talented evader, monsieur. Perhaps that's a key con-struct in the life of a writer——an ability to evade. On which note . . . please excuse me, but I have a rendezvous chez moi with Mehmet in just under half an hour. Which means——unless you want to hear us in action . . ."

"I'll take a walk."

"I thought you'd say that. I know your type all too well. Liberal, creative, open-minded, even a couple of faggot friends. And privately repulsed by it all."

"You mean, reading minds is another one of your manifold talents?"

"Absolutely. And what do you have planned for the afternoon?"

I reached inside my jacket for my pouch of tobacco and rolling pa-pers, and noted that my American passport was lodged next to my smok-ing materials. I glanced at my watch. It was only twelve thirty.

"Maybe I'll go to a foreign country," I said.

"You mean . . . *over there?*"

"Well, it is just five minutes away."

"But if you've ever been over there . . ."

"I haven't."

"Then go on, have a look at it. But I promise you that you'll be back here by six p.m., thinking there's no need to ever set foot in that place again."

"It's that bad?"

"I suppose if you're a member of the Dublin or London branch of the Workers Revolutionary Party, the People's Paradise across the way is a many-splendored thing . . . especially as you also possess a Western passport that allows you to jump ship anytime. But for the rest of the internees over there . . . as I said, go have a look. Perhaps I simply have a problem with all things excessively monochromatic——and am not seeing the virtues behind the relentless drabness. Perhaps I am simply not as insightful as you are."

"Irony noted."

"But, by the way, if you do meet some fraternal socialist brother from Cuba or Angola who's selling decent grade smack . . ."

"You're hilarious."

"So I've been told. But do get back safely. And now if you will excuse me . . ."

He was out the door.

Was this the most opportune moment to make my first crossing to "the other side"? Perhaps not, given that I had already lost the morning and the sky was pregnant with impending snow.

Still I took the U-Bahn up to Kochstrasse. I could have made a far more convenient border crossing just down the street from here at Heinrich Heine Strasse. But thinking as always about the future narrative I would be writing, I knew that I really did have to commence with the essential Cold War experience: the border crossing at Checkpoint Charlie. As the U-Bahn slowed into the Kochstrasse Station a wave of apprehension hit me——rooted in nothing but the fear of the totalitarian that had been embedded in me since the days when Russian missiles had been pointing at us from Cuba, and later on in high school, when we read Solzhenitsyn, and even on into college when the films of Andrzej Wajda articulated the Stalinism of Polish society. But most of all there was the voice of my father during the height of the Vietnam War protests:

"These peaceniks haven't got a clue about how easy they have it here, how, if this was Moscow and they dared assemble on the streets to protest something, they'd all end up in some Siberian slave labor camp. They play rough over there. They know how to shut people up."

Even if I felt at the time that Dad's comments were nothing more than knee-jerk banalities, something did take hold in my imagination. It's a bit like the time when I was eight and we visited the house of one of my mother's aunts near Ossining. It was a very Grant Wood house—— and besides being unnerved by the *American Gothic* style of the place and the fact that my aunt Hester looked like a walking mummy, my father decided to really unnerve me by saying that if I opened the door to her attic I might be in for a nasty surprise. Perhaps the parental logic behind this warning was to scare me off from poking around her things. Perhaps Dad just wanted to creep me out. Whatever the reason I did begin to imagine an entire plethora of horrible things *behind that door*. From that moment on a fear was instilled in me about entering places that had been deemed off-limits.

At first sight Checkpoint Charlie had an "off-limits" aura. As I emerged from the U-Bahn I saw that much-photographed sign——"You Are Now Leaving the American Sector"——directly in front of me, the clear subtext of this message being: *Abandon All Hope Ye Who Enter*. To its immediate right was a storefront museum in a small building——the Haus am Checkpoint Charlie——which, given the displays in its window, memorialized all those who were shot or apprehended trying to make it to this side of the Berlin terrain. I glanced at my watch. It was just after one. I marched toward the American guard post, removing my green American passport as I approached the window. A uniformed officer was there. He noticed that I already had my passport out for him to inspect it.

"Afternoon, sir," he said. "What can I do for you?"

"Do I need to register with you before crossing over?"

"No need, sir. And if you have any problems on the other side, well, we do have an embassy there. But you're just going over for the day, right?"

I nodded.

"Well, unless you're planning to meet with dissidents or give away Bibles on a street corner."

"Not my thing."

"You should have no problems then. And as you will have to be back over here by midnight . . ."

"You ever been over there yourself?"

"That's forbidden for those of us who wear this uniform, sir. You have a good day now in East Berlin."

I moved on toward the checkpoint itself and found myself approaching a huge gate. It stretched the entire width of the street, both sides of it dead-ending into The Wall. Barbed wire shaded all open areas. There were two members of the Volkspolizist stationed immediately on the far side of the gate. As I approached, they nodded to me and swung open this portal.

"Passport," one of them asked in German.

I showed them my American passport.

"You go there," the Volkspolizist said, pointing to a booth up ahead, speaking now in fractured in English.

"*Ich danke ihnen,*" I replied and walked forward, hearing the gate close behind me with a dull clang. Up ahead was a prefabricated booth. There were several heavily armed officers standing by it. Behind the Plexiglas was another uniformed Volkspolizist. He took my passport and asked if I spoke German. When I replied in German, he nodded and informed me that I would be receiving a one-day visa that would expire at midnight tonight.

"You must leave the German Democratic Republic before midnight and you must also leave by this border station. You cannot leave by another border. And you must now change thirty westmarks for thirty GDR marks."

I knew that this exchange rate was absurdly inflated, that a GDR mark was worth nothing more than twenty Pfennig in Western money, thereby making it a 5:1 rate. But I had read in several guidebooks and articles about crossing over into East Berlin that this was a way in which the GDR regime could gain hard currency. It was one of the many non-negotiable components of a GDR visa, the other being the "you must be out by midnight" clause. Trying to actually travel in the country for any greater length of time was profoundly difficult, as the government preferred if you came on an official tour or part of a group with the correct left-leaning credentials. A writer like me would have no chance of getting a visa for independent travel, so an official in the East German embassy in Washington told me in an exchange of letters prior to my arrival, when I was thinking that I might be able to have an entire section on my adventures in the other Germany. The counsel made it very clear that I would only be given an extended visa if I was invited officially by the GDR Writers Union. But as my one book to date (he'd evidently gone to the trouble to find out what I had written) didn't display the sort of socialist credentials that would win me favor with the people at the GDR Writers Union, I would be wasting my time pursuing this avenue of inquiry.

Now, as the Volkspolizist official relieved me of my thirty westmarks (noting how he didn't call this hard currency deutsche marks) and opened a large book, turned to the section marked "N," and spent several minutes seeing if my name and passport number were registered therein, the thought struck me that, perhaps, the GDR counsel in Washington had dispatched my details to East Berlin, informing the authorities that I was a snoopy author, and therefore would be visiting the GDR to defame it.

But the officer evidently found no such black mark against me, as he closed the Book of Non-Desirables and inked his entry stamp. As it landed on a fresh page of my passport I found myself considering, yet again, the dread that all officialdom raised in me. Then he pushed the document back to me and, with a curt nod, informed me that we were finished.

Now one of the armed officers by the booth tapped me on the shoulder and pointed me toward a simple barricade, of the sort seen in parking lots. There was another handful of armed Volkspolizisten standing by this lone divider, beyond which stretched a city thoroughfare: Friedrichstrasse. As I marched toward this final hurdle prior to my entry into East Berlin the relative low-level security of this barricade on the eastern side of the frontier made it very clear that the authorities knew that any citizen committing the crime of "trying to flee the Republic" would be mad to try it at this, the most notorious border post in the city.

A final check of my passport. Another reminder by this new officer perusing my travel document that I needed to be crossing this check-point, "and this checkpoint alone," by midnight. Then, with a nod between these officials, the bar was raised and I walked into the German Democratic Republic. As I did so I couldn't help but wonder what test of fidelity to the state was needed for a Volkspolizist to work here; what emotional ransom was exercised on all the officers stationed at such a sensitive border; whether they were informed, in no uncertain terms, that their families would be severely penalized if they ever dared flee the Republic themselves; what unspoken complicity, or lack thereof, existed in this special cadre of officers assigned to this checkpoint. Most tellingly, what were the unspoken thoughts of these men as they watched Westerners freely coming and going across this most contentious of ideological divides? The captors were possibly even more imprisoned than their fellow citizens whom they were helping keep captive. Because every working day they found themselves just a few steps away from a world where travel wasn't restricted and a large degree of individual liberty was allowed. Or were these men the ultimate true believers, indoctrinated to consider the West a heartless mercantile machine that imprisoned its citizenry in an endless cycle of consumerist want and misery?

And then——in the midst of all this ideological tug-of-war, backed up by two major military-industrial complexes and the omnipresent shadow of mutually assured destruction——there was this thing called day-to-day life. As in: the stout, fifty-something man in a shapeless anorak crossing in front of me as I left the checkpoint. He was carrying a vinyl brown briefcase and a plastic bag with two bottles of beer. An imitation brown fur hat was on his head, He was heading toward the grim concrete block of apartments located on the street behind Friedrichstrasse. What, I wondered, was this man's occupation? He'd evidently been working on a very early shift, as he was heading home with beer at 1:16 in the afternoon. Did he live alone in a tiny apartment? Was he regarded as a citizen of such unquestionable loyalty that he could be housed so near The Wall? Once he was home, would he kill the time watching television or reading or perhaps heading out to some sports center nearby? Did he have a hobby that helped pass the time? If there was a woman in his life, did they live together? Or perhaps they worked together in the bottling plant where they both did the four-a.m.-to-noon shift daily and, as she was married to a cop, they had to meet clandestinely at his apartment for a few stolen hours twice a week. And look over there at that hunched woman in a plain gray cloth coat, following right behind this guy. She had a drab paisley scarf covering her head, a cigarette between the fingers of her left hand, a bag with some sad-looking daffodils clutched in her free fingers. Was she the cop's wife, keeping a discreet distance behind her lover as they headed back to his place for their hurried assignation?

Or was I just having a moment's imaginary improvisation on my first sight of street life in East Berlin?

As he disappeared around a corner, followed by the woman with the head scarf, I found my attention diverted by a squat stone building to my immediate right. A sign above its doorway read: "Bulgarische Handelsbank." The Bulgarian Trade Bank. The building——nineteenth-century, in need of patching up and a coat of paint——had two storefront windows. They were both streaked with dirt. Taped directly onto them from the inside were yellowing photographs of happy peasants in the field, cheerfully bringing in that season's wheat crop. Over these circa 1957 socialist realist snapshots were hand-painted slogans, the rough translations of which were: *We Believe in the Five-Year Plan . . . Together We Can Build the Socialist Future!* Snow began to fall, so I thought it best to keep walking. Friedrichstrasse was, historically, one of the main thoroughfares and shopping precincts in Berlin. But the street I looked up was shuttered, empty. An occasional Trabant car crept up the road. There were a few heavily bundled up citizens in drab coats walking with their heads down against the snow. There was a clothes shop that was noteworthy for the paucity of items on show, the elderliness and shapelessness of the fashion, and the fact that this emporium looked so much like one of those charity shops I occasionally saw on the Lower East Side of Manhattan. The difference here was that it was the only shop of note on this street. In fact, all of Friedrichstrasse appeared to be a testament to civic neglect. Cities are, on one level, visual exercises in façades. It's all architectural window dressing——and, as such, an immediate, if superficial, conduit into the spirit of the place. Paris exudes elegant gravitas. Manhattan informs you constantly of its altitudinous ambition. However, these are merely first-glance observations. Surface scratches. Urban shorthand. But just as all clichés are rooted in a basic, crude verity, so it is also true that initial visual impressions do tell you plenty about a newfound terrain. What so gripped me about Friedrichstrasse——especially as I turned left onto Unter den Linden——was the realization that this was a city in thrall to the communal aesthetic that stated: all optics must be drab, spiritless, devoid of color. A world of grainy black-and-white.

Unter den Linden. The great processional boulevard of Berlin, leading to the Brandenburg Tor, the Reichstag, and the forested playing fields of the Tiergarten. As soon as I stepped out on its wide thoroughfare, I turned west. How did I know this geographic direction? Because The Wall brutally clipped the flow of the avenue, with the Brandenburg Gate appearing above it. The shell of the Reichstag——long since abandoned by the Bundesrepublik when it began its postwar reconstruction in the quiet functionary environs of Bonn——hovered on the far side as well. I stared long and hard at this prospect from the center of Unter den Linden. From here The Wall so dominated everything. On the side streets in my own corner of Kreuzberg, you could be forgiven for thinking that The Wall was simply a dead end, an interference, the world's biggest *No Trespassing* sign. But that was a perspective informed by the fact that I was on the western side of the edifice. But here, in the East, on this most ceremonial of Berlin boulevards, The Wall took on the status of an obscenity. By placing it directly at the end of Unter den Linden, the East German authorities were informing its citizens and the rest of the world: *We are barricading ourselves in here and we celebrate this. We are happy to flaunt the extremity of this measure. Happy to remind you that this is a closed place.*

I had always been suspicious of the sort of standard issue anti-Communist rhetoric spouted by Reagan and his cronies. Just as I also was unnerved by the "America: Love It or Leave It" doctrine of the so-called Moral Majority who accepted the flag-hugging claptrap enunciated by every ambitious conservative American blowhard from the appalling Joe McCarthy onward. But standing here, looking at that Wall . . . it's not that I had an immediate Pauline conversion and would vote for Reagan's reelection in November of this year. Perhaps the heart of the matter was to be found in my own fear of restrictions, of being closed into a life I didn't want. That's how The Wall impacted me, as a symbol of confinement and limitation. The Wall said to me: *We will circumscribe you. We will demand allegiance to a doctrine, a set of social rules, that you have no choice but to obey. If you choose to play the dissident, if you dare act out the dream of simple mobility beyond*

*the frontiers with which we have enveloped you, if you dare publish (or just utter) out loud
thoughts that run counter to our doctrines, we will be merciless.*

Perhaps The Wall was just that: a tabula rasa on which your own
fears and internal contradictions could be reflected. No doubt there were
those in this world who had accepted the official creed that The Wall
existed to shut out impure capitalist/imperialist influence. Perhaps they
needed to believe this creed, as it allowed them to tolerate the limitations placed upon them. Perhaps there were those who rationalized it as
simply the way the world was. Perhaps there were those who didn't care
about freedom of movement, freedom of expression. Perhaps there were
those who were also convinced: *we had no other alternative.* Even though, to
this outsider, this Westerner, such a viewpoint was the height of self-de-
lusion. But don't we frequently perceive our lives through a blurred lens
that masks all the painful truths we prefer to dodge? Even when we tell
ourselves that our point of view is *the* accurate one we are not acknowledging the fact that it is simply *our* own singular way of considering our
lives and the world around us. Everything is subjective, including the
way you choose to look at the Berlin Wall.

I walked down Unter den Linden right to the edge of this blockade.
There were no guards here, no sentry towers. I knew from some reading I had done that while climbing over the wall itself was not difficult (it stood only around fifteen feet high), the would-be escapee then
encountered a no-man's-land, laden with trip wires and patrolled by
guard dogs. Hardly anybody ever made it through this death strip, as the
surveillance was too formidable and the trip wires too densely planted.
Then there was the well-known "shoot to kill" policy that all East German border guards followed when it came to firing on anyone who did
not halt when ordered to. To continue running after being caught in no-
man's-land was to invite death. Even though the standard jail sentence
for the crime of "attempting to flee the Republic" was three years——and
the subsequent loss of all employment or housing status in the GDR (in
short, an even more circumscribed and bleak life)——the vast majority of attempted defectors now tended to bow to the inevitable when
caught. The number of attempted escapes had plummeted massively in
recent years, as the authorities had become so ruthlessly thorough when
it came to closing off all possible avenues of egress. How strange to ap-

proach this edifice with the understanding that you were closed in by it, that the idea of, say, picking up and moving to Paris for a year to write that epic verse novel you always promised yourself you'd tackle was simply beyond the realm of possibility. How strange to have a barrier placed around your state as a means of reinforcing your immobility.

But I had grown up with the absurd idea that the world was my playground; that, as long as I didn't entrap myself, I was free to explore it as much as I wanted. That was the curious thing about life in the West. So many of us with the right educational and socioeconomic opportunities chose to close ourselves off into lives we didn't want, complaining how we had become enslaved by mortgages, car payments, children. Whereas over here . . . well, entrapment had a rather different meaning in East Berlin.

I turned an about-face and spent the next few hours exploring the thoroughfare that ran from Unter den Linden to Alexanderplatz. Just beyond the Komische Oper I wandered around a large, sparsely stacked Buchhandlung named the Karl Marx. It largely seemed filled with yellowing political texts and GDR editions of East German writers like Heiner Müller and Christa Wolf. But there was a small section of foreign literature in German translation——again, all official East German editions, and works that had evidently passed the stringent censorship hurdles set here because they held up a critical mirror to the bourgeois, capitalist systems in which they were written: all of Dickens, Flaubert's Madame Bovary, Dreiser's An American Tragedy, Hawthorne's The Scarlet Letter, James Baldwin's Another Country, Norman Mailer's An American Dream, Ralph Ellison's Invisible Man.

There was a rather fetching young woman seated at the main information desk of the bookshop. She looked about my age, mid-twenties, with long black hair that had been carefully braided and piled up on top of her head in an immense bun. She was slender, wearing a simple black turtleneck, a somewhat short brown corduroy skirt, black tights. Despite her lithe frame, I immediately noticed the fullness of her breasts, the pleasing curvature of her hips, the absolute clarity of her flawless skin, the small granny glasses perched on the edge of her nose that gave her an air of attractive bookishness, the seriousness so apparent in her eyes. She reached for a packet of what I presumed to be local cigarettes. They were called f6——the packet looking like a throwback to the Second World War. As she fished one out, I could see they were filterless and loosely made.

"Would you like to try a Marlboro?" I heard myself asking.

She looked up at me, surprised by the question, surprised by my German. I could see her taking me in immediately. Before crossing I had stopped by the little corner store near the Café Istanbul and bought three packs of Marlboro, thinking they might come in handy on "the other side." I could see her taking me in, noting the leather jacket I was wearing, the heavily soled English black boots, the thick scarf around my neck, and immediately sizing me up as an *Ausländer*: a foreigner. Then I saw her eyes darting around the store, seeing if there was anybody there. There wasn't, so she nodded and whispered, "Why are you offering me a cigarette?"

"Because I want to offer you a cigarette."

I came over and proffered the pack. Again a nervous glance around the shelves and even outside to see if anyone was peering in through the window. Again the coast was clear. She reached over and pulled a cigarette from the pack, then took a box of matches and touched the flame to her Marlboro and the one I had placed between my lips. She took in a deep long lungful of smoke, the smallest of smiles forming on her lips. Then she exhaled, asking me:

"So let me guess: you figured the way to chat up a woman in East Berlin was by playing the GI in 1945 and showing up with some American cigarettes. So before coming over this morning . . ."

"How do you know when I arrived?"

"Because you *all* arrive over here in the morning, and are all gone by the witching hour. That's how the system works. Unless, of course, you are here on official business, in which case you would not be here, trying to get me to spread my legs out of gratitude for letting me smoke one of your *so American* cigarettes."

"Who says there's any sort of ulterior motive here?"

"You're a man. There is always an ulterior motive. And you're an American——so you are an exploitative instrument of Western imperialism as well."

She said this last part of the sentence with such delicious irony that I found myself even more smitten. She noted this, saying:

"Ah, look at the shock on your face at talking with a Communist with a sense of humor."

"You're a Communist?"

"I live here. So I am what the system tells me to be. Because that's how I end up in a good bookshop like this one, in the capital, with a nice little apartment in Mitte which, I'm certain, you'd like to see."

"Is that an offer?"

"No, just a further commentary on the 'ulterior motives' . . . isn't that what you called them? . . . going on in that American mind of yours."

"How can you be sure I'm American?"

"Oh please. But your German is rather good, which is a surprise."

"My name is Thomas."

"And my name is of no consequence here because my boss, Herr Kreplin, will be returning from his lunch in less than fifteen minutes. If he sees me talking to you . . ."

"I understand. Any chance I could see you later?"

"Where shall we meet? In a café in my quarter where everyone will notice that I am seated with an American? Or perhaps at my apartment? You'd like that, wouldn't you?"

"Yes, actually I would."

My directness gave her pause for thought. Again a fast glance through the plate glass window into the street beyond.

"Perhaps I might like that, too, even though I doubt my boyfriend would approve. Not that he is that worthy of fidelity. But the problem with anything happening beyond this casual conversation in this book-shop is: when word got back to the 'authorities' that I was seen with a foreigner, an American, in a bar or had the audacity to invite him back to my apartment . . . and, trust me, someone would see us, someone would inform . . . well, good-bye to my nice job in one of the best bookshops in Berlin. And all because I was seduced by a Marlboro."

Another deep drag on her cigarette.

"But it is a very good cigarette."

"Keep the pack," I said, putting it into her hand. As I did so she covered my hand with her free one and said:

"You must go. Go right now. Because if Herr Kreplin spies me here with you . . ."

"No problem. But please tell me your name."

"Angela."

"Nice meeting you, Angela."

"Nice meeting you, Thomas. And I won't say 'See you around.'"

"That's a shame."

"No," she said, her voice suddenly hard. "That is reality. And now, *Auf Wiedersehen.*"

I wished her good-bye and left. As I looked back, I saw Angela quickly secreting the Marlboros in her bag, her face radiating anxiety. A man in his fifties, carrying a vinyl attaché case and wearing a gray vinyl jacket, came walking toward me. He had thick Coke-bottle glasses. He looked me over with clear distrust. Once he had passed me, I turned around and saw that he had headed into the Karl Marx Buchhandlung. Was that Herr Kreplin? If so, Angela was right to shoo me away so quickly. He looked like such a functionary, such an informer.

And how the hell could you surmise that from a once-over glance on the street? Because Angela indicated that he wasn't someone who would look kindly on her conversation with an American. And therefore . . .

We all make instant summations like this, don't we? Especially when there is the edgy realpolitik of the East-West divide heightening the tension. And yes, I did feel an exhilarating tension while walking the streets of East Berlin. The tension of being in a largely forbidden place, where the undercurrent police state paranoia was already tangible. East Berlin: the bogeyman of all Cold War nightmares.

I pushed north, past the once-ornate, Hapsburgian-style collection of buildings that housed Humboldt University. I approached the front portals, thinking it might be interesting to wander inside, see if I could fall into conversation with some students, get an atmospheric whiff of life in an Eastern Bloc university, maybe even talk my way into a few beers at a local *Stube* with whomever I met. But as I got closer to the entranceway, I saw a uniformed guard checking the ID cards of everyone entering the premises. He glanced in my direction. From the look on his face he made it very clear that he'd immediately clocked me as a Westerner and was wondering why I was walking toward the entrance to this East German university. I smiled at him in a manner that hopefully hinted I saw myself as a thoroughly ditzy tourist who had wandered into the wrong place. With a quick about-face I headed back toward Unter den Linden.

I was in an area that had evidently not been flattened by the Allied bombing raids that had leveled Berlin. The western sector of the city, on the other hand, had been devastated beyond any sort of repair. The few historic buildings that remained in the West——the graceful apartment blocks around Savignyplatz, the occasional fin de siècle hotel——were somewhat akin to the two passengers of a jumbo jet who walked away alive when the rest of the flight went down. The ravaging was so thorough, so scorched earth, that little remained. Perhaps that was one of the stranger ironies about the postwar division of the city. The Western powers were handed the most leveled of landscapes and, in conjunction with the emerging new Bundesrepublik, reconstructed a city in a mishmash of modernist styles that radiated a certain raffish energy. Though the eastern sector also suffered dreadful bombardment, many of its quarters remained semi-intact, while the great ceremonial buildings leading up to Alexanderplatz also managed to largely survive. The problem was, the East couldn't afford the funds needed to restore them back to their original splendor——and the prevailing Communist aesthetic was brutal and based in reinforced concrete.

So after the decayed splendor of Humboldt University and the Staatsoper and the extraordinary sight of the Berliner Dom——that vast variation on the St. Paul's school of ecclesiastical architecture, its charred black dome reflecting certain historic realities——the German Democratic Republic had constructed perhaps the ugliest public works building I had yet to encounter. A squat concrete box stretching over several acres, angular and blunt in its lines, ashen gray breezeblock in color, and finished in a pebble-dash style. It was a profoundly Stalinist civic monument——the most striking statement yet of the way the hierarchy of this state saw the world. For this was Der Palast der Republik: their parliament and the administrative nerve center of the Socialist Workers Party that always won every rigged legislative election with 90 percent of the vote. Aesthetically, the People's Palace reflected the visual barbarity that was The Wall. It informed all onlookers: In this People's Republic there is no belief in the redemptive power of beauty. There is just this stark vision of life as harsh, callous, unkind.

Further up Unter den Linden the boulevard intersected with one of the great geographic locations in twentieth-century German literature, Alexanderplatz. For here Alfred Doblin set his famous 1929 novel, *Berlin Alexanderplatz*. It not only painted a panoramic portrait of low life in this, the actual physical center of Berlin. It remains one of the great novels to have emerged during the Weimar Republic: that German golden age between the two world wars when the country underwent nothing short of a creative revolution and reasserted itself as the great artistic innovator of its time. So much that emerged from the Weimar Republic——from the Brecht and Weill collaborations, to Walter Gropius and the Bauhaus School of Architectural Modernism, to Thomas Mann's dense bildungs-romans, to the visionary early films of Fritz Lang——let it be known that Germany (and, specifically, its capital city, Berlin) was so cutting edge, so out there when it came to redefining the global artistic landscape. The arrival of Nazism at the end of the 1920s was the jackboot forcibly crushing this brief, short interregnum of wild creative freedom and easy mores.

And I knew from photographs that Alexanderplatz had been largely leveled in the last war. Just as I also knew that the East Germans had chosen to build an iconic symbol——a looming television tower——right in the center of the bomb site. But what I wasn't prepared for was the way they had also turned the entire area into a bleak high-rise ghetto. Concrete canyons. Bleak apartment blocks. Empty shopping precincts. No color. No vegetation. No sense of anything geared toward making this urban landscape livable, tolerable.

I ducked into a café just opposite the Alexanderplatz tram stop. It was all linoleum and lit by fluorescent tubes. There was a lingering smell of grease and overcooked cabbage. I sat down at one of the tables. A lone woman——big hipped, an overplump face, her hair in curlers——was behind the counter.

"*Ja?*" she asked tonelessly.

"Coffee, please," I said.

As I waited for it to arrive, I took out my notebook and started jotting down all that had happened to me in the hours since crossing Checkpoint Charlie. I also fished out a Marlboro and lit it up.

"Can I have one, too?" came a voice from a corner of the café.

I looked over and saw a guy around my own age, sitting in a corner. His complexion was copper colored, he had close-cropped black hair, he was wearing a distressed brown leather jacket and the sort of jeans that had been so bleached they were a mishmash of blue denim and white rivulets. He had a packet of f6 cigarettes and a cup of coffee on the table in front of him.

"Help yourself," I said, tossing the pack of cigarettes over to him.

He caught the pack and fished one out, immediately lighting it up.

"We can buy Marlboro back in Luanda," he said, his German decent, if heavily accented (like my own).

"You're Angolan?" I asked.

"That's right. How did you know Luanda? You've been there?"

"Not yet. But I like reading maps. So what are you doing here in East Berlin?"

"Sitting in this café and bothering people, as always."

This was the voice of the woman behind the counter as she came toward me with my cup of coffee, adding:

"I always tell him I don't want his kind in here, but he keeps coming back."

"He's not bothering me," I said. "And explain what you mean when you say 'his kind.'"

The woman glared at me, shoving the coffee in front of me and causing some of it to spill over into the saucer.

"Thirty pfennigs," she said.

"Cigarette?" I asked, proffering the pack of Marlboros. She instantly took one and stormed off into the kitchen behind the counter.

"She hates me," the guy said.

"I'd say she hates everyone."

"You've got that one right," he said. "Can I . . . ?"

He motioned to the seat next to mine.

"Of course."

I now made the mistake of sipping the coffee. It was the color of light brown urine. The taste was commensurate.

"You're American?" he asked.

"That's right."

"You over on a day pass?"

"Something like that."

"West Berlin must be cool."

"Haven't you been over there?"

"Not allowed."

"But surely, as you're not East German . . ."

"Part of the deal with my scholarship. They won't let me leave the country, except to go home to Luanda. And as my course is three years long . . ."

"What are you studying?"

"Chemical engineering."

"Is the course good here?"

"The professors know what they are talking about. The rest of the students . . . I have no friends, except two other Angolans. Before I came here, I was told the German Democratic Republic loves Africans from 'fraternal socialist countries.' The women will throw themselves at you. The truth: I show up here and everyone acts as if I don't exist. I want to go back to Luanda——but my father tells me his standing in the Party back home will be undermined if I quit now. I want to get a visa for West Germany, but my two Angolan friends here told me we are watched all the time. Anyway, the East German border guards have instructions to turn us back if we ever try to approach a border crossing. That's the thing about being a citizen of a 'fraternal socialist country.' You are as entrapped here as everybody else. At least, back home, I am among my own people. And the sun is in the sky most of the year. Here . . . it's all dark."

He said this all in a low voice, the woman, who had re-emerged from the kitchen glaring at us from behind the counter, trying to see if she could discern what he was saying. Why he had chosen me to impart this information so suddenly and freely was evident. Like the person you meet sitting next to you on a plane who unloads onto you his darkest secret and you realize that (1) he has a burning need to articulate that which is gnawing at him constantly; and (2) he knows you are completely outside his realm of contact, let alone someone with a degree of influence or power over his life. Were he to get friendly with a German classmate at his university here and inform him what he truly felt about life in East Berlin he could find himself next talking with the Stasi and representatives of his embassy. But a complete stranger and one who he had established is an American over on a Cinderella visa? I was the ideal candidate, especially as I had a packet of Marlboros on the table in front of me.

"Mind if I . . . ?" he asked, pointing to the pack.

"Go ahead. Why don't you keep them?"

He looked genuinely surprised.

"You sure?"

"I'm sure."

The woman behind the counter scowled some more.

"She will tell someone about this. I live across the street. I usually come in here for coffee, even though the coffee is shit. But it's the only place to have coffee around here. But I know she will now report me for speaking with a foreigner. Maybe, if I get lucky, they will deport me."

He stood up, scooping up the pack of cigarettes.

"Thanks for the Marlboros."

And he was gone.

Once he was outside the door, I returned to my notebook, letting the terrible coffee go cold, occasionally glancing at the woman behind the counter. She was sitting on a stool next to the fridge, smoking and staring blankly up at the yellowed and mold-ridden ceiling tiles. Her eyes were heavy, her expression one of blank exhaustion, a visual expression for which the Germans have a word: weltschmerz. World-weariness. How I wanted to know what was eating her. A bad marriage? No man in her life? A divorce, and a new boyfriend who drank too much and occasionally lashed out with his fists? Loneliness? The futility of this job, with no further horizons beyond this café, this city, this highly regulated society? A sense that, in the great time-space continuum, what did someone who worked in an Alexanderplatz café leave behind? (Then again, unless we were that once-in-a-generation shape shifter of the human landscape, what did any of us leave behind?) Or, perhaps, just perhaps, I was being far too absurdly existential here. Perhaps she was just having a bad day. So I asked her just that.

"Bad day?"

Though she clearly heard me she didn't turn her gaze away from the ceiling tiles. And her reply was nothing more than a simple shrug. I gathered up my things and, with a simple *Auf Wiedersehen*, headed toward the door.

"Could I have another cigarette?" the woman asked.

I came over and put my spare pack of Marlboros in her hand.

"Keep them," I said.

"Not necessary," she said, handing them back to me. "Just one cigarette. That's all."

I opened the pack. She pulled out a single Marlboro and acknowledged her thanks with a small nod. Then, placing it behind her ear, she stared up again at the overhead tiles. The interaction was finished. I had to hit the street.

I spent much of the remaining afternoon walking around two districts: Mitte and Prenzlauer Berg. Proper neighborhoods with an interesting architectural stock. The Allied bombs had also spared much here. Though nearly four decades of civic indifference to their upkeep had left most of them in a blistered, shabby state, the apartment buildings and houses here were built on a nineteenth-century human scale. Unlike the faceless Stalinist blocks that so defined Alexanderplatz and environs, here there was a sense of ordinary life not subservient to the state. Yes, everything needed a paint job. Yes, the paucity of goods for sale in the few corner shops I passed was striking. But in Kollwitzplatz, in the heart of Prenzlauer Berg, there was a small park and playground, in which mothers pushed children in swings and sat on benches, smoking and gossiping. It didn't matter that their clothes matched the grayness of the cityscape, or that the playground equipment was, at best, austere. And it didn't matter that there was a huge billboard on the side of a building, exhorting the people to embrace the Five-Year Plan and featuring a Socialist Realist portrait of the longtime head of state, Erich Honecker, a man whose thick black glasses and drab silver hair and plain dull countenance gave him the look of a merciless tax inspector.

No, what mattered here were children running around and mothers talking among themselves. It reminded me that, whatever about the stark surface realities of East Berlin, the reassuringly humdrum still asserted itself here. There were meals to be prepared, beds to be made, children to be dropped off at school, buses and trams to be taken to work, jobs to do, the commute home, the dinner that night, the book or television or maybe even some external divertissement (a film, play, concert) to chew up the evening, and then bed——and perhaps the pleasures (or, for some, the torments) of sex, followed by whatever sound or broken sleep to which you were accustomed. The accumulation of days like these——with their rarely deviating routines——so constitutes, for the vast majority of us, the broad outlines of our sentient existence. The happy couple, the bad marriage, the profession that excites, the employment that stultifies, the intimacy that is transcendent, the intimacy that is pedestrian or nonexistent . . . all such pleasures and dilemmas, the entire spectrum of human experience, exist in all social landscapes, whether they are walled in or not.

As night began to fall, I found a dingy little restaurant off Kollwitz-platz——which, like the café I patronized earlier, was all linoleum and fluorescent tubing. There was a smell of boiled cabbage everywhere. I drank two shots of Polish vodka (very agreeable). I ordered a schnitzel, which was heavily coated in batter and largely tasteless. I washed it down with two bottles of local beer. Very drinkable——and when combined with the two preceding vodkas, germinating a nice buzz. The entire cost of the booze and the bad food was one mark fifty. I checked my watch. It was now eight. I walked back to Prenzlauer Alle and caught a tram to Al-exanderplatz, changing for the U-Bahn that stopped at Stadtmitte. Had this been a unified city, the station following this one would have been Kochstrasse. But the East Berlin U-Bahn system dead-ended at Stadt-mitte. There was nowhere to go now but up onto the street——which, as before, was Friedrichstrasse. Again I turned and faced west——and saw the gates of Checkpoint Charlie in the very near distance. I wondered where I could go next. But East Berlin at this hour seemed shuttered, closed down for the night. I knew I would return here soon again and go to the opera or a play at the Berliner Ensemble or find my way to a jazz joint, and see if I could penetrate the city's inaccessibility a little further. But with a heavy snow now falling——and nowhere now to go on this side of The Wall——I continued to sludge westward toward the checkpoint. By the time I reached it I was frozen. I was the only customer at the frontier. A guard emerged out of the little hut located next to the barricade and raised the arm that allowed me to enter the customs area. Even on this blizzard of a night I noted the three heavily armed soldiers standing out in the cold, eyeing me carefully as I walked into the customs booth.

I handed over my passport to the uniformed official in the customs booth.

"Are you carrying anything contraband on you?" he asked.

Do I look that crazy? I felt like asking him. But instead I just shook my head and said:

"No, sir."

"You bought nothing?"

What's to buy?

"No, sir."

He scanned my face, trying to see if I was in any way nervous or anxious. I was just cold. Then, inking his stamp, he brought it down on my passport. Handing it back to me he said:

"*Auf Wiedersehen.*"

I nodded back. Passport still in hand, I passed through the final two security checkpoints before reaching the big gate that fronted the "American Sector." Once there, I noted that there were three guards on duty: one to make a final verification of my exit visa and open the gate, the other two (I surmised) to watch their colleague as he let me out. Was this how they guaranteed no flights over the border by those guarding the border? Was everyone, in some way or another, watching each other and, as such, ensuring that they all remained within?

Perhaps the guard was reading my thoughts. Handing me my passport he said, in a flat, hard voice:

"You can go."

Then swinging the gate open, he motioned for me to move forward. I walked back into the West. When I reached the entrance to the U-Bahn I turned back to look at Checkpoint Charlie. But it too had vanished, the snow purifying everything——as it always does——by erasing all that we prefer not to see.

SIX

FITZSIMONS-ROSS WAS AT work when I walked in the door. He had a paintbrush in hand and was vigorously applying a blue undercoat to a blank canvas. He had some sort of free jazz on the stereo——which was as cacophonous as it was wildly animated. And he currently looked like a member of some Touareg tribe, as he was half covered in aquamarine paint. But watching him dip and sway to this full-frontal jazz——wielding the paintbrush with such fluidity, such technical expertise——I found myself marveling at his sense of complete immersion, the pleasure, the release, the solace to be found in losing oneself in the canvas, and being actually able to control the trajectory of something. That's the great consolation lurking behind all art: the fact that, during the act of creation, you have power over things. Once the painting is in the hands of your gallery owner——or your manuscript with your editor——you no longer own it or possess command over its destiny. But when you are at work, it's still all yours. You own it. Every so often there is a here-and-now in the realm of creative work like the one I was currently witnessing. A strange switch is thrown in your brain. You are not pondering or cogitating or thinking about what happens next. You are simply doing. The work has taken you over. You are so totally immersed in its epicenter, so absorbed in its trajectory, that you almost feel possessed by this force that is currently driving you forward.

Watching as Fitzsimons-Ross now attacked the canvas, all I could think was: *That's it. The moment. The most unbridled form of romance imaginable. Pure mad love.*

I crept upstairs, not wanting to disturb the flow of his work. Once I entered my rooms, I saw a scrap of paper left on my table, on which had been scrawled:

Was in the Café Istanbul this afternoon and His Eminence Omar said that the secretary of a Herr Wellmann called for you today. She asks that you call her back.

And below this was scrawled Alaistair's name.

The music blared on downstairs. Though I was deeply tired after my long day on the other side, I knew that to ask Fitzsimons-Ross to turn it down would be to kill the moment. So I opened a bottle of wine and my notebook and got the rest of the evening down on paper. The music snapped off at four. Still awake, I wandered downstairs. Fitzsimons-Ross was seated at the kitchen table, a vodka bottle and a glass on the table, looking spent, punch-drunk, and so covered with paint it was as if he'd been in the line of Jackson Pollock's fire. He was lighting a Gauloises and refilling his glass. I stared over at the canvas on which he'd been at work. The sharp lines of his boxes and rectangles which so characterized the previous canvases had suddenly blurred at the boundaries. The effect was instantly hypnotic, as if his crisp geometric world was now becoming less distinct, more progressively edgy. The blue undercoat was no longer that bright azure or lazuline shade that so called to mind Santorini on a white-hot midmorning in summer. Rather this blue was more darkly hued, more troubled, more inclement in its chromaticism. A blue that reflected a worldview closer to Berlin than to Greece——though unless I wanted to be subject to a torrent of abuse, I wouldn't dare voice such an observation to Fitzsimons-Ross. Anyway it was he who started the conversation, looking up from his vodka with eyes that, despite their late-night, post-work-marathon heaviness, still had that strange, focused incandescence, a radiance that only dimmed after he had given himself his twice-daily fix.

"Didn't see you come in," he said.

"You were busy."

"You didn't tell me to turn off the music."

"I didn't want to disturb you. You looked rather involved."

"So you were spying on me."

"It's good, that canvas."

"It's not 'a canvas,' it's a fucking painting."

"I still like it."

A shrug from Fitzsimons-Ross. Then he picked up an object from the shelf behind him.

"Just been reading this rubbish."

He tossed the object across to me. It was my book on Egypt.

"Where did you get this?"

"I actually bought a copy."

"Really?" I asked.

"Don't sound so fucking surprised. There's an English language bookshop not far from The Café Paris in Kantstrasse. And, voilà, Thomas Nesbitt on Egypt."

"I'm pleased."

"That doesn't mean I liked it."

"You didn't?"

"Actually I thought it pretty damn accomplished for a first book—and that is not damning with faint praise. You're talented. You're a first-rate observer . . ."

"I hear a 'but' on its way . . ."

"The 'but' isn't a criticism. Rather, an observation . . ."

"Which is . . . ?"

"You haven't been fucked over enough by life as yet. Maybe you believe you have. The unhappy parents, a couple of relationships that went nowhere, largely because you couldn't commit . . ."

"I never said that."

"No need to, Tommy Boy. It's tattooed on your bloody forehead. *Please love me . . . please don't crowd me.*"

"That's not fair," I said, thinking: *how the hell did he get me so damn well?*

"Perhaps not—but it's spot on accurate. Bull's-eye. And how can I ascertain that? Because I am cut from the same flinty cloth, my child. You need to let yourself get hurt, Tommy Boy. It will move you out of cleverness—of which you possess a great deal right now—and into darker realms. But don't take my word for it. I depend on smack twice a day to level the playing field on which I operate."

"You've never been in love?"

"Repeatedly."

"I mean, 'seriously.'"

He motioned to the vodka bottle and the empty chair at his kitchen table. I went over to a cabinet and took down a water glass, then joined him. He poured me a shot and pushed the packet of Gauloises toward me.

"Seriously?" he now said, repeating the word in a mock version of my accent. "Have I *seriously* been in love?"

"That was the question, yes."

"Well, *seriously,* yes."

"And?"

He downed his shot of vodka and poured another.

"The facts. I thought I'd met the person with whom I wanted to spend my life. A gallery owner in London. Not *my* gallery owner. I never mix those worlds. No, Frederick had his premises elsewhere——and he stayed well away from my commercial concerns. He was twenty-six years my senior to boot. Old Harrovian, Oxbridge, very posh, very aristo. Everything I hate, and secretly admire, about the fucking Brits. Being the scion of a rather well-known family, he kept his queerness out of sight. Married some unfortunate and rather stupid aristo girl——who, of course, was blond and named Amanda. Was flayed alive legally when she found his 'dirty little secret.' By this time I had come into his life. When I met him he was caught between the desire to live the life he wanted and the need to live the life he had told himself he must live. 'Must keep up appearances, old chap' and all that other Terence Rattigan sort of *dreck*.

"But then I came into his life——and he into mine. And it was just so bloody right. On every damn level. I'd met my match, so to speak, and he his. After a few weeks, *shazam*. He decided to leave the family home and live with me. I had a studio in Hackney——dreadful place, but cheap. Frederick being Frederick, he found us a flat in Mayfair. Small, but rather wonderful. We set up house together. We were seen together publicly, and very much as a couple. This was seven years ago when things were much more closeted. Frederick did pay dearly, both financially and so-cially, for taking up with me and not bothering to hide it. 'Why should I hide the fact that, for the first time in my life, I am happy,' he told me the day before he died. And this from a man who, even with me at the outset, was so bloody buttoned up about his emotions."

"How did he die?" I asked.

"Cleanly. A coronary at his desk at the gallery. He was in the middle of a phone call when . . . *snap*. His heart simply gave up. A lifetime of cigarettes and red meat and all the complexities with which he struggled. It just finally caused his heart to give out. He was only fifty-three, and we'd been together just eight months. Eight sublime months. God knows Frederick had his tetchy side. And *moi* . . . well, I sense you know by now I am not the most balanced and straightforward man to have ever walked the planet. But, how can I put this? In those months together I woke up every morning thinking: I am with Frederick and life is bloody wonderful. It was the first and last time I ever embraced such an absurdly positive view of things. Frederick's death killed that. Killed it permanently."

"Don't be so certain of that."

"Oh, I am, I most certainly am. I know too damn well the truth of the matter, which is that I had my so-called moment in the sun, and now . . ."

"He mightn't be the last love of your life."

"There you go again on some Pollyannaish riff. That part of my life is truly dead and buried. I won't be going to that place again. And I am happy to have an arrangement like the one I have with Mehmet——thrice weekly, no strings, no ties that bind."

"Meanwhile, your paintings are getting darker."

"Possibly because I have reconciled myself to my overall condition. I have my work. I have a lover who means little to me beyond the nuts-and-bolts stuff. I sell just enough work each year to pay for my vices. And courtesy of your rent each month, I now have subdued the rants and threats of that shyster landlord. So——as lives go——it's a rather reasonable one . . . for a junkie."

He stubbed out his cigarette, saying:

"On which note . . . it's a bit after your bedtime, young man. As you well know, in order for me to sleep I need my 'medicine.' And since I sense you are rather queasy about needles, you pansy . . ."

"Say no more," I said and headed up the stairs.

I slept in until noon that morning——and woke to the telltale sounds of Fitzsimons-Ross and Mehmet making love. I blared the radio to block out their soundtrack. After making breakfast and showering I waited until I heard the slam of the door downstairs announcing Mehmet's departure. Then I ventured out. As always, after his encounter with Mehmet, Fitzsimons-Ross was mixing paint or stretching canvases or sketching——what he called "prep work that was also back of the head work." When I came downstairs that morning, about to head out to the Café Istanbul and the nearest phone, he looked up at me with considerable wariness that also carried with it a hint of embarrassment.

"I think I was hit with an attack of garrulousness last night," he said, looking up from a paint tray in which he had been mixing colors.

"Really? I hadn't noticed."

"Talking about oneself . . . it's so tedious. So American."

"And so Irish. Get you anything while I'm out?"

"Two packets of Gauloises and another liter of Stolichnaya," he said, mentioning the Russian vodka he always drank. "There's thirty marks in my jacket hanging up by the door."

The jacket, a battered brown leather item, was suspended from an old Victorian bentwood coat stand. I reached inside the jacket pocket and found the cash alongside a small packet of white powder, tightly bound up in a tiny plastic sack.

"Looks like you forgot something," I said, holding up what was so evidently a bag of heroin.

"Oh fuck," he said, dropping his stirring stick and marching over. "I thought I'd lost that."

He held out his open hand and I dropped the sack into it.

"Well, it's been found," I said.

"And in the one obvious place I didn't look. Jesus, I'm a catastrophe."

I hit the street. Once inside the Café Istanbul I ordered a coffee and asked Omar if I could use the phone. He put it on the counter. Having previously copied down the Radio Liberty number in my notebook, I pulled it out and dialed Jerome Wellmann's office. The same officious woman answered the phone. When I told her who was calling, her reply was as dictatorial as ever:

"Herr Wellmann will see you tomorrow at eleven a.m. Do you have our address?"

"Yes, I *am* free at eleven," I said, "and *no*, I don't have your address."

"Well, write this down," she said, "as we are certainly not in the phone book. You will need to bring your identity papers with you. No admittance without them. Do not be late, as Herr Wellmann has a very busy schedule tomorrow."

The next morning I arrived at the offices of Radio Liberty a good ten minutes before my appointment. I wore the one slightly dressy jacket I'd brought with me——brown corduroy with brown suede patches on the elbows, a black turtleneck sweater, and dark blue jeans that I had bothered to press for the first time that morning. I sensed I looked very Greenwich Village circa 1955 and only needed a well-thumbed paperback copy of the collected Edna St. Vincent Millay sticking out of my pocket to complete the picture.

The offices of Radio Liberty were in a bleak industrial corner of the city with the decidedly ironic name of Wedding. The pharmaceutical giant, Bayer, had a massive 1930s office block near the U-Bahn station where I emerged. It towered over a landscape of grubby apartment blocks and industrial buildings. Chauseestrasse——a onetime border crossing, now closed——loomed up ahead, as did The Wall which defined the immediate eastern horizon. Radio Liberty was located two streets away on Hochstrasse, not far from the Volkspark Humboldthain. It was housed in a low-lying, unmarked plain brick building. You could have easily imagined that the premises once housed a small precision tool factory. There was nothing on the outside stating that this was the West Berlin home of a well-known broadcasting outfit. But it was clear to anyone walking by that the enterprise contained herein was rather security conscious. There was a high wire fence of the type that surrounded school playgrounds in New York. Topping it was barbed wire. A bolted swing door had been fitted into a lower corner of the fence. There was a security camera focused on the street side of the entrance. As I approached the doorway and pressed the bell that was to its immediate right, a hefty man in a blue security uniform emerged from a small hut just inside the fenced-off area.

"Ja?" he asked, staring at me warily.

I had my passport at the ready and explained that I had an appointment with Herr Wellmann. He relieved me of my travel document, saying: "You wait." Then he went into the hut, leaving me outside, hopping from one foot to another, my gloved hands plunged deep into the pockets of my jacket, as a way of staving off the bitter subzero cold. After about ten minutes he reemerged and opened the gate, telling me: "You walk straight ahead to the door marked 'Reception.' Frau Orff will be there to meet you."

"Who's Frau Orff?"

"Herr Wellmann's secretary."

Oh, great. Her.

"Could I have my passport back, please?" I asked.

"You collect it on the way out."

He pointed toward the reception area.

I had expected to find myself face-to-face with a gaunt, highly angular woman with the demeanor of a prison guard or a mother superior. Instead Frau Orff was a most striking woman in her mid-forties: tall, slim, with long flowing chestnut brown hair and an ironic smile on a face that could have easily graced a French movie actress. She was chicly dressed in a black leather skirt and a red silk shirt. I immediately noticed the wedding ring on her left hand. She saw me take that in. Just as she could also see that I was thrown by her beauty——hence the ironic smile——as she proffered her cool hand and said in an ultra-dry voice:

"Herr Nesbitt. What a pleasure."

She led me out of the reception area, which looked much like a doctor's waiting room, and in through an open plan area of several dozen desks, alcoved off with moveable dividers. This open area must have covered three thousand square feet, and we were walking far too briskly (I had to stop myself from watching the sway of Frau Orff's hips as she strode ahead of me) for me to take in the inhabitants of this rabbit warren of desks. Up ahead, at the end of this open area, were several broadcast studios walls of soundproof glass allowing everyone in the immediate area to see who was in front of the microphone at a given moment. Between these two studios was a wall with a door. Outside of it was a sign:

Jerome Wellmann, Direktor

Frau Orff opened the door. We were now in an anteroom with a series of historic Radio Liberty posters dating back to the 1950s adorning the walls. Frau Orff's ultra-tidy desk was positioned right next to a second doorway, upon which she now tapped twice with her knuckles, and then entered once a voice from inside said:

"Kommen sie doch herein."

She went inside, then emerged a moment later to say:

"Herr Direktor will now see you."

I'd dressed correctly for my interview with Jerome Wellmann, as he too was in a corduroy jacket (dark green) with suede patches on the sleeves and a dark brown turtleneck. He was in his early fifties, with a long narrow face and a well-sculpted beard. His office was book lined, with framed photographs of Wellmann with major politicians (Ford, Carter, Helmut Schmidt) and key cultural figures (Ayn Rand, Mstislav Rostropovich, Kurt Vonnegut, Leonard Bernstein) who'd evidently visited his operation while on a trip to Berlin. I found it intriguing that Wellmann would intermingle pictures of evidently left-leaning Americans like Vonnegut and Bernstein with the Philosopher Queen of the Libertarian Right, Ayn Rand. It informed all visitors that the occupant of this office was no mouthpiece for orthodox American conservatism. The fact that Wellmann himself looked like he'd be very much at home giving a tutorial on Kant at Columbia also sent out a signal that he wasn't your typical Cold Warrior.

"As I'm certain you know," he said after motioning for me to sit in the chair opposite his desk, "there are Radio Liberty operations in Vienna, in Hamburg, in Trieste, in Munich. In these facilities they often have separate divisions for, say, Polish or Bulgarian or Czech language broadcasts. But here, given our unique position in this city, we concentrate solely on programs designed for our listeners in the German Democratic Republic. Now an important question: *Wie fließend ist ihr Deutsch ist?*"

How fluent is your German?

For the next half hour Jerome Wellmann probed that question, speaking exclusively to me *auf Deutsch*. I managed to keep up with him. He quizzed me about my college years, about my book on Egypt, about my life in Kreuzberg (I was rather selective about the details of my life chez Fitzsimons-Ross), and most specifically about my primary reactions to the day trip I made into East Berlin. Here the storyteller in me took over. I wove a tale about the woman I met in the bookshop, the Angolan engineer, but most of all my rather visceral response to The Wall as seen from the other side of the divide. Eventually he put up his hand and said:

"All right, you've sold me. We have a slot after the main nine o'clock evening news entitled, quite simply, *Notes from Abroad*. It's an essay——in which we give a journalist, a writer, free rein to comment on a journey, a current event. We put it out on our two services: in German and in English. We have several translators here who will work with you once you've delivered the text and we use several local actors to read the text in German. But you'll also read the original text yourself on our English-language broadcast. What I want you to do is essentially write something along the lines of what you just related to me——'Crossing Over for the First Time,' or whatever you want to call it. I never tell writers how to do their job, and you pretty much have carte blanche, especially as your take on things in East Berlin chimes in with our point of view. Make it smart and always know that we talk up to our audience. Instead of taking a Manichaean viewpoint of things——we're right, you're wrong——we prefer to see things in a more complex shade of gray. Of course this gets us into all sorts of trouble with the sort of rabid patriots back home who think we should be playing 'God Bless America' every five minutes. What they don't get is the fact that we are a much stronger propaganda tool by not being so righteous about life in the West, by showing that we can look critically at ourselves.

"Anyway, if this works out, we can discuss other possible assignments with you. But do understand our budget isn't the most robust imagin-able. We pay public broadcasting rates. I can give you two hundred dol-lars for the piece——but that will also include your fee for recording it. If that isn't enough, I'm afraid . . ."

Two hundred American dollars was around five hundred and sixty deutsche marks at current exchange rate. Rent and most of my living expenses for a month.

"That's just fine," I said.

"Excellent. Can you deliver this time next week? I'll check with the producer I'm assigning you, Pawel Andrejewski. He's Polish, as you may have gathered, but like everyone else who works here, his German is ex-cellent. Anyway, he's recording a program right now, but should be free in five minutes. If the two of you hit it off . . . and, I'm going to warn you now, Pawel can be tricky, though he is one of my best producers . . . but if you can work with the man, we have many slots that need filling. Our pool of contributors is, at best, erratic. So make a good impression with him and . . ."

The phone on Wellmann's desk began to ring. He reached for it, answering it with a *Ja?* and then immediately said: "*Schicken sie sie herein.*" Send her in.

At which point the door opened and a young woman walked in. I guessed she was in her early thirties. Medium height. Short brown hair cut in a simple pageboy style. Wearing a denim skirt with black tights and a long sleeved black T-shirt. She was borderline thin, and currently had a lit cigarette in one hand and a sheaf of papers in the other. I quickly noticed that, like mine, her fingernails were rather chewed up. Just as I also noticed that there was a slight tear in the right knee of her stockings and that the black calf-high boots she wore really needed a shine. Her skin was clear, well scrubbed. Though there was a hint of sleeplessness in the slight dark moons beneath them, what struck me most about her brown eyes was the way they radiated need and sadness and a definite softness within. This was a woman who, I sensed, had known pain but who wanted to present a dignified face to the world. The very fact that she didn't see the need to worry about minor sartorial details like a torn stocking——or could show her vulnerability by keeping her bitten nails unvarnished——immediately appealed to me. Possibly because I found her so beautiful. Not the sort of conventional beauty you associate with a model or a particularly winsome actress. Rather, a beauty that instantly emanated intelligence, vulnerability, a strong sense of self, a profound sense of loneliness.

And her reaction to the sight of me? I saw her fix on me. I saw her register the same brief moment of seismic surprise as we looked at each other for the first time. Then she immediately turned away and said to Wellmann:

"*Herr-Direktor hier ist die Übersetzung die Sie wollten.*" Here is the translation you wanted.

"Thank you, Petra," he said, accepting the papers. "And I want you to meet someone. An American writer——and a good one at that."

I was now on my feet.

"Thomas, meet one of our translators. Petra Dussmann."

She turned to face me. She took my extended hand. There was a brief instant when our eyes again met. She didn't look at me with rapture or romantic longing. But in that very moment of having her hand in mine and facing each other for the first time . . . well, quite simply, *I knew.* Just as, I sensed, she knew, too.

Then she disengaged her hand and turned back to Wellmann, saying:

"*Wenn Sie Fragen zu der Übersetzung haben, Herr Direktor* . . ." If you have any questions about the translation, Herr Direktor . . .

"I doubt I will," he said. "And you'll probably be working with Thomas here very soon."

Did I detect the smallest of smiles on her face as he said that? If so she masked it quickly and simply responded with a quick nod to Herr Direktor.

"I look forward to that," I said.

"*Ja*," she replied. Not looking back at me, she headed for the door.

As it swung behind her all I could think was: life as I know it has just changed.

PART THREE

ONE

L IFE AS I know it has just changed.

I wrote that line later that night in my notebook, nursing a beer on my kitchen table, my pen flying across the page. When I woke late the next morning and reread it my initial reaction was: *Oh please. It was a glance between you, nothing more.*

As I kept telling myself this while waiting for my coffee to percolate, another competing voice between my ears was asking: *. . . then why are you still rerunning that first meeting, frame-by-frame, inside your head? Why can't you wipe her face clear of your mind's eye?*

After Petra left the office, Wellmann was all business——making me immediately think that either he hadn't seen all that had just passed between us, or he chose to not comment about it, or it was all in my head, and I was guilty of an overactive romantic imagination. Picking up the phone, he summoned Pawel Andrejewski to meet us. As we waited for him, Wellmann informed me that, prior to my arrival, he'd had to put me through another security clearance.

"I'm not obliged to inform you of this, but I prefer to be as transparent as possible about such matters. I'm certain you know that no one works for us, even on a freelance basis, unless they have been cleared by the powers-that-be at our local branch of 'the brethren.' If you ever happen to meet around here anyone who identifies himself as connected with the United States Information Agency, do know that you are also dealing with spooks. Why am I telling you this? Because why should you work for us and not know this?"

There was a knock on the door. Frau Orff put her head in to inform us that Herr Andrejewski was awaiting us outside. Wellmann informed her that she could send him in.

Pawel Andrejewski appeared in the doorway. He was a fantastically tall, thin man with dense black hair and tinted rectangular glasses, dressed in black jeans and a black turtleneck sweater. He had a lit cigarette in one hand——and I could see him immediately sizing me up with a certain ironic detachment.

"I am needed, Herr Direktor?" he asked, giving a certain acerbic weight to the expression, Herr Direktor (unlike Petra, who used the title respectfully).

"Meet Thomas Nesbitt. I will pass on to you his book about Egypt. It's actually rather good. He's here in Berlin writing another book . . . about what exactly, Thomas?"

"About Berlin, I suppose."

"You mean, you are not certain what the book will be about?" Pawel asked me.

"I'm never certain about such things until I've done time somewhere."

"'Done time,'" Pawel repeated back to me. "It sounds like a jail sentence."

"Is that your way of looking at Berlin?"

"I am just repeating what you said."

"And I am thinking that you are misreading what I'm saying."

"You have written how many books?"

"Just one."

"So you are still a neophyte."

"Sorry?"

"One published book hardly makes you a proper author."

"Do you always play the agent provocateur on meeting someone for the first time?"

"Absolutely," he said with a smile.

"Well, as I am assigning you to produce Thomas's first essay for us," Herr Wellmann cut in, "I expect you to be professional and collegial. And I now want you to take Thomas around the operation, Pawel, and show him the proverbial ropes."

"Whatever you demand, Herr Direktor."

"One of these days you will lose your acerbity, Pawel, and the world will be a better place for it. I've told Thomas that he is to write us an essay about his first day in East Berlin."

"Shall we call it 'I Meet the Communists'?" Pawel asked.

"That's a brilliant title," I said. "You're a most imaginative guy."

"And I can see that this is a marriage made in heaven," Wellmann said.

"No, in Wedding," Pawel added.

"Now, both of you, get the hell out of here and leave me in peace. Thomas, welcome aboard. Don't let Pawel capsize you."

"As if I would do such a thing," Pawel said. "Okay, neophyte. I now show you the ropes."

As we left the office, Frau Orff stopped me, clipboard in hand.

"Your contract, Herr Nesbitt."

I was going to ask her how she knew what I had agreed with Herr Wellmann while in his office. But Pawel posed that question for me:

"Have you been listening in again to Herr Direktor's conversations, Frau Stasi?"

To her credit Frau Orff responded to this comment with a shrug and a sneer.

"You are the ultimate oxymoron: a Polish comedian."

"And you are a humorless woman."

I took the clipboard from Frau Orff, glanced at the sections about the fee, the delivery date, and the fact that Radio Free Europe would have first broadcast rights for this "on-air essay," then signed it.

"You are a very trusting fellow, signing *anything* this woman hands you."

"I regret, Herr Nesbitt, that you have been assigned to this 'gentleman,' who is anything but a 'gentleman.'"

"You still cannot get over me, can you?" Pawel asked, his tone bone-dry. Frau Orff shook her head and seemed to be suppressing a laugh.

"Let us be definitive about this, Herr Andrejewski. I have never slept with you."

"Are you sure?"

"Good day, Herr Nesbitt," she said, relieving me of the clipboard.

As soon as we were out the door, Pawel turned to me and said:

"Even if the Stasi were interrogating her, she would deny having slept with me."

"That makes it sound like an experience she wants to forget at all costs."

"She has a husband who's a serious fascist; that's why she can't say a word about it."

"Describe 'a serious fascist,'" I said.

"A Christian Democrat who is a senior executive for Krups, and who bears a striking resemblance to Wotan."

"You've evidently had the opportunity to check him out."

"He came to our Christmas party last year. I was very tempted to approach him and tell him that his wife is a rather robust fuck. But executives like him . . . they always have hit men working for them."

This repartee, I came to discover, was classic Pawel. He always spoke in a low, rational voice. Even when he was furious at the world, which he frequently was, he had a surface calm that was preternaturally spooky. As I later came to discover——like so many of the other denizens of Radio Liberty——he was also obsessed with the idea that there were others conspiring against him and that he was a possible target for assassination.

"Now, this is a woman you need to avoid at all costs," he whispered to me as he steered me into the main open-plan work area adjoining the studio. With a rapid movement of the head he pointed to a rather large and puffy woman in her forties with shock black hair, wildly rouged lips, and a gold ring on every finger. She was dressed in something that resembled a caftan and had a cigarette attached to a plastic gold filter. She looked like she belonged in some souq. Seeing us approach, she favored Pawel with a deep and profound sneer.

"Hello, lover boy," she said to him as we approached, her German heavily accented.

"Soraya, always a pleasure."

"You are, per usual, a dreadful liar."

"Say hello to one of our new contributors, Herr Nesbitt."

"Is he a friend of yours?"

"Does that matter?"

"If he is, I will have nothing to do with him."

"I've known Pawel all of two minutes," I said.

"If I were you, I would avoid his acquaintance from this moment on."

"That will be a little difficult, as Herr Direktor has assigned me to be his producer."

"My condolences," she said to me.

As we moved off, I turned to Pawel and said:

"Another of your big fans. Don't tell me you slept with her as well."

"Now that would be a taste crime. Though it will not surprise you to discover that she is Turkish, her husband is a Bulgarian midget who used to be secret police."

"And now?"

"He runs a business leasing portable toilets to building sites. I am certain it is all a front."

"For what?"

Pawel gave me an all-encompassing shrug, indicating a wide range of conspiratorial possibilities.

"Soraya is the Middle Eastern monitor around here. Speaks Arabic into German and Turkish, and was allegedly sleeping with an Ethiopian diplomat last year . . ."

I found myself laughing, as I began to sense a theme-and-variation developing in Pawel's repartee. Everyone around here ended up at this station not simply because they were in the market for a broadcasting job. Rather they were here because they were questionable characters with past or present histories that were, at best, shady.

"How is Robert today?" Pawel asked, approaching a rotund, jovial man with a huge Johannes Brahms-style beard and a formidable beer belly. He was dressed in a style that the Germans refer to as *länder*——i.e., the sort of green tweed jacket with leather collar and heavy green tweed pants that made him appear to be a cross between a Westphalian pig farmer and a Bavarian leprechaun.

"Robert is good," he said, stuffing tobacco into his pipe with the sort of vehemence that I imagined a chicken sexer applied to his chosen craft. "And my Polish friend, he is good?"

"Your Polish friend, he is *sehr gut*," Pawel said, faultlessly mimicking Robert's accent. Robert himself seemed to take no notice of this or, if he was cognizant of it, he seemed to be willing to ruefully ignore it. "And your Polish friend has a new colleague to whom he would like to introduce you."

After exchanging names, I watched as Robert Mütter pulled out a single match from the brown leather vest he wore beneath his jacket, struck it against the corner of his jacket, and ignited his bowl of tobacco, puffing away happily as he asked:

"A real American?"

"One hundred percent," I said.

"We only have one of those around here——Herr Direktor——unless you count our 'friends' from USIA."

"They are not our friends," Pawel said. "They are our secret masters."

"Are you certain our young friend isn't one of them?" Robert asked, all smiles.

"He writes books," Pawel said.

"So did Bukharin."

"Until he was purged by Stalin."

"And all because he opposed agricultural collectivism," Pawel said. "They shot everybody back then for speaking up against anything collective, even collective in-grown toenails, of which there were more than a few cases, especially in the Urals."

"Do you oppose agricultural collectivism, young man?" Robert asked me.

"Not if I am going to get shot for it," I said.

"A smart chap," he said, using the German for this anglicism——*ein Bursche*. "Welcome to our little club."

As soon as we were out of earshot, Pawel said:

"Don't let his Village Idiot fool you. He is the editor of all German news for our service——which means that, outside of Herr Direktor, he is the final frontier when it comes to deciding how and what we transmit in terms of 'Bundesrepublik' and 'Deutsche Demokratische Republik' news to our avid listeners in that prison across the street from us. With a job like that——and the fact that he's a Franz-Joseph Schmidt-style Catholic from Garmisch-Partenkirchen, the spiritual home of repressive Gemütlichkeit——it's clear he is also in the employ of the *Bundesnachrichtendienst* . . . not that a new arrival like yourself would know of such organizations."

"The West German Secret Police?"

"Most impressive. Let me guess——you are here in Berlin to gather material for that most specious form of postwar literary entertainment, the spy novel."

"I'm not a novelist, and I do think that your fellow Pole, Mr. Conrad, would object to your wholesale dismissal of espionage fiction, as he wrote *The Secret Agent* in . . .'"

"1907. And I now also acknowledge a certain autodidacticism on your part."

We approached the next desk. Sitting there was a young woman with spiked hair and a face that had been covered in white pancake makeup. She was listening to a reel-to-reel tape recorder on a pair of oversized headphones, the connecting band of which seemed to float atop the highly gelled peaks of her hair. She was smoking a cigarette and had three open bottles of Coca-Cola on her desk. Pawel addressed her in Polish. At first she glanced at him with a smirk, but then deliberately closed her eyes and began singing along, in jagged English, to whatever she was listening to on tape. It took a moment for me to decipher the lyrics: "Is She Really Going Out with Him?" by Joe Jackson. Again Pawel tried to address her. Again her smirk broadened as she closed her eyes even tighter, choosing to ignore him further. Now he tapped her on the shoulder. With great deliberateness she removed the headphones and made a big deal about letting her finger slowly descend onto the button that stopped the tape reels from turning. There followed a rapid-fire exchange in Polish between them, the young woman regarding Pawel with the amused look one possibly gives to a reprobate. Then Pawel nodded toward me and broke into German:

"And now you must meet my compatriot, Malgorzata."

"That's Margaret in your language," she said in very good English.

"But we speak German here," Pawel said, *auf Deutsch*. "And how did you know that Herr Nesbitt was an Anglophone?"

"He looks so American. The okay kind of American."

"You hear that, Thomas? Thirty seconds after meeting you, my *Zlota Baba* is flirting with you."

Malgorzata immediately said something back to Pawel in Polish——a slight edge creeping into her voice.

"Did I miss something here?" I asked.

"He called me his *Zlota Baba*," Malgorzata said.

"What's a *Zlota Baba*?" I asked.

"His 'golden woman.'"

"It is a term of endearment," Pawel said in German.

"No, it is a term of annoyance. But I am now going to do the intelligent thing and ignore you and ask your nice American friend . . ."

"We're not friends," I said, interrupting her.

"Then I like you more and more. I do rock and roll around here. I get to program all the degenerate music we send over The Wall. And what do you do around here?"

"I scribble."

"I'm certain you scribble interestingly. Hope to see you again."

Then the headphones covered her ears. Swiveling around in her chair, she showed Pawel her back.

"You really have a way with women," I said as we moved on from Malgorzata's desk.

"Actually I do, as she was another of my conquests."

"Let me ask you something. Who haven't you slept with around here?"

"Her," he said, nodding toward the woman now crossing the office floor and heading into one of the studios. Petra. I doubt she heard Pawel——but at the precise moment that he said "her," she glanced over in our direction. Seeing me she seemed a little taken aback. Then another smile seemed to cross her lips before she quickly inhibited it and simply acknowledged me with a nod. Again, a curious electrical charge ran through me at the sight of her. Even though our moment of eye contact only lasted seconds, I found I couldn't take my gaze away from her as she turned away and headed into one of the studios, a sheaf of papers in her left hand. This time I noticed the slenderness of her legs, the graceful movement of her hips, the way she tossed her hair as she moved forward. Then, just as she reached the studio door, she turned around quickly and glanced my way again, giving me yet another nod. It was a look that meant nothing and everything. Nothing insofar at it was just a look. Everything insofar that she turned back and made a point of regarding me again. I found myself beaming at her. Her response was to lower her head and turn directly into the recording studio. Immediately I wondered if I had made the wrong move by giving her such a large smile——perhaps showing my hand far too soon, or stepping over some invisible boundary, the limits of which I had yet to discern. Whatever the reason she had ducked and turned at that particular moment, it threw me. And I knew immediately that it was going to continue to gnaw at me in the days ahead. *Knock it off, knock it off now,* the rational part of my brain told myself. *This is an invention, a fantasy you are playing out on a romantic theme——and with someone with whom you have exchanged less than a dozen words. You are weaving a fiction from nothing more than a look across a room.*

Pawel, meanwhile, didn't seem aware of this momentary glance between Petra and myself. Instead he just kept talking. But what he was saying interested me.

"She is untouchable," he said, motioning toward the studio where Petra was now conferring with a man seated behind a microphone.

"I see," I said, my eyes glued to the soundproof glass on the other side of the room. Petra seemed to be laughing with this not unattractive thirty-something man, touching his shoulder as he apparently said something amusing. *That's her boyfriend,* my bullshit meter hissed. *So much for your romantic reverie.*

Pawel kept talking:

"Not only that, nobody knows a thing about her, except that she's from the East and got expelled from the GDR for some political bad behavior——which, in this place, counts as very good behavior. I heard a rumor once that she had a man on the other side who was also 'political' and is still locked up over there. But outside of Herr Direktor and our benevolent spooks in USIA nobody has the actual goods on Petra Dussmann."

"Is she seeing anybody?" I asked, trying to sound as casual as possible.

"No idea. But if you are thinking about asking her out, don't waste your time. She is the most closed off person here. Always punctual, always professional, always thoughtful and intelligent when asked to comment on her translation work. Beyond that, *nothing*. Never socializes with any of us. A few months ago, at the Christmas party, she stayed for an hour, chatted with a few people, then left. I gather she lives in Kreuzberg."

Now this was news, but I decided not to share with Pawel my pleasure in discovering that she resided in the same neighborhood as me. Instead I kept my eyes fixed on the recording studio. She finished conferring with the man behind the microphone, then headed to the door, shooting him an ironic wave good-bye as she left. *Surely if they were involved she would kiss him or——even if she was working very hard at keeping her private life out of public view——shoot him a look that was meaningful.*

Oh God, how pathetic. Trying to gauge meaningful glances from a distance of around thirty feet. And wildly interpreting banter between colleagues as having some other overriding meaning. What on earth has sent you down this distracted cul-de-sac?

The door to the studio opened. Out came Petra, head down, not looking anywhere toward me, turning left and leaving the office area entirely. All I could feel was a jumble of thoughts, most of which centered around a sense of longing that had never entered my consciousness before. Though I kept telling myself this was all the stuff of silly instant infatuation, I refused to accept such a facile explanation. Something else was at work here. Something formidable and unfamiliar. I was in a new landscape, a terrain wholly different from anything I had ever experienced or traversed before . . . and it was still only minutes after seeing her.

And why the hell didn't she look my way as she left the studio?

"Of course, I asked her out once," Pawel continued on. "Not even a glimmer of interest. Everyone——even Big Soraya——engages in a bit of flirtation, even if it never intended to be anything more than that. Not our *Ossie*——our East German. She is a remote fortress. Back in Poland we always used to joke that the only thing worse than a Soviet practicing Communism was a German practicing Communism."

"But if she was ejected from the GDR, she evidently wasn't practicing Communism the way a German would."

"Perhaps——but she was still indoctrinated in the system. So it is there, within her."

"Not that 'within her' if she ended up a dissident."

"The thing about most dissidents is that they start out as true believers, then become so profoundly disillusioned that they go down the opposite path. It's a bit like excommunicated priests. They always end up the biggest heretics, fucking as many women as possible."

"Is that what happened to you?" I asked.

"Ah, you have that typical American view that everyone who fled a Warsaw Pact country is Ivan Desinovitch. Or that we are so oppressed that we simply dream of fleeing westward."

"You did."

"But for far more ordinary reasons. I was accepted at film school in Hamburg and received permission from my government to attend."

"With no strings attached?"

"Of course there were bloody strings. There are always bloody strings. But that is not a conversation I am interested in having just now. Perhaps later, when we know each other a little better. But for the moment I want to know about your idea for the essay."

By this point we had reached Pawel's desk. It had a large Solidarity poster covering one corner of his divide, with photographs of himself in dark glasses and a leather jacket, standing next to an older man, fifty-something, also in a black leather jacket and square dark glasses.

"Know who that is?" he asked me.

"A fellow compatriot?"

"You have your intelligent moments. Ever heard of Andrzej Wajda?"

"Your greatest living film director."

"You do know a thing or two. And Wajda was something of a father figure to me, and even pulled the strings necessary to get me the scholarship to the Filmschule in Hamburg. The directing program and all. The full ticket."

"So how did you end up here?"

"You mean, why am I making programs for American propagandists instead of making my own films?"

"That's more of a harsh assessment than I would have made."

"But, perhaps, it's what I think every day. Making films takes work, my friend. Work and big money and an ability to cajole and schmooze and promote and play all those games that I find anathema to me. I am lazy. And it suits me to be lazy. Which is why I am here at Radio Liberty, churning out programs so people in Leipzig and Dresden and the other Frankfurt——the eastern one on the Oder——can feel they are connected to the bright, shiny little world we allegedly have over here, and our bright, shiny sad little lives. I've now said enough, as you've sidetracked me away from the subject of our conversation: your essay. As I have been assigned to be your producer, I need to know the parameters within which you plan to work."

He locked both hands behind his head and rocked back in his chair, signaling that he was all ears. I cleared my throat, took a deep breath, and essentially repeated the same pitch that I had given to Jerome Wellmann. Pawel sat impassively as I spoke, his face a mask of indifference. When

I finally stopped speaking, he shrugged his shoulders, ran his fingers through his thick hair, and finally said:

"So you cross 'the great divide' and find that the food is bad, the clothes are synthetic, the buildings gray. *Plus ça change*, as they say in the spiritual home of the bourgeois left. The thing is, my young American friend, what have you to say about East Berlin that hasn't been said before? What are you going to tell your listeners in the People's Paradise, which somehow makes them think: for once here is an *Ausländer* who doesn't throw clichés at us. Nothing you've told me so far sounds like it has its basis in original thought or observation——and, as such, it doesn't interest me. Come back in, let us say, four days with something original and perhaps I will consider putting it on air. However, come back with something as banal as you have outlined . . ."

The effect of his words was akin to a full frontal slap across the face. Whatever about Herr Direktor's enthusiasm for my ideas, Pawel Andrejewski was going to act the role of traffic cop, standing in the way of any forward progress I made here. More tellingly he was informing me that he had the power in this newfangled relationship between us. I wanted to say something back to him, along the lines of: "Herr Direktor thought the idea was just fine." But I knew what the reply would be: *"Herr Direktor isn't producing this slot. I am——and I think your ideas are trite."* At moments like these——when I was coming up against a formidable opponent——I often thought back to my dad, who had this habit of telling people to go fuck themselves whenever they did something to cross him. The result was a career that was all false stops and starts with no purchase, no lasting success. As such, at a moment like this one—— when I could have easily informed Pawel that I was a published author, that his boss had already given me the green light, and that I was certain that this whole business was a head-trip game on his part to see if he could throw me——I knew that the best tactic was to say nothing except:

"So what length do you want and when do you need it by?"

"Ten double-spaced pages due in four days, no later," he said. Turning away from me and picking up a pile of papers, he let it be known the conversation had ended. So I stood up, saying:

"See you in four days then."

Pawel gave me the smallest of nods. I walked off, scanning the office floor in the hope of catching sight of Petra. But she was nowhere within range. Zipping up my coat I headed out to the reception area, handing in the badge they gave me, and picking up my passport from the security officer. Then I hit the street. I was home in Kreuzberg within an hour. Back in my apartment I opened my notebook and went to work. Petra kept looming everywhere in my thoughts. I kept trying to reason with myself, insisting that I be realistic about such matters. *Listen to what Pawel told you about her. She's closed off, an ice queen——and intensely private. Why on earth would she be in any way interested in you? And even if she did smile at you, that was either her being polite or simply being embarrassed by your evident display of interest. You've blown it, my friend. She is just one of many women upon whom you have laid eyes and felt that strange rush of emotional adrenaline, as you have wondered: might she be the one?*

But I lie here. I'd never before had that strange, overpowering sense of certainty that came with the first sight of Petra. Though I tried to tell myself otherwise, a louder voice was overcoming the sardonic one that was counseling caution. And this voice was telling me: *Everything you think and feel right now is true. She is it.*

But how could I know that without even knowing who or what she was? How could I think such a definitive thought without any proof other than sheer instinct? What did it say about my inherent aptitude for such things that I hadn't a clue whatsoever about whether she'd even deign to have a cup of coffee with me, let alone play Tristan and Isolde in Kreuzberg?

Having finished writing up my contorted thoughts about all this, I closed my notebook with a decisive snap, recapped my fountain pen, and pushed them both away——with the knowledge that when I came to read these pages tomorrow I would cringe loudly at the naked naïveté of my longings.

I stood up and reached into the fridge and pulled out another bottle of Paulaner——my beer of choice at the moment, and at seventy-five pfennigs a bottle, very much within my budget. I rolled up three cigarettes to have at the ready. Then I walked over to a shelf on which I stored writing supplies and brought down my red Olivetti typewriter. I checked my watch. It was 12:33 a.m. The sooner I got this damn essay delivered to goddamn Pawel the sooner I might have a chance of contacting Petra again. Though part of me wanted to call her tomorrow morning and ask if she'd like to go out one night, I sensed that Pawel's assessment of her wasn't far off the truth——that, indeed, if I showed interest too soon the door might be abruptly slammed in my face. I had to attempt to play this coolly——and to prepare myself for the likelihood that this little reverie of mine was just that: a reverie with no future beyond the inside of my head.

Anyway there was an essay to write, which, if accepted, could possibly open a regular source of income while in Berlin. The less I had to spend on my advance now the less outside work I would need to take on when finally writing the book.

I took the bright red cover off my Olivetti and popped up the V-shaped stays that held paper upright, then rolled a clean sheet into the typewriter, and sat up in my chair, positioning the machine directly in front of me. I lit a cigarette, drawing the smoke down deep into my lungs, and wondering how the hell to begin. In the version I delineated in Jerome Wellmann's office, I was going to start with my experience of passing through Checkpoint Charlie——and the way the world suddenly shifted from Technicolor into a particularly grainy monochrome. But Pawel's critical blitzkrieg put the kibosh on that. Sitting here now, wrestling with that most daunting of tasks——the first sentence——I ran through Pawel's comments again. With great reluctance I found myself now agreeing with him. Why inform the East Germans what they always knew? Why trundle out the usual clichés about the grayness of life under Marx-Engels? Why spew forth the usual spy novel bromides about The Wall and the East German surveillance state? The trick here, so Pawel was telling me, was to somehow find a way to state the obvious without stating the obvious, to take an approach that sidestepped the standard-issue platitudes . . . even though I never damn well intended to be banal or platitudinous. But one of the tricks of working with an editor or a producer is to gauge early on what they don't want to read from you, or what gets up their nose and vexes them. With Pawel it was a Westerner going on about Eastern European glumness, so I would only mention all that in passing, and in as obtuse a way as possible. Instead of relating my encounter with the rather attractive bookshop assistant on Unter den Linden or the glum Angolan in that godawful café near Alexanderplatz, I would write about . . .

Suddenly my fingers began to pound out a first sentence.

Why does snow silence the world? Why does snow purify everything and transport us out of the existential despair that characterizes so much of adult life and back to that realm of childhood: that magical kingdom where, as Edna St. Vincent Millay noted, nobody dies . . . and where nobody builds walls.

I paused for a moment, wondering if Pawel would let me get away with the existential despair comment, then also thinking that, at this stage of the game, I really shouldn't be fretting about the occasional phrase that might upset the man who now stood between me and an ongoing relationship with Radio Liberty. When in doubt, when worried about how others will view your work, there is only one solution——get it down on paper and fret about it afterward.

So I finished my cigarette and ignited another. As I exhaled another deep intake of smoke, I started to type, bearing down on the keys. For the next three hours I simply wrote, rarely looking up from the page, except to roll the next piece of paper into the machine, and reach occasionally for a swig from the nearby bottle of beer.

Then the last word was typed, and I pulled the paper out of the roller with a decisive yank, and tossed the final page onto the pile in front of me, and lit up a cigarette, feeling giddy and wired. I checked my watch. It was close to three in the morning. Collating the eight pages that I had written I put the cover back on my typewriter, then stored the essay underneath it as I placed it back on the shelf. I grabbed my jacket and headed downstairs. As I turned to head to the front door the voice of Fitzsimons-Ross stopped me.

"Productive bugger, aren't you?"

"Evening," I said.

"Middle of the fucking night is more like it. And you have been driving me spare with the rattle of your typewriter keys."

"Now you know what it's like when you blare Archie Shepp. Anyway, why weren't you wearing your headphones?"

"Because I can't listen to music if I can't paint. And tonight I definitively couldn't paint."

"Any reason why?"

"Because I fucking couldn't, that's why. I mean, do you get asked twenty fucking questions when you have writer's block?"

"I don't get writer's block."

"Of course you don't. Because you're an *über-mensch* American who can do no bloody wrong, who has not a shred of doubt in his entire being, who believes entirely in everything to do with himself, who . . ."

"Why don't you shut the fuck up and come out and have a drink with me?" I said, my voice a sedate contrast to Fitzsimons-Ross's rant. This gave him pause for thought for a moment.

"I'm being a cunt, aren't I?" he said.

"Something like that."

It was almost four when we rolled out onto the street. A dry night—— no snow, the sky as clear as any Berlin sky could be. The mercury was well below zero——but I was still feeling so heady, so bound up in the sheer exhilaration of having written for nearly three hours without a single need to alter my attention from the page, that I was still oblivious to such climatic extremities as minus ten degrees Celsius. Instead, I quoted Brecht, as set to music by his fellow Berliner, Kurt Weill:

"Oh show me the way to the next whiskey bar . . ."

A laugh from Fitzsimons-Ross——who, to my great surprise and pleasure, sang the next line:

"Oh, don't ask why, oh don't ask why. For if we don't find the next whiskey bar I tell you we must die. I tell you, I tell you, I tell you we must die . . ."

I came in here.

"Oh, Moon of Alabama, we must now say good-bye, we've lost our dear old mama, and must have whiskey, oh, you know why."

Fitzsimons-Ross suddenly waved his hands like a referee, signaling the end of play.

"That's it," he said. "The Moon of Alabama."

"By which you mean?"

"The bar to which I am dragging you."

"There's a bar here called the Moon of Alabama?"

"Of course there fucking is. We're in Berlin."

The bar in question was located a cab ride away. We found one prowling the streets within thirty seconds of deciding to head to this dive—— near Tempelhof Airport.

"Tempelhof: Albert Speer's last will and testament," I said, when Fitzsimons-Ross mentioned, as a geographic marker, the Moon of Alabama's proximity to the great extant architectural objet d'art from

Hitler's master urban planner. I'd already done a brief day trip to Tempelhof——because every damn book on Berlin waxed lyrical on its amazing Third-Reich-Goes-Art-Déco aesthetic, and the fact that it remained such a remarkable design artifact from an era that everyone on both sides of the German divide would rather forget.

"Ah, but all the Nazis had a faggot sensibility," Fitzsimons-Ross said. "It was the most closeted political movement in history, which is why they grouped shirt lifters alongside Jews and Gypsies as enemies of the state. Because from Hitler on down they couldn't accept their inherent campness. I am so fucking surprised that Hugh Trevor-Roper and all those other Oxbridgey Nazi specialists failed to make more of the fact that all the horror of World War Two emanated from the fact that Hitler and his cronies were a bunch of bum bandits. Look at the warped documentary masterpieces of his resident dyke film auteur, Leni Riefenstahl. Triumph of the Will and Olympia are two of the greatest pieces of homoeroticism ever consecrated on celluloid."

Fitzsimons-Ross delivered this monologue at the top of his voice—— and in a haranguing style that made him sound like he'd been mainlining Dexedrine (which, knowing Fitzsimons-Ross, wasn't beyond the realm of possibility). I must admit that I found myself highly amused by his rant, and was simply thankful that it was being delivered in English and not auf Deutsch, as the cabbie was one of those late-twenties Berlin toughies who probably wouldn't take kindly to the thesis which my fellow passenger was expostulating.

"Well, stop sitting there with that fucking smug Big Buddha grin of yours," Fitzsimons-Ross said to me, "and tell me I'm full of shit or something."

"I actually think you should go on the lecture circuit with this idea of yours. And start here in the Bundesrepublik, where you will undoubtedly win so many people over with your historical interpretation."

"Go on, mock me."

"But how can I mock someone so amusing, Alaistair?"

That was the first time I had ever called him by his first name. He acknowledged this with a raised eyebrow.

We pulled up in front of a doorway on a deserted street. Over the doorway, painted in Day-Glo paint, were the words, Der Mond Über

Alabama——the calligraphy fashioned so it looked like graffiti. The street was shabby. No shops, no residential buildings, no cars . . . just a few warehouse-style buildings, the moonlit night bathing them in a spectral glow. But what hit me immediately as we emerged from the taxi back into the frigid Berlin night was the wail of sound that came from within. A cacophony that was beyond loud, beyond extreme.

"I meant to tell you," Fitzsimons-Ross said. "This place is just a little out there."

We plunged inside. The sound was instantly deafening. We were in a corridor painted black, lit by purple tubes, with a biker guy——shaved head, bulging biceps, serious tattoos——acting as bouncer on the door and relieving us both of ten deutsche marks. I was almost surprised that he didn't pat us down for weapons. But as I came to quickly discover, *Der Mond Über Alabama* wasn't a biker joint, or a gay bar, or a heavy-metal outpost, or anything easily catagorizable. Rather it was an amalgam of all of the above——but also deliberately, wildly, absurdly excessive. We were in a room around the size of a basketball court, with a ceiling that was no more than ten feet high. It was painted jet black, the only illumination being more of the same long fluorescent purple tubes. There was a bar stretched along one wall. There was a narrow stage on the far side, on which were five black musicians——a trumpeter, a saxophonist, a pianist, a bassist, and a drummer——ranging in age from mid-twenties (the saxophonist) to early seventies (the pianist)——and all of them producing the sort of clamor and wild sonorities that one associates with free jazz. At least half the crowd——and the place was so dense with people that movement was tricky——were pushed up near the stage and seemed to be very much in a near-catatonic state brought on by the five musicians and their unbridled sonic howls. Everyone else was engaged in whatever form of escapism or indulgence or hedonism they had decided to practice——or for that matter, bump into——tonight. The bar seemed to only serve vodka and beer, and there were some very seriously drunk people crushed up against its confines. A low-level, sweet aromatic cloud of grass and hashish hung over everything, intermingled with an even far more dense fog of cigarette smoke. Just about everyone I saw had a cigarette to hand——that is, except the people who were shooting up in one corner of the warehouse, and the others who were disappearing, always two together, behind a black curtain. I looked around for Fitzsimons-Ross, thinking he'd make a beeline for his fellow junkies. But I saw him up against the bar, cigarette and vodka in one hand, deep in conversation with a rather short but very muscular skinhead. He saw me catch sight of him but didn't acknowledge me, instead returning to his conversation with the gentleman who also had an Iron Cross dangling from one ear lobe.

I turned away, trying to survey all that was around me. The music was assaulting my eardrums, the smoke making my eyes tear. The part of me that despises crowds wanted to turn and flee. The place had all the telltale makings of one of those public catastrophes where somebody sets fire to a curtain and panic ensues, with the result that several hundred people trample each other to death. But that was the ultra prudent, *always look both ways before crossing the road* side of me. The other part——the guy who loved being in the middle of extremity——looked around and marveled. What splendid decadence. What mad, collective hedonism, especially as everything here was out in the open. The junkies were shooting up openly. The coke aficionados, both the freebasers and the snorters, were congregated in an adjoining corner of the room. The heavy boozers were up against the bar, blotto. Joints and hash pipes and bongs were being passed freely. When a pipe came my way, I took two hits off it and immediately felt as if my head had been cleaved. Or as if I had walked into the hallucinogenic equivalent of an empty elevator shaft.

"You like that shit?"

The voice belonged to a diminutive woman in her early twenties. She had insanely long hair——it stretched to the middle of her back and was elaborately braided. Her face was made up in an equally elaborate way——the left side in a Kabuki-like white, the right in Goth black. Her lips were tinted purple, or perhaps that was the effect of the fluorescent tubes and the two hits of the herbal trouble that I had just inhaled and that was now making me feel outside, this madly congested place, and which also had the effect of turning the music even more violent.

"It's . . . interesting."

"Have another hit."

She passed me the pipe again. I drew down another small cloud of smoke. But this time I coughed it straight out again, the narcotic effect now robbing me of peripheral vision and turning all sound into an emphatic drone.

"What's in the pipe?" I asked.

"Skunk."

"What?"

"Skunk. Let's go."

She took me by the hand.

"Go where?"

"In the back."

I allowed myself to be led by the hand through the crowd, all ambient noise now reduced to a surreal monotone. After spending several minutes negotiating our way through the crowd we reached the black curtain. My companion pulled me through. There——on a series of mattresses——were assorted couples, all naked (or, at least, from the waist down), in varying stages of what a Victorian pornographer might have described as sexual congress. Perhaps it was the effect of the skunk. Perhaps it was the extremity of this scene. Perhaps it was the fact that there's a part of me which, even when under the influence of a mind-contorting substance, still backs away from the lunatic fringes of excess. Perhaps I am simply someone who doesn't like having sex with a stranger in public——and amidst twenty-four other naked heaving couples (not that I was making an exact count). And perhaps there was also something just a little off-putting about this tiny young woman with the weirdly two-toned face. Was she a member of some would-be coven of Wiccans? Another thing crossed my now thoroughly addled brain. Petra. What was I doing, about to fall onto a grubby, much stained, much overused mattress, with this rather strange person, if my heart was elsewhere?

"*Scheisse*," my companion said. "No free mattress."

I blurrily scanned the immediate vicinity. She was right. No room at the inn.

"Another time," she said, and drifted out of this area.

Well, that makes things easier, I told myself. Followed by another thought: *I really need to get the hell out of here.*

I don't remember much that followed this decision to leave, except that, as I turned away from all those naked, heaving bodies, I heard one woman say in a distinctly American accent: "They won't believe this back in Des Moines."

But when I scanned the room, trying to put a face to this voice, all I could see was a darkened, expansive congealment of the naked human form. No discerning features, no individual characteristics. Just a copulative phantasmagoria. It was something of which I wanted no further part. Maybe that was the skunk talking as well, as I was beginning to feel actively paranoid. So I found myself pushing my way through the crowd, making it down that long, endless black corridor and literally falling out onto the street, whereupon I was certain that secret policemen . . . agents of the Stasi, who had somehow already read my thoughts about East Berlin . . . these agents were going to bundle me into the trunk of a car and speed across Checkpoint Charlie and hold me for months, eventually using me as a bargaining chip to get one of their own operatives out of CIA detention. Then, when I was finally exchanged, the agency would wonder if I had been brainwashed and turned into a Stasi stooge operative . . . and, oh fuck, that skunk was too damn potent, and the car lights so damn bright out here, even though I don't see a fucking light in sight, and . . .

Suddenly, out of nowhere, a cab. I threw myself inside, managed to mumble my address——the driver, a Turk, getting just a little peeved when he asked me to repeat it three times——and then curling up in the backseat and beginning to sob like a fool. All the sorrows of my little life pouring out of me, all triggered by that insane substance I had inhaled into my lungs, and which had sent me over the edge of the emotional cliff, hurtling toward . . .

Finally, my front fucking door. I threw money at the driver, I staggered inside, upstairs, stripping off everything when I reached my bed, falling atop of it, shivering like the naked moron that I was, somehow negotiating myself up again and between the sheets, clicking off the bedside light, then holding to the pillow for dear life, as I was suddenly being taken on the roller coaster ride from hell. I felt the bed, the room, spinning out of control, sending me down a black slope toward a huge tree, the airborne pillow (don't ask) just about dodging this fatal dead end, and sending me flying, then hurling me straight down toward the ground, and vomit rising in my gorge, and me on my feet and careening toward the bathroom, just reaching the doorway as, out of nowhere, I begin to projectile vomit everywhere, and the regurgitation going on interminably and spewing in all conceivable directions, and me staggering out of there and into the kitchen, and turning on the tap in the sink, and putting my face under its frigid stream of water, and cursing myself, and feeling so utterly toxic and beyond redemption, and staggering back to the bedroom, and falling face-first onto the bed, and then . . .

Morning. Or, at least, there was light coming through the window next to the bed. I opened an eye. A bad mistake, as the very act of attempting to reemerge on Planet Earth was accompanied by a migraine of classic proportions. I touched my lips with my tongue and tasted the vile flavor of dried vomit. I tried to move but felt that enervating chill and fever that come with sweating profusely throughout the night, as the sheets were sodden and also stank of nausea. Standing up took some work——my equilibrium virtually nonexistent. Each step forward was an experience in disorientation. When I reached the bathroom, I nearly began to retch again, as I saw the remnants of my handiwork from the night before. Splattered vomit everywhere.

There are moments in life where you just simply want to curl up into a ball on the floor, press the palms of your hands against your eyes, and will away the after-effects of your stupidity. But Dad's Marine Corps legacy——the way he always insisted that I make my bed at home with perfect hospital corners and keep my shoes well shined, and clean up any mess I made——forced me to stagger into the kitchen, put my head under the sink's tap (didn't I also do this last night?), and allow all that arctic Berlin water to snap me into reasonable consciousness. Then I withdrew from the tall kitchen cabinet the mop, a bucket, several rags, rubber gloves, and a bottle of the German equivalent of Mr. Clean that I had bought when first moving in here. Over the next hour I mopped up the mess I made, disinfecting the entire bathroom, making certain that no visual or olfactory traces of my stupidity remained. It was slow, grubby work, during which I told myself: *now you know why they call it dope.* The events of the night before began to reassemble in my head. *You're lucky to have just gotten away with projectile vomiting and the mother of all hangovers.* Once the bathroom was spick-and-span and smelling of lemon disinfectant, the bed stripped and remade with clean linens, my body placed under a very cold shower, my teeth brushed repeatedly, two cups of coffee ingested (and held down) . . . after all this imposition of order upon personal chaos, I proceeded to spend the next hour getting all the gory details of last night down on paper. Only halfway through this exercise——in which I was thoroughly merciless——did I remind myself that I still hadn't bothered to check the time. Glancing at my watch, I saw it was two thirty in the afternoon. Jesus Christ, much of the day lost. I immediately began to map out what I would do to make up for it. Finish the diary entry. Head out to the local laundry with the soiled sheets. A very late lunch at the Café Istanbul. Then back here to start editing the essay——though I also told myself that, given the current state of my brain, it was best to simply read through the piece and consecrate tomorrow to whipping it into presentable shape.

Discipline, discipline. The only antidote to life's helter-skelter tendencies. But the more I pushed forward in my notebook with my account of that crazed, lost night, the more I also knew that I was so damn pleased to have bumped into such mad decadence. Just as I also couldn't help but wonder what everyone who had assembled there were ultimately looking for. On a certain level it was simply a fix, a fuck, communal inebriation, and a general flaunting of society's standard operating mores. *Der Mond Über Alabama* was all about collective subversion——and embracing the sort of sybaritic things that would land you in jail outside of its confines. I was pretty damn certain that the majority of my fellow attendees were as bourgeois in their backgrounds as I was. As such, I couldn't now help but wonder if we were attracted to a place like *Der Mond Über Alabama* for precisely the same reason everyone there had also chosen West Berlin as a place of temporary or permanent residence. Here you didn't need to be meeting the right people at the right parties. Here you didn't have to push yourself onto the world. Here you could sleep with whomever you wanted and not have people talking about it. Here you were ignored, as everyone was ignored in Berlin. We were separate and isolated, and I sensed that you only stayed here if that suited your temperament.

I finished my diary entry on this thought. As I recapped my fountain pen I noted that my general physical condition had upgraded itself from catastrophic to merely terrible. I gathered up the bag of soiled sheets and clothes I was going to drop off at the laundry. I put on my coat and opened the door to head downstairs. But as I began to descend I heard two noises that threw me: the *ca-chink, ca-chink, ca-chink* of a needle stuck in a record groove, and the more profoundly disconcerting sounds of someone moaning in pain. But the moan was so low, so guttural, it was almost as if they were gagging on something. Like their own blood.

Which is exactly what was happening——as Alaistair was lying in a broken heap on the floor, blood cascading from his mouth, his breathing irregular, contorted. His studio had been subjected to a cataclysm. Paint had been splattered everywhere, brushes snapped in two, his worktable turned upside down, a window smashed, and . . . this was too devastatingly awful . . . the three big canvases he had been working on shredded with what must have been a knife.

"Alaistair, Alaistair," I hissed as I made my way toward the debris toward him. But the pool of blood was engulfing him, making it difficult to get even close to him. I was instantly charging down the stairs, racing out into the street, into the corner shop, screaming at the startled man behind the counter.

"*Polizei! Polizei! Sie müssen sofort die Polizei rufen!*"

The man did as ordered, and when he informed me that the dispatcher at the emergency services said that an ambulance would be there in three minutes I ran in helter-skelter fashion back up the stairs, ascertained that Alaistair was still breathing, then dashed into his bedroom, opened the drawer on the bedside table where I knew he kept his heroin gear, ran into the kitchen, found a plastic bag, rushed back to the bedroom, dumped everything——his needles and hypodermics and tourniquets, a burnt spoon and three little packets of white powder——into the bag. Then I threw it all out the back window. At that very moment there was a pounding on the door. The paramedics and the cops had just arrived.

What happened next was wildly choreographed confusion: the paramedics diving in to stabilize Alaistair and stanch the flow of bleeding, the cops immediately deciding that, as I had phoned in the crime, I must be the perpetrator. They shouted innumerable questions at me, demanding to see my papers, demanding to know what my relationship with this man was. When I explained that I had been asleep upstairs, they demanded to know how I could have slept through such an assault. *Ever smoked skunk?* Instead I tried to explain that I was a rather heavy sleeper.

And no, I had absolutely no problems, no issues with Fitzsimons-Ross, no past history of violence, no entanglements with the law, no . . .

"For God's sakes," I finally yelled at the cops. "He's my friend. I found him here ten minutes ago and ran screaming into the shop downstairs. Ask the guy behind the fucking counter."

"You watch your mouth," one of the cops shouted back at me.

"Then stop fucking accusing me."

"You want to be arrested?"

The officer grabbed me by the shirt and began to shake me.

The other cop——the older of the two——put a restraining hand on his colleague's arm and said in a manner that made it clear it was an order, "You go downstairs now, corroborate his story with the guy in the shop. I'll stay with our 'friend' here. What's your roommate's name?"

"Fitzsimons-Ross. Alaistair Fitzsimons-Ross."

"You hear that?" the officer asked his colleague. "You find out if the guy in the shop knows Fitzsimons-Ross."

As soon as the other cop had headed off at speed, the officer asked me manifold questions about Fitzsimons-Ross: his nationality, his profession, his lifestyle. I painted a fairly benign portrait, saying that he was a well-known painter, quiet, low-key, and that our friendship was not one where we knew intimate details of each other's lives.

"But surely the fact that you were living here . . ."

I explained that we kept different hours, had very separate lives.

As this interrogation was going on, another two officers were scrounging around the apartment, pulling open drawers, pulling books down from shelves, heading upstairs to my lair to undoubtedly search everywhere. Thank Christ I had managed to get all evidence of his addiction off the premises——and was quietly holding my breath, wondering if Alaistair had stashed away some other drug paraphernalia (or, worse yet, the junk itself) elsewhere.

In the middle of all this, one of the paramedics shouted over to the cop that "The patient is stabilized" and they were going to move him.

"Will he make it?" I asked.

"He lost a lot of blood, but we have managed to stop the hemorrhage. If you hadn't have found him when you did, he'd have died ten minutes later."

I looked at the cop after the paramedic said this. He merely shrugged and continued pounding me with questions: "What do you do? Are you working here illegally? Where can I see proof that you write books?" Meanwhile, the paramedics lifted Alaistair onto a gurney, a transfusion bag suspended above him, a tube connected to his ravaged veins. They pushed him toward the front door, the wheels streaking the floor with blood as they headed off.

"One last thing," the paramedic told the cops. "Check this out."

Lifting the sheet that was covering Alaistair, he pointed to the track marks that were running up and down the nook of his arm.

"A junkie," the paramedic said.

"Did you know this?" the cop asked me, his tone now indicating that he was incensed.

"Not at all."

"I don't believe you."

"It's the truth."

The cop shouted at his colleague to search the place even more thoroughly, as they were now on the hunt for Class A drugs. Then he turned to me and said:

"Show me your arms."

I did as ordered. He inspected them carefully, clearly disappointed that they were so clean.

"I still don't believe you didn't know he was . . ."

But the officer was interrupted by the arrival of his colleague, together with the man from the corner shop. The accompanying cop pointed to me and asked him:

"Is this the man who ran in to your shop, yelling at you to call for the police?"

The guy knew me, as I made a point of stopping in there at least once a day to buy something. He was Turkish, in his mid-fifties, always downcast, but now wide-eyed as he surveyed the smashed-up studio and the blood that was everywhere.

"Yes, this is the man," he said, nodding toward me. "He's a regular customer."

"And was this the man you saw returning with Herr Fitzsimons-Ross last night?"

"No, not him."

"Are you sure?"

"I know the other man, because he is a regular customer, too. But this man wasn't with him. In fact, I've never seen them together."

"So who was the other man with Herr Fitzsimons-Ross?"

"That is his name?" the shop owner asked.

"You say he was a regular customer and you don't know his name?"

"I don't know the names of most of my customers."

"Describe the other man with Fitzsimons-Ross."

"Short, shaved head, with a tattoo on one cheek."

"What kind of a tattoo?"

"Some sort of bird, I think. It was dark."

"Was this the first time you saw this man with Fitzsimons-Ross?"

"I think so. The times I did run into him early in the morning he was usually with some man."

Now the officer was looking at me.

"So Fitzsimons-Ross often picked up men and brought them back late at night?" he asked.

"As I told you before, though we were friendly, I had little in the way of contact with him."

The officer shook his head, displeased with my response, while tapping my American passport against his thumb.

"Get a full statement from the shopkeeper," he told his colleague. "And meanwhile, Herr Nesbitt, we will see what the search of the premises uncovers."

A very nervous hour passed, while the two policemen assigned to the task pulled the place apart. Meanwhile, the officer took a full deposition from me. One of the officers came down with the one and only copy of my Egyptian book that I had brought with me——and showed the investigating officer my author photograph on the inside jacket flap. The officer also read my biographical sketch on the same flap and even opened the book to the first chapter and scanned the opening page.

"So you are who you say you are," he finally said. "And you are evidently an observant man, given what you do for a living. That is, if you make a living at it. Yet you still try to tell me that you hadn't a clue that

Herr Fitzsimons-Ross was an addict who had the habit of picking up stray men and bringing them back here."

"As you can see, sir, I live in a self-contained unit upstairs. I come and go at different hours from Herr Fitzsimons-Ross——and we barely see each other. But honestly, sir, I can't say that I know much about the man beyond the fact that he is a very fine artist with whom I have shared a beer perhaps twice since I moved in some weeks ago."

The officer wrote this all down, his skepticism still so apparent. When his colleagues finally finished their controlled ransacking——and informed their superior that the place was clean——I could see the officer's disappointment was acute.

Again he tapped my passport against his thumb, pondering his next move. Finally he said:

"If Herr Fitzsimons-Ross survives, we will be naturally taking a deposition from him. If all this checks out, then you will be ruled out of our investigation, and the passport will be returned to you."

"But as the shopkeeper has clearly stated I wasn't with Fitzsimons-Ross."

"Do you have any need for the passport immediately? Are you planning to travel in the coming days?"

"Not in the next week or so, no."

"Well, hopefully, we will have this matter cleared up by then."

He then reached into the pocket of his jacket and took out a hefty notebook. Opening it he wrote out an official receipt for my passport, informing me it would be kept at the *Polizeiwache* in Kreuzberg. And if he needed to phone me?

I explained that there was no phone here at the apartment, but that messages could be left at the Café Istanbul.

"Ah yes, artists do not need phones," the officer said dryly. "We know where to find you when we need you, Herr Nesbitt."

"Can you tell me to which hospital Herr Fitzsimons-Ross has been taken?"

"Not until we have interviewed him. Good day, sir."

And he left, followed by his colleagues.

In the immediate aftermath of his departure, I found my head reeling. As my brain played cartwheels——a reaction to all the adrenaline that had been charging through my system from the moment I found Fitzsimons-Ross on the studio floor——another thought quickly took over: where was the essay I wrote for Radio Liberty . . . and why the hell hadn't I made a Xerox copy of it at the local corner shop (and, by the way, God bless its owner for clearing my name)? The reason my fear about the essay so instantly flooded my thoughts was simple: if it had been torn up, confiscated, or destroyed during this search, it would have taken me another day or so to rewrite it. Or, worst yet, the police might approach Radio Liberty, informing them that this would-be contributor was under suspicion of a violent incident with his gay junkie roommate. Once word got around the studio, I doubted if Petra would even bother to say more than two words to me——"No, thanks"——when I finally got up the courage to ask her out.

So moments after the cops were gone, I found myself charging up the stairs to my apartment and moving immediately to the shelf on which I kept my typewriter. It had been moved to the worktable, the cover taken off it, several keys depressed——as the cops were evidently verifying the fact that I hadn't secreted a small packet of some psychotropic substance inside its frame. My essay had been placed underneath the typewriter on the shelf——and though my first view of the empty shelf was just a little heart stopping, a quick glance at the floor showed that all eight pages had been randomly strewn about the place. I gathered them all up, reordering them according to page number and stacking them neatly on my worktable. Then I double-checked that all my assorted notebooks were still there. Again they had ended up on the floorboards——and several of them had been opened and rifled through. But these were not the thought police, interested in my perceptions of Berlin life. They just wanted to find drugs.

I spent the next two hours slowly putting my rooms back together again. All my clothes had been dumped out of the chest of drawers or pulled off their hangers in the wardrobe. Every kitchen utensil and item of cutlery and all the cleaning supplies under the sink had been haphazardly tossed around. Even my espresso maker and my kettle had been opened and inspected. At least they hadn't done that cheesy Greek restaurant stunt of smashing up all the plates, as these had been stacked on the floor by the sink. Still it took time to rearrange everything, and tackle the medicine chest in the bathroom, given the fact that they squeezed out the entire contents of my toothpaste tube and smashed open a very ordinary bottle of body powder and dumped its contents on the floor, and emptied the entire can of shaving cream, and upended the shampoo, and everything else in which I might have hidden some sort of contraband.

And to think I had just cleaned the bathroom of all that vomit.

Still, nothing important was missing or damaged (they even left the batteries to my radio/cassette player near the machine itself). And I certainly hadn't suffered the same fate as poor Alaistair. Coming downstairs, I saw that the walls were splattered everywhere with blood and paint, the worktable and chairs also covered with this amalgamation of gore and synthetic color. I walked into the bedroom. The attack had evidently started here, as the sheets were also stained crimson and the cops had just added to the chaos by dumping his clothes everywhere. I started surveying all that needed to be done here when I was taken aback by the sound of a key in the front door lock. Hurrying back into the front room——and grabbing a chair as possible protection——I found myself face-to-face with Mehmet. He was taking in the catastrophe and also eyeing me——and the fact that I had a chair in one hand——with alarm.

"Sorry, sorry," I said, dropping the chair. "Something terrible has happened."

"Where's Alaistair?"

"In the hospital. There was an attempted robbery last night. And he was stabbed repeatedly. I was upstairs asleep when it happened——and had drunk so much last night that I slept through it all."

"Is he alive?"

"Just about. When I found him . . . well, put it this way, if I hadn't found him he would have died within a half hour. Or, at least, that's what the ambulance team told me."

"And the man who did this? Did they catch him?"

"No. But I gather he climbed in through an open window while Alaistair was asleep. There was a struggle. And . . ."

Mehmet began to shake his head very slowly. Turning away from me, he said in a voice barely above a whisper:

"There is no need to lie to me. I know it wasn't a thief who broke in here and did this. I know how Alaistair lives."

I looked squarely at Mehmet and saw in his face the same look that a constantly betrayed wife often has, especially if she has decided to accept the fact that her husband is someone who has repeatedly strayed and will continue to do so for as long as they are together. Anyway, who was I to speculate what the nature of their relationship actually was, or whether there were any bonds beyond the three afternoons they spent together every week? What was clear was that Mehmet was so profoundly shaken by the sight of such destruction, and by the fact that I couldn't tell him more about his lover's condition.

"Why didn't they tell you the name of the hospital?" he demanded.

"Because the medic rushed him off and the cops spent all their time getting a deposition from me."

"How will you know where to find him?"

"I'll start phoning around. Once I've found out, we can go see him together."

"No, that is impossible for me," he said.

"I understand," I said.

"No, you don't understand. Nobody understands. If it was to be made public——our 'friendship'——my life would be over. I would be finished. A dead man."

We fell silent. Mehmet reached into his jacket and fished out his packet of cigarettes. Flipping one into his mouth, he tossed me the packet. I took a cigarette and tossed the pack back to him, hunting around my pockets for my Zippo and lighting up. After a few deep drags, I said:

"One thing we could do for Alaistair . . . we could repaint the studio and deal with the blood on the floor and the furniture."

This idea immediately caught Mehmet's attention.

"You know, this is my part-time job. I run the family dry cleaning business, but I have a sideline in home decoration. Of course, I can't bring any of my crew around here to help."

"I'm handy with a paintbrush," I said.

"Can you get up early tomorrow?"

"After the night I had last night, I think I'll fall into bed around nine tonight."

"Okay, I'm here at eight tomorrow morning with everything we need."

"I'll be up and ready."

"Thank you."

"There's no need to thank me," I said.

"Yes, there is. Because I know I can trust you. Because you have his best interests at heart. And because he told me he liked you——and Alaistair likes very few people."

Before he left, Mehmet inspected the bedroom and informed me he'd order a new mattress in the next few days. He also gathered up all of Alaistair's blood-splattered clothes and dumped them into a large plastic bag, saying he'd get his laundry to handle it all. Then he headed off into the night.

I was suddenly hit with a wave of tiredness——not surprising, considering the manic events of the past twelve hours. I checked my watch. It was now seven p.m. Though I hadn't eaten all day I felt no hunger, no need for food, drink, or anything else except sleep. I got myself upstairs, took a long very hot shower, and then fell into bed, setting my alarm for four that morning.

I slept a sleep so deep, so sound, that when I awoke with my alarm clock well before dawn, there were a few delightfully befuddled moments when all I could think was: *my God, I feel positively born-again.* Then the events of the previous day came flooding in, and I found myself haunted by the idea that Alaistair might not have survived the night. What had happened to him had been so monstrous, so unfair——and, truth be told, I did think of him now as my friend. I so wanted to ring the cops and demand to know the state of his condition——whether he'd pulled through and, if so, when I could see him. But as it was in the middle of the night——and phoning the police right now might just make them regard me as a crank, or someone with an obsessively guilty streak (that is, if I could find a working phone on a chilly street corner, as all the public phones in Kreuzberg were inevitably out of order or recently vandalized, and the Café Istanbul didn't open until six)——there was only one solution: go to work. So I made coffee and ate some cheese on pumpernickel bread, and then, sharpened pencil in hand, went to work on my essay——attacking its descriptive excesses and its badly drawn observations, smoothing over its passages of stylistic roughness, and honing its readability. By the time I worked my way through it again it was just after six a.m. Making myself a fresh pot of coffee I set up my typewriter, rolled a clean sheet of paper into it, lit my first cigarette of the morning, and began to hammer away. It took just under two hours to retype the revised eight-page essay——which included the time needed to dab Wite-Out on the paper and wait for it to dry whenever I made a typo. I had just finished when I heard a key in the door. Mehmet had arrived.

"Can you please help me in with a few things from my van?"

The few things included four gallons of white emulsion, paint trays, rollers and brushes, a larger sander for the floor and a small handheld one for furniture, a dozen industrial-strength garbage sacks, and two ladders.

"Good God, how did you manage to round all this up since yesterday afternoon?" I asked.

"I have a cousin who owns a paint shop near here."

As I made us coffee, Mehmet told me that he felt it best if we started with the walls. But first there was the matter of cleaning up the debris from his studio. I excused myself for a moment to change into the shabbiest T-shirt and jeans that I owned, then returned to find that Mehmet was already stuffing all the snapped brushes and upended paint cans from Alaistair's worktable into one of the sacks. I joined in——and we had much of the rubble cleared up in a half hour. When it came to the ripped canvases, Mehmet wanted to throw them out, insisting that Alaistair wouldn't want them around——that it would be too much for him to bear. But I finally convinced him to leave them stacked in one corner until I spoke to Alaistair about them.

"Let him decide whether he wants them here or not," I said.

Mehmet thought that idea over, eventually giving his consent.

"No news?" he asked quietly.

I shook my head.

He fell silent again and began to open a gallon of paint, pouring it into two trays. For the next three hours little in the way of dialogue passed between us. I asked him once if we could listen to some music while we worked. He said, "No problem," and I worked my way through his four-record set of Glenn Gould playing Bach's *The Well-Tempered Clavier* as we managed to get two of the four walls painted.

At ten, I took a ten-minute break, running out to the Café Istanbul to call Pawel at Radio Liberty. He answered on the fifth ring.

"To what do I owe this honor?" he asked dryly after hearing my voice.

"I have your essay."

"My, my, you are the eager beaver."

That's because I cannot get Petra Dussmann out of my head.

"You told me you wanted it quickly."

"Can you bring it over this afternoon?"

"No problem."

"Say three."

And he hung up.

Then I asked to borrow a phone book and called all of the six hospitals located within the confines of West Berlin. Every time I spoke with someone at the reception desk I was told that they could not confirm if they had admitted someone named Alaistair Fitzsimons-Ross. And I was told that I would have to present myself in person with my papers in order to be told whether or not they had a patient by that name with them. "This is how the system works," I was told repeatedly when I complained that I simply wanted a yes or no that he was in their hospital. "We cannot change the system."

I returned to the apartment and told Mehmet about my hospital ring-around and how it yielded no results, no information about Alaistair. He just shrugged and we continued painting until noon——when Mehmet announced he now had to get to work but would return here tomorrow at eight for another redecorating session.

"We should have everything done within three, four days," he said.

"If I hear anything from the police before tomorrow . . . ?"

"It will have to wait until I arrive in the morning. No one can know anything about my presence here. No one."

"You have my word on that."

After Mehmet left, I went back upstairs and showered, changing into blue jeans and a black turtleneck sweater. Then I reread the essay one more time, thinking to myself: *He'll probably hate it, and that will be the end of things. And word will get back to Petra that the essay was no good, and why would she want to go out with a would-be contributor whose work was rejected?*

A few hours later, however, as I emerged from the Wedding U-Bahn station and began to cross the street, there walking toward me was Petra.

She was dressed in a beat-up black leather jacket, zipped up against the cold, a short black corduroy skirt, black tights. A rare sighting of a mid-winter sun caught the auburn wave of her hair and made her look luminous. She didn't initially see me. Instead she was walking along with her head bowed and a look on her face that hinted at some terrible distress within, a deep preoccupation that was causing her considerable grief. I wanted to shout her name. Instinctually I knew this to be a bad idea, given whatever she might be grappling with at this very moment. But as we both approached the entrance to Radio Liberty, she caught sight of me and immediately favored me with a shy, hesitant smile.

"Ah, it's you," she said. "And what brings you back here?"

"Delivering my essay to Pawel."

"You work fast."

"A deadline always focuses the mind."

"Nice seeing you again," she said, walking ahead of me.

"Listen, I've got a pair of tickets for the Philharmonie tomorrow night. It's all Dvorak, conducted by Kubelik, who being Czech, knows his Dvorak . . ."

"Sorry, I'm busy," she said, walking on. "But thank you."

And turning a corner she was gone.

The sense of letdown, of utter disappointment, was vast. There it was. She was telling me in a clear, transparent manner: *I'm not interested.* Or: *There's somebody else in my life.* Or, quite simply: *No thanks.* As much as I tried to rationalize this comment——*maybe she is genuinely busy tomorrow, maybe she was rushing off to a meeting just now, which is why she was so abrupt with you*——I couldn't get around the fact that I had just been given the kiss-off. Perhaps the hardest thing to come to terms with in life is when another person punctures a fantasy that you have been building up in your head. What makes this even more painful is when said person is the subject of said reverie, and you now have to face up to the death of a dream. And you simultaneously wonder why you had such absurd romantic thoughts in the first place.

Because we all want to love and be loved. And, more tellingly, because we are all so in love with the idea of being in love.

"You look morose."

I glanced up as Pawel walked into the reception area, smiling. As I came to know him, I realized that the few times Pawel ever smiled was when he saw other people's discomfort.

"Momentary *weltschmerz*," I said.

"In my experience it's never momentary. Follow me."

I did just that, walking with him toward his office cubicle, keeping my head lowered in case I caught sight of Petra again. When we reached his lair, he motioned for me to sit in his spare chair.

"The copy?" he asked,

I handed it over. Much to my bemusement he immediately started reading it. Now this was a first. Though I kept trying to avoid staring at him, I did find myself repeatedly glancing over in his direction, attempting to gauge his reaction. But his was a true poker face. It revealed nothing. Until, after ten long minutes, he tossed the pages onto his desk and said:

"Okay. You can write. In fact, you can write well. But I have a few suggestions . . ."

It took him exactly three minutes to outline the changes he wanted me to make. Most of them had to do with my observations about East German society——which he felt were a little too "broad-stroked" and needed to be more subtle. And he also wanted me to cut down on "the sub-le Carré stuff" upon my departure via Checkpoint Charlie.

"I've heard that all far too often," he said. "Otherwise, it's fine. Can you get these changes to me by tomorrow morning?"

"Sure."

"If you could hand them in to the security guard before nine a.m. . . . then I'll be in touch when we need you for the recording. And I'll also get the translation started."

"No problem. You'll have it by then."

Actually he had it by seven that next morning. Having done the rewrite upon arriving home——and having again fallen into bed early——I was up and on the U-Bahn by six thirty. After delivering the copy to the security guard at the front entrance, I hopped the underground train back to Kreuzberg and was atop a ladder by eight, covering bloodstains with white primer. As before Mehmet worked opposite me and refused all attempts at conversation. So, bar two breaks for coffee and cigarettes and a general chat about the redecoration progress, little talk passed between us. He was, as before, gone by noon. After a shower and a change of clothes, I was at the Café Istanbul by twelve thirty.

"I have a message for you," Omar said when I entered his premises. "A call about twenty minutes ago from a Fraulein Dussmann."

"Are you serious?" I heard myself saying.

"Of course I'm serious. I took the message. She wants you to call her back."

While handing me the phone, he also gave me the scratch pad on which was written her name and number.

The phone answered immediately. It was her. She'd given me her direct line.

"So they did give you my message," she said after answering. "Pawel told me this was the only way of contacting you."

"One of these days I really must get a phone."

"But then you will be contactable. And you will lose the romance of a Turkish café answering service."

Her tone surprised me. It was light and wry. Again I found myself thinking: *she is wonderful.*

"Pawel also gave me your essay to translate. I have a few questions. Do you have a couple of minutes now?"

"Have a cup of coffee with me."

"But my questions aren't that many."

"Have a coffee with me, Petra."

A long silence followed. *It's just a cup of coffee,* I felt like telling her. But it was hardly just that. The length of this pause now indicated to me that she knew what I knew, that this was momentous. Or, at least, I kept trying to convince myself she understood this, too.

I let the silence linger, not daring to rush the moment, waiting for her response. A good thirty seconds must have passed before she finally spoke.

"All right," she said, her voice barely above a whisper. "Let's meet for coffee."

TWO

WE AGREED TO meet in a café on the other side of Kreuzberg——"my side," as she informed me when I mentioned I wasn't far away from Heinrich Heine Strasse.

"Can you come over to the wrong side of the tracks?" she asked, an amused dryness underscoring the delivery of that question.

"Always."

"I was, of course, referring to geographical matters. You live in the more chic part of Kreuzberg."

"Now that's news to me, as my corner of this district isn't exactly the Rue Saint-Honoré."

"Never been to Paris. Never been in any cities except Berlin and Leipzig and Dresden and Halle."

"The latter of which I never even heard of."

"Nor have most people outside the German Democratic Republic. Even most people in the GDR have never been to Halle, for good reasons."

"But you *have* been to Halle."

"Worse than that. I was born and raised there."

"And it's worse than even the wrong side of the tracks in Kreuzberg?"

"What is the worst city you've ever been to in the United States?"

"There's quite a competition for that prize, but I would have to say Lewiston, Maine——a depressing mill town with ugly architecture, a flatlined economy, and a general air of decay."

"Sounds like Halle, though being the GDR, it was always promoted as a great triumph of proletariat-industrial productivity."

"In Lewiston there were just French Canadian Catholics who drank."

"Oh, everyone drank in Halle, which was the only antidote against the toxic chemical fumes that were exhaled by all the factories there."

"In Lewiston there were just smelly paper mills."

"But you didn't grow up in Lewiston."

"I never said that I did. In fact, I only know the place because, when I was at college, I ran cross-country against a college that happened to be in Lewiston."

"A Manhattan long-distance runner who ends up living in Kreuzberg. Is that what's known in English as 'slumming it'?"

"Except I'm not that sort of Manhattan boy."

"And you can tell me what sort of Manhattan boy you are later, as I am on deadline for a translation and have spent far too long on the phone with you."

"Is that a complaint?"

"Just an observation."

Then she gave me the address of a café called the Ankara.

"I presume you don't mind exchanging Istanbul for Ankara?" she asked.

"Well, Istanbul to Ankara really is crossing over to the wrong side of the tracks."

"Don't forget to bring your passport then. Does eight o'clock tomorrow evening work?"

"Absolutely."

"Enjoy your Dvorak tonight."

She rang off. Of course I felt elated, especially as she had lost a little of the distance that characterized our brief earlier contacts, and I was intrigued and delighted to discover that she could be smart and ever-so-acerbic. Most of all, she had agreed to meet me for more than just a professional chat, and I found myself now thinking that the wait until tomorrow would be a damn long one. Impatience is such a curious emotion. We want the next day to arrive now in the hope that we will get what we are seeking, even though we privately know that there is no guarantee that things will ever turn out the way we desire. Impatience is about wanting validation long before you have any idea whether it will be granted. By showing your hand too quickly——by letting it be known you are already so smitten——you risk rejection. You have to demonstrate interest, but not zealotry. You have to exercise patience.

I had another small problem on my hands. When I suggested going to hear the Berlin Phil, I had no idea whether I would be able to score a pair of standing-room places for the concert——and now I felt obliged to somehow find a ticket for tonight, so if (and, more like, when) she asked me how was the concert, I could talk about it. Also: Kubelik conducting Dvorak was something of an event. So I immediately planned to leave the apartment at six, take the U-Bahn up to Potsdamer Platz, and hope to find somebody selling a spare ticket out front.

But during the course of the afternoon a loud, authoritarian knock came on the door. Opening it I found myself staring at the police officer who had interrogated me after the assault on Alaistair.

"May I come in?" he asked.

"Of course," I said, opening the door fully. "Any news?"

He stepped inside.

"Your friend had a lucky escape. The medics managed to stop the bleeding just in time. He proved to be rather robust for a drug addict. He responded well to the transfusions. As one of the doctors at the hospital told me, he seemed to resist the temptation to surrender to death. He's still in a serious condition, but he is expected to make a full recovery. Of course, he is now in the throes of withdrawal due to the absence of his 'substance,' but you wouldn't know anything about that, would you?"

"You and your colleagues tore the place up, in search of that substance. And what did you find?"

"This is no longer an interrogation, Herr Nesbitt. I just came by to return you your passport. I was able to interview Herr Fitzsimons-Ross this morning, and he not only exonerated you, he was also able to give me an address of the gentleman who assaulted him. It seems that they'd had 'dealings' with each other before, though not of such a violent nature. Your friend had the bad luck of running into him in some bar two nights ago. But, again, you've never been to this bar, or any place like that?"

"I'm afraid not."

"Of course, of course. You are the innocent abroad. You know nothing, you see nothing. And fortunately for you, we found nothing."

He reached into his jacket pocket and withdrew my American passport, along with that hefty notebook he had the last time.

"I need you to sign a document, confirming that the passport has been returned."

I signed where requested.

"Can you now tell me at which hospital I can find my friend?"

He mentioned a hospital not far from the Zoologischer Garten. Trust Alaistair to end up in a hospital near the zoo.

"And he said he would appreciate a visit from you this evening."

"Thank you for that."

"I do hope and trust our paths will not cross professionally again."

"I'm planning to stay out of trouble, sir."

"Of course you are——being such a trouble-free person."

After the officer left, I had to resist the temptation to track down Mehmet and tell him the splendid news that Alaistair had pulled through. Realizing that my evening out at the Berlin Phil was now not going to happen, I instead made my way up at six that night to the Zoologischer Garten. Then I walked the five minutes to a drab 1950s building, with the hospital sign, "Krankenhaus," at the head of the driveway that led to the front entrance.

I was in luck. Evening visitor hours had just started. In the gift shop off the lobby I bought a box of chocolates to go with the assorted magazines and books I had gathered up from my rooms before leaving. The woman at the reception desk checked the Rolodex in front of her and——after I showed her the required ID——confirmed that Herr Fitzsimons-Ross was in Ward K, Block B, giving me directions on how to find it.

Ward K, Block B was a public ward on the fourth floor of the hospital. En route I passed a pair of exhausted, sallow-looking parents pushing a young emaciated boy——he couldn't have been more than seven——in a wheelchair, his skin the color of faded parchment, his head bald from evident chemotherapy treatments. Then there was a hugely overweight man in his forties, standing in a hallway, his face pressed up against one of the institutional green walls, crying uncontrollably. Just beyond him was a woman, around thirty, hunched over a walking frame on wheels, trying to negotiate her way slowly down a corridor.

The writer in me wanted to take everything in, focusing my eyes on all the infirmity and despair and sadness around me, making mental notes, knowing I would, one day, use it all. But the other part of me——

the man without the icicle in his heart——also had to lower his eyes at times (especially the sight of that child in the throes of cancer treatment) when it was just too damn hard to bear. When I finally reached Ward K, Block B, I kept my vision trained on the linoleum, only looking up occasionally to see if I was approaching Bed No. 232, which, as the reception clerk informed me, was the bed occupied by one Alaistair Fitzsimons-Ross.

"Don't you know I hate fucking chocolate?"

His first words to me as I approached his bedside. He had shrunken in the days since the attack: his cheeks hollow, concave, his complexion beyond pale. There were two large intravenous blood bags hoisted above him, dripping slowly into his two arms. There were assorted monitors and screens surrounding him, metronomically registering the beep-beep of his heart. He looked so cadaverous. Yet, as always, his eyes shone bright.

"And I don't want to read any fucking novels," he said as I unpacked the reading material I brought him. "I hate novels. Imitations of life, written by wankers. Almost as bad as travel books."

"I'm delighted to see you're in the process of making a full recovery."

"I think I might turn vampire after all this, given how I have been feeding on other people's blood for days."

"At least you're alive."

"And the police informed me that I owe my life to you, for which I will never forgive you."

"The police say they know who the attacker is."

"Correction: I know who the attacker is, as I was foolish enough to make his acquaintance previously. Mind you, as he didn't stab me on the previous occasion we spent the night together, I thought it was safe to hook up with him for another little dalliance. The problem is, Horst paints."

"I wondered."

"What do you mean, you wondered?"

I paused for a moment, knowing that there was no way around what I had to tell him and that it was best to get it out and done with.

"The man who attacked you also attacked the three canvases you were working on."

Alaistair's lips tightened and he shut his eyes. I felt terrible for him.

"How bad is the damage?"

"Very bad."

"Define 'very bad.'"

"Irreparable."

He shut his eyes tighter, his head sinking deeper into the pillow. We fell silent. I could hear him working hard at muffling a sob.

"I'm so sorry," I finally said.

"Why the fuck should you be sorry?" he asked, suddenly angry. "You're not the talentless little shit who did this to me."

He fell silent again.

"You should have let me die."

Another silence.

"Thank you," he said.

"For what?"

"For letting me know now. Had you waited until I was on the mend I would have despised you."

"I saw Mehmet the other day."

"Did you tell him?"

"He came by the apartment and saw what happened."

"Oh Christ. Did you tell him the circumstances?"

"I said that a thief broke into the place while you were asleep. You woke up. There was a struggle . . ."

"I'm sure he didn't believe a word you said."

"He's currently helping me redecorate your apartment. In fact, it was Mehmet who organized all the paint stuff, the sanders, the . . ."

"Why the fuck are you repainting the place?"

"Because your blood is everywhere. But it will be all gone by the time you're released. And by the way, I really am pleased you're still with us."

"I'm not. Those paintings . . . don't you *ever* fucking call them canvases again . . . those paintings, they were good."

"I know a writer who once lost an entire manuscript of a novel he'd been working on for over a year. A fire in his apartment in Manhattan. He'd fallen asleep in bed with a cigarette and was lucky to escape with his life. But his two copies——the original and the carbon——were burnt to a crisp. And what did he do?"

"Let me ask you something: in your spare time do you give those ghastly motivational speeches that your country so adores?"

"Sorry for trying to cheer you up."

"Nothing will cheer me up now. I am beyond cheerless."

"And you will start those paintings again, and they will be good. Maybe not as good as you will always think the destroyed ones were. But . . ."

"You're far too fucking nice. How is Mehmet?"

"Very concerned about you. So concerned that he's there every morning, painting away. Any idea when they might release you?"

"It's not just the loss of blood that's keeping me here. It's my little 'problem' as well. They have me on the 'substitute.' The quack in charge of me has said that he won't sign off on my release until he is certain I have been weaned off smack."

"How's it going with the methadone?"

"Considering that I have been in a fucking coma, no problems. But now I can already tell that the withdrawal, even with the methadone, is going to be monstrous. I have several close junkie friends who went down the substitute route. They all reported back the same thing: absolute hell."

"Well, at least you will get off it now."

"Stop sounding like I've been spending my entire adult life waiting for the moment when I could be near-fatally stabbed by a fourth-tier artiste in some sordid fuck bar so I could finally free myself of the dreaded drug which had so crippled my life. The fact is, I love smack."

"But since they won't let you out of here until they're sure you're off of it . . ."

"Mind you, I could try to check myself out of here once I have enough blood coursing back in my veins. As the quack and the investigating cop explained to me, the fact that I am Ein Ausländer—a bloody foreigner—presents all sorts of complications, in that it's clear they have physiological proof I am a junkie. Which means they could legally throw me out of the country. But the Germans aren't as rigid as the Brits or the French on such matters, though. Thank fuck, they didn't search the apartment."

"Who told you that?"

"I just surmised that, as it was a case of attempted murder——"

"You're a junkie. They tore the place apart."

"And did they find——?"

"No, I got it out the window and into the trash the next morning."

"You threw it away?"

"What the hell was I supposed to do? Keep it warm until you came back? Say the cops had done a sweep and found your shit?"

"That was seven hundred deutsche marks of 'shit.'"

"A small price for not getting busted and evicted from the Bundesrepublik."

"We don't live in the Bundesrepublik. We live in Berlin."

"They'd still deport you. Now you can wean yourself off your addiction at their expense."

"Stop sounding so fucking *pragmatic*. When are you next seeing Mehmet?"

"Eight a.m. tomorrow, when we sand your floor."

"Will you ask him to visit me?"

"I'll ask, but you know he can't be seen with you."

"He told you that?"

"Yes, he told me that."

"Then can you come back tomorrow night and give me an update?"

"On what?"

"On everything outside this fucking lonely hospital."

"Tomorrow night's impossible."

"Why is that?"

"Because I am otherwise engaged."

"What's her name?"

"I'll tell you if it amounts to anything."

"It will amount to something."

"How can you be so damn sure?"

"Because you know it will."

"The day after tomorrow then?"

"Of course."

"And tell Mehmet he's missed."

I did pass on that message to Mehmet the next morning. The walls were all repainted, and we spent the four hours he had set aside to work here dealing with the messy business of sanding the floor of the studio. The wood dust was torrential, Mehmet pointing out that the parquet flooring was of the cheap variety and seriously brittle when attacked with a sander. Of course, when he arrived that morning I immediately informed him that Alaistair had pulled through——and, judging from the acerbity of his repartee last night at the hospital, had not been too mentally scathed by this attack. Mehmet took this information in with a modest nod of the head, then fell silent until he started telling me what we needed to do to get the floor stripped of blood. Halfway through this dusty job, we took a break for coffee——during which he suddenly asked me:

"You are telling me the truth about his condition? He really will live, yes?"

"It does look that way. And he did ask about you many times. Why don't you just go to the Krankenhaus and visit him? I mean, it's not like we live on the other side of The Wall and have every move we make monitored. Anyway, even on the wild chance that you did run into someone you knew there, big deal. You're visiting a friend, nothing more."

Mehmet simply shook his head and said, "It's not as simple as that."

We carried on working in silence until noon. Mehmet helped me sweep up all the sawdust, then washed his hands, straightened his tie, and said, "Tomorrow at eight."

Once he was gone I glanced at my watch. Realizing that I still had the afternoon to kill before making my way to meet Petra at that Turkish café near her apartment, I decided to do something that had been anathema to me since my last year in college: I was going to go for a run.

A true confession: at one time in my life I actually saw myself as a marathon man. Or, at least, a marathon man in training. I ran cross-country in school. My specialty was the 10K and I actually came in third once in an intercollegiate track meet. I also spent two years on my college's running team until my love affair with cigarettes put an end to all that.

Jogging out onto Berlin's hard, arduous concrete, I was struck immediately by how quickly the old training kicked in again. Setting off I heard again the voice of the taskmaster track coach at school in New York, an ex-Marine name Mr. Toole who always exhorted me:

"Four paces run, then four exhalations, then four paces, then four exhalations. And you never, *never* deviate from that rhythm. You forget the four-four rhythm, your breathing will go all over the place, and you will lose pace, velocity, staying power. You start doing something goofy like even occasionally holding your breath . . . and I've seen even experienced long-distance runners inadvertently make that mistake, because they simply forget the four-four pattern . . . and you will find yourself winded, flagging, lost. In running breathing is energy——and I am going to come down so damn hard on you, Nesbitt, if you forget that."

But I never forgot that, and jogging through Kreuzberg I kept repeating the same mantra:

Four paces, four exhalations. Breathe back slowly through your nose. Four paces, four exhalations. And never, never, hold a breath longer than needed.

Youth is such a great gift and one which we never really see until years later, when we become aware of the body's increasing lack of forgiveness for our excesses. As I hit the first kilometer mark, all I could think was: *So I can smoke and run at the same time.*

A city changes when you run through it. Distances that always seemed lengthy when walked are now surprisingly close, the jaunt from my front door to the U-Bahn station at Heinrich Heine Strasse no longer its usual ten-minute stroll. Then there's the simple fact that you are rushing past everyone——and, as such, are dodging pedestrians and cars and, in this case, heading northward, using The Wall as a directional marker. But even though my route zigged in toward this barricade and then away down nearby streets, the fact was: The Wall now appeared to be an endless impediment. I could turn left, but simply could not jog to the right. When I followed its northward trajectory, it eventually dumped me out in front of the Brandenburg Tor and the ruin that still was the Reichstag. A left-hand turn and I was now running through the Tiergarten——that big public park through which Hitler's mob marched when they torched the parliament, and which, prior to that infamous night, was best known during the exalted decadence of the Weimar Republic as a favored place in which to encounter prostitutes of both sexes. Now it was shadowed by the ghosts of an imperial and fascistic past, and by the biggest line of ideological demarcation constructed during this most terrible of centuries.

But these thoughts came later. For the moment the Tiergarten was simply a patch of green to be traversed at a reasonable clip . . . that is, before my stamina began to wane and I started to feel a heaviness in my legs. My throat was arid and my chest heaving. I slowed down to a panting halt, my head bowed, my hands on my knees, my throat now raw, smoky phlegm filling my mouth. But I also did remind myself that after a five-year hiatus, I had just run for forty minutes without let-up. Glancing at my watch, I put my hand out and grabbed a taxi home.

A few hours later——freshly showered and shaved and wearing black jeans, a black leather jacket, and a black turtleneck——I walked the twenty minutes down to the Café Ankara. Petra was right: compared with my own grubby but energetic corner of Kreuzberg, hers was thoroughly down-at-heel and lacking streetwise vitality. This was an area noteworthy for its faceless blocks of low-income housing, a few extant left-behinds from the late nineteenth century, and a smattering of sad-looking shops: a grocer's, a laundry, a place that sold elderly-looking housewares, a clothing shop aimed at Turkish women who (judging from the strange mannequins in the window) didn't seem to mind wearing the chador.

At the end of this street, the equally ugly tower blocks of East Berlin peered down at me. Though the closest ones were less than one hundred meters from The Wall, they appeared to be near-neighbors to this corner of Kreuzberg. Again I found myself wondering what it must be like to live in such a Stalinist aerie, with a clear panoramic view of the Forbidden City from all western-facing balconies. Did you have to be a senior Party apparatchik to get such a privileged view? Or did the authorities deliberately house political misfits there as a way of sticking in the proverbial knife and reminding them that though they were geographically close to the longed-for Other Side, they were also so damn far from it.

The Café Ankara was the Café Istanbul gone even more downmarket (and that took some work). Even shabbier floral linoleum. Even darker tobacco-cured floral wallpaper. The same Formica tables. The same fluorescent lighting. The same intermingling aroma of bad cigarettes, overcooked Turkish coffee, and grease. And no customers when I walked in.

I slid into a booth, checked my watch, and saw that I was about five minutes early. I felt so damn jumpy, so eager for this to all go so right, so concerned about making a good impression, so desperate to appear calm and not over-eager, that I quickly pulled out my pouch of tobacco and papers and rolled a cigarette. The guy behind the counter shouted over, "What you want?" I ordered a Turkish coffee "medium" (i.e., with a half teaspoon of sugar, rather than the three teaspoons the Café Istanbul usually put into their "sweet" version of this highly caffeinated and thoroughly addictive liquid). Then I pulled out my notebook and started writing down some thoughts about jogging alongside The Wall. The coffee arrived. I lit up my cigarette. I continued to write——trying to let the accumulation of words quell my anxiety. My pen flew along the narrow pages of my pocket-sized book. The combination of caffeine and nicotine kept the nervousness in check. In the middle of an extended sentence about running out of physical steam while in the Tiergarten, I heard her voice:

"*So viele Wörter.*"

So many words.

I looked up. There she was. Petra. Wearing a dark gray tweed overcoat with a brown turtleneck, a short green corduroy skirt, and black tights with——as before——a small tear around the left knee. I forced myself to appear casual as I said:

"*Ja, so viele Wörter. Aber vielleicht sind die ganzen Wörter Abfall.*"

Yes, so many words. But perhaps all the words are crap.

She laughed and sat down opposite me. I saw that she was also carrying a black vinyl shoulder bag, out of which she pulled a packet of HB cigarettes. I reached for my tobacco pouch and papers.

"I never knew Americans smoked roll-ups," she said, tapping out a cigarette and reaching for the lighter I had left on the table. "That is, outside of novels by John Steinbeck."

"It's a habit I got into in college. Especially as it was cheaper than real cigarettes."

"But not as nice. Then again, having grown up with the things that passed for cigarettes over there . . ."

"Like f6s?"

"Ah yes, I forgot you mentioned this brand in your essay. I liked the 'industrial strength' image. Very apt."

"And the rest of the essay?"

Again she smiled at me.

"We'll get to that later. First, I need a beer."

"I could use one, too. I just attempted to run for the first time in more than five years."

"Run from what precisely?"

"Run from the fact that I smoke far too many cigarettes a day, and I used to be able to run 10K in less than an hour."

"You actually did that?"

"For a very brief time in my adolescence."

"Personally, I could not imagine life without smoking."

"That's a serious statement."

"I'm a serious smoker."

"How many every day?"

"Two packets."

"You've never tried to quit?"

"It's the second biggest love of my life."

"What's the first?"

She paused for a moment, inhaling deeply.

"I'll tell you when I know you a little better. But I do need that beer."

I waved over to the waiter.

"Now I'm rather partial to Hefeweizen," I said.

"Each to his own taste. For me, it's far too Bavarian, far too gemütlich. I'm a Berlin girl by adoption, anyway. So for me it's always a Berliner Pilsner."

"You mean, they didn't make beer in Halle?"

"My father did . . . at home. He was talented at it as well. Learned from his father, who'd worked at a brewery before the war."

"And your father did what?"

"He worked as a producer at the regional station of Der Rundfunk der DDR——the national radio station. A very cultured man who was never that ambitious, and therefore seemed to miss out on the promotions that would have sent him to work in Leipzig or Dresden or——the great prize——Berlin. Of course, he was a Party member because, even in a place like Halle, you couldn't get work at that level in DDR Rundfunk without having pledged fealty to the Workers Party. But his heart was never into it. I think his superiors knew this. Which is why they kept him stuck in the provinces, when his interests——classical music, books, the theater——were all elsewhere. Occasionally, he would get a trip to hear the Staatskapelle in Dresden or the Gewandhaus in Leipzig——two of our great orchestras——and he would come back to Halle a little melancholic. Because he felt as if life was passing him by and . . ."

She suddenly shook her head, scowling.

"I am now angry at myself," she said.

"Why's that?"

"I have talked too much about my small, little life."

"But I want to know about you."

"You do not have to humor me, Thomas."

The first time she ever said my name.

"I'm hardly humoring you, Petra. I'm interested. Genuinely."

"We need that beer," she said, cutting me off.

"And your mother?" I asked.

"You pose far too many questions. A professional habit, I suppose."

"I'm interested."

"You keep saying that."

"Because it's the truth. And your mother?"

She looked at me quizzically, as if she was trying to convince herself that I wasn't trying to be polite or faux-interested, that, verily, I *was* interested. Seeing her regard me this way——wary, yet hopeful——made me wonder: is she as smitten and nervous as I am right now?

"Okay, in brief, because we have work to do . . . my mother. A woman from Berlin who could read and write four languages, and wanted, I sensed, to write or edit or be a journalist. But then . . ."

She broke off to stub out her cigarette and shouted over to the waiter:

"*Eine Berliner Pils und eine Hefeweizen.*"

As soon as she had finished giving him our order, she turned back to me and said:

"Love."

"Sorry?" I said.

"My mother. She fell in love. As she told me many times in the year before she died, it was the love of a good man, but one who also brought her to Halle and a life that was not what she envisaged."

"What did she die of?"

"What most people in their forties die of: cancer. In her case, ovarian."

"When was that?"

"Six years ago."

"Around the time my mother died."

"How old?"

"Forty-two. Cancer, too. Brought on by these."

Now I stubbed out my cigarette.

"I'm sorry," she said, momentarily touching my hand with hers. Her fingers were warm, but as soon as she covered mine with hers she pulled them away, as if she was worried about overstepping a boundary or perhaps sending out the wrong signal. How I wanted to reach over and thread my fingers in hers and pull her toward me . . . and simultaneously ruin everything in one badly judged nanosecond.

"She wasn't the happiest of women," I said.

"That sounds familiar. And your father?"

"A complicated guy. A businessman. An ex-soldier. Very rule conscious. Very 'chain of command.' Yet someone who always, I think, wanted to live a different life."

"What does he think about his writer son?"

"I sense he doesn't know what the hell to make of me. Just as, privately, I sense he thinks I'm having the life he wanted to have."

"Ah, but he didn't write books."

"A book. That's it, so far."

"But a very good book."

I looked at her with care.

"You've read it?"

"Don't sound so surprised," she said, reaching again for her cigarettes.

"How'd you get a hold of it?"

"Pawel had a copy. I asked him if I could borrow it."

"That must have amused him."

"He's far too über-cool to show amusement. But he said the book was 'not bad.' Coming from Pawel, that is wild praise."

"And coming from you?"

"Not bad," she said with a small laugh, then added, "What does it matter what I think? You are the published writer. I am just a functionary."

"That's hardly the case."

"Now you are humoring me."

"But translators are hardly functionaries. You're doppelgangers."

"What a triumph——to be a shadow of someone else."

"You put morning words into evening words."

"Not a bad metaphor. But I bet a translator thought it up."

Now it was my turn to laugh.

The beers arrived. We clinked glasses.

"And now, before we get talking any more about parents and professions," she said, "we must deal with your essay."

With that she reached into her shoulder bag and dug out a typescript in German, the margins annotated——in very precise, small handwriting——with multiple notes.

"It looks like you have a lot of questions," I said.

"Mainly questions about word choice——mine for yours. We can dispense with these very systematically. But before we get to that . . . a few critical observations, if you don't mind . . . and I should point out that I discussed these with Pawel this afternoon before meeting you, as he is the producer and I am the mere translator. But as an *Ossi* . . . and given that you are writing about the city in which I lived for ten years . . . well . . ."

"Go ahead. Tell me what you think."

"It's an intelligently argued piece. But let me say this one basic criticism——and then we can get down to the more mundane, semantical questions. The way you paint East Berlin as gray, barren, lacking in any human nuance or color . . ."

"All true."

"But predictable."

"It's what I saw, what I observed, to use your word."

"It's what every Western writer *observes* about East Berlin or Prague or, God help us, Bucharest, which, thanks to that madman Ceaucescu, makes the GDR look like Sweden. My point, Thomas, is that you should rethink certain parts of the essay, and perhaps sidestep the usual 'life in monochrome' clichés which all our listeners in the GDR will have heard before."

"But my essay doesn't attempt to sell itself as anything but what Jerome Wellmann asked me to do: play 'the American abroad in East Berlin for a day.' The fact that I actually chose to center the whole piece on the idea of snow as metaphor . . . well, surely, you can't accuse me of spouting clichés."

I said all this with a certain vehemence that again surprised me. When I reflected on it much later on, I realized that it wasn't just my need to defend my corner that spurred me into a debate with her, but also an instinctual sense that this conversation was part of the entire mating dance that was taking place as we sipped our beers and smoked our cigarettes and kept trying not to gaze too long into each other's eyes. Or, to put it another way, I didn't want to seem to be a pushover——because I also sensed that she didn't want me to capitulate to her criticisms so easily.

"Sorry, but lines about 'the Stalinist architectural blights that now decorate Unter den Linden' or the description of the tasteless meal you had off Alexanderplatz . . . Thomas, your listeners in the East live it every day of their lives. But what you didn't see——and how could you, given this was your Warsaw Pact loss of virginity——is the life that goes on behind the bad architecture, the poorly stocked shops, the life without easy access to Marlboros and cars that don't sound like something with which you mow your lawn. Where I used to live with my husband . . ."

Did I noticeably flinch when I heard those last two words? Absolutely. And Petra saw me flinch, as she said:

"I'm no longer married."

"Were you married for long?"

"Six years. But that's another story, and not for now. What I was trying to say is: where I used to live in East Berlin——an area called Prenzlauer Berg——"

"I was there."

"You were? Why?"

"I just walked up Prenzlauer Allee from Alexanderplatz because the architecture looked different."

"Of course, it's different. It survived the war. Where did you visit there?"

I explained the hour I spent poking around its environs. Every time I mentioned a street name, Petra's face brightened, and she mentioned some landmark there——a little shop, an interesting building, even a quirky street lamp that was a holdover from another time——which she evidently remembered with great vividness. But when I told her about the playground at Kollwitzplatz——and how it was jammed with mothers and their children and how I found this scene of parent-child activity rather touching——her face tightened and she turned her gaze downward.

"Yes, I know that playground," she said. My mentioning of this place threw her and naturally made me curious. But the way I could see her forcing herself out of this moment of darkness hinted to me that—— along with further questions about the man who no longer was her husband——this too was, right now, a no-go area. So I tried to redirect the conversation back to safer territory.

"So . . . you were saying that when you lived in Prenzlauer Berg, not everything was gray and reinforced concrete?"

She exhaled a lungful of smoke, so evidently relieved to be back out of "the playground."

"Actually it was the East Berlin *rive gauche*. If you knew how to play the system——and most of our artist and writer friends worked it out——you could get a big old apartment up there for next to nothing. It was like those lofts I once read about in Lower Manhattan. Of course, this being the 'gray,' the 'ascetic,' the 'no comfort' GDR, the basic amenities were just that. But we all knew somebody who knew somebody who was a plumber or an electrician and who would——for a modest sum——make the toilets flush and the lights work and get the heat up to a certain level where January indoors was tolerable. Still, there was an actual creative community in Prenzlauer Berg. The fact was, even if you couldn't get your writings published or performed, or your canvases exhibited, even if you were simply doing art for yourself, the community there would support you. We staged readings of plays. We had private showings in apartments of photographs and paintings. We passed around each other's manuscripts. And we had fantastic parties. Mad, crazy parties that would often start Friday night after work and continue until six a.m. Sunday. It was a proper bohemian existence, on our own terms, or as much of 'our own terms' as we could have given the way of things over there."

"And you were a translator?"

"Yes, I did that sort of work, English to German, for a state publishing house. Of course, as I was not a Party member and was also considered to be part of a 'quasi-degenerate' group up in the wilds of Prenzlauer Berg, I was never given the big assignment: the new angry black American novel that the publishing board decided was sufficiently bleak about life in the US, or some English Communist's rants against Mrs. Thatcher. No, they had me translating wildlife books, or geologic studies about the North American continental shelf, or technical manuals. Deadening work, but it filled the time. And now I've said enough about myself. I still can't figure out why on earth you're interested in me."

"Because I think you're wonderful."

"Why did you say that?" she asked, her voice quiet and free of reproach.

"It's what I think."

"How can you think that? You've known me for half an hour, no more."

"I can still think that——and know it."

"Now you are embarrassing me."

"No——I'm just telling you what I feel."

At that moment I could see her briefly smiling. But she wiped it away with a shake of the head, a sip of beer, a fresh, steadying cigarette, and the directive:

"Can we please return to your essay?"

For the next twenty minutes we argued the points that she raised. All credit to Petra——if she disagreed with you, she did not yield to your point of view easily. In the end I gave way on six of the nine "observations" that were plaguing her, using more ambiguous language to make my critical points. Then we turned to her translation queries, all of which were bound up in semantic issues about certain Americanisms I used and how she was going to need to find a parallel phrase in German for an idiom like "out of left field."

"We don't play baseball in the GDR," she said after I explained the etymological origins of the expression. "But, again, I like the way you use words."

"Unless they're directed against the architectural charms of Ost Berlin."

"Which is when you descend into platitude. And you are far too smart a man for that."

"Now you're flattering me."

For the first time during this entire dance of a conversation, she met my gaze straight on.

"But it's how I feel, Thomas."

"Good."

"And now."

She glanced at her watch.

"Now I have to go."

"You what?" I said, sounding shaken.

"I have plans for this evening."

"I see."

"You sound disappointed."

"Well . . . yeah, I'm disappointed. But if I was to suggest dinner sometime this week?"

"I'd say of course."

"And if I was to come across as far too eager and suggest tomorrow night?"

"I'd say: there is a cheap and good Italian place two streets from here on Pflügerstrasse. It has an idiotic name: the Arrivederci, which isn't a selling point for a restaurant, now it is?"

"Okay, the Arrivederci then. Say eight?"

"That's fine."

I threw some money down on the table.

"You don't have to pay for me," Petra said.

"But I want to."

We stepped outside into the early evening.

"So what do you think about this dreary little quarter I call home?" she asked.

"It's no worse than my corner of Kreuzberg."

"I shouldn't be living here. It's all too gray."

"Then why stay?"

She glanced briefly at the looming tower blocks of Friedrichshain on the far side of The Wall.

"I have my reasons," she said.

Then, suddenly, without warning, she reached for me and pulled me close and kissed me on the lips, and then gently detached herself from me before I had a chance to pull her back toward me. But she did reach for my hand again and held it tightly, saying:

"Until tomorrow."

"Yes, until tomorrow."

She let go of me and turned away, walking quickly off. I stood there, my head still swimming from the brief but telling kiss, and watched her disappear down the street. When she reached the next corner, she turned back. Seeing me there, she looked relieved, but also as befuddled as I was right now. Still she smiled. And touching her fingers to her lips she blew a kiss toward me. Before I could respond, she turned a corner and was gone.

In the moments that followed, one thought haunted me: *it will be a whole day before I can see her again.*

THREE

ONE OF THE complexities of falling in love is that you cannot help but look for subtext in everything said between the two of you. In that very early stage of a romance——when you know you are infatuated, when you sense (but don't have definitive proof) that it's mutual, and you so desperately want it all to come right——you turn into a specialist in advance semiotics, trying to decipher every meaning behind the words that pass to and fro.

Or, at least, that's what I found myself doing after that hour with Petra in the Café Ankara. All that evening——as I headed back to my apartment, tried to read, then headed out and nursed a few beers in Die schwarze Ecke——I kept running through the gestures and counter-gestures that passed between us, the wordplay exchanged, the inherent tension of two people circling each other. And within all this their needs and desires and hopes——both shared and disparate——counterbalanced by self-protection, the fear of overplaying one's hand, the dread of disappointment, the dread of getting burnt.

Surely the fact that she was more than willing to meet me tomorrow showed that, for her, this is serious.

But what about all the enigmatic talk regarding her ex-husband . . . if, that is, he was, indeed, her ex. And the way she went all sad when I mentioned the playground at Prenzlauer Berg. Had she wanted to get pregnant, but it never happened? Did her husband refuse to have children with her . . . and was it an ongoing sadness? Or did she have a miscarriage and was still subsumed with grief about it all?

And why the hell are you making such wild speculations when her reaction could be linked to a dozen different things, and might simply have sparked homesickness?

That was something that was so evident in Petra's conversation about East Berlin——it was the city that she still regarded as her own. She referred to it in such intriguingly affectionate and defensive terms, with more than a whiff of nostalgia for the life she once had there amidst her fellow bohemians in Prenzlauer Berg. She missed all she had left behind, and yet she was also an émigré who had fled a repressive regime. Why she had left, how she had left, and how much all that still haunted her were questions that still begged answers and which I had no right to pose just yet.

The next afternoon, after restripping all the floors with Mehmet and preparing them for restaining, I headed out in my track gear to pound the pavements. The running went reasonably well. Though I was a little stiff from yesterday's jog, the fact that I had limited my intake yesterday to seven roll-ups and a mere three beers (a light evening for me back then) aided my progress. I was also simply now more conscious of how to pace myself, how to recalibrate my breathing, how to maintain a steady stride as I again followed The Wall north, turned left at the Brandenburg Gate, then made a U-turn and retraced my path all the way back to Kreuzberg. I was drenched and thoroughly winded by the time I fell into the Café Istanbul for a bottle of fizzy water and a coffee. As soon as I settled in Omar said, "A Mr. Pawel called for you at ten this morning."

I checked my watch. It was now just before one p.m. I might just catch him before lunch. I asked for the phone and dialed Pawel's number. He answered on the third ring.

"Ah, Thomas. I'm glad you called. I have a free studio slot at four this afternoon. I'm recording the German translation of your piece at three fifteen, but if you could be here by four, I'm certain we can get you on tape within forty-five minutes . . . that is, unless you make many mistakes reading your own material."

"Well, I've never recorded anything I've written before."

"Then it will, no doubt, be a disaster. So I will hold a two-hour slot for us."

As it turned out, Pawel only needed an hour of my time to get the thing down on tape——because I went home after my coffee at the Istanbul, dug out the manuscript of the essay, and practiced reading it out loud five times before heading all the way up to Wedding for the recording. When I got there, I was kept waiting in reception for more than ten minutes, and naturally spent much of the time peering into the open-plan work area, trying to see if I could catch sight of Petra. No such luck. Eventually, Pawel emerged, accompanied by a dour-looking man in his mid-fifties, wearing a green anorak.

"Ah Thomas, meet Herr Mannheim——who has just recorded your essay in German. Herr Mannheim——here is the face behind the words."

"A pleasure," I said.

Herr Mannheim just gave me a shrug, then said something quickly to Pawel about being available for more work next week. With a curt nod, he headed for the exit.

"Is he always so charming?" I asked.

"Actually, you saw him in one of his better moods. The man is chronically depressed, but with the most wonderful speaking voice. He really should be playing Schiller at the Deutsche Theater, but he's so spectacularly glum all the time no one wants to put him in front of an audience. Nonetheless, he did do a rather good job on your text——and I do think the changes Petra suggested improved it enormously. Then again, as an *Ossie*, she's a little more invested in it all than I am."

An *Ossie*. Again he used that pejorative term for an East German. I decided not to question his use of local argot, but instead asked, "Was she around for the taping with Herr Melancholic?" trying to make this question as casual as possible.

"She's out sick today."

Oh fuck.

Fortunately, Pawel imparted this information as we were walking toward the studio. As he was a few paces ahead of me he didn't see the way I flinched at this news, then quickly masked it as we sat down in the studio and he asked me to read through the piece. He had a stopwatch with him and timed me. When I finished, he depressed the button on top of the watch, glanced at its face, and informed me: "We have to lose two minutes, eight seconds." This required going line by line through the script, excising a paragraph here, a sentence there, then me reading it out loud again and discovering that we were still thirty-eight seconds long, and cutting another two paragraphs.

It was rigorous work, and Pawel was extremely no-nonsense, announcing to me that he wanted the job done and me out of here in forty-five minutes. We succeeded in hitting that deadline. I was grateful to him for pushing me so hard, as it took my mind off of the fact that my date with Petra was undoubtedly off for tonight. At such an early stage in things, of course you want everything to move forward smoothly. When it comes to love, none of us takes a canceled evening lightly. Telling myself that I needed to stop into the Café Istanbul on the way home, I was certain that once I put my head in the door Omar would say, in his inimitable deadpan style, "A woman called. Said she can't see you tonight. Bad luck, American."

But when I reached the Istanbul at six, Omar shook his head when I asked if there were any messages.

"Do you mind if I pop in again around seven to check again?" I asked him.

"Why should I mind how you waste your time?"

Might the evening not be a write-off? Petra had left me a message at the Istanbul once before. Surely if she was ill she would get word to me . . . and why the hell didn't I ask her for her phone number yesterday? More tellingly, maybe she had simply decided to play hooky from work today and used the "I'm sick" excuse as a means by which to give herself a little time off. So, feeling a little more optimistic, I headed home and showered again and shaved. I changed into a dark blue work shirt, jeans, my biker boots, and my ever-reliable black leather jacket. Then I returned to the Istanbul.

"No message, American," Omar said. So I headed to the U-Bahn, then found my way to Pflugerstrasse: a street that must have been named back when there were still agrarian bits to Berlin, as a *pfluger* is a ploughman, though around here the only green space was a small rectangular park that had been bisected by The Wall.

The Arrivederci was one of two restaurants on an otherwise half-abandoned street of boarded-up buildings, many of which looked like they were being used as squats. Graffiti adorned most of the corrugated fencing that had been pried away from the entrances to these dwellings. The two or three elderly apartment blocks that appeared occupied here were in dismal condition. Outside of the Arrivederci and a small sad-looking grocery store the only other business on this street was a takeout kebab place. It had a huge rancid slab of lamb on a revolving spit in its front window. It looked like a rotating penicillin culture.

The Arrivederci was your standard-issue local Italian joint. There were around nine tables, all of them empty when I arrived. There were framed yellowing touristic posters of Napoli and Rome and Pisa and Venice on the walls, Chianti bottles with candles on the Formica tables. Woven bread baskets with packaged breadsticks, and a Muzak system playing Neapolitan favorites on the accordion. There was one waiter——a man in his forties, wearing a white shirt and bow tie that were both dappled in food and wine stains. He had lost most of his hair, but the four large strands that remained had been pasted across his otherwise bald pate with some heavy-duty adhesive. But he smiled as I crossed the threshold and told me to take any table. I parked myself in a booth upholstered in red Naugahyde. The waiter asked if I was waiting for somebody. I said I was——and was relieved when he didn't make mention of a message that had been left for a Herr Nesbitt, but instead asked if I'd like an aperitif of Prosecco "on the house." I asked if he could hold it until my friend arrived. Then, checking my watch and seeing that I was about seven minutes early, I pulled out my notebook and began to scribble away.

I was on the fourth page of notes and the second roll-up when I heard the door open and saw Petra come in. She was dressed in the same tweed overcoat, jeans, and a chunky brown cardigan beneath which she wore a white T-shirt. Though she managed a smile as she came in, when I leaned over to kiss her, she turned to make certain that it landed away from her lips and on her cheek. Looking into her eyes, I could tell that she'd had a very bad day.

"I'm sorry to be late," she said.

"You're hardly late," I said. "In fact, I was wondering if you would make it tonight."

"I told you I'd be here."

"Yes, but when I was at Radio Liberty this afternoon, Pawel mentioned you'd phoned in sick."

"You didn't tell him we were meeting tonight."

"Of course not."

"Sorry, sorry. It's just . . . well, I don't like him. As such, I don't like him knowing my business out of work."

"Fear not, he knows nothing. But are you all right? I mean, if you're not feeling well, we can do this another night."

"You're very sweet. But I'm here because I want to be here. And because I can be here now. A few hours ago . . . well, things did not look so good then."

"That sounds serious."

"Not serious. Just life. And I could use a drink, please."

I mentioned that the waiter had offered us two Proseccos on the house. Petra nodded her ascent, then fished out her pack of HB cigarettes and lit one up, telling me that when she woke this morning, she felt as if someone had pierced the cornea of her left eye with a particularly sharp needle, a pain that was so virulent, so excruciating, that she couldn't even make it to the medicine cabinet in the bathroom where she kept the ultra-potent pills that her doctor had prescribed as an antidote to these ferocious attacks.

"They only happen once or twice a year," she said.

But the vortex of pain kept her pinned to her mattress for a good hour. When it subsided for a few minutes, her equilibrium was restored enough for her to make it to the medicine cabinet. A further half hour after downing the requisite pills, the horror began to subside.

"And now, having bored you with this dreary little tale of my absurd, thermonuclear headaches, you are thinking: my God, this woman is troubled."

"I'm just glad you're better."

"You're being too nice."

"Is that a problem for you?" I asked with a laugh.

"It's just unusual. It makes me wonder what you do with all the dark stuff stalking you."

"How do you know there's a great deal of shadowy crap following me around?"

"Everyone has their dark recesses. Especially writers. But something I noticed about your book intrigued me——the way the reader comes away knowing so much about Egypt and the stories of the people you met while traveling. You tell all those stories wonderfully, and frequently with great compassion. Especially that young woman——the university lecturer——you met on a bus in Cairo who'd lost her husband and three-year-old son in a car accident. You had me in tears. But what surprised me was how, coming away from the book, I knew so little about the writer."

"But that was the strategy behind the book. My little life is less interesting to me than the lives of those I meet."

"Now, you don't really believe that yours is a 'little life'?"

"Hardly. But a reader picking up a narrative travel book about Egypt doesn't want to read about my parents' unhappy marriage."

"Was it an unhappy marriage?"

"We'll talk about that some other time."

"Why not now?"

"Because I don't want to bore you with . . ."

". . . the details of your 'little life'?"

"Precisely."

"But I'm interested."

The two glasses of Prosecco arrived. She clinked hers against mine.

"You let me talk on yesterday. Now, it's your turn. Are you in Berlin just to write a book, or to run away from something?"

I asked her if I could take one of her cigarettes. She pushed the pack toward me.

"A final cigarette before facing the firing squad?" she asked.

"I just don't want to bend your ear with personal stuff."

"I'm asking you because I'm interested, Thomas. But, my God, we do share a certain natural reticence, ja?"

"I like that."

"And I'd like to know why you mentioned that your parents' marriage was an unhappy one."

I lit up my cigarette and took a deep drag off it. Why was I feeling anxious? Perhaps because Petra was right——I kept my past out of the public domain. Fitzsimons-Ross complained about this on several occasions——the way I revealed so little of me. Even when it came to past girlfriends, I was always judicious about giving away too many details about myself. But now, sitting across from the woman with whom I was so smitten——and who, like myself, also evidently struggled with talking about herself——I had one of those strange epiphany-like moments that arise ever-so-rarely in life where I thought: *If you don't trust her with your stuff——the difficult, shadowy things that make you what you are——there's no future here. So take the gamble, expose yourself to a little danger by actually letting Petra inside your past.*

So I started to talk. Telling her about my mother's intrinsic unhappiness, and the way she and my father baited each other endlessly, and the accusations that would emerge repeatedly that the only thing holding them together was their only child . . . and how this knowledge just made me want to hide myself away further. By the time I was in my final year of high school, I was spending most weekends by myself, hiding out in cinemas and theaters and bookshops and not minding it at all.

"And your parents, they never suggested you do things en famille?"

"Not really. By the time I was in my last year in high school they were essentially living separate lives. Dad would be 'traveling on business' most weekends——which, I know now, was a euphemism for seeing one of the many girlfriends that he had. Occasionally, he'd be in town——and would suggest a movie and a late lunch at an Italian place. The thing about my father was, he was never authoritarian or one of those 'my way or the highway' dads like his own father. On the contrary, when I was sixteen he gave me my first cigarette and my first glass of wine, telling me he wanted me to learn how to drink and smoke properly."

"Sounds like a man's man."

"That he was, except when it came to the question of my mother. She made his life awful, as he did hers. But they still couldn't do the sensible thing and separate."

"It sounds like my parents."

"They were unhappy?"

"Not exactly. It was as if they had worked out a way of living together and not being together. I know my father had a girlfriend who worked at DDR Rundfunk in Halle. Just as Mother was involved with the director of the middle school where she taught——though I only accidentally discovered this when I was walking home from school and took a shortcut down an alleyway, and saw her locked in an embrace with her boss in the front seat of his Trabant . . . the director of the local middle school being a Party member of such standing that he could jump the queue for a much-desired car——"

"Did your mom see you?"

"Fortunately, no. She was far too locked in the embrace of Comrade Koelln to notice me."

"And you never said anything to her?"

"Are you mad? Even at this early age——I was fourteen at the time——I understood a basic principle of life in the GDR: in a society where the motto of the secret police is 'to know everything,' the one thing you learned very early on was keeping information to yourself . . . especially if you were beginning to question the way things worked in your country."

"What did you first question?"

"My God, they so indoctrinated us into looking upon the GDR as a great humanistic project. A workers' paradise. An egalitarian dream.' The thing was, I bought into it all. Because from age seven onward, I spent several weeks every summer at a Young Pioneers camp. We also had ideology classes every day in school, in which we were taught about the evil capitalist world that existed to the west of our frontiers, where children were forced to work in sweatshops, and where the majority of Americans were so indoctrinated into a culture of insane consumerism they were all wildly fat and killing themselves by endlessly feeding their faces . . ."

"You know, there's more than a little truth to that last comment."

"Of course. That's what Orwell said about clichés: they are all, on a certain level, true . . . not that we were ever permitted near Orwell in school or university or at any other point in our lives as good citizens of the most humane country the world had ever spawned."

"So when did you first read Orwell?"

"When I started living with Jurgen."

"Who was Jurgen?"

"My husband."

So he finally has a name.

"But you were asking me when I started to question things," she said, stubbing out a cigarette and reaching for another while quickly shifting the conversation back to safer terrain. "That was when I spent a weekend with a school friend named Marguerite. Her parents had a cabin in the country. A tiny place, three rooms, very basic. But they did have a television. Because we were twenty-five kilometers from the border with the Bundesrepublik I had my first introduction to West German television. All the commercials for all the things we never saw in the GDR. All the color. All the cool clothes. Then there was this film, dubbed into German, but set in Paris. I'd heard of Paris because of geography classes and our antifascist history courses, where we learned that the Nazis invaded France in 1940, and where (so our teachers informed us), outside of a few brave French Communists, the majority of the population collaborated with the fascists. But here, for the first time, I saw Paris. The movie was some love story——I forget its name——and the city looked so beautiful. I remember being enraptured by it all.

"But when I got home the next night and told my father that I wanted to learn French and move to Paris when I was eighteen, he did something very uncharacteristic: he got angry at me. He asked me who had placed such ideas in my head. When I tried to say I had been reading picture books about Paris, he said that he knew I was lying, for where would I have found picture books about Paris in Halle? That's when he asked if Marguerite's parents had such books. Again he was so furious. It was so unlike my father to be this way, I felt I had no choice but to tell him the truth: that we had been watching Western television during the weekend at their cottage. Now Papa was livid. He said that I must never, *never*, tell anyone about having seen Western television at the house of Marguerite's parents, and that I must stop being her friend immediately. I started to cry——not just because I couldn't understand why he was telling me to end things with my best friend in school, but also because I'd never seen my father like this."

"And then?"

"He told me that if word ever got out about any of this, it could severely harm us. He swore me to secrecy, swore me to never tell a soul about this, and instructed me to begin cold shouldering Marguerite the next day at school.

"'But all we did was watch television,' I cried.

"'You watched television that was *verboten*.'

"'But I'm always hearing kids in school talk about their parents letting them watch Western television.'

"'Their fathers don't have an important job with DDR Rundfunk. Can you imagine the difficulties I would find myself in if it was discovered that my daughter was watching capitalist television? You must promise me you will never have anything to do with Marguerite again.'"

"Did you keep that promise?"

Petra hung her head and fell silent for a moment. Then:

"I don't know why I told you this story. I've never told anyone this story."

"Really?"

"Not even my husband."

"So what happened?"

"Papa went off immediately to speak with Mother. And she then came to me, very shaken, very worried, and told me that I must do everything my father asked of me; that what Marguerite's parents did was very wrong, very dangerous. I remember saying to her:

"'But they aren't going to tell anybody that they let us watch Western television. It was just a silly movie. And I do really want to learn French now and visit Paris soon.'

"'That will not be possible,' Mother said flatly. 'If you are a good citizen, you might be allowed to go to Warsaw, or Prague, or maybe even Budapest. But Paris? That is the other side. We cannot go there.'

"It was the first time I was made aware of the fact that travel as people in the West know it——buying a ticket and getting on a plane to another country and coming back when you like, or, indeed, not coming back, or simply deciding to live elsewhere for a while——this was beyond the realm of possibility for us. In fact, like Western television, it was *verboten*."

"What happened to Marguerite?"

She stared into her empty glass.

"I don't know."

"By which you mean . . . ?"

"She didn't show up at school the next day. Or the day after. Or the day after that. My parents, meanwhile, never once questioned me whether I had seen or spoken to Marguerite——which struck me as strange, considering how vehement they were about me promising to have no further contact with her. But then, at the end of the week, I asked my form teacher what had happened to my friend. I can still remember the momentary look of unease on that woman's face as she said: 'I hear her father was transferred to a new job elsewhere.'"

"Did your parents denounce them?" I asked.

Her eyes didn't move from her glass.

"I don't know."

"Did your parents ever talk to you about it?"

"Never."

"Did you ask them?"

"How could I?"

"Did you ever see Marguerite again?"

She shook her head, then added:

"But something interesting did happen around six months after all this. My father was promoted to become head of cultural programs at DDR Rundfunk in Halle. Four years later, when I applied to study French and English at Humboldt University in Berlin——which I considered a long shot, as I was from the provinces and I was a half percentage point off their entrance exam requirements——I was offered a place."

"They could have simply decided, on the basis of your application, that you were worth taking a risk. And your father's promotion . . . who's to say it wasn't due to merit and many years of hard work?"

"Again, you are being far too nice. But nobody who hasn't lived in the GDR understands how the system works and how everyone denounced each other. I don't have definitive proof that my parents said anything to the Stasi about Marguerite's family, but why else did they suddenly 'move to another town'? The thing is, everyone lived under the ongoing creeping fear that some minor infraction could be reported to 'the higher powers' and used against them. As such, we were all self-censoring and knew there were limits to things we could discuss. Which is why, after it happened, I never brought up Marguerite again with my parents."

"You said your mother passed away. Are you still in touch with your father?"

She shook her head slowly.

"Have you tried to make contact with him?"

"You don't understand. The fact that I crossed over, got out . . . God knows what happened to his career in the wake of all that. But I also knew that, were I to try to contact him now, the implications for him could be grave."

"Has he ever tried to contact you?"

"You still don't comprehend. For him to survive over there, he must now regard me as dead. A nonperson. I no longer exist."

"I'm so sorry," I said, covering her hand with mine. She didn't pull it away. Instead she entwined her fingers with mine and said:

"I shouldn't have told you all that."

"I'm glad you did."

"But now you think me 'compromised,' a destroyer of other people's lives."

"You were a kid. You'd never seen Western television before. How were you to know? What's more, surely Marguerite's parents knew they were taking a risk."

"I betrayed them," she said, pulling her hand away.

"You did nothing of the sort. You have no concrete proof that your parents went to the authorities and——"

"Please, please, stop trying to cast everything in a reasonable light. The problem with that place is you had to betray others in order to survive. But in doing so you betrayed yourself."

I felt like saying: we all betray ourselves, but knew it would sound naïve and simplistic. Seeing her so distressed——yet also being so heartened by the fact that she trusted me enough to want to share this painful secret with me——simply deepened everything I felt for her. So what I did do was extend my right hand and placed it on her own. It was still kneading the napkin——and when I first touched it, she stiffed and continued agitating this piece of overwashed linen. So I clutched it tightly——and after almost instinctually trying to pull it away, Petra slowly tightened her fingers around my own. I looked up at her and saw that she was fighting tears.

"I'm sorry," she whispered. "I'm so sorry."

"There's nothing to be sorry about," I said. "Nothing."

"You are a lovely man," she said, still not able to look up at me.

"And you are a lovely woman."

"No, I'm not."

"I'm telling you: yes, you are."

"But you hardly know me."

"You are wonderful."

"Thomas, please."

"You are wonderful."

"You said that yesterday."

"Well, I haven't changed my mind since then."

She laughed a small laugh, then fell quiet for a moment, grasping my hand tighter.

"Nobody ever said that to me," she finally said.

"Really?" I said, trying not to sound shocked.

"My marriage . . . it was a curious business."

I said nothing, waiting for her to continue. But she suddenly reached for the menu and her cigarettes.

"I'm starving," she said.

"Let's order then," I said, smiling at her.

"Thank you," she said, and I knew that what she was actually thanking me for was not asking any further questions about her marriage.

The waiter came over. We both ordered pasta. I suggested a bottle of white wine. She nodded her okay, adding:

"I only discovered Italian food after I was evicted from the GDR. Parmesan cheese, linguini, clam sauce, real meatballs——all foods from another planet. But you, growing up in New York, you must have had access with every possible food on offer."

For the next half hour or so she quizzed me intently about my childhood in Manhattan——wanting to know all about my neighborhood, the little restaurants (like Pete's Tavern or Big Wong King on Mott Street in Chinatown) where I ate regularly with my dad, the sorts of Broadway shows I was taken to as a kid, the funkiness of the East Village in the early seventies, even getting me to demonstrate the difference between a Brooklyn and a Bronx accent, making her laugh as I mimicked my father saying expressions like *Howyadoin'?* in his original Prospect Heights intonations.

Petra relaxed considerably during the meal——eating the very good spaghetti carbonara and matching me, glass for glass, with the house white. When I once pointed out that she'd gotten me talking about New York for far too long, and surely it was my turn to bombard her with questions about her childhood, she said:

"But I want to know everything about you . . . everything except your past girlfriends. Or, at least, not yet."

"There's not much to tell in that department."

"When it comes to that part of life——the intimate part——there is *always* much to tell. And yes, this is the wine talking now."

"But you said we weren't going to talk about that just yet."

"All right, be mysterious."

"No more mysterious than you."

"Ah, but I sense your story is a happier one than mine."

"Is your story that sad?" I asked.

"Yes. It is that sad."

And fishing out a cigarette she said:

"And I wouldn't say no to another half liter of wine if you don't object."

"Object?" I said, reaching over and stroking her face with my hand. "This is so . . ."

But before I could finish the sentence she put her index finger on my lips.

"You don't have to tell me, Thomas. I know. I truly know."

Then, without warning, she put her head in her hands and looked stricken, as if everything was suddenly too much to bear.

"What's wrong?" I asked.

"I can't . . ."

I heard her shudder. She pressed her fingers to her eyes. I reached for her again, but she pushed away my hand.

"I can't . . ." she said again, her voice now a whisper.

"Can't what?"

"Thomas, please do yourself a favor and leave now."

"What?"

"Just go and spare yourself."

"Go? There's no way I'm going. There's no way I'll let you push me . . . us . . . aside. Not when I know . . ."

"And I know, too. I knew it the first moment I saw you. That's why I have to ask you to go. Because this can't be——"

"Why can't it be? Why? You are everything to me."

She suddenly stood up, grabbing her cigarettes. Out of nowhere she said three words:

"Ich liebe dich."

I love you.

Then she raced toward the door.

Immediately I threw some money down on the table and ran out into the street. But Pflügerstrasse was empty. I shouted her name several times. I charged up and down the street, checking in the few doorways that weren't boarded up, peering down alleyways, still calling out for her. But there was no response. Just the wind blowing up against the corrugated iron sheeting covering all the condemned buildings. I charged down to the main thoroughfare, scanning the street. But, like everywhere else in this no-man's-land of a neighborhood, there was not a soul to be seen. Petra had vanished.

My head was swimming, not just courtesy of her abrupt departure, but all that had transpired in such a mad rush beforehand. Then there were those three words she had spoken to me before fleeing. She meant them——of that I was absolutely certain. Just as the way everything that had come suddenly spilling out between us——"*I knew it the moment I saw you last week*" . . . "*You are everything to me*"——was simultaneously irrational and so profoundly true.

Sleet began to fall——insidiously cold and glutinous. I needed shelter in a hurry, but I didn't want to head to the U-Bahn and home. I wanted to find Petra. But without her address, without her phone number . . .

There was only one solution: I had to return to the restaurant and hope that she too would make her way back there, that, somehow, this running away was . . .

What? An overreaction? A fear of the enormity of it all? Or was it pegged to a lot of hidden stuff that I had yet to discover and, now, maybe never would? Certainly I was punch-drunk by the wild intensity of those last few moments and how, when we started expressing what we had been pondering, cogitating, feeling for days . . . the immense tactile realization that, yes, this was love . . . even though we both still knew so little about each other . . . well, I for one had never known anything like this before. The fact that Petra had run off into the night, that perhaps I had lost her, lost this mad reverie that was still grounded in a very cogent reality; the thought of this all just slipping away, the idea that she had now run out of my life for good . . . it was devastating, unbearable.

I returned to the restaurant. It had remained empty in my absence. The waiter watched me come in, looking desolate. He raised his eyebrows in my direction, as if to ask: "Any luck?" But he already knew the answer to that question. When I slowly shook my head in response, he pointed me toward a table. I sat down and pulled out my packet of tobacco and started to roll a cigarette. He walked over with a large thick bottle of Vecchia Romagna brandy and a small, thin glass. He poured me out a shot, patted my left shoulder in a fraternal, reassuring way, and said one word:

"Drink."

Leaving the bottle on the table adjacent to my glass, he left me to my cigarette, my booze, my thoughts.

Over the next hour I smoked four roll-ups, drank four small glasses of the Italian brandy, and waited for Petra to walk back in here. But that never happened. During this time I didn't resort to the usual comfort zone——my notebook, my excessive scribblings——that I usually reached for when I was nervous, troubled, trying to find something to do with my hands. Tonight I simply stared at the ceiling and kept seeing Petra in my mind's eye, telling myself that I had met the woman of my life, that everything about her——her beauty, her intelligence, her cunning wit, her immense vulnerability, her sadness, her all-encompassing sensuality, the way her hair gently lilted in the air as she shook her head from side to side, the half-surprised peal of her laughter, the way she so quickly cascaded into tears——represented a terra incognita.

And now . . .

I stubbed out my fourth cigarette and downed the last of the brandy and stood up, expecting to feel shaky after all that low-grade Roman alcohol. But all I felt was sadness. *She's not coming back. She's run from me, run from us. It's all over. Over before it even started.*

"What do I owe you for the brandies, my friend?" I asked the waiter.

"On the house."

"You must let me pay you."

"You threw down enough money when you went chasing after your friend. You have paid enough tonight."

"You're too kind."

"I hope to see you back here. And now, let me call you a taxi."

I was suddenly feeling beyond tired. So I nodded my assent. When the cab showed up five minutes later, the waiter again touched my shoulder and said:

"You love her, don't you?"

"Is it that obvious?"

"You are a lucky man to feel that. Me——I've never felt that. Never once."

"And you're still single?"

"No——married to the same woman for twenty-five years. So I envy you."

"But say it doesn't work out?"

"At least you now know what it feels to feel *that*."

Cold comfort. I let the waiter help me on with my coat. I shook his hand. I staggered out into the street and the cab.

I was home within seven minutes. I climbed the stairs to the apartment. I surveyed the clean, freshly painted, freshly sanded space that was Alaistair's studio. I staggered up to my room, tossed my jacket into a corner, kicked off my boots, and fell onto the bed.

The next thing I knew there was a ringing sound in my ear. It took a moment or two for me to work out where I was, how I had gotten there, and that——according to the watch on my wrist——it was two eleven in the morning.

Brnng.

The downstairs doorbell was ringing. Loudly. Incessantly. As if someone was holding it down. Insisting that I wake up. Insisting that I let her in.

The penny dropped. I was instantly on my feet, rubbing the tiredness out of my eyes, racing downstairs in bare feet, running across the cold flagstones of the entrance foyer, flinging the door open, and . . .

There she was. Petra. Drenched. Her hair matted down from the still-omnipresent sleet. Her eyes red, as if she had been crying for hours. Her body shivering as she fell into my arms.

"I'm cold," she whispered, clutching me tightly, her head so close against mine, her hand running through my hair, then touching my face, as if to prove to herself that I was real, tangible, *here*. I closed my eyes and felt tears.

"Don't let me go," she whispered. "Never let me go."

FOUR

S EVERAL HOURS LATER—IT was five twenty according to my bedside clock——I drifted back into consciousness, my arms around Petra. She was lying next to me in bed, dead to the world. I sat up on one arm and simply looked at her, thinking: *she is so beautiful*. As I stared down at her, I recounted the last few extraordinary hours, moment by moment, how, as soon as we were upstairs in my rooms, she pulled me toward her. Within seconds we were kissing so deeply, and with such vehemence, it was as if we were two lovers who had been separated for years——and had been so yearning for each other during this long absence that when the moment of reunion finally happened, we were insatiable.

Then we were pulling off each other's clothes and tumbling back into the bedroom. As soon as we landed on the mattress, she pulled me atop, letting out a sharp cry as I entered her, then throwing her legs around me to take me as deep as possible. Holding my face in her hands she looked up at me with an expression of such desire, such need, such hope, such ardor, that I immediately blurted what I had known, felt, days earlier at the specific moment when she first came into my field of vision.

"*Ich liebe dich.*"

"And I love you."

These words were whispered, as if we were exchanging a vow. Then, slowly, with a passion that was as outright as it was absolute, we began to make love. As it built——as our want for each other became almost vertiginous——the passion turned unbridled and just this side of crazed.

Afterward we both lay entwined, gazing into each other's eyes, be-dazzled, shell-shocked, alive to the realization that, perhaps, everything in our lives had just been transformed.

"Oh my love," she whispered, her arms so tight around me. "Oh my love."

"I'm yours," I whispered back, stroking her face.

She buried her face in my shoulder and sobbed.

"It's okay," I said, holding her close. "I promise you, all is good now."

"You cannot know . . . cannot begin to know," she said, her voice hushed.

"Know what, my love?"

"When I vanished tonight, I wandered the streets for hours, frightened."

"Frightened of what?"

"Frightened that I had lost you because of my craziness. Frightened that I could not accept the happiness which I thought might be possible with you."

"But that fear . . . it was due to . . . ?"

"So much. Things I will, in time, explain to you. But for now, please . . . I just want to be in this moment. This incredible moment. With you. So hold me as tight as you can, as I want to sleep in your arms tonight and tomorrow, next week, next month, next year, the next decade, the next century . . ."

"By which point you will have been sleeping in my arms for more than sixteen years. A beautiful thought."

"I love you, Thomas."

"I love you, Petra."

After turning her head to kiss me deeply, she placed it again on the pillow. As my arms encircled her, she closed her eyes and was quickly asleep.

I followed moments later, the intensity, the madness, of all that had transpired rolling over me with punch-drunk force. With my lips touching the back of her neck, I too surrendered to the netherworld of night.

Then it was five twenty in the morning——and I had that moment of befuddlement where I didn't know where I was, until I felt Petra stir pleasantly in her sleep. Sitting up on one arm, I simply stared down at her, my mind racing. Until you've experienced it——and I would hope you have at some juncture in your life——you can never really be prepared for the overwhelming nature of falling madly in love for the first time. You find yourself thinking things you never thought possible until now. Just as you so desperately want all to come right, especially as you are now living in a wonderfully heightened world where all seems so extraordinarily propitious. And the American in me——that part of me that believed in "can do," overcoming obstacles, getting the barn rebuilt in the wake of the tornado——now thought: whatever it was that had so hurt and tortured Petra in the past, I would make it right. I would be there for her completely and utterly. I would never let her feel alone again in the world. I would calm her fears and make certain she realized she could talk to me about anything. I would be the person she knew would be the one fixed and solid point amidst life's complex unpredictability. I would be her man.

Yes, I was dwelling in that elevated reality known as *superbia*——in which I found myself seeing life itself in a wholly new and extraordinary way. As I lay there, looking at Petra so happily asleep, so snug against me, so wonderfully omnipresent, I was astounded by the change that had come over me. The way I wanted to give everything to Petra——and how our love was rooted in a sort of instinctual truth. Yes, it was all very sudden, very overpowering. But so what if it had the force of a thunderclap? I knew. Just as Petra told me, she knew, too. For the first time in my life, I understood certainty. You can spend your entire life searching for the person for whom you are destined. Most of the time you will engage in compromises——some reasonable, some catastrophic, some often edging into quiet desperation and the sadness of limited horizons. But when, if, you come face-to-face with the person with whom there is a chance at transcendence, then you have to change everything, if necessary, to make it all come right. For this is your instant, your hour——and such an hour might only arise once or twice during that spell of time known as your life.

After around thirty minutes, I eased myself quietly out of bed and picked up all of Petra's wet clothes, putting them on assorted radiators to have them dried by the time she awoke. Then, going into the bathroom, I collected my robe off the back of the door, catching sight of myself in the mirror. I am someone who is never cheerful when viewing his reflected image. That morning, however, I did find a smile on my face——and one that was overlaid with true wondrous bewilderment.

I returned to the bedroom, leaving the robe on a chair near Petra's side of the bed, in case she woke up before me. Then I crawled in beside her, encircling her again with my arms.

"Is that you?" she mumbled, half-asleep.

"It's me."

"Come closer."

And locked together we retreated back to sleep.

When I awoke, I heard a voice humming in the near distance. Light was streaming through the sides of the window blinds and the clock by the bed said eleven twelve. The humming became more distinct as the world came into focus. With it was the smell of fresh coffee percolating. The space beside me in bed was vacant, as Petra was singing to herself in the kitchen, a song in German which sounded vaguely lieder-ish and familiar. I sat up in bed, feeling extraordinarily rested and——now this was a new sensation——actually happy.

"Good morning, my love," I said.

Petra came in from the kitchen, dressed in my bathrobe. She seemed so luminous, so incandescent, her eyes simply glowing.

"Good morning, my love," she said, putting her arms around me and falling beside me. We kissed deeply. Then, slipping off the bathrobe, we began to make love again. This time we moved even more slowly, with great sensual deliberateness, feeling the sheer intimate pleasure of being so physically amalgamated, so bound together.

Afterward, she took my face in her hands and said:

"This is so . . . God, I want to say 'revolutionary,' but it sounds so Communist! But that, for me, is the word. Revolutionary. Because what I feel now, for you, for us . . . this is a new country . . ."

". . . and one which we are creating for ourselves. And that's all that matters. Us. The rest is noise, Petra. Us."

"The most wonderful pronoun in the world. And one which I've never really used before."

"Nor have I, which, as you say, is what makes this, for me, so, yes, revolutionary."

"And I'm never getting out of this bed."

"I won't hold you to that."

"But you will hold me always?" she asked.

"You have my word on that."

"And I am the happiest woman in Berlin this morning. So happy I want to bring us breakfast in bed."

"You don't have to go to work?"

"I left them a message last night with the security man in the guard post, telling them I was still unwell. And then I came to find you."

"And when I opened the door and saw you there. . . ."

We kissed for a very long time. Then we lay, side by side, again simply looking at each other. Until external reality intervened: the sound of a sander at work downstairs.

"Oh, damn," I said. "I totally forgot."

"Fear not," Petra said. "When I heard movement down below, I went out onto the staircase and found myself face-to-face with a Turkish gentleman. He asked for you, said you were doing some work on 'Mr. Alaistair's studio.' When I explained you were still asleep, he told me not to wake you——that he would come by tomorrow to find out if Mr. Alaistair's condition had improved. I presume 'Mr. Alaistair' is your landlord?"

"You could call him that. You could call him many things. A man of many parts, 'Mr. Alaistair.'"

"Now you have me totally intrigued."

"It's a long story."

"I have all the time in the world. And I want to know everything about you."

"What about the breakfast together in bed?"

"You have a deal. I bring the breakfast, then you tell me all about this 'landlord' of yours."

"Let me help you organize things."

"No——I want the pleasure of bringing *meinem Mann* his breakfast. You will allow me to play *die Hausfrau* just this once."

She disappeared off into the kitchen, humming the same song that greeted my ears as I awoke this morning.

"That sounds like Schubert."

"Bravo. It is Schubert: *An die Musik.* Schubert in a characteristically reflective humor."

"It's beautiful. And the way you sing it . . ."

"Don't tell me I am a nightingale, *please.*"

"You're not a pigeon either. But you do have a very agreeable voice."

"I accept the compliment. But I have a pressing question. Do you take your espresso black or 'con leche,' and marmalade or cheese with your bread?"

"Black and cheese, please."

"Just like me."

She came back into the room five minutes later, a tray in her two hands, still humming the Schubert, her smile even more radiant. After placing the tray on the bed, she first leaned over and kissed me fully on the mouth, then poured us each a small demitasse of espresso. She raised hers to mine, and we clicked them together.

"To us," she said.

"To us." And I kissed her again.

The coffee tasted wonderful. I was famished, as it was now well after midday. So the pumpernickel with Munster cheese was quickly eaten.

"All right," Petra said as I finished the second piece. "Now your end of the bargain. 'Mr. Alaistair.' The whole story. Warts and all."

"All right," I said. "No holds barred." And I took her through the Fitzsimons-Ross saga. When I finished Petra said:

"You sound like you actually like him."

"Well, he has grown on me. Though he is an individual who lives life in extremis, I don't think there is much in the way of malevolence to him. On the contrary, he strikes me as a curiously moral and decent man. Though he can't articulate such things, I sense he and Mehmet are rather attached to each other. But if word was to get out about their relationship, I doubt Alaistair or Mehmet would survive at the hands of his wife's family. My hope, however, is that this near-death experience will have perhaps changed him. The hospital is weaning him off heroin. If he manages not to relapse . . . well, it will either be the start of a new phase of his life or a catastrophe. The addict-artist usually believes that his creativity is linked to his habit, which makes it ten times harder to break."

"So he's rather all over the place."

"Bizarrely, he does happen to be supremely disciplined when it comes to his art and orderly when it comes to his home. But one of the many good things about the geography of the apartment——and Fitzsimons-Ross's work and drug habits——is that we tend to live separate lives. Ever since I convinced him to listen to his blaring music on headphones while painting, we coexist without impinging on each other."

"That's good to know," she said, smiling.

"So if you do move in with me, you won't also be moving in with him."

"That's also good to know."

"Am I getting way ahead of myself here?"

"Yes——and I like it."

We kissed.

"For the rest of the day I simply don't want us to leave here," she said. "The door to the outside world remains shut."

"That sounds like a very acceptable idea."

"And I checked your cupboards. We are fine for food and drink. In fact, it was surprising and rather nice to see such a well-stocked larder."

"Well, I am a New Yorker. We all have a bunker mentality."

"I've already planned dinner: spaghetti with tomato sauce and anchovies. There's even some fresh basil and garlic and parmesan in the fridge, and two bottles of white wine. Most impressive, Thomas. I will move in."

We kissed again. Then, ridding ourselves of the breakfast tray, we slid back beneath the sheets and were once more entwined within moments. Desire at its most pristine has an insatiability that is both intoxicating and happily berserk. The need to be constantly tactile was only matched by the equal need to constantly declare our love for each other with the sort of epithets that were both absurdly romantic and absolutely genuine. Thinking back on that first day together, what now strikes me so forcibly is how I was using an amatory language that I had always sidestepped——because, if you have never fallen madly in love, even the expression "madly in love" can be dismissed by most sardonic metropolitan types like myself as mawkish. But when you cross that frontier, you find yourself saying "*Ich liebe dich*" so often that you have to wonder: are you trying to reassure yourself that this extraordinary place in which you've found yourself is actually real, that this sort of happiness has genuine tangibility?

Petra was clearly thinking the same thing. Later on in the afternoon, after we had fallen asleep again for an hour or so, I awoke to find her sitting up in bed and looking down at me——as I had done at her in the middle of the night.

"Hi there," I said quietly, reaching out for her nearby hand. "Everything okay?"

"I keep asking myself . . . can this be? Is this real?"

"I wonder the same thing myself."

"And I keep asking some supreme being——who's clearly never listened to me in the past, as he knows I'm rather skeptical about his existence——please, please, let this last. Let this always stay the way it is right now."

"Why shouldn't it? Nobody else is pulling the strings when it comes to our life together."

She bit her lip, looking sad.

"Did I say the wrong thing?" I asked.

"Have you had much luck in your life, Thomas?"

"Luck? By which you mean . . . what? Born in Manhattan? Never wanted for anything materially? I suppose in the great scheme of things, it's been a fairly lucky existence to date. Especially since I get to lead the life I want to lead."

"Well, luck has been something that has often seemed to sidestep me. There have been times when I've thought: why so much trouble, so much difficulty?"

"Like what sort of difficulty?"

"The thing is, when you haven't had much in the way of luck, you begin to think that if anything good comes into your life, it has to be taken away."

"It doesn't, and it won't be."

"Promise me that."

"Of course, I promise you that."

She buried her head in my shoulder and again held on to me tightly.

"Thank you," she said.

"And thank you."

"For what?"

"For being you."

"But you still don't know me, Thomas. I could turn out to be an impossible woman, a nag, a bitch."

"Now stop trying to sell me on your good points."

"Please always make me laugh when I get too serious, too dark."

"With pleasure."

"And never vanish on me."

"I would never do that."

"But you have in the past, yes?"

"Guilty as charged. But the truth is——and I've never admitted this before——I have always been looking for an excuse to stand still."

"We're crazy, you know that."

"Why do you think that?"

"Because we are saying all these big things to each other after a single night together."

"I find that rather wonderful."

"You've honestly never felt this way before?"

"Never. And you?"

"There was a marriage. But it was . . . well, not this. Not what I feel now. But what am I feeling now? Madness. A wonderful madness."

"There is nothing wrong with this sort of madness."

"As long as it lasts."

"It will, my love, it will."

Sometime toward sunset, we took a long shower together——soaping each other up with sensual slowness, kissing constantly, clinging together under the cascading water. Then we dried each other and got dressed, and lounged on the sofa, opening the first bottle of cheap Pinot Grigio and smoking cigarettes. Petra browsed through the twenty or so records I had bought since moving in.

"So you like all this jazz of the fifties. And you like Beethoven quartets. And Bartók. And Bach played on the piano. And lots of Brahms, which means you must have a melancholic streak. And two Frank Zappa albums, just to prove that you actually live in the 1980s. But no other new music. No Clash, no Sex Pistols, no Police, no Talking Heads . . ."

"All of whom I like."

"All of whom I worship——as I've only discovered them all in the last year. But I'm not criticizing your taste. It's just all a bit refined. All very New York intellectual. I'd like to see New York."

"That's easy to arrange."

"Now it's me getting ahead of myself here. I should be more reserved, more diffident. My mother used to tell me that when I first got interested in boys. Do not let them know you're interested in them. Always play distant and coy."

"And did you?"

"I tried to but did so very badly. I don't like roles. And I don't like being coy. It's not me. But nor is being the great romantic. Until now. But we are getting off the subject of you."

"Why don't you choose a record?" I said.

"Okay, Brahms. The clarinet trio. But you have to continue telling me about your father."

She pulled out the record——an old Benny Goodman recording——and put it on the turntable. The record player was just that——an old-style Victrola encased in a box. I'd bought it fourth-hand in a nearby junk shop for fifteen marks and the proprietor even threw in a set of spare needles for the tone arm.

"I am impressed," Petra said.

"By what?"

"By the fact that you don't have an elaborate stereo system."

"I wouldn't mind one. But as I am living on a budget . . ."

"And this book you are writing. What will it be about?"

"Berlin, I suppose. But I won't know that until I actually begin to write it. Which I won't do . . ."

". . . until you leave Berlin?"

Petra placed the record on the long rod that could house up to four LPs. Then she pressed the requisite lever, the disc dropped down with a decisive thud onto the turntable, and the tone arm automatically positioned itself over the edge of the record and lowered itself into the first groove. After a few moments of the usual *kachenk-kachenk* the opening wintry chords of the Brahms began to play.

"I'm not planning to leave Berlin," I said.

"Sorry, sorry. That must have sounded like a loaded question."

"The only way I'd now leave Berlin is if you were leaving with me."

She reached over and kissed me.

"I like the fact that you can know that after one day."

"I knew that the moment I saw you."

"As did I, as frightened as I was of it all. The prospect of happiness . . . it can be daunting. You've read Graham Greene?"

"I think everyone who travels and writes about it loves Graham Greene."

"There was a statement in *The Heart of the Matter* that hit me so hard when I read it about a year ago that I underlined it three times: 'He felt the loyalty we feel to unhappiness——the sense that is where we really belong.'"

"That is so damn good——and the reason why Graham Greene *is* Graham Greene. And it kind of sums up my parents. But when you read that . . . ?"

"I thought to myself: can I ever find myself in a place outside of sadness?"

"Was that before or after you came over?"

"Just before. But . . ."

She let the sentence die, indicating yet again that we had reached a frontier in the conversation——in *that subject*——which she wasn't ready to traverse. So I simply put my arms around her and said:

"You don't 'belong' in that place anymore."

We cooked dinner together, collaborating on the spaghetti sauce, agreeing to differ on the number of garlic cloves we should add to the sauce (I was in favor of five, Petra was certain that any more than two would overwhelm it), but concurring that the anchovies lifted the sauce out of the mundane and gave it a necessary kick. I offered to run to a small Italian grocer's a few streets away and buy a baguette to go with the meal, but Petra said:

"I don't want you away from me tonight, even for five minutes. Don't worry. I won't always be so clingy. But grant me that one little wish."

"Of course," I said, simultaneously wondering if there was a man in her past life who told her he was going out for a packet of cigarettes and simply never returned.

The sauce was a collaborative success. As the pasta boiled in the big pot, I lit candles and uncorked the second bottle of wine while Petra grated the parmesan and dimmed the lights. And yes, all these small domestic details——the way the candlelight illuminated her in silhouette as she brought the cheese to the table, the discussion about what was the right texture for *al dente* pasta, and (this was most intriguing) the artful manner in which Petra turned two paper napkins into origami——still stay with me, remaining as vivid in my mind's eye as if it all transpired just a few days ago. Is that the lingering effect of happiness——the fact that even the most minor details linger in the memory decades later?

"You are a woman of many talents," I said, as Petra created two multi-winged and very elegant birds out of two very ordinary pieces of paper towel.

"It's a little pastime of mine, this origami. Actually it's something of a private compulsion——which began around four years ago when I was working at this state publishing house in East Berlin and found a book on origami by accident in a pile of rejected texts. It had been published in the Bundesrepublik——*Do It Yourself Origami*——and had been tossed aside by some editor who decided it wouldn't pass the ideological purity test. So I snuck it home and spent weeks studying it. Paper was something of which there was never a shortage in the GDR——and I used copies of *Neues Deutschland* to practice my origami. We had so little in terms of pretty things——the GDR aesthetic never being one to embrace beauty——that the origami was, I came to conclude, an attempt at cheering things up, trying to make an artistic little object out of very basic materials. I got so good at it that Jurgen insisted I do a private exhibition of my 'pieces' at our apartment in Prenzlauer Berg. We must have had at least fifty people in our little place and all my 'sculptures' were bought. Of course, we charged negligible sums——four or five ostmarks, less than one deutsche mark per piece. But the exhibition meant a great deal to me. I'd been living around all these writers, all these artists——and, finally, something I made, something genuinely creative, was recognized by my peers.

"And now I must be the only person in Kreuzberg who can turn a napkin into a Japanese folding rendition of a swan. Mind you, so many of my friends in Prenzlauer Berg picked up these weird talents due to the starkness of life over there. I knew the best abstract painter in East Berlin——Wolfgang Friederich——who was also an expert at repairing toilet cisterns. His own cistern in his apartment had broken down. When he couldn't get a state-sanctioned plumber for weeks, he simply took the whole apparatus apart and worked out how to make it functioning. After that, word spread that Wolfgang was the man to call if your toilet wasn't working. He must have been doing thirty house calls a week, pocketing

five ostmarks a time. More than one hundred and fifty marks a week——
the same pay I was making a month as a translator. Not that I ever be-
grudged him the money. Five ostmarks was a small price to pay to get your
toilet fixed——and Wolfgang could get to you in an hour after calling him.

"Of course, he was eventually denounced for profiteering and was
taken away for a while. But the man——besides being the de Kooning of
East Berlin——really knew his toilets."

"Bon appétit," I said, ladling the spaghetti and sauce onto our plates.
"Our first proper meal together."

"With thousands more to come."

"Absolutely."

She raised her glass.

"To us."

"To us."

We talked nonstop all that evening——about everything. Our childhoods. The teachers we liked and despised in our respective schools. The
first dance we ever attended. The first person we ever kissed. The curious position of being an only child with parents who had fallen out of
love with each other. What was most intriguing about this conversation
was the way we both had experience of bullies and shrill homeroom
teachers, and the shame of being the wallflower at some dance, and
the growing realization that ours was not a happy family. But when it
came to cultural references——the films we saw growing up, the books
we read, the fashions we tried to ape——we found ourselves in separate
universes. What struck me most forcibly was just how isolated and cut
off Petra was from an entire world of seemingly nonideological material:
like the films of Hitchcock and Bergman and all the French New Wave,
or the vast majority of Western pop music. When it came to the realm
of the material——the realpolitik of an ultra-consumerist society versus
that of a Communist world where there was no such thing as mercantile choice——what fascinated me was how fashion still counted for a
great deal in Halle; how Petra's mother made a faux-denim jacket for
her daughter out of some Romanian wool that she dyed a deep blue,
embossing it with steel buttons "so it looked almost like a Levi's jacket
that Mother saw in some Western film. All my friends at school asked me
where they could buy this jacket, it was that wonderful."

The conversation flowed with an ease, a fluency, a pleasure, that was just dazzling. We were so eager to exchange details of our lives before now——so fascinated by how, despite the massive geopolitical difference of our upbringings, we shared such similar perspectives on everything from the inanity of religion, to the dreariness of most hyperintellectuals, to the primacy of storytelling in fiction, to a tendency to cry at "good sentiment" (Petra's expression) like *La Bohème*, and an equal belief in the pantheistic pleasures of the great outdoors . . . though Petra informed me that she had never seen mountains before in her life.

"Well, the Alps are only a few hours by train," I said. "Ditto the Dolomites. So we'll have to organize a week off for you very soon and jump a Trans Europe Express down there."

"But it will all cost money."

"Let me worry about that."

"I will pay my way."

"All the subject of future negotiations."

"No negotiations," she said. "Only unconditional surrender to my point of view."

"So you are a secret Stalinist."

"What I am is happy."

"Well, here's something that I hope will make you happier," I said, reaching into a side drawer of the kitchen table and pulling out a key.

"Move your stuff in tomorrow," I said, sliding the key over to her.

She stared down at it for a very long time.

"Are you that sure already, Thomas?" she finally said.

"Absolutely."

Another long pause during which I could see her biting down on her lip, her eyes filling up.

"You are a wonderfully mad man. And yes, I will move some things in tomorrow."

"That's very good news," I said, also understanding that the term "some things" also was a gentle hint to me not to push her too far too fast.

"Oh God, look at the time," she said, glancing at her watch, then showing me the dial. It was one thirty-three in the morning.

"And look at the ashtray."

It was brimming with the twelve or so cigarettes we had smoked over the last few hours.

"And look at the two empty bottles of wine."

"Not to mention the half bottle of schnapps we've drained," I added.

"Why don't I feel drunk?"

"Guess."

She stood up and came over to me, sitting down in my lap, arms around my neck.

"When I wake up in a few hours, do you know what I am going to think? The world is now a different place. And the worst thing about waking up this morning will be knowing that I will be away from you until after sunset."

"It will be a very long wait for me, too."

We fell into bed a few minutes later, falling asleep in each other's arms. The next thing I knew the alarm by the bed was ringing. I glanced up and saw that it was just after nine. As I hit the off button with my hand, Petra reached over and pulled me toward her.

"Work can wait another hour."

As we made love, we never once looked away from each other——my face above hers, our mutual gaze constant and bottomless, our bodies moving with a shared rhythm that was so natural, so passionate.

"I want to start every morning with you like this," she whispered to me as we clung to each other afterward.

"I could live with that," I said, smiling.

I got up to make breakfast while Petra showered. The coffee just finished percolating as she came into the kitchen, her face freshly scrubbed, her hair still wet, looking at the set table, the bread and cheese on the wooden cutting board, the glasses of orange juice, the espresso cups at the ready.

"Good morning," I said.

"Good morning. And do you know what I kept thinking while in the shower?"

"Tell me."

"Luck has finally decided to pay me a call."

FIVE

*L*UCK HAS FINALLY *decided to pay me a call."*

Some hours later, sitting on a park bench in the Tiergarten, that sentence——and, specifically, Petra's beautiful enunciation of those nine words——took up occupancy in my head and wouldn't go away. Because I knew she was speaking for both of us.

So this is what it's like.

That was the other realization now so overwhelming me——and one that allowed me to sit on this bench in subzero temperatures, oblivious to the cold. Love. For all those days after first seeing Petra, I kept trying to temper the emotional wave that had blindsided me with the thought: it just can't happen. I told myself a dozen reasons why things would not work out, why Petra would get cold feet and push me away. After she ran off into the night during our first dinner together, I felt an acute loss. With her vanishing came the realization that this just might never be, that a door had been slammed shut on something so tangible, so electric, so possible, so enormous.

But now . . . *now* . . . this was actual, concrete. Again I found myself running the film of the last thirty-six hours over again in that screening room that occupies the back of my head: the immense passion, the profound intimacy, the sense of total complicity, and, of course, the knowledge that I had met the woman of my life. As I sat there, staring up at the wintry Berlin sky, I had a moment of dread when I wondered: say she panics today and does what I did with Ann, runs away from someone who just wants the best for her, for us?

Trust her, trust it, I tried to tell myself. *You are no longer alone in the world. You have someone who not only sees in you what you see in her——but who wants what it all represents as badly as you do.*

The cold finally got me moving again——and as I had already jogged up to the Tiergarten I now headed farther west toward the Krankenhaus. I had a small daypack on my back this morning, containing all of Alaistair's mail as well as several newspapers and a few back issues of *The New Yorker*. When I reached his bedside and proffered assorted letters and the magazines, his first comment to me was:

"What's that old line about 'shooting the messenger'? I mean, did you really have to bring me every fucking demand for money that assorted bloodsucking banks and companies are making upon me?"

"Life, I'm afraid, does go on, and I sensed that when they spring you from here, you might not want to walk back into a room full of creditors."

"Did you bring my checkbook?"

"It's in the file with all the bills."

"You're even more organized than I am. And I hate the fucking *New Yorker* magazine. All those patrician, anglophile New Englanders writing about fucking their neighbor's wife in the nursery while snow falls on Boston and everyone downstairs is singing 'O Come All Ye Faithful.' Then there was that eighty-page dirge I was reading the other day about the origins of the Swiss Army knife. I know it makes a certain sort of East Coast American feel worldly and literate, but Jesus, the sclerosis that simply leaps off the page . . ."

"So the withdrawal symptoms are behind you?"

"You're catching me on a good half hour. Still, the substitute, though dreary, is making the days slightly less intolerable. The doctors think I will be banged up here for at least another fortnight, until they're certain I'm thoroughly detoxed, born-again, and all that. But let's get off the all-encompassing subject of me and address the blinding glimpse of the obvious which I see before me."

"By which you mean?"

"Oh my word, he has gone all coy on me. Coy and demure and bashful . . . and now, my word, he is blushing."

"I don't know what you're talking about," I said, trying to stop a thoroughly goofy smile from spreading across my face.

"Her name, monsieur. Her name."

"Petra."

"Ah, *eine Deutsche* . . ."

"That's right."

"And it's love, isn't it?"

"Is it that obvious?"

"My son, you are as transparent as water. The moment you walked in here, I thought: *Bastard . . . it's happened to him.* I'm not going to say anything more, except . . . and this is the voice of experience talking . . . guard it with your life. Because what you are feeling right now . . . it happens once or twice during a lifetime."

"Is that what you felt with Frederick?"

"My word, you remember his name."

"Of course, I remember his name."

"Let's not continue talking about him, otherwise I might jump ship and head out into the night in a few hours and score the first bag of smack I can find. My goal for the future is to live in that zone that is somewhere beyond the unbearable. Or to put it another way, this is a subject I wish to sidestep in the future. Because . . ."

He fell silent for a moment, then turned away and looked out the nearby window, a shaft of winter light illuminating his face and highlighting a sadness that was tempered by an interesting incandescence—— as if the discovery of all that had hit me brought back, for him, the same glow, the same sense of possibility and emotional immensity.

"Get out of here now," he then said. "What I need to do right now is embrace the mundane and dodge all that you're feeling, as bloody envious as I am of it all."

"Understood," I said.

"But you will come by tomorrow, yes?"

"Of course."

"Any news of Mehmet?"

"He had another job today, so he couldn't make it over. But outside of a final varnishing of your floorboards, your studio is essentially back to what it used to be. In fact it's spanking new and improved."

"And when they finally end this incarceration, I plan to show the world just how fucking resilient I am. Everything destroyed by that talentless wanker I can redo in a matter of days."

"I've no doubt about that."

"One last thing I'm going to say to you before the powers-that-be tell you that visiting hours are over: enjoy your good fortune. You've been dealt four aces, my friend. Play them."

On my run back home, Alaistair's words kept ricocheting around my head, the way that sage advice always lingers. That is, if you allow it to take up residence in your psyche and gain purchase. And when you begin to trust your heart for the first time in your life.

I got back to the apartment and stripped the bed of its wildly contorted, soiled sheets. Then I remade it with fresh linens——and headed out to the Korean laundry two streets away and dumped off the dirty ones. From there I went to a butcher and bought an entire chicken, then stopped by the Turkish corner store for French beans and potatoes and two more bottles of that Pinot Grigio which we so easily drank yesterday. Back home I prepared the chicken and the potatoes, then scrubbed down all surfaces, putting out clean towels, making everything immaculate. As six p.m. approached, I began to obsessively glance at my watch every five minutes. Then I heard the key turn in the lock of the main door below. Bounding down the stairs, I got there just as Petra came in, the beret on her head wet with that evening's sleet, a suitcase in one hand and a bag of groceries in the other. But what I saw before all these secondary details was the huge beaming smile on her face, the electricity in her eyes, the way she quickly shifted the groceries to a chair, tossed her suitcase to one side of me, and threw herself into my arms. We kissed deeply, clutching each other so close, Petra then taking my head in her hands and pulling her lips off mine for a moment to look at me and say:

"Thank God you're here."

"Of course, I'm here."

"All day long, I was afraid you'd be taken away from me."

"And I had the same fear, the same dread. But now . . ."

"Take me upstairs," she whispered.

Once there we fell onto the bed and taking off each other's clothes, whispering "Ich liebe dich" over and over again, Petra again pulling me into her immediately, letting out a sharp moan, digging her fingers into my back, our lovemaking turning wild, without abandon.

Some time later——I'd lost track of the minute, the hour, the day itself——Petra said:

"I want us to be making love like this twenty years from now."

"I want us to make love like this when we decide to have a child together."

Petra looked at me with surprise.

"Do you really mean that?" she asked.

"Have I jumped the gun?"

"Hardly."

"It's not like I'm suggesting we do this next week. It's just . . ."

I broke off, worried that I was entering delicate territory.

"Go on," she said, stroking my face.

"If you love somebody, then you do want, eventually, a child with them. I can't believe I'm saying such things because . . . well, I've never thought this before."

"And if I told you you're the first man with whom I've ever wanted a child . . . well, I hope you won't now be running off in fear to join the French Foreign Legion."

"I would never run away from you. On the contrary, I want everything possible for us. Everything."

"As do I, as do I. And you must know I would never stop you from moving around the world for your work, as long as you always come back to me."

"I'm not even thinking about travel right now."

"But it's what you do, Thomas. I don't want to change you. I just want to be a part of your life."

"And I want our life to be just that. Our life. And that could also mean us traveling together."

"But I'd be in your way."

"You will never, *ever*, be in my way."

"All those hours away from you today . . . it was almost intolerable. But I left work early and went back to my room and brought some clothes with me."

"Yes, I was very pleased when I saw the suitcase with you."

"But what's so *me* is the fact that I kept thinking, all day, the moment you saw the suitcase you'd change your mind, think I was moving in far too quickly."

"And I kept thinking, all day as well, that you might get cold feet about us, and would run off again into the middle of the night."

We stayed in bed for another hour, lying side-by-side, never taking our eyes off each other, talking, talking.

"You know that Rilke poem which begins: 'Be ahead of all partings'?" she asked.

"Rather ominous advice."

"But when you read it in the context of the poem——which is one of his sonnets to Orpheus——you see that it's all about the need to accept the transient nature of everything."

"But this love is not transient."

"That is a wonderful sentiment, Thomas. But we are both mortal. Like it or not, eighty years from now neither of us will be here. We can't sidestep the transience that simply is temporal life. But the thing about Rilke's poem, he actually asks us to celebrate the impermanence with which we struggle. And for non-hereafter types like ourselves, there are these three lines that, when I first read them, struck me so forcibly."

"Can you remember them?"

Not taking her eyes away from mine, our hands entwined, she recited, in a soft but wonderfully articulate voice, the following lines:

"Be——and yet know the great void where all things begin,
"The infinite source of your own most intense vibration
"So that, in this only time around, you may give it your perfect assent."

"'. . . in this only time around,'" I said, repeating the line. "That is so damn true."

"It's why the poem has such heft——because it's alive to the need to make the best of this thing called life."

"Which we will always do together."

"Always remind me of that, if I ever get overwhelmed by things."

Hunger finally got us out of bed. I put the chicken in the oven, then helped her unpack her groceries. I also showed Petra the space in the wardrobe that I'd cleared for her. She had brought just three changes of clothes——two skirts, a simple hippie-ish floral dress, her leather and tweed jackets. Seeing all these items hanging on the wardrobe rail—— along with the two sweaters and underwear she stacked on a shelf——so pleased me, as did the sight of her toiletries in the bathroom. She was installing herself here now. Our story together was truly beginning.

Over dinner that night, she said:

"Now here is a question I have never asked a man in my life before: how on earth did you learn how to properly roast a chicken?"

"That's a skill just about every American boy is taught. My father——despite being a hard-drinking advertising executive——could actually cook rather well."

"And your mother?"

"A total princess when it came to the kitchen. Her father——the Diamond District jeweler——could afford a housekeeper, which was just as well, as my grandmother did very little except play canasta, talk about how disappointing her life was, and tell my mother that she was worthless."

"Did your mother believe her?"

"Absolutely, which was a big part of her tragedy. She was educated at the right schools. She was literate and by no means stupid. But she also married the wrong man as a small act of rebellion, then hated the fact that we were living in what was, for her, diminished status, though even telling you this makes me feel ridiculous, compared with the way you had to live in East Berlin."

"You know, Thomas, there's no need to feel you have to downplay the sorrows of your childhood because they don't match up to the perceived horrors of the GDR. I knew friends who had very wonderful childhoods there. I knew friends who had unhappy ones. Decency, cruelty, happiness, unhappiness . . . all those facets of the human emotional palette, they are rather borderless, aren't they? The important thing is how your childhood ends up making you feel about yourself. Are you someone who comes away furious at the world or able to handle everything it throws at you? Do you believe you deserve to be happy, or do you quietly do everything in your power to upend all possibilities of contentment? And if yours was difficult, sad . . ."

"I still believe in the possibility of happiness."

She slid her fingers through mine.

"So do I, or, at least, I do since you walked into my life."

"*Walked into my life.* That's lovely."

"And so accurate. It's largely how life works, and, more specifically, how it changes. You're going through your life——the day-to-day stuff, business as usual, all very routine. You're trapped into thinking that this is how life is now. Then you walk into somebody's office at work and there you are. I guess, the hardest thing for me was actually not knowing if you felt the same way about me."

"You mean, you knew immediately, too?"

"Don't sound so surprised."

"But I am surprised. You were so reserved, so distant."

"That's because I was so anxious, so nervous that it might not happen, or that I'd run away from it because I feared it not happening, which, of course, I did in that restaurant."

"But you came back. You chose happiness."

"And now," she whispered, "let's go back to the bedroom."

We could not get enough of each other. This was complete mutual intoxication, a physical totality that served to express the immense emotional totality of what we were both feeling. This is what they all talked about when using the phrase true love.

We fell asleep early that night. When I woke the next morning all the dishes were washed, breakfast was laid out on the table, and Bill Evans was on the Victrola.

"You didn't have to do all this," I said, wandering still half-asleep toward the table and kissing Petra good morning.

"Yes I did, and I am stopping by my room today and bringing back some records. So tomorrow you'll be waking up to Stop Making Sense."

We talked about the day ahead, and how she had to deal with a very long and dreary translation of an essay on Heinrich Böll: "A wonderful writer, but in the hands of the dry little English academic who wrote the piece, The Lost Honour of Katharina Blum comes across as the seven stations of the cross."

"It's an interesting choice of piece to discuss on Radio Liberty, given how it so thoroughly criticizes the Bundesrepublik, especially the intelligence services."

"I think that was the point of commissioning the essay, showing how you in the West . . ."

Suddenly she caught herself and flinched.

"We in the West," she said.

"You don't have to correct yourself. You're in exile."

"Maybe one day I'll feel part of this place."

"Or elsewhere."

"Would I like America? Would I fit in?"

"Now, if I were from some small town in Indiana or Nebraska, I think the culture shock would be extreme. But you and Manhattan? It would be love at first sight."

"I adore your absolute certainty, Thomas."

"I am going to bring you to Manhattan."

"Can we leave today?"

"Absolutely."

"You'd do that right now?"

"Say the word and I'll get on the phone and find two seats."

"Now I feel embarrassed."

"Why?"

"Because even if I wanted to, I couldn't just leave Berlin. My contract with Radio Liberty is, at least, for another year. The government department that deals with the integration of GDR citizens into the Bundesrepublik found me this job. Just as they also found me my room and gave me three thousand marks——a small fortune to me——to buy clothes, bed linens and towels, and generally ease my transition over here. To break the contract now . . . it would seem ungrateful, wouldn't it?"

"They'd get over it. But hey, my book means I need to be here for many months to come, and I can stay in Berlin as long as you need to stay. So if Manhattan has to wait . . ."

"But not for too long," she said, kissing me. Then starting to gather up the breakfast dishes she said, "After I deal with these, I'd best get off to work."

"You go do what you have to do. I'll take care of these."

"A man who shops and cooks and does the dishes."

"That's not so wildly unusual, is it?"

"It's just . . . my husband was rather 'traditional' in the domestic arena. He was a writer. He wrote plays that rarely got performed. One of them did get done a great deal in assorted theaters around the GDR. Another got him into considerable trouble. But that's another story. And for all his talk of *kameradschaft*——comradeship——he was a very conservative man when it came to so-called sexual roles. I was his wife. He expected me to keep the apartment clean, and to cook and do the laundry. It didn't matter that his plays were no longer getting staged anywhere, or that he was not even permitted to work . . ."

She cut herself off.

"But I really don't want to say anything more about it, okay?"

Her tone had shifted to defensiveness, and she caught herself immediately, saying:

"Oh God, listen to me. I reveal all this to you of my own volition and then get cross at you."

"You were hardly cross."

"And you must stop being so *reasonable*, Thomas. You can call me on things when I get difficult, which I do from time to time."

"I will never press you for details about your life over there. But, obviously, I do want to know everything about you, or at least everything you want to tell me . . . but in your own time. No pressure. None at all."

"Except to go to work. What are you going to do today?"

From downstairs, there was the sound of a sander being fired up.

"It looks like Mehmet has already started. So I'll help him. And then, well, I do need to start nosing around this city some more. So I might make a call to Tempelhof."

"Oh God. I was there once, and it spooked me."

"But it's only an airport, albeit a Nazi one. And everyone says that, architecturally speaking, it is stunning."

"That it is. But the place still is a throwback to a national horror which we in the GDR were told was perpetrated by the other Germany. Yes, we were told about the death camps, the madness of the Nazis. But in the eastern part of Germany——according to the teaching of the GDR——our victorious Communist brethren vanquished them all in the final days of the war and cleansed our blessed Democratic People's Republic of the scourge of National Socialism. When I came to live in West Berlin I naturally read all I could about the era. The fact is, we were all guilty——and the horror done in our name was unspeakable. But I suppose what was most unspeakable for me was the discovery that we, *das Deutsche Volk*, allowed this monstrosity to happen. The entire division of Germany——the fact that more than fifteen million of its citizens ended up imprisoned in a totalitarian system——finds its origins in our embrace of Nazism. It's strange, isn't it, how when one nightmare is killed off, another replaces it immediately. It's the way of the world, I suppose——but also a reflection of ourselves. We create nightmares. And so often we drop others into them."

Is that what happened to you? I so wanted to ask. Just as I simultaneously sensed there was a part of Petra that wanted to blurt out everything but perhaps feared how I might react to this story. I felt like saying: "Just get it over with and tell me. Because I love you. And because whatever happened over there happened under extreme circumstances."

But, again, my instincts told me not to push here. Petra would tell me when she was ready to tell me about this dark recess of her life.

"I just want you to know one thing," I heard myself saying. "Life will be better now. Or, at least, that's what I want it to be for you, for us."

She came over and buried her head in my shoulder, holding on to me tightly, whispering: "Thank you." Then she took my face in her hands and kissed me.

"Another nine hours away from you," she said. "That idea appals me."

"I'll be here when you walk in tonight. We could go to the ten p.m. gig at the Kunsthaus," I said, mentioning an edgy jazz place a few streets away.

"Only if you let me cook us dinner first."

"Absolutely. But if you give me your shopping list now, I'll pick everything up this afternoon."

"But half the pleasure of cooking is doing the shopping beforehand. Just be here at six, please."

"Where else would I be?"

We kissed again with such desire that we tumbled back into the bedroom and were naked within moments. Is there anything ever so extraordinary as the first months of a love affair? The rueful among us (and we are all, on a certain level, rueful) always talk about how love inevitably changes, how that initial burst of ardor downgrades, over time, into something more muted, more routine. But when you are in the midst of a new love that feels so right, so total, so very much your destiny, how can you think about five years on, when you are awake at four in the morning with a new baby in the throes of colic; when you haven't slept in two days; when making love is, at best, a weekly event; when you are both beginning to fray a bit about the work-family balance and *Why aren't you doing more on the baby front?*

But now all I was thinking was: love is actually possible. And it's all due to this extraordinary person now in my arms.

Just as Petra was pondering the same thing. As we lay next to each other, she said:

"I never realized something until now."

"And what is that, my love?"

"Happiness exists."

SIX

MEHMET WAS DOWNSTAIRS, sanding the last corner of the studio floor, as Petra and I emerged from my rooms. Seeing us he immediately turned off the raucous hum of the machine, removed the safety goggles, and smiled shyly at Petra. I introduced them.

"But we met already the other morning," Petra said.

Mehmet nodded, his timidity in her company noticeable.

"You've done a beautiful job here," she said, pointing to the refinished studio space——and, indeed, it really did look pristine.

"It's Thomas's work, too," he said.

"He's a man of many talents," she said, squeezing my arm and then sliding her hand down to my own. "Very nice to meet you. No doubt we'll be seeing each other around here."

"Back in a moment," I told him as I stepped outside the door with Petra.

"I want to drag you upstairs again," I said.

"If it wasn't for the fact that I am now thirty minutes late for work I'd happily let you drag me upstairs. However, there's a lot to be said for *Vorfreude*."

"Now there's a word I've never come across."

"It means: the anticipation of pleasure that must currently be postponed."

"That is a very German word."

"Indeed it is——but in our case the *Vorfreude* will only last nine hours."

As always, it was hard to let her go. As always, we told each other over again how much we loved each other. As she headed down the stairs, she turned back toward me and beamed a smile of such radiance, such felicity, that I simply found myself considering the vagaries of luck, how if Petra hadn't walked into Pawel's office that day, the entire trajectory of my life would be a different one and that fortune had smiled on me.

Back in the apartment Mehmet had turned on the sander again and was finishing the last small corner of the floor. As I walked in, he clicked off the machine.

"We can put the first coat of varnish down in a few minutes," he said.

"No problem. Just let me get changed into some work clothes. But afterward, why don't we head up to the hospital and see Alaistair?"

Mehmet immediately tensed.

"Everyone will see," he said.

"Everyone will see nothing except two men visiting a friend in a hospital ward. And he really wants to see you. I'm sure you want to see him. Anyway, there is a divider between his bed and the ones on either side of him, so there's no chance that you will be spotted by anyone."

"The world is sometimes very small."

"The world is also very large. But, okay, say the strangest thing happens and you meet someone you know. So what? The man who asked you to redecorate his studio is in the hospital. You have visited him to discuss the progress of the work. End of story."

"They would never believe me."

"Why is that?"

"Because they would see the shame in my eyes."

"They will not see that if you don't show it to them."

Mehmet shook his head, looking dubious.

"Do you want to see him?" I asked.

"Of course, I want to see him."

"Then we're going right after we finish the first coat of floor stain . . ."

"Thomas, please. You don't know my family, her family."

Then, lowering his head, he suddenly began to pace around the room, whispering to himself. I wasn't at all thrown by this behavior as I talk to myself all the time (it's a tic that many writers possess). I could also see that Mehmet was using this self-directed monologue as a way of calming himself down. After about a minute he seemed to shake himself out of his distress. Then turning to me he said:

"You get into your work clothes, I finish sanding."

When I returned five minutes later, Mehmet had already set out the pots of stain and brushes and was using a vacuum cleaner to remove the remaining dust. As I walked into the main body of the studio, he snapped off the vacuum cleaner and said:

"Okay, I go to the hospital with you. But first we finish this."

Two hours later we were on the U-Bahn, heading toward Zoo Station. Sitting in the smoking carriage, Mehmet puffed away on an unfiltered Lucky Strike, wolfing it down in less than three minutes, then lighting another off the end of the one he'd been smoking. His head was lowered, his apprehension palpable. When his shoulders began to shake——and I could sense him beginning to feel overwhelmed——I put an arm around him and said one word:

"*Tapferkeit.*"

Courage.

He nodded several times, then took a few long deep drags off his cigarette and whispered:

"It's impossible, it's all impossible."

Of course, it's easy to think, But it's not impossible. All you have to do is act in your own best interests and walk out on a life you don't want. But that's so profoundly facile and sidesteps not just the huge social ramification of this decision, but also the way we talk ourselves into lives we don't want, largely out of fear of change.

Even if Mehmet couldn't, in the end, bring himself to run away from all that his society expected of him, at least he was making love three times a week with Alaistair, and that was a great act of defiance. We're always answering to a larger authority, aren't we? Social expectations, familial expectations. As such, to even dabble in the zone of dangerous personal liberty——as Mehmet was doing now——required extraordinary strength of character. Just as to somehow cross an impenetrable political divide as Petra had done.

Well, I didn't know all the details of her flight as yet. But I knew that she had paid some sort of huge price by getting out. This, in turn, also made me think that she too had phenomenal courage. As such the choice she made was a huge, impacting one, riddled with regret and infinite sadness. Is change——especially of the most primal and personal variety——ever anything less than cataclysmic?

As we emerged into the pale light of the street, Mehmet proffered his pack of Luckys.

"You should marry that girl," he said as he held a match to my cigarette.

"What makes you think that?"

He just shrugged, his face his usual mask of seriousness.

"You just look happy together."

Walking into the hospital ward ten minutes later, Mehmet eyed every person we passed as if they were a member of the Turkish secret police sent here to find out his terrible secret and upend his life. He was so agitated as we approached Alaistair's bedside that I stopped him and put my hand on his arm and said:

"Have you seen anyone so far who knows you?"

He shook his head.

"Well, we are now ten steps away from Alaistair's cubicle. Once we are inside it no one will see you. So you are scot-free. Please, for Alaistair's sake, pull yourself together and get that look of terror off your face. He needs to see you in reasonable shape. So please . . ."

Mehmet nodded many times and went into another internal monologue for several moments, pulling out his pack of cigarettes and twirling it between his fingers, evidently desperate for a smoke and using the pack as a form of substitute worry beads.

"You okay now?" I finally asked.

He nodded again many times, and I pushed him toward the cubicle. When we reached its entrance I stuck my head in and found Alaistair sitting up in bed, reading *The New Yorker*.

"Back again?" he asked. "You *are* a glutton for punishment."

"That I am, but I'm not staying. Because I've brought a visitor."

I reached behind me and literally had to pull Mehmet into the cubicle. Alaistair looked genuinely stunned to see him, while Mehmet's eyes kept darting from him to the floor.

"I'll come back in an hour," I said. Before Mehmet could raise a nervous objection, I turned and walked quickly down the ward corridor.

I left the hospital and found a little Italian café on a neighboring street. I drank two espressos and worked on my notebook, writing down all that had happened in the last twenty-four hours, Mehmet's comment, "*You should marry that girl*" still ringing in my head. After writing for fifteen minutes, I asked the guy behind the counter if there was a phone I could use.

"One mark for ten minutes," he said, placing a phone on the counter.

"That's expensive," I said.

"No," he said. "That is the price."

I shrugged, pushed a mark toward him, and dialed the number for Radio Liberty. When the switchboard operator answered, I asked to be put through to Petra Dussmann. Her line rang and rang——and by the seventh ring I was beginning to lose hope of speaking with her when, suddenly, she answered.

"Dussmann," she said, sounding out of breath.

"Did I make you run across the office?"

"You did."

"I hope you don't mind me calling you at work."

"It is lovely to hear your voice," she said in a near-whisper, "but if I am sounding clandestine, it's because Pawel is hovering around."

"No problem. The only reason I called is that I can't stand the idea of not hearing your voice until tonight."

"I love you," she whispered. "In fact, if I could, I'd dash out of this damn building right now and run into your arms."

"I could be in front of the Wedding U-Bahn station in fifteen minutes."

"I have a lunch meeting with two producers in twenty-five minutes."

"Well, that would give us five minutes together."

"I'll be awaiting you outside the station."

I actually made it to the Wedding U-Bahn station in eighteen minutes. She was standing at the top of the stairs as I headed up them——and raced down toward me, meeting me on a landing halfway below the street, throwing her arms around me, pinning me against a wall as we kissed. Finally, she broke away.

"You . . . ," she whispered. "You . . ."

"And you . . . and us."

"I'm now late," she said.

"Then you really should go."

"The fact that you came up here for just five minutes . . ."

"I'll come here for five minutes every day if you like . . ."

"Tell me you love me."

"I love you."

"And I love you."

Then, after another very long kiss, she stepped back from me and ran up the stairs. I leaned against the wall, feeling like one of those cartoon characters who gets to kiss the girl and, in the aftermath, is hit with a visual swirl of stars and exclamation points over his head. I forced myself back onto the U-Bahn, wearing an absurd lunatic grin all the way back to Zoo Station. Half-jogging my way to the hospital, I reached Alaistair's ward just fifteen minutes shy of the end of visitor hours. Mehmet was no longer in the cubicle, but Alaistair was seated up in bed, his hands behind his head, staring up at the ceiling.

"Lover boy returns," he said as I entered. "Let me guess. You slipped away for an assignation in a room above a Chinese laundry to avoid detection by her Iranian fascist husband, Abbass——who drives a cab by day, but has a flourishing career as a professional wrestler by night."

"You should really be writing novels, Alaistair."

"So you *did* have an assignation?"

"Not exactly. But . . ."

"Oh I get it. A quick cuddle in a public park. She dashed out from work to meet you, and within moments the earth was moving."

I felt myself blushing. Alaistair's smile widened.

"I've evidently hit the bull's-eye. So, young man, *details, details*."

"You'll meet her eventually."

"Mehmet certainly has, and he informed me she was rather lovely. Very tall——which, for Mehmet, means anyone taller than him. And rather beautiful, with . . . how did he put it . . . sad eyes. Is Petra sad?"

"Aren't we all, to some extent, sad?"

"Ah, I share an apartment with a philosopher prince. But you dodge the question. Mehmet——who is always sad——also said that you both looked most in love."

"We are."

"Congratulations."

"You don't exactly look dejected today."

"Perhaps because some American writer did me a good turn. Thank you."

"He loves you."

"That's a rather presumptuous thing to say."

"It's just the truth."

"In matters of the heart there is no such thing as the truth. There are only moment-to-moment realities. And it can all change tomorrow, especially given the complexities of Mehmet's situation."

"It's only impossible if you let it be so. The struggle I saw Mehmet go through to visit you today——the way he was so clearly at conflict with what his heart was telling him and what his entire culture was telling him——makes it clear he wants this, you. The question is . . ."

"Can you now shut the fuck up?"

He looked away from me, chewing on his lower lip.

"Sorry if I overstepped," I said.

"You see too much, Thomas. What you forget is that there are those of us who don't want to look too closely at ourselves. In fact, the vast majority of people don't want that. And perhaps you yourself——always thinking in terms of narrative——feel the need to seek resolutions, tidy endings, in situations that are anything but tidy."

"I hardly see life as tidy."

"But you do want to live happily ever after with the divine Petra?"

"Of course. Don't we all want that? Don't you want that with Mehmet?"

Alaistair shut his eyes.

"What I want is a cigarette. As soon as you are off the premises—— and no longer raising such vexacious questions——I am going to shuffle down to the room they have consecrated for us nicotine addicts and try to block out the echo of your interrogatory voice with an HB Filter. Then I will get back here for my afternoon fix——another highlight of the day."

"And how is that going?"

"The medicos and the shrink they've assigned to me are pleased with my progress. They feel I am almost ready to be set loose upon the world."

"Fantastic."

"Unless you see the world as vindictive and evil."

"You'll go back to work."

"And then Mehmet will get rumbled by his people, and I'll end up getting stabbed again. Only this time I'll end up on a mortuary slab, not a hospital bed."

"Always the drama queen, Alaistair."

"That's me. But one good piece of news. The police finally captured the lunatic who slashed me and my work. As soon as he was apprehended a few days ago——nabbed while on the run in Munich——he was diagnosed as paranoid schizophrenic and has been indefinitely banged up in some very secure mental hospital deep in Bavaria with all those insane Christian Democrats. So when I am finally given my walking papers out of here, I will be able to stroll the streets of Kreuzberg without the fear of running into that talent-free but very violent nutter again. Meanwhile, when am I going to meet this love of your life?"

"You'll meet her as soon as you are installed back at home. By the way, your studio is pristine again."

"So Mehmet told me. When are you going to present me with the bill for services rendered?"

"All I ask in return is that, once you're finally sprung from here, you actually try to stay clean."

"Why do you even care if I fall back on my old junkie ways?"

"Because, idiot that I am, I happen to like you. And the world, for me, would be a far less interesting place if you were no longer in it."

"Sentimental rubbish," he said as the bell announcing the end of visiting hours sounded. Then, shutting his eyes again, he said:

"Now get out of here before I do something foolish like become emotional. But you will drop by tomorrow?"

"I suppose I have no choice."

"But if you could do it around noonish, as Mehmet will be coming at eleven."

"He is? But that is such good news."

"Perhaps it is," he said, staring back at the ceiling. "Perhaps this is, for both you and me, one of those rare interregnums in which all the fucking stars really are in fucking alignment."

Some hours later, when Petra came rushing through the door and threw herself into my arms, I reflected again on Alaistair's last comment and agreed that there are rare moments in life when everything really does fall into place, when the gods, the stars, the guiding hand of destiny, the nature of happenstance (and all the other non-empirical forces we occasionally cite when discussing the ways our fate plays out) really do seem to be in one's court. Certainly, thinking back on the three months or so that followed this pronouncement, this was a time when all seemed well in the world. Being in love——and having that love so reciprocated——is, perhaps, the closest I've ever come to sheer, unalloyed wonderment. That's what I remember so vividly about this initial time with Petra——the way life was lived at such a heightened level that it was as if we had created a bulwark against the world at large. We were inseparable, and so totally committed to the project that was our life together. This was unknown territory for me. Having previously always told the girlfriend of the moment that I needed space, privacy, a bit of distance to get on with my work, now, I simply couldn't imagine an evening without Petra. I always endeavored to have the day's writing finished by the time Petra was home from work. And she was always rigorously on time, as I was whenever it came to meeting her somewhere outside of the apartment. Then again, we always treated each other with great respect and saw each other as nothing less than equals. In our domestic life together, we had already ascertained that we both liked order. What was wonderful was the way we both, without ever discussing it, always tried to make life easy for each other. For the first time in my life, I was actually playing house with someone else, someone whose arrival in the evening I awaited with the best sort of impatience, someone whose sheer presence in the rooms we shared, across a table from me in a restaurant, with her hand in mine as we sat side-by-side in a cinema or a concert hall, made me so happy.

That was the other overwhelming memory of those first months together: the absolute felicity of our life together. Even Alaistair——when he finally was allowed out of the hospital——noted the "changed atmospherics" in the apartment.

It was a Saturday when he was granted permission to return to life outside constant medical supervision. Mehmet and I arranged to collect him, Mehmet telling his family that he had a decorating job that morning. Before he was released into my "care" (Mehmet was adamant that he not talk to any doctors, that I was to tell anyone at the hospital who asked that he was the taxi driver I'd organized to take Alaistair home), I had to spend half an hour in the company of a Dr. Schroeder. He explained to me that Herr Fitzsimons-Ross had to maintain the strict regime of methadone under which he had been functioning for the last three weeks. It was explained that he would be given no more than a week's supply at a time——sachets to be dissolved in water and then ingested before all meals——and that he would be required to present himself at the hospital every Monday morning at nine o'clock for a blood test to ascertain that he hadn't backslid into heroin. Dr. Schroeder asked me if I had ever seen Alaistair after shooting up. "Don't worry," he said when I hesitated in answering. "You are not his legal guardian, so you will not be held responsible if he does begin to 'use' again. But as you share the apartment with him, you will be more aware than anyone else should he resume, and you must phone me instantly."

"I really don't like the idea of playing Big Brother here," I said, "since it could run him into problems with the law."

"You would also be saving his life at the same time. If he does start to 'use' he will not go to prison, but he will be brought to a secure hospital where he will be put back on methadone and kept there until the doctors are certain that he is fully clean."

"But that means he could be locked up against his will for months."

"It also means that he will be finally off heroin. But, as I said, if he keeps to the methadone regime now, there will be no problem. Here is my card. I know this will all be a question of conscience for you. But if Herr Fitzsimons-Ross really is your friend, then you will be a good friend to him by calling me the moment you see he has embraced heroin. All right?"

He proffered the card. I took it, thinking: actually, no, this is not "all right." In fact, it puts me in a major moral dilemma. Alaistair functioned pretty well as a junkie, and only ended up in the hospital because of his unfortunate choice of pickup. And the libertarian in me basically thought: he's a big boy, and I am not going to play health cop here.

On the way back to the apartment, Alaistair raised this subject with me in English to make certain that Mehmet——who was driving us back in his van——wasn't cognizant of his thoughts on the subject.

"Let me guess: Herr Doktor lectured you on my fragile state, the fact that I am 'teetering on the edge between addiction and cure,' as he put it to me a few days ago, and asked you to play the Stasi and report to him when I started inserting a spike in my veins. Is that about right?"

"That's absolutely right," I said.

"What are your thoughts on the subject?"

"It's a very simple thought. It would be good if you were to remain clean. But it's none of my business if you choose to do otherwise."

"Thank you for that. I know I am very much under surveillance already. If I fail to show up every Monday morning for my weekly appointment——and if I fail the blood test——they can incarcerate me for as long as they see fit. And the bastards have my passport."

"It looks like you have to play by their rules."

"I hate playing by anybody's rules."

"Look at it this way: all junkies die prematurely. If you beat it now . . ."

"Cigarettes or ennui will then kill me. Still, one thing the doctor did say to me which made a little sense: with the Bundesrepublik paying for the substitute, I will be saving myself the three hundred deutsche marks a week it was costing me to fund the habit. And my gallery in London is making noises about those three paintings that they were expecting from me this month. In fact, in the pile of mail you brought me last week, there was a letter asking me when they could expect delivery . . ."

"Did you tell them what had happened?"

"Are you daft? The fastest way to lose a commission is to state that all the work you've been spending months on has been destroyed. Rule Number One of the Creative Life, Thomas, is: never, *never*, tell anyone in authority or with cash in his pockets how long it took you to paint or write something. What I wrote back to the gallery owner was the work was taking longer than expected, and that the reason he was getting this letter on hospital notepaper is that I was suffering from exhaustion. When it comes to extending a deadline, the artist must always hint at *la souffrance* behind the creative process. I am awaiting his reply from London——but I've no doubt it will have bought me some time . . . not that I really have much of that right now, as I have bills to pay."

"So you're going straight to work?"

"Well, give me an afternoon to settle in. But tomorrow I will visit my other dealer in Berlin——the one who supplies me with paint and brushes and stretches canvases for me——and will arrange for a delivery of everything within two days. Then, yes, to work. Though, of course, the very idea of starting again, and painting without smack, well, to say that it's a tad daunting is to engage in understatement."

When we got to the apartment, Alaistair spent several minutes walking around the freshly painted, freshly sanded and stained space. It really did look pristine, and I saw him blink back tears as he surveyed his refurbished domain. When he spoke, his voice was just above a whisper.

"I don't deserve such kindness."

Mehmet shook his head, a hint that he had heard such heart-on-the-sleeve self-loathing from Alaistair far too many times before.

"You're right," I said. "You deserve shit. But me and Mehmet are such fools that we . . ."

"All right, I'll shut up. But not before saying 'thank you.'"

At which moment I heard footsteps coming down the stairs. Petra was standing there, looking wonderful, dressed in jeans and one of my faded blue denim work shirts.

"Welcome home," she said to Alaistair.

"What a pleasure to meet you, Petra."

"You know my name."

"Thomas told me your name. Just as he intimated that he was the happiest man in the world."

I found myself shaking my head at such blatant chutzpah. But Petra came over and put her arm around me and said:

"Well, he has made me the happiest woman in the world."

"And thank God we will be living on separate floors," Alaistair said, "as such blatant bliss is far too difficult to bear. I need negativity, melancholia, dejection in order to——"

"Shut up," Mehmet suddenly said, and with an edge to his voice that caught us all by surprise, most of all Alaistair.

"My, my," he finally said. "I must have misspoken."

"You did," Mehmet said. For the first time I could see that the entire balance of power in his relationship with Alaistair had changed.

"Noted," Alaistair said quietly. "As you will come to discover, Petra, I do talk shit all the time."

"Language," Mehmet said.

"It seems I am being reined in by my associate today."

"I have to go," Mehmet said.

"You mean, you won't stay for lunch?" Petra asked. "I've got a spaghetti sauce brewing upstairs."

"Really?" I asked.

"I just thought, with Alaistair coming home, it would be nice if we could all sit down and have lunch together."

"I'm liking you even more by the minute," Alaistair said.

"So I'll go and put the spaghetti on now," she said. "And Alaistair, you'll see I picked up some bread and cheese and milk and coffee for you."

"Marry this woman," Alaistair told me.

"I probably will," I said, staring right at Petra.

"I'd best go upstairs. I hope you can stay for lunch, Mehmet."

"Not possible."

"See you soon then," she said. Squeezing my hand she whispered: "I'll hold you to what you just said," then headed upstairs.

"Aren't you the lucky bastard," Alaistair said. "She *is* lovely."

"I agree."

"And I hope you didn't ask her to make lunch for me."

"Some people are actually just nice," I said, glancing over at Mehmet.

"I'm aware of that," Alaistair said. "And some people are foolish enough to stay with the wrong person."

Mehmet's response to this was to shake his head several times, then mutter "I have to go," and head to the door. Alaistair immediately chased after him. I took this as a cue to head upstairs. As I reached my doorway I heard something that I had never heard: the sound of Mehmet getting angry, shouting something at Alaistair in his gruff German and Alaistair trying to soothe him. As I opened the door Petra was standing in front of the stove, a huge pot of spaghetti on the boil next to a most aromatic pan of sauce. She immediately came over and put her arms around me:

"It sounds like Alaistair said the wrong thing."

"That he did."

"We'll never say the wrong things to each other, will we?"

"Of course, we will. But then we'll apologize profusely and make mad, passionate love and . . ."

She kissed me, and we stumbled backward against a wall, Petra throwing one leg around me, sticking her hand into my jeans, and whispering:

"If it wasn't for the spaghetti, I'd take you right now."

"To hell with the spaghetti."

"But Alaistair will be arriving any moment."

"To hell with Alaistair."

As we stumbled toward the bedroom, there was the sound of knuckles rapping on the door.

"*Scheisse*," Petra said, straightening out her clothes and rushing to a spaghetti pot that was about to erupt, while I rebuttoned my jeans and staggered over to the door. As I opened it I found Alaistair outside. His eyes were red.

"You okay?" I asked.

"No," he said, coming inside. "Trust me to ruin everything within five minutes of getting home."

"What happened?" Petra asked.

"I pushed Mehmet over the edge, and he just stormed out and said he wasn't coming back."

"That could just be an overreaction," I said.

"No, it's been building up to this for a very long time."

"Let him calm down. He'll be back tomorrow."

"Wishful thinking. The truth is, I've lost him."

"I think you could use a drink," I said.

Alaistair rubbed his hand against his very wet eyes. I'd never seen him quite like this before——so open, so vulnerable, so sad.

"I could use twenty drinks."

I uncorked the cheap Italian white that Petra and I always drank. Alaistair downed two glasses quickly with two accompanying cigarettes. Then, as if a switch had been thrown, he discarded the sorrow and amused us over lunch with tales of the art world, bombarding Petra with questions about her painter friends in Prenzlauer Berg and impressing her with his knowledge of East German artists while downing a bottle of wine by himself before suddenly announcing:

"Oh fuck, I forgot my bloody methadone."

Then he roared down the stairs, clearly drunk.

"Well, that was a first," Petra said.

"Yes, he does tend to deal in extremity."

"I was talking about never having had lunch with someone before who had to dash off and take his methadone."

"At least he doesn't shoot up anymore."

"I actually like him. He is mad and charming and evidently desperate for love and unable to receive it."

"That sounds pretty accurate to me. But I am amazed you gleaned all that over one lunch."

"I was married to a man like Alaistair. Not gay like him. Life was complicated enough between us. But very much a man whose entire life was an extended public performance. Someone who had to take over a room as soon as he walked into it. Who loved to blurt out completely outrageous things, and would frequently tell people what he thought of them without any regard whatsoever for the consequence. Of course, you tell me that Alaistair is highly disciplined, that even when he was using heroin he did so in a very controlled, orderly way. The thing about Jurgen . . . he had brilliance galore. He was wildly cerebral, wildly imaginative, and fantastically entertaining, which, I suppose, made him a very attractive man at the outset.

"But then, once we were settled together, once the shine came off his act, he was impossible to be around. Especially as he was a profoundly talented and undisciplined man——and one who decided to take on the powers-that-be.

"If there was one great rule to life in the GDR it was that you had to somehow find an accommodation with the system, work out a way of paying lip service to the strictures under which we all lived, but also create a private world which the authorities couldn't really penetrate, as much as they wanted to.

"I thought we had created that sort of world for ourselves in Prenzlauer Berg. Our very own Ossie version of Greenwich Village. Unlike all those struggling artists in nineteen-sixties New York we had the one great benefit afforded all citizens of the GDR: we paid nothing in rent, we didn't have to be serious about our jobs, we could allow the state to fund our bohemian existence as long as we didn't question the raison d'être of the regime. But that was the problem with Jurgen. He wasn't satisfied living a relatively easy life. He had to be the eternal provocateur. Even though he wasn't exactly against the regime, the fact that they banned one of his plays——largely because they thought it so extreme in its anger at everything——sent him into a spiral. I told him repeatedly: write something clever, but performable. If you are subtle and intelligent about it you can say all you want, but not land yourself in further trouble. But he would never listen to me. I even pleaded with what few good friends he had left to talk sense to him. But there was something rather monomaniacal about Jurgen. A jazz pianist we knew——and who had been something akin to Jurgen's older brother for about ten years—— told me he felt my husband had turned into a kamikaze, and was determined to crash and obliterate himself and those closest to him."

As she paused and reached for her cigarettes, I asked, "And did he do just that?"

"Absolutely. He also took me down with him, even though I was someone who had no interest whatsoever in the crazed political games he played toward the end. It didn't matter. Guilt by association is a major offense in the GDR, especially if the 'association' is someone with whom you share your bed."

"Was he arrested?"

"What do you think?"

"Were you arrested?"

"That's another conversation," she said. "And now I need you to hold me."

I came over to where she was sitting and picked her up and walked us over to the sofa. We fell onto it and lay there for a very long time, simply holding on to each other, saying nothing. Eventually Petra broke the silence.

"I hate talking about the past."

"But it's what shapes us——and anyway I want to know everything about you."

"And I want to shed everything to do with the last year of my life over there. Eradicate it all from my memory."

"It was that awful?"

She just shrugged, then said:

"You know that Robert Grave's book, *Goodbye to All That*. I keep telling myself to follow the advice of the title. Slam the door on that whole episode of my life and not look back. This is why you are so precious to me. Because for the first time in years I actually see a future that is not tragic."

Interestingly, after this conversation the subject of her husband, of whatever sad or wrenching things befell her before coming west, was dropped. It wasn't as if we stayed away from the subject of our lives before we met each other, or that we didn't touch on difficult things we had weathered. Rather, Petra never seemed to return to that state of bleakness which seemed to envelop her whenever she mentioned her ex-husband or all those things that happened "over there" that she still couldn't bring herself to discuss. And the reason she was no longer dwelling on desolate memories of the recent bleak past was, I sensed, the fact that she was happy. And because our life together had an ease and a rhythm that were simply matchless.

With a book to write, I spent most of my days loitering with intent around the city. I used a letter from my publishers in New York as a bona fide to talk my way into spending a day with one of the US Army guys who manned the checkpoint on the American Sector side of Checkpoint Charlie. I had a fascinating afternoon with a Swiss architectural historian based in Berlin. He knew everything there was to know about the bricks-and-mortar legacy of Albert Speer and while also revealing that his wife had just run off with an émigré Bulgarian poet who wrote "unreadable modernist East European shit." Just as the Army guy dropped the fact that he had a wife and child back in some Kentucky hole that he wasn't planning to see again. Just as I got talking with an elderly black American jazz pianist, Bobby Blakely, who played every night in the bar of the Hotel Kempinski. He'd been living in the same small room near Spandau since coming over in the late 1950s and was one of those rootless expatriates who had no ties that bind, few friends, but had never missed one of his six-night-a-week gigs at the Kempinski since first landing the job in 1962.

These tales interested me, not just because every life is, in its own way, a novel——but also because, little by little, I was beginning to realize that the way to build up an idiosyncratic portrait of Berlin was through the stories of the people into whose path I threw myself. Just as I also knew that I would write about Omar and the Café Istanbul and would probably reinvent Alaistair, turning him into a lifelong Londoner, making Mehmet perhaps Iranian, and setting the scene of the apartment we shared in another corner of Kreuzberg, maybe even in that faceless no-man's-land where Petra lived.

Of course, everything to do with my existence with Petra also went into my notebook. Was I looking upon it as material? I told myself at the time that keeping such a close record was just a way of articulating this most important sea change in my life. But the truth was a little more basic than that. If you write, *everything* is material. And part of me felt that, by getting it all down, I could also convince myself that, yes, this was real, that, yes, I had met the love of my life.

I would wake up every morning to find Petra beside me and simply stare at her, still asleep, marveling. And then she would stir awake and look at me and smile and touch my face and always whisper, "It's you." Once she had finally gone off to work I would spend the balance of the morning writing, then join Fitzsimons-Ross in what became a new ritual for us——an early lunch at the Café Istanbul. The day after he came home from the hospital, he went out and reordered all the necessary brushes and paints, spending hours forcing the man in a nearby artist supply shop (his "paint meister" as he called him) to remix a multiple palette of blues until he achieved the shades of azure, aquamarine, cobalt, and turquoise that Alaistair demanded. Three newly stretched canvases also arrived in his studio space. On his third morning home, I wandered downstairs to see Alaistair, his back to me, headphones on his head, a dripping paintbrush in one hand, circling the canvas like a matador approaching his malevolent prey. Then, in a flash, a streak of cobalt blue was slashed across the canvas. From my hidden vantage point halfway up the stairs I watched as the white of the canvas disappeared under a controlled assault of blue. Watching Alaistair diving headfirst back into the work, all I could think was: he has more courage than most men I know. Resiliency is something you only realize you possess when you demand it of yourself.

"If it wasn't for the fact that I'm three hundred deutsche marks better off a week, I'd jump back on the smack tomorrow," he said loudly one lunchtime, in earshot of Omar and his staff at the Istanbul.

"Why don't you say that a little more loudly so the cop outside can hear you?" I said.

"The last time I looked, you couldn't get busted for expressing an illicit desire. Anyway, the city fathers in Berlin believe junkies give the place a certain edgy cachet. In fact, they should really pay us to shoot up in picturesque locations. And you are now hearing one of the side effects of methadone: a need to spout rubbish at all times. As in: how does it feel to still be so disgustingly in love?"

"Disgustingly wonderful."

"So I can see. I'd advise you to be careful. Too much happiness is catastrophic for an artist. No sense of loss, no sense of creative frisson."

"That's a bunch of theoretical bullshit, and you know it."

"How many genuinely happy people do you know who work in the so-called creative professions?"

I thought this one over for a moment.

"None," I finally said.

"My point exactly."

"Then again," I asked, "how many genuinely happy people do you know outside of the so-called creative professions?"

Without hesitating, Alaistair said:

"None. But look at you. You're actually in the process of becoming happy, even though you still have all that childhood *merde* shadowing your every move."

"I'm sure it will recede in time."

"No, stay angry at it all. It will help you counterbalance all the sunshine that you will have with Fraulein Dussmann. From my very passing acquaintance with her over the past few weeks, I sense that you, sir, are actually doing a great deal of good for her as well. She does have shadows, doesn't she?"

"We all have shadows."

"I'll say no more."

"Good," I said——because unless the relationship is disintegrating and you need to talk things out with a good friend, one of the key unspoken rules of love is that you never discuss the anxieties, the distresses, the fears of the person you adore with anyone else. Not only is it a betrayal of trust, it also subverts a key facet of love at its most profound: the fact that the two of you create a rampart against the world's attendant malignancies. Or, at least, that's the romantic hope.

But this hope found reality in the life that Petra and I shared together. Whenever she returned home in the evening——frustrated and bored by the work at Radio Liberty——I would hand her a glass of wine and she would slam the door on that increasingly fraught and contentious workplace. Just as, if I'd had a bad day at the desk or was worried that the book seemed rudderless, the moment she arrived home I would be transformed out of my funk, and by the end of the evening, I'd also be edging back into an optimistic frame of reference about my work, perhaps because, with Petra, I simply was reminded of the fact that life was also about possibilities.

One ongoing topic of conversation was Pawel. Petra had continued to be very insistent about keeping our relationship quiet within the confined little world of Radio Liberty. So on those occasions when I would show my face there——either for a meeting or a taping session with Pawel——we would acknowledge each other with a friendly formality if we happened to run into each other in a corridor or an office.

"People have so little to talk about," Petra said, "they'd love to spend hours gossiping about how I was involved with a contributor and all that sort of petty stuff."

"Well, unless someone sees us kissing in the street, who's to ever know that we are a couple?"

But that's exactly what happened. One evening we went to see a showing of Billy Wilder's The Apartment at the Delphi near Zoo Station. Afterward, as we stepped out onto the street, I pulled Petra close to me and we kissed, at which point I heard a voice behind me say:

"How charming."

Pawel was standing right by us, on his way into the cinema. Immediately we disentangled. At first Petra looked caught out, a deer in the headlights. Then her shock turned into profound discomfort, as Pawel was regarding us with an enormous smirk. He appeared rather drunk.

"How very interesting," he said. "And here I was thinking that dissidents had no talent for the clandestine."

"That's enough," I said.

"Ah, the macho American defends the sad émigré."

"We're out of here," I said to Petra.

"'*We're out of here,*'" Pawel repeated, imitating my accent. "Thus spake the writer of glossy magazine prose who thinks himself serious."

"You're a shit," Petra said.

"And you are a mediocrity who thinks herself——"

That's when I hit him. Directly in the stomach. My action stunned me. I'd never hit anyone before. As he doubled over and began to retch up all the booze that he'd been evidently imbibing most of the evening, Petra and I hurried off to the U-Bahn. We said nothing until we were seated on a train, at which point I shook my head and said:

"Jesus Christ, I can't believe that just happened."

"You pack a punch," she said.

"I hope he's okay."

"He deserved it."

"I'm still a little shocked."

"He's a petty little despot, and thank you for hitting him on my behalf."

"Do you think he'll try to . . ."

"Get me fired? I doubt it. Herr Wellmann knows that Pawel made advances at me and harassed me repeatedly when I wouldn't sleep with him. Wellmann cautioned him at the time and the harassment stopped. He wouldn't dare do anything against me. Against you, however . . ."

"I don't need Radio Liberty to survive."

"That you don't, and I've never had a man defend me before. So if that bastard Pawel does try to get you dropped as a contributor, I'll talk to Wellmann. Of course, the fact that we are together will now be the talk of the office."

"Is that such a bad thing?"

"I don't care who knows now. If anyone asks, I will tell them the truth: you're the man I love."

As it turned out, there was no need for Petra to make such proclamations at the office, as Pawel called in sick for several days after this incident. When he did return to his producing duties and did knock on the glass of Petra's office cubicle, he was all business, handing her a script to be translated, telling her he'd been out with "a bad gastric flu," asking if she was well, and essentially showing her a professional cordiality that he had never demonstrated before. That same day he left a message for me at the Café Istanbul, asking me to call him back. When I did, he was civility itself, wondering if I could turn around an essay on the von Karajan legacy at the Berlin Philharmonic in three days. The fee he offered was two thousand deutsche marks——almost four times what he usually paid me.

"That's a most generous sum," I said.

"Well, I think you merit it," Pawel said, not a hint of sheepishness or contrition in his voice. "Anyway, you are such a regular and first-rate contributor."

Of course, I did the von Karajan essay. Petra translated it. When I came up to record it at Radio Liberty with Pawel, I just happened to pass Petra in the corridor. We all exchanged pleasantries. That night, back home, she said:

"I think you hitting him was the best thing that ever happened to Pawel. Even though no one at the office knows what happened, everyone is still saying the same thing: the man has become civilized, for the moment anyway."

"Well, when that two thousand deutsche marks comes through, why don't we blow it all on a trip to Paris?"

"You mean that?" she asked, sounding amazed.

"Of course, I mean it," I said. "We're together three months today. It's an anniversary of sorts. And we should do something extravagant and special. So tell me when."

"It would be great to do four or five days there. So maybe I could take a few days off."

"Just let me know and I will get it all in motion."

"Paris. I can't believe it."

The next morning——it was a Saturday——Petra was up early. When I awoke the entire apartment had been cleaned thoroughly——a task we usually shared together——and she was back from the laundromat with the clothes I had dropped off yesterday, now ironing our spare set of sheets.

"There was no need to do all this," I said as I stirred awake and was handed a demitasse of espresso.

"I just couldn't sleep and needed to keep busy."

Now I was wide awake, reaching for her.

"Is something wrong?" I asked, taking her hand. She sat down on the edge of the bed but didn't seem able to look at me.

"Just worried about work, that's all," she said, digging out a cigarette in the pocket of her work shirt and simultaneously biting down on her lip.

I sat up and reached for her.

"This isn't about work."

"It's something that I should have told you weeks, months ago, but was too afraid to discuss."

"But why?"

"Because I was scared that, if you knew . . ."

"Scared if I knew what?"

Now she stood up and walked to the other side of the room, sitting down in an armchair, her eyes welling up, shaking her head as she tried to forestall the sobs that were welling up within her. Immediately I raced over to her, taking her in my arms, rocking her back and forth.

"I'm sorry," she whispered through the tears. "I'm so sorry."

"Sorry about what?"

"The reason it's all so hard this morning . . . it's because . . ."

"Yes?"

"It's his birthday."

"Whose birthday?"

She pulled back from my embrace, looking away from me.

"It's the birthday of my son, Johannes. He's three years old today."

SEVEN

FOR THE NEXT hour Petra spoke nonstop——the entire story coming out in a long and terrible cascade.

"I need to first tell you about me and Jurgen. Yes, he was my husband. Yes, we lived together for five years. I was very young when I met him. I had been in a relationship for two years prior to this with a man named Kurt, who was twenty years my senior and produced classical music programs for the state radio station. Kurt was very quiet, very cultured, very married. I had just finished university. I had just been awarded the post of translator at the state publishing house. I was living in a tiny room in Mitte. My room was no more than nine meters. One minuscule window. An alcove with a hot plate, a sink, and a very small fridge. A bathroom the size of a narrow closet. No natural light. A single bed. A table and a chair. I had a radio and some books and little else. But it was my first place. I found someone who got me a few small pots of paint and some brushes——never easy to find——and painted my very own mural——very Alice in Wonderland——on one wall. But even with this dash of color, the place was drab, sad, a cell, and only enlivened when Kurt came by three days a week from six to eight. Kurt was hugely intelligent——a near concert-grade pianist who should have gone on to great things, but always seemed to come up short in life. He was sent to the big music conservatory in Moscow, but his teachers there considered him just 'moderately gifted' and not destined for the great concert halls. So when he returned to the DDR he got a job in the state broadcasting system and occasionally played recitals and concertos in small provincial halls. He also met a rather overbearing woman named Hildegarde. They had three children. They all lived in three rooms way up near Pankow. He felt trapped. Then he was introduced to me when he had to come to the state publishing house one day to consult on a book of musicology by a Canadian academic. Over a cup of tea in a café on Unter den Linden, I remember Kurt telling me he was brought in to make certain that the book's 'interpretative analyses were ideologically acceptable.' I remember laughing and being rather amazed at such blunt sarcasm. I was just twenty-two and didn't have a boyfriend.

"It lasted two years. Like all such arrangements, it was a half-life for the third party——which was me. Kurt was, in the end, far too melancholic and permanently stuck in his bad marriage. You know how it is with so many people. They believe there is no way out, even if life is hell. And I was wondering how I could get myself out of my terrible one-room life and this sad affair with a very bright, but very sad man.

"Then I met Jurgen at a *vernissage* in someone's apartment up in Prenzlauer Berg. He wasn't the best-looking man in history. Stocky, a big beard, a big appetite, and, oh my God, how he smoked. Three packs a day. But at the time, he was an important young playwright in the DDR. I'd read an article about him in *Neues Deutschland* and one of the literary magazines about this brilliant first play of his——*Die Wahl*——which, as the title indicated, was all about human choice. It was set in a munitions factory after an explosion that has killed several workers. And it turns out the manager——under pressure to fill quotas——had cut corners when it came to safety.

"Though it didn't come out and say accusatory things directly, it was clear that Jurgen was pointing a big finger at state bureaucracy and the maniacal need to meet quotas in order to convince everyone that the Five-Year Plan was working. The thing was, the play worked brilliantly as a character study, also showing the way everyone attempted to abnegate responsibility for actions that resulted in the death of ten workers. That was the cleverness of the play. It played the proletarian card, yet also was a riveting study of individual versus collective choice. It made Jurgen, for a time, hugely regarded.

"Naturally I'd seen the play in its original Berlin production. Given how much attention he'd received——and how he had any woman he wanted——I was rather surprised that he would be interested in me.

"But, much to my amazement, he was. He also had a rather big apartment for Berlin——sixty square meters——in Prenzlauer Berg. Of course, he had no talent for housekeeping, and the place was rather squalid. But after my cell of a room, Jurgen's apartment on Jablonski Strasse seemed like a villa. And he had all these interesting artist friends who lived nearby. So, suddenly, I was part of a community. These friends of his had almost created a state-within-the-state. Yes, we knew we were being frequently observed. Yes, we sometimes privately wondered who among us might be informing to the Stasi about our lives, because in any group you could be sure that several people had been turned. It was an accepted fact of life.

"Anyway, I loved this new life in Prenzlauer Berg, loved being part of this artistic group. There was only one problem. I never really loved Jurgen. Nor, truth be told, did he love me. He made a fuss about me at first. Then I moved in. We shared a bed. We had sex the nights of the week he wasn't drunk. Beyond that, it was as if we were two people who had fallen into a life together that was strangely utilitarian but not unreasonable. One thing about our bohemian existence in Prenzlauer Berg: it was never boring.

"But then, out of nowhere, I was pregnant. It was an accident. My diaphragm had a tiny tear in it which I had never seen. 'Must have been manufactured in Halle' was Jurgen's only comment about it. After making that bad joke, he just shrugged and said: 'If you want to keep it, that's fine, but it will be your responsibility entirely.'

"The thing was, in the GDR abortions were used all the time as an alternative form of birth control. They were very simple to obtain. I wrestled with this idea for no more than five minutes. I was pregnant. I had so little in my life. As sad and hurt as I was by Jurgen's reaction——he called our baby 'it'——I so wanted this child.

"'I'm keeping the baby,' I said.

"'That's your business,' Jurgen said in response.

"As it turned out, he meant what he said. For the next nine months, he acted as if this pregnancy was an ancillary event in our lives. When I had morning sickness, when I had to go in for a test to see if I was suffering from jaundice, when I was so pregnant that getting up the four flights of stairs with our groceries was a major burden, when my waters broke and I had to be rushed to hospital, when the delivery was complicated and our son spent his first five days on a respirator and there were fears about his survival . . . during all these dramas and anxieties that accompanied the birth of our son, Jurgen was largely elsewhere. Yes, he was still in the apartment. Yes, he was still eating the meals he expected me to cook for him and wearing the clothes he expected me to wash and iron for him. And yes, one Saturday when I was three months pregnant, we went to the registry office on Unter den Linden and, with all our friends from Prenzlauer Berg present, were legally declared man and wife. Why did we go through this charade when there was no real love between us? I insisted on it, because it guaranteed me residence in the apartment we shared and also gave me certain maternal benefits that I would have otherwise been without had I remained single. Yes, I put on a happy face for the ceremony. Afterward, this wonderful sculptor named Judit——who lived near us and did brilliant abstract work that was never officially sanctioned——had a party for us in her apartment. Again I acted happy, even when Jurgen drank so much that he fell asleep on the sofa and began to snore wildly.

"I remember two men in our crowd——they were both novelists who could no longer get published——having to help him home that night. I accompanied them as they literally struggled to keep Jurgen—— who was, at this point, turning fat——belching and singing absurd songs and, at one point, shouting: 'I'm too young to be sentenced to father-hood!' They blanched at such drunken awfulness, whispering to me: 'Don't listen to him. He's just being stupid.' But I knew there was more than a profound grain of truth in what he said. When they finally got him home and he pitched forward into bed, I remember curling up in this broken-down armchair we had and crying nonstop for about an hour. Why was I shedding tears? Because I realized that I was alone in the world, in this farce of a marriage, in this farce of a country that had to keep its citizens imprisoned and under constant surveillance because, at heart, it knew that it was a sham, a counterfeit version of a state. Even my father couldn't be bothered to come up to see me getting married. He had a program he simply had to produce that day. I didn't even put up a fight about it. I just accepted his disinterest, which had only increased since my mother's death. Just as I accepted Jurgen's disinterest. Just as I accepted my small limited life over there as nothing less than my due. That's what really troubled me: the realization that my choices were all against happiness, against possibility. Yes, it's true the horizons were hardly limitless in the GDR. But I knew people, friends, who had happy marriages, happy relationships. What did I choose? Indifference, apathy, aloofness——all for sixty square meters in Prenzlauer Berg.

"Judit became my savior. She all but got me through the pregnancy. She was a shoulder to cry on. She even confronted Jurgen on two occasions and forced him to do the shopping once a week or pick me up at the hospital after an examination. But on the night that Johannes arrived, my husband was down in Dresden at the opening night of a local production of his play. Judit, however, was at the hospital with me.

"The birth itself was complicated, and they gave me an anesthetic that made me so groggy I couldn't recall the moment when my son actually arrived in the world. When I was cognizant of the world around me again, I panicked, for there was no child by my side. One of the nurses came in and informed me that during the delivery, the umbilical cord had wrapped itself around my son's neck. That was the first time I learned what sex he was and that he was on a respirator. I insisted on being taken to see him. This was the middle of the night and Judit had already gone home. They brought me to this machine that looked like something out of a mad scientist movie, with this tiny creature sucked into its vortex, a tube down his throat and his nostrils, the machine heaving so loudly as it kept my baby ventilated, alive. When they insisted I return to my ward and get some sleep, I refused. The nurse on duty was a hugely officious type who essentially ordered me back. When I said I wasn't going anywhere, she threatened me, telling me she could have me reported for antisocial behavior. That's when I began to scream at her that she could bring the fucking Stasi in here, but I would still not leave my baby alone.

"Fortunately, there was a young doctor——his family name was Mühl——who walked in just as this bitch of a nurse threatened to denounce me to the secret police. He immediately ordered the nurse into an adjoining room. Once they were there, I could hear her getting angry, informing the doctor that, though he was 'hierarchically senior' to her, this had been her ward for the past twenty years and no young medico was going to give her orders. The doctor turned out to be made of sterner stuff. He said that she'd behaved in a completely reprehensible way toward——and I always remember the language he used——'a brave young woman who has given our Democratic Republic a new son.' At that point I sensed that this doctor was very clever when it came to the sort of ideological attack language that intimidated people and allowed you to get your way. Because he then informed the nurse that she was being reactionary and bourgeois, and he would report her to her trade union for 'authoritarian behavior.' Immediately she acted contrite. The doctor returned to the ward and informed me that, from this moment on, a bed would be brought in so I could sleep next to my son, and that he thought he would pull through.

"Well, Johannes——that was the name I gave him——did pull through. Five days later we were home. Bless Judit. She herself had no children. But she'd found me a crib that belonged to one of her neighbors and an old baby carriage. While I was in the hospital she arranged for a bunch of her artist friends to come over and paint little stars and moons in the tiny alcove that was to be Johannes's nursery.

"But when I came home with our son, Jurgen was still nowhere to be found. He only showed up three days later, unshaven, dirty, smelling of other women, looking like he'd been drinking for around a week. He also didn't seem to have slept in a very long time——and perhaps that's the reason his emotions were so raw. When he saw his son——and took him in his arms for the first time——he burst into tears and couldn't stop crying for around half an hour. I decided not to say anything or do anything, as he was holding Johannes correctly. When he finally subsided, what did he do? He handed me the baby and kissed me on the head and told me he knew he had acted atrociously and would now change his ways. Then he went into our bedroom, left his sweat-soaked, booze- and lipstick-smudged clothes everywhere on the floor, crawled into our bed, and slept for the next twelve hours.

"When he awoke, it was five in the morning and I had been up already with Johannes for three hours, as he was suffering from colic. Jurgen insisted I go back to bed, especially as I had just finished feeding Johannes. He said he would stand watch with him for the rest of the night. I actually slept five hours straight——a new record since the birth of my son——and woke to find Jurgen passed out on the sofa and Johannes curled up in his arms. Seeing this father-son scene——and how peaceful Johannes was next to him——I couldn't help but hope that Jurgen had come to his senses, that paternity would make him assume just a little responsibility, that we could find a way of becoming a couple, a family. Maybe I also hoped that the tears he shed when he first saw his son were a reflection of some sort of love he had for me but could never express. That's the most dangerous dream you can have in a relationship that you know is fundamentally flawed——the belief that someone will come to love you and that you will come to love that person. Such thinking is catastrophic, because you are grasping at a hope which, in private, you really know is an illusion.

"Still, I did have this hope. For around four weeks, Jurgen started to show signs of finally wanting to be a father and a husband. He even cut down the drinking and tried to lose a little weight and actually began to pick up after himself. He seemed to relish, for a while, taking his son for walks in his carriage and playing house with us and making love with me again. I can't say that sex with Jurgen was ever very satisfactory. He was fast; he didn't understand tenderness or sensuality. Even when he wasn't drinking heavily, he smelled. But I knew this all from the first night I ever spent with him. Yet I still decided to stay put. Why is it that we so often refuse to trust our instincts——and instead talk ourselves into situations we know are defective, impossible?

"But when you have a new child in your life——a child you simply adore more than anyone you have ever known, a child who has become the best thing ever to happen to you, and without whom you know life simply has no purpose——you can put up with all the defects and short-comings of his father. Or, at least, that's what I felt. Just as, during those four weeks of good feelings between us——I also felt that we had turned a corner, that we were becoming a family.

"Then a film that Jurgen had been writing for the state film company, DEFA, was suddenly halted two weeks before shooting was due to begin.

"The script was very brilliant and completely subversive——about a socialist writer who is imprisoned in the final months of the Nazi period and is so badly beaten by two SS guards that he goes into a coma and wakes up seven years later to find himself in a new country called the GDR. And he comes to find the socialist paradise of which he once dreamed a rather flawed one.

"I remember reading the script for the first time shortly before

Johannes was born and telling Jurgen that I couldn't imagine DEFA approving it for production. But this was a moment in 1981 when there was a hint of liberalism by the regime, and they seemed to be encouraging writers and directors to be a little critical of life as we lived it in our 'humanistic system.' So Jurgen was very confident the film would happen. They had a director and actors chosen, and locations scouted, when, suddenly, someone in the Ministry of Propaganda got hold of the script and the head of DEFA was called in and formally carpeted for even thinking that such a piece of 'virulently anti-DDR propaganda' could ever be made. The minister then turned the whole thing over to the Stasi. Jurgen suddenly disappeared for six days. I was frantic, thinking he'd had an accident or had gone on another bender. Out of nowhere, he showed up at dawn one morning——telling me that he had been held incommunicado in what he was certain was Hohenschönhausen, the famous Stasi prison. But he couldn't be that certain of its location. As he explained to me, when they came for him, they put him into the back of a van, which had a small cell contained within it, and drove him around for several hours in an attempt to disorient him. We both knew about this Stasi strategy for confusing the people they arrested. Jurgen said that they kept him locked up in that van for hours, arriving at some prison well after nightfall. Beyond that he wouldn't talk too much about what happened over the next few days, except to say he was interrogated twice daily——always during daylight hours, as 'befits a "humanistic" police state'——and then he was kept alone in a cell with nothing to read, no paper and pen to write with, no stimulation whatsoever. When I asked him what they demanded of him during the interrogations, he became very tight-lipped, refusing to say anything. Everyone knew that the only way the Stasi would let you out so early is if you denounced somebody. When Jurgen informed me that I must never tell anybody that he was picked up by the Stasi——and did so in a manner that hinted he now regretted even mentioning this to me——I knew that he had been forced into naming names, even if there were no names to name. In fact he became so vehement, so paranoid about any word getting out whatsoever regarding his detention, that I had to promise him repeatedly I would stay silent about his arrest. Which, of course, I did.

"After this, two things happened. The first was that, over the next year, Jurgen discovered that he had gone from being the hottest young playwright in the GDR to someone who couldn't get his work put on anywhere. He approached several theaters about commissions they had promised him in the wake of the success of *Die Wahl*. Not one of them would now go near him. Nor would any television or radio drama producers, with the result that Jurgen had his professional identity——the writing that maintained his fragile equilibrium——taken away from him. At first he went all inward, not talking to anybody for days. Then, right after some tiny theater company refused him a commission, he disappeared again and didn't return for two weeks, showing up in the same bloated, disheveled, catastrophic state as when he had disappeared before. When I demanded to know where he was, his response was: 'Everywhere.' And he recounted fourteen days of simply drifting around the country, sometimes crashing on the floors of a friend's apartment, sometimes sleeping in cheap hotels, sometimes sleeping on trains, sometimes not knowing where he was, sometimes thinking about throwing himself in front of the next oncoming train. But then, so he told me, he had an epiphany while standing on the platform in Frankfurt an der Oder, right on the Polish border. He was going to write his own epic Ring Cycle on the history of the GDR. It was going to have a cast of one hundred and would play out over five nights at a length of around four hours per night. For the better part of an hour he described, in incessant detail, just how all the parts would weave together. He was on creative fire and spoke with such passion, such ferocious commitment, that I felt as if he was in a trance. Every time he could corner me over the next week, he would continue going on about the masterpiece, the East German epic that was assembling itself in his head. As this monologue became more and more of a rant, I really began to fear for his sanity.

"Around this time we celebrated Johannes's first birthday. I'd been back at work for nine months, leaving Johannes every day at a nursery in Prenzlauer Berg and picking him up after work, as Jurgen was now writing every night from ten until just before dawn, and drinking a bottle of vodka each evening in the process, as vodka was cheap in the GDR. He got even more wildly fat, and he rarely left the apartment. When he awoke at three in the afternoon, he started eating. The deeper he got into the plays, the more detached from reality he became, to the point where he virtually stopped acknowledging his family's existence. I found him a camp bed he could put in the little alcove he called his study. As he retreated completely from his wife and child, I basically created my own wall between us. I would leave food for him to eat. I would wash his clothes. Once a week I would attempt to clean the chaos that was his alcove, remaking the bed with clean sheets. Other than that I was with Johannes. Bless my son. His presence in my life saved my sanity that year. He was such a quiet baby——and one who occasionally appeared withdrawn. But when I held him he always smiled, always cooed. Outside that first bout of colic, he was such a good little man. As his father had now taken over the alcove that was supposed to be his nursery, I was very happy to have him in our bedroom——and would so often put him next to me in bed and talk to him and make him laugh and help him play with the few stuffed toys that we had, all of which were made for me by the very wonderful Judit——who was always around the apartment, always happy to take him to her place for an evening if I wanted to go out to the theater or a cinema, always incredibly supportive when it came to Jurgen's increasingly deranged behavior.

"The thing was, I knew my husband was acting out some Prenzlauer Berg version of the Myth of Sisyphus, that this entire mad dramatic enterprise——'The most important piece of German dramatic writing since Goethe's *Faust*,' he announced one evening when he was relatively sober, which made it all the more unnerving——was, at best, doomed. Everyone in our circle in Prenzlauer Berg largely began to steer clear of Jurgen—— because it was clear that he had entered some zone where it was impossible for him to accept that he was on the blacklist. Unless he was willing to do a major public self-criticism and turn into a Party sycophant, his career as a writer was over. I was pretty damn certain that he privately knew the reality of his situation. Yet, like most of us, he retreated into a scenario——'I will write a masterpiece . . . every theater in the country will produce it . . . I will be proclaimed a genius and win the Lenin Prize for Literature and be rehabilitated and publicly loved again'——that allowed him to dodge the terribleness of his situation and simultaneously function on a daily basis. Jurgen really spent that year working. I never saw him. We hardly talked. But his industry was wild. Each play ran to more than two hundred and fifty pages in manuscript, and he was compulsive about getting to his desk every night.

"He finished the fourth part of this epic at three in the morning. It was around eighteen months ago. He started screaming at the top of his lungs when he wrote the last line. I know this because I was asleep with Johannes in the next room when he let rip. He woke us up, the yelps turning to hysterical sobs, Jurgen crying and telling me how we were now saved, how the brilliance of this work would change our lives, how we would be living in one of those dachas they gave to important writers by the Grosser Müggelsee on the outskirts of the city. 'I will be the first GDR writer to win the Nobel Prize for Literature!' he proclaimed to me one night when we had a few friends over. 'You will all brag about knowing me.'

"What I knew was going to happen did happen. Jurgen did begin to unravel. Over three months rejection after rejection hit him. Not only that, but some of the theaters to which he submitted the play cycle felt duty bound to tell the Stasi about this 'ill-disciplined, but profoundly antisocial piece of trash,' as the policeman who first interrogated Jurgen told him. This time he was 'invited' to come in and speak to the police. This time they simply cautioned him to stop trying to get his play even read. 'You should think about another line of work,' the cop told him.

"Afterward Jurgen came home and drank a bottle of vodka straight down. Then grabbing the huge manuscript of his plays he took the tram and the U-Bahn to the Berliner Ensemble——the theater that Brecht himself created in the GDR. It was the first night of a new play by Heiner Müller and there were a considerable number of high-level people in the theater, including the minister for culture and several ambassadors of 'fraternal socialist states.' Our neighbors Susanne and Horst——both actors in the ensemble, but not cast in this play——were there. And Horst said that Jurgen had arrived with a wooden box and stood up on it outside the Berliner Ensemble, screaming at the top of his lungs: 'I am a great German writer! I have written a masterpiece! I am being censored by the Stasi!' Horst came over and begged him to stop this act of professional and personal suicide, but Jurgen shouted him down, stating that he was going to stand on this soapbox and read his play out loud until the directors of the Berliner Ensemble accepted it for production. Just then a big car drove up, accompanied by two police vehicles, and the minister of culture came out. At which point

Jurgen unzipped his fly and began to urinate on the wall of the Berliner Ensemble, screaming:

"'I am a great German writer and I piss on the house that Brecht built!'

"Then he turned and sprayed the minister with his urine. At which point the police tackled him and, according to Horst, beat him senseless right there on the street.

"I learned about all this from Susanne and Horst, who came straight home, clearly distraught, and told me I should borrow their car——they were among the privileged few who had a Trabbi——and get out of town with Johannes immediately. They had a cottage on the Baltic Sea and they told me that I needed to pack and disappear, as the Stasi were bound to arrive before dawn. That was always the way when somebody committed a grievous offense against the state——their spouses or live-in lovers were inevitably picked up. The thing was, even if I did flee north to their cottage in Mecklenburg-Vorpommern, it would only be a matter of time before the authorities found me. I insisted that it was best if I stayed put and answered their questions and explained to them that my marriage to Jurgen was a sham, and that he was——as far as I was concerned—— someone in need of psychological and medical help. Also I knew that if I took Horst and Susanne's car and borrowed their cottage, it would implicate them. Anyway I had led a blameless life to date. No political or dissident activity. No questionable behavior. No applications to 'leave the Republic.' I had always been a good citizen. Surely the authorities would see that.

"Of course, I was horrified by what Jurgen had done. Horrified and depressed. But I knew it was coming——and there was also part of me that wished I had been strong enough to have reported him to our local doctor some time earlier, when it was clear he was heading for a major breakdown. But I also feared ratting on him and being the one who put him in the hands of the authorities. Now, however, I regretted not having taken such action earlier, as I knew that his fate would be, at best, one of those horrible asylums I'd heard about where 'extreme' political dissidents were kept.

"Anyway the Stasi never came that night, which I took to be a good sign. The next morning——after just a few hours of bad sleep——I awoke and fed Johannes and got him changed, then showered and prepared to go to work. Again outside my door there were no unmarked cars, no men in trench coats awaiting me. When I reached the nursery with my son, the woman in charge, Frau Schmidt, greeted me with the usual pleasantries she exchanged with me every morning. Then I turned and started walking toward the tram at Prenzlauer Allee. That's when a plain gray van suddenly pulled up alongside me, screeching to a halt. Two men in suits got out. They asked to see my papers. I demanded to know what this was about. 'Crimes against the Republic,' one of them told me. The other one said: 'And we know exactly the nature of your betrayal, Frau Dussmann.' This was before I had even shown them my identity papers, and a chill ran through me. The next thing I knew the two men were frog-marching me into the rear of the van. I can remember its interior very clearly. Very low——less than one meter in height——and inside there were two small cells. I began to protest, saying I had done nothing wrong, never did anything wrong, that I was a loyal citizen. That's when one of the men spat in my face. 'You dare call yourself loyal after what you've done.' He literally shoved me so hard into the cell that I twisted an ankle as I hit the floor. I screamed in pain, but he simply threw the cell door closed and attached a padlock to it, then told me:

"'Now you will see what happens to people who betray their Republic.'

"I still had my watch on my wrist——and for the next eleven hours the van was in virtual nonstop motion. Occasionally, we'd park somewhere for ten or fifteen minutes. But largely it just kept driving around. As there were no lights in the interior of the van the effect was completely disorienting. There was also no toilet in this tiny locked cubicle——and they didn't bother to offer me any food, let alone water, during all the hours I was being driven to . . .

"Well, that was the big question. To where was I being driven? I knew from Jurgen's recounting of this experience that I would probably end up in some prison at some hour of the night. But where exactly? Was I still in Berlin? Or down in Saxony, where I knew they had a women's prison? And who was picking up my son tonight? That's what was really terrifying me. The idea that five p.m. would come around and there would be nobody there to collect Johannes. I remember screaming repeatedly that I needed to speak to somebody in charge, that they had to call one of my neighbors——like Susanne or Judit——and tell them to pick up Johannes. But my screams were met with silence. So I screamed some more, literally asking that they stop the car and make a phone call. I even started shouting out Judit's phone number, my screams mixing with a growing hysteria that came out of the realization: I was in a very bad place.

"Finally, I could no longer hold my bladder anymore, and I used a bucket that had been left in the corner of the cell as a makeshift toilet. But then the van hit a pothole and urine went everywhere. This is when I started to weep. Because I knew that if I was being given this treatment early on, God knows what awaited me when they got me to prison.

"My mind was racing wildly, wondering what horrible scenarios now faced me. But behind all this was also a crazed, absurd hope that somehow they would stop driving me around, drop me off in front of my apartment, tell me that I had now learned a lesson about marrying the wrong sort of man, and order me to go upstairs and comfort my son. That's how deranged I was at this point——somehow thinking that they would let me go. I read somewhere that prisoners on death row often go through the same delusion. They're being walked to the execution chamber and they still believe it's not going to happen. I felt that as the van finally stopped and I heard a heavy door being pulled down behind me. Then the rear of the van opened and this yellow light streaked in. After eleven hours in the dark, even these fluorescent tubes stung my eyes. I was stinking of urine and my own sweat, so dehydrated by lack of water, and so frightened and so desperate to see Johannes, that as soon as they brought me out of the van I started to scream wildly again. These two women guards——they had faces like old cement——strong-armed me immediately, one of them yanking my hand halfway up my back while the other slapped me hard across the face and ordered me to shut up. Which I did immediately.

"Then they marched me to some reception area where they took the few valuables I had——my watch, my wedding ring. They handed me a drab gray prison uniform and rudimentary underwear, and told me that I now had a number instead of a name, and said that if I cooperated with the authorities, my stay here mightn't be a long one. Then I was marched to a shower. The two women guards watched me as I stripped off my clothes and stood under the lukewarm water. Suddenly I started to break down again, screaming for Johannes, begging them to let me see my son. One of them told me to shut up, or she'd have to slap my face again. I finished my shower. I dressed in the rough, sandpaperlike underwear and prison uniform. I was led to a cell, perhaps two square meters in total. There was a lightbulb that was on all the time. There was a single mattress on a concrete platform, a blanket, a pillow. There was a sink and a toilet. The guards told me to sleep. But I couldn't sleep. I paced the small floor all night. I had nothing with which to occupy myself except my thoughts. All I could think of was Johannes . . . and who was watching him right now and when I would be able to see him again and why . . . my God, *why*? . . . was I being held here? Trying to calm myself down I said: *I'm certain once I talk with the interrogator all will be cleared up and I'll be home with my son by nightfall.* I kept telling myself, *They will be fair. They will be, as they always told us on news broadcasts and in the pages of* Neues Deutschland, *humanistic.*

But the next morning——having not slept at all and having been given a hard roll and a cup of weak tea for breakfast——I was brought down a series of corridors to another corner of the prison. They had this system of pull-cords in the corridors. The woman guard who was escorting me would pull a cord and then wait for someone in a nearby area to respond by yanking it back and thus ringing a little bell on the end of the cord. It took me a few days to work out why they used this rudimentary system of communication before walking me to my daily interrogation. They were letting other guards know that they were leading a prisoner down the corridors——and, as such, ensuring that there were no other prisoners in the hallways at the same time. That was the thing about this prison. As a captive you had no idea of anyone else who was being held there. We were all kept in isolation. Just as you had no idea if this prison was the infamous Hohenschönhausen——the Stasi's remand center in Berlin——or another of their places of interrogation.

My interrogator was named Colonel Stenhammer. He was a man in his late thirties. Short but well built. And evidently very conscious of his appearance, as his hair was always slicked back, his face smooth, his fingernails immaculate, his uniform perfectly pressed, his boots shined to such a high gloss that the few rays of light that passed through the barred windows lit them up. He smoked Western cigarettes——Marlboros——and would keep them in a gold cigarette case that looked like a family heirloom. When I was first brought to his 'office'——as he referred to this interrogation room——he was seated behind a desk and I was told to place myself in a chair that was located around two meters away from him and positioned so whoever sat there found himself in a corner. Officer Stenhammer informed the guard that she could leave us be. Once the door was closed behind her, Officer Stenhammer opened a sizeable file and ran through a basic checklist of questions about where I was born, my parents, my education, everywhere I had ever lived, every job I had held, even every man I had been involved with. I interrupted him once, telling him I had no idea why I was here and how worried I was about my son Johannes, especially as my husband Jurgen . . .

"'Do you really think that, given our humanistic system, we would think of allowing a thirteen-month-old child to be left on his own?' he asked, his tone cool, unnerving. 'Despite the fact that his mother is under suspicion of espionage and treason?'

"'What?' I screamed. 'I have never, never . . . '

"'Be quiet now,' he ordered, his voice as lethal as a wielded scalpel. Then he informed me that if I continued to interrupt him, he would have me brought back to my cell. And I would spend at least five days there without any contact or exercise as a punishment for being uncooperative and antisocial.

"I hung my head and started to weep, whispering 'I'm so sorry, sir' while trying to control the tears that were now flowing. 'I just so miss my son and don't understand . . . '

"'And you have interrupted me again, so now I have no choice.'

"'Please, please, please . . . ' I was wailing now.

"'Will you remain quiet and cooperate fully?'

"I nodded my head many times.

"Stenhammer said nothing. He just sat there and stared at me for a good two minutes. I felt myself becoming unhinged again——unhinged because I was so frightened. But I also told myself I had no choice but to try to maintain a veneer of sanity——and meet Stenhammer's clinical gaze. Then he did something unexpected. He smiled at me and said:

"'Perhaps you would like a coffee and a cigarette. In fact, I am certain you could use both.'

"I didn't know how to reply to this act of kindness, except to say: 'That would be very nice, thank you.'

"He stood up and opened a cupboard, within which was a Western-style coffee machine. It looked very fancy.

"'How do you take your coffee?' he asked. I told him milk, one sugar. He poured me a cup, added milk and a teaspoon of sugar and actually brought it over to me. Then he offered me a cigarette——and slyly added:

"'You won't tell anyone I smoke an American brand, will you?'

"'No, sir,' I said. 'And I am very grateful to you for . . .'

"He held his hand up.

"'I do not need your gratitude, Frau Dussmann. I need you to tell me what you think of the coffee.'

"I took a sip. The aroma of the coffee was overpowering. So too was the sheer richness of its taste. In the GDR such coffee was unobtainable. It was like nectar. The cigarette, too. I'd smoked Western cigarettes a few times before. They were such rarities in the GDR, especially among my crowd, none of whom had contacts in the hard currency shops or in the higher levels of the Party. Of course, part of me knew that Stenhammer was now playing the Good Cop. But the other part of me that was desperate to get out of this nightmare, to get home to my son, also knew that this Stasi man was my one hope of salvation. The coffee and cigarette were meant to make me feel good at a terrible moment. Even though he was my captor, I was nonetheless beholden to him right now. So I said:

"'The coffee is wonderful. So too is the cigarette.'

"'Then we are finally off to a good start,' he said and turned on a tape recorder. I noticed immediately that on the wall to the left of the chair in which I had been ordered to sit, there was a microphone positioned toward me. 'Now I want you to tell me the story of your marriage. And I want all the details. Everything. Even the painful ones.'

"For the next hour I told him all that I sensed he wanted to know. Because I realized that I was doomed if I didn't speak frankly and directly. Anyway, the person who had already most betrayed Jurgen was himself. I made it very clear to Stenhammer that I was never someone involved in political movements, and that Jurgen was a crisis waiting to happen.

"'So your marriage was what exactly?' he asked.

"'A mistake, but with one great gift: my wonderful son.'

"'And when, precisely, did you begin work as an American spy?' he asked. His tone was absolutely conversational, calm, unruffled. I felt myself flinch and had to fight another sob escaping from my throat.

"'Sir, I have never met an American, let alone ever had any contact with their security services. I have lived a quiet life. I am a loyal citizen. I have never . . .'

"'Joined the Socialist Workers Party, for example, which is what most 'loyal citizens' do. And though your parents did join the Party, according to my colleagues in Halle, they have lived rather disreputable private lives. Would you agree that your parents didn't exactly set you the best example when it came to being a "loyal citizen"?'

"I remember taking a very long drag on my cigarette and wishing the ground would open me up and swallow me whole. The bastard was asking me to denounce my own parents as inadequate. And yet I knew that if I fought this, I would be digging myself into deeper trouble. So I said:

"'I think they could have been more positive about the achievements of the GDR.'

"'I don't believe you mean that.'

"'I love my parents, sir.'

"'Even though they were both unfaithful during their marriage . . . your mother having had a long affair with . . .'

"He rifled through my file until he reached a document. Then he read out loud the name of her school's head teacher.

"'Were you aware of this affair?' he asked. I shook my head. He reached for another document. 'Now I know that you are lying to me—— as one of our men in Halle was observing this gentleman and your mother having an assignation near the school. For reasons of state security, which I will not divulge here, their meeting was photographed.'

"He held up a grainy black-and-white photo of Mother and the man locked in a fervent embrace. 'And he also photographed a teenage girl watching them from behind a parked car.'

"Now he held up another photograph——and there I was, an adolescent girl, looking shocked and saddened as she watched her mother in the arms of a man not her father.

"Seeing those photographs sent a jolt of horror through me because I realized: *they really do know everything.* And because Stenhammer had just cleverly checkmated me. He could now accuse me of being fast and loose with the truth.

"'With you having just denied something for which we have proof, how can I begin to believe anything else you tell me?'

"I hung my head. And felt tears well up in my eyes again.

"'I was just trying to protect my family, sir. Surely you can understand.'

"'Actually I cannot. You are under investigation here for treasonous activities against the Republic that has raised you and educated you and looked after you far better than the two crypto-bourgeois parents who were both ungrateful to the humane society that has allowed them to flourish, and who betrayed each other the way they betrayed their fealty to the state. Look at the daughter they produced——someone with the same bourgeois tendencies who admits that she started living with a self-destructive, narcissistic writer because the man had a large apartment. When your husband was off writing his anti-GDR ravings you knew the vile content of his "Ring Cycle" . . . isn't that what he called it? . . . and said nothing. A loyal citizen would have talked to her shop steward or made a phone call to us about his recreant scribbles. But you stayed silent. You allowed him to push forward with his manic endeavors.'

"'Sir, the man was living in a state of advanced solipsism. He had sealed himself off from me and the rest of the world.'

"'Not true. Every day he was at a bar on Prenzlauer Allee, drinking with three of his friends. We have their names here.'

"'But if you ask any members of our crowd in Prenzlauer Berg . . .'

"'Ah yes, your crowd. The "artistes" of Kollwitzplatz. A group of unconstructive, unproductive dilettantes, living off the state, and complaining endlessly in private about the unfairness of their lives. Your crowd.'

"He reached for his cigarette case and fished out another cigarette. He didn't offer me one.

"'Now let me ask you this: you said earlier that your husband shut himself off from the world, talked stupid politics, but really had nothing to do with the forces that would happily destroy our Republic. And you also said that his proclamations in front of the Berliner Ensemble were the ravings of a lunatic. But did you know that this "lunatic" informed us that he was an American spy?'

"'Of course not. And given his fragile mental state, it's clear that this is more of his ravings.'

"'I didn't realize I had asked you for your interpretation of the situation.'

"'Excuse me,' I said, hanging my head lower.

"'The fact is, your husband may have been outwardly delusional to you——but we also know that he contacted a member of the United States Information Agency staff at the US embassy in Berlin; an agency that is a front for the CIA. And they did have two or three meetings at an allegedly secret location near Friedrichshain.'

"The sense of shock I was feeling had now deepened to alarming levels. I raised my hand, asking to speak. Stenhammer nodded his assent.

"'I just don't see what sort of information Jurgen could have given the Americans, given that he hardly moved out of Prenzlauer Berg and . . .'

"'That doesn't really matter here. The fact is, your husband had made contact with agents of a foreign power hostile to the German Democratic Republic. He was observed and photographed meeting this "gentleman" here within this city. That makes him a foreign spy who has committed treason against the Republic.'

"He let that sentence linger in the air, then reached for his Marlboro and took a deep drag off it, allowing a tense theatrical silence to fill his office. Then he finally said:

"'But I don't believe that this information is actually news to you. On the contrary, I am certain you are now feigning shock and horror because it allows you to cover up the other major "truth" of this situation——and one that your husband admitted under interrogation yesterday.'

"'What truth is that, sir?'

"'The fact that you too are an American spy.'

"I felt a horrified shudder rumble across me.

"'That's a complete lie, sir. A total, terrible lie.'

"'You are accusing me of lying?' he said, his voice remaining insidiously calm.

"'Of course not, sir. I am accusing my husband of lying.'

"'Naturally, you would accuse him of that. And let me guess, you are going to now tell me that this comment was that of a deranged lunatic who is divorced from reality, except that we do have photographic evidence of him meeting American agents.'

"'But that doesn't mean that I . . . '

"' . . . was in any way involved in such a business?'

"'Do you have any evidence that I was? Photographs of me meeting an American agent?'

"'What did I tell you about not interrupting me, or acting like it is you who has the right to pose questions? You have no right whatsoever. And as someone accused of treasonous behavior . . . '

"'I don't know what you are talking about,' I wailed.

"'Our interview is now over,' he said, pushing a button on the nearby telephone console.

"'What is happening with my son? I have to see Johannes. I simply must.'

"'As I said before your son, Johannes, is being cared for by the state. And he will remain in the care of the state until you reveal everything to us about your dealings with the Americans.'

"'There were no dealings with "the Americans." I've never even met an American.'

"'And your husband says otherwise.'

"'My husband is demoniacal.'

"'You husband is an American spy. And so are you.'

"'I am not an American spy,' I screamed.

"There was a knock on the door. Stenhammer said, 'Enter.' The same hardened woman prison guard was there. 'I am done with this prisoner,' he told her. 'But she needs to be properly photographed now.'

"'Please, sir,' I cried. 'I beg you . . . my son is the only thing I have in my life.'

"With a dismissive wave of the hand, Stenhammer signaled that the woman should take me away.

"'I have to see him, sir. I can't live without him.'

"'When you give me the answers I demand, we can further discuss this. Until then . . . '

"'But I've done nothing wrong!'

"Stenhammer swiveled his chair away from me, showing me his back. I cried again, 'You have to believe me!' But the guard was now strong-arming me and marching me out the door. I was weeping hysterically. Once we were in the corridor, with the interrogation room door closed behind us, she slapped me hard across the face.

"'You stop that hysterical self-pity now,' she said, digging her fingers into my arm. 'I hear another squeal out of you, there will be serious trouble.'

"She kept the pressure on my arm as she steered me along the corridor, stopping only to pull the cord and let the other guards know we were en route. We turned up some stairs and I was brought into a room, bare except for a stool on a small wooden box, behind which was a gray curtain. In front of this was an old-fashioned camera on a tripod. An officer in a uniform came out and ordered me to sit on the stool. He then stood behind the camera and told me to face front, barking at me to sit up straighter and look more directly at him. Then, his hand on a long cord, he depressed the shutter release. At that very moment I felt a strange wave of heat hit my back. It was so disconcertingly warm that I found myself squirming on the seat. The officer ordered me to be still, then had me turn sideways for a profile photograph. Once he depressed the shutter release the heat hit me again, this time on the side of my body facing the curtain. Now he commanded me to swivel around so he could photograph the other side of my face. Again the shutter button was depressed. Again there was this whoosh of heat enveloping the side of my body away from the camera.

"When I was returned to my cell ten minutes later I lifted up the top of the uniform and saw red welts on both sides of my midsection. Craning my neck I could also see a pronounced redness stretching down my spine, or, at least, as far down my spine as I could see. What had been done to me during that photographic session? But this concern was overridden by a far larger fear——the fact that Jurgen had set me up as his accomplice. And what I couldn't figure out was whether this was an act of maliciousness on his part, or just a further example of his derangement. What I did know was that the Stasi would now use our son as a negotiating tool, and that I would have no chance of seeing him unless I gave them what they wanted. What Stenhammer wanted, no doubt, was the names of all the alleged American agents with whom Jurgen told him we were consorting. The problem was: as I had never made contact with any American agents, how could I give him names or details of what they demanded of me in the way of information or intelligence? Yet I also simultaneously knew that, even if I invented an entire fictitious scenario about secret rendezvous with CIA operatives, they would run scrupulous checks of everything I told them. And they would undoubtedly use my 'treason' as a way of keeping me apart from Johannes. Stenhammer understood I had already grasped this scenario; that I had figured out there was no way out of all this; that even if I gave them everything they wanted, it would be a lie, because I was never a CIA stooge. I am pretty damn certain he had ascertained that I had no espionage credentials whatsoever. But Jurgen had said something that had incriminated me. According to Stasi logic, you were guilty *even* if you were innocent. They had decided that my cohabitation with a mentally unstable man who peed on the Minister for Culture——and may have tried to contact the Americans——was cause enough to ruin my life.

"I also realized very quickly that Stenhammer was determined to break me down and make me malleable in his hands. How did I know this? Because after our first 'interview' I was locked up for three straight days without any contact, except the occasional visit by a guard with a food tray. Yes, I was allowed one hour of exercise per day, but this entailed being led outside and locked up in a concrete cube, around five meters by two meters. The walls of this cube were three meters high, and were covered by barbed wire. I was left to my own devices during this hour in the great outdoors. I was never one for exercising in the past. But now I started running back and forth like a lunatic, deliberately trying to exhaust myself, to sprint so hard in this limited space that I would——so I imagined in my delirious moments——burst through the walls and be free of this place. This reverie was simply one aspect of the psychological meltdown I was experiencing. Besides locking me up for twenty-three hours a day, they were also denying me any outside stimulus. No radio, no books, no writing materials. Nothing but my thoughts. I did devise strategies for keeping my mind active. I would replay films, frame by frame. I tried to mentally categorize every word in English I had learned to date. But my thoughts were endlessly dominated by my son. You cannot begin to imagine what it is like to be deprived of contact with the child who is the center of your world. The sheer visceral, tactile need to hold him close, to smell that still new-minted, *undamaged by life* aroma which seemed to emanate from Johannes's every pore, the inability to hear him cooing, to bring him into bed with me when he cried in the middle of the night. For me this was the most extreme punishment imaginable.

"When, after three days, they finally brought me back for my second interview, I was so psychologically destroyed, so manic from lack of sleep and rampant claustrophobia, so desperate to do anything necessary to get myself free and back with my son, that I sat down and accepted one of the colonel's very good cigarettes and his excellent coffee, and asked him to turn the tape recorder on, as I had a confession to make. He obliged, and I launched into this highly researched spiel about being approached in a bookshop on Unter den Linden by a man I called Smith who informed me that he would be willing to pay me fifty dollars a week in hard currency if I would slip him information.

"The story sounded ridiculous. As soon as I opened my mouth, I knew how implausible it seemed. After five minutes, Stenhammer quietly said, 'That's enough,' and turned off the machine. Then, turning to me with an amused smile, he said:

"'You want your son back, don't you?'

"'More than anything in the world.'

"'Then you have to tell me the truth.'

"'But you know the truth, sir.'

"'Do I?'

"'Yes, I think you do. And the truth is: I never had any contact with any Americans.'

"'Then back you go to your cell.'

"'You have to believe me,' I said, my voice straining.

"'You keep telling me this. I don't have to believe you at all. In fact, I don't believe you whatsoever.'

"Another three days in the cell, twenty-three hours a day locked up, no reading material, no outside stimulus whatsoever. I started thinking about killing myself, how I read somewhere that if you drenched a bed-sheet it wouldn't snap when you fashioned it into a noose. Maybe the

Stasi had ways of reading my mind as well, as the morning after I first thought of this a guard came and took away the thin sheet covering the bed. When Stenhammer saw me again three days later, he smiled and offered me a cigarette and a cup of coffee. He was back in Good Cop mode. As always they both tasted wonderful and slightly lifted my mood.

"'Now I am certain you are wondering how you can get yourself out of here,' he said.

"'What I am wondering most of all is about the welfare of my son.'

"'That is not a worry, as I told you before. He is being looked after by an excellent family.'

"'Who are they?'

"'That's confidential information. But I know the family——and I can reassure you that Johannes is receiving all the love and care that he needs.'

"I felt a chill run through me. 'But I know the family.' That could only mean one thing. He had been placed with a Stasi family. This, in turn, meant that they would be even more loath to ever return him to me. And Stenhammer——still smiling sympathetically at me, the bastard——knew that this little tidbit of information, couched in such vague language, would be a knife to the heart. When I bowed my head and started weeping, he acted all concerned.

"'Have I said the wrong thing?' he asked.

"'I'm never seeing him again, am I?'

"'I've never said such a thing.'

"'But it's true, isn't it? He's been adopted by a Stasi family, hasn't he?'

"'I advise you to lower your voice and stop making such extreme accusations.'

"'Even if you get what you want from me——which is impossible, as I never had any contact with agents of the United States——you'll still deny me access to Johannes.'

"'Now you are inventing things.'

"'Bullshit,' I screamed. 'My husband is a traitor and you have decided, without any proof, that I am one as well. So how could your "humanistic" system allow a young son of this extraordinarily democratic republic——which locks up its citizens on trumped-up charges and removes their children as punishment——to be raised by a woman who, though completely innocent of everything of which she has been accused, is still ideologically tainted by her association with a man who has lost his reason and . . . '

"'That will be enough,' Stenhammer snapped.

"'Because you can't stand to hear the truth,' I wailed. 'How the fuck do you sleep at night, knowing you have denied an innocent mother the child who means more to her . . . '

"Stenhammer stubbed out his cigarette, hit a buzzer on his desk, and interrupted my rant by slapping me hard across the face. As he did so, his face was contorted into such a violent and frightening expression that I was immediately covering my head with my hands, screaming and crying and begging him not to hit me.

"'Shut up now," he hissed.

"I fell silent, trying to suppress the scream that was still lodged in my throat. Stenhammer, clearly shaken by what had just transpired, walked around the office, his breathing indicating that he was trying to steady himself and muffle the fury that had overtaken him. After a moment he grabbed his cigarette case and fished out a Marlboro and lit it up, taking a deep drag off it before speaking again . . . only this time his voice was back to its usual eerie coolness.

"'You have just overstepped the boundary of no return, Frau Dussmann. And you are right: given your evident psychological instability, your treasonous behavior, your thoroughly tainted character, there is no way that this *very* democratic and *very* humanistic republic could allow one of its children to be raised by such a compromised, contaminated individual. So, yes, you will not be seeing Johannes again. Since you don't want to tell me the truth about your collaboration with capitalist agents, I am ordering that you remain locked up constantly——except your one hour of exercise per day and your own weekly shower——until you are ready to tell me everything I want to know about your so-called bohemian circle in Prenzlauer Berg. Until you inform one of the guards that you are willing to give me the information on these subversives that I require . . . '

"'That I will not do, because none of them are subversives and because I won't betray my friends.'

"'Then you will simply rot in here.'

"He hit a button on his desk. Within moments a woman guard was in the room, strong-arming me up out of the chair.

"'Why don't you just take me out and shoot me?' I hissed. 'Save the Republic the cost of keeping me locked up here.'

"'But that would be far too easy a way out for you,' he said.

"That was the last I ever saw of Colonel Stenhammer. I was returned to my cell. Thus began the three longest weeks of my life. Stenhammer remained true to his threat. I was never brought back to his 'office.' I was kept locked up twenty-three hours a day. I continued to be deprived of anything that might allow me to escape the inside of my head. I was on constant suicide watch, as the light burned in my cell day and night, and the sliding panel on the solid steel door slid open every half hour as a guard checked that I hadn't indulged in any form of self-harm.

"After a few days I fell into a sort of walking catatonia, in which I lost the will to reflect or play the sort of cerebral gymnastics that would keep my faculties intact. Instead I slipped into the sort of malaise that saw me lie motionless on the bare mattress for hours on end. I ate little. I had no appetite for anything. When I was brought to the exercise block, I simply sat slumped against one of the walls——and the morning guard on duty (it was a young man——and less harsh and cruel than his female counterparts) would always slip me a packet of f6 cigarettes and a box of matches, and allow me to smoke. But I didn't have the will to exercise or even walk back and forth within this cement cage. I just sat there, smoking as many cigarettes as I could during this one hour outside, staring at the sky through the barbed wire overhead, still telling myself that, somehow, I would be reunited with Johannes. How could I kill myself when I knew that my son was out there in the world beyond these walls, and that some sort of general decency and humanity would have to prevail, and he would be restored to me?

"The weeks went by. My waking catatonia deepened. It got to the point where I had to be physically hauled off the bunk and all but carried outside. I had lost a shocking amount of weight. I didn't care. I was happy to waste away, as nothing mattered anymore. I had been sentenced to live in this limbo, this nonlife, forever.

"Then late one evening——or, at least, I thought it was the evening, as I could see nothing but darkness outside the tiny aperture that served as my window——the cell door opened and two men in suits stood outside, accompanied by two women guards.

"'Frau Dussmann,' one of the suits told me. 'You will get up now.'

"I shook my head slowly, and whispered one word: 'No.' One of the suits nodded to the guards and they approached me. But when they began to manhandle me off the bunk in their usual rough style, he shouted at them to be 'gentle.'

"The next thing I knew I was being escorted down the corridor to the showers. The suits waited outside as the guards helped me off with my clothes and handed me a bar of soap and a bottle of Western shampoo. I was so weak that I found it difficult to even work the shampoo through my hair. But I somehow managed to finish the shower. The guards then brought me the street clothes I had been wearing when arrested. All freshly laundered and pressed, but now——given all the weight I'd lost——far too big for me. The skirt was so large one of the guards disappeared with my belt and returned a few minutes later with three new holes punched in it. As I dressed, one thought kept hitting me: What is happening? Is some justice minister showing up for an inspection and they want me to look relatively normal? I asked one of the guards if she could tell me what was going on. She just shook her head and told me——politely, I should add——to hurry up. Then I was brought down a few more empty corridors and up a flight of stairs to a small dining area. I was told to sit down at one of the tables. I could hear the noise of pots and pans close by. A door swung open and a woman in a white chef's tunic emerged with a plate, on which were an omelette and some brown bread. The eggs tasted real——so often, we had to make do with powdered eggs in the GDR——and the bread was fresh. She brought a pot of good coffee, and one of the guards put a packet of f6 cigarettes by me and said I could smoke.

"The food was the first solid meal I'd had in weeks——and, again, the question *What does all this mean?* was haunting my every thought. After I'd wolfed down the omelette and bread and lit up the cigarette, the door swung open and one of the suits was there.

"'It's time,' he said.

"'Time for what?' I asked.

"'You'll see.'

"One of the guards tapped me on the shoulder, indicating I should stand up. Five minutes later I found myself in a garage, being placed in the same sort of van in which I had been brought here. They put me in the same interior cell as before, locking it shut. Then the back door closed, I heard the hum of machinery as, I presumed, a garage door opened. The van backed up. With a distinctive change of gears, we headed off.

"We must have driven for an hour. The van came to a halt. I could hear another few vehicles pulling up to meet us. The van sat there for the better part of another hour. I could hear several different voices outside, but there was a wind blowing and I couldn't discern a word of what they were saying. Then, suddenly, I heard a bolt being thrown and the rear door opening and the headlights of a vehicle facing our own filled the interior of the van. One of the suits climbed up and crouched down as he walked the few steps to the cell in which I was being kept. He undid the padlock and said two words——'We're here'——and escorted me outside.

"A sharp blast of cold air hit me as I climbed down off the van. Snow was falling. I could tell that we were in the middle of a bridge. Next to the beaming headlights of the vehicle facing us were several men and women in plainclothes and uniforms. One of the suits took me by my arm and led me toward these waiting figures. A woman came forward. The suit literally handed me over to her. I was so blinded by the headlights, the snow, the confusion of everything that was happening to me, that I couldn't discern who she was, what she looked like. My steps were tentative. I felt so desperately weak. Immediately she put a protective arm around me and said:

"'Petra Dussmann, I am Marta Jochum of the *Bundesnachrichtendienst*,' the West German intelligence services. 'Welcome to the Bundesrepublik.'

"'I don't understand,' I said.

"'Let's get you out of the cold,' she said.

"She escorted me into a very large car. There was a policeman standing by the door. As he opened it for me, he touched my shoulder with his gloved hand and said one word: '*Willkommen.*'

"I sat in the back of this huge car with Frau Jochum. There was another policeman behind the wheel. A man in a very fine overcoat got in beside him. He turned around. He was around thirty and very good looking. He smiled at me.

"'This is Herr Ullmann. He is from the American mission here in West Berlin.'

"'It is wonderful to see you here, Frau Dussmann,' he said in fluent German. 'We've been following your case for many weeks now.'

"'You have?' I said.

"'I know this is all very confusing,' Frau Jochum said. 'But all will be explained tomorrow after you've had a good night's sleep and a decent breakfast.'

"'But why am I here? I'm nobody.'

"'Don't say that,' Ullmann said. 'You're exactly the sort of person we've been working to get out.'

"'But I'm not a dissident, not a politico. I never did a political thing in my life.'

"'We know all that, Petra,' Frau Jochum said.

"'Just as we know how ruthless those bastards have been, vis-à-vis your son,' Ullmann said. 'And excuse the bad language, but having followed your case . . . being deprived of your child like that . . . well, it beggars belief.'

"'Not only have I been denied him access, but they have put him with another family. And my psychotic husband informed the Stasi that we were American spies.'

"'We need to talk to you about your husband,' Ullmann said.

"'But it can wait until tomorrow morning,' Frau Jochum added quickly.

"'Has something happened to Jurgen?' I asked.

"'There is a great deal to discuss, Petra,' Frau Jochum said. 'And as it's now three in the morning . . .'

"'If something has happened to Jurgen, I want to know now.'

"'We have a very nice place for you to stay,' Frau Jochum said. 'A most modern apartment which is yours for the next month or so, as you adjust to . . .'

"'Tell me what happened to my husband,' I said. 'I want to know now, please.'

"Ullmann and Frau Jochum exchanged a nervous glance. Then

Ullmann gravely nodded his assent. That's when I knew. Frau Jochum reached over and took my hand.

"'Your husband hanged himself in his cell several days ago,' Frau Jochum said.

"The news didn't blindside me. On the contrary, it made terrible sense. Jurgen was, at best, a fragile man——and one who would not have withstood the horrors of isolation and lack of stimuli visited upon him in a Stasi jail. But though I wasn't overwhelmed with grief, I still felt a profound despair——because I also knew that, with his father dead and his mother ejected from the Republic, Johannes would now become a ward of the state and the child of whatever family they had placed him in.

"'Was Jurgen's death the reason I was expelled from the GDR?' I asked.

"'Jurgen was never working for us,' Ullmann said, 'though he did make contact with several people we have on the ground in East Berlin. To be blunt about it, we didn't consider him psychologically reliable enough to use as an intelligence contact. But we were aware of his false implication of you.'

"'How were you aware of that?'

"'We have our sources of information within the Stasi. In essence, the Stasi knew you had nothing to do with us. But they were using you as leverage against Jurgen. Just as we know that they were using your son as leverage against you.'

"For a moment a wild thought came to me: could it be that Colonel Stenhammer was their mole inside the Stasi? Was he interrogating me and Jurgen and was he then reporting back, via some clandestine route, to Ullmann? Though I had never loved Jurgen——nor he me——the fact that he was now dead . . . that his death was such a lonely and terrible way out of the nightmare into which he had dropped all of us . . . oh God, I was so angry at Jurgen for having ruined our lives and so desperately sad at the thought that he was no more. That madly talented, furious, brilliant, far too complex, so self-destructive, so crazed, so unhappy man . . . who also happened to be the father of my son. The son who had been taken away from me. The son who would now grow up as the child of other parents. The son who would be told that this false mother and father were his own, and would never have any knowledge of my existence. The son who was now lost to me forever.

"I lowered my head as my eyes filled up with tears. I could feel Frau Jochum's hand pressing harder against mine.

"'I know how difficult this news must be. That's why I wanted to wait until morning.'

"'You got me out,' I said. 'Now you have to please get my son out.'

"I could see an anxious glance pass between Ullmann and Frau Jochum.

"'We'll discuss all that tomorrow, Petra,' Frau Jochum said once more.

"'In other words, it's hopeless,' I said.

"'We will explore every avenue possible,' Ullmann said. 'Of that I can assure you.'

"'I'm never getting him back, am I?' I said.

"Another nervous glance between Ullmann and Jochum.

"'We'll do our best, Petra,' Ullmann said. 'But we are up against certain realities here. The biggest reality is that those people do not play by the same rules as we do.'

"They brought me to a compound, located in the far west of the city. Frau Jochum was right. The apartment into which they ushered me was, by the standards of what I had known until now, the most luxurious imaginable. There was a woman there named Frau Ludwig, in her mid-forties. She informed me that she was going to look after me in the weeks ahead. Frau Jochum turned me over to her and said that, after a medical appointment I was to have tomorrow morning, she would be back with Herr Ullmann in the late afternoon to have an extended chat with me.

"Once she was gone, Frau Ludwig informed me that, in the coming weeks, I was to call on her for anything——and that right now I probably needed a shower and a good night's sleep. There was a living area with a sofa and a big reading chair and a television——all very modern, very much like a deluxe hotel. There was a bedroom with a massive bed, made up with the most wonderful sheets and the softest duvet imaginable. She asked if she could run me a bath——and I spent almost an hour soaking in this deep tub filled with scented bath salts. She had fresh pajamas awaiting me. Once I changed into these, she insisted on using a tape measure to take some basic measurements so she could order me some new clothes, as the ones I had on not only were too big for me, but were, of course, the only set I now had in the world. She wished me a good night, I climbed into that massive bed and couldn't sleep for more than an hour. All this cocooned luxury. I was also still so traumatized by the last three weeks of isolation and sensory deprivation that it was hard to cope with such changed circumstances. Then there was the overwhelming sadness and strange guilt that I felt about Jurgen's death, coupled with the deepening horror at the realization that Johannes was lost to me forever. Staring at the ceiling, trying to still fathom why I had been released so suddenly, and how I would never be free of the longing I had for my lost son. It was all just too confusing, too wounding.

"But I finally did surrender to sleep. When I awoke the next morning it was just after noon and Frau Ludwig presented me with two pairs of jeans——actual real Levi's——and a corduroy skirt and a very nice double-breasted dark blue military-style overcoat and assorted underwear. I remember all this not just because I was overwhelmed by the quality of the clothes and the generosity of my benefactors, but also because, again, I couldn't understand why all this goodwill was being visited upon me.

"After breakfast I was walked across a spacious courtyard——so beautifully landscaped——to a medical facility where a very efficient but kind doctor ran all sorts of tests on me. He said that the now-fading red welts on my body——which happened during that alleged 'photographic session'——were, in fact, radiation burns, and that I wasn't the first person he'd examined upon release from a Stasi prison who had suffered such burns.

"'But why would they expose me to radiation?'

"He hesitated for a moment, then said:

"'Our theory is that they use radiation as a way of marking certain dissidents, in order to be able to trace them in the future.'

"'Or to make them deathly ill.'

"'There is that,' the doctor said. 'But it all depends on the level of radiation with which they hit you.'

"'If it caused such burns on my body . . .'

"'Yes, it is a great worry. But the lasting damage to your health——if, that is, there is any——will only be discerned many years from now. And there is the good possibility that you will be spared any illness.'

"'Just as there is the possibility I will get very sick from what they did to me.'

"'Yes, that is a potential outcome. But the physical scars——the welts——should fully disappear within weeks.'

"That afternoon. Herr Ullmann and Frau Jochum both interviewed me. I learned that the reason they wanted me 'out' of the GDR——and the way they traded me for two GDR spies who had been imprisoned in the Bundesrepublik for many months——was twofold. I had been interrogated by Colonel Stenhammer, a 'gentleman' who interested this pair intensely. They had targeted me as a potential bargaining chip because the GDR authorities knew that I was essentially blameless—— and therefore, as such, had nothing to share with agents of 'the other side.'

"'The fact is, we need to question you extensively about Stenhammer,' Frau Jochum said. 'Because he has been a key interrogator of many dissidents and you are the first of his "subjects" that we have been able to get out. So, over the next few days, if you are agreeable . . .'

"'Of course,' I said, knowing that something would have to be given back in return, and that the only hope of being reunited with Johannes would be through Frau Jochum and Herr Ullmann.

"'There's something else you need to know,' Ullmann told me. 'This is something we also need to question you about. Within your circle in Prenzlauer Berg there was a Stasi informer. This informer did you and Jurgen a considerable amount of damage, as she was reporting back to them all your conversations. As you trusted this person, as she was your closest confidante . . .'

"As soon as he said the word she, a chill ran through me. A chill followed by disbelief. Surely it wasn't she. Surely she would never do that to me.

"'Your friend Judit Fleischmann has been a longtime informant of the Stasi. From what we can gather from our source within their organization, she reported everything you confided to her back to them.'

"I felt as if I had just walked into an empty elevator shaft and was on a long downward plunge. Frau Jochum saw this and reached over and gripped my shoulder with one of her hands, saying:

"'I know how betrayed you must feel right now. But you need to remember that the more information you can give us about what she told you, the more leverage we can bring when attempting to negotiate the return of Johannes to you.'

"'He's with a Stasi family now, isn't he?' I said.

"I watched as Frau Jochum and Herr Ullmann exchanged another uncomfortable glance.

"'We have reason to believe that is so,' Ullmann said.

"'Do you have the name of that family?'

"'If you attempt to somehow contact them, Petra,' Frau Jochum said, 'it will throw all our efforts into . . . '

"'I just want to know the name of the family who have my son.'

"'Herr Stefan and Frau Effi Klaus.'

"'Where do they live?'

"'We don't have the exact address,' Ullmann said.

"'Just tell me the district.'

"'Friedrichshain.'

"'And my "friend" Judit. Was she rewarded for such a "patriotic" betrayal of her best friend?'

"'Our contact on the other side informed us that your friend had something of a breakdown after you were arrested and Johannes was placed with another family. I'm certain you despise her now, but the Stasi knew that she had been having an extramarital affair with a woman for some years and threatened her with exposure to her husband as a lesbian if she didn't cooperate. We have learned that since her breakdown, she's been institutionalized.'

"My head was reeling. Jurgen dead. Judit in one of those psychiatric hospitals from which few people ever emerged unscathed. And the knowledge that my best friend had been forced into informing on me. But overriding everything was the realization that Johannes was now being brought up in a Stasi family. Would a Stasi couple——undoubtedly childless——really return a baby to his lawful mother when that woman had been expelled from their 'democratic, humanistic' republic? Never.

I knew that immediately. Frau Jochum saw that I knew it——and tried to comfort me some more by saying:

"'This could be a long process, Petra, but you have my word that we will move mountains to get Johannes back to you.'

"'You don't need to "move mountains," I whispered. 'Just The Wall.'

"I spent the next few weeks cooperating fully with them, answering all their questions. I accepted their offer to help me find a small apartment and the job at Radio Liberty. When they offered me three thousand deutsche marks to buy furniture and clothes, I didn't say no. Frau Ludwig became like a big sister to me, taking me out clothes shopping, bringing me around West Berlin so I could get my bearings, making certain I ate well, keeping me in reasonable spirits, and evidently monitoring my moods to see how well I was coping.

"The fact was that the shock I was feeling, the profound grief and anguish, translated into a silent resolve to simply try to get through the day. When it came time to find a little apartment somewhere, Frau Ludwig raised a concern when I insisted on finding something in Kreuzberg very near The Wall——because she knew why I was choosing this location.

"'Is this a good idea, living so close to where Johannes is now?' she asked me.

"'I need to be near him.'

"'But knowing that you can't be with him, aren't you allowing the wound to stay open?'

"'Do you really think it will ever close?'

"'Speaking as a mother, no, I doubt it will. But speaking as someone who cares about you, you are going, in time, to have to find some sort of accommodation with it all.'

"'That will never happen,' I said.

"A year on, the wound remains as fresh and as raw as ever. The love I have for you, Thomas . . . the love you have given me . . . the love we share . . . of course, it has changed my life. And I have begun to know happiness again. But before you the only real happiness in my life was Johannes. No matter how hard I try to negotiate with myself——to try to accept that he is lost to me, that I simply will never get him back and I need to mourn his loss as if it was his death——I still cannot find a way of accepting this reality. It so haunts everything. I know it always will.

That's why I have to say that for your own sake, it's best if you walk away from all this, from me. Because as long as my son is being raised on the other side of that monstrosity by people not his own——people who were rewarded for their dirty work for the regime with the gift of my son——a part of me will always be so damaged, so sad, that a life together will be impossible.

"So, please, Thomas, get up right now and walk away. Save yourself from all this. Save yourself from me."

EIGHT

AS SOON AS Petra finished talking, I stood up and took her in my arms. But her reaction to this embrace, this attempt to comfort her, was disconcerting. She was limp, lifeless——as if the telling of this terrible tale had depleted her entirely. I held her close to me, saying:

"When you first came here——that night we first spent together—— you asked me to never let you go. I promised you I wouldn't. And that promise holds——even more so after what you've just told me."

"You really mean that?"

"You know I do. Just as you know there's nothing I wouldn't do for you, for us."

"Us," she said, pronouncing the pronoun carefully, as if it was foreign to her or——worse yet——a word that had been proscribed. "I so want that. But . . ."

"I won't accept the word 'but.' What you've been through, what you've survived, it would have broken most people. It didn't break you. Now, together, we have a real chance at happiness."

"But, as I told you, how can I ever be happy if Johannes is with those people?"

"You can have another child. With me."

"It won't bring Johannes across The Wall. It will never end the sense of loss."

"True, but it will mean you will be a mother again."

"But do you really want that, Thomas? You, who live this vagabond existence, who love to wander, to roam. Surely you don't want to be changing diapers or forced to stand still for a while . . ."

"I want this, you, us. And, yes, I want a child with you."

"Please don't say that just to make me feel better."

"I'm saying that because I mean it. And because I will also do everything I can to get Johannes back to you."

"You're being far too romantic, Thomas. What Herr Ullmann told me a year ago was correct: there is no way you can negotiate with these people."

"They got you out."

"Because they had a bargaining chip: Dieter Mettel, a high-ranking officer in the *Bundesnachrichtendienst* who turned out to be a Stasi operative. He was such a big catch for the West Germans that they traded him for three East German dissidents and me. The only reason they wanted me out was that they could learn all about Stenhammer's interrogation techniques. He was someone who had broken many of their own people over there. And I was able to give them a very comprehensive account of his strategies when it came to breaking his victims."

"But he didn't break you."

"I didn't tell him anything he wanted to know. But yes, he still broke me. Just as they broke Judit."

"But she betrayed you. Betrayed you utterly."

"I got a letter from her five months ago. A letter that had been smuggled out by a second cousin who teaches at Tübingen and was visiting her in the East. According to the letter, Judit only spent a few weeks in the psychiatric hospital——where she was administered electric shock treatment that, as she said, mentally neutered her. She said the horrible feelings she had for betraying me, for betraying our friendship, have been neutralized by the treatment. She said she's almost grateful, as the horror became unlivable after I was arrested and Johannes was taken away. She said her 'nervous breakdown'——that was the official word for it, as everyone is too happy in the People's Republic to even contemplate taking their own lives——was an attempted suicide. She turned the gas on in her stove, stuck her head in, and passed out, only to be found by a neighbor. Judit told me that she had been blackmailed into informing on me because she had a secret that she was terrified of being made public. And since she had a job teaching art in a grammar school, she was certain that the revelation about her lesbianism would mean the end of her career. She told me she wasn't trying to make excuses for what she had done or ask for my forgiveness——because what she did she found unforgivable. But she did want me to know that on the morning of my arrest, she made a sweep of my apartment, taking several photograph albums and some letters before the Stasi's people came and turned the place upside down. If there was any way I could ever get them collected from her . . ."

"And the photographs were of . . . ?"

"My parents, my childhood, my friends in Prenzlauer Berg. But most of all, they were all the photos I took of Johannes during that first and only year we had together."

"Is Judit teaching again?"

"Not at all. In her letter she's on indefinite sick leave. From what I could gather, she spends most of the time at home in her little apartment, her husband having left her for another woman while she was in the hospital."

"So if I was to show up on her doorstep, saying I had come for the photographs . . . ?"

Petra looked at me with care.

"But you could get arrested, thrown into jail."

"For what? Collecting a couple of volumes of family photos?"

"They'd find a reason to arrest you. It's too dangerous, too risky."

"Not from where I sit."

"You'd actually do this?"

"I'm doing it. Tomorrow."

"But it's not necessary."

"Do you have any photographs of Johannes with you?"

"None. When they arrested me they took my wallet, along with the photographs of my son that I had with me. When they expelled me, they kept the wallet."

"You'll have some photographs tomorrow by nightfall."

"I want to say, 'Yes, please, go.' But if anything happens to you . . ."

"Do you think Judit is still being watched?"

"Given that I am out of the country and her life has been ruined, I doubt it."

"Then I'll get up early and cross Checkpoint Charlie by eight. I presume I can take the U-Bahn up to her."

"You get the U-Bahn from Stadtmitte——that's the first East Berlin station after Checkpoint Charlie——up to Alexanderplatz. Then you switch for a tram heading to Danzinger Strasse. You get off at Marienburgerstrasse and cross the tramline and walk two streets until you reach Rykestrasse. Her apartment is in number thirty-three——and her name, Fleischmann, is on the bell. I will write a letter explaining very little, except the fact that you have come for my photographs. Once you've gotten what she can give you, you need to somehow not be seen carrying them back here."

"I'll bring a daypack with me, big enough to carry a few photo albums."

"What if they search it on your way out?"

"The worst they can do is confiscate the photos."

"That is hardly the worst they can do."

"I'm an American."

"And like all Americans, you think yourself indestructible."

"Absolutely. I also know that if I'm not back by nightfall, I will get someone to make a call to my embassy and they will send in the Marines."

"You don't have to do this."

"Yes, I do."

I now finally understood the horror and the sorrow that shadowed Petra's every move. The very fact that she had somehow managed to survive all that had been visited upon her struck me as extraordinary and made me want even more to put things right for her. As we clung to each other in bed later that night, I told her:

"This will all work out. It may take months, maybe a few years. But you will get Johannes back."

"Please stop this sort of talk now," she hissed. "I know you mean well. I know you want to fix everything. But all this positive talk, all this hope . . . it has a contradictory effect on me. It just underscores the hopelessness of the situation. And now, if anything happens to you over there . . ."

"Nothing's going to happen because I plan to be very careful."

I glanced over at the clock by the bed. It was just after ten. I set the alarm for six-thirty tomorrow morning, telling Petra I wanted to get an early start to Checkpoint Charlie and try to be at Judit's apartment before eight-thirty, in case she was heading out for the day.

"From what I could gather from her letter, she hardly ever leaves it and is a virtual recluse," she said.

"Does she smoke?"

"Everybody over the age of thirteen in the GDR smokes——except the athletes they develop in those battery farms of theirs. So, yes, a packet or two of Camels would win her over immediately."

"And the letter of introduction?"

"It will be ready by the time you wake up."

"I love you, Petra."

"I love you, Thomas."

After a long, extended kiss, I turned over and surrendered to sleep. When I awoke eight hours later it was to the sound of the alarm going off and the smell of a smoldering cigarette.

"Want a coffee?" Petra asked.

"When did you get up?" I asked.

"I never got to bed."

"But why?"

"Just was worried."

"About me making this trip?"

She shrugged, then nodded, then shrugged again, turning away from me, her eyes suddenly filled with tears. I was immediately up out of bed, but when I attempted to take her in my arms, she stood up and reached for her coat, saying:

"I think I should go back to my place for a while."

"Petra, there's really no need to . . ."

"I just need to be by myself."

"I'm going to be fine."

"I don't want you to do this. I don't need the photographs. I don't need reminders of . . ."

"Did you write the letter to Judit?"

She pointed to a sealed envelope on the table. It had the name——Judit Fleischmann——written on the front of it. Next to it was a piece of paper, covered with Petra's neat handwriting.

"I've written down Judit's address and all the necessary instructions for getting to her apartment. I'll be awaiting you here tonight with dinner ready. Please try to get back by six, otherwise I'll be . . ."

"I will be back by six."

"I am not going to be able to think until then."

She kissed me deeply, grabbed her coat, and headed for the door.

I wanted to give pursuit, to take her in my arms and again reassure her that all would be fine. But another part of me knew that when Petra was having one of those moments when sorrow and worry were clouding everything, it was best not to crowd her. If the death of a child was the worst thing that could befall anyone, then the idea of having your child physically removed from you and placed with a family had to be nothing less than a living death, especially when coupled with the realization that you could never see your son again.

Add to this the knowledge that with each day, each week, each month, this baby would become further attached to his new parents, and that he would have no memory of the mother who brought him into this world, who adored him from the moment he breathed for the first time, whose entire life was centered on him. I, for one, would have gone mad with grief and rage by now. Not only was it as cruel and vindictive a punishment imaginable, it was also so maniacally unfair.

Did I think that bringing back some photographs of Johannes would somehow ease Petra's agony? I doubted it——but I still had to cross over to the other side and retrieve them. Because, yes, in that very American way of mine, I wanted to somehow try to do good, to make up for all the terrible things that had been thrown in her path. And my mind had already been thinking about scenarios and strategies for somehow reuniting Petra with her son.

But another thought struck me as I got dressed. I had not discussed with Petra what she should do if I was apprehended by the GDR authorities——as, perhaps, they were still keeping an eye on Judit and might immediately bring in for questioning someone visiting her from the West. There was also the possibility that if I was searched on my way back through Checkpoint Charlie, I could find myself being asked a lot of awkward questions about the photographs in my pockets. I knew that any lame excuse about me bringing these snapshots over to show my friends in East Berlin would be completely upended by the fact that the photos were so clearly not printed in the United States.

If such an arrest came to pass, and I didn't show up, Petra's panic would be enormous. Even if she did call the embassy, then what?

As I dug out my passport——and wondered if I should just leave a note for Petra, explaining what to do if I wasn't home by mid-evening——I heard movement downstairs, specifically, pots and pans being rustled and Alaistair shouting "Oh fuck" as something hit the floor. A thought came to me: for all his bluster and extremity, he was a strangely good man. Someone I could trust.

So gathering up my daypack, the letter to Judit, and the paper on which Petra had written her address I headed downstairs. Alaistair was on his knees by the stove in his kitchen, sweeping up the remnants of an omelette into a dustpan.

"Fucking inept, *comme d'habitude*. I was far steadier on smack."

"It doesn't seem to be affecting the work," I said, nodding toward the three canvases that were half-finished along the back wall of his studio. Though they resembled the geometric studies in varying hues of blue that he was working on before the attack, they were not reproductions. On the contrary, these new paintings had a fluidity and complex depth of coloration and perspective that marked a real departure from his previous work. Gone were the primal blues and pellucid lines that defined the others. These were troubled, yet supremely confident——a real mastery of shape and hue amidst moody abstraction. Alaistair saw me studying them——though perhaps the right verb would be "drawn in" by them, as they had that visceral effect on me.

"You approve?" he asked.

"Enormously."

"Coffee?" he asked.

"Please."

"I just saw Petra leave. Anything wrong between you two?"

"Let's have a coffee and a cigarette."

"No problem."

The coffee percolated as I accepted one of Alaistair's Gauloises.

"You're up very early," I said.

"Working all night. Been on one of those manic jags the last few days. Which has also been a reaction to a little change in my life."

"Something serious?"

"Now here's a question for the American writer: is a breakup of an arrangement serious?"

"You and Mehmet?"

Alaistair nodded.

"But I thought after that last little rupture things had settled down again."

"They had. But then his wife became——as they used to say in Victorian music halls——'in the family way' and he feels he simply cannot risk seeing me again."

"When did he tell you this?"

"Two days ago."

"You should have said something," I said.

"And break the Fitzsimons-Ross Code of Stoicism, passed along for centuries by generations of rigid Protestants on horseback? I knew this would happen one day. But like most things that you know are going to eventually arrive in your life and leave you distressed, you tend not to dwell on their inevitability. Even when we had that little contretemps a few weeks ago——and Mehmet finally showed up here again after a few days——I knew that it was only a matter of time before the inevitable happened. If you ask me how I'm feeling, I will become homicidal."

"It's that bad, is it?"

"You never know your real feelings about someone until that someone is no longer in your life. Think of all the people who stay forty years married to the wrong person——and feel trapped most of the time. Then the hated spouse dies and they are bereft."

"Or those who let somebody go, and then discovered that they had fired the love of their life."

"I didn't let Mehmet go."

"I know that."

"Yes, it's all bothering me bloody more than I'd like it to. But . . ."

I could see his eyes fill up as he turned away from me and stood up to collect the now-percolated coffee, rubbing away his tears with the paint-stained sleeve of his sweatshirt. Then, taking a deep steadying breath, he turned to me and said:

"And now we're getting off this fucking subject."

I nodded while glancing at my watch and noticing that the time was now 7:08.

"Hurrying off somewhere?"

"Can I trust you with something, Alaistair? Something very private that must never be discussed with anyone else but me?"

Without pausing to think this one through, he said:

"Of course." I could see in the clarity of his gaze that he meant it. So I told him that I was about to cross over to East Berlin and explained the purpose of my journey. I also told him about Petra's arrest, her appalling incarceration, the suicide of her husband, and the way her son was "adopted" by a Stasi family. Alaistair listened in silence. When I was finished, his response was to reach for his cigarettes, light one up, and stare off into the distance for a few moments.

"You never really know the horrors that other people carry around with them, do you? There I was, thinking that Petra was sad, and perhaps the sadness had to do with a bad love affair in the past, or that buyer's regret which many émigrés have after they've landed in the West. But this nightmare she's been forced to live . . . it's unspeakable. Fear not, I will never breathe a word I know anything about this to a soul, let alone to Petra. But thank you for entrusting me with it all."

"I don't have any contacts at the US embassy——and I definitely don't want anyone called at Radio Liberty, as it might put Petra's post there in jeopardy. But if I'm not home by eight tonight at the latest . . ."

"I will keep Petra calm. And I will make certain that the man on call at the US consul——I think they call him the duty officer——is fully briefed. But do try to get back in one piece . . . with the photographs."

Half an hour later I was emerging out of the Kochstrasse U-Bahn station, passing the "You Are Leaving the American Sector" sign, and heading toward the barriers up ahead. As I reached the gate, a guard looked at me. I nodded, indicating that I wanted to cross over. He nodded back. The barrier was raised. I walked in. I was the only customer this morning. The uniformed Volkspolizist officer in the booth accepted my passport and asked me the usual questions: "Purpose of visit?" ("Tourism"). "Anything to declare?" (I shook my head). "You are aware that this is a day visa and you must cross back through this checkpoint——and only this checkpoint——by 23:59 tonight?" ("Yes, I am aware of that"). Then he asked me for the obligatory thirty-deutsche-mark entrance fee. I had it ready in my pocket——and after handing it over, he pushed back to me thirty ostmarks, Lenin's jutting chin filling up half of the bills. Then he asked me one final question:

"Are you bringing in any goods that you plan to leave in the GDR?"

Actually, I had five packets of Camel Filters and six bars of Ritter chocolate in my daypack but decided to take a risk and simply said: "No." The guard studied me, decided not to press the matter further. With a nod of the head toward the East, he indicated I was in.

On to the next barrier. My passport was checked again, the barrier raised, and I headed up a near-empty Friedrichstrasse to the Stadtmitte U-Bahn station. The day was bright, sunny, almost warm. I blinked into the unforgiving light, peering up this bleak boulevard, still devoid of people, cars, signs of life. The U-Bahn station was just up ahead. I went down its narrow stairs and found myself in a subterranean world of harsh lights and the stench of a very powerful disinfectant. I bought a ticket. Then I waited for the train to Alexanderplatz, sharing the platform with two other people. They were a young couple in their twenties, both wearing nylon jackets——his gray, hers a curious shade of maroon——holding hands awkwardly, occasionally smiling when their eyes met, but looking tentative and a little shy. Had they just spent the night together for the first time? Were they edging their way into love and still unsure how to negotiate it? He had long, slightly greasy hair and a moustache that was just one step beyond peach fuzz. She had a pretty face but was already a little heavy in the thigh. For the entire five minutes as we waited for the next train, they exchanged plenty of shy yet affectionate glances, but not a word passed between them. New lovers, without question, in the disinfected netherworld of the East German U-Bahn.

Just as we were about to board the arriving train, I looked to my right and saw that now standing on the platform was a man in a blue suit that gave off a serge-like shine. He was half-hidden by a pillar, reading that morning's copy of *Neues Deutschland*. He wore a porkpie hat and slightly tinted oversized black glasses. When he saw me catch sight of him, he adjusted his body ever so slowly to disappear behind the pillar. Immediately I wondered if he had followed me from the border checkpoint. As the train rumbled into the station, I walked further down the platform away from him and boarded the second carriage.

The train only took ten minutes to reach Alexanderplatz——and Mr. Undercover (as I now deemed him) never appeared in the carriage where I was sitting. When we arrived I bolted up the stairs and emerged in the shadow of that overbearing and very looming television tower that so dominated this barren square. I checked my watch. I needed to keep moving. So I walked to the tram station right by the big S-Bahn station and was in luck: a tram toward Danziger Strasse was just leaving. I climbed aboard and could see my fellow passengers eyeing me warily. Was I that identifiably a visitor from the West? Even in my beat-up army desert jacket, was it so damn obvious? I was also just a little disconcerted to see the man in the tinted glasses and porkpie hat at the far end of the tram. Was I being followed? Or was this one of those strange coincidences, and could he also just be another man in a porkpie hat and 1950s style eyewear?

I got my answer when I stepped off the tram——as instructed by Petra in her note——at Marienburgerstrasse. Mr. Undercover followed. Then I did something extreme and potentially stupid. I started to run. But instead of crossing the tracks to my left, I made a beeline down a street on which there was a church in bad repair. The signpost of this street——Heinrich-Roller-Strasse——flashed by as I sprinted, my old cross-country training coming back, as I glanced around behind me and saw that Mr. Undercover was giving pursuit. But he was a little on the hefty side and possibly hadn't been running as much as I had been recently——so I lost him within moments, cutting into an alleyway and hiding behind a parked car. Three minutes later he came jogging by, his face beetroot red, muttering "*Scheisse*" under his breath, glancing everywhere, clearly panicked. I waited another minute before peering out of the alleyway, seeing him now at the bottom of the street, wildly glancing left and right, then dashing rightward. As soon as I was certain he wasn't doubling back, I ran across the road, down a side street, then back up to the tram tracks. Fortunately, there were no police around. And the few passersby just looked on with mild bemusement. Perhaps they thought I was just running for a tram.

As soon as I reached the tram tracks——which bisected a boulevard

called Prenzlauer Allee——I stopped running, especially as there were police here. Looking right and left——and very much behind me——I saw
no sign of Mr. Undercover. I wondered if he had ducked into a phone
booth or a shop to make a call to his superiors, telling them to be on the
lookout for a Westerner in a dark green desert jacket, now in the vicinity
of the Marienburgerstrasse tram stop. I took off my jacket and bundled
it into my daypack. Then I crossed the tram tracks quickly, but not at a
speed that could call attention to myself. Keeping my head down, I continued moving until I found Rykestrasse——a street of imposing nineteenth-century apartment blocks, all badly in need of a paint job, yet still
redolent of a certain bourgeois solidity. There was a Martello-like tower
at the end of the street——blackened by coal and other pollutants, its
masonry chipped, frayed, like a crumbling holdover from a Grimm fairy
tale. I pulled out Petra's note. Judit lived in number 33 Rykestrasse——a
building that had a dilapidated quasi-Gothic portico, into which had
been placed a grim steel door. It opened at a push——there was no security system——and Petra's note informed me that Judit's apartment was
on the ground floor, just to the left of the stairwell that led to the higher
floors. The stairs were in dangerous condition, with large chips missing
from their once-solid stone construction. There were two fluorescent
tubes, unevenly suspended from a skylight with cracked glass, casting
the foyer in a strange orange glow. And the aroma of scorched grease and
overcooked cabbage intermingled with the same toxic disinfectant that
I smelled in the U-Bahn. The door to Judit's apartment was also made of
steel, but looked as if it had been repeatedly attacked with a hammer or
some other hefty object. I could hear a radio playing inside, a voice intermingled with a considerable amount of static. I knocked on the door
several times. No response. I knocked again, this time louder. The radio
snapped off and the door opened a tiny crack. I was looking down at a
set of eyes, from behind which came a hoarse voice:

"Ja?"

"Are you Judit Fleischmann?"

"Who are you?" she said, sounding accusatory and a little fearful.

"I am a friend of Petra Dussmann's."

"I don't know any Petra Dussmann."

"I have a letter here from her to you."

"I don't believe you."

"My name is Thomas Nesbitt, and I live with Petra in Kreuzberg."

I said this in a low voice, just in case there were nosy neighbors or listening devices planted around here.

"This is no lie?" she asked, her voice trembling.

I dug the letter out of my pocket and held it up to the crack in the door.

"She wrote you this," I said.

A small trembling hand shot up and grabbed the letter from me. The door suddenly snapped shut. I waited outside, cursing myself for allowing her to snatch the letter and not let me in. But after a moment the door opened and I found myself staring at a most diminutive woman——she couldn't have been more than five feet tall——with short cropped hair that had turned gray, a face that, though once possibly attractive, was already heavily lined. She had a cigarette between fingers with heavily chewed nails. She was dressed in a shabby floral bathrobe. She looked thin to the point of emaciation. Her eyes were underscored by deep rings that gave her the look of the perpetual insomniac. I could tell that she saw I was disconcerted by her appearance, so I lowered my eyes as she hissed:

"Come in, come."

I stepped inside. She quickly closed the door behind me. I was in a room of around fifteen square meters. It had a high ceiling——and that was the only thing to recommend it. It was squalid. Yellowing linoleum on the floors, a stained cream blind half-covering the greasy window. A double bed in a corner, unmade, with a blanket dappled with cigarette burns. A hot plate, a small fridge, a sink stacked with dirty dishes, empty bottles of schnapps and brimming ashtrays, a small stack of books next to a folding card table that served as a makeshift desk, and clothes strewn everywhere. The smallness of the place didn't get to me——I'd lived in plenty of tiny apartments. Nor did the basic nature of the furnishings, as only the privileged few on this side of the ideological divide had access to decent household goods. No, what was truly unsettling about this place was that it was the apartment of someone who had chosen to live in a doleful way. I could only wonder if this sense of self-flagellation had begun to rise when she was forced to rat on Petra and increased radically after Johannes was taken away.

She reached over to the radio and turned it up a few notches. The announcer's voice was now blaring.

"I do that so they can't hear us," she said, her voice leathery and wheezy from far too many cigarettes. "If, that is, they are even bothering to listen to me anymore. Since my husband left, I have been here entirely on my own, so if they are listening they've been hearing the radio and no other conversations. What did you say your name was?"

I told her again.

"You sit here," she said, pointing to a folding chair. "You want tea? I don't have coffee, because the coffee is never good here."

"I have coffee," I said, opening up my daypack and pulling out the two bags of pre-ground coffee I'd picked up alongside my other gifts.

"You brought this for me?" Judit said, wide-eyed.

"And a few other things," I said. "Petra told me you liked a strong cigarette, but filtered."

I brought out the five packs of Camel Filters. Judit began to shake her head, as if in considerable distress.

"Why did you do this?" she asked.

"Because I thought it would be nice to bring you a few things. You like chocolate, I hope?"

I now placed the six bars of Ritter chocolate——two mint, two marzipan, a yogurt, and an almond——on the table next to the cigarettes and the coffee.

"Take them back. I don't deserve them."

"I'm not taking them back."

"Did Petra tell you?"

"Yes, she told me everything."

"Everything?"

"Absolutely."

"And yet you still bring all this to me?"

"She forgives you."

She lowered her eyes as they filled with tears.

"How can she forgive me?"

"What does it say in the letter?"

She picked up a pair of battered wire-rimmed glasses, one corner of which was held together with black electrical tape. Putting them on the edge of her nose, she opened the letter. From what I could see it was short and covered less than one side of the page. Judit moved her lips as she read. When she finished she lowered her head and began to sob quietly. I stood up and found a battered percolator on a shelf near her sink. I opened it and found the hardened remains of old coffee grounds embedded within. I pulled out the tin filter and ran it under the tap until the hot water finally began to erode the congealed grounds. It took around five minutes to loosen it all and dump its soggy remains in the trash basket. Then I rinsed out the base of the percolator, reassembled it, and carefully measured out three tablespoons of coffee. As I did all this Judit sat at the table, lost in thought. When I placed the now reassembled percolator on the hot plate, my host snapped out of her reverie and said:

"I would have done all that."

"Yes, but I was already up by the sink."

"You are being far too polite. May I have one of those cigarettes?"

"They are yours, so there's no need to ask me."

"I just feel . . . awkward about all this."

"Don't."

"In the letter Petra says very little——except that she would like me to give you some photographs of her and Johannes. She also said that she had heard about my stay in the hospital and hoped I was now in a better place. And she concluded with one sentence: 'Despite all that has happened I still consider you my friend.'"

She lowered her head as her eyes filled up again.

"The problem is, I can't forgive myself."

"Maybe the fact that Petra does forgive you . . ."

"They still took away her son. And she will never get over that."

"Perhaps, in time, it will get easier."

"You're a young man. And, I sense, one without children. Though you may possibly be able to imagine what it must be like to lose a child——or, in Petra's case, have one taken away from you——you still cannot imagine the true horror of it all."

"Did you lose a child?"

"I never wanted children. Because I knew that they would just bring loss, pain. Like the pain Petra is suffering now. The pain I caused."

"You weren't the reason she was arrested."

"Please stop trying to be nice to a stranger."

"Should I try to be horrible instead?"

That raised a small smile.

"What do you do, Thomas?"

I told her.

"So Petra's found herself another writer," she said with more than a hint of irony.

"It looks that way."

"Not that I would ever try to compare you with Jurgen."

"That's good to know."

"Believe me, it is. Because that man . . . he was, at one time, brilliant, extraordinary. *Ein Wunderkind.* But then he had a few setbacks and he came completely unstuck. And started doing mad, irrational things. That's when the Stasi moved in on me. Because someone had informed them that I was Petra's best friend. And they had this information on me. Did Petra tell you about that?"

I nodded——noting how Judit was imparting this information in a sort of rote style, as if she had told herself these facts (*"he came completely unstuck . . . and that's when the Stasi moved in on me"*) many times over, as a way of reassuring herself that other people, larger forces, had so compromised her.

"Yes," I said, "she did tell me about the information they had on you."

"So you now know my dirty little secret."

"I don't think it dirty at all."

"My husband thought otherwise. He found out via the neighbors and he's gone. That woman I was involved with . . . she ended things between us when the Stasi visited her and said they knew all about our 'relationship.' She had a husband, too. But he either never found out or chose not to react——as I gather they are still together. Whereas I am, as you can see, alone."

The coffee had finished percolating. When I stood up to get it, she insisted on playing host. She brought out two elderly yet rather fine china cups——floral in design, but harking back to a more elegant moment in time. She also brought out a sugar bowl and a small jug, all in the same design. Seeing these rarefied objects in the midst of this personal squalor was strangely touching. Judit must have noticed me taking them in, as she said:

"They belonged to my grandmother. Dresdner Porzellan. The best, unless you are from France and think that the world of fine china ends at Limoges. Grandmother died in 1976 at the age of eighty. She survived the destruction of her home city. She refused to leave the GDR when it was still possible in 1960. She adjusted to the austerity of life here. Even toward the end she remained the very proud *hausfrau* who polished twice a week what little silver she had left, and actually managed to rescue a full set of Dresdner china from the family house that was destroyed by Allied bombing, and which killed her two parents, her unmarried sister, and two of her three children who were staying with their grandparents on the night the city was leveled. A very dignified woman, my grandmother."

"What was her name?"

"Lotte. But now you are getting me to tell stories. And we have this excellent coffee to drink."

"It might not be that good."

She poured out a cup and lifted it to her nose, taking in its aroma with a deep sigh.

"It is so good."

She carefully reopened one of the packets of Camel Filters, tapping two out and offering me one. I accepted it and lit both cigarettes. Judit took a long drag off of hers, letting the smoke out with a low pleasurable groan. Then she took the first sip of coffee and smiled.

"Thank you," she said quietly. "It's been quite some time since any-one has been this kind to me. Tell me about Petra's life in West Berlin."

Immediately I thought: *Danger. Maybe, for all her sad talk about the ruination of her life, she might still think she could win a privilege or two if she supplied the Stasi with any information that comes along her way.* Or perhaps I was just being far too overcautious.

"Petra is doing well. We are very happy together."

"Is she working?"

"Yes, she's working."

"What kind of work?"

"Translations."

"Ah, that makes sense. She was always so good with languages. Is she working for a government organization over there?"

"Why does that interest you?" I asked, my tone deliberately letting her know I didn't like where this line of questioning was going. She caught the edge in my voice and quickly said:

"I just wanted to know if she had a job she liked."

"She has a job she likes."

"Good."

An uncomfortable pause followed. Judit broke it.

"You now think I was digging for information, don't you?"

"Not at all."

"I have nothing to do with those people anymore. *Nothing.*"

"It's really not my business."

"Were you followed here?"

"Actually I was. But I managed to lose the guy on Prenzlauer Allee."

"How did you do that?"

"I ran."

"Didn't that draw attention?"

"Not so far."

"They are probably now scouring the area for you."

"That thought did cross my mind."

"You think I am going to call them the moment you walk out of here," she said, her voice suddenly overwrought.

"I honestly don't know what to think right now."

"I swear to you, I won't do that."

"All right, I believe you," I lied.

"In fact, I will show you a side way out of the building that will bring you down an alley and into a backstreet. From there you have to walk a bit, but you'll reach, in ten minutes, the U-Bahn at Schönhauser Allee. It will get you back to Alexanderplatz, then you change for the line to Stadtmitte and the border crossing."

"I think they will get suspicious if I am crossing only a few hours after coming over."

"They won't care."

"How can you know that?"

Again my tone was challenging, yet the question was an evident one. How the hell could she have such knowledge of what questions they posed at Checkpoint Charlie?

"Of course, this is mere speculation on my part," she said.

"Of course."

"This cigarette . . . it is like nectar. And the coffee. Petra is lucky. A generous American."

"How did you know I was American?"

"I just guessed."

"I see."

"Well, your German. It sounded American."

I switched into English, asking:

"And do I sound American now?"

Judit tensed, looking like someone caught out in a possible lie.

"I don't speak English," she said, turning away from me. "I speak nothing but German, and have never been out of the GDR. You must forgive me. Please . . ."

"When I leave here . . . ?"

"Nothing will happen. As I said before, I am useless to them now."

Is anyone ever entirely useless to "them"? I wondered.

This was the problem in sticking your toe into the murky waters of a highly surveilled society that operated according to the principles of fear and paranoia. You could never really know whom to believe, what to believe. Ambiguity and doubt and mistrust were the holy trinity here—— and watching Judit become increasingly agitated as she sensed I was on to her signaled the fact that it was time for me to leave.

"Those photographs that Petra mentioned in her letter . . ."

"Of course, of course," she said, standing up with the cigarette still in her lips. "I have them in a special hiding place. So if you wouldn't mind shutting your eyes for a moment . . ."

"Why should I do that?" I asked, my voice edging into controlled anger. "I mean, who am I going to tell about your hiding place?"

I could see her entire body tense up again. I suddenly felt terrible for snapping, but I also couldn't help but think how this woman had denounced Petra for years, while simultaneously being her best friend. Still, I had to remember Petra's own comments about Judit being put under the worst sort of psychological strain——and remind myself that I could not engage in armchair moralizing about a system under which I fortunately never had to live.

"You're right, you're right," I said. "I have no business seeing your hiding place. So I'm going to turn around and shut my eyes and open them when you say so."

I did just that. Less than thirty seconds later she said, "You can open them now."

As I did, and turned back toward her, I could see that she was crying.

"Thank you for that," she said.

"I'm sorry if I was a little abrupt before."

"Please, please, do not apologize. It is me who should apologize . . . for everything."

I saw that she had a book of photographs in one hand——a small ring binder with a gray vinyl cover.

"Here," she said, extending it toward me. "I managed to get a mutual acquaintance to send Petra a letter after she had crossed over, explaining that I had been able to get her photographic albums out before the Stasi sealed her apartment. I put them all together into one book. I wish I had been able to claim more of her possessions, but I had so little time and they arrived six, seven minutes after I was there. I hope she will take some comfort from——"

Once more she broke off, shaking her head, muttering to herself. I opened the book. There were snapshots of Petra holding Johannes close to her in the hospital bed, evidently just after his birth. There were photographs of him asleep in a small crib. Of Petra breast-feeding him. Of Petra tickling him on a sofa. Of Johannes holding a stuffed zebra. Of Petra pushing Johannes in a stroller along a street. Of Petra with him in a local playground——perhaps the one I happened upon in Kollwitzplatz on my first trip here some months back. Of Johannes and Petra in the middle of a double bed. Of Johannes standing up and looking bemused at being able to do just that.

Of course, he was a cute baby. What baby isn't? But what struck me immediately about this collection of twenty or so photographs was the fact that not one showed Johannes with his father or Petra with her husband. Judit must have been reading my thoughts as she said:

"I pulled out all the photographs with Jurgen, as I know Petra wouldn't want to see them."

"Well, maybe we should let Petra be the judge of that. So why don't you give them back to me and . . ."

"I can't give them back to you. I burned them. Burned them all."

"But why?"

"Because it was Jurgen's insanity that brought on this catastrophe."

"You still should have let Petra decide if she wanted them."

"Jurgen was like a cancer that infected us all. And what do you know of anything over here? *Anything?*"

She was shouting——and she was clearly surprised that she was shouting, as she now turned shamefaced.

"Listen to me, listen to me, idiot, idiot, idiot. You bring me lovely things. You love my friend. You tell me my friend forgives me. And how, *how*, do I behave? Like the complete, total, pathetic, useless . . ."

"Enough," I hissed. "I thank you for the photographs. I will tell Petra——"

"Tell her I hate myself for what I did. I tried to communicate this in the letter I sent her months ago. But it was all coded, not direct and honest. Tell her I am grateful for her forgiveness, and that I don't merit it."

"All right, I'll tell her all that. Now, tell me about the back alley way out of here, please."

She gave me very detailed instructions, informing me exactly how to negotiate the maze of nearby side streets and make it undetected to the Schönhauser Allee U-Bahn station.

"Thank you," I said, putting the photo album in my daypack and standing up.

"I hope you can forgive me," she said.

"Forgive you for what?"

She hung her head, like a convicted criminal on whom sentence had just been passed.

"For everything," she said.

When I left a few moments later, I waited until Judit had closed the door behind me, then I took the photo album out of my daypack, spent several minutes removing all the snapshots, placed them in an envelope I had brought with me, pulled out my shirt, stuffed them in the back of my pants, and covered them again with the tail of my shirt. Then I dumped the empty photo album in a trash can and hesitated for a moment, wondering if I should follow Judit's clandestine route to the U-Bahn or simply brave the public way back to Prenzlauer Allee. Part of me thought that if I left now I could possibly count on the Stasi awaiting me at the U-Bahn station by the time I arrived——that is, if she had already made a call to them. Whereas if I simply walked down to Alexanderplatz, using side streets to avoid the tram stop at Marienburgerstrasse which might now be under surveillance, they might still be awaiting me at Checkpoint Charlie. But I could refute any of their accusations that I was in Prenzlauer Berg this morning. That is, of course, if there wasn't already a police car awaiting me outside Judit's front door.

I touched the back of my shirt to make certain the photographs were tucked away. Then I spent a few moments calming my nerves by rolling a cigarette, grimly thinking this could be my last smoke for a while if the Stasi were out front awaiting me. But when I stepped out into the street there was nobody there. I looked both ways. Outside of a few parked and empty Trabbis, the street was devoid of cars. I began to walk, heading down Rykestrasse toward the ruined tower, then around a side street, snaking down a street that ran parallel to Prenzlauer Allee. Once again I kept expecting a car with tinted glass to drive up beside me and men in dark suits to hop out and bundle me into the backseat. But I walked on unencumbered, without anyone on my tail (or, at least, not to my visual knowledge), all the way down to Alexanderplatz. I checked my watch. It was just after eleven in the morning. I knew I simply wanted to jump the U-Bahn back to Stadtmitte and walk the hundred yards to Checkpoint Charlie and cross over. But I sensed that I would be inviting far too many questions about why I had only chosen to make a three-hour crossing into the GDR. So I bypassed Alexanderplatz and continued walking south, killing two hours in Das Alte Museum near the Berliner Dom, looking at a profoundly dispiriting collection of Socialist Realist art on themes such as *The Workers Strike Against the Prussian Oligarchy* and *Children of the Democratic Republic Sing Songs of Peace Against Capitalist Oppressors*. There was also an entire section of the museum consecrated to "Photographic Work from Fraternal Socialist Nations," in which I gawked at happy peasants bringing in the wheat harvest in Bulgaria and the Cuban baseball team helping bring in the sugarcane crop on a collective farm east of Havana.

Propaganda always casts off a spectral, sinister glow——a sense of trying not just to preach to the submissive, but also to dress up terrible realities in the raiment of gaudy fabrication. Two hours amidst such totalitarian kitsch left me stupefied, and finally made me decide: *To hell with the risk. I'm crossing back over now.*

I ducked into the bathroom and stuffed the photographs deeper into my jeans, so they were hidden completely. Then I headed off into the sun-drenched early afternoon. Twenty minutes later I approached Checkpoint Charlie on foot after a stroll down Unter den Linden and a turn left on Friedrichstrasse.

As soon as I arrived there, I saw a figure standing by the guards at the first checkpoint. He wore a blue serge suit, tinted glasses, a porkpie hat. *Shit, shit, shit.* Mr. Undercover. Since losing me in Prenzlauer Berg he had evidently doubled back here and was probably ordered to position himself at this checkpoint, through which I was obliged to pass, until I returned. From the surprised and pleased look on his face, it was clear that he was relieved I wouldn't be keeping him loitering until 11:59 p.m., the last possible moment I could cross back into West Berlin without overstaying my Cinderella visa and landing myself in all sorts of trouble.

Which I was about to do just now.

Mr. Undercover motioned toward the uniformed guard and whispered something in his ear. I saw the guard place his left hand on the revolver holstered next to him. Though terrified, I knew I had no choice but to submit to their questions and, I hoped, be granted access to the thirty yards that separated their world from mine.

The border gate swung upward. I walked toward Mr. Undercover and the guard. As soon as I had crossed the painted line on the ground, the guard had his hand around my right arm.

"You will come with me," he said.

I was ushered into a prefabricated hut just after the border. As the guard led me in, he was joined by Mr. Undercover and an older uniformed man with several medals adorning his two breast pockets. There were no chairs in this tiny space——just a long table in front of which I was ordered to stand.

"Papers," he said. I handed them over.

The officer studied them, then turned to Mr. Undercover and asked, "This is the man who ran away from you?"

"That is him," he said.

"Are you sure?"

"Absolutely."

The guard stared down at my papers and said, "So, Herr Nesbitt, this gentleman says you started running when you left the tram at Marienburgerstrasse in Prenzlauer Berg."

"That's right. I started running."

"Why did you start running?"

I took a deep steadying breath, trying to tamper down the fear that had seized me.

"I ran because I am a runner. I have a run every morning. And this morning I thought it would be interesting to have a run over here."

The guard looked at me as if I were mad. Which, perhaps, I was.

"That is a ludicrous story. This gentleman said you were acting suspicious on the tram."

"And what does this gentleman do?" I asked, my tone simultaneously challenging and nervous.

"We are posing the questions here."

"I am bemused at why I am being questioned for deciding to go for a jog in Prenzlauer Berg."

"You're not dressed for running."

"I have a pair of sneakers on," I said, pointing to the Nikes on my feet.

"You live in West Berlin?"

"Yes."

"And what do you do there?"

I explained that I was a writer of books.

"What kind of books?"

I told him about my one and only book.

"So you are in West Berlin doing research?"

"No, I'm writing a novel."

"About what?"

"The first girl who broke my heart."

Again he gave me a withering look.

"What brought you over here this morning?"

"I wanted to see the exhibition at the Das Alte Museum."

"And why did you want to see it?"

"Because it interested me."

"But why did it interest you?"

"Because that sort of artwork interests me."

"Even though it has nothing to do with the romantic novel you are writing."

"Who says my novel is romantic?"

"If you were going to the Das Alte Museum, why were you first in Prenzlauer Berg?"

"As I'm certain your records show, I made an earlier visit here more than four months ago. I discovered Prenzlauer Berg during that day over here. And I found it very agreeable."

"I think you were seeing someone there."

"I wasn't."

"You're lying."

"Do you have proof I'm lying?"

As they hadn't seen me enter Judit's apartment, I was fairly certain I was in the clear on this issue, unless she had called them. But had she called them, she would have landed herself in deeper trouble, as she did give me the photographs now hugging the small of my back.

"I just know you are lying," the officer said.

I shrugged, trying to appear unruffled, even though I was profoundly nervous.

"I would like to inspect the contents of your backpack."

I handed it over. He pulled out each item: a blank notebook, a copy of *The New Yorker*, my tobacco pouch and rolling papers, assorted pens and pencils, a paperback edition of Graham Greene's *Our Man in Havana*, which I was reading for the first time, and a half-eaten bar of Ritter marzipan chocolate. The guard examined each article intently. Then he asked me to empty my pockets. I did as ordered, putting keys, money, and my wallet on the table. He was greatly interested in my wallet, reading every card I had stored in its assorted pockets.

"Now take off your jacket and hand it to me. And I want your watch as well."

As I did this I could see Mr. Undercover eyeing me up and down. Fortunately, my shirttail covered the back of my jeans. But if they did make me take off the shirt, I was pretty certain the bulge in the back would be noticeable.

The guard searched every pocket of my jacket and also examined the black 1950s Omega watch I had inherited from my grandfather many years earlier. I was now beginning to feel sweat gather under my arms. My verbal cockiness with the guard masked a profound fear that I could end up being held for, at best, several days on suspicion of espionage, smuggling, whatever.

"Wait here, please," the guard said.

Gathering up my personal effects, he shoved them all into my day-pack and headed off with Mr. Undercover, locking the hut door behind him. I found myself wondering: *What next?*

I was left alone in that hut for more than two hours. Or, at least, I sensed it was two hours, as he had also disappeared with my watch. Having been left with no reading material, no pen and paper, I could do nothing but sit down on the floor and lose myself in thought. I pondered the fact that Petra, when held for weeks in that Stasi jail, also spent day after day without any distraction whatsoever. Judging from the few hours I was left alone, it was a physically noninvasive yet profoundly effective form of torture——especially when augmented by the fact that I so desperately needed to pee, and the ever-enlarging fear that I was in way over my head. I wondered what nightmare scenario they were now devising for me.

But then, out of nowhere, the door opened and the guard came in, alone. He was carrying my backpack. He dumped it onto the table and said:

"Get up."

Once I was on my feet he pointed to the pack and said:

"Here are your things. Please check that they are all there."

I did so, confirming that nothing was missing.

"Now put your jacket on, put your things away."

Again I did exactly as asked. Once I was finished, he handed me my passport.

"You are free to go."

There were so many questions I wanted to pose right now. Why had they decided I was no longer a risk? Did they ever get a tip-off from Judit? Why didn't they strip search me if they were concerned that I was carrying something compromising out of the country? But I also knew that I was being allowed to leave, which was actually all I needed to know.

So I followed the guard outside. He handed me over to a subordinate who walked me to the western side of the barrier and signaled that it be raised. He tapped me on my shoulder and pointed forward. As I headed toward the Kochstrasse U-Bahn station, the gate lowered behind me with a clank. Once downstairs in the underground I pulled the bent photographs out of my jeans and spent much of the ride back to Kreuzberg trying to flatten them out.

As soon as I approached the outside door of my apartment building and fished for my keys, I heard footsteps racing down the stairs and the door swinging open, and Petra threw herself into my arms.

"I've been standing by the window for the last hour, worried, desperate."

"Hey, I'm early."

"Did you see her?"

I reached into my jacket and handed her the envelope with the photographs.

"They came back here concealed against my back, so they got a little bent."

Now Petra raced inside and sat down on the steps and frantically shuffled her way through the stack of snapshots, stifling sobs as she looked at image after image of Johannes. When the sobs escalated, I sat down next to her and put my arms around her.

"I shouldn't have made you go there," she said. "I shouldn't have so wanted to see . . ."

But she could not finish the sentence and buried her face in my shoulder, weeping. When she subsided I got her upstairs. Once inside our apartment she kissed me with such passion, such need and desire, that we fell straight into the bedroom.

Afterward I was blindsided by fatigue, a delayed shock hitting me. So I nodded off for almost an hour. When I stirred awake Petra was sitting up in bed next to me, smoking a cigarette. The photographs were in her hand and she was staring with profound wistfulness at a snap of Johannes enraptured by a balloon.

"Hi there," she said, leaning down to kiss me.

"You okay?" I asked.

"A bit better, yes. It's just so hard."

"I'm sure."

"But what you did . . . to have these photos of Johannes . . . tangible evidence beyond all the memories inside my head . . . it means so much."

"Good."

I accepted the offer of a cigarette.

"And how was Judit?"

"That's a long story. In fact, everything about the day was a long story."

"Tell it to me."

Petra said nothing throughout my recounting of it all. When I got to the end of my tale——how the senior border guard finally let me go after several hours of incarceration——she finally spoke.

"I'm so sorry."

"Don't be. I knew the risks involved in crossing over. I'm just glad I'm back here, and with the photographs. But as for Judit's role in all this, do you think she called the Stasi as soon as I was out her front door?"

Her face became as hard and angry as reinforced concrete.

"Of course, she did. And, of course, she will spend the rest of her life denying that she did. Because that's what Stasi informers do. They convince themselves to live a lie and pretend that they 'have no choice,' that it is all out of their control. Whereas the truth is, they inform because they are afraid. And they are afraid because they inform. Once you are caught in that conundrum, you never get out of it with your sanity intact. It destroys you. Utterly."

NINE

PETRA KEPT FOUR of the snapshots of Johannes in a small photo book she carried with her everywhere. She kept two in her wallet. She kept two tucked away in the leather-bound writing case in which she always kept a large pad of lined paper on which she first drafted her translations in longhand. On the few occasions I ever ventured to her apartment——as she found it depressing and cramped and so preferred the space and airiness of my place——I saw a couple more of the photos adorning a bulletin board that was hung over the table she used as a desk. After my trip across The Wall she never again talked about Johannes or Judit or any further details of her former life over there. The only reason I knew about the photos she carried with her was that I saw them when her writing case or wallet was left open on the kitchen table. But she never mentioned them again. I could sense that, having told me all about her imprisonment and the loss of Johannes, she now didn't want to enter that terrain with me again. And she seemed to be working very hard at keeping the titanic emotional distress of it all out of my field of vision.

Of course, the morning after I arrived back from East Berlin——and once Petra had gone off to work——I had a coffee with Alaistair. I'd poked my head into his studio the night before to tell him I'd made it back alive. Now I filled him in on my adventures at the border. I didn't talk much about Judit, nor did I ever mention to him the fact that she had betrayed Petra to the Stasi. But I did ask him not to mention a word to Petra that he knew about my journey on her behalf.

"As I said before, I never betray a trust," he said. "Especially because I myself have had my trust betrayed——and it is never less appalling. But poor Petra——the photos must provide cold comfort."

Yet a week later, as we were having lunch in the Café Istanbul, he remarked, "Petra seems rather happier. I ran into her on the street yesterday. She was all smiles, as if she's no longer carrying some sort of terrible grief."

Alaistair's assessment was a correct one. A change had come over her——a sense of lightness, an absence of those dark moments when she seemed to recede into herself, and an increasingly articulate optimism about the future. When that check for two thousand deutsche marks arrived for the Radio Liberty essay and I suggested five days in Paris she said, "I'll let you know tonight." When she came home that evening, she informed me that her boss had given her the entire following week off.

"I'll go to the travel agent tomorrow," I said. "Do you want to fly or take the train?"

"The train has to go through the GDR. Even though it doesn't stop there and I now have a Bundesrepublik passport, I still couldn't bear the thought of being within their borders."

"Don't worry," I said. "We'll fly."

I booked us a pair of seats on Air France to Paris, and six nights in a cheap one-star hotel on the Rue Gay Lussac in the Fifth Arrondissement.

"I have to tell you something," Petra said as we boarded the flight at Tegel Airport and she stared around the jet with something approaching wide-eyed wonder. "I've never been on a plane before."

She gripped my hand for most of the flight, staring out at the empty green fields of the country from which she had been exiled as we flew at the prescribed, bumpy 10,000 feet over the GDR. We knew that we had left their airspace as the plane banked steeply, achieving cruising altitude. For the next hour it was a smooth ride before our descent into Paris.

"It's mad, isn't it, thinking that there are even borders up here in the clouds," Petra said.

"We love drawing lines of demarcation," I said. "It's always been one of the great human preoccupations——marking our territory, telling others this is my turf and you can't cross into it."

"Or, worse yet, you can't leave it. Or if you do, you lose everything."

She lit up a cigarette and added:

"But listen to me sounding so bleak while on my way to Paris. I don't want to dwell on the impossible."

And she didn't again during our time in Paris. Those six days there were such heady, amorous ones. The little one-star hotel on the Rue Gay Lussac had a small double bed with a profoundly soft mattress. When we made love, the bed heaved and screeched like some wounded animal. The room was classic *Rive Gauche louche*: peeling floral wallpaper, a carpet with multiple cigarette burns, a wooden writing table on which someone had perhaps attempted to open a vein (it had a long deep crimson stain across its midsection), a shower in a corner of the room which was simply a small platform covered by an oily green curtain, a tiny shared toilet at the end of a badly lit hallway, an all-pervasive aroma of one hundred and fifty years of accumulated cigarette smoke, the endless soundtrack of fighting from the downstairs kitchen, a diminutive woman at the front desk whose style of makeup veered toward Kabuki theater, whose voice was a Gitanes-cured rasp, and who never had a smile for any of the guests.

We loved this little dive of a hotel. Especially because, once inside the thin door of our *petite chambre sans pretension*, we could not keep our hands off each other. There is something about a shabby hotel room——especially a shabby Paris hotel room——that seems to heighten need and desire.

Then there was Paris itself. Two days after our arrival Petra turned to me and said, "Let's move here . . . tomorrow."

We were sitting in a café on the Carrefour de l'Odeon in the Sixth, having just watched a new print of *The Big Sleep* at the Cinéma Action Christine nearby. It was a perfect day in early summer. We were drinking a serviceable and (for the Sixth Arrondissement) cheap glass of something Burgundy and red. Sharing cigarettes. Holding hands. Looking out at the pedestrian parade——the chic and the intellectually nerdish, the highly overdressed and the waiflike. The sense of urban life as stylized theater. The mutual realization that we were having one of those shared sublime moments because we were together, wildly in love, in this city, at this magical hour of early evening where the street was bathed in an Armagnac-like tint of receding light, and everything was just so damn perfect. So when Petra suggested we move here immediately, I countered with another thought:

"I'm all for that. But why don't we get married as well?"

She was caught off-guard by this proposal and took a minute or so to absorb it all. Then she said, in a voice as hushed as it was considered:

"I'd like that. I'd like that more than anything. It's just . . . are you sure, Thomas? Of course, I want to say 'yes' on the spot."

"Then do so."

"I just fear . . ."

"What?"

"I fear . . . letting you down."

"I could also let you down," I said.

"No, you couldn't. Or, at least, not like I could."

"But how?"

She suddenly stood up and said, "Give me a moment."

She disappeared into the café, heading for the toilets. As I waited for her to return, I fretted that I had overplayed my hand, that, given all she had gone through, this was too much too fast. But, damn it, I knew. Just as she had let me know repeatedly that she knew, too. Now my great fear was that part of her so understandably distrusted other people that the prospect of happiness with someone else was beyond her. As I always thought that it was beyond me, until I met Petra.

But when she returned to the table a few minutes later she was all smiles.

"I was just . . . overwhelmed. The idea that you want me as your wife . . ."

"More than anything."

"And I want you as my husband more than anything."

"Then what's stopping us?"

"Nothing, I suppose. But . . ."

"We're brilliant together. You want to live in Paris, we can live in Paris. You want to live in New York, we can live in New York——and as my wife you'll have immediate right of residence. You want a child, we can have a child. As I told you before, I want a child with you."

"You paint the most seductive pictures, Thomas."

"But not based on some skewed sense of reality."

"I know, I know. Okay then," she finally whispered.

"Okay then."

And we sat there looking at each other, absorbing the enormity of it all.

"I think this calls for champagne," I said.

"And the East German girl in me worries that it might break the budget."

"It won't. Even if it did . . ."

"You're right, you're right."

So we ordered a bottle of house champagne. When the waiter brought it over and I told him, exuberantly, "We've just gotten engaged!" he gave us both a small, sage nod and said one word:

"*Chapeau.*"

We toasted ourselves and drank the bottle of champagne. Somewhere between the second and third glass, I said that we should think about a trip to the States sometime soon.

"Will your father like me?" she asked.

"I've no doubt about that . . . though when I tell him we're engaged he will initially say something charming like, 'Giving up your freedom so young.'"

"Might he not have a point?"

"Not at all. And I only mentioned that to underscore the fact that my dad is a rather gruff customer. But once he meets you, he will envy me."

"What I said before——about wanting to move to Paris or New York tomorrow——I truly mean it. And even though I know 'tomorrow' really means a few months from now . . . please, Thomas, take me out of Berlin."

"With pleasure," I said.

Much of that night——as we moved on to dinner in a brasserie on the Rue des Écoles——we began to talk seriously about our future life together. Petra knew about my studio apartment in Manhattan——and I said that, if we moved back, we could easily camp there for a couple of months while we found something bigger.

"For around seven hundred dollars per month we could probably get two bedrooms up near Columbia University."

"Could we afford that?"

"I'd need to get one more book review or magazine article a month."

"But say I couldn't find any work?"

"You'll find work——teaching, translating. I bet you could talk your way into the German department of some private school, even find something at Columbia."

"But I have no advanced degrees."

"But you have been a professional translator for years."

"That doesn't mean I can teach."

"Why not?"

"You really are relentlessly optimistic."

"It's an optimism for us."

"I don't want to be dependent on you in New York."

"But say, five years from now, when you have a full-time post at some college or at the UN, and I can't get a book published . . ."

"That will never happen."

"It happens all the time in the wonderful world of letters. Two or three books into a career——bad sales, indifferent reviews——and suddenly nobody wants to know you anymore."

"But that is not you."

"How can you be so sure of that?"

"Because I read your book——and all the essays of yours I've translated . . ."

"*'You really are relentlessly optimistic.'*"

"Ouch."

"You take my point?"

"It's the old East German indoctrination kicking in. One should be optimistic about the future of revolutionary Communism. But when it comes to oneself . . ."

"You'll learn to be easier on yourself."

"Only when I finally get out of Berlin. Staying there has all been about being near Johannes. Now I realize that it's all futile. I've lost him forever."

"I think that's a very brave thing to admit."

"What? Accepting that there is no hope?"

"Yes, that is exactly what I mean."

We fell silent.

"Paris," she finally said. "It once seemed as remote as the far side of the moon."

Three days later——as we boarded the bus to Orly and the flight back to Berlin——Petra held on to my hand so tightly it felt as if she was in desperate need of ballast.

"You okay?" I asked.

"I don't want to go back."

"But it will only be for a couple of weeks."

"I know, I know. It's just . . ."

"We can expedite our exit by me booking an appointment with the US consul as soon as we're home and finding out what we have to do to get you a green card."

"How long do you think that will take?"

"I haven't a clue, as I haven't exactly had a string of foreign fiancées in the past."

"Let's see if they can get it done as soon as possible."

"You mean, before you change your mind?"

"I'll never do that."

"Nor will I. So there's nothing to worry about."

"I hope you're right."

Back in Berlin that afternoon we found Alaistair sitting alone in his studio, staring at the three canvases that had been preoccupying him for weeks. The depth of color, the edginess of their geometric conceits, the darkness visible within them, the way they worked as a triptych that invited you to contrast the azure tonalities that enveloped the viewer and made you ponder the infiniteness so inherent in the color blue. They were clearly finished and clearly remarkable.

"You're done?" I asked.

"As done as I can be," Alaistair said.

"Fantastic."

"That's one point of view. But maybe I'm just suffering a touch of the postpartum blues."

"They're brilliant, Alaistair."

"And the fucking London art vultures will write them off as 'Yves Klein Light,' not that there can be anything lighter than Yves-fucking-Klein and his fucking blue. And apologies, Petra, but I am usually like this when I cross the finish line."

"Thomas is right. They are wonderful."

"Well, considering they were done in the throes of withdrawal."

"People will see how astonishing they are," she said.

"Not the people who dictate taste."

"We got engaged in Paris," I suddenly said.

Alaistair genuinely looked thrown by the way I dropped this little tidbit of news.

"Let's have that again?" he said.

"We're getting married."

"So you've now said twice. But Mademoiselle is curiously silent on the issue."

"That's because Mademoiselle isn't as gregarious as Monsieur," she said with a smile.

"'Gregarious' being a synonym for 'American,'" Alaistair added.

"But as I love this American . . . ," Petra said.

"So, you confirm that what our gregarious friend says is true?"

"Absolutely true."

"Well then . . . somewhere around here, I think in the back of my fridge, there is a bottle of French fizz I have been saving for an event of note. Like this one."

"That's very kind of you," I said.

"Proper and right, given the momentousness of the occasion. Being a closet romantic, I must say that I do envy you both this, and only hope you won't bloody squander it."

The bottle of champagne turned into a lengthy and very boozy dinner at some local Italian joint, during which Alaistair turned to me when Petra stepped away to use the bathroom and said:

"What makes me happiest——and yes, this is the fucking drink talking——is the fact that you so wanted this. Needed this. That's not a reproach or a criticism. Just an observational truth. Because, for years, I was like you. Singular. Solitary. Not willing to let anyone come too close. Then I met the right man. And it was totally mutual. And if the bastard hadn't had the bad taste to die on me . . . The thing is, *mein Freund*: you've found her."

The next day I called the US consul and spoke with a surprisingly pleasant secretary with a flat, Midwestern accent who told me that, yes, if I was planning to marry a German woman and we were intending to settle in the States, it was best if I came by with her to meet one of the assistant consuls who could get the immigration wheels moving. Once we were legally married, as long as there were no snags, she should have her green card within a month tops.

"So if you want to expedite things," she said, "I'd get married as soon as possible!"

When I mentioned this to Petra that night, she laughed and said:

"We can ask Alaistair to officiate."

"I was thinking of asking him to be my witness."

"And mine, too, as there aren't exactly a horde of people I'm close to here."

"Then let's go to the registry office or whatever they call it here sometime next week," I said.

"I'll research all that tomorrow."

"We have the appointment with the consul at one fifteen. If you can make it down to the Ku'damm by then."

"I'll be there. As soon as the consul informs us my green card is cleared, I'm giving notice at work, if that is okay with you."

"Absolutely. And I'm calling the guy who's subletting my place in Manhattan tonight and telling him I'm back in a month. He might not like it——but four weeks' notice was the deal we agreed on both sides, so if all goes well, we'll be in New York just in time for August. Heat and humidity on a level you cannot imagine until experienced firsthand."

"I'll be free of this place and with you. So, believe me, the heat will be a minor detail."

The next afternoon I dropped by the main Kreuzberg post office and asked the woman at the switchboard to put a call through to a New York number which I supplied on a piece of paper. It was eight in the morning on the East Coast of the United States. My subtenant was a fact checker for *Newsweek* named Richard Rounder who had already published a story in *The New Yorker* and seemed to have checked into the creative deep freeze since then. Unusually for a writer, he was an early riser, so he was up when I called. And he was surprisingly cool about vacating the apartment in a month, as he had just been accepted for a three-month residency at the Yadoo arts colony and would be heading there in early September.

The US consul was a woman in her late thirties named Madeleine Abbott. She wore a severe civil service gray suit and was pleasant in an administrative sort of way. Petra had come to this meeting dressed soberly in a white blouse and a black skirt that stopped just above the knee. She seemed genuinely nervous when we met in front of the main entrance of the US Consulate in a wealthy suburban area called Zehlendorf.

"Not having second thoughts?" I asked after kissing her hello.

"I always get edgy whenever I have to deal with bureaucracy. They have such control over you."

"This will be very straightforward."

"I hope you're right."

Actually the meeting was exceptionally businesslike. When I told the consul we were getting married, she offered perfunctory congratulations, then pulled out assorted forms that needed filling out. She asked Petra about her background. When she mentioned that she had been expelled from the GDR last year, the consul's pen paused for a moment and she looked at her with interest.

"Were you expelled for political reasons?" she asked.

"That's right."

"You will need to explain that on the application form. In fact, I would suggest that you write a statement explaining the details of your expulsion, not that this will count against you when the case is reviewed by the Department of State in Washington. On the contrary. But you must be very transparent about the whys and wherefores of your case. Are you okay with that?"

Petra nodded, but I could see that her anxiety level had just jumped a notch or two.

The consul then took down assorted details, studying both our passports, asking us both assorted questions about our professions, our parents' birthplaces, any criminal convictions.

"I was never convicted of anything," Petra said. "But I was held in prison for several weeks in the GDR because my then-husband was engaged in political activity."

"Activity against the Communist Party?"

"That's right."

"And you were arrested in the wake of his activity?"

"I think it's called guilt by association."

"Is your husband is still in prison?"

"He is no longer my husband because he died in prison more than a year ago."

"I'm sorry to hear that. As I said earlier, I suggest you include all this information in the statement you will attach with your application form. One question for you both. How long have you known each other?"

"Six months," I said, staring directly at her.

"I don't think that should present a problem, as I will note in my letter to State that you met in Berlin. Had you met Miss Dussmann while she was visiting the US, the fact that you are getting married after such a short amount of time might lead the people in charge into questioning whether this was a marriage of convenience. Of course, they still might raise a few questions about that. But the very fact that you are, if I am not being presumptuous, planning to get married before arriving in the United States . . ."

"Absolutely," I said.

"Well, I naturally cannot give you one hundred percent assurance that your application will be approved. But unless anything untoward is found in your background, I sense it will all be rather straightforward. Of course, the sooner you get your application back to me the sooner it will be processed."

And she wished us both well.

Outside Petra immediately lit up a cigarette and seemed to be in the throes of a near-anxiety attack. Shaking her head rapidly, her shoulders scrunched up against her head, all *sturm und drang*, so evidently unnerved by it all.

"My love," I said, trying to take her in my arms. "What's wrong?"

"They're going to find a reason to turn me down," she said.

"That's not what she said."

"But that's what these people do all the time. They work out an excuse to ruin your life."

"Maybe in the GDR. But in the States . . ."

"They'll think I'm a Communist."

"No, they won't. And here's why: because those people who debriefed you when you were expelled have an extensive file on you. What did that file say? Everything that you told them——and all the other details they had on your case, including the way that your son was taken away from you. Trust me, these people are Cold Warriors. Given how you were treated by the other side and the fact that you are marrying an American . . ."

"Sorry, sorry. I just am so frightened of something going wrong now. Right when everything seems so happy, so possible, when there is finally a future for me, for us."

"Nothing, *nothing*, will go wrong. The consul was pretty damn clear about that. Let's look at the absolutely worst-case scenario. If they found some sort of stupid technicality not to grant you a green card, we could still get married. As I would then be the husband of a European national we could easily get me a *carte de séjour* for France in a nanosecond. So we'd do Paris and appeal like hell to get you into the States. But this simply isn't going to happen. If I may say so, I think you are understandably haunted by what they did to you over there."

"You're right, you're right. I'm just being absurd."

"No, you're just reacting to bureaucracy in the same way that some-one who has been butchered by a dentist reacts when told that he has to get another tooth filled."

"Thank you, thank you," she whispered, putting her arms around me.

Petra had to return to work that afternoon. I stopped by the Café Istanbul and found I had an "urgent" message from Pawel. I rang him. He answered immediately.

"Is this 'good urgent' or 'bad urgent'?" I asked.

"Always the catastrophizer," he said. "Actually it's a plum assignment for you, but one I'd prefer not to discuss on the telephone. I am looking for an excuse to duck out for a late afternoon beer, as I am working late tonight. So you can be my excuse for the beer. Do you know that café around the corner from the station? Could you be there in forty-five minutes?"

"How plum an assignment?"

"Very prestigious——and I'll even make it lucrative again. Forty-five minutes."

And the line went dead.

Naturally I was intrigued. Naturally I continued to be amazed at Pawel's ability to pretend that our relationship had always been a most collegial one.

Even when he was being atrocious, the man maintained the most calm of outward expressions. Today was no different. A fast greeting, two beers ordered, and he got right down to business.

"What I am about to tell you is highly classified. Last week two very leading East German dancers——Hans and Heidi Braun, they're brother and sister——managed to get themselves smuggled out of their fair city by being loaded into two duffel bags that were part of an entire armory of gear that had been brought into the GDR by a Bundesrepublik dance troupe. The directors of this troupe have impeccable socialist credentials, and were therefore granted permission to tour the Workers' Paradise. However, it seems that one of the directors fell in love with Hans. The fact that Hans had already been harassed over there repeatedly for being such a high-profile dancer and gay . . . well, the GDR authorities are now furious and embarrassed that this dancer and his sister were smuggled out in duffel bags piled up among all the scenery and gear of this company from Freiburg. Then there's the whole 'homosexual persecution' dimension to the story——which will also have the GDR stooges squirming. And Hans Braun is something of a garrulous character who just loves to talk. So far he's still here in West Berlin with his sister. He insisted that she be brought along. They are still being debriefed. So we'd like you to be the one who first interviews them. It was Wellmann's idea, as you fit the bill perfectly: American, fluent in German, and a New Yorker who, I hope, knows his dance."

"I grew up with Ballanchine and the New York City Ballet."

"That's what we reckoned. And that's perfect, as it turns out that Hans Braun has been offered a place at the City Ballet. Of course, Hans's lover wants him in his company in Freiburg. But New York . . . how can he say no? Anyway, can you get here at five tomorrow? We'll have a car arranged to take you to the place where they're being put up. You'll do the interview and then we'll get it all transcribed and back to you on Sunday, as you'll need to start making some suggested cuts——as I will simultaneously do——and also write a spoken introduction, which we'll then record on Monday morning. So you will have a long weekend. But I will pay you fifteen hundred deutsche marks, if that is acceptable."

"Most acceptable."

"The plan is to go public with their defection exactly a week from now——and ruin the weekend of the GDR propaganda people. Of course, not a word about this to anyone."

Petra didn't get home until well after eight that night.

"Bloody Pawel kept me late on some translation he said was absolutely urgent," she said. "Then I got a summons to Herr Wellmann's office, asking me if I could accompany him to Hamburg this weekend. All very last minute, but there's a big Radio Liberty conference there and the usual translator he brings along on these things, Frau Koenig, is down with a very bad flu. He needs someone who can do a simultaneous translation of the speech he's giving there. And though Hamburg says they can supply someone, he's very picky about such things. Personally, I think his German is more than adequate, but he feels that, though he can hold his own conversationally, the idea of talking for an hour *auf Deutsch* truly worries him. As such, he was very emphatic that I travel with him. Believe me, I don't want to go."

"Then don't. You'll be leaving that job pretty soon anyway."

"I owe Wellmann this favor. He's been incredibly kind and decent to me."

"Then you have to go. But, as it turns out, I am going to have something of a busy weekend. Ever hear of Hans and Heidi Braun?"

"The ballet dancers?"

"You know them?"

"Everyone in the GDR knows them. They're the brother and sister stars of the Berlin State Ballet. When did they get out?"

"Just a few days ago."

"But I've read or heard nothing about it."

"I gather they're being very much debriefed, as you were. And the authorities here don't want to release anything about their defection until they're ready to go public with it, which I don't think will be until the end of next week. But guess who's been given the job of doing the first interview with them?"

Then I told her all about how I would be brought to them "at an undisclosed location" late tomorrow afternoon and would have to work on the transcript of the interview over the weekend.

"And Pawel handed you this?"

"It was Herr Wellmann via Pawel."

"Well, it's a fantastic coup. You say you'll have the transcripts Sunday?"

"That's right."

"That will make interesting reading. And if you wouldn't mind a few suggested questions you might want to pose to Hans . . ."

With that, Petra gave me a long list of queries, telling me I should ask them about the alleged special camps to which gifted young dancers were shipped at the age of nine onward, in which they were groomed to become "immaculate state artists." Then there was the gay bar scene in East Berlin——of which Hans Braun was undoubtedly an habitué——and which was frequently raided by the police. I took extensive notes as she talked, always impressed at the angry vehemence that took over her voice whenever she spoke of the inequities of life over there.

"I so wish I could be at home all weekend to hear about it all," she said.

"You will get a blow-by-blow account Sunday night," I said. "I'll even let you see the transcript."

"Pawel will kill you."

"Pawel will never know."

"That's the truth."

"I'll miss you every minute you're away."

"And I will be here, back in your arms, by early afternoon Sunday."

On the morning that she left, the alarm went off at eight. Before I was even able to reach for the button to shut the damn thing off Petra was all over me, pulling me immediately inside her, making love with such vehemence and need, as if we were about to be separated for months.

"I don't want to go," she said afterward.

"Then don't. I mean, what's the worst that can happen? He fires you. But since you're about to give notice . . ."

"And then, when I am in the States with you and a future employer asks him for a reference, he'll say I'm no good."

"It looks like you're convincing yourself that you have to go."

"You're right. I am."

"So make your boss happy and translate him in Hamburg. Then hurry back to me. And have you checked out where we might get married next week?"

"The Rathaus in Kreuzberg does marriages. They just need three days' notice."

"So if we were to stop by together on Monday morning, we could set a date for Friday."

Petra bit down on her lip, her eyes brimming.

"You're too wonderful, Thomas."

"Is that a 'yes' then?"

She nodded, then dried her eyes and said:

"I will always love you. Forever."

An hour later——after seeing Petra off out the door with a long kiss good-bye——I threw on some clothes and headed out to the Café Istanbul for breakfast. Her departure had left me feeling empty and a little anxious, perhaps because it was our first time apart. Even though I was telling myself she'd be back in just over forty-eight hours, there was that low-lying fear that always accompanies love: the fear of it all being taken away from you.

But the day was bright and clear. I kept replaying the way Petra told me, when she broke off the endless kiss in the doorway of the apartment, "I will marry you next week because I so want to be your wife."

I had a slow morning at home. After a run and a few hours at the desk, I showed up at Radio Liberty, as requested, at five p.m. When Pawel met me at reception, he was accompanied by a man I'd never met before. He was borderline short——around five foot seven——stocky, but with the build of a onetime linebacker now edging into fleshiness in midlife but still maintaining the gruff demeanor of a defensive lineman who had been schooled to maul the opposition. Or at least that's what popped into my head the moment I was introduced to this gentleman, taking in his crew cut, the ultraconservative blue pinstripe suit, the button-down blue shirt and rep tie, the small American flag in the buttonhole of his left lapel. Then there was the way he smiled at me with a hint of superiority and lightly veiled contempt. Who was this guy?

"I want you to meet a great fan of yours," Pawel said. "Walter Bubriski."

"A fellow Pole?" I asked.

"In name only," Bubriski said in an accent redolent of the empty lowlands of the Midwest.

"Walter is number two here at the USIA."

"I presume you've heard of us?" Bubriski asked me.

Of course, I remembered what Wellmann told me when he first hired me as a Radio Liberty contributor: if I was ever to encounter someone who said he worked for the USIA, I should immediately assume he was a member of intelligence services. Because everyone knew that the USIA was, by and large, a front for the Central Intelligence Agency. And this Bubriski guy certainly looked like a spook.

"Yes, I know all about the USIA," I said in a deliberately neutral voice.

"Then you also know that we take a great interest in the output of Radio Liberty and its contributors. I have to say that I have been most impressed by your contributions to the service."

"Thank you."

"We're very pleased that you're the guy doing the first interview with the Brauns. But things are running a bit behind schedule, so we now have an hour or so to kill before going up to see them. And since I like to get to know our contributors, how about you letting me buy you a beer?"

"You coming along?" I asked Pawel.

"I have to get something finished before the weekend."

I immediately wondered if, from the outset, Pawel knew the interview with the two dancers wouldn't be until after six, but called me in here early because Mr. Spook wanted to meet me. The reason he wanted to meet me, no doubt, was that he objected to something I had written and had decided to give me a directive about my content. Or maybe he just wanted to augment the file they had on everyone who contributed here and decided to sound out my sociopolitical thoughts over a couple of drinks.

As much as I wanted to turn tail and tell him I wasn't in the mood for such a conversation——that I would come back here at six to head off to the interview——the writer with a book to write simultaneously thought: *but this could be a fantastic incident on which to report . . . the moment when my own side——in true Cold War style——decided to investigate where my true loyalties lay.*

"I'm happy to have a beer with a fan," I said. "Especially if the fan is paying."

"You said he was a real New Yorker," Bubriski told Pawel.

"Where are you from, sir?" I asked.

"Muncie, Indiana. That part of the world which you people back east call 'the flyover states.'"

Oh, this was going to be a very interesting conversation.

The bar to which we adjourned was located just across the street from Radio Liberty. It was your classic Berlin *Bierstube*. Simple, unadorned, with no customers and a booth in a far corner to which Bubriski directed us, making me immediately think: so this is where he always has these "talks."

The waitress came by and we both ordered Hefeweizen. As we waited for them to arrive, I pulled out my tobacco pouch and cigarette papers.

"That makes sense," Bubriski said.

"What makes sense?"

"The fact that you roll your own."

"And why does it 'make sense,' sir?"

"It just fits in with the image I've been building up of you."

"Why have you been 'building up' an image of me?"

"Because, as our Polish friend said before, I'm a big fan of yours."

The drinks arrived. As soon as the waitress had returned to the bar, he hoisted his and took a long sip. There was to be no clinking of glasses between us. I finished rolling up my cigarette and lit it, wondering what was coming next.

"So you've read my book?" I asked.

"Not only that. Like any fanatical reader I've found out so much about my newfound favorite writer."

I noted the irony that underscored those last two words. I took a sip of my beer. I asked:

"And what have you found out?"

"Lots. Such as his unhappy Manhattan childhood. The mother who was the frustrated *hausfrau* and always resented his presence in her life. The distant father who always considered his son a little too artsy. The way this kid spent much of his adolescence thinking of himself as some Parisian intellectual in the making. And when he got into that oh-so-elite eastern college up in Maine, how he was considered an uppity New York smarty-pants, marching around campus in his trench coat with his smelly French cigarettes, talking Proust and Truffaut and Robbe-Grillet . . ."

"Your knowledge of twentieth-century French culture is impressive."

"You mean, for a guy from Muncie, Indiana, who went to Ohio State?"

"I never said that."

"Yeah, but it's there in the way you regard me. I've dealt with types like you my entire life. All those guys and gals in DC with their New England noblesse oblige and their big-deal diplomacy degrees from Woodrow Wilson and Fletcher and Georgetown."

"I'm not from New England, and I never went to Princeton."

"But you applied to Princeton, didn't you?"

I felt a shudder run through me. This man was an operative, and one who had subjected my life to extreme scrutiny.

"What's the point of all this, besides letting me know you know a great deal about me?"

"Hey, as I said before, I'm just displaying my keen interest in the life and times of my favorite writer. And one who, in his Egypt book, refers to the Voice of America as 'middling propaganda.' A nice turn of phrase. The way you denude its mission——and the fact that, like the broadcasting system which has helped pay your bills in that apartment you share with that junkie faggot in Kreuzberg . . ."

"This conversation is finished," I said, stubbing out my cigarette.

"You mean, you can't handle a little banter?"

"What I can't handle is the sort of shit you peddle."

"Ever heard of radar?"

"What?" I asked, thrown by this conversational change of direction.

"Radar. Ever heard of it?"

"Of course, I've heard of it. But what does this have to do with——"

"Know how radar works?"

"What's the point of this?"

"It's just a 'general knowledge' question——and one which a smart guy like you must know."

"I'm leaving."

"Just hear me out. Radar. Do you understand its basic principle?"

"Something to do with an electromagnetic field, right?"

"My, my, they did teach you well at the elite eastern college of yours——even if you never took a science course there. Radar is an acronym created by the US Navy in 1940: Radio Detection and Ranging. But it was the Brits who perfected it once the Krauts starting bombing the shit out of them. What they discovered——and I want you, in that writerly way of yours, to consider the subtext of what I am about to tell you——is that radar works when a magnetic field, almost like a field of attraction, is set up between two objects. One object then sends out a signal to another object in the distance. When that signal hits the other object, what is transmitted back is not the object itself. Rather, it's the image of that object."

"Very interesting. I still don't see the point of this little scientific lecture."

"You don't?" he said, all smiles. "You really don't?"

"Not at all."

"Now that surprises me, Mr. Nesbitt. Because as a man profoundly in love with a woman, so profoundly in love with said woman that the happy couple have approached the US consul in this great city to inform the authorities that they are planning to marry . . . well, you should really think long and hard about radar and its 'subtextual meanings.' I mean, my first marriage collapsed after ten years and two kids. I fell in love at the same stupid age as yourself. But in the wake of the divorce a decade later, what I realized was that, from the outset, I wasn't looking at who this woman really was. Rather, what I was seeing was the image of this woman that I had projected onto her amidst all that magnetic headiness that comes with thinking you're in love."

"I've had enough of this," I said, standing up.

"You still don't get it, do you?"

"Get what? Besides the fact that you have so little to do here——and you people are so obsessed with knowing everything about everyone who even tangentially comes into your field of vision——that you have to go through their lives with the proverbial fine-tooth comb."

"You're a man in love, Thomas."

"My, my, what brilliant intelligence-gathering operations you run."

"But the thing is, you're in love with an image. An image that, in your adolescent romantic way, you've projected upon . . ."

"How dare you."

"How dare I?" he said with a smile. "I *dare* because I *know*."

"Know what?"

He paused and took a long sip of his beer. Then, fixing his cold gaze directly on me, he said:

"I know that Petra Dussmann is an agent of the Stasi."

TEN

FOR A MOMENT or two afterward, I experienced what could only be described as complete manic disorientation. I was in shock. But it was the shock that accompanies disbelief, a refusal to accept the news that had landed on me like a kick to the stomach.

"You asshole," I hissed at Bubriski. "You lying, sadistic asshole."

His smile grew wider. The smile of a chess player who has just made a sudden Black Knight move and checkmated you before you could even see what was coming.

"I figured you'd react this way," he said. "It doesn't surprise me. Because you're in stage one of Kübler-Ross's five stages of grief——and I bet you never expected some Ohio Stater to know cerebral shit like that. But I'm sure you remember——from the one sociology course you took at that fancy eastern school of yours——that stage one of grief is denial. That's what you're dealing with right now: the belief that what I've just told you is nothing more than a malicious falsehood designed to mess up your afternoon and generally destabilize you."

I shouted back:

"They taught you this crap at spy school, right? How to put 'the subject' in a position of psychological disadvantage. Undermine their belief in the most important thing in their life."

"And Frau Dussmann is certainly that. Especially given the way you never received much in the way of love from your two parents and couldn't exactly commit to that lovely willowy thing from Juilliard."

"I've had enough . . ." I said, standing up.

"Sit down," he ordered.

"Don't go fucking telling me . . ."

"I could have your passport stripped off you tomorrow," he said in an even, level voice. "I could have you deported back to the United

States and held in a detention center indefinitely. I could have your name put on the blacklist of every Western European country. And the reason I could wreak such havoc with your life, your *career* as a roaming man of the world, is that you have been linked with an enemy agent. You can hire an entire truckload of lefty ACLU lawyers and they still won't be able to get you traveling again——which, let's face it, is what you live to do——because you will be classified a major security risk. So sit down *now* before I get really pissed and make good on my threat."

I sat down.

"Smart guy," Bubriski said.

I felt my hands shaking. Bubriski saw that. He reached into his jacket pocket and tossed a packet of Old Golds onto the table.

"Here, have a proper smoke——not one of those backpack specials you call a cigarette."

I reached for the packet, but my hands kept shaking.

"*Fraulein,*" Bubriski shouted at the waitress. "*Zwei Schnaps. Wir Möchten Doppelte.*"

Two double schnapps duly arrived. I managed to fish a cigarette out of the packet and accepted a light from Bubriski's outstretched Zippo.

"Get that into you," he said, pointing to the schnapps. I lifted the little shot glass and tossed it back, wincing as it went down but welcoming its immediate balming effect.

"Did that help?" he asked.

I nodded.

"Now, just to get one thing clear," he said. "I don't think you're in cahoots with this woman. If anything, I consider you nothing more than an innocent dupe——and your reaction just now reinforces my opinion. But that doesn't mean you aren't tainted by your association with Frau Dussmann——especially since, from what we can gather, you carried back microfilm in those photographs you collected on her behalf from her friend Judit."

"They were pictures of her son."

"That they were. And how many of them has she displayed to you?"

"I don't know . . . ten, twelve."

"And how many did you bring back?"

"Maybe twenty."

"So where are the others?"

"I don't know."

"I'll tell you where they are. They are with her boss over here——a Stasi man named Helmut Haechen. Herr Haechen has been on our radar for the past two years——as he has been running three women agents in West Berlin, one of whom happens to be Petra Dussmann. And he also has been sleeping with Frau Dussmann since she was allegedly 'expelled' from the GDR just over a year ago."

I shut my eyes, wanting to black out the world.

"Let me guess: you're telling yourself right now, 'I can't believe that . . . because she told me again and again that I was the love of her life.' She did tell you that, didn't she?"

"How do you know that?"

"The same way I know about the one and only sociology course you took at college, and the fact that your dad smokes Old Golds. It's our business to know lots. And we do know lots about you."

"I need proof that Petra . . ."

"Ah yes, why believe a representative of his own government when it comes to matters of the heart and the betrayal of trust? What you need is something factual, if not downright empirical. All right then. Can you remember the night you first had dinner with Frau Dussmann, the night when she first stayed at your apartment? It was January twenty-third, ja?"

"How did you know that?" I asked, sounding shocked.

Bubriski just shrugged and said:

"Can you confirm it was January twenty-seventh when you had that first dinner with Frau Dussmann?"

I nodded.

"And can you confirm that halfway through the dinner, she raced off into the night without any apparent reason?"

"Were you watching us?"

"We were watching her. You just happened to be there. Why did she run off in the middle of dinner?"

"She gave no reason. She just got all emotional and . . ."

"She was checking in with her controller, Herr Haechen."

"Bullshit."

"Ah yes, the man needs proof."

He reached for the attaché case by his chair, hoisted it onto the table, and flipped it open, bringing out a hefty manila file. Then, after closing the case, he flipped open the file.

"Proof the man wants," he said, pulling out a photograph, "proof the man gets."

He pushed two grainy eight-by-ten black-and-white photographs toward me. The first showed Petra hurrying out of the restaurant where we had that first dinner——and the time signature imprinted on the left-hand corner indicated that it was on the date in question at 21:22. The next shot showed her entering a hotel at 21:51.

"The hotel was up near Tegel Airport," Bubriski said. "She had to run off because she had a liaison with this man."

He tossed another grainy photograph in front of me, showing a stocky man leaving the hotel at 22:41. It was hard to see his face, though I did note that he had a goatee.

"So she was entering a hotel," I said, "and this man exited the same hotel sometime later. That doesn't mean she was seeing him there."

"Then why did she leave your dinner so abruptly? And when she did leave, did she inform you she was heading to a sleazy hotel on the other side of town?"

I shook my head.

"The man at the hotel was Helmut Haechen. As to why she ran out of the restaurant . . . we don't read minds, Thomas. Or, at least, not yet. And yes, that was my attempt at a bad joke. So all I can do is speculate. Maybe she had to get clearance from Haechen to sleep with you. Maybe it was all part of an elaborate ploy to make her seem troubled and complex and, as such, all the more desirable. That's my theory. They decided to reel you in by letting you sense that she had some hidden tragedy in her life. Then, when she realized that she had you, she sent you across the border to collect the all-important photographs of her lost son, on which was embedded microfilm containing something rather crucial for Haechen's attention."

"But her son was taken away from her."

"She gave the kid up for adoption at birth."

"That I can't believe. The pain she expressed when talking about him——"

"The man needs more proof."

The file was flipped open again. He handed me a photocopy of a document which, judging from its slightly blurred imagery, might have been originally photographed. It was an official document from the *Deutsche Agentur für das Wohl das Kinder*——the State Agency for Child Welfare in the GDR. The names of the child, the father, and the mother were clearly visible. The word *Tote* (Dead) in brackets next to Jurgen's name. In the semiblurred but still visible legal text below I read that the undersigned, Petra Alma Dussmann, was hereby giving her son, Johannes, up for legal adoption; that she waived all further legal rights over this child; that she was signing this document without coercion or any outside pressure, and was allowing her child to be adopted out of her own free will and in the best interests of the child. The document was dated 6 May 1982.

"We have an operative over there who, at great personal risk, managed to photograph this document for us. Let me guess what you're now thinking. What mother agrees to have her child adopted at a year old? A mother who has been informing on her mad husband to the Stasi for years."

"That I cannot believe."

"More proof needed," he said, digging around in the file. He handed me another grainy photographed document. It was from the MfS—— Ministerium für Staatssicherheit: the Ministry for State Security, better known as the Stasi. There was Petra's photograph, her date of birth, home address, and two telling words:

Spitzelaffäre seit . . . Informer since. And the date: 20 January 1981. She must have been pregnant with Johannes.

"The operative who scored us this document, along with dozens more, is now doing twenty years' hard labor for his pains. They play rough over there. Then again, so do we. But, as you can see, she was working for them for several years before she crossed over. What was the story she gave you about Johannes?"

"Could I have another schnapps, please?"

"After you answer the question."

"She told me that Johannes was taken away from her because her husband went mad, tried to make contact with American agents, and screamed at the minister for culture before peeing on him."

"All true——except that, as you see from that earlier document, she voluntarily gave up Johannes for adoption. As for all her crocodile tears to you about having the kid taken away, my theory is a simple one: the Stasi offered her an opportunity for promotion if she would go west and spy for them. They gave her the perfect cover: the unjustly persecuted spouse of a dissident whose son was forcibly wrenched from her hands by the heinous, demonic forces of the Ministerium für Staatssicherheit. They had her whisked away from her life in Prenzlauer Berg for months before trading her over to our side as a victimized innocent. We appeared to buy it, whereas the truth was we were certain from the outset that she was being 'run' by Herr Haechen. We directed her into the job at Radio Liberty to let her seem to have a big score. The people we have there, they left out certain 'allegedly' classified documents as bait——which she later photographed. And if you'd like proof of that . . ."

He was about to reach into the file for another photograph. I waved it away. I knew it would confirm what he was alleging. I knew that it would just have the effect of even more acid dropped into a pair of eyes that had been forced wide-open by all this terrible visual evidence.

"Well, do you want to have a proper look at the man she's been fucking all this time?"

"Not particularly."

"I insist," he said, pulling out a new photograph from the file and tossing it in front of me like a croupier dealing a card that he knows is going to cost a player big.

The image that landed in front of me was of the same man seen in the earlier photograph, only this time the image was far too crisp and vivid. Helmut Haechen was a diminutive, bloated man with greased-back black hair, thick black glasses, a terrible goatee, bad teeth, and a complexion that was oleaginous.

"Now I could definitely lose twenty pounds," Bubriski said. "And I wouldn't call myself a pretty boy. But this thug . . . and that's the only word to describe this vicious little bastard . . . well, 'physically repulsive' are the two words that come to mind when I have to stare at his picture. This is the man whom your beloved started to sleep with around a month after she was 'settled' by us in her room in Kreuzberg and her job at Radio Liberty. All during your 'romance,' she saw Haechen at least twice a week——and his debriefings of her always involved sex. I can't imagine that Frau Dussmann enjoyed having this garden gnome inside of her."

"Please stop that."

"I'm just imagining what it must be like for you to discover that you had to share her with that grotesque——"

"You've made your damn point."

"Now, as I was hinting before, we do need to give Frau Dussmann a little bit of sympathy here. Because when you are being run by a Stasi agent——and you have all the benefits of life in the West——the deal is: you have to fuck him on a regular basis. Which is what she was doing."

He dug into the file and pulled out a written report, scanning it as he spoke.

"According to our surveillance team, they fucked twice a week. They never met at his apartment, by the way. He always organized a room in some cheap hotel, usually near the Hauptbahnhof, but he changed the location all the time. I doubt she thought she was being observed, given how she'd been made to feel by our people from the outset that she was a heroine. But Haechen was very careful about changing U-Bahn stations, dashing out and jumping into taxis just to make certain he wasn't being followed. He did manage to lose us occasionally——but the rest of the time . . ."

He dealt me photograph after photograph——all time-signaled in the corner——of Haechen entering some sleazy hotel and Petra following seven to ten minutes later.

"Where do you think your beloved is right now?" he asked.

"En route to Hamburg as a last-minute translator for Mr. Wellmann."

"That was her story, huh?"

"And you knew she was about to head out of town with her puppeteer."

"Nice turn of phrase, Thomas. I might steal that."

"So you got Pawel to call me in. I bet it's Pawel who has been leaving out bogus classified documents for her to copy, right? I mean, he's the sort of opportunistic shit who probably thought being your lackey was the way up the propagandistic ladder. What's his payoff for his services rendered going to be? A green card?"

"You are so way out of line, mister. But, like I said before, you're in the 'denial' phase right now. You're thinking: *She had to have been set up. There were bad people leaving classified documents around, just tempting her to photograph them. And, of course, she so loved me——and fucked me so passionately.* I bet she said you were the man she always dreamed about, but thought she'd never find. When you talked about marriage, children, the life together in New York that you were about to start next month——"

"Shut up," I hissed.

"The truth is an uncomfortable conundrum, is it not? I mean, we never taped your conversations. But you don't have to be a clever writer like yourself to imagine the sort of intimate postcoital dialogues you had together. Because we've all been there, chum. '*I've never felt this way before . . . the passion we have will never ebb . . . I will always be there for you . . . You are the one. The only one. I trust you with my life.*'"

I put my head in my hands, wanting him to stop, yet also perversely wanting him to continue berating me for my stupidity, my naïveté, for the love that I so craved and which I had thought I had found. And now . . . now . . . even if only part of what this bastard was telling me was correct . . . and he had so much terrible, overwhelming proof in that fucking file of his . . . I couldn't sidestep the fact that he was speaking a terrible truth: I had been deeply and profoundly duped. Even if part of her really did feel the things she had articulated to me.

Oh please. She sent you across the border on a mercy mission for the photographs she craved of her lost son. And now you've seen proof that she willingly gave up the child for adoption while also getting you to unknowingly smuggle out microfilm for that repulsive pig whom she was sneaking off to service twice a week, while telling you that she had never known love before you walked into her life.

"Evidently all those sentiments I just expressed——those emphatic expressions of love and devotion——ring true," he said. "As I said earlier, you were a man in love. And she wanted to feed that desperate need of yours to be loved. Because she knew that once she gave you the image of that love you never received before, you'd walk over hot coals for her. Radar, my friend. It all comes back to *radar*. She and her handler worked you out so quickly. *Give him the image of love, but also make it hard to win. Play up the idea that you are a woman who can't fully commit because she has been so damaged by the monolith of a Communist state. Let him in on your tragic secret. Talk eternal devotion* and marriage. And then get the unsuspecting errand boy to collect and carry documents across a foreign border for you."

"And you have no idea what might have been contained on those photographs?" I asked.

"Not a chance. Herr Haechen is a clever operator. He's either burnt the evidence or so carefully hidden it all that we'll never know what level of espionage those microfilms revealed."

"And the way I was treated on the GDR side of Checkpoint Charlie upon my return?"

"Oh yes, I heard you were detained there for a couple of hours."

"Your sources are impeccable. And do you think——knowing what you know——that this semi-arrest was designed to . . ."

". . . make you believe that you were in jeopardy because you visited Frau Judit Fleischmann, a discredited Stasi informer? Absolutely. You came back from this experience rather shaken, didn't you? But a little proud about having been held for several hours by the forces of a police state, yet having still managed to deliver the snapshots of the child seized from Frau Dussmann's arms."

"So they did stage that all for me?" I said, cutting him off. I could see Bubriski smile the smile of a psychological grandmaster who knew that he'd just "turned" somebody.

"I can't one hundred percent confirm that, but yes, I do feel that the detention was a final theatrical flourish to make you think that you had just been in your very own Cold War thriller. Like I'm certain you were followed from the moment you stepped into East Berlin, again just to heighten the drama of the situation. Had we not finally decided to call time on Herr Haechen and his band of female operatives, I've no doubt that before you and your beloved went to New York, she would have asked you to make one more foray to the other side and collect more souvenirs of Johannes for her. I bet she would have told you about another friend who had all the dolls she once bought for him——and back you would have come with a teddy bear stuffed with more microfilm. One aspect to this story does intrigue me: What are the ulterior motives of Herr Haechen in allowing her to move with you to the States? Might they have considered her useful over there to them? Perhaps finding her some high-level translating job at the UN? Or was this all an elaborate setup?"

"A setup for what?"

"We've gathered, from our people in the GDR, that Haechen's superiors aren't happy with the level of intelligence he's been feeding them through his operatives, that he needs a big score. We need to catch Haechen red-handed to both interrogate him and use him as a bargaining chip for three of our own people——including the man doing twenty years' hard labor——whom we want to get out of assorted GDR prisons. The problem is, we sense that Haechen and your beloved have started to wonder if our man at Radio Liberty is feeding them bogus documents. What we need to do is catch her actually photographing a classified item."

"But you could have probably done that many times over the last year."

"True, but we didn't want to arrest her. Because we wanted to create the illusion that she and Haechen were getting away with their little espionage operations, as we also wanted to see their so-called game plan. Now we have come to the conclusion that they are both, at best, lower-echelon operatives but useful to us under arrest for all the reasons I just explained. The thing is, we don't want a public scene at Radio Liberty when it comes to arresting her. Whereas if we were to stage the arrest at your apartment——"

"No damn way."

"Hear me out, Thomas. I know there is a part of you that is still refusing to believe that all this about Frau Dussmann is possible. It's understandable, given how much you have invested in this relationship and the profound trust you placed in her. Everything that I told you, all the evidence that I have presented to you, must be difficult to absorb. Like anyone who's been told the person they thought to be the center of their existence is a fraud——"

"Could you please spare me the fucking editorializing?"

"You still don't trust what I'm telling you, do you?"

"Proof is always flexible, especially in the hands of people like you."

"Very elegantly put and, yes, quite true. We share with 'the other side' the capability of bending the truth to suit our purposes. But how am I bending anything here?"

"She could have just been meeting this man for debriefings," I said.

"Good point," he said, all too brightly and with the sort of ironic undercurrent that a teacher might bestow on a pupil who has made a particularly naïve comment. "But we can show you photos——taken from a distance, but still pretty damn clear——of the two of them in bed together. Taken as recently as three weeks ago. Feel like a peep?"

He flipped open the file again, thumbing his way through the eight-by-tens.

"You really have got me checkmated, don't you?"

"And why do you say that?"

"Because if I offer up any hypothetical alternative to the reality you are presenting me . . ."

". . . we have visual veracity on our side? All right, say she was just going to meet Haechen in those crummy hotel rooms for debriefings. The fact remains: she's the agent of a totalitarian regime, and she tricked you into thinking——"

"I know what I thought. I know what was said between us. I know . . ."

I fell silent. A new double shot of schnapps arrived. I downed it. I thought: *just get up and walk out the door and don't come back. Go home. Pack everything up. Get the last train out of town . . . only that would probably be the night train to Hamburg, the city where she is allegedly shacked up with the troll who has been running her life for more than a year.*

"I need proof that she isn't in Hamburg translating for Wellmann," I said.

"Easily arranged," Bubriski said. "Herr Wellmann is taking his wife to hear the Berliner Philharmoniker tonight. You're quite the classical music nut, aren't you? So you'll approve of the fact that it's that Italian guy, Abbado, conducting Mendelssohn and Schubert. Given that we are rather cultured people at the USIA, I happen to have a spare ticket for the concert. The seat is just two rows back from where Wellmann will be sitting. So if you want proof . . . ?"

He reached into his pocket and slid a Berliner Philharmoniker ticket toward me. I covered it with my hand.

"So after you see Wellmann there tonight . . . ," he said.

"I still need proof that she is actually working for the Stasi."

"I would demand the same thing if I were in your position."

"But you're not. And you want something from me. And I am not willing to set her up."

"But here's the thing. You told her that you were interviewing those two East German dancers who just defected, right?"

"That's none of your damn business."

"I will take that as an 'affirmative.' So if you told her about the interview, you also told her about the transcript you'll be receiving over the weekend of the conversation you were supposed to have with these two dancers."

"You fucking set me up," I hissed.

"The fact is, it is you who set yourself up, sir. Now I must tell you: this interview is never going to take place. But say we were to give you a copy of this alleged transcript, all marked 'Classified.' Say you were to leave it out on a table for your beloved——"

"Stop calling her that!"

"Sorry, sorry, I can see why you're now a little bit touchy."

"Fuck you, 'chum.' Fuck your mental head games and your Good Cop/Bad Cop routine. I don't like you. I don't like who you are, what you stand for, or the shitty little games you play in the name of God and country. Just as I don't like the contempt you feel for anyone who isn't a 'team player,' 'plainspoken,' 'a real American.' And the thing is, though you spout neocon nastiness about any compatriot who doesn't embrace your black-and-white worldview, you live in the biggest fog of moral grayness imaginable."

"And you, sir, are someone whose worldliness on the page is not mirrored by that in real life. I may talk a sardonic game, Thomas. I may needle you with my Midwestern bluntness. But I am also sympathetic to the dilemma into which you have been tossed. Which is why, instead of trying to convince you any more of the 'truth' of this situation, I am proposing a simple test that will either incriminate or exonerate Frau Dussmann. It will give you a definite yes or no as to whether she is what I am alleging her to be. Will you allow me to outline this plan, please?"

I lowered my head. *You want proof. Here's the possibility of proof.*

"Go ahead," I said quietly.

"When Frau Dussmann returns to your apartment on Sunday, you must muster up what few clandestine bones you have in your body and pretend that all is as it was before. Can you do that?"

"I don't know."

"That's an honest answer. But for your own sake——by which I mean, in order to get the answers you need——you are going to have to act a role for a few days. The role you have been playing up to now. The role of the man who adores her. And yes, that means pulling her into bed, making love to her, telling her, as always, how much you adore her, acting as if nothing has changed. But then, the subject of your interview with the two dancers will come up. What you will then need to tell her——besides saying how interesting the two dancers were, and how disoriented but pleased they were to have escaped——is that the transcripts of the interview make fascinating reading . . . and it's going to be quite the coup for Radio Liberty to break this news first. Then you say no more about it. You have a nice evening. You take your lady to bed. I bet the two of you fuck every night."

"Shut up."

"I mention this simply as a tactical consideration. If you do make love every night, then do so again here. Afterward do you usually fall asleep straight away?"

"Is this necessary?"

"Yes, it is. And I will explain why. Because Haechen is a major security risk——"

"Whom you've allowed to operate here for more than two years."

"We've been hoping he'd lead us to even bigger fish. But he's a thug. Used to work in a special Stasi division at Hohenschöenhausen prison breaking down detainees through extreme psychological torture. Last year he picked up a prostitute near the Tiergarten and roughed her up so badly that she lost an eye. Her face is disfigured for life. And he's been targeting genuine defectors in the Bundesrepublik——one of whom was found dead on the InterCity express train tracks near Hamburg last year. The authorities ruled it a suicide, but our forensic people said the man was clearly thrown in front of the train. This is the man your friend has slept with repeatedly, and for whom she has photographed more than two dozen bogus classified documents. And if you dare say anything about her being forced into this role . . . there are thousands of dissidents in East German prisons who could have chosen the informant role but didn't. Everything in life comes down to two things: choice and interpretation. We make decisions——and then we generally fashion our interpretations of these choices in a manner that allows us to live with them. Which is what Frau Dussmann has been doing. Loving you and betraying you at the same time, and telling herself it's the only way she can maintain the huge plum assignment of living in the West. But remember this, Thomas——she *chose* this role. Just as she *chose* to deceive you."

Considered now, years later, I see that Bubriski was such a master at poisoning me by cleverly ratcheting up my sense of outrage at having been so wronged that I did come to see him as a difficult but essential ally. Though, again, a competing voice within me urged: *run away from this now*.

But my distress and mounting rage kept me rooted to the vinyl chair in that *bierstube*, listening intently as Bubriski plotted out, step by step, the scenario I was to act out. The specificity of his instructions——the way it was already so clearly thought through——made me realize that, like the sort of novelist who needs everything plotted out before putting pen to paper, he'd been working out the mechanics of it all for a very long time.

"So we are back in the bed you share with Frau Dussmann. It is now late Sunday night. You have just had sex. I repeat my question of before: do you usually fall asleep straight afterward?"

"If it's late, then yes."

"Don't get into bed before midnight then. When you've finished, I want you to fake falling asleep——but under no circumstance should you surrender to sleep. That would throw everything out of kilter. My hunch here is that once she is certain you have passed out, she will get up and find the briefcase . . . no, you carry some leather satchel, don't you? . . . the satchel in which you have kept the interview transcripts which we will supply you with that afternoon. Leave the satchel in your living room on that big table of yours."

"I don't ever remember inviting you up to my apartment."

"We are aware of its layout," he said. "Just as we know there is a sizeable keyhole in the bedroom door——and one which, when squinted through, gives you a clear line of vision onto the living room table.

Once she has shut the door behind her, count to sixty, then creep out of bed and put your eye to the keyhole and see if she is photographing the documents. My guess is she will use the little camera that she carries everywhere. Then she will return to bed, so make certain that you are back under the covers with the lights off before she returns. If, however, she does decide to steal away to Herr Haechen while you are asleep, you do nothing——as we will have someone posted near your doorway who will follow her from there. If she comes back to bed, make certain you wake up with her that morning——and, again, you must act as if nothing is out of the ordinary. Then, when she leaves, I want you to simply go to the window in the kitchen, the blinds of which are always open, if I'm not mistaken. All you need to do is lower the blinds. That will be the signal to our people that she has photographed the documents. If nothing has happened, don't touch the blinds and we will do nothing. But my great hope, Thomas, is that having seen proof that she is who we are alleging she is, you will not let her get away with it. I cannot emphasize how important it is that we capture Haechen red-handed. He has destroyed so many lives. And his work against GDR refugees who have settled in the Bundesrepublik . . . put it this way, if you help us here, you will also be doing a great service to your country, and that will be noted."

"I don't need any of your blue ribbons or your patriotic pats on the back. If I do this, it's because . . ."

But I couldn't get to the end of the sentence. Because I still didn't want to believe it all.

"Just remember this, Thomas. You won't be betraying her. Because she betrayed herself years ago when she——"

"You don't know when to stop, do you?"

He knew he had me. By playing on the betrayal theme, he was tapping into a fundamental part of my psyche, the part that believed love was, at best, an elusive notion. Was that also in his file on me——the fact my parents acted as if I was the weight that had dragged them down and, as such, left me thinking I could count on nobody in this world? Until, that is, I met Petra——and her love for me made me think that trusting someone else emotionally was finally possible. Which made the discovery that she had completely deceived me, that she was all that time working for the people she told me had destroyed her life . . .

I had to bolt this place now. So I scooped up the Berliner Philharmoniker ticket and pocketed it, then stood up.

"I'll go to the concert. I'll think things through."

"And then I'll see you tomorrow."

"What makes you think I will want to see you?"

"If you choose not to cooperate with us, then we will have to presume that you are aiding and abetting a foreign agent. I have already outlined for you the blowback resulting from your refusal to aid us: loss of passport, possible detention back home, possible border difficulties in the future."

"In other words, I have no choice, do I?"

"But you forget my earlier comment, Thomas. We all have a choice in everything we do. But that choice inevitably invites consequences. The question you must ask yourself: is this duplicitous woman worth it?"

Now he stood up and proffered his hand.

"I am certain you will make the intelligent choice——as hard as that choice is. See you tomorrow at the Café Istanbul. Shall we say breakfast at nine, seeing that it is a Saturday?"

"You know the Café Istanbul?"

"I know that it's your outer office. Until then, enjoy the concert. Abbado really shows up von Karajan's need to beautify everything. He defogs the music and lets it truly live. But what do I, a guy from Indiana, know about such things, right?"

I didn't hear a damn note of the Berliner Philharmoniker that evening, even though I had a seat in the center block just six rows from the platform. Jerome Wellmann was in the row directly in front of me and turned around when I sat down.

"What an *interesting* coincidence, finding you right behind me."

"I was given a ticket at the last minute," I said.

"You must know somebody with real clout," he said, then quickly introduced me to the small, hawk-featured woman seated next to him.

"My wife, Helen," he said. "And this is the famous Thomas Nesbitt."

What did he mean by that? Was he nudging her to say: *here's the guy I was telling you about who's been sleeping with the East German spy we allowed to be hired by us, never once revealing to her that, from the outset, we were on to her game.* Was that comment about me "knowing someone with real clout" his way of telling me that he knew exactly who had supplied me with this seat tonight? All I could feel as Wellmann smiled hello at me was desperation. Did he know, via Bubriski, that Petra had used him as an alibi this weekend? The very fact of his presence here in front of me slammed home the truth that Bubriski had confronted me with only an hour or so earlier. She had lied to me about being in Hamburg on professional translation duty with her boss.

Could she actually be with that fleshy creep Haechen? Had she slept with him throughout our love affair? How could she profess that I was the man of her life, then sneak off to that greasy little man and spread her legs for him?

Listen to you, sounding exactly like the betrayed lover.

I was still at that stage of disbelief where I wanted to find some sort of other interpretation of events, where Petra knew she was supplying him with false information, where she wasn't sleeping with the guy, where she was only doing his bidding to . . .

What exactly? She'd given up her child for adoption. She had to play the game in order to . . . ?

The concert passed in a blur, as I kept trying to tell myself: this is all smoke and mirrors. The photographs were only half-incriminating. The faces of the couple in bed were blurred. She only went to Hamburg this weekend because . . .

When the concert ended——amidst an eruption of bravos——Wellmann turned around and said:

"May your weekend be an interesting one."

He knew. The bastard had been fully briefed. Yet his comment was also designed to be laden with ambiguity. After all, he could just be telling me to have an "interesting" couple of days.

Again I was faced with the ongoing quandary of this shadowy realm into which I had been dropped. Was there anything called truth within its clandestine frontiers?

It was a mild night——so I walked home, thinking, thinking, trying to reason this all out, telling myself that when Petra came home on Sunday there would be a logical explanation for it all, that all the pieces would fit, all the doubts would be quelled, and we'd be on our way to the States in a few weeks, married, happy, with Petra ready to find some sort of accommodation with the nightmares of her past.

Enough, the voice of reason shouted in my inner ear. *You are weaving a romantic fantasy in your head——and one that ignores documented facts.*

But when the facts are too difficult to bear . . .

I reached the apartment by midnight. Alaistair was up as I came in, a bottle of vodka open on the table, a glass in front of him. The three canvases were no longer there——and he was staring at the now blank wall where they once lived.

"Feel like a shot or three?" he asked as I walked in.

I shook my head.

"Something wrong?" he asked.

"Just a lot on my mind," I said.

"Where's Petra?"

"Off in Hamburg."

"Business?"

"Something like that."

I could see him studying me with care.

"What's happened, Thomas?"

"Nothing."

"Bullshit."

"Where are your paintings?"

"Shipped this afternoon to my gallery in London. And you're changing the subject. Something is seriously amiss with you."

"I'm going to bed."

"You're being evasive, and that is not like you."

"Good night."

"Thomas . . ."

"I don't feel like talking right now."

"Fine, fine," he said, studying me with considerable care. "But whatever is going on——and I sense it has to do with Petra——don't be imprudent or careless. She is wonderful and you need her."

"Thanks for the advice," I said, sounding far too sharp and angry.

I went upstairs and slammed the door. And dug out my own bottle of vodka and drank shot after shot until intoxication sent me reeling toward my bed. But the five percent of my brain that was still rational somehow remembered to set the clock for eight before throwing off my clothes and climbing in between the sheets.

Then it was morning. The alarm was ringing. My head felt cleaved by all the clear Polish spirit I had imbibed. While subjecting myself to an arctic shower——and then forcing three cups of coffee down my throat——I decided on the course of action I would take when I met Bubriski in just less than an hour.

He was awaiting me in a corner booth of the Café Istanbul, stirring a glutinous cup of Turkish coffee with one of the tiny bent demitasse spoons that were a feature of the place. And he was dressed in his version of casual: a red Lacoste shirt and yellowish khakis. It didn't sit too well with his entire ultra-alert demeanor. It was as if he was trying to dress for a round of eighteen holes at a midscale country club and maintain surveillance on anyone who ventured near him at the same time. As I approached the booth in which he had parked himself, it was clear that he was eavesdropping on the Turkish guy and his very blond, very emaciated German girlfriend in the adjoining one.

"She's a junkie, he is her dealer and her occasional pimp," he said as I slid in opposite him.

"Beg your pardon?"

"The couple behind you. She turns tricks and he keeps her supplied with the little white powder that fueled your roommate for so many years. But hats off to him for going clean and finishing that triptych of paintings. I always like 'triumph over adversity' stories——especially involving gay, drug-addled painters who still work in Abstract Expressionism, though he hates the Rothko comparison, doesn't he?"

"Am I now supposed to wonder if he too is working for you?"

"Now you *have* finally amused me. I can categorically state that Mr. Fitzsimons-Ross has no connection with us whatsoever. But I am impressed by your concern that all the walls have ears."

"Well, in your world, they most evidently do."

"If I may say so, you look as if you have had one terrible night. What choice of substance rendered you unconscious?"

"That's my business."

"Indeed it is. And what did you think of the concert?"

"Impressive."

"In other words, you didn't hear a note. Who could blame you, considering the news you had to grapple with? Did you see Herr Wellmann?"

I nodded.

"Did that give you the proof that you needed?"

I said nothing but reached for his packet of Old Golds and fished out a cigarette.

"Just to further corroborate everything, I've brought along these photos of Frau Dussmann and Herr Haechen arriving on separate trains in Hamburg yesterday."

He reached for the file on the table in front of him.

"No need," I said. "I'll do what you want, but on one condition: I want to spring the trap tomorrow."

"And why do you want to do that?"

"Because I know I won't be able to playact this role for very long."

"That's an honest answer."

"You ask me to take her to bed and pretend that nothing has transpired. How can I even touch her after this?"

"If you don't make love with her immediately, she'll suspect."

"I'll feign food poisoning or something."

"She still might wonder."

"No, she won't. Because she has no reason to wonder if I am on to her. I'm the dupe here, right? So why should she even begin to think that I know her dirty little secret?"

"And you will mention having the transcripts?"

"Absolutely."

"And you should mention that someone at Radio Liberty transcribed the interviews for you yesterday. Tell her it was Frau Koenig. She's one of the people who does that sort of work over there."

"And if, as I suspect, Petra doesn't photograph the documents . . ."

"If Frau Dussmann later mentions in passing to Frau Koenig the work that she allegedly did for you over the weekend, Frau Koenig will know what to say. So the setup is the same as before. She arrives back at five forty-three off the Hamburg–Berlin express. She will be tailed to your door. Another of our operatives will be posted down your street and will move opposite your front door once she has gone inside. I suggest you feign illness early on and tell her that you are so unwell you are going to bed early. But somewhere during the course of the evening, after asking her about her weekend in Hamburg——"

"I think I can take care of all details. When can I get the transcript?"

"It will be waiting for you here tomorrow after eleven a.m."

"Is that a good idea?"

"The owner . . . he's a friend of mine."

I shut my eyes. Was this man——and his people——everywhere in my life?

"You have many friends, don't you?" I finally said.

"That's because I'm a very friendly guy."

I spent the remainder of the day hiding in movies. A cinema off the Ku'damm that started showing films at one in the afternoon and the program changed constantly. I shuffled in and out of its three screening rooms for the balance of the day (and night), trying not to think, trying to steel myself for the moment when Petra returned tomorrow.

When I got home it was just after one in the morning. Thankfully, Alaistair was not yet in——and the residual hangover and lack of sleep from the previous night sent me pitching into bed immediately. When I awoke it was ten. Another fine, clear morning. Dread hit me instantly. So I threw on some track clothes and went for an hour-long run through the still-empty streets. Kreuzberg on a Sunday morning always looked hungover——the pavements dappled with rubbish and empty beer bottles and the occasional used condom. The few stragglers out now appeared themselves to be careening home after a long night's journey into day. I was moving at a ferocious clip, trying to block out all thought through physical speed. Within twenty minutes I was in the Tiergarten. I circumnavigated the park twice, then slowed down to a jog for the return to Kreuzberg. When I reached the Café Istanbul I checked my watch and realized I had been running for more than an hour. Though now drenched from the exertion of it all, I still hadn't been able to expunge the apprehension that I felt about seeing Petra tonight. Would I be able to play everything with a poker face? Would she immediately sense that something huge was troubling me? How would I react when she started lying about the weekend? And if she did photograph the documents?

I stuck my head into the Café Istanbul. Omar, as usual, was behind the counter.

"Somebody left you a package," he said.

He handed over a thick manila envelope. I slid into a booth, asked for a coffee, and opened the flap, sliding out a neat pile of twenty-two pages. The first page was on Radio Liberty letterhead——and the translator's name, Magdalena Koenig, was marked in the upper right-hand corner. My name featured at the start of the transcript——and then, after its first entry, was abbreviated as T.N. The transcript was completely in German, it was dated yesterday, and it detailed an interview I had allegedly made with a certain Hans and Heidi Braun. I read through the entire transcript, trying to absorb the details of their lives in the GDR, their political activities, the plot that surrounded their escape, the way they were now planning to speak out against the repressive regime of Erich Honecker. I thought the way the interview detailed their escape plot something of a masterstroke. Once mentioned to Petra, it would grab her attention, if, that is, she really was working for them.

That was the "truth" I still couldn't accept——the fact that she was their agent. After all she had said about the horrors of her incarceration, her hatred of the regime, the agony of losing her son, the way she always seemed privately haunted by recent terrors . . . no, it was impossible to imagine that she had actually collaborated with them.

I went home to find Alaistair up and staring again at the blank walls of his studio. He looked me over, taking in my sweat-stained track clothes, my disheveled hair, the envelope under my arm.

"You must be in a bad way, charging through the streets at this time of the morning."

"It helps keep all the demons at bay," I said with a smile.

"And what, precisely, are those demons?"

"The demons we carry with us everywhere."

"Thank you, Hieronymus Bosch. But let me ask you something: do you always go running with a large manila envelope under your arm?"

"It's some work stuff left for me at the Istanbul. I have an essay to finish by tonight."

"And I am heading out tonight for some dinner at the apartment of some very queeny art critic whose father was something very important at BMW and left him a very large inheritance. The gent seems to have taken a shine to me and is talking about a commission. So I might not be home until rather late. And when is Ms. Petra due back?"

"Early evening."

"I'm glad to hear it."

"I've got to get on with things now."

"Thomas, if you are thinking about doing something cataclysmic . . ."

"I am thinking about writing," I said, then headed upstairs and shut the door behind me.

Was I that transparent? At least Alaistair would be out tonight. And if, as he was hinting, this potential commission also involved sexual favors, he might not be back here at all.

I stripped off my track clothes, took a shower, dressed, checked my watch, and realized that I needed to do something to chew up the hours between now and Petra's return. So I brought my typewriter down off the shelf and positioned it at one end of my kitchen table, bringing over typing paper, a pad and a pen, and a desk lamp. Then I opened the cupboard where I had been storing all my Berlin notebooks. I pulled down the first one, flopped into my armchair, rolled up a cigarette, and read through the detailed notes I had inscribed about the conversation I had with the woman on the flight from Frankfurt to Berlin all those months ago——and the story she told me about jumping out the window of the building in Friedrichshain. Because she mentioned the word "Kreuz-berg," I ended up here on one of my first nights in Berlin. Because I happened to stop in the Café Istanbul, I saw an announcement on a bulletin board which led to this apartment——and the acquaintance of Alaistair. And on the day that I visited Herr Wellmann, if Petra hadn't walked in at that specific instant . . . ?

Is this what is meant by the random trajectory of things? Happen-stance, coincidence, being in a certain place at a certain moment, the end result of which is that now you find yourself in the middle of a terrible scenario you could have never imagined . . . but also after knowing, for the first time in your life, the full extraordinary force of real love.

There had to be an explanation to all this. Or perhaps a hidden agenda here that Bubriski was keeping out of sight. Yet I knew that if I did confront Petra the moment she walked through that door——and if she was innocent——then the landscape between us would be irrevo-cably changed. Just as I also knew that if I said nothing . . . well, only a deranged optimist would think, *perhaps it will all go away.* But isn't that always the Last Chance Saloon hope of anyone facing a terminal situation? *Tomorrow I will wake up and the tumor will be gone. Tomorrow I will wake up and she will be in bed next to me.*

How we always hope for something to contradict the most terrible truths we have to face. How we all privately believe in anything to counter reality at its most concrete.

But, again, what was the truth here? I simply wanted to believe another interpretation of this narrative, a version that wasn't so chilling, so bleak. A version I could live with.

I glanced at my watch. I still had six hours before she arrived. I needed something to fill the time, kill the hours, keep my hands and brain occupied. So after reading my first Berlin notebook straight through, I moved myself to the kitchen table, opened the notebook back to its first page, rolled a sheet of paper into the typewriter, and——after a sharp intake of breath——began to attack the keys. Part of me knew it was foolhardy to start writing the opening chapter of my Berlin book while still here, that I really shouldn't even think about beginning work on it until after I had left the city, for all the evident "critical distance" reasons. But work right now was the only answer.

I wrote in a controlled fury, breaking after two hours to make myself a pot of coffee and roll another four cigarettes. Then I settled down for another lengthy sprint at the typewriter. It lasted until sometime after four, at which point I had more than twelve pages in front of me. I read through them, making a few minor adjustments with my fountain pen, knowing I wouldn't even begin to think about doing any significant rewrites until the entire manuscript was done. Then, checking my watch, I decided I had time to slip out for a beer in a local *Stube* and gather up my jumbled thoughts before Petra arrived home.

Home. That's what I considered this apartment, the home I shared with the woman I adored. The first of many homes we would share together. The start of a life together, with all its attendant possibilities. And now, all was in the balance. And I still didn't know if I could do Bubriski's bidding, even if I discovered that she really was who he said she was.

Suddenly the front door opened. Petra walked in.

"I know I was due back later, but I so wanted to get home to you."

She smiled at me with such love, such sheer pleasure in seeing me, that I was up out of my chair and in her arms immediately. We were in bed moments later.

"Oh God, how I missed you," Petra said afterward as we lay together, drained, spent.

"And I you."

"I never want to be apart from you again."

"You mean that?"

"Can't you tell?" she said with a smile. "And while in Hamburg, I thought: in just a few days I will be your wife."

"A nice thought," I said, making certain I smiled. But as I said this I was so conscious that I was now acting out a role, and one that I hoped wasn't too transparently different from usual. The fact that she was displaying no outward signs of guilt, of concealment . . .

"Did you have a good weekend?" she asked.

"It would have been better if you were here. How was Hamburg?"

"My first time there. I was surprised by what a beautiful city it was. But the conference was boring. And Herr Wellmann's speech was on the dry side. Still I had time to go to the Museum of Modern Art and take a boat across the lake. But I wished you had been there with me. In fact, I wished that all the time."

I had to fight the urge to tense up and burst out with an accusation that I knew she was lying. Just as part of me kept thinking: *But surely there is an explanation for all this that doesn't involve . . . him. The man with whom she actually spent the weekend. The man to whom she reports and hands over clandestinely photographed official documents.*

"But tell me all about Hans and Heidi Braun," she said.

I went into the spiel I had been preparing for the past thirty-six hours——how I was brought to the place they are being kept in an official car with blacked-out windows, so I hadn't a clue where it was. But I had two hours with them. Heidi was rather shy and nervous. But Hans was absurdly outgoing, and said the most outrageously funny things about life in the GDR——especially when it came to gay life over there. But it all turned serious when he described how one of his lovers had been brutally beaten by the police and was still in a coma.

Then I mentioned how we brought the tapes back to the Radio Liberty office and Magdalena Koenig spent the whole of the weekend transcribing them all.

"They were sent by courier to me this morning, and I've been reading them through. I must say that when the interview is broadcast, it's going to be much talked-about. I'm meeting Pawel tomorrow to listen again to the tapes and to decide what we can and cannot use. We have to cut all the material down to half an hour."

"And they're planning to broadcast the interview when?"

"As soon as the authorities give us the all-clear——but they want it out by this Friday. Hans Braun has been offered a job with the Freiburg dance company. The New York City Ballet is also interested. The big question is whether his sister will get an offer from either company as well."

"And how did they get out?"

I told her about how they were snuck out in a van transporting the scenery and lighting equipment of the Dance Theatre of Freiburg.

"They're quite a politically radical company, aren't they?" she said.

"Very leftist. In fact, so leftist that they had troubles getting visas for a US tour. But they still decided to help two East German dancers get their freedom."

"And the Brauns talk about all this in the interview?"

"Yes and in great detail."

"And the transcript?"

"There are only two copies, and I have one. In fact, tonight I'm going to have to find an hour to work on it, if that's okay with you, as they need my proposed cuts by tomorrow morning."

"No problem," Petra said, her face expressionless. "No problem at all."

We eventually got out of bed around seven and went to a nearby Italian place for a bowl of pasta and a shared half-liter of their house red. Petra talked excitedly about New York, telling me she'd drafted the statement she had to write for the green card application on the train back to Hamburg, and she was going to type it up tomorrow, and would I read it and correct her "bad English."

"I'm sure the English is excellent," I said.

"Will you start speaking with me in English once we get to the States?"

"How about half the time in English, the rest *auf Deutsch*?"

"A good compromise. And do you know what I'd love to do . . . and I have some money saved up, so I'd be able to do this for us . . . is buy a cheap car and spend a couple of months driving across America. We could decide to stay somewhere for a while or move on. You could work every day on your Berlin book. The rest of the time it would be *On the Road with Thomas and Petra.*"

She reached out and put her hand to my face.

"All is going to be wonderful once we are out of this city."

I nodded many times, hoping she didn't see how shaky I now was. Why was she painting such a romantic picture of us bombing down a two-lane blacktop in a Chevy if she had been off with him all weekend? And what was the subtext behind that comment, *"All is going to be wonderful once we are out of this city"*? Had she found a way out of the clandestine world in which she had been allegedly operating? But if this was the case, could I live with the knowledge that, at the outset of our relationship, she had lied so comprehensively to me about so many things? Is that what the subconscious meaning of her statement was really about——telling me (without telling me) that she was finally breaking with the past?

I excused myself to go to the bathroom. Once there I found myself having to grip the sink or else collapse mentally and physically.

How can you even begin to think that an East German operative would be granted her freedom from any further espionage activity——and given a blessing to marry an American and emigrate to the States?

Then why is she telling me all this?

Throwing cold water on my face, I managed to quiet myself with one simple thought: *at least you will have answers very soon.*

When we got back home, I excused myself to spend an hour working on the transcript. Not once did Petra approach me. Not once did she look over my shoulder or ask if she could peruse the transcripts. Instead she sat on our bed, editing the statement she was writing to support her green card application. I pushed on until ten o'clock, then gathered up the transcript pages and deliberately left them on the table. I went into the bedroom. Petra looked up from her notepad.

"Done already?"

"I'll get back to it tomorrow before I go in to work on the editing of the actual tapes with Pawel."

"You must be tired."

"That I am."

"But not too tired, I hope."

She opened her arms to me. We pulled off each other's clothes again and made love with a deliberateness so slow, so intimate, that I couldn't help but sense that Petra's love for me was still as deep and as profound as mine for her. Afterward, she whispered in my ear:

"I will always love you, no matter what happens."

Then, turning off the light, we fell asleep in each other's arms.

Except, of course, I was wide awake with my eyes shut. I was actually damn tired, but I fought the urge to pass out, while simultaneously hoping that in ten or fifteen minutes I would open my eyes and find Petra there beside me, fast asleep. Then I too would drift off into unconsciousness, knowing that I had the answer I so wanted.

If she sleeps, life goes on as planned.

But if she gets up . . .

Ten minutes later, she did just that. Disengaging herself from my arms. Sitting up in the bed and then not moving for at least sixty seconds (was she making sure I was fast asleep?). Then I heard her quietly scooping up her clothes and heading out the bedroom door, closing it behind her as soundlessly as possible.

I counted to sixty before silently getting out of bed. I pulled on my jeans and a T-shirt, relieved that the bedroom blinds were partly open and the room half-lit by moonlight. I waited another five minutes, standing absolutely still, my eyes focused on the second hand of my watch. When the three hundred seconds had passed, I crept toward the closed bedroom door. But during those five motionless minutes, I tossed aside Bubriski's directive to squat down and put my eye to the keyhole. To do so would be to spy, to engage in the surreptitious. Instead I just opened the door as quietly as possible.

There was Petra, leaning over the kitchen table. My work light was now focused down upon several transcript pages that had been spread out across the sanded pine surface. And she was using a tiny camera to photograph each page. For several moments I didn't move. Even though I expected this from the moment I felt her get up and leave the bed, the shock of seeing her engaged in this "work" . . . all I could do was stand there and watch everything disintegrate. Love is, among other things, about hope. Hope is such a fragile entity——so charged with meaning, so delicately balanced on the frontier between great possibility and an even greater sense of loss——that you always fear the moment when you have definitive, concrete proof that things are now hopeless.

"You need to leave," I heard myself saying.

Petra was so caught unaware by the sound of my voice that she lost her balance, breaking her fall by hitting the table with her hand and sending the lamp crashing to the ground, its bulb smashing on impact.

"Thomas . . . ," she whispered.

"Get out," I said, my voice still quiet.

"There is an explanation for all this."

"I know there is. You work for them, don't you?"

"Thomas . . ."

"Don't you?" I now shouted.

She put her hand to her mouth, her eyes filling up with tears.

"You have to let me explain."

"No, I don't. Because you've betrayed me, you've betrayed us, you've betrayed everything."

I could hear her strangle a cry in her throat.

"I love you," she whispered.

"And you were with another man this weekend in Hamburg."

Now it was she who looked as if she had been slapped across the face.

"How did you——?"

"*Know?* That's my business. But I found out. Just as I found out that you've been fucking him all the time that you were telling me——"

"You are the man I love, Thomas. And you have to let me——"

"What? *Explain? Give* me some excuse *why* you had to *service* that evil little monster?"

"Please, *please*, let me try to——"

"Did you fucking hear me?" I screamed. "I want you out of here, out of my life *now.*"

When she came toward me, weeping, her arms open, repeating just one word, "*Please . . . please . . . please,*" I found myself edging into the sort of irrational anger where all past grievances——all the accumulated personal betrayals dating back to childhood——coalesced into a rage that

I had never experienced before, a rage that terrified me. But I couldn't apply the brakes, couldn't quell the fury that propelled me toward her, Petra crying wildly, cowering in a corner as I scooped up the transcript, flung it all at her, yelling:

"Take it, take the fucking thing! You'll probably get the Order of Fucking Lenin for it!"

"Please . . . please . . . please . . . ," she cried again, the words hardly getting out.

"You destroy everything, and you want fucking mercy? Out."

As I screamed that last word, I lashed out, flinging a kitchen chair across the room, watching her howl with grief as she still managed to scrabble together all the pages of the transcript.

"You see! You see!" I shrieked at her as I saw her gather up the pages. "You've got what you wanted, now fuck off and . . ."

She raced for her shoulder bag, stuffing the camera and the pages into it, then ran for the door, hysterical, frightened, crying uncontrollably. The door slammed behind her with a huge thud. I went charging to the window. The rage still in full throttle, I pulled the cord, lowering the blinds immediately, sending whatever operative posted outside the agreed signal that she was coming downstairs. That action——it was if I had given the firing squad the order to shoot——instantly sent me in a different direction, as I started barreling down the stairs, yelling at Petra to stop, to wait, to . . .

What was I thinking? I had no idea, except that having gone mad with fury I now suddenly found myself overwhelmed by the realization that I had acted irrationally, logic scrambled in the middle of wrath, so enraged at her that I didn't even let her explain. And now . . .

I ran as fast as I could, slamming myself against the main door of the apartment, careening out into the darkened street, screaming Petra's name as I saw her being bundled into a car by two men in suits. As I raced toward the car, which was now pulling away at speed, yelling at them to stop, to let me explain, someone stepped out of the shadows and, with a fast right to my stomach, sent me flying toward the pavement. As my knees hit the concrete, I was suddenly yanked up by the collar and found myself face-to-face with Bubriski.

"The fuck are you doing?" he said.

"You didn't say you were going to arrest her on the street!" I yelled. "You said you were going to use her to get——"

His fist slammed again into my stomach. This time he hauled me up, dragged me inside the lobby of my building, and pushed me against a wall, hissing:

"You shut up *now* unless you want to end up in indefinite custody, and I am totally fucking serious about that. *Understand?*"

I nodded my head, many times, thrown by the ferocity of his tone.

"Your role in all this is finished. You did the right thing. Now it is over. Here's the deal I am willing to cut you. You pack your bags and you get out of Berlin now——and if I never read or hear anything by you about any of this, I will let you get on with your life. But if you make trouble . . . if you start raising shit . . ."

"I'll make no trouble," I said.

He let go of my shirt.

"Smart guy. Now go upstairs and start packing your bags. There's a BA flight to Frankfurt at seven tomorrow morning. It connects with a Lufthansa flight at ten twenty-five a.m. to New York. You have an open round-trip ticket, don't you?"

He knows everything about me. Everything.

"I am going to have my people call the two airlines and book you on those flights. No objections?"

And no choice in the matter.

"No objections," I said.

"You're a truly smart guy. On behalf of the US government, I thank you for your sterling work. She was a piece of shit, and you got duped and then you settled the score, which is the way I like to see these stories turn out, not that they ever really do. Still . . ."

I lowered my head and said nothing. All I felt right now was shame and horror. "*Please, please, please,*" she'd said to me over and over again, begging me to let her tell her side of things. Instead, all full of righteous rage, I had thrown her into the clutches of these men whose games were as dirty as those played by the other side.

"If you're feeling guilty——and I'm a good read of these things," Bubriski said, "lose it now. She knew what she was getting into when she got into bed with those people. She'll be traded in a few weeks for some people they have imprisoned over there and will probably be awarded with a bigger apartment and a Trabbi. Until then we won't deprive her of sleep or try to break her down——because there's little she can tell us that we don't already know. She's just a minor pawn in all this. Just like you."

"And how about Haechen? Will you be arresting him?"

"That's confidential. My advice to you is: go back to New York. Write your Berlin book. Find some interesting neurotic junior editor at the *New York Review of Books* to sleep with. Never mention any of this to anybody, but I told you that already, and I sense you're a fast learner. Just be thankful you walked away relatively unscathed. My report about you will praise your cooperation and the fact that you delivered the 'package' to us. But it will also insist that a close eye be kept on your literary output. By all means continue to be somewhat snide about your country in print. It shows we don't clamp down on creative types who play the critical card. But if word ever reaches us that you have told this story . . ."

"What story?"

"I'm actually beginning to moderately like you."

"If my roommate asks why I'm leaving in a hurry?"

"Tell him you broke up with your girlfriend and it's too hard to bear remaining in Berlin. Then be on that plane tomorrow morning at seven."

He stepped back from me.

"So this is where I wish you *Auf Wiedersehen und gute Reise*——as I doubt our paths will ever cross again. Once again, good work, *comrade*. You're one of us now."

And he turned and disappeared back into the shadows.

I went upstairs——my brain so rattled that I had to grasp the railings all the way up to keep myself steady. But when I reached the door to the apartment I found Alaistair standing outside it. He looked at me with cold contempt.

"What have you done?" he asked, his voice hard, disdainful, full of scorn. "My God, Thomas. What have you done?"

"I don't know what you're talking about."

"I was in my bedroom. I heard everything upstairs. I was about to in-tervene when Petra ran down the stairs. Then peering through the blinds

I saw what happened in the street. And when that compatriot thug of yours dragged you back in here I quietly stepped out onto the landing and eavesdropped. I got it all. Everything."

"And what are you going to do about it?"

"Nothing . . . except to tell you that if you weren't being ordered to leave Berlin in a few hours I'd be ordering you to clear out of my apartment. I want nothing to do with you again."

"You don't understand what she did, how she betrayed——"

"The biggest betrayal here——after turning the woman you loved over to those bastards——is the one you have perpetrated on yourself. You've ruined your life, Thomas. Because you'll never get over this. *Never.*"

Three days later I sat up half the night with my mathematician friend Stan in his tiny apartment near MIT in Cambridge. With several weeks left to go before my subletter vacated my place in Manhattan and in desperate need of a friend, I rang Stan from Kennedy, saying I needed refuge. He said the lumpy pull-out bed in his living room was mine for as long as I needed it——and I grabbed the bus to La Guardia and the shuttle to Boston. I showed up at his place around ten that night, having not slept in more than thirty-six hours. He saw the exhaustion etched on my face and asked no questions. He just made up the bed for me and managed to leave the next morning without waking me up. When I finally came to, it was approaching one in the afternoon——and though rested I felt as if I were locked into some manic vortex without exit. For the next two days I never left the apartment, terrified of the world beyond these secure walls. Stan let me be, never trying to engage me in too much conversation or find out why I had turned into an agoraphobic. Then, on the third night, I turned to him and said:

"If I tell you a story do you promise . . . ?"

"You know you don't have to ask," he said.

So I told him everything. And when I finished, he said nothing for a very long time. Then:

"Don't blame yourself. That Bubriski fellow was right when he said that you and Petra were just minor pawns in a very large game."

"But I went crazy and destroyed everything."

"You went crazy because you loved her more than you have ever loved anyone. She will know that. Believe me, for the rest of her life, she will not think that you were a demon for going mad when you found out the truth about her. She will think: 'That man so loved me his whole world was upended when he found out who I was.' And it will haunt her forever."

"And will it haunt me forever?" I asked.

"You already know the answer to that question."

I hung my head. I said nothing. But Stan filled the silence.

"You're never going to get over this, Thomas. Try as you might, it just won't happen."

When Stan died suddenly many years later, his words filled my inner ear and refused to be dislodged for days. Not that they had ever really vanished from my consciousness in the decade and a half since they were first spoken. On the contrary, they were always there. Just as she was always there. Every day. That part of my past which I shared with one good friend and then banished from any further mention. Because to share it with another person would be to admit the one thing I didn't want to articulate, even though I knew it to be so profoundly true.

I had never gotten over it.

ELEVEN

THE MANUSCRIPT ENDED there. As I turned the last page over, I pushed it away. Just as I had done back in December 2000, when I finished writing it all——six breathless weeks of solid work for a book that would never make its way into print, because I would never let it. And having gotten it all down on paper, I immediately locked it away in my manuscript cabinet, certain that I would never read it again. It wasn't as if, at the time, I was still taking Bubriski's threat of retribution seriously. After all, The Wall had fallen eleven years earlier. The Cold War was in the past tense. The city——to which I had never returned from the moment I was ordered out of it all those years earlier——was now a reunified construct. And, of course, I had published, in mid-1986, a book about my time in Berlin . . . but one that dodged all that I knew could never be made public.

In fact, I started that book just a week after my atrocious exit from Berlin in the summer of '84. After spending a few catatonic days at Stan's place in Cambridge, he said, "I'm ordering you out of Dodge and to somewhere where you can recuperate while looking at wide open spaces." He threw me the keys to his family's summer cottage on the shores of Lake Champlain just outside of Burlington. His parents had died two years earlier in a car accident. He was their only child. Since he was now back finishing his doctorate at MIT while teaching there full-time, the cottage was empty.

"Hang out there as long as you like," he said. "If you even try to pay me rent I won't ever talk to you again."

I took the bus north to Vermont. The cottage was simple but livable. It was three rooms right on the shores of the lake and just a ten-minute bike ride from downtown Burlington. It had a decent bed, a decent desk, a comfortable chair for reading, books, records, a shortwave radio, and a small desk with an impeccable view of the lake and the looming presence of the Adirondack Mountains that defined the far shoreline. There was even a bicycle with panniers——which meant I could bike down into Burlington to buy groceries, sip coffee, haunt bookshops, watch a movie, and generally fill the time that I wasn't spending writing.

Yes, I started writing immediately. Within a day of getting there, I set up my typewriter on the desk in Stan's cottage. In that mad rush to get to the airport for that seven a.m. flight I had taken with me just some basic clothes, my typewriter, and my all-important notebooks. Everything else I had acquired in Berlin——books, records, additional clothes——I left behind with two hundred dollars on the kitchen table and a note to Alaistair with my New York address.

> If you can bring yourself to pack up what remains for me, please ship it all. The $200 should adequately cover costs. If you decide to simply dump it all into the nearest charity shop, I will understand.

I could have gone on, saying how this was not the ending I wanted. But I simply signed it and stuffed what remained in my two suitcases, then hauled everything downstairs. Alaistair was there, an open vodka bottle on the table, a cigarette in hand, staring at the empty blank walls behind him.

"So you really are running away," he said.

"That's right."

"Story of your life, isn't it?"

Then he swiveled around in his chair and showed me his back, letting me know that there was to be no further conversation between us.

I struggled with my bags onto the street, waiting more than twenty minutes until a cab came along. At the airport I discovered that, yes, I had been reserved a seat on the seven a.m. Frankfurt flight and the onward connection to New York. Some hours later, well over the Atlantic, I locked myself in one of the toilets and lost it for the better part of ten minutes. I was crying so loudly that one of the flight attendants banged on the door and asked if I was all right. That snapped me out of my sobbing jag. I opened the door. The attendant eyed me with concern.

"You had me worried," she said. "Such grief."

"I'm sorry," I said in a half-voice.

"Was there a death in the family?"

"I lost somebody . . . yes."

Back in my seat, I stared ahead of me and kept hearing a line of an Oscar Wilde's poem over and over again in my head: "*All men kill the thing they love.*"

But she betrayed me.

And then you betrayed yourself.

It was like a death. During those early days back——after collapsing with exhaustion the first night——I hardly slept, hardly ate, and never left Stan's apartment. Even after spending an entire night with him talking it all out, there was no sense of purgation, no chink in the grief and the guilt I possessed. On the contrary, all I felt was a deepening of the despair, the sense that Alaistair nailed it when he said that I had ruined my life. I kept replaying those final moments in the apartment, when she pleaded with me to listen, and I couldn't help but wonder what would have happened if I had heard her out. Yes, the fact that she was clearly working for the other side would have precluded her from entry into the US. But——and this was the ongoing but——there would have been some way through this. Especially as everything she said, everything that her grief showed me in those final moments, confronted me with the fact that, yes, she did love me.

And yet, how could she love me and so deceive me? How could she profess I was the man of her life, tell me these horror stories about her time in a Stasi prison, the way they cleaved her son away from her, and then turn out to have been one of their people all along? Were love and betrayal always so closely allied?

Writing the book was a diversionary tactic——a way of keeping occupied, of accomplishing something, of pushing time forward in the hope that its onward momentum would balm the wound or, at least, allow me to reach an accommodation with it all. I worked like a man possessed——which, I suppose, I was. I went for a run along the lakeshore every morning. I found time to bike into town most afternoons and buy a newspaper and kill time in a café. Once or twice a week I went to the local art house cinema and watched a movie. Otherwise, I stayed inside Stan's cottage and wrote. When my tenant left my apartment in Manhattan, I dropped down to the city for a few days and met with a teacher friend who was looking for a short sublet. So I tossed him the keys, my rent covered until the end of November. Stan was true to his word when it came to letting me stay in the cottage for as long as I wanted. So I hung on there until Thanksgiving——when a first draft was finished. Stan showed up on Thanksgiving Eve with a turkey in tow.

"You've lost weight," was his first observation. He was right, as I had dropped fifteen pounds since returning from Berlin.

"And I've gained four hundred pages," I said, pointing to the manuscript now stacked neatly on a shelf.

"The consolations of art."

"I suppose so."

"What next?"

"New York. Delivering the manuscript. Another draft or two, given my editor's predilections to get me to rewrite everything. And then . . . well, I was thinking about a book on Alaska."

Stan thought that one over.

"Well, that place is about as extreme as they come. And if it continues the distancing process . . ."

I said nothing. Getting all the subtexts behind my silence, Stan simply gripped my arm and said:

"You will find a way of living with the sense of loss."

There was some truth in that comment. My editor thought the Berlin book "very accomplished, very Isherwood-esque" in its portrait of modern Berlin as a rakish city of shadows, and "full of larger-than-life characters." (Alaistair was reinvented in the text as Simon Channing-Burnett, and I made him a sculptor from English aristo stock.) But she also found it "curiously detached" and "emotionally distant" and wondered out loud in our editorial sessions whether the book could be given more heart.

"It's Berlin," I argued. "And Berlin is about decadent surfaces."

"I sense there is, lurking behind all your decadent surfaces, a story you don't want to tell."

"We all have stories we don't want to tell."

"And I want to see more emotion in the book."

I did attempt to meet her demand by building up the relationship in the book between Simon and his married Greek Cypriot lover, Constantine, using much of the Alaistair-Mehmet breach that never healed. But my editor was right about the book's inherent detachment, the way the "I" in the book was very much an onlooker: wry, ironic, closed off from the larger human dramas going on around him.

"You are one hell of an actor," was Stan's take on the book when he first read it, whereas the majority of the reviews noted that it was diverting, readable, and just a bit shallow: a verdict with which I couldn't argue.

Yes, I did follow that book up with one based on the three months I lived in Alaska. When that came out I ventured immediately into the vast open spaces of the Australian bush, then spent a few months in western Canada writing my outback book. Of course, there were other women, other adventures. A photojournalist in Sydney with whom I spent three months——but who, toward the end of things, told me that I was always "elsewhere." A jazz singer named Jennifer whom I met during my stint in Vancouver——and who, when she announced she was in love with me, sent me running back to Manhattan. A stockbroker in New York who thought that sleeping with a writer was exotic for a while, but eventually said she didn't want to be with someone who seemed to be always thinking about the next flight out of town.

Then I met Jan. Smart. Confident. Sexy in a controlled way. Well read. My age. Willing to deal with my frequent absences. Wanting a life with me. Telling me that, yes, I was so different from anyone she'd been with before, but she liked the challenge that was me. Just as I was intrigued by her intellectual cogency as a lawyer, her organizational rigor, her need to exercise control over life's inherent messiness. We'd met at a reading I'd given in Boston, and she'd been brought along by a college classmate who was a partner at the law firm where she was still an associate. We all went out to dinner afterward. I was impressed with her smarts and her dry wit. Just as she seemed genuinely interested in everything to do with me. Before I knew it, she'd convinced me to come live with her for a while at her very nice apartment on Commonwealth Avenue. Then I invited her down on a trip to the Atacama Desert of Chile. And then on an assignment to the Tunisian island of Djerba. Around six months into our romance, she forgot to put her diaphragm in one night when we were having a weekend at some Cape Cod inn, and when she discovered she was pregnant, she did tell me that, as much as she wanted to keep the baby, if I strenuously objected . . .

But I didn't object. Though I told Jan that I did love her, I quietly knew that the love I felt for her was qualified, perhaps because it seemed like a pale shadow of all that I had once known with Petra. And though I never mentioned Petra's name to her, Jan still knew that ours wasn't the great love story of the century. When she was five months pregnant, we rented a house for two weeks in August on the Maine coastal island of Vinalhaven. One night, sitting on the deck that faced the ever-choppy waters of the Atlantic, she turned to me out of nowhere and said:

"I do know, Thomas, that your heart is elsewhere."

"What?" I said, thrown by this out-of-left-field statement. Jan trained her sights on the breaking waters of the Atlantic, never once looking toward me, as she said again:

"I know you may care very much for me. And I sincerely hope that you will adore the child that I am carrying right now. But I also understand, deep down, that I am not the love of your life. As hard as it is for me to say it, I do accept that."

This comment was spoken with no lethal edge. It was just a cold, hard statement of fact. And it caught me so unaware that my reply was a lame one.

"I don't know what you're talking about."

"Yes, you do. And if you'd like to tell me all about her . . ."

I looked over and saw that Jan's eyes were brimming with uncharacteristic sadness. I reached out for her hand, but she pulled away.

"What was her name?" she asked.

"There was no one important."

"Please don't try to placate me, Thomas. The truth I can handle. Bullshit I cannot."

But to tell her about Petra, to admit the fact that, even when we made love, I saw her face superimposed on hers, would be to invite grief. So all I said was:

"I want to spend my life with you."

"Are you certain about that? Because . . . and this is the truth . . . I can handle raising this child largely on my own."

"I want this child more than anything."

That was the truth. Because I was tired of the shifting nature of perpetual motion. Because I thought that being a father was one of those things in life you really regretted not doing. And because I instinctually understood that I needed to put down roots and try to properly build a life with someone else. Here was a hugely bright, intelligent, capable woman who wanted the same thing, who grasped so much about me, and seemed to want to accommodate my wanderlust while also providing me with the domestic ballast I needed. She also saw in me (I sensed) a man who wasn't intimidated by her intellect (as so many others were) and could handle the flinty side of her nature.

Stan didn't like her from the outset——warning me that there was an inherent coldness to Jan, and that he could see that, while I admired her, I was not wholly in love with her.

But, like Jan, I was at a stage in life when I no longer wanted to be adrift. Moreover, there was cognitive and domestic compatibility between us. We could talk books and interesting movies and current affairs and what we heard that day on National Public Radio. We shared the same aesthetic. And we weren't outwardly competitive with each other, never forcing each other into roles we didn't want to play.

Though everything on paper made us seem like the stuff of a very good match, there was one huge disconnect between us: a lack of true love.

I now see that at the time, I was willing to talk myself into a position of compromise about all this. *All right, your heart never sings when you see her. All right, there is companionship, but no sense of complicity or shared destiny between you. But surely, that will come in time.*

It was a way of papering over all the silent doubts that I was unwilling to confront. Are so many marriages forged this way——hoping that the fundamentals you know are missing will eventually arrive, desperately accentuating the positive to close the deal, because you feel somehow that you really should be grounding yourself at this moment in time?

In November of 1989, with my wife now eight months pregnant, I headed off solo to a movie theater at Harvard Square to see a new print of "The Third Man" (Jan having to work late at her office on a case that she was determined to close before our baby arrived in the world). After the film, I dropped in to one of the few good old-fashioned dingy saloons that still remained in this increasingly gentrified corner of Cambridge. While I was sitting at the bar with three drunks, a news bulletin came on the overhead television. And I watched static-laden images of the Berlin Wall being breached, the correspondent from CNN standing at the now wide-open gates of Checkpoint Charlie as thousands of East Germans swarmed Westwards, getting choked with emotion as he stated: "The Berlin Wall has finally fallen down today . . . and the world is a different place."

I remember being so overcome by this statement——and the images of Berliners from both sides of the frontier embracing and crying——that I stepped outside into the darkened night and found myself in a mad reverie, wondering how long it would take to get myself from here to Berlin. Then, if I could somehow find Petra in East Berlin, how I would take her in my arms and tell her that not a day had gone by in the past five years when she had not loomed large in my life, when I had continued to blame myself for letting my rage kill my compassion, and how if I could turn back the clock . . .

But the clock can never be turned back. What had happened had happened, and I was now a married man with a child due momentarily. Anyway, even if I had been free, why would she want anything to do with me after what I had rained down on her? With any luck she had met somebody over the past few years and was now a mother again. And here I was . . . haunted. Overshadowed. Never unburdened by all that was unresolved.

The Wall might have come down, but it still enclosed my heart.

Certainly, when Candace finally arrived in the world, my love for her was overwhelming, unconditional. And because we shared responsibility for this wonderful person, Jan and I were able to evade, for a time, the growing realization that ours was a relationship lacking the essential propulsion that love provides.

Thinking back to that night on the deck of that cottage on that off-shore island in Maine, when she said she knew she was not the love of my life, when she showed greater perception than me about the emotional landscape between us and what were to be its increasingly profound limitations . . . why didn't I tell her the truth? Why did I not admit

that——seven years on from my ignoble departure from Berlin——the
loss of Petra had never really dulled? Yes, I had reached an accommodation with it all——the way you eventually accept the death of someone
central to your life. But its lingering presence——the fact that no romance since then had ever come close to matching the absolute and profound certainty that Petra and I shared——served as a quiet but persistent
reminder of all that was lacking in my marriage . . . and, most tellingly,
of all that I had lost.

Still, I reassured Jan that night that I loved her, that I would be there
for her and our child, that we had a great future together. For the first
years of Candace's life, we did manage to have a sense of shared purpose.
We bought a house in Cambridge. I found a part-time teaching post
at Boston University——from September to December every year——
and scaled back travel during the other months to no more than eight
weeks per year. I continued to turn out books. During the ten months I
was home I very much shared, and enjoyed sharing, responsibility for
everything to do with Candace's daily life. Watching her discover the
world was so interesting and pleasurable that it compensated for the
ever-growing distance between her mother and me. Increasingly, Jan's
controlling nature, her flintiness, her inability to nurture——the root
coldness I always knew was there but could never bring myself to properly consider——pushed me deeper into my own shell. According to Jan,
I was the sort of man who lived most of the time in my own head, who
was far too singular, too much the loner, to be able to accept "the sense
of mutuality" that must accompany a good marriage and that, in truth,
my love for her was never anything more than a fragile veneer with no
real substance to it whatsoever.

Still, we soldiered along, making increasingly passionless but ongoing love with each other at least twice a week, very much a team when
it came to Candace's needs and her future, but otherwise increasingly
estranged. *Things fall apart, the center will not hold.* And once Candace hit adolescence and began to need us less on a full-time basis . . . that's when
the real drift began.

It was also in the year 2004 that——following a book I wrote about
the theoretics of travel and the very human need to escape day-in, day-
out reality——my editor suggested I consider a memoir of a life spent

ricocheting around the world. This proposal arrived at a moment when I was pretty certain that Jan was having an affair with a colleague——a truth that was admitted some years later during the endgame moments of our marriage——and I had fallen into an occasional thing with a magazine editor in New York. She was a most independent woman named Eleanor who was pleased to see me whenever I was in Manhattan. She would accompany me two or three times a year on a weeklong trip somewhere and was very clear about the fact that she wanted nothing more from me than this "collegial arrangement" (her exact words). Eleanor was forty, hugely smart, funny, clever, and exceptionally passionate. But she had been badly singed in a relationship prior to meeting me, and had decided to erect a barrier around her heart, even though she once admitted that we were so right for each other. But the man who had so hurt her had also been married. On a trip together to Costa Rica, six months into what she described as "our erotic friendship," I admitted that I was in love with her. Her response was to slam on the emotional breaks.

"Don't go there," she said, turning away from me in bed and reaching for a postcoital cigarette.

"But it's the truth. And I sense that you yourself feel the same way about——"

"What I feel," she said, cutting me off, "is that you are very married and living in a city two hundred miles away with a teenage daughter who, from everything you've told me, is clearly crazy about you."

"She will still love me——and she will still see a very great deal of me——even if I am living in Manhattan."

"You want to move in with me?"

"I would not be so presumptuous. But I want to be with you, yes. And not once every six weeks for a weekend, with the occasional interesting trip thrown in. I want a life with you, and would be willing to rent a place in Manhattan."

"This can't be," she said, sitting up and actually getting slightly agitated in her body language.

"I love you. I know that."

"And I know that you are a wonderful man, and one who deserves to be happier than you are. But I'm not the person with whom to collaborate on such a project."

"But we're so great together, so right for each other."

"And there are limits beyond which I am not willing to venture."

"Wouldn't you be willing to, at least, see how things developed if I were nearby?"

"I'll be blunt here, Thomas. I love seeing you when I do. I love sharing a bed with you. I love walking a beach with you. I love talking into the night with you, but only on the basis that you then vanish for a few weeks. Perhaps that might strike you as self-limiting. But I believe the reason we have such a good thing between us——besides the fact that you never complain to me about your wife, even though it is clear to me how unhappy you are——is that we are not in each other's lives all the time."

"But if I did move to New York, we wouldn't have to see each other every night."

"But I might want that, and that spells trouble for me. There is only so far I'm now willing to travel romantically with you, or anyone else for that matter."

"Even though you have just intimated to me that you might want that life together?"

"That's right. And if that sounds like a major contradiction . . . well, it is. And so it goes. But as a real traveler, surely you know there are certain places you refuse to venture."

"I did once turn down an assignment to Lagos."

"Very witty. But I know that you understand what I'm talking about. Because I sense, like me, you were so hurt by something, or *someone*. You have spent much of the years since then in mourning for her, because you also realize that what you had might never come your way again."

"Am I that transparent?" I asked with a sad smile.

"Intimacy does that, doesn't it? And yes, when we are together——and especially when we make love——I feel that loss you carry, and your desire to have it erased by the love of someone else."

"My love for you."

"I know. I see it in your eyes all the time. But, sorry, I just can't cross that line. I have my reasons, and I am also going to reserve my right not to explain them. Except to say I wish it were otherwise."

Nothing more was said about this during the forty-eight hours we had left in the Costa Rican rain forest. When we returned to the States, and I kissed her good-bye at JFK before jumping a connecting flight back to Boston, her eyes welled up, she buried her head in my shoulder, and she said three words:

"I'm so sorry."

The next morning I woke to an email written by Eleanor in the middle of that night, informing me that she had decided to "call time on us before it gets too serious, before it cuts too deep."

I wrote back, telling her that love was always a risk but, in our case, so worth taking. I never received a reply. As this flash of possibility, this willingness to risk my heart again, was extinguished right at a moment when I knew that Jan was sleeping with a hard-driving mergers-and-acquisitions lawyer named Brad Bingley (in all American stories there is always a guy named Brad), I felt the loss even more acutely . . . even though, as someone who had also stepped beyond the "forsaking all others" boundaries of my marriage, I couldn't exactly feel manic jealousy at the thought that Jan was twice a week in the arms of another man.

In the wake of Eleanor ending things between us, Jan informed me that she had been offered a two-month transfer to her firm's Washington office. "Maybe it would be a good idea if we had a small break from each other, a period of reassessment," she said. I spent that time she was away playing Dad to Candace. When she was at school or doing the half-dozen extracurricular activities that filled her afternoons, or spending half the weekend with a friend, I wrote the Berlin memoir that I had been ordered by Bubriski not to write all those years ago. I wrote it with a speed and a need that surprised me. Reading through all the notebooks again, what so amazed me was not just what a younger man I was back then——young not just chronologically, but also in terms of my understanding about life's larger questions——but also just how, in my day-to-day accounting of the love that Petra and I shared, I never once expressed a doubt about the veracity of our feelings toward each other. Yes, the notebooks were filled with worries about the shadows in her past. Yes, I often articulated my fear of losing her. And yes, I detailed——with an almost forensic attention to detail——that horrible final night in Berlin, when my rage and hurt destroyed everything.

But most of all what emerged so profoundly from these notebooks, which I hadn't opened in the eighteen subsequent years, but which I also kept locked up in the big fireproof cabinet I had in my office, was the sense of wonderment at the love I felt, the love I received, the belief that everything together was possible, the sense of hope permeating so much of our time together, and then the way it all just imploded in the most appalling and tragic of circumstances.

As I now reconstructed on the page all those extraordinary months in Berlin, I was very conscious of looking upon this time with the more weathered eye of a man in his forties——who, like anyone who has made it into his middle years, has been both bruised and deepened by everything that life has tossed in his path.

When, after six feverish weeks, I completed this memoir——stopping at that very moment when I wrote the words, *I had never gotten over it*——I got a call that same evening from my wife. She told me she was coming home earlier than expected from Washington and said that she had missed me while she was away.

This was a somewhat bemusing revelation, made all the more curious by the way she arrived back at midnight and essentially threw me onto the bed and made love to me with a passion that had been absent for more than a decade. Afterward she turned to me and——without saying that her fling with Mr. Mergers and Acquisitions was over——told me that she herself realized that many of the shortcomings in our marriage were down to her and that she wanted to make a strong effort to try to see if we could "find again the love that was once there."

I felt like saying: *"But the problem is, it started as a companionable romance with no real passionate depth. And can we now, after fifteen years together, really believe we can find untapped reserves of affection for each other?"*

This was the thought that first came into my head as we lay sprawled and——for a change——satiated on the bed we had shared so distantly for so many years. But I stopped myself from articulating it as I was still stinging from the end of my involvement with Eleanor, and because, for the first time ever, Jan was displaying vulnerability and worry about losing this edifice of a life that we had built together. Perhaps part of me—— the part that always traveled away from discomforting truths——thought that after all these years, we could find a proper fondness for each other.

We were so used to each other's quirks, and there was a wonderful fourteen-year-old daughter whose stability in the midst of the usual hormonal roller coaster of adolescence we both wanted to preserve. Surely, this was a moment of great possibility between us.

The Berlin memoir was the first thing to get shelved. I locked the manuscript away in my fireproof cabinet and took Jan and Candace on an assignment that brought me to Easter Island. I returned home and spent six months writing a travel memoir called *The Door Marked Exit*——which talked about the need to escape that had so shaped my life. During this time my marriage reverted back to the icy construct that it was, our era of good feeling lasting around six weeks before all the old habits and pathologies (both individual and shared) began to rear up again. When the book was published a year later, my father——now living in Arizona——wrote me a three-line letter after receiving his copy:

> Glad to hear your screwed-up parents made you the writer you are today. I commend you for your lack of self-pity. Just as I am relieved that your mother is not around to read your drivel about your childhood.

I wasn't surprised by this reaction——even though I thought myself pretty even-handed in the book about my father, painting him as a rather robust, larger-than-life mid-century American ad guy, trapped into doing what was expected of him but nonetheless blessed with a certain independent streak and no-bullshit charm. Mom came across as Mom: frustrated, disappointed, always thinking the denouement of her life should have turned out differently. And later on in the book, I also talked about a certain inherent loneliness that I always carried with me and never seemed able to shake.

Intriguingly, Jan had little to say about the book when it came out, though when we were out to dinner a few weeks later with some mutual friends and someone commented how we were one of the few couples they knew who had managed to remain married, given all my travel and Jan's high-powered and professional legal career, my wife's reply to this was:

"The reason we're still together is that, over the past sixteen years of marriage, Thomas has only been here for a total of five of them."

That certainly cast a momentary pall over the dinner. On the drive back home, when I tried to raise the issue with her, she said:

"Why even talk about the obvious? You have a life. I have a life. They are separate entities. We share a house. We share a bed. We share a daughter whom we both adore and who remains the only plausible reason we are still together."

"What a romantic picture you paint."

"I am just stating facts, Thomas."

"So what do you want?"

"I'm too damn busy right now to think about major personal upheavals. But if you want to go, I won't stop you."

But I didn't "go." I just kept voting with my feet. Once Candace was accepted at college——and effectively away for eight months a year——I too was barely seen. Jan, having made senior partner and having all sorts of new high-end pressures to deal with, raised no objections. When I was in town, we would share meals together, make love on occasion, and do the family thing at Thanksgiving and Christmas, and the three weeks every August when we took a house in a remote corner of Nova Scotia. The curious thing about this detached marriage was that the era of withering looks and unspoken emotional frustration and the episodic blow-up had been replaced by an era of indifferent civility. Even the sex was conducted along the lines of two people who were fulfilling a need, but no longer had much in the way of any amorous connection with each other.

Of course, Candace——being a more than perceptive young woman (and also someone who, from the age of fifteen onward, sparred constantly with her mother)——picked up early on the fact that her parents' marriage had become putative. The summer before she started college I bought her a transatlantic air ticket and an InterRail pass, handed her two thousand dollars, and told her to knock around Europe for a month. I received an email from her on the Greek island of Spetses, telling me she'd finished my travel memoir and "though I was, of course, flattered by everything you wrote about me, what really got to me was the way the whole book was really about trying to cope with the idea of being alone in the world, which, I suppose, we all are. But I do want you to always remember that you have me, just as I always remind myself that I have you."

I actually teared up upon reading that email. Just as I also had a moment's pause some weeks later when an email arrived from my father, saying that his new girlfriend had just read my memoir, "and she thought the way you depicted your old man was both affectionate and interesting . . . so what the hell do I know, right? And yeah, I guess I went for the jugular the last time I wrote you. My hard-ass style, right? What can I say, son? I've never done touchy-feely very well. So don't expect me to start now. Holly——that's the girlfriend's name——thinks you can write, but also that you tend to show off your smarts for all to see. But, hey, she isn't exactly Madame Curie."

I had to smile while reading this. My father——who never apologized or paid me a compliment in his life——was doing both in that backhanded way of his. Though our contact was nominal in the subsequent years——a phone call every few weeks, an annual three-day visit to the tacky retirement village to which he had retreated in the Arizona desert after things went all wrong for him professionally in New York——his death in 2009 rattled me so deeply that on the way home from his funeral, I jumped in my car and ended up in some hotel outside of Edgecomb, Maine.

And thus began the trajectory of events that saw me buy this cottage, lose my marriage, and fall into a melancholy that I refused to acknowledge for months afterward and which I only accepted after I stopped myself, at the very last minute, from a fatal encounter with a very large tree while on a cross-country ski hill in Quebec. And upon returning from Canada——psychically and physically bruised, but quietly relieved to be alive——the box from Berlin was waiting for me. The box with her name in the upper right-hand corner and her address in Prenzlauer Berg. Though I couldn't go near the box after bringing it home, the fact that I noted that her address was in Prenzlauer Berg made me want to know everything about her life since that final night together in Berlin some twenty-six years earlier. Then again, that desire to make contact had never left me. Why hadn't I fulfilled it? For the same reason I had never once returned to Berlin in all those years. Perhaps because I had known something so extraordinary with Petra——and once it was taken from me, once I learned of her treachery and then felt propelled to respond with an act of willful destructiveness (which, I realized only moments after it was perpetrated, was also an act of self-destructiveness), I couldn't bear to set eyes on the place again . . . let alone on the woman with whom I once thought I would spend the rest of my life.

Over the years, whenever the ache returned, I would try to reason that, of course, it had all just been youthful intoxication, passionate infatuation at its most open-throttle, something that was too fever-pitched, too intense, to survive on a long-term basis. Just as I would also remind myself that she was a woman living a double life and, because of that, all further trust between us would have been impossible.

But these statements were designed to dull the unresolved ache of it all. Why then did I feel compelled today to pull the Berlin manuscript down off the shelf and, for the first time in ten years since its composition, sit down and reread it?

Because of the goddamn box from Germany, that's why. Because of the sight of her name and her address. Because . . .

I checked my watch. It was well after midnight now. I'd been reading for more than six hours. Moonlight lit up the bay. I went into the kitchen, poured myself a small Scotch, opened the side door that led to my deck, braved the night-time boreal wind coming off the water, downed the Scotch, and told myself: *There's no use trying to dodge things any further. You have to open the damn box.*

So I went back inside and did just that. Reaching in I found myself first in possession of two large notebooks, of the type used in schools. Brown cardboard covers, spiral bindings, thinly lined inexpensive paper. On each cover was drawn in ink a large number indicating their sequence——and in the space that allowed the owner of the notebook to write his name were simply two initials: P.D. I opened the first notebook and saw page after page of her tightly wound handwriting. Each entry was undated, a series of asterisks indicating the end of a statement, a thought. Many of the pages had a residual gray smudge, hinting at fallen cigarette ash that was embedded on the page when the notebook was closed. Occasionally there was the long-dried watermark from a glass that had been used to prop the book open. The sight of her immaculate penmanship unsettled me further. It was all so intimate, so private, that I could only begin to wonder what had possessed her to send me these notebooks so many years later.

Until, that is, I pulled the second of the notebooks out and found myself staring down at a newspaper clipping attached to a single sheet of paper on which a brief letter had been written. A woman's face filled half the clipping. Picking it up I could see that the woman looked well into her sixties, given the grayness of her hair, the puffiness of her face, the deep lines that even the graininess of the newspaper print seemed to accentuate. The face of a woman I had never seen before.

But then my eyes moved to the name above the photograph. And I realized that I was staring at a recent photograph of Petra.

And below this was a small headline:

Petra Dussmann Stirbt am 2 Januar in Berlin.

Petra Dussmann dies in Berlin 2 January.

Her death notice.

My eyes swam over the few short German sentences that followed:

. . . daughter of the late Martin and Frieda Dussmann of Halle. Mother of Johannes Dussmann. Worked as a translator at Deutsche Welle in Berlin. Died at the Charité Hospital in Berlin after a long battle with cancer. Funeral at the Friedrichshain Crematorium at 10:30 am, 5 January.

And behind this clipping was a line scrawled in German on a piece of plain white paper:

Mother wanted you to have these.

Below this——after a home address, an email address, and a phone number——there was a signature: Johannes Dussmann.

I sat down slowly in my desk chair. Have you ever noticed how—— when first presented with dreadful news——the world goes so profoundly quiet? It's as if the shock of the appalling deadens all ambient sound and forces you to hear the great empty chasm that it the beginning of grief.

Only in this case, the grief had begun twenty-six years ago.

And now . . .

Three words kept repeating themselves in my head:

Petra. Meine Petra.

I sat in that chair motionless for I don't know how long. I simply had no cognizance of time. Just:

Petra. Meine Petra.

This can't be.

But there it was. In black and white. Like the inked words that cascaded across the thin watermarked lines of the two notebooks in front of me.

Mother wanted you to have these.

Because she wanted you to read these. Now.

PART FOUR

NOTEBOOK ONE

L IPSTICK. THAT'S THE first thing she handed me when she welcomed me. She introduced herself as Frau Ludwig——and said she would be looking after me during my stay here. And then Frau Jochum and Herr Ullmann——who had collected me from the hand-over point——wished me a good night's sleep and said they would see me tomorrow afternoon.

I had no idea where I was. I had been turned over to Frau Jochum and Herr Ullmann in the middle of some bridge——what I learned later was the Glienicken Brücke, which spans the River Havel between Potsdam and Berlin, and which I found out later from Herr Ullmann is known as the Bridge of Spies, because that's where they often trade agents who've been imprisoned by "the other side." Frau Jochum introduced herself as a representative of the West German intelligence service. Ullmann——thin, tall, dressed in a severe suit, wire-rimmed glasses, very American looking——introduced himself in good German. He said he was from "the American mission here in West Berlin" . . . but I knew that, if he was in this car with an agent from the *Bundesnachrichtendienst*, he was definitely CIA. What surprised me was how he told me that he was so pleased to meet me, as he had been following my case for several weeks now. He also said that I was the sort of person they were working to get out. I emphasized the fact that I wasn't a dissident, a politico. They said they knew all that——and that they had much to talk about with me, but would wait until I had a good night's sleep.

Though I was still trying to appear bewildered——as I had been instructed to appear——so much about all this was genuinely bewildering. The glare of the headlights turned on me on the bridge. Was that to ensure that the agents on the GDR side could not see the faces of their Western counterparts awaiting me? The fact that Frau Jochum was so well dressed. The leather interior of the most luxurious car I had ever entered (of course, it was a Mercedes). The low murmur of its engine as we drove off. The way Frau Jochum and Herr Ullmann spoke in low, comforting voices, designed to put me at my ease. But when I asked them about Jurgen I could see them exchanging glances, looking ill at ease, trying to communicate to each other with their eyes. That's when I knew. When I pressed them to tell me what had happened to my husband. they said they'd rather talk to me after I'd had a good night's sleep. *He's dead,* I told myself. And those bastards over there——in the prison where they kept me——told me nothing about this. Nothing.

I pressed Frau Jochum again. This time she told me that Jurgen had hanged himself in his cell. It was strange, my reaction. Yes, I was shocked. But because she had first hesitated before telling me, I was already prepared for such extreme news. While it still had a certain kick-in-the-stomach impact on me, it didn't cleave me the way the death of a spouse should. Perhaps because, though he was officially my husband, he was a man with whom I shared an apartment and little more. But I sensed Frau Jochum and Herr Ullmann knew this from my file. Just as they would also know that it was his insane behavior that landed me in prison some weeks ago . . . or, at least, I thought it was weeks ago. They kept me so disorientated I could never work out how long I had been locked up. Whenever I asked Colonel Stenhammer——the Stasi man who interrogated me daily——if my husband had been saying mad things about me, he would always tell me not to ask questions, and then demand to know if I had something to hide.

"If you come clean with us, the path back to Johannes will be an easier one."

But as I had nothing to confess . . .

Weeks this went on. All the while they were keeping the light on in my cell twenty-four hours a day, letting me out only for a half hour of exercise in a concrete block topped with barbed wire, and for the five hours of interrogations that took up the mornings. In other words, they were rapidly grinding me down. All I could think about, day and night, was the fact that they had now taken Johannes from me and were telling me——as I was now classified as a traitor to the State——that they would never let my polluted influence infect "this child of our People's Republic."

You will never see him again unless you cooperate with them, I told myself so many times. And the knowledge that Jurgen——his self-importance, his childishness, his lack of responsibility when it came to his wife and, most especially, his child——created this catastrophe that had seen Johannes taken away from me . . . well, when Frau Jochum told me of his death, all I could think (after the initial jolt that accompanied the news) was: *at least you now do not have to live with the pain and consequences of your aberrant behavior.*

The windows of the Mercedes were tinted, which meant that all the neon of the city——neon like I had never seen before——appeared refracted through a darkened prism.

Eventually we drove into a compound. Gates. Men in uniforms. Bright lights. Security everywhere. We pulled up in front of what seemed to be a small house within these grounds. A woman was standing outside. This was Frau Ludwig. Forties. Quiet. Professional. Kind in a professionally competent way.

"You must be Petra," she said as Frau Jochum handed me over, saying good-bye after informing me that we would continue our conversation tomorrow afternoon. I was suddenly feeling an exhaustion and a fear that almost matched the exhaustion and fear that I felt all those weeks locked up in that prison, being told I had to cooperate with the Stasi or I would be left dangling in this limbo for years, with no hope whatsoever of my son being returned to me.

In the end, I did everything they asked of me. Including signing those fucking papers, allowing them to place Johannes with another family.

But it was all entered into as "a deal." A deal that would involve me doing some work for them.

"Greatly serious, important work," Colonel Stenhammer told me.

"Work that will be of such benefit to our Democratic Republic that I can see no reason why you shouldn't be honored to do it."

And then he presented his proposition to me. A proposition that, as he put it, "offers you the possibility of hope."

How could I say no, knowing that if I did, all hope would be quashed?

So I said yes——and so quickly that Stenhammer insisted I be returned to my cell for forty-eight hours to truly ponder whether I was up to the task. Forty-eight hours in that cell without any contact. With the knowledge that my one and only chance was by doing exactly what he demanded?

That's when I broke down completely in front of him, begging him not to lock me up again, promising him my full and utter cooperation, my complete fealty. I even used that word, "fealty"——which in German is *Lehenstreue*. Stenhammer smiled when he heard it.

"A very medieval word, Frau Dussmann," he said. "Yet one with strong semantical connotations. Knights swore *Lehenstreue* to the realm. And although the feudalism of the medieval system runs so contrary to the democratic tenets of our Republic, I do acknowledge and appreciate——as one who has sworn to defend the Republic from its capitalist enemies——the metaphoric resonance of *Lehenstreue* as regards your response to our proposition. Just as I can also see that, having finally accepted your duty to the state that has given you so much, you wish to get to work as soon as possible, knowing that the faster things progress, the closer you will be to . . ."

He didn't finish this sentence, because he knew it was more effective to let this "payoff" dangle. It was the bait——and I had no choice but to swallow it.

Perhaps that was what was so unnerving about these first hours in the West. The civility of Frau Jochum and Herr Ullmann. Their evident decency. The way they were so solicitous toward me. And all the while, me feeling like a bad provincial actor forced to play the role of Faust at the Deutsches Theater in West Berlin——and wondering endlessly if they were accepting my performance.

Frau Ludwig also could not have been more hospitable——and, in her own controlled way, truly compassionate. The apartment into which I had been ushered was so plush, so beautifully furnished, so redolent of security and safety, that I was nothing less than overwhelmed by the way they were trying to cushion me. Then, after telling me she was going to run me a bath, she said that she had a small gift for me——and placed in my hand a very elegant chrome lipstick. My eyes immediately welled up. For I remembered instantly something I had read once in a book about the Second World War by an English academic, a book that had been briefly considered by the state publishing house where I worked as a translator. It was only considered, I learned later, because the man had impeccable socialist credentials. But it was tossed into that pile of books that had been rejected and were to be incinerated, for that is what we did with foreign books from outside the fraternal socialist nations which we knew we wouldn't publish and which we didn't want to fall into the wrong hands. I saw this book at the top of one of those bins. It looked interesting and——from a GDR perspective——revisionist. So I took a risk and snuck it into my shoulder bag and brought it home, hiding it in a hole in a kitchen cupboard in my room. This was just a month before I moved in with Jurgen. Late at night, when I couldn't sleep, I would take the book out and learn that everything we had been taught about Nazis coming from the west of Germany was a fantasy. They came from all corners of *Das Vaterland*. Although we knew certain things about the concentration camps, the details were never spelled out in all their horror. This historian did so graphically, but with great technical control. He didn't try to embellish the monstrosity perpetrated there. He simply let the facts speak. Just as he also made the parallel with the much less documented horrors of the Stalinist gulags which, of course, we only knew about in a sort of hearsay way.

It's strange, isn't it, how, amidst all the accounts of children being forcibly separated from their parents, and the hideous medical experiments (women having liquid concrete shoved up their uteruses) and the gassings, and the harvesting of teeth for their gold fillings, a small detail suddenly illuminates everything. And it was the mention, made by this Oxford historian, that when the British troops liberated the concentration camp at Belsen, they handed lipsticks to all the surviving women inmates. Those women broke down at this small gesture——a materially tiny but psychologically huge bit of luxury that acknowledged the femininity of women who were, at best, lice-ridden, emaciated.

So when Frau Ludwig handed me that lipstick, I was so overcome that I had to excuse myself to go to the bathroom. Once I had the door closed I began to weep. I cried because I couldn't bear being separated from Johannes, because the ache I felt without him was limitless. But I also cried at the simple humanity of the gesture that Frau Ludwig just made to me—and all that it implied.

But the weeping was also bound up in the fact that I would now have to betray everyone I encountered in this new world. To realize that in the face of such a simple act of kindness . . .

I can't live with myself.

I have to live with myself. It is the only way back.

*   *   *

I can lie to others. I cannot lie to myself. Jurgen lied to himself constantly. He told himself he was the great playwright. The great radical thinker. The great subversive. What he was—what he saw in those sad moments when I could see him catch furtive glances at himself in the mirror—was a man who had squandered his early success. Instead of taking steps to recapture the brilliant spark that illuminated that one extraordinary play of his, he gave in to all those voices that told him he was a genius and that simultaneously whispered to him that he would never fulfill the promise he briefly showed.

But who am I—a woman of no creative talent whatsoever, a minor little translator who hasn't ever even been given the privilege of applying her craft to a major novel—to disparage a man who did write one significant play that, until he landed himself in trouble with the authorities, was performed everywhere in our strange little country.

So yes, I see myself with a certain hard clarity. Just as I know that this is but a half truth, that a very large part of the human condition involves having to modulate truth in order to make living with yourself possible.

So I try to justify my actions to myself all the time. Just as the other more brutal side of me grabs me by the scruff of the neck, shoves me in front of a mirror, and says: stop the self-deception, the pretense, the fraud. Look at yourself——and don't be magnanimous.

That voice——it's my mother's. She always had the hard words for me. Praise, she once told me, is an overrated tendency. It creates narcissism and self-absorption. Whereas self-criticism, fault-finding, keeps you grounded, bona fide, principled.

I could have added one last word here: joyless.

Am I joyless? I think back to all the joy I had with Johannes—— how he made every day worthwhile, and his presence in my life so counterbalanced everything else. It's what I once said to Colonel Stenhammer: *Johannes is my entire reason for living.* To which he dryly replied: "Then you will, I am certain, do everything in your power to convince the state that you merit his return to your care and custody."

Of course, I said I would do whatever was asked of me.

I can lie to others. I cannot lie to myself.

And so I must admit a chronological truth here. I am writing this four weeks after that first night I was handed over to Frau Jochum and Herr Ullmann. Before tonight I never put pen to paper and attempted to assemble my thoughts about all that had happened to me, all that I had to hide. A day or so after I was brought to the West, Frau Ludwig had asked me if I wanted "writing materials." Perhaps she understood——given everything I'd been through——the need to write things down, to set out my version of events on the page and, in the process, try to sort out my feelings about everything . . . even vent my anger, my agony at having lost my son, and the fury I felt at Stenhammer never telling me, before my departure, about Jurgen's suicide . . . if it really was a suicide. But he knew that to inform me of that before I left would have been destabilizing——and, perhaps, I might not have accepted the Faustian bargain he proposed. He also knew that, once handed over, I would ask his Western counterparts——or they would have to tell me——about my husband's fate. This would undoubtedly devastate me——even if my feelings toward Jurgen were, at best, mixed ones. Stenhammer was counting on this devastation to make me feel even more isolated even more fearful of the fact that, if I didn't now cooperate . . .

So . . . the truth. Or, at least, my version thereof.

I am writing this in a room they found for me in Kreuzberg. Before now I scribbled banal things in another notebook I left closed on my little desk here in my room. I had inserted three hairs in the pages of this closed notebook——and every day, when I went out for a few hours, I always returned, prepared to discover that Frau Jochum's and Herr Ullmann's people had been snooping around my room and reading what I had written.

But the notebook remained closed and untouched.

Once convinced that my room wasn't being swept on a regular basis, I then did a little inspection of the basement in my building—— and found a disused ventilator shaft in a particularly dark corner of this cavern. Reaching up into the shaft I discovered there was a small shelf just above its point of entry, one that could comfortably house a few journals.

That same day I went out and bought a second similar notebook to the one I had been leaving on my desk as a decoy. That night I began to write the journal I am scribbling in just now, trying to get down on paper everything that had happened to me since I was brought to the West. Every few days since that first night, I retrieve the journal from its hiding place and commit to paper all that I can never tell anyone.

I am vigilant about the fact that this journal never leaves this building, that when I finish writing in it, I always bring it straight down to its hiding place in the cellar, and do so after midnight when there is nobody around. And I keep on writing that rather prosaic decoy journal, jotting down thoughts about my work, my impressions of West Berlin, my loneliness and (yes) how much I miss my son. Once I start work, I plan to make a point of bringing it out with me and also continue to leave it on my desk at home.

And the hairs I continue to hide in its pages remain unmoved.

And when it comes to my "actual" journal, the one in which this sentence is being written right now, the journal I keep stashed in the basement . . .

Despite so carefully hiding it away——and never allowing it to re-main in my room for longer than the period in which I am writing in it——I know I am still taking an immense risk in chronicling the lie I am forced to live. But writing it down means it is not just existing inside my head, that there is a place in which I can disclose what is happening to me, the deceit and fraudulence that now underscore everything about my life here. If I didn't have the refuge of this journal, I would go under. I don't seek absolution, but I do need confession.

I only write in this journal every few days. I always do it late in the evening——retrieving it from the basement after ascertaining that no one is in the hallway, secreting it under my shirt or sweater as I head back to my room, then returning it to its ventilator shaft hiding place as soon as I have finished my entry. I never go near it during daylight hours, no matter how much I want to get something down in it.

Kreuzberg. It is such a sad place. But I insisted on living here because, during one of our many daily "conversations," Frau Jochum revealed, after I demanded the information, that Johannes had been placed with a Stasi family who lived in Friedrichshain. That's when I also demanded a map of West Berlin and saw that the district closest to Friedrichshain was Kreuzberg——The Wall cleaving the two areas like a surgeon who had the shakes when making an incision, leaving a scar that looks like a demented crescent moon.

"I want to live here," I said, pointing to Kreuzberg.

"Is that, psychologically speaking, a good idea?" Frau Jochum asked me. "After all, you will be in proximity to where Johannes lives."

"That's the idea," I said. "I want to be close to my son."

"Personally, I do not think this wise."

"Personally, I think it essential for me," I said.

I could see Frau Jochum pondering all this, then saying:

"All right, in time, when you are ready to go out into the world . . . yes, we will help you find an apartment in Kreuzberg."

The "apartment" was this room. Frau Ludwig brought me out apartment hunting the next week. She said she just wanted to help me find my way around the city, but my feeling is they felt they had to chaperone me, to make certain I was stable, capable of being out on my own. I couldn't help but wonder if they were thinking about keeping me under surveillance for the first weeks that I was an independent entity.

That's the reason I didn't accept Frau Ludwig's offer of a notebook in which to record my thoughts in the weeks that they were interviewing me. I worried that they might read the notebook when I was away from the apartment. After all, they were the intelligence services——and as I was warned many times before being handed over, they would be both warm and welcoming, while privately wondering if I was "kosher."

"The fact that your story is so horrible," Stenhammer told me. "The fact that you can tell them about your wrongful imprisonment, and the way we took your child away from you . . ."

"But you did wrongfully imprison me," I said. "And you did take my child away from me."

"Then why did you sign an agreement here yesterday, offering up your child for voluntary adoption?"

I wanted to scream and shout and say: "Because you forced me to, telling me that if I didn't agree to have Johannes adopted, you would start a criminal proceeding against me as an unfit mother and would make certain the judge at the trial ensured that I was barred permanently from contact with him."

"At least this way," he argued, "once you have proven your worthiness to the Republic again——once you have redeemed yourself——the return of Johannes to your custody will be a relatively straightforward business. All going well, he will be back with you within eighteen months. But this will all be based on your effectiveness for us after you are traded. Do understand: you will have to lie to people who will show you kindness, who will treat you as a heroine who was indecently abused by a 'totalitarian regime,' which is how they regard our highly egalitarian society where no child wants for hunger, where there is universal health care for all, where a superb standard of education exists, where artists are valued and subsidized, where merit, not money, advances all . . ."

As he spouted these propagandistic banalities, all I could think was: *Everything you described——the lack of poverty, the free hospitals, the excellent free schools——can be found in every Scandinavian country. But, unlike our little Republic, they allow their citizens the right to travel freely and they don't imprison people for daring to voice an opinion against the state. Nor do they take away children from a citizen whose only crime is that her erstwhile husband has gone crazy in public.*

But I said nothing, except: "I will do what you ask. And I will trust you when you say that if I fulfill my role, you will return my son to me."

A large part of me knew this outcome was highly unlikely, that with Johannes having been placed with a couple who I guessed were Stasi *and* childless, they would be loath to part with him. I also knew that I couldn't trust Stenhammer—that he was an arch manipulator who knew he held all the cards. That was the hardest part of the equation—the recognition that it was all a game of power for him, and one predicated on the fact that he also held out hope. A favorable resolution if I cooperated. What else did I have but this hope?

I'm not going to write too much about the three weeks of daily "interviews" that I had with Frau Jochum and Herr Ullmann, except to say that theirs was a very polite and civilized form of interrogation. Again there was a Faustian bargain here—a nice cushioned landing in the West, in which I was put up in a luxurious apartment, bought real Levi's and nice clothes and makeup, given a place to live and a possible job (the interview is in two days' time), and given enough money to tide me over until I started earning. What they wanted in exchange was information. They quizzed me about everything—from Stenhammer's interrogation techniques to how many Marlboros he smoked a day. Their interest in detail was extraordinary. They wanted to know the color of the walls in the prison in which I was kept, the type of linoleum on the floors, the height in meters of the cage in which I was allowed to exercise, the sort of recording equipment they used when questioning me, even: *Was there a specific brand of coffee that Stenhammer brewed for himself?*

Information, they say, is knowledge. But after three weeks of such excruciating attention to detail I wanted to scream: *information is ennui.* But I couldn't. I needed these people on my side. Though tedious and pedantic, they were also both so decent, so courteous, so careful never to be officious.

But they also saw me as a conduit of information. I was their entree to a closed world—someone who had been dropped into its vortex, and could now give them a firsthand account of everything I had seen and experienced.

How I wanted to break down in front of Frau Jochum and confess everything. How I wanted to make a clean breast and throw myself at her mercy. But I feared that, perhaps, they would immediately label me "damaged goods" and throw me back—at which point my destiny would be prison. Stenhammer threatened me with this, were I to be returned by "the enemy." And the end of any hope of Johannes being returned to me. And he did promise me . . .

There are moments when I just feel like dying. Literally walking out of this room and heading to the U-Bahn station and throwing myself in front of the first oncoming train. I rationalize this decision by simply telling myself it will be the end of all pain, that it is the only way to silence the agony. For that is what I feel, hour after hour. The agony of being forced into living this double life. The agony of knowing that I am now completely alone in the world. Most of all, the wrenching agony of losing my son—and having him dangled in front of me as the prize I will receive if I give them what they want.

But what stops me from making that journey off the U-Bahn plat-form is Johannes. I tell myself that as long as there is even the slight-est possibility of him being returned to me, I must somehow keep myself afloat.

I cannot give up hope. Because it's all I have. Because *he* is all I have. There is nothing else in my life but my son. *Nothing.*

*   *   *

This room. I didn't want to move here. I wanted to stay in the plush, cosseting world of that intelligence compound, where somebody made the bed every day and picked up the towels and did my laundry and cooked wonderful food (the vegetables alone were incredible—I had never had any access to such fresh foodstuffs), and kept a basket of fruit topped up for me every day. Apples, peaches, bananas, straw-berries—all exotica back across The Wall, but so evidently abundant here. I kept wondering if, being in a special compound, I was also being granted privileged access to special delicacies, like the senior party apparatchiks back home who, rumor always had it, were al-lowed into special shops where hard-to-get items—like fresh fruits and Marlboro cigarettes——were accessible. What an extraordinary system. "The dictatorship of the proletariat," as Lenin put it, in which an elite——the people who administered the dictatorship in the name of social egalitarianism——insisted that everyone accept material deprivation and profound restriction on personal liberties, while they themselves acted like a feudal ruling class and granted themselves privileges denied to all those they kept enslaved and imprisoned. No wonder poor Jurgen went mad. He actually thought his creative brilliance would be a bulwark against the system's implacability. Those people hated artists——even the ones who paid lip service to the Republic. Because they knew that a streak of subversion always clouded their hearts. Anyway, who trusts a writer? Not only do they "sponge off life and those close to them" (a Jurgen quote), but they so often articulate the things we're all thinking but don't want to be made public.

This train of thought started with a comment about fruit, and how I was certain that the sweet, ripe, wildly red strawberries I was eating every morning were only being provided to me because I was a special status "guest" with information to impart. But then, one afternoon, Frau Ludwig suggested we take a walk in the area near the compound. I discovered we were a little out of town, near Spandau Prison. But the area was residential and green, with fine houses and well-maintained apartment blocks. Frau Ludwig said the area was largely working class——but the shops were still stocked with the most extraordinary range of things to buy. Just rereading that sentence I know how naïve, how *Communist provincial,* I sound. But the truth is, my eyes went wide at the sight of huge clumps of broccoli, the tomatoes the size of a clenched fist, the twenty types of chocolate on sale just by the cash register. All this choice, all this plenty, and accessible even in a small corner shop. I wanted to be thrilled by all the options that now awaited me. But all I could think was: I may have crossed over, but I am in no way free. Because they have me beholden to them if I want to see Johannes again.

But, God, the apartment in that compound, it was so lavish, so comforting. And so outside of the world——which is what I loved most about it. I was still safe here. Once beyond its secure walls, I would be back in a world I knew would close in on me shortly thereafter. Because the call would one day come from their "contact" in West Berlin. And then . . .

So I really did talk up my fear of the world beyond theirs. But it wasn't playacting. It was an absolute terror of what lay in store for me. Frau Ludwig and Frau Jochum together did their best to reassure me that what I was feeling was profoundly normal, given the number of political prisoners they had welcomed here and shepherded toward integration in Western society. Frau Jochum said:

"I've often seen people who, like you, have been released from the most psychologically damaging detention——and then simply cannot cope with the sense of choice, the sheer liberty, that life over here provides. You must learn that you can have a conversation with somebody and make a sardonic comment about Chancellor Kohl——and you will not lose your career on account of it."

Unless you happen to work for Chancellor Kohl's party.

"You are just going to have to be patient with yourself," Frau Ludwig told me. "It's a steep learning curve, I know. But, in time . . ."

I was able to stay in the compound for more than four weeks. As tedious as I found the interviews, I cooperated fully. Because I knew that as long as I was proving useful to them, they would let me stay. Around the end of the third week Herr Ullmann informed me that, as I had been a translator back east, he had found an opening for me at Radio Liberty.

"It will allow you to keep in contact with the land of your birth by doing something positive for your compatriots. And it will also allow you to meet an entire group of fellow refugees in West Berlin."

Is that supposed to please me? To be tossed in with the other lost souls from the Eastern Bloc, all harboring sadness and resentment and all the psychic scars that come with the territory. The thing is—— and I explained this to Stenhammer so many damn times——I never wanted to be a dissident. I didn't have extensive grievances against the state. I didn't long for a life in the West. I never once took part in a political activity that compromised my loyalty to the German Democratic Republic. Yes, I wanted a nicer apartment. Yes, I would have liked the opportunity to go to Paris in my lifetime. But I accepted the limitations, and I loved the community we made for ourselves in Prenzlauer Berg. When Johannes arrived, it didn't matter that his father virtually ignored him. It didn't matter that he was going off the rails. All that mattered was this new life, this child whom, if I had been in any way religious, I would have called a gift from God. Because his presence in my life changed it utterly. I had never felt such unconditional love before toward anyone. Whatever about the drabness of our material lives. Whatever about the tedium of my job. Whatever about Jurgen's increasing withdrawal from our lives——to the point where we stopped sharing a bed and I didn't really care if he went off whoring for days at a time——I had my son there. He was the center of my existence, my future, *our* future. He made everything else that was dismal and joyless in my life seem less significant. He gave me an *Existenzberechtigung*——a reason to be. A reason to live.

And without it I have nothing. I am nothing.

*   *   *

I moved in here last week. Five days ago to be exact. Frau Ludwig went apartment hunting with me. Or, rather, she told me she'd found a nice *Einzimmerwohnung*——a bedsitting room, or what is called in French a *chambre de bonne*——in the area I had requested. She'd even gone ahead and put a deposit down on it, and was getting the landlord to repaint it and retile the shower. When we visited it, I was impressed by the fact that it smelled new. White walls. Brown painted floorboards. A plain single bed with a wooden headboard. A desk in matching dark wood with a bentwood chair. A small kitchen table with two chairs. A galley kitchen with a new fridge, a cooker, a hot plate. A tiny shower in a far corner of this fifteen-meter room. One window, with a simple but new white blind, that looked out on a rather grubby alley——but at least was away from the main road, down which traffic rumbled day and night. After the sumptuousness of the compound, this was a return to reality. Still this *reality* was still more comfortable and well equipped and airy (despite its small size) than anywhere I had ever lived before. What's more, two days before

I moved in here, Frau Ludwig took me shopping. They'd already supplied me with several pairs of Levi's and T-shirts and underwear, a double-breasted dark blue military overcoat, even a leather jacket. Now she brought me to this extraordinary department store on the Ku'damm called KaDeWe which we had, of course, heard about back in the GDR——but which surpassed my expectations. I had never seen a place so opulent, so crammed with goods. And the choice, *the choice,* was overwhelming. We went to buy plain white sheets. But Frau Ludwig stated that I would probably not want to have to iron them all the time, so she suggested we buy two pairs of a style called "easy care." She also told me about a duvet that was "good for all seasons." And she insisted on buying me a small set of pots and pans that, she said, you never had to clean too thoroughly as they all had something called "a nonstick surface."

We also bought a set of white crockery, a box of cutlery, a wooden chopping board and a few kitchen knives, a coffee press, and (because it was the one appliance I had always craved) a toaster. She even brought me to the hi-fi department to buy me a radio and a little record player with two speakers. I felt like a child being spoiled by a rich aunt——and both loved it and felt profound guilt, as I knew I would be called upon to betray such generosity and had done so already. Because I'd not had the courage to come clean with them about . . .

Enough. You know why you have to follow their command. You know it's the only possible way back to Johannes. Stop the soul searching. The sooner you give them what they want the sooner this waking nightmare will be over.

*   *   *

I left the room today for the first time in three days. After moving in here on Monday I went to the local store——it's a small supermarket——and bought enough food to last me several days. They'd opened a bank account for me in the local Sparkasse——two thousand marks. So much money. Enough to cushion me until I receive my first month's salary from the job that I don't want to start. Herr Ullmann told me that the director of Radio Liberty, Herr Wellmann, would be expecting a call from me this week. But I decided that "this week" could also mean Friday. Once I arrived here on Monday——and found everything that Frau Ludwig had bought for me at KaDeWe already delivered here and piled on the bed and kitchen table——I just ventured out the one time to shop. I bought the food and carted it home. Then I spent the balance of the first day and night organizing the apartment. Once it was set up, I made one last trip outside, as I had seen a used record and book shop on a side street near mine. I bought a record by Wolf Biermann. *Chauseestrasse 131*. Jurgen had a copy of this album. It was a prized possession, as it had been banned and Biermann stripped of his citizenship while on a tour of the West in 1976. The great irony of this action by the state was that Biermann himself had been born in the West and emigrated to the GDR because he was a socialist idealist. And then, when he became far too critical of his adopted land, they threw him out. Like the son rejected by the father whose love he always craved.

I also bought *Sgt. Pepper,* letting out a little excited yelp when I saw it in one of the bins, as this too was so hard to find at home. Judit had a copy, and we listened to it together on several occasions, drinking vodka, smoking, trying to imagine what London must be like, wondering out loud if we would ever see the world beyond the sealed borders within which we lived.

Back in my room I played the Biermann and the Beatles over and over again. I found myself crying several times. Biermann's sarcastic, sardonic lyrics bringing me back to Prenzlauer Berg and twenty friends crammed into a tiny apartment. A few candles burning. Bad Romanian wine and cheap vodka. Biermann on the record player. Everybody talking, talking. A real sense of animation, of engagement. Me still feeling out of my depth around so many proper writers and artists. Me going into the alcove every fifteen minutes to make certain Johannes wasn't crying amidst all the music and talk and laughter. Judit joining me there once, looking down at my sleeping son and starting to sob that she knew it was now too late to have children, and how I was the only real friend she could count on in the world.

Judit.

When Frau Jochum revealed that it was Judit who had been reporting on me to the Stasi for months, maybe years . . . no, I didn't
feel hatred. Just desperate shock, then the most crippling sort of
sadness. Whom could you trust? Who *wasn't* in their pocket? Who
wouldn't betray their closest friend to maintain some sort of détente
with those bastards?

But she told me repeatedly that she valued our friendship more
than anything. *"We are sisters——and we will always look after each
other."* And I believed her and told her everything. Now it turns out
she was meeting her Stasi man and telling him everything I told her.
It was all taken down and used against me——even though I can't remember a truly subversive comment I made in front of her. But Stenhammer was able to quote to me things that I had allegedly said——but
they were all passing sarcasms about life in our little Republic, and
all very Berlin in their sardonicism. The sorts of things we all said all
the time during those long, alcohol-driven evenings in somebody's
apartment up off Kollwitzplatz. When I heard them quoted back to me
during my daily interrogations, I realized that somebody among our
group had been the Stasi's eyes and ears into our little bohemian circle. But Stenhammer was clever. He never quoted me anything I said
that was so specific, so intimate, as to make me realize it was Judit
who had been their mole. So when Frau Jochum told me, I couldn't
bring myself to believe it. And still don't. Even finally writing it down
doesn't lessen the blow, doesn't make me feel any less alone. Which
I am. That's why I haven't been able to go outside. Seeing people on
the street just emphasizes my feeling of total sequestration. I have
no family. I have no friends. I am living a lie in the hope of undoing
a monstrous wrong. And this room——it's clean and well heated and
nicer than anywhere I've ever lived, albeit tiny. Much of the time I
envisage a crib next to my bed and my son sleeping in it. I worry that
the people he has been placed with will not give him the love that he
needs, that they will be formal and distant with him. He loves to be
cuddled. And I could never stop holding him, touching him.

And now . . .

Now I keep hoping that writing about it will allow me to understand it. To accept it. But it just heightens the nightmare. Every

morning I wake up from a restive night and there are about ten, fifteen seconds when I am not aware of things, of all that constitutes my life. The world does not look bad at all. But then the daily re- alization hits——they have taken away my son——and I understand that this is a sorrow without frontiers. A sorrow that will never be excised.

*   *   *

I finally got up the courage and went out today. A snowy day. Snow—— the great temporary purifier. The world goes silent and is baptized white. Even Kreuzberg——ugly Kreuzberg——takes on an aura of wonder under snow. Even the sad-eyed Turks I see everywhere—— their dislocation and homesickness so etched on their faces——seem less forlorn in the face of all this cascading *Schnee*.

I went to a phone booth on the corner of my street and dialed the number for Radio Liberty that Herr Ullmann had given me. When the switchboard answered I asked to be put through to Herr Wellmann's office. A very officious woman came on the line. Introduced herself as Frau Orff and said she was Herr Wellmann's secretary. When I told her my name she said:

"We were expecting to hear from you sooner."

"I was told to call you this week."

"So you leave it to three p.m. on a Friday afternoon? Not very professional, if I may say so."

"I am still finding my feet here," I said, sounding so lame.

"Eleven a.m. Monday," she said. "Unless your schedule is so busy that you cannot find the time to meet with your prospective employer."

"Eleven a.m. Monday is fine."

"Be prompt, Frau Dussmann. In fact, be early."

*   *   *

I bought food again after the phone call and went home. The thought struck me: I still haven't heard from *him*. The man they said would contact me. *Their man*. I have a momentary reverie. He will never contact me. Maybe he's been picked up by the police, or they have decided not to use me . . . and I am free.

But if they don't "use" me, I never see my son again.

*   *   *

I am such a coward. Another two days locked up inside. And a sleepless night Sunday out of fear about the interview. The insomnia was murderous.

I must have smoked twenty cigarettes before the sun squinted awake. And the reason I could not surrender to sleep? Worry about not getting the job——and displeasing my masters who would then simply tell me I hadn't kept my end of the bargain. So now they weren't keeping theirs.

But if I did get this job, I was certain their man would come calling. Cause and effect. They would be highly pleased, no doubt, that I was working in what was essentially the propaganda department of the enemy.

After I showered I took a long look in the mirror and didn't like what I saw: Big deep rings under my eyes. My skin ashen. Lines already forming in my forehead. I've aged ten years in the past few dreadful months. I look worn down, world-weary. No man will ever come near me again. Because I exude too much sadness. A woman carrying far too much troubled baggage behind her.

I applied copious amounts of makeup to my face in an attempt to mask the sleeplessness, the damage. I drank five cups of coffee and smoked a commensurate number of cigarette. Then I put on my boots and my new leather jacket, conscious of the softness and quality of the leather, and took the U-Bahn up to Wedding.

Radio Liberty. A bland industrial building with serious security. I had to hand over my newly minted papers to the uniformed functionary at the gates, then wait until clearance was given. Once I was ushered inside, Frau Orff——severe, contemptuous——was there to meet me at reception.

"So you deign to come and see us," she said.

"I was having some difficulties."

"You people always do," she said.

I said nothing, though I felt a certain rage inside. *You people.* Yes, I am an Ossie—an East German. Yes, we are a thwarted race. Yes, our country is a repressive tragedy. So, by all means, be contemptuous of me if it makes you feel better about your own little life. Because all our lives are, in the great cosmic scheme of things, so minute, so ephemeral. Who will know any of this one hundred years from now? The fact that my child has been taken from me; the fact that a secretary at a radio station that broadcasts Western programming to Eastern Europe was rude to an insignificant translator; the fact that I am shrieking inside all the time with grief; the fact that our personal dramas mean nothing beyond this moment when we are sentient and playing out our minor destinies.

But when you are engulfed in loss, how can you detach yourself from the transience of everything? How can I take a theoretically long view of things when every waking moment without Johannes is agony? And how was I to explain all this to the bumptious, overbearing Frau Orff—who, like any little functionary, had her own tiny bit of power and was determined to wield it? I simply made one comment: "I thank you for your understanding," knowing that this would unsettle her, as she was being anything but understanding. As expected, she gave me a pinched smile and said she would see if "Herr Direktor" was free to see me.

She kept me waiting a good half hour before I was ushered into Herr Wellmann's office. A rather bookish, unattractive man. Intellectual turned administrator. But decent and reasonable. He must have sensed how nervous I was and tried to put me at ease immediately. Told me he'd been briefed about my "personal circumstances" and "it must be a difficult thing to bear." Again I felt a desperate stab of guilt and wanted to scream, "Stop being so damn nice. You don't know who and what you're dealing with."

Then he opened a file, in which my curriculum vitae—which Frau Ludwig had helped me write one afternoon—was present, along with other substantial papers on me. He asked me many questions about my work at the state translation company and seemed genuinely interested in what kind of English-language books made it into print "over there." At one point he switched into English and seemed pleased when I was able to converse with him for more than fifteen minutes in his own language. Then he handed me a page-long document——an English commentary someone had written on an antiques dealer in Berlin who specialized in Prussian memorabilia——and asked me to translate it out loud, on the spot. I did as requested, even though my voice was very shaky at first. But I managed to bring my nerves under control and got through this oral exam without stumbling over words.

"Impressive," Herr Wellmann said. "And I like the fact that the German you used was conversational, not at all too formal."

"Thank you, Herr Direktor."

He then handed me another document——two pages long, something to do with a speech President Reagan just gave about Iran—— and told me to go outside to Frau Orff and she would direct me to a typewriter. "Consider this translation a rush job," he said. "So get it back to me as fast as you can."

As soon as I emerged from his office, Frau Orff immediately pointed me toward a desk with an electric typewriter. IBM. A round ball on which were all the letters. I had never used such a sophisticated piece of technology before——and was a bit daunted at first. But I knew I had another test to pass and wrote quickly, translating the entire two pages in just less than half an hour. Then I reread my work, made some corrections with a pencil, and retyped it all in around ten minutes. After pulling it out of the machine, I headed back toward the door to Herr Wellmann's office. Immediately Frau Orff ordered me to halt.

"You never enter Herr Direktor's office without first letting me call him."

"Sorry" I said quietly.

Frau Orff picked up her phone, hit a button, and spoke briefly to Herr Direktor. Then she turned to me and nodded that I had her permission to enter.

"That was fast," Herr Wellmann said. He accepted the two pages I handed over to him, studied them, and complimented me on both "the fluidity of the translation" and the cleanness of the copy. When I explained that I had retyped my first draft, so he could read it without corrections, he smiled and said:

"Well, I suppose I have no choice but to hire you."

Then he informed me that I would be on a weekly salary of five hundred deutsche marks——more money than I could have ever dreamed of. With tax taken at source and with the standard social insurance deductions, I would receive around three hundred and seventy-five deutsche marks in my hand every week.

"Is that acceptable?" he asked.

"Very," I said.

I spent much of the morning filling out paperwork and being sent to a room to be photographed for an identification card. I was also interviewed by a man named Stüder who, I am certain, was their security chief, as he asked me many leading questions about my contacts with other East Germans here in the West. "I know nobody" was my honest reply. He informed me, with stern clarity, that there were strict regulations about all documents remaining on the premises and no work allowed to be taken home.

"Nothing we do here could be classified as high security. But the fact that we do broadcast specifically to the GDR . . . put it this way, their people would love to know in advance the content of our programs for all the obvious reasons. So you may occasionally have your bag searched by our security men when you leave the premises. We need you to sign a security agreement, stating that you will not discuss any of your work here with anyone outside of the organization, and that you will never bring documents out of the building or do anything to compromise our work here. Any objections to signing such a document?"

"None at all," I said, hoping he didn't catch the anxiety I was feeling.

I signed the document. I waited while my identification card was laminated. I was shown a cubicle in the main work area. I was introduced to several colleagues, including a Polish guy named Pawel who is one of the producers here. Not bad looking, but an aggressive flirt. He made a point of staring at my breasts and legs and giving me a sardonic smile while asking me if I had a boyfriend.

"I had a husband, but he's dead," I said, my tone letting him know that I wasn't going to play the coquette. But my comment only seemed to encourage him further as he said:

"What a foolish man, dying like that."

I wanted to lash out and slap his face. From the smile on his lips, I could see that this was exactly the sort of response he wanted from me. I immediately characterized him as a provocateur with a cruel streak and realized that this was unlikely to be the last such encounter with him.

Fortunately, I was called back into Herr Wellmann's office. Herr Direktor had an urgent translation needed of a talk someone would be giving on a writer I had never heard of before: Sinclair Lewis. It was a long document—twelve double-spaced pages—and Herr Direktor wondered if I could have it finished in two hours, as the other resident translator scheduled to do it was off with one of her usual migraines today, and the actor coming in to read it had been booked for three p.m. And as it was now just one . . .

Of course, I said yes. Work gave me something to do. Work helped block out all the wild contradictory emotions crowding my head. Work kept me focused.

As I walked back to my cubicle, Pawel passed me by. I kept my head down.

"Don't think you can ignore me," he said. "I won't allow it."

*   *   *

Work. I have just finished my first seven days of work. As one of the other translators, Magdalena Koenig, has been suffering migraines repeatedly, the large bulk of translation work has landed on my desk. Half the writers for the station—they're all freelance—are Anglophones. So the work load is constant and, as befits a broadcast organization, always pressing. Everyone here is under pressure. The staff should be twice as big—as Pawel keeps telling me—but the funding isn't what it used to be, even given Reagan's virulent anti-Communism.

"Reagan and his cronies speak about the Evil Empire," Pawel noted one day when he dropped by my cubicle to bother me, "but they also believe in no government, no public broadcasting, paying for nothing in the fight against the Red Devils except ballistic weapons. No need to talk to the head. Just train a nuclear warhead at the Soviets' collective testicles."

Pawel. Intellectually clever, and he knows it. Otherwise, at best, a nuisance. Every day he attempts to engage me in conversation. But it is the sort of conversation in which the sexual is omnipresent. He keeps ogling me while trying to force details out of me about my life. I refuse to tell him anything. Just as I don't enter into much in the way of conversation with anyone else on the staff. I went out to eat the other day with a contributor named Monica Pippig. An American writer in her late forties living here, who writes and presents a program twice a month about books. I'd been translating all her stuff. We met one morning to discuss some problems I had with an essay she'd written on Philip K. Dick——and how many of the science fiction terminologies she used were difficult to translate into German. We worked for two hours, then she suggested lunch at a nearby café. I heard all about her childhood in Manhattan, and the parents who didn't love her, and the two terrible men she married——one of whom turned out to be gay. And how she came to Berlin after her last serious relationship broke up. And the fact that she can't now seem to meet available men. And how, at her age, no one will ever employ her again, so she's stuck at Radio Liberty, and "it isn't exactly the BBC World Service." And never allow yourself to be invited out for a drink with Pawel "because I did that and woke up next to him the following morning, and he told me that he wasn't in the habit of sleeping with women so much older than him, but he decided to take pity on me."

I certainly learned a great deal during that lunch with Monica—— and, happily, she asked so little about me that I was never forced to be evasive. But I also decided afterward that if she proposed lunch or a drink again, I'd find an excuse to say no. That's my rule with everyone here. I will be a diligent and helpful colleague. I will always be pleasant and courteous and on time and completely professional. Beyond that I will not let anyone near me. Nor will I talk about my life, the circumstances that brought me to West Berlin, the horrendous shadow that stalks me night and day. Just as I will also not be drawn into any friendships or after-work social activities because that could also leave me vulnerable to the interests of others.

I want no one to be interested in me.

*   *   *

There is a playground near my building. I only discovered it the other day when I took a different route home. It was a bright, unseasonably pleasant midwinter's day——and the playground was packed with mothers my own age and their children. The moment I happened upon it I turned and started running, tears cascading down my face, a scream in my throat. When I got home I couldn't stop crying for more than half an hour.

It just never goes away. Try as I do to negotiate with it, it refuses to leave me in peace. And I can't mourn it like a death because my son is so very much alive. And just ten minutes' walk from my front door. If only that wall wasn't in the way.

*   *   *

I work. I come home. I cook something. I drink a few beers. I smoke cigarettes. I play records. I read. I sleep badly. I go to work. The pattern repeats itself. Day in, day out. I found a used bookstore near the Heinrich Heine Strasse U-Bahn station that has a very good English-language section. I've made a point of trying to read the American writers whose works have been under discussion in the broadcast essays I've translated for the station. Sinclair Lewis. Theodore Dreiser. John dos Passos. James Jones. J. D. Salinger. John Updike. Kurt Vonnegut. Writers I never knew existed. Because there is that bimonthly program, written and presented by Monica, which is all about American literature, I have treated it like a university course and an escape hatch. The very nice Herr Bauer who runs this vast used bookshop near me has been able to find me just about every novel or short story collection I've requested and all in the original English.

"Either you've fallen in love with an American or you're planning to move there," he told me one day.

"I should be so lucky," I said.

Those books kept me sane during my first weeks in Kreuzberg. Occasionally, I would go out at night and see a movie or sit alone in a bar where some jazz group was playing, nursing a vodka and fending off any man who tried to have a conversation with me. But largely, outside of work, I sat at home and listened to music and read, all the while wondering when *he* would be in contact, when everything would begin to change.

That happened my fourth week at Radio Liberty. I was heading out of the office and into the U-Bahn station when a fat man in a green parka with a fur hood bumped into me. As he did, he thrust a card into my hand and then moved on. I pocketed the card immediately, waiting until I was home to read it:

Meet me tomorrow at six p.m., Hotel Claussmann. Room 12. Londoner Strasse.

I stared at the card for a very long time, knowing what would happen if I didn't show up.

I had no choice. I had to meet that man in that hotel room. And I had to do whatever he asked of me.

*   *   *

Londoner Strasse was a shabby street in an outlying area near Tegel Airport. Dreary apartment blocks. Scruffy streets in which trash had gone uncollected for some days. Some fast food cafés. Graffiti. Bad lighting. A sense of neglect. Sleet falling. And a man asleep at the reception desk of the Hotel Claussmann. He had a heavily pockmarked face. As he snored, an emphysemic wheeze was discernible. The hotel lobby was painted a garish maroon and had a carpet that was heavily stained and dirty. This was a cheap hotel. Very cheap.

I sidestepped the desk clerk and went up a flight of stairs to discover a narrow corridor, lit by fluorescent tubes. Room 12 was at the end of the hall. I knocked on it lightly, hoping against hope there would be no answer. But a thick voice said:

"*Ja?*"

"It's Dussmann," I said.

The door opened, and there he was. The fat man who bumped into me at the U-Bahn station yesterday. He was short, around five foot six, with a significant potbelly and a half-shaven face with a decidedly oily patina. He was in some indeterminate corner of middle age——his graying hair and brown teeth possibly making him appear more the wrong side of fifty. He had a cigarette in his mouth when I walked in. He was stripped down to a dirty white T-shirt that stretched over his distended stomach and a pair of yellowed Y-fronts.

"Shut the door," he ordered.

"If I'm getting you at a bad time . . . ," I said.

"Shut the fucking door," he ordered, his voice level but very threatening.

I shut the door. The room was small and as shabby as the rest of the hotel. A sagging double bed, a naked lightbulb suspended from the ceiling, floral wallpaper peeling off the walls, a stench of mildew and cigarette smoke and male sweat.

"Anyone follow you here?" he asked.

"I didn't notice."

"In the future you notice."

"Sorry."

"Take off your clothes."

"What?"

"Take off your clothes."

Instantly I thought: *flee*. He gauged this immediately, as he said:

"You leave now, you can forget ever seeing your cute little son again. I will make an anonymous call to those *Bundesnachrichtendienst* spooks who debriefed you and tell them you're a double agent. And if you don't think I'm serious . . ."

He reached over to the scarred metal table by the bed and picked up an envelope, tossing its contents out onto the bed. I gasped when I saw a half dozen snapshots of Johannes. All recent. All of him being held up and clutched by a couple. Both fair haired and young and smiling. The man in the formal uniform of a Stasi officer. I immediately dived for the photographs, but the man grabbed my arm and wrenched it behind my back with such force that I let out a scream which he silenced by pulling me toward him and slapping his free hand across my mouth.

"You *never* do anything without my permission. *Never.* You understand?"

Now he yanked my arm up so high it felt like he was about to dislocate it. I nodded agreement many times. He let me go, simultaneously throwing me down on the bed on top of the photographs. I jumped up immediately, not wanting to crease them.

"Now take off your clothes," he said.

I hesitated, still wanting to flee.

"Now."

Awkwardly I took off my jacket, my sweater, my skirt, my tights, my underwear. I covered my breasts with my arms, shielding them.

"On the bed," he ordered.

I reached down to first tidy up the photographs.

"Did I give you permission to do that?"

I began to sob.

"You stop that crying now," he hissed.

I worked hard at stifling my sobs.

"May I please pick up the photographs, sir?"

"You're learning. Yes, you may."

I scooped up the snapshots, looking for a moment at one of Johannes alone, clutching a teddy bear.

"Did I give you permission to look at the photographs?" he yelled.

"Sorry, sorry," I said, scooping the rest up and dropping them on the side table.

"Now on the bed."

The mattress sagged as I lay down on it, creaking loudly. I curled up into a fetal position, wanting so much at that moment to simply die.

"On your back," he yelled.

I did as ordered.

He approached me, pulling my legs apart with his two hands. Then he yanked down his Y-fronts and licked his hand, touching the head of his erect penis with it. I shut my eyes tightly as he barged into me. I was dry and so desperately tense that it felt as if he was ripping directly into me. I lay there, inert, as he thrust in and out. Happily—and that's the wrong adverb to use here, but the only one that comes to mind—he never tried to kiss me. And he was fast. A minute or so of his thrusts and then he came in me with a groan that sounded more like an expectoration. He turned flaccid within moments. He stood up almost immidiately, pulled up his Y-fronts, and ordered me to get dressed, then said:

"We are going to meet twice a week—and I am going to fuck you both times. If you don't want to do that, just tell me now—and I will get word to East Berlin that you want the adoption of Johannes to be permanent."

"I don't want that."

"Then you will do exactly what I request. If you behave like a good operative, our masters back home will get a decent report from me about you—and that should help your case. Of course, if you don't follow orders . . ."

And orders involve fucking you.

"I'll follow orders," I said, thinking: *I have no cards to play here.*

"Then put your clothes back on."

As I got dressed, the man reached for his packet of Camels and lit one up. As an afterthought he tossed the packet onto the bed, saying:

"Take one."

"Thank you."

"You on the pill?" he asked.

I shook my head.

"You get knocked up, you deal with it."

"My period's due tomorrow."

"Then you go on the pill this week. Understood?"

I nodded.

Once I was fully dressed again, he opened a wardrobe and pulled out a cheap-looking suitcase. He squatted down and flipped it open. He pulled out a small zipped bag.

"This is for you," he said, handing it to me. "Go ahead, open it."

Again I did as ordered. Inside the bag was a tiny camera—so small it could easily fit in the palm of my right hand.

"This is the tool of your trade. Also in the bag you will find twenty-four miniature rolls of film, each with sixteen exposures. Your task is simple. You photograph both the original copy and the translation you make of everything handed to you. You find a way of secreting this camera on your person—and you bring the film back here to me twice a week. You also work out a way of getting up here without being followed."

"What makes you think I'm being followed?"

"You're a new arrival. They always keep a close eye on recent political émigrés. Why do you think I waited a month before contacting you? I was simply making sure they had reached a moment where they were becoming less vigilant about tracking you everywhere. But we still can't be too cautious. So you must find a route that will lose them."

"Who's to say they didn't follow me up here tonight?"

"Because we have our sources and you are now considered, by them, to be clean. Even so, we will never meet just here. And the way I contact you will be very simple. There is a bar near you in Kreuzberg called Der Schlüssel. A dive—and patronized by a young, druggy clientele. It is atrocious at night, but just about tolerable during the day. You will make it your local. I want you to stop in there at least five times a week for a beer, a coffee. You will always go to the bathroom while there. In the one and only stall in the ladies', you will notice a loose floor tile just to the right of the toilet. I will always leave a note under this tile, stating the time and place of our next rendezvous. It will always be two days in advance. You must memorize the details, then flush the card away. You must always make our appointments promptly. You must always bring the film with you. And I will always expect new film from you twice a week."

He then gave me a fast lesson in how to load the film, how to photograph the documents, and how to hide the camera within my clothes.

"Best in the crotch of your jeans when you are coming to work. There's no metal detector at Radio Liberty, but the security people there do make random searches of bags and desks. So you should only bring the camera two, three times a week and photograph your work at that time. The station is usually working on everything but the news a week or so in advance, so it is critical that we have your film promptly. Do remember: failure to make our appointments, failure to have photographed all the translations you have worked on, will be reported back. You do not want that, do you?"

"No, sir."

"You really are learning. Maybe you will convert to being a true believer——which, trust me, is the fastest way back to your son."

"Whatever it takes, sir," I said. "Whatever it takes."

"I'm Haechen, by the way. Helmut Haechen. It's not my real name, but it's what I adopted years ago. Who needs a past, *ja*? You check the toilet at Der Schlüssel in two days——and there will be instructions where we meet next. Now get out of here."

*   *   *

As soon as I was out on the street, I doubled over and began to retch. I must have vomited for a good five minutes, sinking down to my knees on the slushy pavement, sobbing and spewing at the same time, feeling beyond violated. A man——elderly, frail, but with deeply alert eyes——came by and asked if I needed his help. His decency only made me cry louder. Instead of talking in the sort of well-meaning clichés——*It's not the end of the world now, is it?*——he did something so incredibly humane, so profoundly powerful. He just put one of his hands on my shoulder and kept it there until I was able to bring myself under control. When I made it to my feet, he touched my face with his gloved hand. His eyes brimming with concern and (I sensed) the understanding of someone who had known life's more extreme horrors, he uttered one simple word:

"Courage."

I got home. I stripped off everything I was wearing. I took a shower so hot it almost scalded me. I wrapped myself in a bathrobe. I stared at myself long and hard in the mirror, trying to see if the woman looking back at me——with her red, exhausted eyes, her expression of deep shock and fear etched everywhere on her face——could provide me with some sort of way out of a nightmare that I knew would just deepen with time.

Call Frau Jochum, call Herr Ullmann. Beg for mercy . . . and never see Johannes again.

And if you do everything Haechen asks you . . . if you spread your legs for him twice a week . . .

They will have to reunite me with Johannes. They will owe me that. They will have to play fair.

The worst lies are the ones we tell ourselves.

But when you have no other options——when any decision you make will lead to grief——what other choice do you have but to hold on to the lie that might miraculously transform itself into the denouement you spend your days pleading for?

I've never had a religious impulse in my life. But tonight, passing by a Catholic church on the way home, I had the urgent desire to go inside and find a priest and lay bare my soul to him and ask for some sort of divine guidance.

Can prayers be answered, Father? I would ask him afterward. No doubt he'd tell me that miracles do happen, that the hand of the Almighty Father works in mysterious ways.

But I also know that this Kreuzberg priest——well schooled like the rest of the populace here in the realpolitik of walls and sentries and armed snipers and secret police——would privately think: *She's up against the Stasi. And when you are up against the Stasi . . . well, even the Almighty doesn't stand a chance.*

*   *   *

I went to Der Schlüssel last night. A dump. I ordered a vodka and a beer. I drank them both down. I studied the other clientele. The usual Kreuzberg mélange of bikers and punks and junkies. I regarded them all furtively for more than half an hour, making certain that none of them was eyeing me with interest, that I hadn't been tailed. I have been obsessed with this fear for days now, always checking if I am being followed. Just as, this afternoon, at Radio Liberty I took the English-language draft of an essay I was translating into the bathroom with me. Sitting on the closed toilet, with the manuscript piled up on my lap, I photographed each of the seven pages of this piece. It detailed an evening spent drinking with a couple of American soldiers who regularly drove to the west side of The Wall on night patrol. I was amazed that Herr Wellmann allowed this piece, as it pointed out the fact that their job was a nonevent, as nobody from the GDR ever made it over The Wall. It also was thoroughly sardonic about the marathon sessions they had in local bars after getting off duty. As I was beginning to discover Radio Liberty liked to show off its ability to send up aspects of Americanness or even let a writer openly criticize the president. Herr Wellmann felt this showed the power of free speech over here in the West, and that was the best propaganda going.

I was photographing the text of this "propaganda" inside one of the two toilet stalls in the ladies', desperately worried that someone might enter the other stall and perhaps hear the rustle of paper, the low click of the shutter release on the camera. Of course, I made a point, the day before I photographed documents for the first time, of spending some time alone in the bathroom during lunch hour—when most everyone else was off the premises—seeing if I could find any hidden cameras there. None seemed to be visible. I also made a point of noting if anyone's bag was searched going in and out of the bathroom. From what I had discerned in my weeks there so far, outside of the occasional spot check from the security guards on the way out of the building, there wasn't hypervigilance at work here. Given that, on this first day with the tiny camera, I made certain I wore a pair of boots that I bought the day before specifically because they were a half-size too large and had enough space in the right toe to hide the camera. Haechen's idea of hiding it in the crotch of my jeans struck me as both stupid and dangerous, as there would be a telltale bulge there whenever I snuck it into work. I could live with the camera rattling around my boot for the entire day. I also never saw anyone being asked to take off their footwear.

Bringing the documents into the toilet was easy. I walked in with a file under my arm, figuring if anyone asked me why I was carrying them in with me, I'd just explain that I was editing while using the bathroom.

But no one questioned me. I was able to photograph all seven pages of the text in the space of five minutes, then store the camera back in the right toe of my boot, flush the toilet, step out, wash my hands, and head back to my desk, thankful that there wasn't a sound detector on the premises that could register the insane pounding of my heart as I sat down in my cubicle, all fear and paranoia, yet also a guilty little-girl pleasure in having gotten away with something bad.

As soon as the workday had ended, I was out the door, holding my breath in case security was about to conduct the first-ever shoe inspection I'd seen at the station. Then I made my way by U-Bahn to Kreuzberg and the Café Schlüssel. I drank my vodka and my beer. I ascertained that none of the scruffy crew there looked like obvious spooks——then again, maybe they had recruited junkies, getting them to follow me around in exchange for drug money. I went into the bathroom. It stank of blocked drains and disinfectant. The toilet itself was disgusting. But I did find the loose floor tile immediately. Beneath it there was a card. I read it quickly. *Hotel Liebermann, Oldenburg Alle 33, Wednesday 7 p.m.* I made certain I repeated the address silently to myself several times, then tore it up, dumped it in the toilet, flushed it away, and fled into the now-snowy streets.

That night——and all the next day——was one of dread. Haechen—— that foul, ugly little man. Repulsive beyond belief. I could smell his toxic breath, the acridity of his sweat, and I could still feel the little erect stump of a penis that he shoved into me as if it were a mechanical tool. Again I told myself that this was beyond all limits of toleration, that I should get word to Stenhammer that his agent was demanding sexual services from me. Would it be best to run before he began to demand more from me? Say he insisted on three rendezvous per week? Or even four?

But I still showed up for my appointment as ordered. And yes, it was another grubby hotel in another backstreet. And yes, he was stripped down again to a similar soiled T-shirt and Y-fronts. And yes, he ordered me to strip. And yes, he mounted me. And yes, it again only took him a few terrible minutes to spurt into me. Then he withdrew and barked some obscenities at me when he saw that his penis was covered in menstrual blood. I dashed into the bathroom to insert a tampon and drench a hand towel in water. I came back out and handed it to him.

He grunted acknowledgment, disappearing into the toilet with it, peeing loudly with the door open.

"You bring the film?" he shouted from within.

"Of course."

When he came out, I handed over the two minute rolls.

"What are the documents about?"

I gave him a rundown of the piece. He seemed genuinely enthused that it involved the American military guarding The Wall and the fact that they liked to get smashed after an all-night tour of duty.

"Good work," he said. "But I will reserve judgment—and will not let them know if it is good work until I see the quality of the photographs."

"Can I have some more film, please? I only have two rolls and if there are more documents to be photographed . . ."

He then quizzed me most intensely about how and where I photographed the documents. Did anyone at the station see me, were any suspicions raised, was I aware of anyone hanging around my street or following me anywhere? He seemed pleased with my responses. And said:

"You deserve a small reward."

Reaching into an envelope on the bedside table, he extracted one small photograph of Johannes. Sitting on the floor, playing with a few wooden blocks. He looked a month or two older now, and was wearing that same charming half smile that always made my heart sing whenever it filled his face. I always sense he inherited that from me—as my friends told me that I was someone who never fully smiled. Curious that my son already shared that same tendency, as if he too was tentative about trusting the world. Of course, that's reading far too much into a baby's smile. But I still wondered if being taken away from his mother—and suddenly finding himself in the arms of strangers—wasn't somehow disturbing to him, that even if he was far too young to be cognizant of this big upheaval in his life, he still nevertheless *knew*.

I felt a sob strangle my throat as I gazed at the photograph. But I quelled it, as I didn't want to allow this bastard the pleasure of watching me cry. Still, from the corner of my eye I could see him studying me, a slightly smug smile on his face—as if he knew that, as long as the possibility of reuniting with Johannes was there, he could virtually do what he wanted to me.

"May I please keep this photograph?" I asked him.

"Not allowed," he said. "Say somebody saw it . . ."

"No one will see it. I would only keep it at home."

"But you might feel compelled to carry it with you at all times."

"I'm more disciplined than that."

"I'm not convinced. And *they* know you were deported to the West without any photograph of your son on your person——because, trust me, *they* made a strict inventory of everything you arrived with. Should one of your coworkers see this photograph by accident, they might tell somebody who might tell somebody, and word would get back to *them* and questions would be asked about how she obtained these photographs, and with whom from over there she was making contact and . . ."

"I would never let that happen. No one ever comes to my room. So, please, just let me have that one photograph of my son. You can trust me."

"You haven't proved yourself worthy of trust yet."

With that he snatched the photograph out of my hand.

"You can see these photographs every time we meet," he said. "It will be your reward for fulfilling your duties as specified. Now go."

*   *   *

I went to a public clinic in Kreuzberg yesterday and met with a woman doctor and said I wanted to go on the pill. She asked me a variety of straightforward questions, including: "Are you planning to have children?" To which I flatly said "No." She just shrugged and told me I might just change my mind someday.

Ten minutes later I was outside with a prescription. I went to a chemist and got it filled. The chemist warned me that full protection would not be "in place" until a full week after I started taking the pill.

"So suggest to your boyfriend that he uses condoms in the meantime."

I asked for a tube of spermicide.

The next day——before having to report to my meeting with Haechen——I stopped in a bathroom in Zoo Station and took the tube of spermicide out of my bag and lowered my jeans and my knickers and inserted the tube and emptied a good third of it into me. He didn't notice the slightly chemical aroma of the spermicide when he was fucking me ten minutes later. I used the spermicide again before the next three visits while waiting for the pill's efficacy to take. The idea of getting pregnant by this man is a nightmare beyond nightmares.

*   *   *

Weeks now since I wrote here. Life is, on the surface, straightforward, unchanging. I do my job. I translate what is demanded. I always meet the deadline. I am always punctual at work. I keep to myself. Twice a week I arrive with the camera in my boots. As winter is fading away, I have bought a lighter pair, also a half-size too big, to secrete the camera on those days when I need to photograph the documents. My system of bringing them into the toilet stall with me has been varied, as I also found a storage room downstairs in which stationery supplies are kept. Nobody ever goes in there at lunchtime. The light is better than the toilets (Haecher told me that he has had occasional complaints from his people that the quality of the photos could be improved). If I leave the door open while getting the photography done, no one can happen upon me, as the storage room is at the end of a long basement corridor. There is a metal door from the staircase leading into this corridor——it's the only point of entrance——and even if you try to open it quietly, it still makes a very discernible noise. The floors are concrete——so even when walking in sneakers, your footsteps can be heard. I scoured the storage room everywhere to see if there were any hidden closed-circuit cameras——or an eye in the sky. Nothing found. So it has become the perfect spot during lunch hour to get my work for Haechen done.

We continue to meet twice a week in variations on the same dingy hotel room. The order of business is always the same. I arrive. I strip. He fucks me for the three minutes it takes him to ejaculate. We smoke cigarettes. I hand him the film. I leave.

I haven't become inured to the degradation of it all. I still find him bestial and gross. But I have also accepted these twice-weekly events as a duty to be fulfilled. He never speaks about anything to do with himself. I know nothing about his own life——whether there's a wife, a girlfriend, an ex, children, where he was born, where he was raised, whether his parents were kind to him or left him feeling permanently alone, whether he has a flat here in the city or moves clandestinely from dive hotel to dive hotel. He, in turn, asks no questions about me. However, he recently did make a point to question me at length about life at Radio Liberty——wanting to know as much as I could report about my colleagues.

Pawel particularly interests him, especially as he continues to plague me, often criticizing my translations on pedantic grounds, always making a point of looking down my shirt, endlessly asking me out for a drink, dinner, alternating flirtatious banter with invective, constantly unnerving me.

"I want to report him to Herr Wellmann," I told Haechen one evening.

"Put up with him," he said. "The more unpleasant he is, the better."

"Why is that?"

"Because colleagues at work will see how detestable he is being to you——and how stoic you are being by withstanding it. It plays to your advantage."

And does anybody see how stoic I am being by spreading my legs for you twice a week?

*   *   *

Time. It just drags along. I live such a circumscribed existence. The translation work is semi-interesting, frequently routine. A few of our writers have flair. A few are in love with their own cleverness. The vast majority are simply dead on the page. But Monica told me that Wellmann is a man who prefers the factual and the dull to the flamboyant and the talented. He is a real functionary, albeit one who will have his avuncular moments, asking me how I'm getting along, hoping that "you're finding your way in this new world and that the past is starting to be a bit more manageable" (his first and only hint that he knew all about my personal situation), along with his reassurance,

"Of course, I mention this only to you and have never and will never discuss this with anyone else."

Granted, Pawel was relentless when it came to trying to get some personal information out of me, once challenging me in front of four other staffers at a lunch in a local pizzeria to explain what "angelic deed" I did to get myself evicted from the GDR, calling me a "tight-lipped Solzhenitsyn who probably wrote mediocre human rights poetry about the bourgeois dominion of her cunt." That's when I threw my beer in his face. His response was to just laugh.

Monica tried to get him fired after this—telling me she confronted Wellmann about him, stating that she was appalled that he would allow such a sexist, nasty little shit to remain on staff when he abused a woman colleague in such a vile, derogatory way.

"Wellmann said that he fully sympathized," Monica told me, "and he would personally carpet Pawel, and insist that he write me a proper letter of apology and promise to never pull that sort of thing again. But he also told me, *categorically,* that Pawel couldn't be fired. 'My hands are tied here'——his exact words."

With a knowing smile on her lips, Monica added:

"We all know what that means."

So he too is an operative. One of theirs. And, as such, untouchable.

When I reported this all to Haechen several days later, he couldn't have been more excited (and this from a man who, despite the vindictive veneer, never showed enthusiasm for anything), wanting to know every detail of the reported conversation between Monica and Wellmann. And when Pawel's very formal—and, it must be said, contrite—letter arrived two days later, I made a photocopy and gave it to Haechen.

Yes, I was always trying to curry favor with him, to show him I was on board and wanting to please him and his masters. I even began to show the slightest bit of reciprocal movement when he fucked me—in the hope that he would, in turn, show a little kindness toward me.

But as the weeks turned into months, as he occasionally granted me five minutes' custody with another snapshot of Johannes, I began to realize what I realized from the outset but kept trying to convince myself otherwise: the fact that he would, and could, string this along forever. On the one occasion when I dared to inquire when this all might end and I would be reunited with my son, he simply regarded his fingernails and said:

"That is not my decision. You should know better than to try my patience with such shit. You betrayed your homeland—and now you are trying to prove your worthiness to return there and, *perhaps,* regain responsibility for your son. Given the level of your betrayal the very fact that you are being offered this opportunity to redeem yourself speaks volumes about our humane system. But do not think for a moment that after a few mere months, you are going to be absolved and get handed the keys to the castle. Not a chance."

After this dressing-down I went into a tailspin for days, suicide looming very large in my thoughts. It wasn't as if Haechen had told me something I hadn't already known from the outset. The truth was . . . there was no possibility of a reversal of fortune, no hope, no possible redemption or way out of this labyrinth of lies into which I had led myself.

One morning, after the third night in a row when I couldn't sleep, my thoughts started turning to suicide again, only this time there was a calm logic to my deliberations. Pills versus slashing my wrists in the shower? Or maybe I should try to scale The Wall and get shot trying to repatriate myself back to the GDR (no, that would give those bastards some sort of propaganda victory: *She was so unhappy in the West, so despondent after having been stripped of her GDR citizenship, that she was willing to go to desperate lengths to return to the fatherland she had betrayed*).

Was I serious about taking my own life? Absolutely. A cocktail of despair, despondency, crushing insomnia, and the acceptance that all was lost, without possibility, *dead.*

Which, I had decided, is what I wanted to be.

On the day in question, I first made a side trip to Kochstrasse and made inquiries about the viewing roof open to the public on the thirty-eighth storey of the building that housed Axel Springer's publishing empire. The woman at the information desk on the ground floor joked with me that if I had fear of heights, I shouldn't go up there, "as the guard rails are low and the view down very vertiginous." The only thing that stopped me from buying a ticket to the observatory tower, and taking the elevator straight to the top and flinging myself off before I had the chance to change my mind, was the desire to write a long explanatory letter to Johannes, which I would somehow find a way for it to be given to him when he was older. It was a letter in which I told him . . .

Well, everything.

Looking at my watch and realizing, in my good German way, that I was going to be late for work, I hurried off to the U-Bahn, pondering a question all the way to Wedding: could I find somebody who would, upon receipt of this sealed envelope after my death, be trusted to carry out the instructions I left him or her to find a way of delivering this letter to Johannes when he turned eighteen?

More specifically, would Monica——the only quasi-friend I had here——do that for me?

I only arrived five minutes late and had a note marked *Urgent* on my desk from Herr Wellmann. It was the translation of a piece explaining Reagan's Star Wars program, which Wellmann said he needed by eleven. I grabbed a coffee from the communal pot. I lit a cigarette. I rolled a piece of paper into my typewriter. I went to work, finishing off this dry, concrete apologia for such an absurd weapons system just before the deadline. Then I proofed it and entered Herr Wellmann's outer office.

"Oh good, you have it done," Frau Orff said, seeing the copy in my hand. "I'll send you right in."

After phoning him, she pointed to the door. I knocked on it and walked in. In the moment I walked in I saw, sitting in the chair in front of Wellmann's desk, a man in his mid-twenties. He stood up as I entered. I liked that. He was tall, with a big mop of brown hair and a very square jaw. Thin, lanky, interesting. A bookish man, but someone who, I sensed immediately, knew a bit about the world. Handsome, too. Very handsome . . . but not too aware of that. But what got me immediately about him were his eyes. They were sharp, observant eyes——yet also ones that radiated a certain forlornness. The eyes of someone worldly yet alone. The eyes of somebody looking for love and having yet to find it.

Then he saw me. And I saw the way he saw me. And, I sensed, he saw the way I saw him. In that instant . . . . it couldn't have been more than a few seconds, but it seemed so much longer owing to the way we held each other's gaze . . . in that instant, I fell victim to something that can only be described as febrile. Something I had never been hit with before. Something that I found perplexing and wondrous and wholly disconcerting at the same time.

Herr Wellmann introduced us.

Thomas Nesbitt. His name is Thomas Nesbitt.

And I have just fallen in love with him.

NOTEBOOK TWO

THOMAS NESBITT. THOMAS Nesbitt. Thomas Nesbitt.

In the hours, days, since meeting him I have said his name over and over again. I like the sound of it. So solid. So mature. So . . . . American.

He smiled at me as I left Wellmann's office. Such a smile. So much behind that smile. Or am I being absurd and delusional here? Am I projecting onto this man——about whom I know nothing——all these possibilities that have passed through my head from the moment I first set eyes on him a few hours ago? What possibilities?

Love. Real love. Something——I have to admit here within the safe confines of this journal——that I have never known. Always felt myself rather unlucky in that department. Then again, for the people I knew who had fallen madly in love, it was either with the wrong person or someone who could not live up to the expectations, the hopes, that had been placed upon them.

As I am placing them on him now. What do I know about him but that he's American and he writes? No doubt there's a girlfriend or a fiancée. Or maybe he's already married but doesn't wear a ring.

No, he strikes me as one of those men who, if married, would wear a ring, would make his commitment to someone very clear.

But there I go projecting again.

Is this what it feels like? Unable to concentrate on anything else but *him,* even though he might just have been naturally flirtatious and always came on to women like he did with me.

But he didn't come on to me. He looked at me in a way that mirrored exactly what I was feeling the moment I first saw him. *He knew.* Just the way *I knew.*

I saw something else there behind that look. A loneliness, a need, a sense of wanting so desperately to connect.

But there I go projecting again.

Thomas Nesbitt. Thomas Nesbitt. Thomas Nesbitt.

I keep saying his name over and over again. Like an invocation, an entreaty, a prayer.

*　　*　　*

I found out he writes books. Or, at least, *a book*. But how many people even write *one* book? And it's a very good book, despite what Pawel says.

I saw it on Pawel's desk this morning as I delivered a translation to him. Since that whole business some weeks ago——and his subsequent letter of apology——Pawel has stopped his campaign of harassment against me. Perhaps he also realizes that I now know who and what he really is, and why he can't be fired——though I'm pretty certain the entire office has been quietly aware of this fact for some time. That's one of the great unspoken rules about Radio Liberty: though we all realize that it's funded by the US Congress and overseen by the CIA . . . and though occasionally we get a visit from USIA people (who are so clearly "operatives") . . . the one thing no one ever discusses (except in very low tones——and in as fleeting a way as possible) is the "security service" aspect of the operation. But it is something I think about every moment I am there, as I cannot help but wonder if I am under surveillance. Then again, after so many months, surely if they knew what I was doing, they would have moved in on me by now.

How can I fall in love with anyone when I am living such a duplicitous existence? How can I even think of a life with Thomas when I have to keep seeing Haechen twice a week?

"Is it any good?" I asked Pawel, pointing to the copy of Thomas's book on his desk, trying to sound casual.

"Superficial, far too self-assured, far too entertaining."

"'Entertaining' is a sin?"

"The jacket blurb says he's a writer in the 'Graham Greene' tradition of travel writers. But he's far too American."

"By which you mean?"

"He shows off his erudition all the time, the way all those New York intellectuals are always letting you know how much they've read. Just like your friend Monica. Her hyperliteracy is underscored by a need to quote Proust or Emily Dickinson at every damn opportunity. This guy, Nesbitt, does the same thing——using Egypt as a way of talking about himself."

"At least he's between hard covers," I said.

"There are many minor writers 'between hard covers,'" Pawel said. "And being a minor writer who happens to be in Berlin right now . . . of course, Herr Nesbitt is doing some work for us."

"Can I borrow the book, then?" I asked.

"Keep it. I have no use for it. But as our fearless leader has assigned him to me, I'll be producing his drivel."

"And you are such an expert when it comes to drivel," I said.

I took the book home and devoured it that night. Of course, Pawel was being his usual vicious self when it came to his criticisms of the book, and I could see why he felt such a stab of jealousy. I loved the way the entire book had the structure and drive of a novel. I loved the way Thomas drew out so many interesting stories from the people he met "on the road." I loved the way he captured the exoticism of Egypt along with its contemporary extremities. More than anything——in the few moments that he dared to speak personally about himself in an otherwise "detached observer" narrative——the book revealed its writer to be a loner who was very good at getting people to talk about themselves, but was clearly rueful about his solitariness.

As I finally closed the book at three that morning two words kept preoccupying my thoughts:

Thomas Nesbitt. Thomas Nesbitt. Thomas Nesbitt.

I don't deserve him.

Thomas Nesbitt. Thomas Nesbitt. Thomas Nesbitt.

I know it's all the stuff of reverie. And like all such romantic musings, the stuff of imagination, not reality.

*   *   *

I saw him briefly on my way into work. We made eye contact. And, oh God, I think he asked me out to a concert, but I was so nervous I could barely hear anything over the pounding of my heart. And now I'm speaking in clichés. I'm sure I was too distant, too diffident. He just beamed at me. Like a man in love.

Stop inventing again. It was another of his nice smiles, that's all. He's new to Berlin and probably casually asks people out all the time. He probably smiles that way at every woman he sees. And I should have smiled back.

*   *   *

His first essay arrived today! And I was asked to translate it.

I read it through immediately. It described a day he spent in East Berlin. The first time he'd ever "crossed over." Of course, I was intrigued by his take on things. I sometimes worried that he stated the obvious a little too often——especially when it came to the fundamental drabness of the place. But I loved his use of snow as a metaphor. The way he described East Berlin in the throes of a blizzard . . . strangely it made me homesick. This is what they don't get in the West, and what Thomas himself didn't pick up: the fact that we accepted the gray, concrete realities of the place as a given. The fact that not all of us dreamed of Levi's jeans and a new Volkswagen. The fact that, despite its limitations, it was *our* city, our society, our world. We loved so much about its peculiarities. It made us form communities. It made our friendships all that deeper.

And it made us inform on each other, too.

Homesick, yes. Heartsick, yes. Full of conflicting emotions about whether I should make a move in Thomas's direction or stay clear of him altogether and keep everything simpler.

I had to see Haechen this afternoon. He couldn't get an erection and made me go down on him with my mouth. Even then, he remained limp, impotent. I took silent pleasure in this.

"I think you need to do better next time," he said as he pulled up his Y-fronts. I wanted to scream and shout and tell him that I found him nothing less than revolting.

But as always, I held my tongue like the subservient creature I must be in his presence. There is nothing worse than knowing someone has you in a place out of which you cannot negotiate, that their power over you is a near-absolute.

But he couldn't stop me from having a life out of these biweekly degradations. And he wasn't——to the best of my knowledge——having me followed.

Thomas, I decided, would be my escape hatch out of all this horror. Thomas would make this other humiliating part of my life somehow bearable.

If, that is, Thomas was even interested in me.

But think about that look he gave you yesterday.

It was just a look. And it could have been nothing but that.

You don't trust others, do you?

Can you blame me?

*   *   *

I decided to be bold this morning. I picked up the phone at work and called the number Thomas had written on the cover sheet of his essay, only to discover I was speaking to a man with a decidedly non-German accent. When I asked for Thomas Nesbitt he explained that he took messages for Thomas——and that he was probably due in later that morning. I gave him my name and number, thanked him, then hung up, feeling rather stupid about having called. Would Thomas think I was harassing him? Would he even return the call? Maybe I overplayed my hand here. How would I react if he called back and actually asked if we could meet? That was a growing concern of mine, the worry that I couldn't handle it if he was interested.

I want him. I fear I can't have him. I fear everything else will conspire to make me unable to even consider getting to know him.

And I am building all this up into something that may not happen at all.

Then, late that afternoon, my phone rang and . . . there he was. All charming and pleasant . . . and did I also hear a certain nervous catch in his voice as well? We bantered a bit. He made a joke about how he didn't have a phone at home. Then when I said I had a couple of questions about his text, he asked if we could meet for a coffee. Instead of saying an instant "yes," I had to go all hesitant and strange. It was a good thirty seconds before I got up the courage to say: "All right." I felt so silly afterward. And so hopeful. And so afraid. Afraid of it happening. Afraid of it not happening.

*   *   *

He agreed to meet me at a café of my choice. I proposed the Ankara, right near my room. I made some lame joke about the place where he picks up his phone messages being called the Istanbul. And how he was now exchanging Istanbul for Ankara.

God, how I hated myself for that stupidity afterward. And my inane banter, as in asking him if he didn't mind coming to the wrong side of Kreuzberg. He must now think me idiotic.

I could hardly sleep last night, wondering, worrying, fretting. The desire for love to be reciprocated is the most quiet sort of agony. I tried to prepare myself for everything from his last-minute cancelation to the discovery that he had a woman back home in the States who was joining him here next month. I couldn't accept the idea that, somehow, what I felt for him——in all its sudden, ferocious force——could be in any way reciprocated. Who would want to fall in love with me?

When sleep finally came it was five in the morning, and I had spent the last three hours going through Thomas's essay several times, outlining the points I felt needed addressing. Then I woke with my alarm at nine. I showered and dressed, wondering if the brown cardigan and the green corduroy skirt I chose made me look like I was trying too hard to play the Kreuzberg bohemian. I somehow got through the working day——and made certain I arrived five minutes later than agreed at the Café Ankara. He was already sitting there, at work in his notebook, so engrossed that he initially didn't see me enter. I was pleased about that, because at the sight of him I felt that exact same surge, that sense of accelerated pulsation, of absolute certainty, which hit me a few days ago. If I wanted confirmation, here it was.

I approached his table.

"So viele Wörter," I said. So many words.

He looked up at me and smiled. God, how I wanted to throw myself in his arms at that instant.

"So viele Wörter," he repeated to me——and reached out to take my hand, covering mine with both of his. The first time he touched me. He sat down and we started to talk about his essay, but he also wanted to know so much about my life in Prenzlauer Berg. He was so interested in *me*——and I found out some things about his life as well, like the fact that his father was a man who didn't live the life he wanted to lead. And he made the most beautiful comment about my work as a translator, saying that all translation was putting morning words into evening words. Far too poetic in terms of the dreariness of my métier, but I loved the fact that he wanted to tell me he saw value in what I did.

And then . . . *then* . . . out of nowhere he told me I was wonderful. I was so thrown by this——so privately overwhelmed——that I did a stupid, coy thing. When he asked me to have dinner with him tonight, I made up some absurd excuse about having other plans. Why did I make that up? What was I thinking? I know the answer to that question. His praise——a near-declaration of love——so disconcerted me that my first reaction was to create a diversion, an excuse, anything to mess it up. Once that stupidity about being otherwise engaged was out of my mouth, I wanted to take it all back, to tell him that, yes, I was free but so scared he might now think me emotionally unpredictable. But——oh, God, what a relief——he asked if I was free tomorrow night. I tried to keep my cool as I said yes.

Once we were outside in the street I did something wildly impulsive. I pulled him toward me and kissed him right on the lips. But then, again, I pulled back before I went crazy. I so wanted him right there and then. Still he took my hand as I pulled back and said:

"Until tomorrow."

And I could see in his gaze that he was as smitten as I am.

*   *   *

Shit, shit, shit.

After saying good-bye to Thomas I went home and ate a sad om-elette by myself, thinking all the time how I could be with him. I was still furious with myself for having pushed him away this evening, still wondering whether——in the wake of that kiss——he might find me the worst sort of tease.

Shit, shit, shit.

I keep seeing his face in front of me. Keep remembering how bright and knowledgeable he is. How he knows his East German writ-ers. How curious and engaged he was. And how I saw again that vulnerability and solitariness in his eyes. How I so wanted to tell him I loved him; that I would, if I could, make him feel less alone in the world; how he could trust me.

Which he could. Utterly. Until it came to the issue of . . .

I knew I had to go to Der Schlüssel this evening to find out my next rendezvous with Haechen. I dropped by the place. Ordered my usual beer and vodka from Otto——the big, heavily tattooed bar man with a shaved head and two enormous circular earrings expanding each ear lobe. Then, after a few minutes, I went to the bathroom and . . .

Shit, shit, shit.

The card he left gave the address of a hotel way up in Wedding, and he wanted me there tomorrow night at ten.

Shit, shit, shit.

I have to see Thomas. And if I don't show up for my rendezvous with Haechen . . .

*   *   *

I didn't sleep again. I phoned in sick. I fretted all day. The restau-rant was the Italian place near me: a little hole in the wall where I had eaten twice before. We arranged to meet there at eight, which gave me just seventy-five minutes with him before I had to meet Haechen.

Say I didn't show up in whatever horrible hotel Haechen was now perching. Say I skipped this rendezvous. What could he do to me? What vengeance would he actually wreak?

I knew the answer to that question. He would, as he always promised, be merciless. I had to work out some sort of way to escape from Thomas in a little while but do it in such a way that . . .

I can't lose him. I won't lose him.

I walked into the restaurant, and there he was. Seated with his notebook open in front of him, the same fountain pen he always has snug in his hand, his head lowered, his concentration total. The longing I had for him at that moment was overwhelming. He looked up at me with such a big welcoming smile, but I could see that he noticed my tiredness, the dark circles under my eyes that I unsuccessfully tried to mask with makeup. He attempted to kiss me on the lips, but I turned and gave him my cheek, again hating myself for deliberately playing distant. I mean, what could he be thinking now after me kissing him so passionately yesterday? As I sat down I suddenly felt so desperately tired, all the sleeplessness finally catching up with me, terrified that I would somehow show all the contradiction raging inside me. But then we started to talk. For the next two hours we couldn't stop. I got him speaking about his Egypt book——and was able to drag out details from him about his parents' marriage and the reasons he was so reluctant to reveal too much about himself in print, preferring the stories of others. Everything I had sensed about him——the lonely childhood, the self-protective need to hide away, the parents who were unhappy and therefore couldn't appreciate their interesting, different son——was also hinted at by Thomas. It was so fascinating to see how we were both drawing each other out, both more eager to hear the other person's story than tell our own. There was a real kinship there——and an unspoken understanding that we both had firsthand knowledge of life's larger disappointments . . . whether it be a mother and a father who took such little pleasure in you, or a husband with whom there was none of the shared destiny that should be such an essential component of a marriage. But mine with Jurgen was never a real marriage——and I see that so desperately clearly now. I even went so far as to admit something I never mentioned to anyone in my life——the way that the parents of my friend Marguerite were (I was so sure) shopped to the Stasi after I mentioned to my own parents that we watched Western television at their little cottage near the border with the Bundesrepublik . . . and how I felt so profoundly guilty about this after Marguerite's mother and father got into such terrible trouble. Thomas could not have been more understanding, more sympathetic. When he covered my hand with his I didn't pull away, even though I got cross at him for being so reasonable. But instead of being offended, he took my other hand and said the same thing he told me yesterday: that I was wonderful. No one's ever said that to me. Not a parent. Not a lover. Not even a friend. And we drank another half-liter of wine at my insistence because I was so unsettled by his decency. Because everything he was saying——his incredible empathy, the way he seemed to be hanging on to every word I spoke, the way he looked at me——made me realize he was in love with me. The panic within me was growing wilder by the minute——the sense that if I gave myself to Thomas, I would never forgive myself for then having to betray him with the man who currently controlled my life. I didn't want to live a lie, but I also knew that Thomas was now everything to me.

When the conversation edged into this——when we both admitted that, indeed, this was now *everything*——I suddenly found myself telling Thomas that he had to go, that he should leave now and spare himself so much grief. He was looking incredulously at me as I kept repeating that it just couldn't be. But then I blurted out what I wanted to say to him from the first moment he came into my life: *Ich liebe dich.*

And I fled.

I raced up the street to the main thoroughfare and got lucky. An empty taxi was coming by. I hailed it and jumped in, just as I could see Thomas dashing into the street. I gave the driver the address in Wedding——and fell back against the rear seat, sobbing uncontrollably. I didn't stop until the taxi reached the grubby façade of the hotel. I was in a terrible place. I sat in the back of the taxi for many minutes, not moving. To the driver's credit, he didn't ask me to get a move on and get out. He just turned off the meter and waited until I was ready to leave. But I wasn't *ready* to leave. I simply had no choice but to go upstairs and deal with that monster again. When I reached for my bag and asked the driver what I owed him, he simply said: "No charge." When I found myself sobbing again at this spontaneous act of kindness, he said:

"Just say yes and I will drive you away from this. Drive you to wherever you want to go."

"You are too kind," I whispered, then got out and staggered into the reception area, where a sad-looking man sat behind the desk (in none of the hotels in which I was forced to meet Haechen did I ever see a desk clerk who looked even vaguely happy——and who could blame them?). When I mentioned Haechen's name he tonelessly said: "Room 316."

Business as usual. Haechen in his dirty T-shirt and stained Y-fronts. I asked him why we had to meet so late. "Because I couldn't meet you earlier" was his reply. He motioned for me to take off my clothes. "You messed up my evening with friends," I said. He just shrugged and said, "The faster you get out of your clothes, the faster you can go back to them."

Tonight was, by far, a new low point——as he insisted on kissing me, and I tasted his acrid breath, the cheap beer I sensed he drank all day, the four decades of cigarettes he inhaled, the diet of grease on which I was certain he subsisted, and, most of all, his supreme vileness. He shoved his tongue into my mouth the way he shoved his pathetic penis into me——like the malevolent yet profoundly insecure bully that he was. A man who, I sensed, knew he was anything but a man——but was willing to use whatever pitiable power he had to force this woman to be an unwilling receptacle for his wretchedness. Did he privately know this, or was he one of those profoundly amoral creatures who had developed the sort of innate, animal mechanisms that allowed them to sidestep any self-reflection whatsoever?

Fortunately, he had no erection problems tonight——which meant that it was all over in a few minutes. I got dressed. I tossed him four new tiny canisters of film, thinking guiltily that among the many documents contained within, were photos of the translation I made of Thomas's piece about crossing over to East Berlin for the first time. Might they stop him at the border the next time he tried to visit, all because of me? Why did I include this? Because Haechen informed me that *they* listened to Radio Liberty all the time. They had day and night monitors. They were aware that I had become the chief translator. Which meant that anything written by a non-German that was broadcast on the station I had probably translated. And Haechen was very menacing about the fact that "they will be most displeased if they hear things being broadcast about which they weren't already aware." In other words: *you give us everything you work on*.

Still, Haechen seemed pleased with double the usual quota of film. Handing me a few fresh rolls he said what he always said at the end of our "sessions."

"Now go."

It was sleeting when I hit the street. I didn't care. I went home. I stood under a shower for half an hour, trying to wash away all traces of Haechen. The idea of climbing into bed now was impossible. So I hurriedly dressed and fled into the night. I walked for hours. Winding my way down from the north of the city all the way to Kreuzberg. It must have taken three hours or so, as I stopped at four cafés along the way to smoke cigarettes and drink vodka, while all the time ordering myself to go home and slam the door on the world and quietly mourn all that could have been with Thomas and reason with myself that it was all for the best.

But I knew his home address, as it was typed on the title page of his essay. As I passed the Heinrich Heine checkpoint——my entire body drenched from the constant sleet——I couldn't stop thinking all the time about Thomas, and the fact that Johannes was sound asleep just moments from where I now stood. Those two thoughts became so overwhelming that I suddenly found myself running, my gait unsteady due to the wetness of the pavement, the lateness of the hour, all the vodka I'd drunk, the emotional havoc of the evening, the fact that as I turned the corner onto Mariannenstrasse I began to run headlong toward his front door, deciding that as soon as he opened it . . .

It took around three minutes for him to come downstairs. He looked as if he had been asleep. But his eyes grew wide with wonder and (yes) relief when he saw me there.

"I'm cold," I said, falling into his arms. As he held me, I whispered: "Never let me go."

*　　*　　*

I wrote the above immediately upon getting to my apartment this morning. I took a risk I never took in the past——retrieving the journal from the basement during daylight hours, so I could get everything else down before heading to work and then (thank God) back to Thomas's tonight. I've closed the blinds in my room, so no one can see me writing. As soon as this entry is finished, back goes the journal to the cellar——and out I go to work.

But first . . .

I don't know what time it was when I reached Thomas's front door. All I know was that it was cold and I was shivering, but so determined to get there, to tell him that I loved him, to fall into bed with him, to ask him to never let me go.

As soon as we were upstairs, we were in bed within minutes. And when he was inside of me for the first time . . . again, I just knew that this was the man of my life. I've never experienced such extraordinary intimacy (it's the only word for it) before. Yes, there was a guy I saw for two years at university——a law student named Florian——with whom sex was rather wonderful. However, there was no love between us. But that first time with Thomas——it was all about love. As were the second, third, fourth, fifth, sixth . . . I lost track of how many times we made love, how often we pulled each other into bed. I do know that, over and over again, we kept saying how much we loved each other, kept our gazes locked on each other, a real overwhelming sense of certainty always there. At some point that first night, before finally falling asleep, I apologized profusely to Thomas for running off earlier in the evening. He was so kind about it, so understanding, that I easily fell asleep in his arms.

When I awoke it was morning. Thomas must have been up before me, as all my once-wet clothes had been hung up to dry on the radiators. My love was fast asleep in bed. Sitting up beside him I simply spent several long, wondrous minutes looking at him, stroking his hair, watching the rhythm of his breathing, thinking how handsome he was, wanting so much to have a life with him, vowing to myself to somehow find a way out of the situation with . . . no, I don't even want to mention his name here.

I got up and had my first proper look at Thomas's apartment. So clean, so airy, so organized, so simple, but urbane in a way I've only seen in magazines. Yet there's no expensive furniture, no big stereo or television (in fact, no television at all). But the walls are very white, all the furniture has been stripped down to the original wood, and everything seems exactly in place. Looking around——noting how all the dishes and glasses and books and records were so carefully ordered and stacked on their respective shelves, how his clothes were all hung on wooden hangers in his closet, how his shoes seemed polished and never run-down——my first thought was: he did tell me his father had been a military man. But I also sensed that this need for order was a form of self-protection——the same self-protection he found when he was allowed to go to the library for the first time (God, how that story has stayed with me). I found myself loving him for that——and feeling such a kinship there, too. For we had both experienced the sort of sadness that comes from strange families and never having connected with anyone before. This is why I couldn't help but think: the gods have, for the second time, smiled on me. The first time was the birth of Johannes. And now . . .

As I went into the kitchen and began rattling around his fridge, his cupboards, his larder (all very well stocked——my word, he is so organized), I found myself doing something that I last remember doing at home with Johannes: humming.

I think it was a song by Schubert——"An die Musik"——which Jurgen (I'll give him credit here) introduced me to. I put coffee in the percolator. I set the table and laid out bread and butter and honey and orange marmalade and anything else I could find. Then, out of nowhere, Thomas was beside me, kissing me, pulling off the bathrobe I had discovered hanging near the shower, pulling me back into bed.

This time was even more intense, more charged and erotic than before. And we talked again about how this was all so revolutionary (the exact word used) for us both . . . how we would not allow this to fail or come asunder . . . how it was the greatest surprise either of us had known.

We never left the apartment. I briefly met the Turkish lover of Thomas's landlord——and then heard the fantastic story of this man named Alaistair who was gay and a heroin addict and whom Thomas nearly found dead and got him rushed to hospital and saved his life (though he was modest about all that——and about the fact that, with Alaistair's lover, he'd redecorated his studio which had been awash in blood). I talked a bit about my marriage and how empty it was. We made our first proper dinner together——pasta with an anchovy and tomato sauce, and he even had real parmesan in his fridge. I showed him my minor talent for constructing origami figures. And we talked and talked and talked. That was almost as electric as the physical passion we shared——the fact that our conversation (all in German, at his insistence) flowed not just easily, but with the same sort of intensity and brio and, yes, delight that underscored everything else about us.

I have to say that yesterday was perhaps the happiest day I have ever experienced. Because, and I understand this now, I never really knew love before this moment. Never knew it at all.

Then, out of nowhere, he asked me to move in. Handed me a key and told me to bring my things over. I was so bemused, yet also so overwhelmed, by this that all I could say was, "Are you sure?" When he reassured me he was, I told him I'd bring some of my stuff by . . . again, my caution getting to me. But there was also a silent fear that if I gave up my room . . . which I now wanted to do immediately . . . Haechen would somehow find out and that would be the beginning of the end of things.

But the important thing was: I would now be living with the man I love. Just a few days ago I was contemplating a plunge from a high building. The capacity for horror in life is counterbalanced by the possibility of the wondrous.

I dreaded having to go to work today. I never wanted to leave Thomas's apartment, Thomas's bed. I can't abide the thought of stopping in at Der Schlüssel tonight to find the card that Haechen has left me, informing me where I have to fuck him next. I dread having to spend lunchtime clandestinely photographing documents in the basement of the station. I must find a way out of all this. I must find a way of not allowing any of this to destroy the incredible gift of loving and being loved by Thomas.

We woke early today and made love slowly, and with such incredible deliberateness, that we could never take our eyes off each other.

"I want to start every morning like this," I told him afterward. And he assured me that we always would.

Before I left to face a world I so didn't want to face, I told Thomas how lucky I knew I was. And luck——as I have discovered——is the big existential variable in life. It can come your way. It can totally sidestep you. Even when Johannes was born I still had to deal with the fact that I was with a man who didn't care for me——who didn't want to share the responsibilities and the pleasures of being a parent. Now I'm with a man who tells me he wants to share everything with me. The question now for me is: can I finally accept happiness? Can I deem myself deserving of it? Can I hold on to it? Can I not push it away, not let it go?

* * *

It's been several weeks now since I've written here. That's largely because I haven't been home much. I moved in half my things the day I made the last entry. And since then . . .

Happiness.

I said something about all that to Thomas recently. "Happiness exists," I told him. For the first time in my life I've actually begun to trust it. Before then I always thought happiness was, at best, a double-edged thing. The wonder of a son like Johannes and the distress of a mess of a husband like Jurgen.

But now, with Thomas, there's a real sense of being part of a shared project. Of wanting the same things. Of being each other's best friend.

Day after day I cannot wait to get home to him. I want him inside me all the time. I want his arms encircling me as I fall asleep. I want to be sitting across from him at our kitchen table——yes, I just used the pronoun "our"——talking with him nonstop. I love talking books with him, and going out to the cinema with him, and simply having a domestic life with him. We also look after each other——whether it be Thomas doing all my laundry most weeks or me always bringing him a coffee in bed most mornings before I head off to work. I love these little shared kindnesses. Just as I love his decency, his sense of wanting the best for me, for us. *I'm lucky,* I tell myself daily. So lucky.

*   *   *

Alaistair finally came home from the hospital today. I'd heard so much about him from Thomas——and, of course, did see Mehmet on the few occasions when he stopped by——that I was naturally intrigued to learn what this larger-than-life character was actually like. Thomas told me that since his near-death assault, he'd been off heroin and was now coming home clean. He also warned me that he had a real edge to him and was probably in a "profoundly misanthropic state," given his lack of drugs.

But what surprised me immediately about Alaistair was that when you scratched away his world-weary veneer, he was so gentlemanly, so amusing, so smart. He obviously thought the world of Thomas——and not just because he saved his life. I liked him immediately and also found his courage admirable. I'd heard about how the paintings he'd been working on had been wrecked by the man who tried to kill him. Yet Alaistair got down to work again a day or so after being released from the hospital. Every morning when I would come downstairs, heading off to work, I would stop to look at the three paintings he now had "in progress." Thomas was right when he told me before Alaistair's return: "He is a truly wonderful painter." Seeing the nascent (I love that word) beginning of these new canvases (as Alaistair was adamant that he was not re-creating the destroyed paintings), I too couldn't help but think that Alaistair had an ability to play with color and dimension and notions of light in a manner so astonishing that it actually humbled me. Thomas can write wonderfully. Alaistair is so gifted, such a natural. What do I have to show for myself?

A few days after first meeting him, we happened to run into each other on the street as I was returning home from work. To my surprise he invited me for a beer. Once seated at a table he talked a bit about the fact that "his friend" Mehmet no longer wanted to see him, that it was definitively over, and it was bothering him far more than he expected. He then said something rather extraordinary to me:

"I am not one who trades in romantic hyperbole. But I want you to know: you are the best thing that has ever happened to Thomas. I also know he just adores you. So I do hope that the two of you can keep your nerve and see how bloody rare this is."

Bloody rare. Of course, I had to write that down——as he said it in English. I looked it up afterward in a dictionary. It is a reference to a style of cooked meat——red on the inside to the point of appearing rather *blutig*. But it also means exceptional, uncommon, singular. Synonyms I like.

Bloody rare. That's us.

*   *   *

An insane thing happened tonight. Thomas insisted (in the nicest sort of way) that we go see one of his favorite films——Billy Wilder's *The Apartment*. It was playing at the Delphi. A wonderful film. Very cynical. Very knowing. And I loved the fact that this native German speaker——a Viennese who made his start as a journalist and screenwriter in Berlin, then emigrated to the States——so assimilated the American sensibility yet still retained that sardonic Berlin worldview. You could see his mordant take on American corporate life, but also his humanity when it came to the fact that even people with small lives have complicated personal stories. I loved the film, loved seeing it with Thomas, kept thinking how wonderful it would be if we lived together in New York, how I could find a translating or teaching job, how we could get an apartment together, how perhaps we could have a child——and maybe that would diminish some of the pain that . . .

No, that pain will not diminish. It will always be there——a stain that never washes away and continues to color everything.

But, perhaps, I could come to learn to live with the stain. Perhaps I had no choice. Perhaps I knew this all along. Perhaps Thomas——and the life we could have together——was the antidote that would, at least, allow me to live with the ongoing grief of it all.

But still. I was in a buoyant mood after the film.

And then, out of nowhere, Pawel approached us. He was going into the cinema we just left——and his eyes grew wide when he saw us. I could tell that he'd been drinking. He smirked at us and made some nasty comment about how he thought that dissidents had no talent for the clandestine. Thomas told him to stop. But Pawel persisted. And when put down Thomas's writing I called him a shit. That's when he said I was nothing but a mediocrity who . . .

But before he could finish the sentence Thomas punched him. Very hard. In the stomach. He doubled over. And we left in a hurry.

I was so shocked, so amazed, and——all right, I'll admit it——so pleased that Thomas defended me like that. And I told Thomas that, though I was relentlessly private at the office, if word got out about us I'd tell everyone the truth: this is the man I love.

Of course, I went to work on Monday, expecting everyone at the station to know about what had happened——as Pawel was a notorious gossip and would have retailored the story to make it seem like Thomas had hit him out of nowhere. But Pawel called in sick for several days. When I saw him next he acted as if nothing had happened, just passing me by with a terse "Good morning." Not that he had ever tried anything since Monica had confronted Wellmann about his treatment of me. But from that moment on, he was distant, coolly polite, and completely professional with me.

Bullies are always cowed when challenged. Or punched.

*   *   *

A terrible, terrible thing happened yesterday evening. I went to my usual rendezvous with Haechen. As soon as I was in the door, he grabbed me by the arm and shoved it so hard up behind my back I started to scream. That's when he told me that if I screamed again he would break my neck. And he informed me that he knew all about my relationship "with the American." I felt panic course through me. He kept pushing my forearm higher toward my shoulders, using such force that I was certain he was going to snap it.

"Did you really think you could keep all this from me?" he hissed. "Did you, you cheap little bitch?"

I was crying so hard I couldn't speak. That's when he threw me on the bed, threw up my skirt, tore off my underwear, and . . .

He had his hands on my neck throughout. It was over, as usual, quickly. After he came, he punched me hard in the stomach. I curled up into a ball, sobbing so loudly that language was impossible. But I could hear him saying:

"You actually deserve to have your face rearranged. But that would leave noticeable marks. Still I have reported your profound insubordination——yet another of your treasons——to our friends over there. They are not pleased. Of course, this completely compromises any possible reconciliation with Johannes."

"I'll stop seeing him," I whispered through the sobs. "I'll do anything you ask. Just please let me . . ."

"Redeem yourself?"

I nodded.

"Why should I trust you?"

"I've done everything you've asked. And gotten everything you've demanded."

"That is true. But you have also become involved with an American——and tried to hide this from me. As you surely realize by now, it is our business to know *everything*."

"I know that."

"So I also know that you are rather smitten——in fact, in love—— with this American. But how deep is your love for your son? Are you willing to sacrifice him for your American writer?"

I shook my head.

"That was the response I was hoping for. By the way, I am not going to make you drop your American lover. Not yet. But you are going to make him useful to us."

*   *   *

I wandered around after all this. I wanted to go and tell Thomas everything. Surely he would understand. Surely his love for me would . . .

No. That would be asking too much of him. His sense of betrayal would be enormous.

But now I also knew that Haechen——or somebody working for Haechen——was shadowing me everywhere.

What do I do here? What moral course of action do I take here? There's no way out. I am about to lose everything.

*   *   *

Thomas was out for the evening at a concert. I got home. I threw away the remnants of the underwear that Haechen had torn off me. I took a long, hot shower. By the time Thomas walked in I had managed, as always, to shove everything I was feeling (the rage, the fury, the fear) into that dark room in which I only dwelled. I took Thomas by the hand immediately and pulled him into the bedroom. We made love. I was so overwrought, so wound tight, that I seemed to be even more fervent than usual, screaming when I came. Afterward I curled up in a corner of the bed, wishing I could confess it all to Thomas. He put his arms around me and asked me what was wrong.

Everything.

But I said not a word. I just told him I loved him, then shut my eyes and feigned sleep. Sleep, however, never arrived that night. At one point I got up, went into the kitchen, poured myself a glass of red wine, smoked several cigarettes, and finally came up with a solution to my checkmated life. The moment that I chose to execute this plan would have to be the right one. Everything else would have to be in place before I made the move I would make. Because that move would be irrevocable. I would have to bide my time——doing all that was asked of me——until that certain moment arrived.

But having decided on this course of action——having finally realized there was a way out of all this——a certain calm came over me. When you have a solution to something insoluble you also have hope.

*   *   *

At our next rendezvous Haechen didn't rough me up. When he kissed me my lips didn't contort with horror. Rather I kissed him back hard——and pumped hard with my pelvis to make him come that much more forcibly.

He noticed this, saying afterward:

"So you have decided to be a nice girl, *ja?*"

"I will do what you ask. For my son. For my homeland."

He seemed to buy this.

"You can demonstrate your patriotism by convincing your lover to run a little errand for me. Not, of course, that he will ever know who the guiding hand behind all this actually is. Do you think you could convince him to collect some photographs of your son from your friend Judit?"

*   *   *

That night I revealed to Thomas the fact that I have a son. I told him the entire story——and Thomas listened in shocked silence throughout the rendering. I didn't embellish. I didn't play up things in an attempt to win his sympathy. I never once cried——though the retelling of it all made me want to on several occasions. I just reported the facts——including the discovery that my great friend Judit had betrayed me. And I told him that life without Johannes was a form of living death.

Thomas could not have reacted more wonderfully. He said that knowing all this explained so much——and he couldn't imagine having endured what I had endured.

I mentioned that I had received a letter some months ago from Judit, a letter smuggled to me. In it she said she was so appalled by her betrayal of me and begged my forgiveness, while also stating that she had a collection of photographs that belonged to me. Thomas immediately said he would go to East Berlin, knock on her door, and get the photographs. I felt such a stab of guilt when he said this. Because there had never been a letter from Judit. And the only reason I knew she had the photographs was that Haechen told me his "people" would be delivering them to her this week and would brief her on what to say to Thomas when he arrived at her apartment.

"All he will have to do is bring back twenty or so photographs," Haechen told me. "Half of them I will keep. The other half you will be able to keep. So, you see, you profit from sending your boyfriend on this expedition. You will finally have photographs of your beloved son——and trust me, the Republic will be most impressed by your assistance. This could be the turning point for you."

Now listening to my beloved Thomas insist that he collect those photographs for me . . . that he just had to do this . . . my guilt was bottomless. How could I do this . . . how could I involve the man I so adored in such a grubby, shadowy business?

But as my panic mounted, it was shouted down by that reasoned voice within me. And that voice said:

"You do what you have to do to get through the next few weeks. Then all will come right. And you will be free."

So——after sounding very reluctant to involve him——I told Thomas that, yes, I would be hugely grateful if he could pay Judit a visit.

*   *   *

He left early this morning for Checkpoint Charlie. I held on to him a very long time before he left, telling him to be careful. Even though Haechen informed me yesterday that I shouldn't worry about Thomas's safety——that it was in *their* interest that his trip to East Berlin was an uneventful one——I still didn't believe a word he told me. Haechen is a man whose entire life is made up of fabrications, lies, falsehoods, the control of others through the threat of blackmail, extortion, physical injury. So who knew what games they might spring on my beloved.

Because they are the Stasi. And their rules defy moral logic.

I ran to the window and watched Thomas walk off. Oh God, please get him back to me tonight. Safely.

*   *   *

He was home before five! He looked tired and a little shaken up——as he had a story to tell. The border guards had held him at Checkpoint Charlie for a good two hours. They gave him no reason for this delay. And though they tore his bag apart, they didn't make him undress—— he had secreted the photographs under his jeans. I cried when I saw all the images of Johannes. He'd grown, of course. He was a little chunkier than when I last held him——which was a relief, as whoever was looking after him was feeding him reasonably. He had more hair, his eyes were more alert, but there was that ever-present half smile. Seeing that smile, seeing my son again after all these months, I couldn't stop myself from crying. And Thomas held me until I finally did

Much later——as Thomas dozed in bed after we had made love——I got up and collated the photographs together, feeling each one, wondering which contained the microfilm or whatever they had secreted within them. I could sense no bulge in any of them. But they were rather professional when it came to such things, weren't they?

*   *   *

Haechen was pleased with the photographs.

"Good work," he said, handing me ten of the twenty that I was allowed to keep. Then: "You won't be hearing from me for a little while. I have business elsewhere. But I might call on you to join me in a few weeks. So keep checking that loose tile in Der Schlüssel. Twice a week as normal. When I need you, I will let you know. Do not believe that this absence is a permanent one."

Afterward the thought struck me that he had somebody here doing part of his dirty work for him. Tailing me. Keeping tabs on all my movements. Leaving his notes. Knowing everything about me.

*   *   *

Thomas has told me we are going to Paris!

Paris. I cannot believe it. All these years when Paris seemed like a distant planet, out of permanent reach. And now . . .

Alaistair's paintings continue to astonish me. I said that to him the other day, the fact that they are so extraordinary. His reply:

"I have no damn idea if they are good or not. And even when I finish them, I probably won't like them. But you can like them for me."

Much later Thomas and I joined him for several vodkas downstairs in his studio. When Thomas excused himself to use the bath-room, Alaistair turned to me and said:

"You seem happier than I've ever seen you. What's happened?"

"Life has gotten simpler."

Because Haechen had vanished. For the moment.

*   *   *

I am just back from Paris.

Paris.

If I die tomorrow I can think: at least I was once in Paris. And with the man of my life.

Paris.

Where to start?

The Rue Gay Lussac perhaps? That's the street that housed the charming little hotel into which Thomas had booked us for several nights. He noted with amusement that it was a little run-down, a little too noisy, a little too impregnated with tobacco, and a little too "French plumbing" when it came to the feeble shower in our room. I didn't care. We were in Paris. And Paris was overwhelming in ways that appealed to me. Yes, it had its majestic moments. Yes, it was all such a visual set-piece. But what I loved most about it were things like the little bakery near our hotel where you could buy the sort of croissants that were akin to a religious experience. Or the little cinemas where you could hide in old movies for a few francs. Or the jazz place near Châtelet where all the musicians seemed to be black American émigrés, wildly gifted and so deeply cool. Or the wonderful little café next to our hotel where all the local workmen seemed to gather for a glass of wine at nine in the morning and where, while sitting there with Thomas, I could pretend for the length of a coffee that I lived the sort of unencumbered bohemian existence that I know is nothing more than the fantasy of somebody visiting this city with a return ticket to elsewhere.

What a wondrous fantasy. Does Paris always seduce with its sen-suality and its image of life unimpeded, even though I know damn well that, like anywhere else, people here are paying rents and raising children and fighting with their spouses and dealing with jobs that leave them unfulfilled, all the *realpolitik* of day-to-day life that we tend to overlook while sitting in a café on an atmospheric street in the Fifth Arrondissement, watching life go by?

I had my decoy journal with me, recording all the films and museums and cafés we loitered in while playacting Parisians. But how I wished I'd had this "real" journal with me, to confess something that has been on my conscience for some time now:

With Haechen absent from my life for the past few weeks, I made a decision as soon as I had my last period——and I knew that I did not risk getting pregnant anymore by *him*.

I went off the pill.

Yes, yes, I should have told Thomas immediately. Yes, yes, I shouldn't be making decisions for the two of us. Yes, yes, I know he has spoken many times about wanting a baby with me. But the word "eventually" has always been there.

So why have I decided to get pregnant without consulting him?

Because I fear all the other shit coming back at me. Because I want certainty. Because I know that Thomas will not be angry about this. Bemused perhaps. Anxious, of course (aren't all men?). But he has told me often enough it's what he wants with me. And I want it now. I want a new child. A new life.

Yet I feel so profoundly guilty at the same time about it all. I should have told him. But I can't. Just like I cannot tell him about the even bigger betrayal I have perpetrated upon him.

Does love——profound love——have to involve a degree of betrayal? I ask myself that question so often now. Had I followed my instincts at the outset I would have pushed Thomas away from me, because I knew I was a mine field of conflicting interests. And because I had to answer to the man who had announced he controlled my destiny.

But if I had pushed him away——if I had chosen the less problematic route (even though there was hardly anything unproblematic about the Faustian bargain that Haechen had offered me)——I would never have known what it was like to feel so certain about another person, and to have that conviction validated by him.

But, damn me, why didn't I just tell him: *I want to have a baby with you now*. Why did I insist on retreating into connivance and deceit when a straightforward statement of fact would have been unquestionably met with the response I so wanted?

Why do I complicate things so? And why do I gamble with the love of the one and only man in my life who has ever shown me real love?

*   *   *

We were sitting in a café in the Odeon, holding hands, drinking wine, when he asked me to marry him. Just like that. Yes, he'd mentioned marriage in the past, but always in the manner that one mentions some place you'll visit in the near future.

This was definitive. It came in the wake of me stating (again!) that I thought we should move here. He then said, "Well, why don't we get married as well?" I thought at first he was joking. But it was clear he was immensely serious. And this threw me. I wanted it more than ever.

But instead of expressing the joy I truly felt, I disappeared into the ladies' room and locked myself in a stall and lit up a cigarette and talked myself out of the panic attack I was having, telling myself once again that there was a plan. Once that plan was followed all would be fine. So I went back outside and said that, yes, I would marry him. He insisted on ordering champagne——and we talked about our possible life in New York and renting a larger apartment there and me finding work . . . and, yes, the fact that I had now given up hope about ever being allowed custody of Johannes again, and Thomas saying it was best to give up hope, as hard a conclusion as that was to reach. And me thinking all the time: the fact that I have finally given up hope has allowed me to begin formulating the plan that will liberate me from Haechen forever.

But things need to move along now. Part of me prays that, if we can expedite things——the marriage, the green card——we might be gone by the time Haechen gets back. He could have me chased to New York. But then what? More threats of exposure? Now that I accept that Johannes is gone, so too is their power over me. My son again was the last bargaining chip they had with me. Of course, they could threaten to eliminate me——but I have an answer to that as well. First things first. I need to see Haechen one more time. Just to definitively close the chapter, end the tale, turn the page, all those clichés we mouth in the hope that things can change. Then life can become good again.

That's the great aspiration behind everything: the vision of life as a happy, positive enterprise. Free from tragedy and pettiness and meanness and disappointment. That too is the great hope behind love: total fulfillment with another person who becomes your bulwark against everything that human existence can throw in your path, or, at the very least, can diminish the pain of it all.

*   *   *

Back in Berlin. We told Alaistair about our engagement in Paris. He insisted on champagne and looked surprisingly touched by our news. I sense he still misses Mehmet.

I was very nervous before meeting the American consul today. Terrified, actually.

But the meeting was straightforward. The consul was a woman. Not someone who smiled that much, but she asked all the appropriate questions. About the reasons for my expulsion from the GDR. About the death of my husband. About how long Thomas and I had known each other. At the end she said she saw no reason why my application wouldn't be approved——but tempered this with the statement that it wasn't her decision.

Afterward, outside, I almost fell apart I was so tense, so frightened. I explained it away to Thomas as my ingrained fear of all bureaucracy. He kept trying to reassure me that nothing would go wrong, that there was no chance they would turn me down for a green card.

But my nervousness was rooted in something else.

I'm pregnant. I bought one of those tests yesterday, and while everyone else was out at lunch, I went into the bathroom at work and peed on the little chemical strip. Then I waited and watched as the paper turned from gray to telltale pink.

I must say that I am ecstatic. But it's a jubilation tempered by the understanding that I must break the news to Thomas at the appropriate moment, explain it away by saying I forgot to bring my pills with me to Paris, and hope that he won't feel too aggrieved by it all. If he does . . . if he feels I've entrapped him . . .

But it's what he wants. He's told me that several times. And he knows we will do this all wonderfully together, that having this child will be the source of so many good things, of such happiness.

Of course, I was relieved that conception happened during that six week window when Haechen was away. I couldn't have come off the pill if I was still being forced to service him.

I mention this because I did have to see Haechen last night. There was a card awaiting me in Der Schlüssel, telling me where to meet him. One of his usual cheap hotels. As soon as I was in the door——and he was inside me——he said:

"So you ran off with your boyfriend to Paris."

I said nothing. He grabbed my face.

"You are never to leave Berlin again without my permission. Do you understand that?"

I nodded, knowing that the only reason I was letting him fuck me right now was to let it seem as if all was just business as usual, that nothing was untoward. I wanted to make my move now——but knew it wasn't the right setting, the right moment. So I just lay there, waiting for him to finish. Then:

"We're going away for a weekend," he said.

"I see."

"Hamburg. I have business there. But I want you along."

"Am I part of this business?"

"You will see. We travel separately, the day after tomorrow. We will stay in different hotels. But I will come and find you. There is an envelope on the dresser with your train ticket and the name of the hotel. Bring your typewriter with you. You will need to do some translation work while there. Then you will have to bring some things back to a contact of mine in Berlin. And I know that Radio Liberty is about to interview those two traitorous dancers who just defected. If you can get me the transcript of that interview well before it is broadcast, it might just be the coup that wins you back your son."

*   *   *

The plan is now moving apace. Being out of town is perfect. Hamburg even more so. So too are the separate hotel rooms——and the fact that in the envelope are two hundred deutsche marks to cover my hotel costs and any basic expenses, as well as a false set of identity papers, stating that my name is Hildegard Hinckel. I have now bought everything I need for the trip——and did it in a shop on the other side of the city, away from my own neighborhood. I have told Thomas that Herr Wellmann's usual translator is off sick and that Herr Direktor has insisted I come along with him on a last-minute trip to Hamburg, where he's giving some lecture at a big conference and needs some-body to do simultaneous translation for him. Thomas seemed to buy this. But then he told me he's the man who's been asked to interview Hans and Heidi Braun, and that he'll be working on the transcript this weekend. All right, I hate doing this one more time. If all goes to plan in Hamburg, I can return to Berlin, see my beloved Sunday night, quickly photograph the transcript while he sleeps, then leave it with Haechen's contact, and then . . .

By the end of the week I will be Thomas's wife. And with these much-craved documents now in their hands, who's to say they mightn't relent?

Thomas commented on the fact that this is the first time we have ever been apart since everything started between us.

And it will be the last time we are ever apart.

*   *   *

I was booked on the 12:13 from Berlin Zoo Station to the Hamburg Hauptbahnhof. I changed my ticket and took the 9:47. There was a strange moment in the journey when we reached the western bor-der of Berlin and reentered GDR territory. The border delineated by armed soldiers and barbed wire. The train didn't stop——but actually seemed to gain speed. Perhaps this was something the GDR authori-ties insisted upon——the train from West Berlin to Hamburg traveling at a certain agreed high speed through their territory so nobody can attempt to jump on it. Has there ever been a state so obsessed with keeping its citizens permanently corralled and controlled?

Hamburg. The hotel was in the red light district. The Reeperbahn. This too was good news. They let me check in early. The hotel was cheap and shabby and very transient. Hookers work out of here. People come and go all the time. The sort of place where the staff are told not to notice anything——unless it involves nonpayment of a bill——and to never ask questions or tell anything to the police.

I went for a walk in the Reeperbahn. I explored side streets and back alleys. I worked out a scenario in my head. I went back to the hotel. My sense of anxiety mounted. I smoked and studied a map of the city and its U-Bahn system. I waited for his call. It didn't come until seven that night. He said he was in a bar across the road.

"Do you want to come up?" I ask.

"Later. I want to eat first."

Perfect.

"I'll be right down."

I picked up my daypack that I had brought along in my suitcase. It was unseasonably chilly, so I put on the denim jacket I traveled in, checking my pockets. All was ready.

As I left the hotel I noted that no desk clerk was there to see me go out. I crossed the street. I entered the bar. It was packed. Haechen was standing at the counter, watching a naked woman on a nearby stage sticking a banana inside herself.

"What do you think?" Haechen asked, nodding toward the stage show.

I just shrugged, then said: "I'm hungry."

"We can eat here. They have food."

"I found a little Italian place not far away. Supposed to have the best pizzas in Hamburg."

"When did you do that?"

"When I arrived."

"I ordered you to go straight to the hotel."

"And I felt like stretching my legs, so I took a little walk. And found this restaurant. And saw in the window some framed review from some newspaper saying . . ."

"I don't like you being insubordinate and disobeying my clear instructions."

"It was a ten-minute stroll, nothing more. I promise it won't happen again. But this restaurant does look good."

"Expensive?"

"No."

I could see Haechen thinking this over.

"All right. But after dinner we go back to my room. And you will need to translate these before you return on Sunday."

He slid an envelope toward me. I immediately put it in my daypack.

"Fine, fine," I said. "And I have some great news for you. I will be able to score the transcripts of the interview with Hans and Heidi Braun by Monday."

"You serious?"

"Yes."

"That *is* good news. You are certain you can get the interview transcript on Sunday?"

"My friend said he would be working on it this weekend."

"Then you must photograph it that night. The timing is perfect. I'm staying on here for a few days, but they told me that getting that interview transcript before it is broadcast was a matter of extreme urgency. So you will need to leave the documents I've asked you to translate—and the photographs of the transcripts of the interviews—this Monday morning behind the cistern in the usual lavatory cubicle in Der Schlüssel. The fact that they will have it at the start of the week . . . believe me, my people will be terribly impressed with this prize you have given us. I think it will help your case enormously."

He threw some money on the bar. The woman onstage was currently doing unspeakable things with an orange. The lights were so dim—and the crowd so tightly packed—that I doubted anyone would ever remember that we were there.

We started walking down some side streets, Haechen looking strangely relaxed, telling me he preferred Hamburg to Berlin, "because here not everybody is spying on each other." He let me lead the way, going deeper and deeper into the labyrinth that was the Reeperbahn, passing numerous prostitutes and sex shops and loud bars, moving further into a quieter corner of the district.

"You sure you know where you're going?" he asked as we turned a corner into an area largely inhabited by warehouses.

"Not far now," I said.

At the next corner I steered him right, saying the restaurant was at the end of this street. I let him walk a few paces ahead of me. As he turned right I could see him realizing that we had turned into an unlit back alley. Suddenly he wheeled around toward me. That's when my right hand sprang out of nowhere and plunged a switchblade into his heart. I'd hidden the knife in the pocket of my jacket, along with a pair of plain black gloves. As he was walking ahead of me, I'd pulled the gloves on, coughed as the switchblade flicked open with a decided snap, then waited for him to turn around toward me as soon as he saw that we'd entered the dark alley from which he'd never emerge.

Only that realization didn't hit him until the knife made a direct hit. Using its now extended handle as a form of leverage, I shoved him up against the alley wall and immediately covered his nose and mouth with my free hand, pinching the nostrils closed, forcibly sealing his mouth with my palm, keeping my gaze fixed on him as he asphyxiated on his own blood. His eyes met mine——and I could see the shock, the fear, the terror. Then he began to vomit blood, and I had to pull my hand away. He collapsed on the ground, writhing for a few moments, before lying very still.

Luck was still with me. No one was around. Nor were there any sounds of approaching vehicles or footsteps. Quickly I reached into his trouser pocket and removed his wallet. I opened his jacket and pulled out his identity papers. I loosened his belt and pulled down his pants and his Y-fronts. Then, with an almighty yank, I pulled the knife out of his chest. Holding the wallet, the identity papers, and the bloody knife in one hand, I stepped out into the side street again, looking both ways. I had chosen this area well. No one was here after dark. I turned right, walking quickly yet calmly down the street, then turned into another side alleyway, this one as dark and unlit as the one where Haechen now lay. Quickly I stripped off the bloody gloves, then my jacket, jeans, T-shirt, and sneakers——all of which were now stained with blood. Opening up the daypack I took out an identical set of clothes bought yesterday in Berlin. I was dressed in seconds, bundling the knife, my clothes, the wallet, and the papers into the bag. Again I looked both ways before stepping out into the street. No pedestrians. No cars. I had the place to myself. Turning right I hit a main thoroughfare and walked on until I found the U-Bahn station I'd discovered earlier. I took a train across the city to Planten un Blomen——a park that, according to the tourist map I had also bought at the Hamburg Hauptbahnhof, had some forty-seven hectares and contained a lake. Emerging from the U-Bahn at the southwest corner of the park I walked into its confines, quickly finding my way to the lake, only passing one homeless man asleep on the grass. There was a bridge over a corner of the lake. The moonlight was noticeable here. I picked up a pebble and tossed it into the water. It sank quickly and, I sensed, deeply. Putting on the fresh pair of gloves that I had previously stuffed into my daypack, I then zipped open my shoulder bag, retrieved the knife, and tossed it into the water. I also pulled out the wallet——which was not that bloodied——removed the cash that was there, walked on until I was out of the park again, and dumped the wallet into a public trash can on the street. A few streets away, the identity papers went into another public receptacle. I was in an area not far from the Hauptbahnhof. Approaching the railway station I saw a huge industrial-sized trash container located in a refuse area behind its main entranceway. Fortunately the cover of this container was not locked, and it was swimming with rubbish. The backpack went in here. I moved on to the railway station. Having already balled up the gloves that had touched all the evidence, I dumped them into the first bin I could find.

Then I turned into the U-Bahn station and took a train back to my hotel, where I stripped off all of my new clothes and had a very hot shower. I checked my watch. It was just 9:09. I had an hour or so before I needed to leave. I messed up the bed, so when the maid arrived tomorrow morning there were signs that somebody slept there. Then I opened a bottle of vodka I brought with me and drank three shots and smoked three cigarettes. I gathered up my suitcase and went downstairs. Again luck was on my side, as there was nobody at the front desk as I left. A quick walk to the U-Bahn, a quick ride to the Hauptbahnhof, and the 11:07 back to Berlin.

I was at home and in bed in my room before two this morning. I didn't sleep well, expecting Stasi agents to burst in here any moment and cart me away.

I hid at home all Saturday and translated the documents Haechen gave me. In an attempt to keep busy I also drafted my essay to be submitted with my US green card application. It's now just after midnight. I snuck downstairs an hour ago to retrieve this notebook and start writing. I will see Thomas in less than eighteen hours. I'll bring my suitcase with me, pretending that I've just arrived back from Hamburg. I must try to appear calm, try to mask all the fear I have right now.

I know that, with Haechen's people briefed, it's obligatory that I photograph the interview transcripts on Sunday night and sneak out with the film while Thomas sleeps. The idea now is to play for time. Dropping off everything they're expecting from me will cover my tracks. Because my story to them, should I be forced to tell it, will be:

I arrived in Hamburg as directed. I waited at the hotel, but Haechen never appeared. I hung on until 10:00, then decided to leave—because Haechen and I had an unspoken rule that if he didn't show up at a rendezvous I was to return home. And since home is Berlin, I caught the last train back. However, being the loyal operative, I still scored for you the transcripts of the interview with Hans and Heidi Braun.

Indeed, being able to proffer these transcripts will be my alibi should the Stasi accuse me of having anything to do with Haechen's disappearance.

Anyway, when Haechen's body is found, the knife wound, the missing wallet, the trousers around his legs will all make it seem like he picked up somebody for a bit of rough sex in a back alleyway and that somebody turned larcenous and homicidal. My hope, though, is that the lack of a wallet or identity papers means the body will go unclaimed. I doubt very much that the Stasi would send a representative to collect it. I checked into the hotel using false identity papers, thus there is also no official record of me ever having left Berlin.

Perhaps, in the weeks remaining before Thomas and I move to the States, their new Haechen will get in touch and insist on meeting me in another sleazy hotel room. This time I will refuse to see him. Would they really expose me as their operative at Radio Liberty? That would be counterintuitive and hurt them, as it would have the American and West German security services on high alert for other operatives in other governmental bodies. Yes, they could kill me, but I gave them the big counter-propaganda coup by leaking them the Braun transcript days before the broadcast. Were they to kill me thereafter, it would probably expose the fact that I had been their mole at Radio Liberty. Again, would they really want that sort of interest around a lowly nobody like myself?

I'm frightened. Frightened and desperate to get through these next few days. Though I feel a great shocked numbness in the wake of murdering Haechen, there is no guilt whatsoever. It had to be done. There was no other alternative if I wanted to be able to walk away, turn the page, start anew. Especially with this new life inside me.

Can I do all that? Can I somehow shove this all into a dark room deep within my psyche and slam it shut, never to be opened again? I doubt it. But I do plan, as soon as I finish this entry, to go down to the basement and place this journal, alongside the first one, on the shelf inside the disused ventilation shaft that has always been their hiding place. Only this time I plan not to retrieve these journals again before Thomas and I leave the city. With any luck, ten, fifteen years from now, when I visit Berlin with Thomas and our two children, I will excuse myself for a couple of hours, make a pilgrimage back to Kreuzberg, loiter outside until someone enters or exits the building, then go downstairs and recover them again——as if they were a time capsule from a part of my life that has always shadowed me and made me what I am but which I have been able to compartmentalize. Not the loss of Johannes. I know that until the day I die, I will never be able to fully block that out of my life. Nor do I want to. Because his loss was such a profound one. But I will now try to slam the door on everything else, most especially the fact that I had to kill a man in order to live again. Haechen would have insisted on a termination as soon as my pregnancy started to show. His death allows me to keep the child that is now inside me. With strong effort I will be able to bury the memory of what I did to gain my freedom. Toss those remembrances into the darkest hole imaginable, cover it all with reinforced concrete, walk away from the burial site, never to visit it again.

Can I actually do this? Can I force myself into willful amnesia about all that I have just done this weekend? Time will only tell.

What I do know right now is this:

All the murder evidence has been scattered. No sign of my ever having been in Hamburg exists.

I've gotten away with it. I've gotten away with it all.

And now . . .

Now I'm free. Well and truly free. Now life with Thomas can really begin. Thomas and our child. I am going to be a mother again.

I'm free.

We're free.

PART FIVE

ONE

THE NOTEBOOK ENDED there. As I shut it and pushed it away from me, I glanced up and noticed darkness had fallen outside. In the few hours it took me to read through it all, I had been oblivious to the world outside of Petra's words.

I'm free.

We're free.

I snapped my eyes shut and thought back to that scene in my apartment one day after she wrote this. When I confronted her with her "treason" against me. When she begged me to listen. When I refused to listen. When I was so enraged I couldn't hear what she was telling me. *Please let me explain.*

But instead, I only heard my own hurt pride, my own sense of outrage. Instead, in that crucial instant, I slammed the door.

I reached for the bottle of Scotch near my elbow, poured myself another shot, threw it back, and stepped outside onto the deck that fronted my kitchen. As always, the Maine night was so black, so impermeable. The mercury was well below freezing, a light snow was falling, but I was indifferent to it all. For I was thinking back as well to that moment in that bar in Wedding and that CIA spook, Bubriski, explaining to me the theory of radar and telling me:

"Radar works when a magnetic field——almost like a field of attraction——is set up between two objects. One object then sends out a signal to another object in the distance. And when that signal hits the other object, what is transmitted back is *not* the object itself. Rather it's the *image* of that object."

Then he revealed all about Petra. And he used the radar metaphor to rub in the fact that I had fallen in love with the "image" that I had projected onto her and, in the process, had failed to see what she really was.

Since then, whenever I found myself wondering whether I had made a desperately wrong call, when my guilt for shopping her to Bubriski and his fellow spooks sometimes loomed up out of nowhere, I tried to console myself with the thought: *but she was projecting an image of herself that didn't tally with the truth.*

Privately I always knew I was trying to validate the angry, impulsive decision I had made, a decision that, as I now learned, had destroyed everything.

One moment. Why hadn't I let her tell me what she was so desperate to tell me? Why had I allowed my hubris, my arrogance, to deny her the chance to explain everything?

What page after page of the notebook told me was . . .

"Love. Real love. Something——I have to admit within the safe confines of this journal——that I had never known."

Those were her words. One of so many declarations of love. For me. *The man of my life,* as she wrote so many times. When I read her thoughts about my vulnerabilities, my defenses, the way she so understood how all the childhood sadness still shadowed me. Had anyone ever really "got" me the way Petra did?

Standing out on that deck, staring out at the tenebrous void beyond, all I could now think was: you lost the one person in the world who ever truly loved you. And you lost her because you killed it. Killed it through self-righteousness. A need to be aggrieved. To punish without considering the circumstances.

In page after page of the notebooks she also informed me of what she so wanted to let me know back then——that her role as a Stasi operative was one that had been imposed upon her, a form of maniacal blackmail that she only accepted because she knew it was the one and only way she might ever be reunited with her son. And I wouldn't let her explain that to me.

Or explain the horror of her indentured relationship with Haechen, and how she had finally resorted to murder because . . .

Because it was the only way she thought she could be free to be with me. And because she was carrying our child.

I'm free.

We're free.

Our child.

What happened to our child? Was it a boy, a girl? And he or she was now . . . ? My God, twenty-five years old.

Immediately I reentered the kitchen, grabbing the cover letter from Johannes that accompanied the notebooks. On it was an email address. I moved quickly to my office, turned on my computer, and sent him an email that read:

I am coming to Berlin the day after tomorrow. Can we meet up?

And I signed my name.

Then I switched over to a last-minute travel site and scored a cheap fare from Boston to Berlin via Munich. The flight would leave Boston tomorrow night at eight-thirty. On the same site, I found a hotel in a district called Mitte.

Mitte. The former East. Once forbidden territory. Now . . .

Radar.

". . . when that signal hits the other object what is transmitted back is not the object itself. It's the image of that object."

I was convinced by that postulation——because, in my outrage at having been cheated on, cuckolded, betrayed, I was thinking only of the image.

But now I realized the "image" was anything but that. The love was not an illusion. It was profoundly real.

Now my sense of shame was only surpassed by the thought: pride is the most destructive force in the world. It blinds us to anything but our hubristic need to be right, to defend our own fragile sense of self. In doing so, it stops us from seeing other interpretations of the narrative we're living. Pride makes you take a position from which you cannot be budged. Pride makes you refuse to even consider the reason someone is begging you to hear them out. Pride insists that you toss away the one person you've met in the course of five decades who offered you the chance of real happiness. Pride murders the love of your life.

I sat down at the table and stared again at Petra's obituary notice——the photograph so cruelly delineating the devastation of the past decades. A devastation that started with Johannes being taken away from her, and continued throughout that horrifying year of servicing Haechen, and then culminated in my wholesale betrayal of her.

Our child.

I delivered her into the hands of the security services when she was pregnant with our child.

Who was now where?

And how did Petra manage to be reunited with Johannes?

Our child.

I was going to Berlin to find our child.

*   *   *

I tried to sleep, but failed. So, as first light broke, I stopped staring at the badly flecked paint on the bedroom ceiling. I got up. I packed a small bag. I checked my email. There was a reply from Johannes:

Café Sibylle. Karl-Marx-Allee 72. Friedrichshain. 18h00 tomorrow. You need to take the U-Bahn to Strausberger Platz, then walk ten minutes. Don't worry about finding me. I will recognize you.

*   *   *

Land. Fields. Buildings. The outline of a city on the curved edge of the horizon. And all refracted through the numbness of a night spent sleeping sitting up in a cramped seat.

Those words came back to me as the flight from Munich banked and headed toward the city below. Only this time Berlin's defining aerial landmark——the structure that cleaved the city in two——appeared to have been simply expunged from its cartography. Up here you could imagine some divine hand wielding an eraser and simply rubbing away that barrier——once so stark, so ruthless, so all-defining. And now? Now down below was just a metropolitan sprawl.

Then we were on the ground in Tegel. When I piled myself into a taxi and gave him my hotel address in Mitte, the driver didn't make any noises about having to go east. Berlin was a construction site. New buildings everywhere. A game of architectural one-upmanship as ultramodern designs competed with each other for audacity and über-style.

Suddenly I was looking at the recently opened Hauptbahnhof——a huge glass and steel box, multileveled, in and out of which trains shunted with metronomic regularity. Then, looming up ahead was the television tower of Alexanderplatz. We were now no more than a kilometer from it. Somewhere within the last few minutes we had crossed the frontier that no longer existed. The remnants of The Wall were nowhere to be seen. All was free flow, unmarked. It was as if that thing had never existed.

Alexanderplatz. As Stalinist and brutal as ever——with a few changes. A big sprawling fitness center on the second floor of the tower. A big shopping complex constructed nearby. There were some of the old GDR apartment blocks——like the one that Petra initially lived in when she arrived in Berlin——but all renovated, modernized. An attempt to make palatable the aesthetically grim. As the taxi swung down a street toward my hotel, I could see that a big pedestrian precinct had been opened, lined with the same brand names and food outlets that you find in any metropolitan concentration of people worldwide these days. In my mind's eye I could flash back to that cold winter's morning in 1984 when I first crossed over to "the other side," when Alexanderplatz was as bleak and as forbidding as a Siberian steppe, when I felt as if I was staring at an emergency edition of life: hard, unvarnished, lacking all notions of beauty or comfort.

And now you could shop here.

Shopping: the great barometric gauge of our times.

My hotel was very designer. Wildly stylized, as if someone was trying to create a brothel in minimalist style. Intriguingly, it looked right out on the concrete precincts of Alexanderplatz, as if you were being given an aerie over reinvented Soviet-era realities from the vantage point of a glossy magazine. I took a shower. I checked my watch. I had several hours to kill. I wandered the immediate area. Mitte had become something akin to SoHo in New York. Interesting galleries. Interesting cafés. Interesting loft spaces. Designer boutiques. Hip tourists. Backstreet cinemas and theaters. Renovated apartment blocks. Discernment and money.

I walked around, bemused. The lack of sleep had something to do with this. So too did the fact that I was still in shock after all that I had absorbed in the last two days, a renewed grief that now made me feel, in every sense of the word, so small.

But the befuddlement was also due to the radical change to the Berlin cityscape, and the sense that, systematically, understandably, the eastern part of the city was expunging all that it could of its past. Even the area of Friedrichshain——with its dense collection of socialist realist tower blocks——was remodeling these grim-looking boxes, using bright primary colors and redesigned finishes to take the harsh, functionalist edge off them.

Coming out of the Strausberger Platz U-Bahn station, I couldn't help but now think that it was in one of these blocks that Johannes lived with the Stasi family to whom he was handed, one year old, as a gift. Just as I remembered that Petra insisted on living only a few streets——but another universe——away in Kreuzberg, because it was as geopolitically close as she could be to the son who had been taken away from her.

The Café Sibylle was something of an anomaly. It was located on the ground floor of a vast building constructed in that proletarian palatial style favored by Muscovite architects in the 1930s. Inside the décor was retro East Bloc circa 1955——as if the current owners were trying to preserve a glimpse of GDR café life as it once existed at the height of the Cold War. The travel writer in me is always taking mental notes——and I immediately spotted a small corner of the café given over to Communist-era souvenirs. There was a quartet of elderly women with severe faces sitting around a Formica table, talking to each other in conspiratorial whispers. There were a couple of menacing-looking skinheads who exchanged civil greetings with one of the old ladies, and a very plump woman with a huge bouffant hairdo seated on a stool behind the cash register, looking as if she had been positioned there for the past thirty years. And sitting in a corner was a rather introverted guy wearing a Manga T-shirt and an electric-blue hooded sweatshirt, his hair gelled into spikes, his skin retaining scars from adolescent acne, his eyes hinting at ongoing preoccupation. He was currently engrossed in some Japanese graphic novel. Something within its visuals or its text amused him, as his lips formed a half smile that hinted at a certain ambiguous and suspicious take on everything.

So this was Johannes.

He glanced up from his book, saw me watching him, and knew immediately who I was as he nodded gravely at me. I came over and extended my hand. He took it reluctantly and favored me with the most feeble of grips before pulling away.

"I'm Thomas," I said.

"I know."

"How did you know?"

"I've seen your photograph in your books."

"You've read my books?"

"Don't flatter yourself."

"I never flatter myself into thinking that anyone reads my books, because so few people do. May I sit down?"

He nodded, motioning toward the vacant seat opposite him. I noticed the empty beer glass in front of him.

"May I buy you another?"

A shrug. Then: "Okay."

"I appreciate you agreeing to see me at such short notice," I said.

"I'm not exactly running between meetings," he said.

"You a student?"

"Hardly. Never went to university."

"Was that your own decision?"

"Yeah, inasmuch as if you don't study and don't really care about passing exams, you generally end up not getting into a university. But did you actually come all this way from wherever you live to hear about my failure as a student?"

He said all this in an unchanging monotone. I also noticed that he never once made eye contact with me, that his vision was always focused elsewhere.

"I wanted to meet you," I said.

"Why is that?"

"I think you know why."

"Your guilt?"

Again, the comment was made without edge or anger.

"Yes, my guilt has something to do with me being here."

"I read the journals. You should be guilty."

"I am."

"You should also know that she always talked about you."

"Really?"

"You sound surprised."

"It's just . . . well, it was more than a quarter of a century ago when——"

"You turned her over to the CIA?"

I fell silent, staring down at the table, thinking, *I deserve this. All of this and more.*

"I won't try to defend what I did. It was wrong. And even though I didn't know the actual story itself before I read the journals——"

"Mother killed a guy. That struck me as kind of cool. Especially as he was a bad guy. A Stasi prick liked the man who had custody of me for five years."

"It was just five years you were with him?"

"Just five years? It felt like a lifetime. But why should this story interest you?"

"Why do you think?"

"So . . . the journals. They really got to you?"

"Are you surprised?"

"I don't know you."

"You know certain things about me."

"I know what my mother told me about you. I know what she wrote in the journals. I know what you did. I know what that cost her."

"What did it cost her?"

"That's another conversation."

"How did she get you back?"

"You are very direct. Are all Americans so direct?"

"This one is. How did she get you back?"

I also wanted to ask: *and do you have a brother or a sister somewhere?* But Johannes's distracted manner made me hesitate. Especially as his response to my last question was:

"Weren't you going to order me a beer?"

I raised my hand. A waitress came by. Johannes asked for a Hefeweizen. I said she should make that two. When she left, he stared ahead for a very long time, never once turning toward me. Finally, he said:

"I didn't want to do this."

"Meet me?"

"Send you the journals. But Mother insisted. One of the last things she asked me. And she made me promise I'd do it."

"What did she die of?"

"Cancer."

"Was it fast?"

He shook his head, then added:

"But she did continue smoking right up to the end, so you've got to admire the courage of her convictions."

"So it was lung cancer, throat cancer?"

"It was cancer caused by the radiation she was subjected to while in prison. Or, at least, that was what the doctors thought——as around one hundred other prisoners who were kept at Hohenschönhausen around the same time as Mother also died of different kinds of blood cancer. Mother said that when she was first arrested, they photographed her in a special room——and after the session she had these red burns everywhere. Radiation. Hidden from view. The fuckers thought they could impregnate their prisoners with radiation, then keep tabs on them afterward with homing devises. It's like something from a bad mad scientist movie. Everyone who got that treatment at Hohenschönhausen is either dead or on their way. Mother was one of the last."

"I'm so sorry."

"Are you?"

"More than I can say."

Silence. Then:

"I ran into my other 'parents' a few days ago on the street. They're in their sixties now. Still together. Still looking as stiff as they always did. Hadn't seen them in twenty-five years. Not since Mother got me back. I saw them walking toward me. I sort of smiled. They walked right on by, didn't recognize me at all."

"Did that surprise you?"

"It pleased me. Because when I was with them I never knew I had this real mother who was locked up somewhere."

"Your mother was locked up after——"

"After you did what you did? That's right. Locked up, then sent off to Karl Marx Stadt as a form of internal exile. That city——it was our Siberia. But you interrupted me. Five years with those people who called themselves my parents. They were very strict. I had to call my alleged father 'sir.' My 'mother' was also an officer in the Stasi and not comfortable with the whole idea of affection. Or, at least, that's what I tell myself I remember from that time. The truth is, I remember so very little, except that my 'parents' were always distant with me, always so formal. But . . . from the start, I thought they were my real parents. So I also thought: this is how parents behave. Then, one day, some men in suits came to the door of our apartment not far from here in Friedrichshain. They were accompanied by two policemen. One of the men spoke with my 'father.' Then he spoke with me. Said he wanted to bring me somewhere to meet a woman who really wanted to get to know me. It was all just a little confusing. My 'parents' stood there, saying nothing, while one of the suits hissed at them and another handed them a bunch of papers.

"What they were doing was telling these people——my 'parents'——that they knew they had gotten this child . . . *me* . . . through illegal means. Just as they also knew that, in their 'professional work,' they were guilty of many crimes against humanity."

He paused, that half smile crossing his lips again.

"Do I talk too much?" he asked.

"Not at all."

"You're lying. I know I talk too much. My teachers all told me that. My friends all tell me that, not that I have many friends. Dietrich tells me that all the time."

"Who's Dietrich?" I asked.

"My boss."

"Where?"

"A bookshop a few streets away from here. I work there. Have been for seven years. We specialize in comics, graphic novels. Especially Japanese stuff. Manga."

"We got off the subject of you going back to your mother."

"You really want to hear it all, don't you?"

"I do."

"My alleged parents——when they understood what the suits were telling them, and which I didn't understand myself at the time—— well, my 'mother' began to sob. My 'father' . . his name is not important . . . stood there all tight-lipped. The man in the suit who had talked to me——he was actually very kind——asked me:

"'Would you like to meet your real mother, Johannes?'

"'But this is my mother,' I said, pointing to the woman who always played that role. At which point she began to cry. Loudly. Her husband hushing her. Telling her to behave.

"'No, the Klauses looked after you while your real mother was unwell. But she is very much better now and she wants to meet you.'

"'But . . . these are my parents.'

"Even my 'father'——who I learned later helped pioneer psychological torture methods against dissidents——sobbed when he heard me say that.

"'I'll tell you what,' the suit told me. 'Let's go meet your real mother and see how you feel after you've met her.'

"They drove me to this place——it was like a school, and there was this room with all these games and toys to play with. I remember coming in with the suit and being met by this woman who was very kind. She got me some juice and asked me what I liked to play with the most. I told her I liked puzzles. She found me a puzzle. I think it was a puzzle of the Brandenburg Gate——big pieces, suitable for a kid. And I sat in a corner, working on this puzzle for a long time. When I looked up, I saw this woman still watching me. She had short hair. I can't say if I remember she was as thin as she always was after that. But I looked up and she smiled at me. I smiled at her. I don't remember much else that happened after that, though when Mother was dying a few weeks ago and I asked her all about that first time she'd seen me after all those years, she told me that she had to work so hard not to cry. Because she was terrified of frightening me. But she did come over and help me make the puzzle. And she then told me things about when I was first born, and how my father wrote stories, and how she herself used to sing me to sleep, and . . .

"The thing is, I remember none of this. But Mother recounted it all just three weeks ago like it was yesterday. She said that the more we talked that first day, the more I seemed to trust her. There was a point, after around an hour, when I got tired and laid my head against her shoulder. She said that even the suits in the room——all of whom were members of the *Bundesnachrichtendienst*——began to sob.

"They put us up in this halfway house for a few nights to make certain I was adjusting. But I just accepted that this was my real mother, maybe because she was so kind and affectionate to me. Then, after around a week, they allowed Mother to bring me home."

"And home was . . . ?"

"Prenzlauer Berg. The same apartment in which she lived with my father. After his death and her expulsion, they gave it to some people. But once The Wall came down and Mother didn't have to stay in exile in Karl Marx Stadt any longer, she became quite the attack dog. Or, at least, that's what I heard from her friends after the funeral. Within a week of the GDR collapsing, Mother had found some very tough lawyers in West Berlin who got me back to her. And the Klauses didn't dare put up a fight. The lawyers also got the apartment back. When she started getting sick around five years ago, they were able to get her a settlement from the state, given that she was made sick by all that radiation in prison. Not a bad amount of money. I think it was one hundred thousand euros. Mother bought the apartment for us, for me. She said she needed to leave me some sort of heritage. What was left over . . . she had free health care from the state and a small pension. But she had no work, so it all went over the five years she was sick. But even so, she also insisted, twice a year, to take me somewhere interesting. London. Paris. Istanbul. A week in Sicily. A week in Marrakesh. We traveled cheaply. But we still saw places. She told me that her dream when she was young——and couldn't travel beyond the GDR——was to move freely around the world. 'Like my Thomas.' That's a direct quote. 'Like my Thomas.'"

I hung my head and said nothing.

"But again I'm talking too much, *ja*? That's what Dietrich always says. 'You talk too much, Johannes. You start and you can't stop. You say whatever comes into your head. You have a problem not shutting up.'"

"I don't have any problem with it."

"That's because you're feeling guilty. When Mother asked me to send you the journals, I said, 'Why? Because all these years later you want the man to feel guilty?' And she said: 'No, because I want him to know how wrong I got things.'"

"Your mother didn't get anything wrong. I did."

"So what are you doing here?"

"Meeting you."

"You traveled all this way just to meet me?"

"How can I put this? You were so much a part of our life together back then. Your mother couldn't bear the fact that they had taken you away from her. Everything, absolutely everything in her life, was about getting you back."

"I know. I've read the journals."

"And what did you think when you read them?"

"What did I think? I thought: 'Mom, you were crazy expending all that energy on me. I mean, I'm a guy who works in a bookshop. I read Manga all the time. I don't have a lot of friends. I don't have a girlfriend. And some shrink told me and Mother that I have this manic disorder where I talk all the time, say whatever comes into my head.'"

"Your mother loved you more than anything."

"Yeah, and that was her problem. Along with loving you."

Again, I said nothing.

"That hurt, right?" he asked.

I just shrugged.

"Tell me the truth," he said. "Did that hurt?"

"Yes," I said. "It hurt."

"Good," he said, his voice still that incessant monotone. "Come on. I'll show you where she lived."

There was a taxi driving by as we stepped out into Karl-Marx-Allee. Johannes told me it was stupid to waste money on somebody driving us. But my head was swimming, the jet lag intermingling with Johannes's unnerving delivery, his uncensored directness, his profound strangeness which also allowed him to sidestep decorum or standard-issue politesse and instead articulate everything that was in his brain at the moment you were speaking with him. What I found most unsettling about all this was the way he was also able to cut to the heart of the matter and express the truth as he saw it. A truth that——though totally subjective——had more than the weight of veracity to it.

I talked Johannes into letting me treat us to a cab. En route, he told me that he was hoping to open his very own cartoon and graphic novel bookshop very soon. He had the premises picked out——on Prenzlauer Allee between Marienburgerstrasse and Christburger Strasse. The east side of the street, a five-minute walk from his own apartment on Jablonski Strasse.

"Prenzlauer Berg is all young bourgeois bohemian families. A great audience for cartoons and graphic novels. Now if I can convince a bank to front me some money."

"How much do you make in the current bookshop?"

"Around two hundred and fifty euros a week before tax. Maybe one eighty to take home. But thanks to Mother, I've got no rent. And I don't spend a lot on myself. I actually manage to save fifty of that a week. I've got maybe four thousand put aside now. If the bank could front me fifteen . . ."

"What would you envisage?"

"Nothing less than the most comprehensive and coolest graphic novel bookstore in the capital. I've got close to fifty meters in the premises I want. The landlord's willing to rent it to me for less than one thousand per month, which isn't cheap. But I've been doing my math. If I make this place *the go-to* bookshop of its kind in Berlin, I should be able to turn over three thousand a week easily."

"And you'd be your own boss."

"Exactly. That would be such a change. No answering to some petty little guy who really knows shit about Manga and is only in it because graphic novels sell. But he has no love of what he's selling. That's what Mother said about your books. They all have love in them."

"She really said that?"

"Love of writing, love of traveling, love of running away."

"That I've done a great deal of."

"She said that, too."

Jablonski Strasse was a street of venerable apartment buildings, all daubed with the ubiquitous graffiti that seemed to be an essential component of the new Berlin cityscape. Though many of the apartment blocks had undergone architectural plastic surgery, there were still several that remained unapologetically rooted in the GDR era. Johannes's building was one of these. A faded brown pebble-dash exterior. Grubby windows, some of which had wood hammered over their smashed frames. A front doorway that was almost hanging off the hinges. A hallway that smelled of unfinished concrete and mold.

"We're all being asked to pay three thousand each to have the entire façade and hallways renovated," he said. "But no one who lives here has three grand to spend."

His apartment was at the top of the house. I approached it, preparing myself for the worst. A toxic shambles. Dishes piled high in the sink. Toilets not cleaned in months. Dirty clothes everywhere. Spoiled food in the fridge.

Certainly, the stairwell up to this fourth-floor apartment boded badly, as it was poorly lit, half-painted, a single bare lightbulb providing the most nominal of illumination.

But as for the apartment itself, Johannes must have also decided that order was a solution against the world's disorder. It was no more than five hundred square feet, half of which was given over to a living room with basic furnishings——a simple modern black sofa and armchair that Johannes told me he found (much to his mother's delight) discarded outside a furniture showroom. Both objects had broken springs and bad padding, but Johannes knew a guy from school who worked in a furniture factory and renovated them both for one hundred euros. He mentioned this sum with particular pride, just as he explained the fifty or so Manga drawings that blanketed the walls. None of them were framed. "I don't have that sort of money," he explained. But they were all affixed to the walls of the apartment with the exact same sort of adhesive that gave the effect of four corners of a frame around each drawing. What was even more fascinating was that the drawings were lined up in immaculate rows, the distance between the cartoons perfectly measured so that none appeared farther apart than the others.

I took this all in, along with the simple kitchen, the piles upon piles of graphic novels on the apartment's many shelves, all completely alphabetized. Johannes showed me his bedroom——a simple single bed, its hospital corners tight as a drum. He showed me his extensive CD collection of strange Scandinavian heavy metal bands. Then he opened a door and said:

"Here's where Mother worked and slept."

What I saw, as the door swung inward, blindsided me. The room was no bigger than a cell. Petra too slept in a simple single bed that took up one wall. There was an equally simple white veneered desk which took up part of the other wall, on which sat a dated computer. But then I looked up at the shelves above her work area. There—— covering two long ledges, each perhaps six feet long——was copy after copy of all fourteen books that I had written. The original English versions——and their subsequent paperback incarnations——took up the top shelf. All the German and French and Italian and Greek and Polish and Swedish and Finnish translations were piled high on the shelves below.

Nearby there were also four big box files, on the spines of which had been written *T.N.: Journalismus*. Opening one of these for me Johannes showed me article after article I had written over the last twenty years for publications as wide ranging as *National Geographic, The New York Review of Books, The Times Literary Supplement.*

How had she managed to track all these down? And why, *why,* did she bother?

As soon as my brain posed that inane question, I found myself reaching for Petra's desk chair, pulling it toward me, and collapsing into it just as I started to cry, my sorrow now without limits.

All these years . . . all that time when I so wondered about her, when I told myself it was all in the grim past, don't revisit it, don't open the Pandora's box . . .

All that time, when I still privately longed for her, when I mourned what we had, what I had squandered and lost, and all the terrible things I knew must have been inflicted upon her in the wake of denouncing her . . .

All that time . . . she was still there. With me. Following my work, my career, collecting my books in as many languages as she could find, tracking down all my journalistic scribblings, making certain she was abreast of what I was always doing, what was preoccupying me professionally, what I was thinking and writing about the world and life as it was happening to me.

Seeing all those painstakingly sourced books and articles——all perfectly ordered, all a testament to the very minor oeuvre that I will leave behind when death finally comes calling for me——one simple but overpowering thought grabbed hold of me and wouldn't let go:

She loved me. And I just couldn't see it.

Johannes sat on the edge of the bed as I cried, watching me with almost clinical detachment. When I finally stopped, he said:

"I used to hate you. Every time Mother managed to spend money she didn't have on one of your books, every time a package would arrive from New York or London or Lisbon with your new magnum opus——and she had to collect all your fucking translations as well——she would sit where you're sitting right now. And she would do just what you've done. She would cry."

He stood up and reached for something on a shelf above me. An envelope. Thick. Manila. He tossed it in front of me. My name was on it. In her writing.

"Mother said if you ever did make it over to Berlin——and only if you really did physically show up *here*——I was to give you this.

"But you can read it elsewhere. Because I don't really want to be around you right now."

He stood up. I picked up the envelope and followed him as he headed to the front door. He opened it. I stepped over its threshold, the envelope now tucked under my arm.

"I'm sorry," I whispered. "I'm so . . . sorry."

Johannes stared into the empty distance. And said:

"Aren't we all."

TWO

DEAREST THOMAS.

So. Finally. At last. *En fin. Endlich.*

Actually, the German synonym works best. *Endlich.* At the end of things. Which this is. A letter I should have written years . . . no, decades . . . earlier. And which I have dodged for so many reasons. Some complex. Some far too personal. Some just so commonplace.

Endlich.

How to start? How to begin?

The facts:

For the past five years I have been in thrall to a form of blood cancer known by its rather long-winded but still impressive clinical name: *Precursor B acute lymphoblastic leukemia.* I have naturally been reading up a great deal on the thing that I have been fighting these sixty months and which seems determined to take my life away from me sooner than I'd prefer. There are about twenty different substrata of the disease, but I found the following definition online some time back. I quote it because it seemed to sum it all up:

"Acute leukemia is characterized by the rapid increase of immature blood cells. The crowding makes the bone marrow unable to produce healthy blood cells. Immediate treatment is required in acute leukemia due to the rapid progression and accumulation of the malignant cells which then spill over into the bloodstream and spread to other organs of the body."

A part of me was blackly amused that it was the *immature* blood cells within my body that wreaked havoc upon me. So much that wreaked havoc on me took place when I was in my twenties, a time when I was rather immature about the ways of the world.

Or am I just striving for a metaphor here when none is needed?

Another thing about leukemia and its causes was listed on that same site:

"Among adults the known causes are natural and artificial ionizing radiation . . ."

Of course, smoking two packets of cigarettes per day, as I have done for the past three decades, can't have helped things either. But the exposure to radiation is——as they say in bad English crime novels of a certain epoch——the smoking gun. I told you about being "photographed" at Hohenschönhausen after my first arrest. When I was deported from West Berlin in '84 they also held me for a while in Hohenschönhausen——not that they ever told me which prison I was in, but I remembered it all from the previous experience. The reason I was held in the prison was the death of their beloved Herr Haechen. The Stasi were certain I was to blame. So when the *Bundesnachrichtendienst* and the Americans tossed me back to the Stasi——after me pleading with them to grant me asylum (but as one of your compatriots told me: "We did that already and look what happened")——I was immediately incarcerated on suspicion of murder. The thing was, I had covered my tracks so well——and Haechen left no record of having arranged to meet me in Hamburg——that there was nothing they could directly pin on me. Of course, they tried all sorts of psychological coercion——denying me sleep, forcing me to endure, during one terrible week, eighteen hours a day of interrogation. But I realized from the moment I was locked up in a cell that I had the trump card. That card, quite simply, was my silence. If I confessed, I was doomed. A life sentence. A nightmare without end. If I refused to talk, if I said nothing, they could not get anything on me.

So that was my tactic——and the war of nerves that followed over the five months I was kept at Hohenschönhausen was desperate. Every three days they brought me to be "photographed" again. Every time I came away with red welts on my back.

Radiation.

I finally outlasted my interrogators. They gave up on me. They also told me that any chance of me ever seeing Johannes again was gone. But you must know something else that happened early on in

my incarceration. I was pregnant——maybe six to eight weeks——
with our child. Upon being handed back, I was examined extensively
by several doctors. A blood and urine test validated the pregnancy.
As they knew——via Haechen's reports about me——that you were
the father of this child, they took action. One day in prison, I was
brought to the hospital wing. I demanded to know why I was here.
They said it was another routine examination. I sensed something terrible afoot. I demanded to see a senior doctor. I demanded a lawyer.
I demanded . . .

But suddenly two male nurses were in the examination room.
When I tried to break away from them, they held me down while the
woman doctor on duty gave me an injection that knocked me out.

When I awoke some hours later, I was strapped down to a hospital bed. From the pain between my legs, I knew what they had done
while I was under anesthetic. The woman doctor——her name was
Keller——came in and actually smiled when she said:

"We scraped that capitalist filth out of you. Scraped it all away."

At that moment I vowed that, someday, I would destroy this
woman. Just as I settled matters with Haechen. Just as I was determined to find out the names of the people who had been given
Johannes and destroy them. It's horrifying to admit this now. But
though I forgave Judit for what she did——because she did it out of
weakness, out of fear, out of pressure so extreme on her to cooperate——I could never forgive those who allowed the system to simply
augment their cruelty. As a woman only a week or so away from her
death I can admit: I have never, for a moment, lost sleep over murdering Haechen. He was killing me slowly with his pitilessness——and
I knew that when and if the order came for me to be eliminated, he
would have executed it without a moment's hesitation. The only reason I think that the Stasi didn't do me in is that the Americans and
the *Bundesnachrichtendienst* were aware of my existence. Even though
they handed me back to them, had I been "suicided," it would have
looked bad. Better to try to break me psychologically. To abort the
child of ours that I so wanted. To then ship me off to the bleakest
corner of this bleak republic of ours——Karl Marx Stadt——as a form
of internal exile.

Karl Marx Stadt was industrial. It had no character, no charm, no culture. But it had an outpost of DDR Rundfunk——the state radio station——and I was given the job of writing book programs. They found me a tiny apartment. I began to sleep with a colleague at the station——a quiet man named Hans Schygula who had been exiled from Berlin as well, only in his case for the crime of propagating free jazz and once playing Stockhausen on the national radio service. Hans was older than me, well into his fifties, divorced, bookish, decent. He helped me get through the day. Especially during those early days when I first arrived in Karl Marx Stadt——and was trying to cope with what they had done to me in that prison hospital. The loss of our child was so devastating that I realized the only thing I could do to survive was blot it out.

No doubt, you might think I hate you for turning me in. Yes, there were moments——especially early on, in the wake of being expelled back to East Berlin, and the months of incarceration, and the forced abortion——when I did hate you. But honestly, my love, I hated myself for not having the courage, early on in our story, to have told you everything. But everything in my background, the social conditioning that was intrinsic in formulating my worldview, taught me to conceal, to suppress. I always saw——and felt——the profound love you had for me. But I couldn't completely trust it. I had to believe that if the truth willed out, you would have screamed betrayal and fled. Whereas by not telling you the whole story——how Haechen used Johannes as the ongoing bargaining chip——I destroyed everything. Had it been me in your position, I've no doubt I would have reacted the same way you did. And my one great hope over all these years is that you have not anguished too much about it all . . . though in each of your books (and I have read them all) you've always somehow made mention of life being a collection of sadnesses one frequently keeps hidden away. Along with all the other hints you've dropped in your more recent books about the shakiness of your own marriage, I always sensed that the damage of what befell both of us back then never fully cauterized.

And as for me . . . bless Hans. He made the years in Karl Marx Stadt just about bearable. Then The Wall came down. Within days of us being able to cross into the West without problem——I literally walked over to Kreuzberg and reclaimed the two journals I had hidden away before my arrest in the basement of my old building——I had also found a terrific civil rights attorney named Julia Koch. She took on my case after hearing me tell her everything about how Johannes was removed from me. I think Julia decided that mine would be a test case——and would demonstrate how the Stasi would be held accountable for their actions. It only took around six weeks of her applying the most relentless sort of pressure before the Klauses——the couple who had been "given" Johannes——were shamed publicly in the local press. There was something of a minor cause célèbre——especially as other people came forward, stating that both Herr and Frau Klaus had been among the most vindictive and excessive of Stasi interrogators. The fact that they had happily adopted a child taken away from a woman wrongfully accused of political activity . . . put it this way, I gather they were hounded out of their apartment in Friedrichshain and I have heard that they both finished their careers in clerical jobs in the local tax office.

And that doctor——the one who told me with pleasure how she had aborted our child——my lawyer also went after her. Once her name was made public, another thirty women——all interred at one time or another in Hohenschönhausen——came forward to say that she had performed abortions or (even in certain cases) sterilizations on them without their consent. The result of all this was that the doctor was struck off the medical record and ended up six months later plouwing her car off a bridge near Berlin while drunk.

I wish I could say I got any pleasure from her demise. All I could think was: people who commit savagery toward others must always justify their actions with phrases like: "I was only following orders." Or: "I was told it was for the good of the Fatherland." Or: "The system made me into the person I was then." It's like the way we believe that by eliminating an entire race of people, or putting up an "antifascist protection device" that walls in an entire country, or locking up anyone who voices a contradictory opinion against the system under which we live, we will solve our communal problems. Whereas the truth is: Walls fall down. Systems are discredited and come asunder.

An entire collective reality is shown to be fatally flawed. And the entire human circus just keeps moving forward.

One day recently, when I could still walk a bit, I asked Johannes to bring me down to the Brandenburg Gate. Growing up I remember how The Wall was always *there*, just before its ceremonial entrance. How we could see the ruins of the Reichstag and the trees of the Tiergarten to the immediate west. How near and yet how wildly far it all was. The forbidden planet into which we would never be allowed to cross.

Then Gorbachev decided he didn't want to prop up our sad little republic anymore. So things fell apart. The center did not hold.

Anyone can walk through that gate now.

So there I stood by the gate, just two weeks ago with my son. The son who was wrenched from me owing to all that Wall represented. Johannes is now nearly twenty-eight years old. A wonderful, original young man——yet also one whom so many people think of as strange, different. Yes, he is singular. Yes, he does live in his own world——a world of comics and graphic novels and Japanese cartoonists that has little to do with the nuts-and-bolts of everyone else's reality. But isn't he far more interesting for being that way? He has few friends, let alone a woman in his life. But he is a good man. A very good son. Every time I look at him, I keep thinking of the horror that took him away from me and the providence that brought us back together. It's been more than twenty years since that reconciliation. He still tells me he remembers so little about the five years when he was apart from me and with "those people." Just as he himself has no recollection now of the GDR.

"There really was a wall here?" he asked me as he held my arm by the Brandenburg Gate.

"You know there was," I said. "I've told you enough times, and you studied all about it in school."

"But they left none of it behind."

"Because it was too horrible to be left behind."

"Then they should have left some of it there," Johannes said, "just so people would remember how bad it was."

I couldn't have put it better myself. I was so impressed with his analysis of it all. But what he will come to realize, when he's a bit older, is that if we keep staring at the wall that divided us, that locked us in, we are still in thrall to the horror that it represents. Perhaps that's the largest overarching question in life. Can we always really look forward, as everyone endlessly advises us to do? Or do we have to hold on to certain key vestiges of our past——as painful, as terrible as they might be——as a way of understanding that there are certain things in life that change us so radically that they stay with us forever? Can we ever really close the door on that which still haunts us?

I so wanted that child of ours. I know I shouldn't have gone off the pill without informing you. And yes, if I had only had the courage to tell you about the shadows trailing me everywhere . . .

But I didn't. Because——and I understand this only now——I didn't believe myself worthy of the happiness you represented, of the life we could have given each other. Perhaps that's been the hardest thing about the last three decades. Knowing that you were the man of my life, that I had never felt that way about anybody before or after. Knowing——and this is the sadness that I will take with me to the grave——that I had a moment, an extraordinary moment, with you.

But if we can't hold on to the moment, it becomes just that: a moment. And life, like recorded time itself, has its own ruthless logic, a forward momentum that is as implacable as it is unstoppable. Until it runs out for you.

The idea that my life is being taken away from me in my fifties . . . I think about those men and women at the prison who were told to train radiation guns on me and, nearly thirty years on, have precipitated my early death.

But fifty years from now——when they too have vanished from this life, when disease and old age and time have snuffed them out—— will anyone even remember the fact that the security apparatus of a vanished state once used radiation to mark its political prisoners and bequeathed to them a fatal form of blood cancer? Do people now ever ponder the effects of mustard gas in the First World War? Or the spread of typhoid in the trenches? Was there a woman in Berlin in 1910 who had her one-year-old son unfairly taken away from her, and who (unlike me) never got him back . . . and for the rest of her life could never really get over her loss? Who is the witness to her story today? No one. Because her siblings, her friends, her work colleagues, her neighbors, the people she grew up with, the cousins she saw once a year, the man who sold her a newspaper every morning, have long since left this life. But think of the pain she carried with her——and how, at the time, it mingled with all the other pain of those who walked the earth during the same epoch as she did. All of them, like us now, struggling with things so difficult, so raw, so forlorn——during the moment in which it was all so lived.

But then, mortality wipes out an entire generation. And all the pain they carried? Vanished. Forgotten.

I do not consider mine to be an unfortunate life. On the contrary. Hans moved with me back here from Karl Marx Stadt and fought his way back into radio in the new unified Germany. Though we kept separate apartments in Berlin——at first because I needed to give Johannes time to readjust, but also because Hans and I were happier not cohabiting together——we remained a couple until his death from pancreatic cancer two years ago. Was it love? Not really. But he was my lover, my rock. When I myself started falling ill, it was he who insisted I again contact my Rottweiler lawyer, Julia. She won me a settlement from the state. Not vast——but enough to buy Johannes an apartment, so I can die knowing that, at the very worst, my son has a fully paid roof over his head for the rest of his life.

And it is the subject of Johannes which I need to raise with you now, my love. With Hans dead and me soon gone, he will be alone in the world.

Though he has enough practical skills to pay his bills and do his laundry and change the sheets on his bed once a week, I genuinely fear that he will be friendless. Isolated. Unable to connect.

Therefore, if it is at all possible, I ask just one thing from you:

Be his friend. He needs someone he can talk to, seek counsel from, lean on. The very fact that you are reading this letter now means you came all the way from your home in Maine to Berlin because you knew that we had unfinished business. And because the sense of loss never went away.

I know I should have contacted you years ago. I dreamed of that, just as I pushed away that hope. Because of my shame at having deceived you. Because I also believed that I deserved not to be forgiven. We're all so preposterous, aren't we? Holding on to our torments, our agonies, our small dramas——and using them to sabotage that which we so want . . . and actually deserve.

Loving you. Being loved by you. What a gift. I deserved you. You deserved me. The moment came. The moment went. And I still think of us and cry.

Ich liebe dich. Damals. Jetzt. Immer.
Deine Petra.

THREE

*I*CH LIEBE DICH. *Damals. Jetzt. Immer.*
I love you. Then. Now. Always.
Deine Petra.
Your Petra.

I dropped the last page of the letter on the desk and sat there, motionless, for a very long time. It was well after midnight. Earlier I had eaten dinner alone in Prenzlauer Berg. I had wandered the gentrified streets around Kollwitzplatz, passing by Rykestrasse 33, where Judit once lived——and where, twenty-six years earlier, I had knocked on her door, inquiring about some photographs of a child taken away from her friend, a woman who happened to be the love of my life. A woman whom this woman betrayed. And whom, in turn, I betrayed. Because I thought she had betrayed me.

But all I had done was betray myself.

Petra. Meine Petra.

I had the letter with me during dinner. It remained sealed in its envelope. It stayed there during a drink in a bar further down Prenzlauer Allee afterward. Only after a slow walk back to Alexanderplatz and a final nightcap in the hotel bar did I go upstairs and dare open it.

I read it once. I stood up and paced the room, feeling overwhelmed, lost. I read it again. I read it a third time——and found myself standing up, grabbing my coat and room key, heading for the door.

It was cold outside. New snow. I turned right and walked on past the old GDR housing blocks, then the building site on which once sat a concrete monstrosity that was called the Berlin City Palace. It was also the East German Parliament building. During its demolition in 2002, it was discovered to have toxic levels of asbestos crammed within its walls.

And exposure to asbestos——like exposure to radiation——causes cancer.

Petra. Meine Petra.

I kept walking, past the renovated Berliner Dom, the renovated Kunsthistorisches Museum, the renovated Staatsoper, the renovated conglomeration of buildings that was Humboldt University, where Petra once studied. The end of Communism always means a new paint job, doesn't it? Unter den Linden——East Berlin's bleak, ceremonial boulevard——was now a touristic, mercantile showpiece. A Guggenheim Museum. A Ferrari dealership. Five-star hotels. Cities can do this. Cast off their onetime identity and——while wearing the same (but now reconstructed) exterior——become something new. We as individuals can also change physical shape. We can lose weight and gain muscle, or go the other way and give in to flab. We can wear clothes that speak volumes about the image we want to present to the world. We can display our wealth, our poverty, our sense of confidence, our sense of doubt. We can, like cities, change all the externals. But what we can never do is change the story that has made us what we are. It's a story completely dictated by the accumulation of life's manifold complexities——its capacity for astonishment and horror, for sanguinity and hopelessness, for pellucid light and the most profound darkness. We are what has happened to us. And we carry everywhere all that has shaped us——all that we lacked, all that we wanted but never got, all that we got but never wanted, all that was found and lost.

Petra was so right: there are certain things in life that change us so radically that they stay with us forever. And we can never really close the door on that which still haunts us.

Petra. Meine Petra.

I turned left at Friedrichstrasse. Here the shops were even more upscale. Swiss timepieces. Parisian couture. Swedish design. Belgian chocolate. Everything was shuttered, closed. The street empty. The city all to myself. I kept walking, all of Petra's words rebounding within me, the sense of loss not just acute but so profoundly immediate . . . even after twenty-six years.

Will I ever make my peace with what happened? Or will it always be there? Happiness found. Happiness lost. Happiness squandered. We control our destinies much more than we like to admit. Even when confronting a terrible tragedy we can choose to be hobbled by it or somehow carry on. More tellingly, we always have the choice to stay or walk away. To want domesticity and simultaneously fear its restraints. To know we are making a fundamentally flawed decision and still go through with it. To accept love or sidestep it.

I've been guilty of all of the above. Only now——with Petra's voice fresh in my ear——do I see how the choices I made brought me here today. Traveling solo along a snow-swept street——bereaved, solitary, estranged from a wife I never really loved, missing my daughter, and musing endlessly about what could have been with Petra . . . and how the entire trajectory of my life would have been a different and (perhaps) sunnier one if I had only listened to her when she begged me to hear her out.

The moment came. The moment went. And I still think of us and cry.

I kept walking, my mind so awash in rumination and regret that I suddenly found myself at the Kochstrasse U-Bahn station. The realization that I was here threw me. How could I have walked down this street——and bumped into this U-Bahn station——without having first traversed Checkpoint Charlie?

Because Checkpoint Charlie had long vanished. Retracing my steps, I discovered that all that remained of that great ideological divide was its famous West Side sign:

"You Are Now Leaving the American Sector."

All the other Cold War paraphernalia——the electrified gates, the barbed wire, the cinderblock bunkers, the sentries with binoculars, the snipers, The Wall itself——was long gone. There was, I noticed, a small museum dedicated to the checkpoint. Otherwise, The Wall was now office blocks——all shiny and mercantile and new. The divide that divided so much, the symbol of all that changed the entire course of my life.

Gone. Expunged.

And I'd just walked right past it, forgetting it was once there.

All personal histories largely vanish. Most geopolitical ones do, too.

*   *   *

When I returned to my hotel it was sometime after two. An email was awaiting me.

> I'm heading out to my local bar——Vebereck on
> Prenzlauer Alle. Will be there until around three . . .
> Johannes.

I hopped a cab and arrived there ten minutes later. Vebereck looked vaguely vampiric——black walls, shadowy lighting, burning candles, and dripping wax at all the tables. Johannes was at a table in the corner, reading a Manga book. He had a beer in front of him.

"So you suffer from insomnia, too," he said as I approached.

"All the time. Buy you another beer?"

"Why not?"

I signaled to the bartender for two more.

"So what's keeping you up so late?" he asked. "Jet lag? A bad conscience?"

"Something like that, yes."

"Did you read Mother's letter?"

I nodded.

"And . . . ?"

"You mean, you didn't see its contents?"

"Mother put it in a sealed envelope around five days before she died, with the request that I never read it, but that I try to get you to come to Berlin to read it here. Guess both her final wishes were fulfilled."

"I suppose so," I said quietly.

"Have you always been so guilty about stuff?"

I laughed and said:

"Absolutely."

"Mother mentioned that often about you. The sense of regret that was everywhere in your books. The way you always seemed to be running away from yourself. She was your most astute critic, my mom."

"That she was. And I loved her more than I have ever loved——"

Johannes put his hand up, like a traffic cop signaling for me to halt.

"I don't need to hear any more of that. Because I've heard it all before. Mother was your greatest fan. Your greatest supporter. Your greatest reader. The way she talked about your books——*'Did you see how brilliantly Thomas described the Costa Rican rain forest.'* . . . *'I so wish he'd say a little more about his cold little wife in this book'*——it was as if you always were in the room."

"She knew my wife was cold?"

"Well, it was there on the page, right?"

"She's soon to be my ex-wife. We're divorcing."

"And Mother just died. Your timing is brilliant."

I bit my lip, my eyes welling up.

"Did I say the wrong thing?" he asked.

"It's okay," I whispered.

"No, it's not. I made you cry. So why not tell me I'm a shit or something like that?"

"Because it's me who's the shit here."

"No——it's you who's the sad man in the room. From what I've been hearing, my impression is that you've been this way for years. Unless, of course, I'm wildly off-beam."

"Anything but that."

"So I'm right. You're sad."

"Yes," I said. "That's me. Sad."

Johannes thought about all this for a moment. Then said:

"Mother always thought that about you, too. It always bothered her. 'He's so smart, so talented, so clever, he should be happy.'"

"I was happy. With her."

"Yet you chose sadness."

The comment hit me like a slap across the face. But I didn't flinch. I just shrugged and said:

"Yes, that is exactly what I chose."

The bartender kicked us out a few minutes later. Once on the street, Johannes said that he wanted to show me where his book-shop would be. We walked south to the next block. There was a storefront——a former salon, now empty, a "For Rent" sign in the window. The place had two large windows and, as I saw squinting in through the dirty window, seemed spacious enough for a good-sized bookshop.

"Tell me again how much they want a month?" I asked.

"Nine hundred."

"That strikes me as pretty reasonable for a neighborhood like this one."

"Yes, it's a good deal. And I have some carpenter and painter friends who would do all the refurbishing stuff very reasonably. Of course, the main outlay would be stock. Because, as I told you, I plan to make this not just the best bookshop of its kind in Berlin, but in Germany as well."

"And you need around fifteen thousand to get the whole place up and running?"

"If I can ever get a bank to listen to me."

"I'll give you the money," I said.

Johannes looked at me with care.

"Are you serious?" he asked.

"Totally."

"Even though the whole thing might fail?"

"It won't."

"How can you be so sure?"

"Because you're the brains behind the operation."

"There are a lot of people in this city who would think because it's my idea it's doomed to fail."

"I'm not one of those people."

"I don't want your charity."

"Then we won't call the fifteen thousand a gift. We'll call it an investment."

"And one which I plan to pay back with interest."

"That would be nice, but it's not essential."

"It's absolutely essential."

"Fine by me then," I said.

"Can you even afford fifteen thousand?"

"I have some savings."

"But you're hardly a rich guy."

"Let me worry about the money."

"You're doing this out of guilt, aren't you?"

"That's part of the equation, yes."

"What's the other part?"

"She would have wanted this."

Silence. Johannes lowered his head. Tears welled up in his eyes. Tears that he wiped away.

"I miss my mother," he finally said.

"And I certainly know how much she loved you."

For the first time since we'd met, Johannes looked directly at me. And said:

"You know what she told me the night she died? 'I was always convinced that life was essentially unfair, especially during all those years that you weren't with me. Then I got you back, and life never struck me as unfair again.' That from a woman dying thirty years too young, from a cancer inflicted upon her."

"You made her life, Johannes."

"So did you."

* * *

I returned to Maine the following evening, picking up my car in Boston and driving northward up the darkened interstate. Fresh snow had fallen while I was away, but the guy who plowed my driveway had also cleared out the path leading up to my door. As I stepped inside, the thought struck me that I hadn't really slept in three days. Along with another reflection: it is still so hard coming home to an empty house.

I dumped the dirty laundry from my travel bag into the washing machine. I stood under the shower for a good quarter of an hour, trying to wash away the ten hours of flying and the three-hour drive. I poured myself a very small whiskey and checked my emails. There was one from my daughter:

> Are you in the country, Dad? I never know. I could
> drive up from college tomorrow if you feel like hav-
> ing dinner somewhere.

I wrote immediately back:

> Let me make it easier for you. I'll drive down to Brunswick. What's the name of that Italian place you like so much?

We arranged a date for seven that evening.
There was also an email from Johannes:

> Talked with the real estate agent today——and I'm signing lease papers for the premises next week. Talked to a lawyer. He'll be drawing up a contract between you and the company that I'm forming—— with myself as the sole shareholder——to open the store. Everything about your investment will be clearly laid out——and I'd prefer if you ran it by a lawyer . . . preferably one who speaks German . . . when you receive it. Like I said the other night, I will only accept your money as an investment . . . and also if you promise me you'll come back to Berlin for the opening of the bookstore.

"I'll certainly be there for your opening," I wrote back. "And if you feel like ever giving me a call——just to chat——here's my Skype address."

"I'm on Skype, too!" he wrote back. "No cost to either of us—— and I can now plague you for hours about the latest Manga stuff I'm going to force you to read."

"Plague away," I wrote back. "And know that you can call me whenever. Day or night. Because, like you, I don't sleep much."

But that evening I did sleep straight through the night. Nine seamless hours. I woke to one of those rare midwinter days in Maine. A hard blue sky. The mercury well below freezing——bracing but not polar. The snow still pristine. The world appearing well ordered and unusually rational on this bright, peerless morning.

I caught up on correspondence. I punched out a few pages of a long piece I was writing on a journey to Mauritania that I had undertaken just before Christmas. Then I pointed the car south and headed toward the Italian joint in Brunswick that Candace so liked. She was already waiting for me when I arrived. She didn't see me at first when I came in, so I caught a glance of her alone at the table: very poised and elegant, dressed simply but stylishly in a black turtleneck sweater and jeans, clearly intelligent and attractive, yet lacking her mother's angular severity. I could see that she was hunched over a book, chewing on the end of a pencil.

"Is it a book worth reading?" I asked as I approached her table. She looked up and gave me the biggest of smiles——albeit one that was tempered by some underlying worry.

"Thomas Mann. *The Magic Mountain*. Great Foreign Literature in Translation. I have an exam on it next Monday."

"And it's very long, but good in its own imperious way."

"'Imperious.' I like that."

"Steal it then," I said, sitting down. "Can I tempt you with a glass of wine?"

"You know I'm still a few months underage."

"I'll take the fall if the cops arrive."

"My father the outlaw," she said with a smile.

"Hey, I remember when I was at college here, the drinking age was eighteen. But that was in the decadent seventies, when we weren't so obsessed with the micromanagement of all social behavior in this country."

"Spoken like a true libertarian."

"Spoken like a man in his fifties."

The waiter showed up and we ordered a half bottle of Chianti.

He glanced at Candace, then shrugged and went off in search of the wine.

"You see, we fooled them," I said.

"Well, a glass is my limit."

"Mine too, as I'm driving back home tonight. And I'm just in from elsewhere."

"Now you know I've been in the country for a good month and a half."

"That must be a new record for you."

"I happened to be in Berlin."

"Your old stomping ground," she said. "You seem a little down tonight, Dad. Something happen there?"

"Lots."

"You want to share it?"

"I do, but not just yet."

I could see my daughter studying me. In that always interesting, always analytical ways of hers, she was also quietly sizing up the situation. Then she smiled and said:

"No problem, Dad. And yeah, when you're ready to tell me . . . of course, I want to hear all about it. But you do look . . . I guess 'pensive' is the word I'd use."

"Pensive about sums it up. But when I was coming in tonight, I saw you looking . . . well, 'pensive' is the word I'd use, too. And it wasn't just due to Thomas Mann, was it?"

Our wine arrived. We clinked glasses. I could see Candace formulating how to tell me something difficult——as she had that look that crossed her face when she was struggling with a big decision. Glimpsing her in the middle of this internal conflict all I could feel was an enormous stab of love for my daughter——as I saw again that she was now beginning to edge into adulthood and all its attendant complexities.

Staring down at the empty plate in front of her, she said:

"Paul asked me to marry him."

Paul was Paul Forbusch. A very nice, very thoughtful guy from upstate New York who was in her class, whom I'd met on several occasions, who majored in philosophy and religion, and was never less than kind and enormously loving toward my daughter. He even told me how much he adored her once when they came and spent a weekend at my house——and I didn't do the Shocked Dad thing when they shared the same bed in my guest room. When Candace went upstairs ahead of him, he said:

"You know, sir, that your daughter, Candace, is——"

"Paul, we're not in a Jane Austen novel, so you can call me Thomas. And I do know that Candace is my daughter."

"Well, all I wanted to say, Thomas, sir, is that Candace is the best thing that has ever happened to me."

"That's a very sweet thing to say, Paul."

"And I think she's also about the smartest person I've ever met."

Part of me immediately wondered if——due to my many absences during her childhood and the rather frosty relationship between her mother and me——what Candace saw in Paul was decency and stability. Admirable qualities——but not exactly the most interesting ones.

"When did this proposal happen?" I asked her.

"Around three weeks ago."

"I see."

"I know I should have talked with you about it earlier."

"Not at all. You needed time to think it through before talking to me."

"I haven't spoken to Mom yet about it."

"Well, are you pleased? Surprised? Horrified?"

"All of the above. You know, Paul's just been accepted at Yale Divinity School. He'll be getting a master's, maybe even a doctorate. And he'll also be eventually ordained as an Episcopalian minister."

"Very nice," I said.

"I hear irony behind that statement."

"Look, Episcopalians are happily not Pentecostalists. And he is a nice guy. But . . ."

"I think I love him, Dad."

"Well, that's kind of essential if you are going to marry him. But look how you qualified the statement with 'I think.' And sorry . . . I know I'm not jumping up and down and telling you 'Fantastic.' It's just . . ."

"He doesn't cut it for you, does he?"

"Like I said, I think him exceptionally nice and thoughtful. And I know he adores you."

"I hear a 'but' coming."

"Well, you know I put fifteen thousand dollars aside for you as a graduation gift. My hope is that you'll take it and vanish somewhere for a year. Go travel across Southeast Asia, then head to Australia. Get yourself one of those working visas they give to people right out of college. Spend half a year on the Barrier Reef or working on a newspaper in Sydney. I've got a few connections there. Then come back——*or not*——and start figuring out what your next move might be."

"In other words, don't get married."

"In other words, find your way in the world first. Don't hem yourself into a corner. Especially when it might not turn out to be the corner you want to be in."

"Paul has told me the same thing. He knows about the fifteen thousand you're giving me. He knows you've encouraged me to go traveling, telling me that his certified public accountant father would never have been so cool. He wants me to do the trip. But then he wants me to come back and marry him."

"That's very progressive of him."

"I'm hearing irony again, Dad."

"I think Paul is right. Head out into the world. Travel. Have adventures. Then if, a year from now, you do want to marry him——"

"I think I want to marry him now."

"Ah."

"You sound disappointed."

"I am never disappointed in you, Candace. Never."

"But you think I'm rushing into something without giving it full thought. The thing is, I've given it a lot of thought. Paul is someone who respects and cares passionately about me. Who won't try to make me into something that I don't want to be. Who will give me plenty of latitude to be myself."

"That all sounds very positive. It's just . . . why not take him up on his offer to let you knock around the world for a year?"

"And maybe meet some surfer dude on Bondi Beach who will show me a good time and convince me that the world is bigger than that offered by a future Episcopalian minister?"

I smiled and told myself: *shut up now . . . no more advice.* Instead, I said:

"I would never tell you what to do with your life, Candace. Just be sure that this is the man you really love, that's all."

"I am sure. I know I said 'I think' before. But that was more an anxious turn of phrase, as I thought if I told you definitively, 'Yes, I know he's the one' you would have . . .'"

"It doesn't, in the end, matter what I think. It matters what you feel. That's it. And if you truly believe this is it . . ."

"You've felt that, haven't you?"

"Yes. I have."

"But not with my mother."

"Did she say that?"

"As a matter of fact, she did. And she also said she didn't ever really feel it with you either."

"Well, your mother can be most direct."

"But she also said you would never talk with her about 'it.' This woman."

"Maybe because, had I talked with her about 'it,' I might have upset her."

"Because she would have known that you were once so in love with somebody . . ."

". . . that I still grieve for it."

"But that's so sad."

"No. That's just life. Anyway, if things had worked out with that other person, there would have been no you."

"So I'm the recompense?"

"You're the best thing that ever happened to me, Candace."

She reached over and briefly clutched my hand, whispering, "Thank you." Then adding:

"But you're still so alone, Dad."

"That might change."

"Only if you want it to."

"We all have to voyage hopefully, Candace. Even when we think all is lost, we still have to try to convince ourselves that life can shift gears——and that it is still laden with possibility."

"So if I marry Paul because I so love him and then ten years from now it all goes wrong and I find myself stuck with two kids and no money . . ."

"I promise not to say 'I told you so.' But say that does happen. Say it does fall apart. Say you do have two young children as well. Everything is about interpretation. You can decide all doors are closed to you. You can decide that crisis is a synonym for opportunity. You can sit in some suburb and be sad. You can take your two kids to another country and start again. That's the great tragedy for so many people. They forget that life is such a flexible construct . . . that, by and large, you choose the limits and the horizons."

"Not everyone is as free as you are, Dad."

"I'm hardly free. In fact, I'm anything but free."

A few hours later, I drove my daughter back to her apartment off campus. As we pulled up, I could see Paul sitting in a rocking chair in their living room, studiously hunched over some very big book.

"Can we drop up and see you this weekend?" Candace asked.

"I'd like that very much."

"I *am* going to marry him, Dad."

Before I could reply, she leaned over and gave me a hug, then left the car.

I waited until she was inside the door before putting the car into gear and pointing it north back home. As I pulled away, I pondered the fact that my very wonderful daughter timed that final declaration with a quick exit from the car. That saddened me——but I also got the gist of her action. We're close, Candace and me. But she's twenty-one——and she has to act out her own life now. Perhaps Paul will be the best thing that happened to her: a man who loves her utterly, who gives her the latitude she needs, but also makes her feel wanted, adored, whole. Or perhaps he will become a self-righteous, persnickety, controlling little pedant who makes her waking hours hell. Or perhaps it will all turn out to be very pleasant and middling. The fact is, we are always taking chances in life. Always convincing ourselves of a scenario, a way forward, that we hope will make things right for us, or at least will make this short little span of time we're given seem worthwhile and somehow complete.

Complete.

Is anything in life ever complete? Or is it all lost and found? Found and lost?

My daughter——my only child——wants to get married. Of course, I will give her my blessing. Of course, I have the most profound doubts about the real rationale behind this decision. Of course, I wonder if, like the rest of us, she's trying to make up for all that she was lacking early on in life. Of course, I feel guilt about that. And, of course, I temper this guilt with the understanding that we are pals, that we can talk, that we "get" each other.

"You're still so alone, Dad."

True——but I have known love at its most unbridled, its most profound. Lost and found. Found and lost.

What a privilege to have found it, if only for a brief, transcendent instant.

And now . . . ?

Now I am on a highway. Now it is as dark and cold a night as they come. Now I am a single vehicle moving northward. Now I am alone.

The road is wide and clear. Dawn will break in a few hours. Another day, another day. So many exceptional possibilities. So many possible banalities. Choice is everything——and choice is nothing. The story can turn out well. The story can turn out tragically. But the road is always there. And, like it or not, we have to travel it.

And how we travel it . . . and whom we find along the way . . .

Love is always the great search. For what is a road without some sort of concrete meaning? How can we plunge through the ever-diminishing momentum of time without someone to slow things down, make it all seem worthwhile, give some true import to the journey?

Petra. Meine Petra.

Will I be haunted by this forever? Will every highway I travel always resonate to those words? Because what we all so want I actually found.

And having then lost it all . . .

There's the road. The new day. The things up ahead. The hope for something revelatory and profound. The thought that it may never come your way again. The need to tell yourself that life is about second acts. The imperative of moving forward. The solitariness at the heart of human existence. The desire to connect. The fear inherent in connecting.

And amidst all this, there is also . . .

The moment.

The moment that can change everything. The moment that can change nothing. The moment that lies to us. Or the moment that tells us who we are, what we search for, what we so want to unearth . . . and possibly never will.

Are we ever truly free of the moment?

ACKNOWLEDGMENTS

I am indebted to my very canny and smart editor, Sarah Branham, for being so canny and smart——and for helping me to immeasurably improve this novel. Just as I also owe an enormous debt of gratitude to Judith Curr for championing my fiction and relaunching me in my home country. At Atria, I also want to thank Mellony Torres, Christine Lloreda, Rachel Zugschwert, and Wendy Sheanin, not to mention the entire Simon & Schuster sales team——in particular, Adene Corns, Janice Fryer, and Stuart Smith, who have given me such outstanding support. My agents——Antony Harwood, Grainne Fox, and Richard Green——are also my friends (and that says it all). Susanne Gerber——my wonderful German teacher in Berlin and a great denizen of the city——served as the novel's fact checker (but I take full responsibility for any misplaced umlauts). And most of all, I want to thank my children, Max and Amelia, for being so interesting, so thoughtful, and, yes, so nice (always an underrated virtue). They are the best raison d'être I know.